The Jewel Series Anthology

Three Novels and a Novella by

Hallee Bridgeman

Published by
Olivia Kimbrell Press™

COPYRIGHT NOTICE

The Jewel Series Anthology
Sapphire Ice, Greater Than Rubies, Emerald Fire, & Topaz Heat

All derivative works Copyright © 2012 by Hallee Bridgeman.

> Sapphire Ice, Book 1 of the Jewel Series
> Greater Than Rubies, a Novella (Book 1.5 of the Jewel Series)
> Emerald Fire, Book 2 of the Jewel Series
> Topaz Heat, Book 3 of the Jewel Series

Fifth edition. Copyright © 2012 by Hallee Bridgeman. All rights reserved. No part of this publication may be reproduced or transmitted in any form or by any means – electronic, mechanical, photocopying, or recording – without express written permission of the author. The only exception is brief quotations in printed or broadcasted critical articles and reviews. Your support and respect for the property of this author is appreciated.

This book is a work of fiction. Names, characters, places, and incidents are either the product of the author's imagination or are used fictitiously. Any resemblance to actual events, organizations, places, locales or to persons, living or dead, is purely coincidental and beyond the intent of either the author or publisher. The characters are productions of the author's imagination and used fictitiously.

PUBLISHED BY: Olivia Kimbrell Press™*, P.O. Box 4393, Winchester, KY 40392-4393

The *Olivia Kimbrell Press™* colophon and open book logo are trademarks of Olivia Kimbrell Press™.

Olivia Kimbrell Press™ is a publisher offering true to life, meaningful fiction from a Christian worldview intended to uplift the heart and engage the mind.

Some scripture quotations courtesy of the King James Version of the Holy Bible.

Some scripture quotations courtesy of the New King James Version of the Holy Bible, Copyright © 1979, 1980, 1982 by Thomas-Nelson, Inc. Used by permission. All rights reserved.

Original Cover Art and Graphics by Debi Warford (www.debiwarford.com)

Boston photo by Robert Lowe (username rmlowe on Flickr) licensed under Creative Commons (CC) license.

Library Cataloging Data
 Bridgeman, Hallee (Hallee A. Bridgeman) 1972-
 Jewel Series Anthology, The / Hallee Bridgeman
  660 p. 23cm x 15cm (9in x 6 in.)
Summary: Three half-sisters, Robin, Maxine, and Sarah, share one nightmarish past. With the world and the scars of the past against them, can the three of them find love and learn to live a life of faith?
 ISBN: 978-1-939603-40-1 (trade perfect) ISBN-10: 1-939603-40-4
 ISBN: 978-1-452492-88-9 (ebook) ISBN: 978-1-476028-18-7 (text only)
1. Christian fiction 2. man-woman relationships 3. love stories 4. family relationships 5. literary anthologies

PS3568.B7534 J494 2012   [Fic.] 813.6 (DDC 23)

Jewel Anthology

THE JEWEL SERIES

The Jewel Series
by Hallee Bridgeman

Book 1: ***Sapphire Ice***, a novel	....	3
Sapphire Ice Reader's Guide	....	149
Greater Than Rubies, a Novella	....	159
Greater Than Rubies Reader's Guide	....	298
Book 2: ***Emerald Fire***, a novel	....	307
Emerald Fire Reader's Guide	....	473
Book 3: ***Topaz Heat***, a novel	....	481
Topaz Heat Reader's Guide	....	639
Master Translation Key	....	647
Afterword, by Gregg Bridgeman	....	650

Hallee Bridgeman

SAPPHIRE ICE – COPYRIGHT NOTICE

SAPPHIRE Ice

Sapphire Ice, Book 1 of the Jewel Series

Fifth edition. Copyright © 2012 by Hallee Bridgeman. All rights reserved.

Words and lyrics from the hymn, SOFTLY AND TENDERLY JESUS IS CALLING, in the public domain. Words & Music by Will L. Thompson, originally published in Sparkling Gems, Nos. 1 and 2, by J. Calvin Bushey (Chicago, Illinois: Will L. Thompson & Company, 1880)

Original Cover Art and Graphics by Debi Warford (www.debiwarford.com)

Boston skyline photo by Nicole Kotschate (username mcfly1980 licensed under agreement by SXC.hu)

Library Cataloging Data

Bridgeman, Hallee (Hallee A. Bridgeman) 1972-
  Sapphire Ice; Jewel Series part 1 / Hallee Bridgeman
    p. 23cm x 15cm (9in x 6 in.)
Summary: The men in unbeliever Robin Bartlett's life have only ever been users. Believer Tony Viscolli's arrival and relentless interest in Robin both infuriates and intrigues her.
  ISBN: 978-1-939603-33-3 (trade perfect) ISBN-10: 1-939603-33-1
  ISBN: 978-1-452416-52-6 (ebook) ISBN: 978-1-476142-00-5 (text only)
1. Christian fiction 2. man-woman relationships 3. love stories 4. family relationships
  PS3568.B7534 S277 2012
  [Fic.] 813.6 (DDC 23)

SAPPHIRE ICE - PROLOGUE

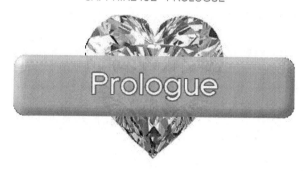

THERE were three of them. Sisters. Half sisters, technically, born to the same mother but different fathers. They lived in bad circumstances, the kind of childhood existence that makes for melodramatic and heart-wrenching movie of the week scripts. There were nights when it was bad, and then there were those nights when it was really bad. The really bad nights they all had to hide.

Tonight was one of those really bad nights.

Robin hadn't gotten out of the way fast enough. Maxine and Sarah had been able to hear her screaming from their closet hiding place, but to go out there, to face him wouldn't have helped Robin. It would have just given him two more targets, or possibly hostages. Eventually, Robin crawled in with them, shaking with fear and rage, not even knowing which was the strongest emotion from one tremor to the next. She'd managed to fight him off this time. He was probably still trying to get his breath back. But Robin needed her strength for the next day … and the next … and the one after that.

Robin was fifteen, blonde, blue eyed, and already beautiful. She was the oldest of the three, the protector of the other two. She had no memory of her father but knew he was doing seven to twenty-one for trafficking cocaine.

Green eyed Maxine was twelve, olive-skinned, with straight, dark hair that testified to the proof of her father's American Indian blood. He had been a warm bed on a drunken night, and only Maxine's features gave evidence of which of her mother's many one night stands had fathered her. She had never learned his name. Neither had her mother.

Little Sarah was nine. She was thin – too thin – pale, and small enough to pass for six. Her brown, curly hair had red streaks that came out in the summer. She needed glasses, but he had already broken them twice, so she gave up on them. When Sarah was two, her father had played lollipop with a loaded revolver and lost.

Robin wrapped her sisters in her arms as they heard the front door open, heard their mother's raucous laughter and a man's answering voice. Then HE started yelling and the sound of breaking glass made each girl flinch.

Their mother's shrill shrieks added to the cacophony, and the new man's voice joined in. The three girls inched farther back into the closet as the fight intensified. Shouting escalated. Words began to become clearer. Robin tried to cover her sisters' ears to block out the quarrel. The adults screamed at each other about a deal gone bad, about drugs, about money. There had been many fights like this in the past, and the three sisters prayed that he would leave this time.

Sarah screamed at the sound of the gunshot. Robin grabbed her and covered her mouth with her hand. Greasy fear churned through her gut at the sound of another shot. And another. And another. Four shots in all, then a deafening, roaring silence that screamed in their small ears.

In the silence, Maxine shifted, but Robin gripped her arm tight enough to bruise, her dirty nails digging into her sister's brown skin. Heavy boots moved through the apartment, entered their room, started toward the closet. They each drew in a breath and held it, surprised their teeth didn't rattle and give them away. Then the screech of sirens penetrated the thin walls and they heard the heavy boots run, heard the door slam.

They didn't move. They waited through the silence, through the banging on the door, through the dozens of footsteps that entered the apartment. They heard the shouts and the buzzing and chirping of hand held radios. They heard the metallic clicks of hammers falling back onto unfired chambers and eager, stiff muzzles sliding forcefully back into worn leather sheaths. They heard muttered curses about wasted lives or scumbags slaying scumbags. The light in their room flicked on and, after a moment, a voice called, "Hey, Sarge, there's toys in here. Little girl toys. Dolls and stuff."

They sat there in the dark, quivering with their backs to the wall, their arms wrapped around each other, and shivered together, terrified of what waited for them outside the closet.

SAPPHIRE ICE - CHAPTER 1

THE wait for a table at Hank's Place spilled out beyond the patio and into the parking lot. Parents stood in cliquish groups, tightly gripping little trophies, pagers for tables, and various beverages from the bar. Throngs of little leaguers dashed around chasing each other, exactly as loud and somewhat rowdy little boys ought to do. They wore white jerseys with yellow sleeves, each bearing the Hank's Place logo, which accounted for the presence of such a large crowd on the last night of the season.

Robin Bartlett balanced her tray over her head and stood on her tiptoes to keep from losing her balance as a pack of nine-year-olds shoved by her. A yellow cap landed at her feet and, with dexterity, she slipped her toe under it and kicked up, catching it in mid air as she continued forward with the drinks. She arrived at her target group of parents and delivered two diet colas, an iced tea, and a water with lemon without dislodging a single drop.

"Do you know how much longer we'll be?" A perfectly groomed and well-bejeweled mother asked, irritation heavy in her tone.

Robin smiled, feeling the headache she'd fought all evening start spearing the back of her right eyebrow. "We're setting up for you in the outside bar area," she answered. Number seventeen bumped into her, knocking her sideways. Seeing a head bare of a cap, she placed the cap in her hand atop the tawny head and gave the bill a quick tug. "Shouldn't be more than five or ten minutes."

The customer pursed her lips but didn't say anything. Robin stepped slightly to the left and addressed the next group clustered around the large potted fern. "Would you like something from the bar while you're waiting?"

One of the women in the group answered. As she shoved the designer sunglasses on top of her head, the diamond tennis bracelet on her tanned wrist caught the light of the setting sun. "We're a church group."

Robin bit her tongue before she blurted out exactly what she thought of "church groups" and instead smiled a bright, saccharine smile. "I can get you water or cola from the bar as well."

The woman actually looked Robin up and down, from the toes of her worn out black sneakers to the top of her tightly bound blonde hair. Once she had concluded her inspection, she turned her back as she spoke, as if dismissing Robin. "No, thank you," she said.

Robin shrugged it off. She met a dozen like her a day. She worked her way through the crowd, taking drink orders and reassuring parents that the wait wouldn't be much longer. Some were rude, some polite. Robin guessed the polite ones had once waited tables. It didn't matter either way to Robin. Robin's boss paid her simply to fill drink orders, not make lifelong friends.

After making her way back into the restaurant and behind the bar to pour wine and beer, she paused for just a moment to roll her head on her neck, trying to relieve some of the tension. She caught her reflection in the mirror behind the bar. She wore her blonde hair wrapped into a tight bun at the base of her neck. Instead of detracting from her beauty, it accented her high cheekbones and long neck and helped the casual observer focus on her deep blue eyes and long lashes. She wore makeup only to hide the shadows under her eyes and the cheeks pale from fatigue, but the light dusting of lipstick simply made her full lips all the more appealing. She wore the standard bartender uniform of Hank's Place, with her starched white shirt and black slacks, which helped to exhibit her thin waist and long legs.

She'd worked in the bar for eight years. Hank had given her the job at eighteen, and from the first day she'd had to fight off the men who made passes on an almost nightly basis. The regulars eventually learned that a date could not be had, and also attained an education on just how badly fingers could ache for days as the consequence of a casual touch. A few times she'd been tempted to take one of them up on the offer for a date, but the truth of the matter was that she didn't have time. She didn't have the time for a date, and she certainly didn't have the time for a man in her life.

Robin simply worked. She slept, ate, and worked. She methodically made drinks and served customers. She was the head bartender now, and while she could have done without the added responsibility, the extra pay helped. The little bonuses Hank slipped into her paycheck from time to time let her know that he appreciated her and the regular crowd who managed to find their way in only on the nights she worked.

Two hours later, her hands burning from the bleach water used to wash the glasses and her feet feeling like they might just fall off, the restaurant reached its peak dinner time. People at the entrance were told that the wait would be at least an hour if not more and the customers, to Robin's continuing surprise, accepted that. Happy hour came to an end and the rush of double orders ended, so Robin just concentrated on keeping the waiting customers happy and keeping the eating customers served. That worked for her because her headache beat against her skull in a thundering rhythm that she kept expecting nearby people to overhear.

Regardless, her smile looked fresh to the new customers who had sidled up to whatever free spot there remained along the bar, and she fixed their drinks with the same efficiency as she had two hours earlier. She took money, pocketed tips, and offered an audible, "thank you," as a mother carted out a toddler who had been screaming for the last forty-five minutes. She turned toward the cash register and barreled into the solid chest of Hank Lamore. Even though she stood nearly six feet tall herself, she barely reached his shoulder, and had to crane her neck to give him a grin.

Hank ran his place as tightly as he'd run his ship when he'd been a Captain in the Navy. He was edging toward sixty now, but discipline over his body and the daily workout regime he put himself through kept him looking early forties. Robin loved him like the father she'd never had, and owed him almost everything.

"Break, Robin," he stated flatly in his gravelly voice.

She snorted and skirted around him, not even bothering to respond.

He turned and snatched the bills out of her hand and stepped between her and the cash register. "I said break. And I mean a full half hour. Not the measly five minutes you try to get away with."

If she sat down for a full half hour, Robin knew she'd fall asleep. Still, it was best not to argue with the boss. She'd get off her feet for a few minutes, drink a cup of coffee, maybe take an aspirin, and then get back to work. Hank might growl at her then, but he wouldn't try to force the issue.

With cup in hand and a be-right-back wave to her regulars, she went through the double doors off to the side of the bar into the kitchen. Casey stood at his place behind the huge stainless steel table, inspecting plates and passing or failing them with his very high standards of sensory appeal. Those approved went onto the warmer shelf in front of him where the wait staff lingered, waiting to pick up their orders. Those rejected were sent back to the minions behind him who then scurried to make repairs and please the legend. Chef Casey stood very short and very thin, thin enough that it always surprised Robin that he could even lift the larger pots off the stove.

He gifted Robin with the grimace that passed for his smile, making his uneven teeth flash startling white against his ebony face. "Hiya."

Robin smiled back, "Hiya yourself." Then she headed to the corner of the big room toward a large table that sat ready and waiting for the staff to sit and relax on their breaks.

"Alright, then."

The greeting was a ritual, and hadn't changed over the past eight years. With a sigh, Robin leaned back in the chair and propped her feet in the one across from her. "How's the world treating you, Casey?"

"Well, now, here and there, mostly." A plate with a ten-ounce steak, mushroom risotto, and some fresh vegetables artfully displayed on the side made it to the finish line. Once Casey topped it with herbed butter, a waiter immediately snatched it up and put it on his tray. "You'll be wanting some of my pie to go with that coffee."

"I would, yes." She'd offer to get it, but she knew not to enter the stainless steel kingdom. The regular staff – regular meaning anyone not trained in the art and craft of preparing fine cuisine – was relegated to the large oak table in the corner. It was the same table Casey used for *mise en place* back when Hank's was nothing more than a glorified one-room burger joint.

She watched him dice some green herbs with such speed and precision that it made Robin's aching head spin. He sprinkled them into a large stainless steel pot and tasted his sauce before he fixed her a slice of pie. Without asking her, he went into the large freezer and returned with two generous scoops of vanilla ice cream to the top, then served it to her with exaggerated movements. "Not quite the fancy feast you used to getting at that Benedicts."

Sighing around her spoon at the explosion of taste of perfectly seasoned apples, Robin could only shake her head. When her tongue finally quit enjoying long enough that she could use it to form words, she chuckled. "They've got nothing on you, Casey. Not a darned thing."

His cackle followed him back to the stove. "Not a darn thing," he laughed while he glanced through a tray of raw aged steaks awaiting his approval before they could have the honor of searing to juicy perfection on the grill.

Neither spoke again. Casey concentrated on perfection while Robin concentrated on quickly devouring as much of the pie as she could. Waitresses and waiters came and went, bringing empty plates to exchange for full ones, too busy to have a conversation during the circle. It didn't bother Robin, though. She enjoyed the quiet, broken only by the opening and closing of the swinging doors.

One of the bartenders, Marissa was her name, pushed open the door and stuck her head through, scanned the kitchen, then looked back behind her. "She's in here."

Robin was just pushing her plate away and was contemplating getting back to work when she looked up and watched her sister Maxine stalk through the doors into the kitchen. "What are you doing here?"

Maxine laughed and glided to the table. She wore some green little sparkly sheath looking thing and shoes with such heels that Robin wondered how she stood without toppling over. Robin had heard people refer to her sister as beautiful all her life, but as adolescence gave way to adulthood, she thought that the word stunning might better apply. Her jet black hair fell thick and straight to her hips. She stood tall and thin with a delicate figure

Robin would have gladly traded for her more generous curves. Her most striking feature was her eyes. They were green, nearly emerald, slightly slanted in the corners with lashes so long and full they required no helping enhancements by way of mascara.

Maxine pulled the chair out from under Robin's feet and sat down, propping her chin in her hands. "I have a date. He's meeting me here."

Robin glared at her sister while she contemplated actually getting back on her feet to step out the back door for a quick breath of fresh, Boston air. "You have to work tomorrow."

Maxine glared right back. "So do you."

"That's different."

"How?"

Robin sighed and rubbed her forehead. "Because I'm working now. I'm not out late playing, so that I'll drag into work tomorrow and have to come up with new ideas on too little sleep."

Maxine sat back in her chair and crossed her arms over her chest. "I've been telling you for a year, Robin, to let me help you, now. You don't have to work two jobs."

"I'm not taking your money, Maxi. You work hard for it, and you deserve to be able to have things."

Maxine grabbed the hair on either side of her head and tugged while she groaned out loud. "Listen to yourself! You've done nothing but sacrifice since the day I got out of high school, and you're talking about me deserving to have nice things! When is it your turn, Robin?"

"Sarah finishes school in two years."

"You put me through four years of school, set me up with a contact from Benedict's, and expect me to sit back and make twice as much money as you and not contribute?" She slapped her palm on the top of the table. "That's nonsense."

Robin took a pull of her coffee and set the cup down hard enough that it nearly broke. "You wouldn't be having this conversation with me if I were your mother instead of your sister."

"Well, you aren't our mother. Besides, don't bet I wouldn't. You're twenty-six years old. By the time Sarah finishes, you'll be nearly thirty. That's when you decide to start living your own life? Almost thirty-years old and never even been on a date?"

Temper surged through Robin in a white flash. She looked into her sister's face, a face that looked nothing like her own. "I refuse to measure the quality of my life based on the number of men I've dated. I will not be like her, dating thirty men by the time she was thirty. Relying on a string of boyfriends for survival, then being shot to death by one of them. Whoopee! Life was one big party."

Robin stood, put her hands flat on the table, and leaned forward until her face was close to Maxine's. "I don't need a man in my life like her to feel my life is complete. I've managed to put one of you through college, our sister halfway through, and if I accomplish nothing else, I will have done more than I had ever dreamed possible. I get great joy out of seeing you successful in advertising, as I'll get when I see Sarah as a nurse. If it means that I sacrifice my youth, then so be it. Neither one of you will ever have to rely on any man for your livelihood, either."

Maxine stared at her for a second, then started laughing. "Is that what this is all about?" She rose from the chair until, in her heels, she stood taller than Robin. "Sis, you can have fun with a man, go out on a date, relax, enjoy yourself, and not have to rely on him for your livelihood. You're allowed to do that."

Robin grabbed the cup and drained the rest of the coffee with one swallow. "I don't need it and I don't want it. My life is good, now."

"Your life is work!"

"Work and you two. It's honest. Clean. I don't need anything else."

"You don't know that!"

"I've seen the other side, Maxi. I'm not going there."

Maxine stepped back and took a deep breath. "Okay. I'm not going to try to argue with you anymore. But, will you do one thing?"

She moved to the back door and Maxine followed. "What's that?"

"Will you go to college when Sarah's done? Will you let the two of us help you do that?"

It was her turn to laugh. "Yeah, right." She laughed. "That's a good one. Me, the high school dropout, go to college at thirty something."

Maxine squeezed her shoulder and turned to leave. "You're the smartest person I know, Robin, and you deserve to be happy."

She pushed the door open with her shoulder and stepped into the cool night air. "I'm happy."

"No. You're just happier. There's a big difference."

Robin snorted. "Go do whatever it is you do on a date. But try to make it an early day. You have to sell tires or something tomorrow."

"Ha-ha. Actually it's peanut butter. We need to convince choosy mothers to choose a different brand."

Robin plunked down on an overturned crate and stared at the gravel on the ground at her feet long after her sister left. She looked up at the night sky, at the stars she could see through the haze of the city lights. Finally, shaking off the dark mood that apparently came out of nowhere, she went back into the kitchen to find Casey waiting for her with a bottle of aspirin and a glass of water. She smiled as she took them from him, then swallowed two of the pills.

"That Maxi. I've always liked that one." Taking the bottle and the empty glass from her, he turned away, heading back to roost. "Smart girl."

Robin stretched her lower back. "Shut up, Casey."

His cackle followed her out of the kitchen.

AT seven-thirty that night, Antonio "Tony" Viscolli opened the door to Hank's Place. He'd done his research. He always did his research. He knew that Thursday nights were the busiest weeknight at Hank's, just as he knew that Tuesdays and Fridays were the busiest days for lunch, and Saturdays were the busiest nights on the weekend.

This visit was unplanned. Tony wanted to know if he would like or dislike the business without them knowing they had a potential buyer peeking under the carpets. He'd liked what he'd seen on paper. He'd liked what he'd heard on the street. He really liked what he saw when he walked into the building.

The house was packed with families. Somehow, despite the understated elegance and four-star menu, it came off as being a family place. That surprised Tony. He expected the same stuffiness found in fine dining all over the city.

"Impressive," Barry Anderson said from well above and right beside him.

"Very," Tony said, moving forward toward the smiling hostess, his towering companion at his side.

"I like it," the giant offered. "I really like it."

The hostess explained that there would be a short wait and directed them to the bar area. Tony was an even six-feet tall, with the stereotypical dark olive complexion that most every Sicilian sported, and eyes so brown they looked black, set in a lean, angular face. Still, even at six-feet, he only came up to Barry's shoulder.

People mistook Barry's size to mean that he was Tony's bodyguard, and the men had shared plenty of laughter over the assumption. He stood at six-nine, weighed close to three hundred pounds of steel hard bone and muscle, with sandy blond hair and ice blue eyes. The massive Super Bowl Ring on his massive right hand sparkled in the low lighting.

Barry served as Tony's attorney, and had done so from the very first business deal Tony had made that required a lawyer. His practice had grown, as Tony's business had grown, until it was one of the largest law firms in the city. While Barry oversaw his own practice with due diligence, he – and he alone – only ever personally handled Viscolli business.

The bar area was busy for a restaurant bar. When a cheer rippled through the bar, Tony glanced up and saw the possible reason for the crowd. A Red Sox game played on the large flat screen television gracing the wall opposite the bar, and the boys had just pulled ahead.

Two stools became available at the end of the bar. They hadn't been seated thirty seconds before the bartender appeared in front of them. She handed the man on the other side of Barry a fresh beer, and as she brought her hand back, she pulled the levers on the tap in front of her to fill another two glasses.

"What can I get you gentlemen?" she asked as she Frisbee tossed cardboard coasters in front of them.

The second her eyes collided with Tony's, he felt like something sucked all of the air out of his chest. Her eyes were crystal blue seas that he was certain would drown him if he let them. Shaking his head to ward off whatever it was that had suddenly struck him, he cleared his throat and gave her his order. "Ginger ale with lemon."

"And you, sir?" she asked, her eyes sliding over to Barry.

"Shirley Temple."

Tony had to give her credit. Most bartenders did a double take whenever Barry ordered. She simply nodded and began to prepare their drinks.

"Hey, Robin. No way will you know this one," the man on Tony's left spoke.

If he hadn't been watching her so closely, he wouldn't have spotted the flicker of annoyance before she laughed and set his drink in front of him. "I'm telling you, Sandy, give it up."

"No way. I got you this time." The man laughed and pounded the bar with his fist. "Straight Law Cocktail."

Her hands were busy while she answered. "Gin and dry sherry." She added an orange slice and a few extra cherries to the glass and set it in front of Barry. "Stirred, not shaken."

An elbow nudged Tony's ribs, making him slosh his drink. "That girl. She's the best."

"Is she?" Tony asked rhetorically, then helped right the man before he sopped up the spill with his napkin.

Robin reached across the bar and took the rest of Sandy's drink. "That's it, hon'. You're done."

"Come on, Robin. At least let me finish my beer."

Her eyes remained sober through her smile. "Sorry, Sandy. You're falling off the stool as it is."

"You can't just cut a man off at the knees like that."

Tony watched with interest as she handled the intoxicated man next to him. She set a mug of black coffee in front of him along with his tab, called a cab, made two more drinks, collected Tony's money for their drinks, and all the while talked to the inebriated man, teased him, kept him happy while he waited for his cab.

Tony could have watched her work all night. The longer he watched, the more he realized that he wasn't the only man in the building upon whom she had such an affect. Several knew her, stopped to speak with her, and more than one stared at her with the same desire Tony felt skirting at the edges of his mind. It irritated him that he could fall so easily into line with a dozen others, and he frowned into his drink while he considered it.

"Well, well. Antonio Viscolli." He looked behind him and saw a man who could easily rival Barry in size. His head was shaved, he sported a mustache and a partial beard, and had tattoos running up both arms. "You officially checking me out Mr. Viscolli?" he asked with a laugh.

Tony grinned and held out a hand. "Hank Lamore. It's good to see you again."

"You should have told me you were coming out. I'd have held a table."

"We were coming in from the airport and decided to swing by." He gestured to his right. "Barry Anderson ... Hank Lamore."

Tony caught one more look at the bartender as she worked farther down the bar before he set his full attention to the matter at hand. "Do you have an office, Hank?"

"Sure. Come on back."

On the way to the seller's office, Tony pushed the blonde out of his mind and turned it fully and completely to the business at hand.

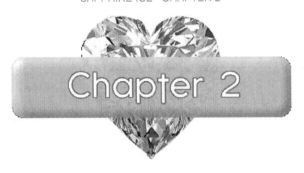

Chapter 2

THE shrieking of the alarm clock finally penetrated the thick fog of sleep that Robin had savored for too few hours. With a groan, she rolled over and hit the button to silence the stupid thing, then forced herself into a sitting position.

She put her elbows on her knees and rested her face in her hands. Three hours of sleep would get her through the day, but just barely. Hopefully, she'd still get a chance this afternoon to take a nap before she had to be back at Hank's.

With another groan, she rubbed her face and stood up. It was five-thirty in the morning, and she had to be dressed and at work in forty-five minutes. She stumbled through the darkened apartment, passed the closed door of the room that housed Maxine and Sarah, and into the tiny kitchen. She stopped short when she saw Sarah already at the table, nursing a cup of tea.

"Why are you up so early?" she mumbled, fumbling for a coffee cup, sloshing in the rejuvenating brew that had perked to perfection the last twenty minutes of her sleep time via the wonderful invention of a timer.

"I have a test at seven-thirty."

Robin collapsed into one of the two remaining chairs and stared at her sister through half-open eyes. Sarah had always been petite and almost delicate, but on the verge of adulthood, she looked nearly angelic. She wore wire-rimmed glasses that subtracted nothing from her hazel eyes. Her hair fell to her shoulders, an auburn mass of curls that no amount of styling could contain, framing a small face sprinkled with freckles. She'd barely breached the five-foot mark, with such a delicate bone structure that Robin sometimes worried a strong hug could break her.

She was studying to be a nurse, and Robin wondered how she'd ever have the stamina to make it through the rigors of the education process. Whenever that particular thought materialized, Robin made herself realize that Sarah had always been tougher than she looked. They all had. Robin just had to constantly remind herself of that fact.

"Why are *you* up so early?" Sarah asked in return. "Seems like you just got in."

A yawn made Robin's jaw pop, and she had to wipe the tears from her eyes before she spoke. "There's a Chamber of Commerce breakfast at the club this morning."

Sarah arched an eyebrow. "Isn't Benedict's a little fancy for a Chamber breakfast?"

Benedict's was a very private, very exclusive dining club, and very picky about not only the patrons, but also who worked on staff. She'd applied every two months for three years, but it was one of the most sought after restaurant jobs in the city. The summer before Maxine started college, Robin finally managed to secure a job at Benedict's. She worked the lunch shift six days a week, and on a slow day made a hundred in tips. She'd been able to put Maxine through college on her tips alone, and managed to save enough from her hourly paycheck at Hank's for the year that she had to pay the tuition and books for both Maxine and Sarah.

She yawned again. Two more years. Then she could rest. "There's some member who's sponsoring it, paying for the whole thing." Which probably meant scrimpy tips, but it would still amount to more than she could earn bagging groceries for two hours, and that was what counted.

"Are you working lunch, too?"

"Just the first shift. I have to be at Hank's at six, so I'm taking off at one and sleeping for the afternoon.

Sarah rose to add more water to her cup. "Oh, that reminds me. Can you get some of Benedict's artichoke dip?"

Robin had her head on the table, quietly dreaming of being back in her bed. "Probably, why?"

"Mom is having some church something or other. I told her I'd try and get her some."

Sarah sat back down as Robin kept her face hidden. She just felt too tired to fight her emotions, and didn't want her all too perceptive little sister to recognize the pain that must have flashed in her eyes. It felt like a knife twisting in her heart.

Little Sarah had been the only one of the three girls who made it through the system into a real family. An older couple who'd tried for years to have children of their own had just recently applied for and been approved for foster care. Sarah had still been young enough for them to want to adopt her, and the house she'd been placed in that terrible night that it all happened was the house she still called home. They'd fallen in love with Sarah on that first night, and immediately went through the motions to make her theirs. It was understood that they could only manage one child.

They felt very protective of Sarah and, because she had no memory of anything until that very first morning in their home, they cut off all ties to her past including her half-sisters. Robin fought for visitation rights and the courts finally granted monthly visitation after Sarah turned fifteen. For one hour a month, Robin and Maxine sat in the Thomas kitchen and drank coffee while reacquainting themselves with their little sister. Every single visit, Sarah's adopted mother hovered near the door unabashedly eavesdropping the entire time.

Because the Thomas couple couldn't afford to send Sarah to college on what was, by that time, their retirement pay, Robin approached them. She offered to fund Sarah's college on the condition that her youngest sister had to move in and live with Robin and Maxine. At first, the Thomas' flatly refused. Ultimately, their concern for Sarah's future forced them accept Robin's terms, but they made it clear that the acceptance came grudgingly.

Robin didn't care. Finally, all three sisters came back together again. Except no matter how she tried to bridge the gap, she had neither the bond with Sarah that she shared with Maxine, nor the closeness that should have come naturally to sisters, even half-sisters.

The emotion that besieged her whenever Sarah talked about her foster parents was nothing but jealousy, pure and simple, which in Robin's mind was on the border of evil. She felt jealous that Sarah had found a home and knew what it was like to get a hug before bed instead of either nothing or a slap across the face. She had a family that was still intact, complete with grandparents and uncles and aunts and cousins, of which Robin and Maxine never would and never could be a part.

Robin swiftly stood and gulped her coffee down. "No problem. I'll check with Carmine and see what I can get."

"Thanks, Robin. You're the best."

ONCE again, she wore her hair in a tight bun. Sometimes, she just wanted to cut the whole mass so that she wouldn't have to deal with continually putting it up for sixteen hours a day. Except every time she started, her hands paused on the scissors and she couldn't bring herself to do it.

Her makeup looked perfect, her lipstick crisp and even. She wore another starched white shirt, tighter and more feminine looking than the one she wore at Hank's, and a short black skirt with dark stockings. A bow-tie hugged her neck, and she draped a trim black apron around her waist.

Working at Benedict's required a good memory. The wait staff was not permitted to write down orders at the table. Carmine, the general manager, felt that it took away the necessity for eye contact with the customers, and created too informal of an atmosphere. It also meant that they were required to memorize any specials, details about all of the dishes (is that made with peanuts?), and the extensive wine list.

Thankfully, memory had never been a problem for Robin. It sometimes surprised her, considering the amount of drugs her mother had consumed on a regular basis, that the three sisters had been born with any brain cells at all. Pure necessity forced Robin to drop out of high school, but she'd always loved to learn. Unfortunately, she never had time to read anything but the daily specials and any book that came out that listed new drinks, and she imagined that's why it was so easy for her to remember everything else.

"You look a little piqued this morning, Robin," Stan Humphrey observed, fiddling with his tie at the mirror in a corner of the kitchen. Clip-on ties were not permitted, and Robin finally brushed his hands away and fixed it for him.

"Three hours of sleep will do that to you."

He stood tall and lanky, sporting dull brown hair speckled with gray and flat green eyes on a face Robin always thought of as uninteresting. At times she liked him, and at times he gave her the creeps. She remembered enough to know the signs of habitual drug use. "You partied last night?" he asked with a grin.

No one knew of her other job. Moonlighting was frowned upon by the management, and they were under the guided assumption that she'd left her position at Hank's to work exclusively for them. "Ughh, if I never see another rum and Coke again, it'll be too soon."

He leaned closer to her ear and she had to restrain the urge to flinch back. "I have a little pick-me-up, if you're interested."

She raised an eyebrow and kept her voice at a normal level. "You ever offer me drugs again, Stan, and I'll probably have to break one of your fingers."

He slouched back, holding up both hands as if to ward her off. "Okay. Sorry. You just looked like you needed something. No offense meant."

"Well, it was taken."

"Robin. Stan. Take your posts, please." The maitre' de's voice singsonged through the kitchen. "Okay, people," Clarence continued, "we have a buffet available, but our guests may order from the menu if they prefer." He looked at his pocket watch as ten waiters and waitresses brushed by him and headed toward the doors that lead to the dining room. "The bar is open, and Billy is ready with pitchers of bloody marys and screwdrivers. Mimosas are available with our normal champagne list." He clapped his hands together twice. "Serve well people."

Robin stopped near him to grab a carafe of coffee. "How did we manage to get the early shift, Clarence?"

He winked and whispered conspiratorially. "Tell me about it. I have my lunch patrons' whole lives memorized, but I only know half the people out there." He looked over her head to the head table. "Boston's royalty is here."

Robin was too tired to even be intrigued by Clarence's abnormal awe. "Maybe we can get Stanley a jester's hat," she whispered back, then pushed open the door to the dining room and forced a serious expression onto her face. The door swinging shut cut off his choking laughter.

The dining room was packed with people, seated at tables of eight. The restaurant was closed for the meeting, and it surprised her to see so many people there. But then, most of the customers weren't members and wouldn't get many opportunities to dine at Benedict's, especially for free.

She was given the head table to serve, and knew some of them as regular lunch patrons. She addressed those she knew by name, and tried to discretely read the name tags of those she didn't. Methodically, she worked her way down the long table, pausing to chat when it was required, fetching drinks as they were needed.

"Mr. Riley, it's good to see you again. I think it's been several weeks," she said, speaking to the president of the Chamber.

"I've been on vacation, Robin. Have you ever been to Greece?"

She smiled and filled his coffee cup. "Not yet, but I want to go someday."

"Beautiful country, dear. If you ever get the opportunity, don't pass it up."

"If a trip to Greece ever falls into my lap, I'll remember your advice." She moved to the next person while Riley continued to speak.

"Tony, if you've never had Robin here serve you, you've been missing out on the best that Benedict's has to offer."

"Yes. I think I've heard something similar about her before."

The smooth voice seemed familiar, but she couldn't quite place it. She took her attention from the cup and lifted her head, her eyes crashing into a pair of black eyes that seemed to look all the way inside of her, instantly learning all her secrets. "I didn't expect to see you here," he said.

Tony felt deep shock when he'd seen Robin enter the dining room. He'd had time to recover as she worked her way to him, and had nearly gained back enough self control to not show any outward reaction as she leaned in from behind him to pour his coffee. He had already had his normal morning quota of two cups, but allowing her to serve it gave him a chance to have her stop at his shoulder. As she completed her task, he caught her scent, something exotic and spicy, entirely feminine. Then she met his eyes and he thought that his heart would beat itself out of his chest.

When she looked away, it broke the spell, but a tremor in his hand that he neither liked nor appreciated remained. He was better prepared when she looked directly at him again, and concentrated fully on keeping his brain functioning.

"Do I know you?" She asked, her voice soft so as not to carry.

He kept his voice as soft as hers. "Not officially."

"I'm sorry, I don't ... " her eyes skimmed his name tag, "I don't recall meeting you, Mr. Viscolli."

His teeth flashed white against his olive skin. "I unofficially met you last night."

Panic skirted up her spine and she looked around the room. Lowering her voice even farther, she leaned closer so that he could hear her. "Please, don't say anything. I ... we can't ... I mean, another job ... "

He placed a hand on her wrist, startling her. His hand felt rough, but warm. Warm enough that it sent heat up her arm, causing her to flush. "So, what you're saying is that your job may be in my hands."

The flush that covered her cheeks was no longer from heat, but from the anger he saw flash in her eyes. "Release me, sir." She bit out.

He didn't think he could. "What would you do to keep your job, I wonder?"

She could never take him on in a game of cards. Every cruel thought in her imagination seared right through her sapphire eyes and bored into his, which he struggled to keep impassive. Still, she maintained her cool façade, something he deeply admired amidst his mirth. Tony carefully bit down on the inside of his lip to keep himself from laughing at her next words. "I don't play those games, Mr. Viscolli. Remove your hand, or else I'll remove it."

He shifted his grip until his fingers encircled her wrist. They overlapped on the thin bones, and this time he did chuckle. "You think you could?"

In a panic, knowing how long she was taking with this customer, she glanced up and spotted Clarence watching her. Baring her teeth, she leaned close to this man's ear and whispered. "I can and I have, on men bigger than you. Are you willing to test me?"

With a grin, he reluctantly let her go. It was that or drag her into his lap, and he didn't think anyone in the room would appreciate that too much. "Perhaps another time I'll take you up on your challenge."

Unable to stand the thought of leaving him with the last word, she leaned forward again, barely speaking above a whisper. "If the thought of seeing you again didn't repulse me, Mr. Viscolli, I'd almost look forward to it."

With that she moved on down the table, ignoring his chuckle that followed her parting shot. She found it especially challenging to keep a polite smile on her face and make inane chatter with the other patrons as she continued to serve while seething inside. How dare he?

She headed back into the kitchen to get more coffee and Clarence immediately intercepted her. "Did you have a problem with that man, Robin?"

Out of earshot of the customers, she was able to slam things around, surprised that she didn't break the glass coffee carafe. "Nothing I couldn't handle," she said, slamming the top back on her serving container.

He gripped her elbow and kept her from reentering the room. "I know that sometimes customers might get a little – well – fresh with some of our girls, but I wouldn't want to think that you might have – albeit unintentionally – insulted one of them."

She bared her teeth at him. "Did he look insulted?"

"No, but you looked insulting, and I'm concerned because I've never seen you act that way before."

She slammed the coffee onto a counter and stepped closer, until she could poke his bony chest with her finger. "I didn't like the way he looked at me, I didn't like the way he touched me, and I didn't like what he implied when he spoke to me." When he flinched, she realized what she was doing and stepped away from him, drawing in a deep breath to calm down. "Now, you've had your little 'chat' with me. Do you intend to speak with him?"

Clarence's face fused with color. "Robin, do you have any idea who that is out there?"

"I don't quite have the approbation for most of our patrons as you do, because I truly don't care." She grabbed the pot of coffee and pushed open the door.

He took insult at her words, as was her intent, though she regretted it the second his face fell. She paused and went back into the kitchen. As she opened her mouth to retract it, he straightened, stiff as a board, and put a regal tone in his voice. "That is Mr. Antonio Viscolli. He is one of the stockholders of this club, and is hosting this morning's breakfast. If you would like to lodge a formal, written complaint, I will entertain reviewing it, but in the meantime, you are here to serve, so I suggest you return to your post." He looked her up and down, his expression hinting that he didn't much care for what he saw. "Unless, of course, you'd like me to have someone else wait the head table. I'm sure that any server out there would be happy to trade places with you."

Oh, what a tempting notion. She considered it, very seriously, for several breaths. Ultimately, she decided that trading tables would most certainly give Viscolli a great deal of satisfaction, a game point. No, she'd serve him, and do a heck of a good job at it. "That won't be necessary, sir. I'm fully capable of performing all of my duties."

His face softened, momentarily. "I know. Now, get back to work."

Not wanting to leave things tense with someone she considered a friend, she paused to make one of her normal parting remarks. "Purple and green," she said. At his confused look, she continued, "with bells. For Stan's hat."

His mouth twitched as he fought the smile and waved her away.

Chapter 3

BARRY gripped the side of the golf cart to keep Tony from tossing him out as he took a sharp turn, and asked, "Have I ever told you how much I loathe this game?"

"It's a necessary evil. I doubt very seriously that much business could get done in a football huddle." Tony skidded to a stop at the next tee.

"How long have we known each other?" Barry asked superfluously as Tony leapt from the cart and snatched the number two driver out of the bag strapped to the back of the cart.

Tony chuckled and took a practice swing. "Too long for you to ask that question."

"In all that time, you've never – I repeat – never, done business on a golf course."

"Sure I have. I've formed relationships, negotiated deals, worked out problems – "

Barry cut him off by laughing. "You could get as much done over a lunch or dinner in half the time. You just want the excuse to be outdoors."

"Maybe," he said with a smile. Tony lifted his face to the sun and breathed deep. "But look at this sunny day! You look like you could use some fresh air anyway, buddy."

In a few short weeks, the skies would loom dark and overcast, sending flurries of snow that would hamper driving, keep people indoors, and dampen spirits. The thought brought memories of shivering in the doorway of an abandoned building at age seventeen, two weeks after his mother's death. He'd survived, thrived even, but he hated winter. His home in the Florida Keys was his normal retreat during those cold months. Recently, however, and all too often, business interfered and forced him to stay weeks at a time in the chill climate of the North.

For now, it was unseasonably warm in Bean Town. The bright blue sky and crisp air gave him extra energy, and he wanted to take advantage of it one last time. He'd met with Barry immediately after the Chamber breakfast, not even going to his office first. The way the day was shaping up, and with the air growing warmer by the minute, he had no intention of going in at all.

He stood back as Barry teed off. The ball landed perfectly in the middle of the fairway, just off the green. "I don't know why you hate this game so much. You've just about mastered it."

Barry threw his driver into his golf bag and watched Tony hit a near identical shot. "There's no challenge." He grinned and climbed back into the cart. "And very little blood."

"Ahh. Honesty." He followed the cart path until they reached the green. "So, Barry, I've been thinking. I want Hank's."

The two men climbed out of the cart and chose their clubs. "Tony, I don't think it's a good idea."

Tony looked at the club in his hand. "You think the pitching wedge instead of the nine iron?"

"Ha, ha." Barry offered drily. "Seriously, Hank is who keeps it alive. He has that touch. Without him, I think it's going to lose whatever it has that makes it so special and become just another restaurant."

"He's going to sell it, anyway." He watched as Barry lightly hit the ball, smiled as it rolled to about two feet past the hole.

"Good. Let someone else take the loss."

A scowling face with a pair of bright, deep blue eyes hovered in front of Tony's vision. Then he remembered her body, her grace, her grin.

"No. Give him his asking price but give him some earnest money up front. Ten percent, maybe. That's in addition to the asking price if he stays on as manager."

"His asking price? He's cushioned that by at least twenty percent."

Tony's ball landed on the green and slowly rolled toward the hole, teetered on the edge, then fell into the cup. He turned his body and looked directly at Barry, his face hard, his eyes serious. "Barry, I have accountants. I need you to be my lawyer. Think you can get the papers drawn up today?"

Barry shrugged before he putted. "It's your money." His ball rattled into the hole. "What about the bar?"

Tony retrieved his ball from the cup. "You know I don't like it. None of my other restaurants have a bar. I'll have to think on it and pray on it, but I'm already ninety percent sure we'll lose the bar."

"With Hank wanting to keep his staff, we'll need to make sure something that extreme is in the contract."

"Whatever you need to do." Tony watched as Barry retrieved his ball and they both replaced their putters and climbed back into the cart. "See, Barry? You're wrong again."

"Again? About what?"

"I just conducted business on a golf course."

"True. But it would have been more satisfying if I could have tackled you to the ground with my bare hands instead of whacking some stupid little ball with a stick."

Tony chuckled for the sake of the gentle giant's sense of humor. He always laughed at Barry's jokes. The men understood each other on many unspoken levels. They approached the eighteenth hole. "As soon as we're done here, I'll buy you lunch," Tony offered.

Barry sighed, understanding that lunch would likely be the special at Hank's Place. He pulled his telephone out of his pocket and dialed his office number. "I'll have the papers waiting on us. We'll need to stop by my office on the way."

THE three men sat in Hank's office in the back of the restaurant, sandwiches at their elbows. Hank had reading glasses perched on his nose and slowly read over the contract one more time. "What's the deal, here? Did someone find uranium under the patio tiles? Am I sitting on top of an unknown oil well or gold mine?"

Tony drained his glass, uncommonly relaxed. "Yeah," he drawled, "your restaurant. This place is its own gold mine."

Hank looked at him over the rim of his glasses. "Don't play games with me, Viscolli. You have a reputation that well precedes you and I'm not as dumb as I look. How come you're giving me my asking price without even trying to negotiate?"

Tony returned his stare. "I want to buy this place. You want to sell it."

"What's this offer of earnest money above the asking price? This ties me in for five more years if I accept it."

Tony shrugged. "It's pretty black and white. Why the questions?"

"Because, suddenly, I don't trust this deal."

"You contacted me, Lamore. I've done my due diligence and this is the only way the place remains profitable."

"What does a small time restaurant outside the city limits have that draws the direct attention of the infamous Antonio Viscolli?" He tossed the contract on the desk in front of him and leaned back in his chair. "I sign nothing until I figure that out."

Barry spoke. "You sell nothing if we get up and walk out, too."

Hank shrugged. "Maybe not to you, but I will to someone, and probably inside of five years."

Tony surged out of his chair and paced to a picture hanging on the wall. He stared at a picture of a younger Hank, looking very different in a crisp white uniform, his arm draped across the shoulders of a woman, presumably his wife, standing in front of their restaurant. A banner across the front of the building read "Grand Opening."

He put his hands in his pockets and rocked back on his heels. "I want to buy this place for the reason that I buy anything – because it's a moneymaking venture. I'm choosing to offer you your asking price for two reasons. First, it is actually a very reasonable asking price, and you could have asked for more. You should have consulted with more people before locking in. Secondly, I like you. I rarely allow emotions to affect business deals, but I do like you, and I figure my offer just might make your retirement sweeter." He crossed the room and stood near his chair, but didn't sit. "But I'm not going to play cat and mouse games with anyone. You decide, now or in your own time, but you decide without the games."

Hank drew his glasses off and rubbed his eyes. "I have a condition that I absolutely will not back away from."

Barry uncapped his pen. "What's that?"

"You keep my employees, without pay cuts and with similar benefits."

"That's a standard clause. If you'll see article fifteen of the – "

"I don't need to read it. I'll take your word." His eyes cut to Tony but addressed Barry. "Because I'm guessing your word is as good as his."

"The bar will be removed. The bartenders will have to be assigned new jobs, and if they choose to quit instead, that will be their choice and not affect the contract."

Hank raised an eyebrow. "No bar?"

Barry answered, thumbing through the stapled contract and marking places requiring his personal touch. "No Viscolli restaurant has a bar. We're also closed on Sundays in observance of the Sabbath."

Hank looked from Barry to Tony. "No kidding?"

Tony gave a slight nod of his head. Hank continued. "Okay. That's intriguing." He cleared his throat. "I'll sign these papers in two weeks. It will give my lawyer time to go over them, and give my wife time to make sure that it's what we want to do."

Tony held his hand out. "Then we'll be in touch in two weeks."

IT was rare for Antonio Viscolli to have an entire afternoon off, alone. It seemed wherever he went, whatever he was doing, business followed, and when business followed, it meant dealing with people: asking, demanding, meeting, negotiating. If it wasn't a lawyer, it was a secretary. If it wasn't a secretary, it was a reporter. On and on, constant demands. It wasn't something he disliked or resented. It was simply his life.

He woke early to pray and meditate on God, to read his Bible, and to have conversations with his heavenly Father. The opportunity to get away in the daytime, during business hours, was a rare treat.

After working almost nonstop for months, Tony was exhausted. It was rare for his energy to be so diminished, but when he thought back, it had been more than two years since he'd truly taken any time for himself. The golf game relaxed him a bit, but he needed more. He needed to pour some energy into something, let his body slow down with his mind.

He needed to sweat.

He'd taken up rowing because it was something kids with his background didn't do. It was a sport in which the blue bloods of the country competed, kids in Ivy League schools and their recent graduates. It was one more step away from his childhood, one more step to discard his past. It was also a sport that required no interaction with another human being. His solitude was something that he treasured.

He let his mind wander as the muscles in his arms worked the oars. Smoothly and cleanly he cut across the water, letting the sun beat down on his head, warming his neck and shoulders. The breeze blew warm, heated by the late summer the state presently enjoyed, and he lifted his face, letting the stress and pressures bleed out of him with each stroke.

In just two short weeks, he would celebrate his thirty-second birthday. All he had striven to achieve in life had been accomplished and then some. He was very nearly bored. Perhaps it was time he set his sites on something new. Something that didn't require contracts or negotiations. The water reflected back at him, as blue as a pair of eyes that hadn't left his mind in nearly twenty-four hours.

Pushing the thought away, he tried to plan for the coming month. He'd spent almost too much time in Los Angeles, but it had been necessary. It had taken him some time to establish himself in the business, to make sure those he left in charge knew that he, ultimately, was the boss. It hadn't been easy, but he had friends who helped him out, helped him sort through the lingo and nuances unique to Hollywood. With their continued help his company would provide good, quality, Christian films and television shows, and it would soar.

Because they all did, all the enterprises he owned. Tony Viscolli insisted on it.

A bird flew by overhead, hunting fish that were foolish enough to swim close to the surface. He heard it cry out, watched it circle back, then dive down and come up clutching its dinner in its beak. Across the river, he passed a small boat with a father and son fishing. The oars occupied his hands, so he nodded to return their polite wave, glad no words needed exchanging. If envy twisted in his gut at the sight of such a simple father and son outing, he ignored it and pushed the feeling away, focused on something else.

Women had always thrown themselves at him. He knew he was physically attractive and actually used his looks to his advantage as he scrambled up the ladder of success.

When it had become necessary, he'd hired consultants and learned how to dress immaculately for whatever the occasion demanded. Learned how to speak without his street accent coming through. Learned what fork to use when, learned how to have polite dinner conversation. He had transformed himself, but his Savior had transformed him even more completely before Tony ever began that process, and Tony admitted that fact and felt humbled by it.

In the process of his transformation, he met women who, five years before, would have turned their noses up at his offer to clean their toilets. None knew he'd been a street rat, as he'd been called on several occasions. They never saw past the charm, the polish. They never saw the kid who had eaten out of garbage dumpsters when he'd been hungry enough. They saw Antonio Viscolli, a man with money, power, connections, and a bit of danger lurking in the background behind those dark brown eyes.

Tony enjoyed women, enjoyed being with them, enjoyed entertaining them. He had scores of women across the country he could call on at any time if he wanted a date or a hostess. It was something that was just part of his life, something he never gave much thought. Most didn't even mind the platonic boundaries of their relationships, always hopeful that he might fall in love and propose, giving away the coveted title of Mrs. Antonio Viscolli.

This one was different. He didn't have a finger on it yet. Something about her, something in her, made her different. His attraction to her had been instant and absolute. Was he listening to God's whispered voice in his ear, or his own human weaknesses? He didn't know. All he knew was that he must see her again. He felt led to get to know her.

Pushing all thoughts out of his mind, he concentrated solely on the rhythm of his strokes. Flexing his arms, he cut the oars through the water, sending the boat sleekly across the surface as a trickle of sweat rolled down his back between his shoulder blades.

THAT insufferable, miserable–. Robin's hand slapped the side of the wall, cutting off the next words in her mind.

Robin stood under the weak spray of the shower, wishing that the wall she slapped with her open palm could be him. His face. No, she changed her mind. She wouldn't give him a full slap on the face. No, she'd curl her hands until her nails would rake some of the handsome off, until they drew blood and left scars.

The nerve of the man.

She slopped shampoo into her palm and started the long process of washing her hair. How dare he? Leaving her a tip under his plate that nearly matched to the penny the tip put on his account that she and ten others split. Who did he think she was? What did he think she was? It seemed like he made it clear what he thought she was, asking what she'd do to keep her job at Hank's a secret from Benedict's.

Oh, and the way that he just smiled that irritatingly polite smile at her through the rest of breakfast. And then there was that stupid trick of the way he held her eyes, giving her the feeling that he wanted to be alone with her in a candlelit room, and the whole time giving some stupid speech about the economic development of Boston. He never even tripped on his words, not when she glared at him, nor when she turned her back on him.

She scrubbed her scalp until it hurt, then finally took mercy on her poor roots, knowing that the strands were going to have to be bound tightly in a bun for another grueling eight hours.

She would just put the bills into a little envelope and mail the money right back to him. She didn't need him or his money.

She closed her eyes and rested her cheek against the tile wall. What she needed was a vacation. "Two more years," she said out loud, then ducked her head back under the spray to finish washing the suds away.

Feeling better after pounding the shower wall some more, she sat at her kitchen table, a tuna sandwich and a cup of coffee at her elbow, and figured out her budget. She'd had a good summer, considering the way business declined at Hank's during the school's off season. That was a good thing about working two jobs. Without fail, Benedict's always had a great summer.

While she had very little money for herself, very little extras, she was able to pay all of the bills without a hitch. She finished balancing her checkbook and found the money that Maxine deposited into her account. She made a note to call the bank and have it transferred. She'd made a vow to do this alone, and she intended to see it through to the end.

Maxine had tried giving her checks, but eventually quit when Robin kept handing them back to her torn up. She had tried cash, but it kept ending up on her bed. Now she'd resorted to directly depositing the money. Robin simply opened her sister a savings account and had the money transferred as soon as she discovered it.

It bothered her that she hadn't been grocery shopping in months, and that was because Maxine beat her to it. If she could take the food back, she would. Of course she couldn't, so she simply added what she guessed Maxine was spending on the food to the amount that got transferred into the savings account.

Robin popped a peppermint onto her tongue and looked at the balance in the account. There wasn't a whole lot left but she would have enough from tonight's tips to fill her car up with gas. Then she wouldn't have to worry about anything for another week.

Just as she finished putting everything away, she heard the apartment door open and close, and watched Sarah come around the corner of the kitchen. She wore a baggy T-shirt that advertised Hank's and a pair of baggy jeans. She stopped short when she saw Robin sitting at the table.

"Hey. I expected you to be sleeping."

Robin shrugged and sucked on her peppermint. "I guess I'm not used to napping." She stared at Sarah while the young woman rummaged in the refrigerator and pulled out salad makings. "How did your test go?"

Sarah groaned as she tore off lettuce leaves and dropped them into a bowl. "Microbiology." She popped a cherry tomato into her mouth and grinned around the fruit. "But, I think I aced it. Whether or not I'll remember anything remains to be seen, but at least I got through the exam."

"That's great." Robin reached across the table and snagged a slice of cucumber from the bowl. "Your dip's in the fridge."

"Thanks, Robin. I appreciate that."

The front door opened and shut again. Seconds later, Maxine footed into the kitchen looking as if she were dashing toward an unseen finish line. She wore a plum colored skirt and a white silk blouse, and somehow had all of that hair contained in a stylish twist on the back of her head. Robin thought that the contrast between her two sisters was almost comical.

"Hi honey, I'm home. What's for lunch?" she grinned, looking over Sarah's shoulder. She snagged a slice of carrot from the bowl.

"If you two want some of this, I can make a bigger salad," Sarah frowned.

Robin winked at Maxine and snuck a tomato. "Don't be silly. We can just eat off of yours."

Maxine kicked her heels off, pulled out a chair, and sat down. "You have any meat to go with that?"

Sarah shuddered. "Do you know the types of hormones and other toxins they pump farm animals full of? How can you eat that?"

Maxine grinned and snatched a peppermint out of Robin's tin. "Luckily, I studied mundane things like art and drafting, and have no need for that kind knowledge. And after my double cheeseburger on my way home just now, I must say that ignorance is bliss." She turned her head and looked at her older sister. "You look tired."

"Don't I always look tired?" She stood and stretched, then threw the checkbook and calculator into a drawer. "I need to get ready to go to Hank's." She lifted her hair and let it fall. It was nearly dry. "What are you two doing tonight?"

Sarah carefully added extra virgin olive oil and a dash of vinegar to her salad. "I have to take that dip out to my parents'. I'll probably just spend the night there."

Maxine propped her feet on the chair Robin had just vacated and grinned. "I am taking the rest of the day off and treating myself to a mini-spa day. I have a hot date."

"You always have a hot date." Sarah grabbed a fork and sat down. "I don't see how you ever made it through college."

"It was definitely a juggling act." She stood and grabbed a glass out of the drainer on the side of the sink, flicking the faucet handle up, letting cool water fill the glass. "I had to work for this one, though. This guy ignored signals for months. I thought I was going to have to get a neon sign." She took a long pull of water as she sat back down.

Robin laughed on her way out of the room. "What? You don't have one?"

Maxine leaned the chair back and stuck her head through the doorway. "You're lucky I already took my shoes off, or I'd be throwing one at you."

The sound of Robin's laughter was muffled as she shut her door. Maxine sighed and looked at Sarah. "I'm getting worried about her."

Sarah reached behind her, opened the refrigerator door from her seat, and pulled out a bottle of water. "I don't think you have to worry about her. She's strong. Stronger than I could ever hope to be."

Maxine frowned. "I don't know. Every month that passes, she's losing something."

"What are you talking about?"

She shrugged, not really knowing how to word it. She thought about her conversation with Robin the night before. "Her spark for life, maybe."

Sarah stared at her while she chewed. She finally swallowed and slowly licked her lips. "Did she ever have one?"

Maxine looked at a spot above Sarah's shoulder and slowly nodded. "Yeah. It used to be there. It only showed when she wasn't paying attention, but it was definitely there."

"I think she just works too hard. I wish she'd let me take out a student loan or get a job or something. Anything that would help her out."

Maxine snorted. "Good luck trying. But, I think it's more than that. I can't quite put my finger on it. When I do, I'll figure out what to do."

Sarah pushed her bowl away and leaned forward. "Can I ask you something?"

Maxine shrugged. "Sure."

"Do you remember that night?"

A chill skirted up her spine, and the memory assaulted her. Suddenly, she was back in the dark closet, listening to the footsteps of the man coming closer. She shook it off and focused back on Sarah's face. "Yeah. Why?"

She looked behind her, then back at Maxine. "I don't remember any of it. Not even her. Sometimes, I get little flashes. Why is that? I was nine years old. How can I forget it?"

Memories crammed into the front of Maxine's mind. Normally, she kept them pushed so far back that she could go for days without remembering any of it. But like a slide show, they popped in front of her vision, one at a time. The dingy apartments, the smell of burning drugs, the rotten food, the odorous men. Ugh! So many men constantly coming and going.

She pushed it all away and realized that her hands had started to shake. "Trust me, honey, you don't want to remember."

ROBIN entered the lobby of Hotel Viscolli Boston. Green marble, elegant brass, high ceilings, starched uniforms, overstated elegance – it all formed together to one impression in her mind. Wealthy power. She swallowed hard, knowing that her black pants and white shirt, her old ugly clunky shoes and her worn canvas backpack made her look like a waif compared to the coifed, tucked, heeled women gracing the lobby. Steeling her shoulders against the aura of intimidation, she crossed the expanse of the marble foyer and found a smiling, uniformed brunette behind the counter.

"May I help you?" She singsonged.

On the wall above her head, scrolling brass read: *Whatever you do, work at it with all your heart, as working for the Lord, not for men. Colossians 3:23*

Robin kept from fidgeting. "I'd like to see Mr. Antonio Viscolli, please."

The woman gestured with her hand. "Mr. Viscolli's offices are on the twentieth floor. The elevators are right around that corner there."

Robin looked to where she pointed, saw the elevator sign, and looked back to her and said, "Thank you."

"You're very welcome," she said with an impossibly large smile. "Have a wonderful day."

Robin lost a little of the confidence she'd stored up to step into the lobby during the elevator ride up. She had almost changed her mind about it when the doors opened. Because a receptionist sitting behind a large half-mooned desk saw her and smiled, Robin felt obligated to step off of the elevator and into the lobby of the office floor. Her feet sank into the lush carpet and her eyes skimmed the leather furniture and black granite tables. While the lobby screamed wealth and power, this floor seemed to radiate it like an actual energy source. Robin's stomach clenched.

"Good afternoon. May I help you?" The receptionist asked.

"Yes." It came out a little hoarse, so Robin cleared her dry throat. Her eyes caught the scrolling brass on the wall behind the desk that said: *He has showed you, O man, what is good. And what does the Lord require of you? To act justly and to love mercy and to walk humbly with your God. Micah 6:8.* What was this place? A church or something?

"I'd like to see Mr. Viscolli, please."

"I'm sorry, but Mr. Viscolli is not in right now." She pulled a pink pad close to her and picked up a pen. "May I take your name?"

What was she going to do now? "Never mind. I'll –"

The woman looked over Robin's shoulder. "Mr. Viscolli!" She said, her voice a surprised gasp.

"Maggie." Robin felt her shoulders tense so tightly that it hurt. She would have recognized that rich, baritone voice without the receptionist's confirmation. "I stopped in the lobby and grabbed a smoothie, so I decided to take the front elevator." Robin turned. He wore shorts and a golf shirt, his tanned legs and muscled arms somehow not looking out of place in the elegant business reception area. "Please hold any –" As their eyes met, his sentence faltered. His forward motion ceased so quickly that some of the drink in his hand threatened to slosh over the side of his cup. He stared at her and his mouth opened and closed once. "I –"

Not waiting for him to demand a reason for her presence there or, worse yet, not recognize her at all, Robin pulled the envelope full of money out of her pocket and slapped it against his chest. "I can't stay. I just wanted to return this."

She let go of it and the envelope fell to the carpet. He still hadn't moved. She ignored it and rushed past him to the elevators, frantically pushing the button and hoping that the car was still on this floor.

"I'm not what you think I am," she said. She looked back at him. He had moved enough to turn and continue staring at her, but the money still lay at his feet. "I never have been and I never will be." Wanting to cry with relief as the door slid open immediately, she stepped into the car and hit the button to take her to the lobby. As the doors closed on his astounded expression, she said, "Never."

While the elevator glided its downward decent, Robin leaned against the mahogany walls and put her hands against her chest. Her heart pounded in her ears. Goodness, but he was a handsome man. Infuriating, but handsome. She closed her eyes and leaned her head back, willing her heart to resume its normal rhythm so that she could catch her breath.

Chapter 4

ROBIN cornered Hank in the dry storage room. "What is this?" she asked, waving the schedule for next week in one hand. The corners were torn from where she ripped it off of the bulletin board.

He looked up from his inventory clipboard and peered at the paper. "It would appear to be the schedule for the week beginning tomorrow." He dipped his head down and looked at her over his half-eyes. "Why do you have it all balled up in your hand?"

"Because, once again, I'm not bartending. Last week, you had me waitress, food prep, hostess. This week I'm doing food ordering and hostessing? I need the tips from bartending, Hank. You know that. What's going on?"

Hank rubbed the back of his neck. "I, ah…" He cleared his throat. "Listen. I need an assistant manager. Marjorie is wanting to be down in Florida more and more, with the kids. The work here, our work here, is really getting in her way of enjoying her grandchildren."

Robin smiled at the thought of Hank's wife, doting on her 'grandbabies' as she called them. "I bet."

He took off his reading glasses and slipped them into his front pocket. "I thought I'd schedule you around the restaurant, give you a feel of all of the other jobs, then offer it to you."

"Offer what to me?"

"The position."

For a moment, she had nothing to say. "Me?"

Hank inhaled deeply then huffed out the air. "I don't really know how to tell you this. Okay. I'll just spit it out." He moved quickly, put a large hand on her small shoulder. "I love you like one of my own, Robin. You and your sisters. Helping you out, making sure you got custody of Maxi was one of the things I know I did good in my life. You're one of the reasons this restaurant has flourished the way it has, one of the reasons that I can retire and know I made a success out of two careers."

She licked her lips and fought panic. "Retire?"

He nodded. "Retire. We're selling out, heading south to be with the kids."

"Selling out?" Her hand trembled in his, so she pulled it away. "You're leaving me?"

He sighed and sat down on a pallet of flour. "The new owner, he's going to close down the bar. I wanted to get you into the assistant manager position before the transition was final so that you'd be locked in."

Robin paced the small room. "What will happen to us? All of us? We just get dumped?"

Color was coming back to her face, so he relaxed and shook his head. "No. It's a condition of the contract. You all stay, benefits and everything."

She whirled around. "Contract? You've already done this?"

"Yesterday."

"Yesterday, as in Friday?" The hurt in her voice was like a tangible thing. She could hear it dripping over every word. She hated showing that weakness. "You didn't even think to tell me?" Robin quickly turned her back and buried her face in her hands. As surreptitiously as possible, dug her fists into her burning eyes. She felt so tired, so very tired. She turned and stared at him. "Sorry. I have to go."

He was off of his perch and in front of the door before she had even turned all the way around. "We'll finish this."

"You've already finished it. You're leaving. You're abandoning me." Her voice trembled.

He put his hands on her shoulders and squeezed. "No, Robin, I'm not. You're almost done. Two more years, right? You have this job guaranteed for at least that long." He gave her a small shake. "I didn't think you could do it. I never told you that. You've held out though, and you've made me proud. As proud as a dad can be for his daughter. But, this is something me and the wife need to do. And I'm leaving you in good hands."

Weary now that the short burst of adrenaline left her, she rested her face on his chest and let his strong arms envelop her. "I'll miss you so much."

He kissed the top of her head and squeezed her tight. "I'll just be waiting for you to take a vacation, come down and visit once Sarah's done."

Her words were muffled against his flannel shirt. "Deal."

SUNDAY was her day off. It was always her day off, and everyone knew it. She knew she had to have at least one day to completely recoup.

She rarely got in from Hank's before one in the morning, and she would fall onto her bed and sleep until at least noon. Eventually she would make it out of bed, drink a cup of coffee, eat a really big breakfast that Maxine usually prepared, then fall back asleep for a few hours.

Sunday nights she reserved for lounging on the couch, watching television or reading a book. Sometimes, her sisters persuaded her to go with them to see a movie, but those times were few and far between. It was the one day she was able to be home, and she rarely liked to leave.

She woke up this Sunday with a horrible headache. It didn't surprise her, considering the fact that sleep evaded her that morning. The last time she'd looked at the clock, the blurry numbers of 6:27 stared back at her. When she rolled back over, 11:13 signaled the end of trying to sleep. Sadness overwhelmed her. Loss of an important part of her life threatened what tiny bit of security she'd managed to build around her over the last seven years.

Hank had never been just her employer. He'd hired her just days after his youngest daughter moved from home, and Robin had easily slid right into her place. Hank's wife, Marjorie, suffering under some severe empty nest syndrome took her under her wing in her own gentle way.

Hank found her in the back alley the day that she received the rejection on her petition to be Maxine's guardian. An eighteen-year-old bartender wasn't a viable candidate for guardianship of an impressionable young fifteen-year-old. That was what the case worker had said. Of course, Robin had retorted back on the phone to her that the foster father who'd raped her couldn't be considered better, but the case worker had turned deaf ears on her pleas, and had given her a flat no.

He'd found her with the letter crumpled in her fist, shaking with rage in the back alley. No tears fell from her eyes, but it was a struggle to contain them when he'd pulled her into his arms and listened to her story. She told him the whole sordid tale. For the first time, she laid her entire life out. It sounded tragic to her own ears, and after he silently listened to every word, his large hands curled into fists and a muscle ticked in his jaw where he clenched his teeth.

So Hank had pulled strings. Retiring so high up in the chain of command in the Navy gave him high strings to pull. He wrote letters to the social services, ensuring that Robin would only work shifts that correlated with school hours as long as Maxine was a minor, and ensured that his own wife would watch over her in the summer months. He made telephone calls, took people to lunch, and – Robin was sure – issued a few veiled threats, until the day Maxine sat in her apartment, finally in a safe, permanent home.

Hank made it happen. Without him, Robin didn't know where her fragile family would be. She loved him only second to her sisters, and knew that she would lose a part of herself when he left.

She'd never really cried in her adult life, couldn't remember the last time a genuine tear had fallen from her eyes. So much had happened in her life that she feared if she started crying about it all, she would never stop. Still, the back of her throat ached as she lay in her bed and stared at the ceiling.

Silence hung over the apartment like a cloak. Sarah was likely at church and Maxine must be off somewhere. She didn't even have anyone to complain to or whine to, and that seemed to make it worse.

She groaned and rolled out of bed. Hank's didn't open until four on Sundays, but he would be there. That was his quiet time, to catch up on paperwork and do whatever he needed to do. Maybe she could talk him into making her lunch, let them have an afternoon like they used to have before she started putting sisters through college.

If the chill last night was any indication, the Indian summer was over and Fall was definitely in the air, so she dressed to suit the weather. She noticed as she buttoned her jeans that she'd lost some more weight, but simply shrugged it off and secured the pants with a leather belt. She added a white T-shirt, a green and blue flannel shirt, and a pair of hiking boots, and was out of the apartment within fifteen minutes.

She lived close enough to Hank's to walk it. The early afternoon air crisply stung her cheeks, but her eyes watered against the bright sun shining against the deep blue sky. As she inhaled the cool air and slipped a pair of sunglasses on her nose, she decided that just being outside in the daylight without deadlines or appointments was enough to lift her spirits.

There were a few cars in the parking lot, one of which was Hank's, but she didn't pay attention to the others. They could have belonged to patrons who'd been too intoxicated to make their way home the night before. They could have belonged to people from the city who had headed to their little corner for antique shopping. Either way, she was unprepared for anyone else to be in the building when she walked inside.

She stepped through the entrance and stood just inside, slipping off her sunglasses so that her eyes could pan the room. She stood near the hostess stand, and looked around. Marjorie had done an amazing job decorating the interior of Hank's. The Spanish tile floor created a stunning terra cotta and beige pattern through the rooms. Black tablecloths covered square tables, and charcoal drawings of turn-of-the-century Boston covered the beige walls. Off to her right and through double frosted glass doors was her former territory. The bar acted as its own entity and was only opened up to the main restaurant when the wait for a table was long enough to justify sending patrons to the bar for a drink. The doors stood closed now, and Robin went in that direction, wanting to take a long look before the new owners took it away.

Twenty black leather barstools surrounded the large circular bar. Ten small circular tables were placed around the rest of the room, providing a place for two or three people to perch on high chairs or stand while waiting for a table. Two large flat screen televisions adorned the small room, one always turned to a sports station and the other always on a 24 hour news station but on mute with closed captioning enabled. The opposite side of the room had access to the patio area, and on warm summer days, half of the wall would slide out and a tiki-bar could be set up to serve drinks and appetizers.

Never again would a warm summer breeze blow on her while she made frozen drinks and laughed with college students enjoying the relaxed summer schedule. Never again would another football season crowd so thick force her waitresses to access her through the kitchen door. Seven years of seasons coming and going suddenly ended. What now?

Tony Viscolli came through the kitchen door and saw her, staring at the patio doors with a mournful expression on her face. He took the opportunity to silently observe her, knowing she would tense up as soon as she saw him.

She'd worn her hair down today. He had never seen it down, had no idea how long it actually was. It shined around her head, a glowing, cascading mass that fell halfway down her back. He almost chuckled aloud at the romantic description, but anything else seemed too tame. He wanted to feel it entwine itself around his fingers.

He was losing his mind.

He'd seen her several times over the past two weeks, at Benedict's and at the bar, and while he made it a point to ensure she did not serve him, he also made it a point to be where he could watch her.

She'd given him his tip money back, every dime. With his confused receptionist watching, he'd observed the elevator doors close on Robin then laughed out loud. If he wasn't already intrigued to the point of obsession, that would certainly have been the trigger.

While he'd contemplated the notion of having her researched several times over the last two weeks, he decided against it. He definitely had the resources, but he decided that he would learn what made her tick the old fashioned way.

When she walked farther into the room, far enough away from the door to prohibit a quick exit, he finally decided it was time to make his presence known. He stepped forward and pretended to cough.

She turned toward the sound, and he watched her face the very second recognition dawned in those blue, blue eyes. Sapphires. She needed a band of sapphires around her neck, encased in platinum.

"You!" As their eyes clashed, her face hardened and she froze. "What are you doing here?"

His eyebrow quirked upward. His lips barely twisted into a sardonic grin. "I could ask you the same question."

"That's none of your business."

"Oh," he said, opening the small refrigerator under the bar and pulling out a tonic water. "I disagree."

She surged forward and slapped her palm on the top of the bar. "You can't be back there." She watched as he reached above his head and pulled down two glasses. "What are you doing? Get away from there."

He poured half of the bottle into one glass and half in the other. "Here. Have one."

He stayed behind the bar. It was better to keep something immobile between them. It kept her from scratching his eyes out, and it kept him from touching her.

She was furious.

And magnificent.

"Don't make me call the police, Mr. Viscolli."

He chuckled. It made her seethe. "And what would you say the charges should be, Robin?"

"Trespassing, theft. I'm sure there's more. Did you break in?"

He took a long swallow of his drink, a diamond winking on his little finger. "Sorry. None of those charges would stick."

She moved behind the bar and snatched the glass from his hand. She dumped both glasses out in the sink and turned the water on. "I wouldn't be so sure," she snapped.

"Oh, I am. You can't trespass on your own property."

The glasses clattered into the sink, forgotten. She turned and stared at him with wide, almost panicked eyes. "Your property?"

He stepped forward and reached behind her. She took a quick step back, then felt color flood her face when he simply turned off the water at the sink. He stood close enough now that she could smell his cologne. "Signed and sealed. They might haul you away for trespassing, of course."

"No," she said. Her eyes darted to the left and right. "Where's Hank?"

He inclined his head toward the kitchen, and she turned and ran without a backward glance.

Robin slammed the kitchen doors open and immediately spotted Hank at the stove. "Do you have any idea what you've just done?"

He turned at the sound of her voice and grinned the second he saw her. "Robin! Come in, come in." He had a spatula in his hand, and waved it toward the stainless steel counter. "Barry Anderson, Robin Bartlett." He smiled at her and turned back to the stove. "You're in time to eat one of my burgers."

She looked at the guy sitting at the counter without actually seeing him. "Hi," she said distractedly, then immediately rounded back on Hank. "Do you have any idea who you just sold your place to?"

With an expert flick of his wrist, he turned the frying meat over on the grill. "Sure. Tony Viscolli. Nice kid. I like him."

"He isn't nice and he isn't a kid."

"You'll like him once you get to know him." He moved to the wall and opened the oven to check on something in there, then shut the door before he turned and winked at her. "He comes across a little hard at first, but then you get to know him."

"Hank," she started, then remembered she had an audience. Then she didn't care that she had an audience. "Hank, I've served him at Benedict's."

He whistled under his breath while he set rolls out on the counter. "I forget sometimes that you know several of the more prominent people in the city."

She wanted to scream. "Hank, listen to me. You can't sell your place to him."

Her tone suddenly reached him, and he stopped all movement and looked full at her. "What are you talking about?"

"I'm telling you. I served him at Benedict's. Hank, he implied that I could be bought."

His expression was blank for a moment, before rage over took it. "What are you talking about?" he bellowed.

She crossed her arms over her chest and lifted her chin. "Just that. He implied he could buy me. You'll just have to tear up the contracts."

"Tony wouldn't do that. You're either mistaken or lying." The man at the counter spoke for the first time, and she whipped her head around to look at him.

"How do you know?"

"Because I know." He rose to his feet and she had to lift her head to keep eye contact. "He wouldn't, and he wouldn't have to."

"He did."

"I seriously doubt it."

She recognized him now. He drank a Shirley Temple one night a couple of weeks ago in the bar. Then she suddenly realized where she'd seen Viscolli that day at Benedict's when she'd been sure that she'd seen him before. They'd come in together, a Shirley Temple and a ginger ale. "He all but said the words."

"That's not the same as saying them."

Dismissing him, because he was clearly Tony's crony, she turned her attention back to Hank. "Listen to me, he – "

"What exactly did he say?" Barry asked.

She sighed, and with an embarrassed flush, she relayed the conversation she'd had with that man.

Hank frowned and looked at Barry then back at Robin. "You could almost read anything into that, Robin."

"You can't read anything into it that isn't there."

Barry interrupted again. "Maybe he was simply flirting."

"Flirting?" She turned and faced him fully. "Mr. Anderson, I've worked at Benedict's for six years. The men who are members there and who dine there do not flirt with the wait staff. They sleep with them, pay them – or some of them anyway – but there is no casual flirting."

He raised an eyebrow. "In the last six years, have you ever served Antonio Viscolli?"

"Not that I can recall, other than that one time."

"Don't be so quick to lump him into a category, Miss Bartlett. You'll find he doesn't fit."

Snarling at the man who was so obviously the greaseball's wingman, she turned back to Hank. "Are you not going to pay any attention to what I told you?"

He glared at her. "Don't be insulting, Robin. I heard every word and I'll look into it."

"But – "

"I said I'd look into it."

She let out a breath and nodded. "Okay. Okay, thanks." She turned and looked at the other man, but didn't speak. Then she started toward the back door. "I'm going back home and going back to bed."

Chapter 5

GROWING up, Tony knew nothing of boundaries or rules. When he gave his life to the Lord, he made a personal vow to always play by the rules. Usually, he did. In this case, though, he felt he had to cross a few boundaries – not necessarily break rules, but just toe a line. Or two. Today those boundaries included looking through personnel files until he obtained a certain home address.

He climbed the threadbare stairs to the third floor, walked down the long hallway, and scanned the apartment numbers on the doors until he came to the one he sought. He paused, took a deep breath and rapped on the door with his bare knuckles.

He expected Robin to open the door, take one look at him, and snarl. To his surprise, when the door swung open, he came face to face with one of the most beautiful women he'd ever seen. She stood nearly as tall as he, with long straight black hair, almond shaped eyes, and dark skin. She was obviously of Native American descent, but her green eyes told a story of mixed blood.

"May I help you?" she asked over the rock music pounding out of the stereo from somewhere in the apartment.

Giving her his warmest smile, he slipped his hands in his pockets and rocked back on his heels. "I'm looking for Robin."

"Robin?" She raised an eyebrow. "Really?"

"Robin Bartlett. She does live here, doesn't she?"

She grinned at him while she crossed her arms over her chest and leaned against the door frame. "My sister Robin? A man is here to see my sister Robin?"

It was impossible not to return her smile. "I would hope that's what I am."

She laughed and straightened. "Please, come in. If you're a psycho with a knife, just don't sneak up behind me. I really hate that." She held her hand out. "I'm Maxine. Call me Maxi."

He gave her cool fingers a slight squeeze. "Tony."

She gestured toward a worn couch as she flipped off the stereo. "Have a seat. I have no idea where she went or when she'll be back, but I'm guessing it will be soon. It's Sunday, and she's always home on Sundays."

He nodded as he sat on the couch and relaxed against the cushions. "Actually, I saw her not twenty minutes ago."

Maxine raised an eyebrow. Tony could tell she wanted to ask questions, but refrained. "Can I offer you anything to drink, Tony?"

"No, thanks." He leaned forward with his knees on his elbows. "I should warn you, though. Robin won't exactly be excited to see me."

Maxine started laughing. "Oh, this is too good," she said. Still laughing, she gestured at her outfit of shorts and an oversized sweatshirt. "Excuse me while I change into something more appropriate for company." Her voice carried to him as she walked down the hallway. "This is just too good."

He stayed where she had seated him, but inspected the room in her absence. It could have fit into his closet, he thought, wondering how two girls lived together in such a small space. There was room for the couch, an overstuffed chair, a scarred coffee table, and crammed into the corner was a small television. A bar separated the kitchen from the living room. The kitchen looked like it was just big enough to have the smallest of tables in it. One person would be cramped living here for any length of time.

Seconds later, Maxine returned, still in the sweatshirt, but now wearing a pair of jeans. "So, what brings you here today, Tony?"

He toyed with the ring on his finger. "I thought I'd try to convince your sister to celebrate my birthday with me tonight." He glanced at her. "Think I could talk her into it?"

Throwing herself onto the couch opposite him, she curled her legs underneath her and grinned. "You say you don't think she'll really appreciate you coming by?"

"Yes, though that may be an understatement."

She laughed again. "Oh, this will be good."

He cut her a look from the corner of his eyes. "You keep saying that."

She reached out with a long arm and playfully poked his shoulder. "Are you sure you're not an ax murderer or a bill collector?"

He frowned. "I'm afraid not. Why do you ask?"

"Because you may wish you had some kind of weapon before it's all said and done." She looked at her watch. "If she's not back by two, I'm going to have to call and cancel a date. I can't miss this."

Remembering the spark in Robin's eyes the last time she looked at him, Tony smiled.

Both heads turned expectantly as the door opened, and Tony watched a woman walk in whose frame was small enough that she could easily pass for a child. She had curly, curly brown hair and an almost porcelain complexion. She made him think of a pixie.

"Hello," she said in a soft voice, staring at him with large hazel eyes set behind a pair of wire framed glasses. "Are you Dwayne?"

Maxine laughed. "No, he's not coming until two." Maxine gestured between the two. "Sarah, Tony. Tony, my sister Sarah." She grinned at her sister. "Sarah, Tony's here to see Robin."

Sarah's eyes widened and she slowly lowered herself into the chair. "Robin? Really?" She looked at Tony again, a closer inspection, and the wonder on her face grew. "Our Robin? Goodness."

Tony began to question whether coming here had been a wise decision. He shifted uncomfortably and leaned forward, putting his elbows on his knees. "Maybe I should just come back another time."

Maxine sprang to her feet. "No. No, don't do that." She looked at her sister and back at Tony. "We're not trying to make you uncomfortable. I apologize. We're just surprised, that's all."

"Why?"

Maxine shoved her hands in her pockets and ran her tongue over her teeth. "Well … " The door opened, cutting off her next words.

Tony felt a little anticipated excitement skirt along his spine. This time Robin entered, carrying a grocery sack, her face flushed from the bite of Fall in the air. "You aren't going to believe this," she said. She had her back to them, securing the locks on the door as she spoke. "I was just at Hank's … "

She turned around and froze. Her eyes darted from Tony to Maxine to Sarah and back to Tony. "Oh, you have got to be kidding me!"

He smoothly made it to his feet. "Hello, Robin."

She bared her teeth at him. "You're like a bad penny. No. A bad dream." She stormed toward the kitchen. "A nightmare."

Wondering if it was wise, especially considering the innumerable weapons that could be found in a standard kitchen, he followed her. He leaned against the doorway and watched her slam the bag of groceries onto the top of a small table. He watched her open and shut cupboards nearly hard enough to break them off at the hinges as she put the items away. The whole time she muttered under her breath.

He flinched a little at her colorful language before he spoke. "I talked to Hank right after you left."

She whirled around, surprised to see him right there. "Did I ask?"

He continued as though she had. "I feel it is important for us to clear the air."

The grocery bag was empty and she suddenly had nothing to do with her hands. Feeling like she was at an incredible disadvantage, she leaned against the small stove and crossed her arms over her chest. "So you invade my house and consume my personal time? If you want to clear the air, you can do it during my working hours."

He straightened and came all the way into the room, filling up the small space, stopping just a few feet from her. "This has nothing to do with business, Robin. It's all personal."

"Nothing between us is personal."

He moved forward one more step. She could almost feel the heat radiating from his body. "I think that there is a very serious misunderstanding between us that needs to be cleared up right away."

She tilted her chin up, almost looked down her nose at him. He had to bite the inside of his lip to keep from grinning. "Are you talking about your implication that I could be bought?"

He held up a finger. "See? There it is. I never implied that."

"Ha!" She straightened and threw her hair over her shoulder. "Now you're a liar and a jerk. Wow. All of the things I thought about you are panning out to be true. And they say one should never judge by first impressions alone." His eyes hardened and for the slightest moment, she felt fear. Then she got mad at the feeling. "Go away."

"At what point did I imply that you would be willing to trade sex for money?"

She stepped forward and put her hands on her hips. He didn't think she realized that they were almost nose to nose. "You implied it when you said my job was in your hands and then asked me what I'd do to keep it. You acted on it when you left me that tip."

Her eyes had darkened to near indigo, and they sizzled with anger. He resisted every urge inside him that screamed to touch her, to soothe her. "That tip wasn't payment to get you into my bed."

"No?" She raised an eyebrow. "Was its purpose not to make me remember you, to fawn after you, to perhaps flirt back the next time you happened to be seated at a table I serve?"

He saw where she was leading and grinned. "Yeah."

"Then I would be flattered that the oh so rich Antonio Viscolli actually showed an interest in little dirt poor me, and then I would perhaps jump at the opportunity for a date with you, which would, I'm sure, be scheduled out to end up with us having sex."

He couldn't take it anymore. Just one touch, whether or not he lost the finger. He reached out and found a strand of her hair, letting it wind its way around his finger. "It isn't quite as cut and dry as that, Robin."

His voice was very quiet. She felt it almost as much as she heard it, and his words sent a thrill through her that she didn't recognize or understand. But she didn't like it, especially coming from him. "Please don't touch me."

For a long time he searched her eyes, holding her stare until she wanted to twitch. Then he let go of her hair and stepped away. Shaking with rage, she pushed past him and stormed out of the kitchen. Maxine and Sarah weren't even hiding the fact that they had been standing at the bar, listening to the entire conversation. "I'm going to bed," she told them through gritted teeth. She stopped just before her bedroom door and threw over her shoulder, "Alone."

Sarah and Maxine cringed at the sound of the bedroom door slamming, but Tony leaned against the bar on the kitchen side. "Well," he said, "that went better than I'd anticipated."

Sarah looked at him with her mouth open. "Are you out of your mind? What was it that went so well?"

"Well," he breathed between clenched teeth, "I'm not bleeding, I still have all of my operating parts, and my voice isn't ten octaves higher."

Maxine started laughing, laughing so hard she had to sit on an arm of the chair. She laughed until tears ran out of her face, then slowly straightened and wiped her eyes. Tony couldn't help smiling in return. "Oh, I like you. Can I keep you?"

Sarah looked between the two of them and shook her head. "Maybe you should leave," she said to Tony. "I don't know you and I don't think that Robin wants you here."

Maxine stood up and brushed Sarah off with the wave of her hand. "Don't be ridiculous. It's his birthday. We must celebrate."

"Maxine," Sarah said under her breath. "Robin … "

"… needs this." She rounded the corner to the kitchen and elbowed Tony out of her way. "Move over. I'm going to bake you a cake."

"You're going to bake me a cake?" He stared at her in disbelief.

"Sure." She turned her head and looked at her sister, who was staring at them both with a mixture of fear and excitement. "And Sarah's going to go to the store and buy the makings of a birthday feast."

Sarah took a step back and held up her hands as if to ward her off. "No way. I'm not having any part in this."

She dug through a drawer until she came up with a pen and a pad of paper. "Actually, Tony may need to go with you. I'm not going to trust you not to come back with tofu or sprouts or soy milk or some other inedible oddity."

She quickly wrote out a list then grabbed her purse off of the kitchen table. "Just around the corner is a little market. It should have everything you need, so you won't even have to drive." She pulled out her wallet and counted out some money. "Here. This should be enough."

He just looked at the money then back at her, feeling out of control of the situation for the first time in fifteen years. "Really, you don't have to do this."

"Don't be ridiculous. I think it's great." Since he wasn't moving, she picked up his hand and slapped the list and the money into his palm. "It's about time things got shaken up a bit around here."

He stared down at their joined hands. He could still smell Robin all around him, and suddenly thought that it was all a great idea. "Okay, but you don't need to give me any money. I can handle it."

"No one's buying their own dinner on their own birthday when I'm around." She turned him around and pushed between his shoulder blades. "Go on. I'll see you two back in a bit."

"Maxine," Sarah said. She was still standing in the same position. "I'm not having anything to do with this."

Maxine grinned at her while Tony held the door open, waiting. "Sure you are. You have to show him where the shop is. Don't be rude to our guest, Sarah."

Sarah tried to stare her down, but Tony watched as she fidgeted with her glasses then let out an uncomfortable breath. "I will accept no responsibility."

Maxine smiled. "What a surprise."

"When it all hits the fan, none of it is going to come back and hit me." She stepped out the door and turned around. "You hear me, Maxi?"

Maxine laughed and shut the door behind them.

SHE dreamt of him, in a very surreal, very light dream. They stood on the banks of a river, dressed in white. The warm sun shone down from a bright blue sky, and the softly blowing breeze caught the hem of her dress, slowly moving it around her bare legs.

He wore white trousers and a white top, making his skin seem darker, his teeth whiter. They laughed and danced on the grass while butterflies fluttered around them. Then his eyes grew serious and his lips touched hers.

Lost in each other, they fell onto the blanket that suddenly appeared on the grass at their feet. His mouth felt gentle, loving, glorious. Her hands moved in lazy patterns across his back, feeling the hard muscles, loving his strength. He raised his head and smiled down at her, and she saw the need inside her reflected in his eyes.

Then his eyes changed. They became light blue, glassy, red-rimmed. The face lightened, widened, hardened, until she was staring at HIM. The bank of the river disappeared, the grass faded, the air chilled. Suddenly, she was in her bed. The single bed with the lumpy mattress and dirty sheets.

A hand covered her mouth, forcing her to breathe through her nose, to smell the gin and tobacco on his breath, the stench making her stomach roll.

She started to fight, but her legs and arms were pinned by his huge body.

"You can't get away this time, little girl," he grunted in her ear.

She screamed, but the sound was muffled by his hand.

"Not a little girl, though, are ya? No, you're a woman. Or you will be, soon as I'm done with you." A hand gripped her breast, squeezed and twisted it until the pain made her vision gray. She realized that her nightgown was gone.

Vomit clawed at her throat. No matter how she resisted, she wasn't strong enough. A single tear rolled out of the corner of her eye while his laughter echoed in her head.

With a strangled cry, Robin clawed her way out of the dream, bolting into a sitting position on the bed. Her whole body quaked in the aftermath. Her hands trembled and her breath came in quick shaky gasps. Sweat poured over her body, and she lifted the damp tendrils of her bangs to wipe her forehead.

Years had gone by since she'd last had the dream. Sometimes, she dreamt through to the bitter end, sometimes she could pull herself out of it in time. It was so much worse if she didn't get out of it in time.

She was about to get out of the bed when she heard a noise in the other room. One or both of her sisters were home, so she stayed where she was, waiting for the effects of the dream to go away. She didn't want to carry the cobwebs of the nightmare out of the room with her.

She drew her legs up and rested her forehead against her knees. Her breathing slowly returned to normal. Her hands slowly stopped shaking, and the sweat cooled on her body.

Finally feeling normal again, she got out of bed, changed back into jeans and a loose top, and felt that she could face her sisters.

Wonderful smells assailed her nose when she opened her bedroom door. Something spicy and tangy was cooking, and her stomach rumbled in response. Every step toward the living room seemed lighter, and she almost had a smile on her face as she walked the last few steps.

She smelled it first; the underlying smell of expensive cologne. Then she heard him; that deep chuckle that sent a shiver over her spine. Maxine had better have a new boyfriend who wore costly aftershave and was annoyingly happy all the time. Then she saw him, sitting forward on the couch, a glass of water in his hand. His attention was on Maxine, and he had that irritatingly irresistible grin on his face again.

"Oh, you've got to be kidding me," she said.

SAPPHIRE ICE - CHAPTER 6

TONY slowly set his glass down while he mentally prepared himself for the attack. He let his eyes casually take Robin in, noting her hands clenched into fists as they rested on her hips, recognizing the flush of anger as it moved up her neck to her face.

God, he prayed silently, in his mind, give me wisdom and patience. I feel like You brought her into my life for a purpose. Keep me from reacting or acting in the wrong way. Keep me strong and keep me pure and tell me what I'm supposed to do here. Amen.

She was magnificent. He wanted nothing more than to see her smile. He wanted to rub the tension away from her face, to hug her in his arms.

He smoothly rose to his feet and walked toward her. Her sisters left his mind. Nothing around him existed except her. He never even paused his advance, his whole focus on her face. Something was there in her eyes. Dark shadows that leapt at the edges, interfering with the angry sparks that were for him alone. He wanted to make the shadows disappear. He wanted to have the right to ask her about them. But it wasn't his right. Not yet.

"This is my house," she spat at him, "and I don't want you here."

He grinned. His bold approach worked. Shadows started moving out of her eyes as irritation replaced them. "You aren't the one who invited me." He'd finally reached her and stood inches away. "What is the matter?" he asked her quietly.

Her eyes widened before they narrowed. "You."

He shook his head. "No. Something else." He reached out and put a hand on each shoulder, squeezing gently. She was too thin. She needed to gain some weight. He felt an overwhelming urge to pull her to him, to shield her from the world, to give her everything his considerable empire could offer. Only, he knew the last place she wanted to be was in his arms, so he squeezed her shoulders one more time and stepped back. "Your sister has invited me to dinner."

As he spoke, the timer went off with a loud, "Ding!" in the kitchen.

Robin looked past Tony to Maxine. "My sister?"

"Looks like dinner's ready," Maxine said, hopping up from the couch. "I'll just set it out and we can eat."

"Why did my sister invite you to dinner?"

Maxine was in the kitchen opening the oven door before she spoke. "We're celebrating his birthday."

Robin felt her jaw drop. "We?" she asked. She moved to the entrance of the kitchen.

Maxine winked. "I am." She pulled a pan out of the oven and set it on the small stove. As she took the oven mitts off her hands, she turned and faced Robin. "Oh, by the way, Tony's my guest. You want to eat what I cooked, you'll have to eat with him. You don't like it, leave."

Robin rounded on Sarah. "And how much of this was your idea?"

"I had nothing to do with it." Sarah sank into cushions of the couch. "I accept absolutely no responsibility for this."

Maxine leaned over the bar. "Dinner's ready."

Robin jumped as Tony's hand came up and squeezed the back of her neck. "Smells great," he said, giving her neck a reassuring squeeze before inching past her in the doorway. It bothered her that his touch actually reassured her. She should feel annoyed that he felt like he could touch her at all.

She entered the room and pulled her chair out. Maxine had pulled the spare chair out of her bedroom and shifted the table away from the wall so that four chairs would fit around it. Sarah squeezed past them and claimed the spot in the corner against the wall and Maxine sat next to her, closest to the stove. That forced Robin next to Tony, who sat between Maxine and Robin.

As he sat, he held his hands out, palms up. "Do you mind if I bless the meal?"

Sarah, whose parents did things like pray before meals, was the one who answered. "Of course. Thank you."

Tony looked at Robin until she, reluctantly, followed Sarah's lead and placed her hand in his. She felt Maxine take her other hand, but could only concentrate on the feel of Tony's palm against her own. She bowed her head and closed her eyes. Soon, the rich tones of his voice flowed over her, and for the first time since her dream, she felt herself relaxing, felt peace edge its way into the corners of her mind.

"Father God, we thank You for this time of new friendship and fellowship. Thank You for Maxine's generous heart that is keeping me from spending this anniversary of my birth alone. Thank You for bringing this family of sisters into my life. Pour out Your blessings into their lives and enrich them, Father. Thank You for my life. Thank You for all of the ways You have brought such joy to my life, including this wonderful meal. Please bless it and bless the hands that made it. In Your precious holy Son's name, Amen."

He let go of Robin's hand after giving it a squeeze. She raised her head and put her hand into her lap, gripping it with the other. What just happened?

Sarah took the lead and picked up the spoon in the dish of potatoes in front of her. "This smells wonderful, Maxi."

Robin had never seen Maxine off balance before and was intrigued by the way she just blinked before shaking her head and coming out of it. She smiled broadly. "Thank you." She picked up a platter of chicken and handed it over to Tony. "Please eat as much as you want. There is more than plenty."

Robin recovered from the prayer and glared at Tony while he loaded his plate and picked up his fork and dug in. Robin had no appetite, but she put some sparse servings on her plate and pushed food around while she listened, refusing to interact. Instead, she forced the anger toward him back, intentionally remembering the insult so that she didn't fall under the spell that he apparently wove around her sisters' better judgement.

They laughed at every inane thing he said and blushed like students at a junior high dance when he looked at them. Robin remained unaffected, though. She knew his game and could see right through it. She might have been a lowly servant to him, but she'd been dealing with the public for years and knew how to read into unspoken words and body language.

He was trying to charm her by charming her sisters. What if she occasionally let her guard down and he did just that? Then she'd remember, and slam the walls right back up.

The comfort in his touch softened her. It unnerved her. She'd admit it to herself, if to no one else.

She'd spent the first half of her life avoiding men. The types of the male species that her mother brought home were always far from respectable, and most had lived their lives in a glorification of evil. Then there were the foster fathers. Two of them had tried the same things that her mother's boyfriends always had. One managed to get to Maxine before Robin could get to him, and she was lucky the foster mother had been disgusted and sickened with her husband, or Robin could have easily been faced with criminal charges after stabbing him in the shoulder with his own hunting knife.

Boys in high school had paid very little attention to her. She guessed, looking back now with an adult's eyes, that she had intimidated them. When she'd finally been settled into a relatively good home for girls – and while she made excellent grades and learned quickly – she was so far behind in school that she went to an alternative all-girls' school until she finally dropped out.

Her defenses were sharpened even further working so young as a bartender. The advances from the patrons would just get worse and worse as the nights wore on and they continued to drink. By the time she'd started working at Benedict's, her defense was a perfect air of disinterest, leaving the customers who might otherwise have been interested with the first impression not even to make the attempt.

So, she was twenty-eight years old and had absolutely no experience in dealing with men, unless it was to serve them lunch or a drink. She didn't know how to interact with a man – especially a man like Tony – on any level. Then he had to go and comfort her as if wanting nothing in return, right at one of those moments when everything was bared naked from her dream. Right when all she wanted was someone else's back to be stronger than hers. There he was. He made her want something she never wanted before.

She hated him and wished she had the energy to tell him. Instead, she just sat at her little table that now seemed too small because he occupied a chair, eating food that she was certain would taste good if it didn't all seem to turn to sawdust in her mouth, and watching him charm the socks right off of her own flesh and blood.

When Maxine jumped up and whipped a cake out of the refrigerator, she was sure she was going to throw up. Not able to take any more, she pushed away from the table. "You'll have to excuse me," she said as sickly sweet as possible, "but I have some things to do."

She refused to meet his eyes, gave Maxine a look that left no doubt about how she felt about the entire night, and went to her room. Not knowing what else to do that would get her out of there at eight o'clock on a Sunday night, she grabbed her bag of laundry and stormed out of the apartment, slamming the door as hard as she could on her way out.

The fact that the laundry room was empty helped. She was in no mood to be pleasant or even cordial. It afforded her the privacy and the opportunity to slam things around, to kick a couple of machines and listen to the satisfying clang of the metal. Only when her laundry was sorted, loaded into the machines, and starting the wash cycle did she feel like she had calmed down somewhat.

The room would have looked small even without the four washing machines and dryers, so the only thing to sit on was a lone table that had been shoved into a corner. Most of the time, she risked the possible theft of her clothes to wait for the wash upstairs in her own apartment, but she had no desire to go back up there. Instead, she tested the strength of the table, decided it would probably hold her weight, and scooted on top of it.

There was a day old newspaper on the table, and for lack of anything better to do, she decided to read it. She skimmed headlines and glanced at pictures without actually retaining anything she saw. Instead, of its own volition, her mind drifted back to dinner.

She tried to get a grip back on the anger, but it had faded away. All she could think about was the way his hand felt as it held hers during his prayer. It was almost as if she could still feel him, the heat of his hand, the strength. Closing her eyes, she thought back and almost completely recaptured the moment.

Was it actually possible to be so comfortable around a man that she could enjoy feeling her hand in his? Had she truly been missing something? Maxine had told her several times she was missing out on the best things in life by pushing men away from her. Maybe Maxine was right. Robin tried but was unable to come up with anything that had ever felt so comforting in such a simple manner.

She knew that not all men were like the ones her mother brought home. It wasn't that. She just simply refused to need a man, and since so many women she worked with and knew fell prey time and time again, allowed themselves to be chewed up and spit out, she really didn't see what she'd been missing.

Except now all she could think about was Tony. If the feelings inside of her were normal, she could almost understand the waitresses she worked with continually falling victim to the men in their lives. Maybe it was time to learn. Maybe Maxine had a point.

She certainly had a willing partner. He was only looking for sex, after all. Perhaps she should just go for it. What could it hurt? Unlike some of the desperate waitresses at Benedicts hoping to score a rich man, she'd be going into it with open eyes, expecting nothing else out of it. She had a feeling that Mr. Antonio Viscolli preferred it that way. He could teach her the ropes, so to speak, and they could go their separate ways soon after. She guessed he'd be around Hank's for another week at the most, then he'd hand the reins over to a manager and that little corner of Boston would no longer hold his attention. Having a physical relationship might even make his constant presence during the transition at least endurable.

A week would be enough time. At least it should. Since she didn't really know what she was talking about, she was going into it rather blindly.

How to approach him, though? She thought about it while she transferred clothes from the washers to the dryers. A direct approach would be best. He wasn't the type to play games, obviously. It had to be soon, too. She had his attention now. Who knew what tomorrow would bring.

Tonight. She should catch him before he left. Leaving everything where it was, she burst out of the laundry room and took the first flight of stairs two at a time. She hit the first landing and rounded the corner, only to slam right into the chest of the man she was in such a hurry to see.

"Whoa, slow down," he said, gripping her arms to keep her from falling backward down the stairs, "Are you okay?"

"Yeah." She pulled away out of habit and cringed inwardly at the brief flash of resignation in his eyes. "You're leaving?"

The corner of his mouth tilted up in a mocking smile. "Yes. Please, though. There's no need to beg me to stay. I can't be swayed."

Oh, no. The sarcasm was so obvious. Maybe it was too late. "Um, listen, could I talk to you for a minute?"

Tony's eyebrow rose a fraction of an inch. "Of course." He turned his body slightly, as if to go back up the stairs, but stopped when she put a hesitant hand on his arm.

"No, not up there. I kind of wanted to discuss something, uh, private." She turned started walking down. "We can just talk in the laundry room, if you don't mind. My clothes are almost dry, and if I leave them in there, I risk someone throwing them on the floor."

Tony couldn't help but feel intrigued. Without a second thought he followed her until they reached a little room on the first floor crammed with machines that had to be as old as he was. Something on the chipped tile floor stuck to the bottom of his shoes, but it was so dingy gray that he could not identify the source. Two of the three fluorescent lights were burnt out, and a bulletin board was covered with layers of advertisements.

Robin turned to face him as soon as they entered the room and stood there with her hands shoved into the pockets of her jeans while she rocked back and forth on the soles of her feet. "I guess I didn't really plan how I wanted to say this," she said. He thought that maybe her face reddened, but with the low light, it was hard to tell.

"Saying something outright usually works," he said. She'd been civil to him for about fifty-seven seconds. He wondered if he should begin to worry.

She huffed out a breath and looked over his shoulder. "I want to sleep with you."

He wasn't quite sure how long it took for the words to sink in. He knew he stared at her, speechless, for several seconds, and managed to remember to close his mouth before he looked like an idiot. After it all clicked in and made sense, once he found his tongue again, he was able to speak. "Excuse me?"

She met his eyes this time. Nothing was reflected out of the blue depths that would make him think this was one big joke. "I said, I want to sleep with you."

"Okay. That's what I thought you said." Did he pinch himself now in order to wake up from this odd daydream, or wait for this to play itself out? "May I ask why?"

Her shutters came back into place. He was almost certain that he could hear them slamming shut. "Look, never mind. Maybe this wasn't a good idea."

She would have brushed by him if he hadn't grabbed her arm. "Nope. You started this. See it through. You couldn't stand me an hour ago. Why the sudden change of heart?"

Not knowing what to say to that, she once again decided the most direct route would be the best. "I've never dated anyone before."

She said nothing else. He waited a beat, then two, before prompting her. "Never?"

"Never."

"Why?"

She closed her eyes and let out a breath. "I don't know. I guess..." She opened her eyes and stared into his. There was no derision. Simply – caring. How she knew that, she didn't know. He cared about what she would say next. "Listen. I had a pretty rough childhood. My mom ..." She broke off and looked at her shoes. "Anyway, when I was fifteen we were on our own and bouncing from home to home and eventually I ended up in a girls' home. After that, I had Maxi to take care of and I've just never had the time or inclination to date."

Uncomfortable, she paced the tiny confines of the room before she whirled back around. "Look, you can either say yes or no. I'm not holding a gun to your head or anything. I just figured, you know, you want sex and I want to learn about all that." She stopped and looked at him, floundering for something else to say. "Anyway ..."

Tony crossed his arms and leaned against a washing machine. "Back up a second. You want me to teach you about sex?"

"Yeah, um, that would be the point."

"I see." He cleared his throat. Lord, help me, he thought. It was a bit of a precarious situation, but he didn't want her to stop talking to him, so he played it out. "And why did you pick me?"

Stay direct, Robin, she thought. She brushed her hair off her forehead in a nervous movement. "Well, you're obviously willing. And I figure that you won't be expecting a lifelong commitment or anything, you know? Just some sex, hopefully pleasant if not good, and then you'll be done with Hank's and done with me."

He lost all feeling in his legs and struggled to keep breathing normally. If he hadn't been leaning against the machine, he would have fallen down as he realized the monumental truth.

Dear God, he was in love with her. He always hoped he'd fall in love. He had prayed God would reveal his true love to him one day. As soon as the realization hit, he knew that he'd known who she was this whole time.

Suddenly spurred with energy, he straightened and stepped forward. "You aren't planning on hiding a knife and plotting a sneak attack or anything, are you? This isn't a tactic to lower my guard, is it?"

Robin huffed out a breath. "You know what? Forget it. This was a bad idea to think of, much less approach you with." The buzz of a dryer made her jump. She grabbed her laundry bag and started shoving it full of warm clothes. "Let's just pretend this conversation never happened."

He waited until she straightened and turned before stepping forward. She'd been in the process of slinging her laundry bag over her shoulder, and it fell unnoticed somewhere behind her as she stared up at him. His hands moved forward of their own accord and cupped her cheeks, his fingers splaying down along her neck. The touch was so incredibly soothing that Robin wanted to close her eyes and lean her forehead against his. She was so tired and out of nowhere wished she had someone to share the burden of her life.

He wondered if she realized that a single tear had escaped out of the corner of her eye and trailed over his thumb. It burned a path across his skin until he feared it would leave a mark. He rubbed his thumbs along the shadows under her eyes. A feeling of tenderness blended with the love that overflowed his heart. He cleared his throat, worried his voice was gone. "You're on."

He felt the muscles under his neck tense right before she opened her eyes. "Excuse me?"

"I said you're on. I'll teach you. All of it."

She gave a small shake of her head to clear it. "All of it?"

"You said that I wanted sex and that you wanted to learn about all of that. I'm going to teach you about all of that."

If her heart would slow down, maybe she could make some sense of what he was saying. "What does that mean?"

"You'll see." He released her face and stepped back while he looked at his watch. "What are you doing tomorrow?"

She rubbed her face with both hands and struggled to keep up with him. "Um, the week begins. I have to be at Benedict's from ten-thirty until three, then Hank's at six to one."

He mentally made all of the arrangements he needed for his schedule and nodded. "Okay. I'll see you tomorrow." He put a hand on either side of her face and kissed her forehead.

She stood there dumbly, staring at the doorway, long after he was gone. The sound of another dryer buzzing finally broke her trance and, for some reason feeling lighter than she ever had in her life, she hummed under her breath while she unloaded her clothes into her bag.

Chapter 7

ROBIN'S car shuddered as she pulled into her parking space and shut it off. As she opened the door, the smell of exhaust stung her nose. The car was made the same year Sarah was born. As Robin rounded the hood she gave the old girl a little pat, hoping that kindness would make it run one more day.

Just as she stepped onto the curb to go into the building, a sleek red sports car whipped into the spot next to hers. She started to smile, bit her lip, then thought better of it and allowed the smile. As Tony climbed out of the low car, her stomach did a nervous lurch.

He wore a brown leather jacket over a button down shirt with no tie, and a pair of khaki pants. He looked like a model showing off the perfect weekday casual look. He slipped off his sunglasses and smiled as he strolled up to her. "Good afternoon," he said.

Robin's mouth went dry. All day long she could think of nothing but the conversation the night before. She felt some excitement at the prospect of what she proposed, but in the light of day, she also felt quite foolish. "Tony, hi. Look –"

He cupped her elbow under his hand and steered her toward the building. "No time. Go get changed. Jeans are fine. Grab your clothes for Hank's and meet me back down here. We need to drive away fifteen minutes from now."

As he propelled her toward the door, she tried to catch up to what he said. "Leave? What?"

He smiled. "Just get changed. Fifteen minutes." He looked at his watch. "Fourteen."

Flustered, Robin went inside and up to her apartment. She couldn't imagine where he thought they were going when she had to be at work in less than three hours, but she followed his instructions until, three minutes later, she locked the door behind her wearing jeans with a cotton top and carrying her Hank's Place uniform in a grocery bag.

She found him where she left him, leaning against the hood of his car, his legs crossed in front of him at the ankle. When he saw her approaching, he straightened and grinned. "Thank you for hurrying," he said, hitting a button on the keys in his hand to release the latch that kept the trunk closed. He took the bag from her and set it in the trunk, then moved to the passenger door and opened it. "We have to be downtown by four."

"Why?" She lowered herself into the car. He shut the door and rushed around the front to the driver's side.

He slid in and started the car in one movement. "Because the movie starts at four."

"Movie? Tony, I have to be at work at six."

Her shoulders hit the back of the seat as he accelerated out of the parking lot and turned the zippy little car toward downtown. "Robin, do you think I didn't hear you last night or pay attention to what you said?"

She felt her face surge with heat at some of the things she'd said last night. "Of course not."

"Then relax. I know what time you have to be at work." He shot her a glance and reached out, capturing her hand with his. "Have fun without worrying about something."

Instead of arguing about the fact that she didn't worry, when she knew all she did was worry, she sat back and enjoyed the way he drove the car. Tony had no fear, had amazing confidence, and it came out in his driving. He zipped through the heavy afternoon traffic without stressing out about the way cab drivers cut people off, about missing a green light. He stayed lighthearted, happy, calm, all the while driving with a skill that leant no doubt that he knew exactly how to drive that powerful machine the way it was intended to be driven.

"How was your day?" He asked while idling at a red light.

Robin turned from looking at the downtown scenery around her and found him looking directly at her. "My day?"

His smile made her heart skip a beat. "Yeah," he drawled, "your day. Tell me about it."

"I served brunch and lunch to some power players and some over indulged wives all morning and afternoon."

He put the car in gear and shot away from the light, changing lanes to get around a bus. "And nothing exciting or interesting happened?"

"What? You want me to tell you who had a two martini lunch?"

She felt her body moving forward against the seat belt as he had to quickly hit the brakes for a cab that jolted out in front of them. "No, Robin. I want to know about YOUR day." He shot her a quick smile. "How about I start? I'll tell you about my day. I was so excited about this afternoon that I forgot about a big meeting. I walked into my office and Margaret, my secretary, told me they were waiting for me in the conference room. I said, 'Who is waiting?' She looked so worried about me that I wanted to hug her."

He stopped talking so she assumed he wanted her to speak. She searched her mind, trying to come up with something interesting to tell him. "After lunch today, when the restaurant was closed, a woman and her daughter came in. They're having her bridal shower there and wanted to discuss menus and staff. They started arguing over what kind of sandwich to serve, and the daughter started screeching at the mom over having chives or no chives in their cucumber sandwiches. She had a total breakdown, and as soon as the mother agreed with her, she immediately calmed down and went on with the meeting." Robin reached up and started pulling pins from her hair. "She made me think of a two-year-old having a temper tantrum."

At another stoplight, Tony looked at her again and forgot what he was about to say as he watched her hair tumble out of the tight bun that had confined it all day. Robin closed her eyes and ran her fingers over her scalp, making Tony wish he were the one doing that. He looked back to the road in front of him in time to see the light change to green. "I imagine you see a lot of temper tantrums there."

"People are people. I like most of my customers."

"You don't mind the excessive lifestyle?"

With a smile, she said, "What do I know of excess? I know of some lifestyles I wouldn't wish on my worst enemies. What I see at Benedicts is just another way of life."

"You don't wish it were you?"

Now she snorted. "Yeah, right. Because I'd fit in as well as a square peg." She turned her body as much as her seat belt would allow. "I don't care about stuff like that. You can't imagine how good my life is compared to what it used to be. I work hard. I work honest. And my sisters are taken care of. That's the only thing that matters to me."

They reached their destination and Tony found a parking space. The ways he could carry that conversation could take hours, could go deep, could go life-altering. Right now, he just wanted to enjoy the next hour or so.

When he pulled into the parking lot of the Museum of Science, Robin was confused. Tony tapped the clock on the dash before he turned the car off. "Ten minutes to spare," he said with a wink.

He was out of the car in a fluid movement and had her door open before she even had her seat belt off. He took her hand and helped her out of the car, but instead of releasing her, he just shifted her hand to his other and walked with her to the museum entrance.

"What are we doing here?" She asked.

He gave her hand a squeeze as he opened the door for her. "Going to the movie. I told you." At the admissions desk, he bought two tickets to the IMAX theater and steered her past the cafe, the store, and to the theater. There he bought a huge tub of popcorn, a box of chocolate covered raisins, and two drinks. Robin smiled as he flirted with the teenager behind the counter and realized that the tension was gone from her shoulders and neck and she felt lighthearted, almost carefree.

Tony turned to hand over her drink and caught her eyes. For a moment he stared at her, then winked and picked up the rest of the goodies. "Shall we?"

They watched a space documentary presented in 3-D. She sat next to him in a darkened theater on a Monday afternoon, two hours before a work shift started, eating buttered popcorn and chocolate covered raisins, and watching a 3-D movie. Her first experience with a 3-D movie, even, which made her duck the first few times a roving comet or an exploding star headed in her direction.

Some time after he set the empty tub at their feet, Tony took Robin's hand in his. She threaded her fingers with his and settled herself as close as the theater seats would allow and just enjoyed it. Enjoyed herself – enjoyed him – enjoyed being there with him.

When the lights came on and the world returned, Robin found herself wishing for just another few minutes. But time wouldn't allow it, especially at rush hour. So they gathered their trash and left the museum.

In the car again, this time headed toward Hank's Place, Tony stopped in the dead-stop traffic and put the engine in neutral. He turned his head and looked at Robin, happy to see the relaxed glow on her face. "Did you enjoy that?"

She smiled as she rolled her head on the seat to look at him. "That was fun."

"Are you interested in space and the cosmos?"

With a shrug she turned in her seat so that she nearly faced him. "I don't know. I've never looked into it before." Not wanting him to think she was trying to discourage conversation, she said, "What about you?"

"I am extremely busy." He inched the car forward. "I have very little free time to pursue any intellectual pursuits. However, anything having to do with the majesty of God's creation interests me on a purely emotional level. A friend saw this show with his kids and assured me that it contained nothing that would insult my belief in Creationism, so I've been looking forward to seeing it."

She nodded, digesting this new information about him. "You're pretty much unapologetically a Christian, aren't you?"

His laugh surprised her. He shook his head while he grinned and let a minivan in before inching forward some more. "Pretty much," he said with a smile.

"Do you go to church and stuff?"

A break in the traffic allowed him to shoot forward three or four car lengths. "And stuff." When he could take his eyes off the road again, he looked back at her. "If you want to come with me some time, just let me know. I'd love to have you by my side."

What little she knew of church didn't hold any appeal to her. "Uh, thanks. But no thanks."

Tony shrugged and found a spot to surge forward half a block. "It's an open invitation. And I reserve the right to ask again."

THE next day, Tony showed up outside of Benedicts in a stretch limo. When Robin climbed in, she saw the picnic he had laid out on the floor of the limo, complete with a red and white checked tablecloth.

"What is this?" She asked, shedding her coat in the warmth of the interior of the car.

"Well," Tony said, sitting on the floor with his back against the base of the seat. "I wanted to take you on a picnic, but it's so cold outside."

Robin laughed and accepted the bottle of water from him as the limo pulled away from the curb. "You're from Boston, aren't you? You're going to let a little autumn air get in your way?"

For a brief moment, he had a flash of the past. The shiver that went through him was more than a memory. "I don't do cold." He opened the picnic basket at his side and dug around until he came out with a bowl of grapes. "Soon it will be time for my annual migration to The Keys."

"Florida?" That sounded so far away to someone who had never been outside of the greater Boston area in her life. "What's there?"

He tipped his water bottle toward her as if toasting. "Not cold."

"Ah," Robin said with a wink. "Got you."

Tony held his hand out. "Do you mind if we bless this food before we eat it?"

Robin paused, hesitated, then placed her hand in his. She politely bowed her head, but didn't listen much to what he said. Instead, she just listened to his voice, felt the touch of his hand, and wondered. Wondered who this man was who was such a huge financial success, but who wouldn't eat until he'd prayed to God to bless it. What did he think of her, if at all, and her lack of prayer, her lack of God?

Having seen the darker side of the world, of humanity, she wondered how there could even be a God. Who let little girls get beaten, starved, terrified, raped? What God would allow that? What God would turn His back on mothers who pumped their bodies full of chemicals, who latched on to any man who would take her and her three children in, regardless of the consequence to the daughters?

Maybe Tony didn't know about such darkness, so it gave him an ignorant faith and allowed him to bee-bop from the Keys to Boston and back again without a care in the world. Maybe that's how he could get by with believing what he believed.

He'd said "Amen" and squeezed her hand. She raised her eyes and realized he hadn't released her hand. She sat in the seat and he sat at her feet and held her hand in his, looking at her face. When she finally focused her attention on him, he smiled. "Thank you for sharing this meal with me."

She ran her tongue over her lips in a nervous gesture. "I don't really know what to do next."

He held her eyes for several seconds before letting go of her hand. "You enjoy your meal," he said, handing her a napkin and a bowl with a lid. "And when we're done, you will be at Hank's in plenty of time to get ready for work. Maxine packed your uniform for me."

ROBIN had about five minutes to spare to get dressed. Tony watched her rush through the back entrance to the staff rest room in order to change. He followed more slowly, stopping inside the kitchen door to get a cup of coffee. As he turned, he met Hank's watchful gaze.

Hank stood on the outside of the stainless steel counter, talking to the kitchen staff through the warming lights and to the wait staff who stood around him. He kept talking while he measured Tony, and never one to be intimidated, Tony returned the stare just as thoughtfully. When Hank finished his predinner rush meeting with the staff, he dismissed them to get back to work and met Tony at the wooden table.

"Robin is like one of my own," he said without preamble.

Tony took a sip of coffee and leaned back against the table. "Glad she has you," he said.

"I'm not going to take a liking to some rich playboy playing games with her."

Tony set his cup on the table behind him and straightened. He reached out and slapped Hank's arm in a masculine sign of agreement. "Neither would I, brother," he said. He looked at his watch. "I have a dinner engagement. Have a good evening."

Chapter 8

ROBIN smiled and headed to the table.

"Hiya."

"Hiya yourself, Casey."

"Alright, then."

After getting a cup of coffee, and with a near groan, she leaned back in the chair and propped her feet in the one across from her. "How's the world treating you?"

"Well, now, here and there, mostly." He lifted a finger to a sous chef and leaned under the heating lamps so that she could hear him over the din of the busy kitchen. "You'll be wanting some of my pie to go with that coffee."

"I would, yes." She stifled a yawn as she brought the steaming cup of coffee to her lips.

A uniformed sous chef handed him a platter, which he slid under the lights and nodded at a waitress. She set the hollowed out bread round filled with steaming chili in front of Robin before returning to wait for her order. "You'll eat that first."

She shook her head. "Really, Casey, I'm not hungry."

"You's looking a bit piqued lately, Robin. You eat that before you get any of my pie." Turning, he put his hands on his skinny hips and barked a few orders to the dinner prep crew.

Feeling a bit like a scolded child, Robin picked up the spoon and took a bite. The spices teased her tongue with just the right amount of heat. Not even thinking about it, she took another bite and another. "Piqued?" she asked with a smile after she had consumed half of the bowl. She broke off a piece of the bread and slowly chewed.

"Ayah. You don't take care of yourself, girlie. Too busy looking after others." He shifted a perfectly fried onion that sat on top of a juicy ribeye and held the plate at arms length, checking the appearance. Only when it visually pleased him did he slide it to the lingering waiter.

"I take care of myself just fine. I'm just tired. I had to work a breakfast shift this morning on top of the lunch." And now she faced a full Saturday evening and night. She looked down, surprised that she had emptied the bowl. With a contented sigh, she finished her cup of coffee and grinned at Casey as he personally set a slice of pecan pie in front of her.

"You's shouldn't be working two jobs. That girl Maxi is working now, and Sarah's mighty capable of it."

The sweet crunch of the meaty nuts satisfied her tongue too much to form speech right away. Instead, she closed her eyes and enjoyed the flavors. Only after she had swallowed did she open her eyes again, and found a newly refilled cup of coffee in front of her and Casey sitting across from her. "You only sound like Hank when he's not around, Casey. Will I look forward to nightly lectures when he's gone full time?"

He threw his head back and cackled while he slapped his knee. He laughed for about fifteen seconds, then he stopped, shook his head, and abruptly stood and bustled back over to his command perch. "Just take care of yerself, missy. I kinda like having you around."

She pushed away the half eaten pie and stood to get ready for work. "Two more years. Then I can slow down." She considered the date and performed a quick mental calculation. "No wait, not even. This semester's half over by now."

Noise from the bar section of the restaurant invaded the room as the connecting door swung open. Robin ignored it, supposing one of the other bartenders was getting supplies before the dinner rush began, until Casey spoke. "You'll be wanting something to eat this early, Mr. V?"

She turned her head and prepared herself for the skip of her heart that suddenly started occurring whenever Tony walked into a room. "No thanks, Casey I'll just grab a coffee."

He strode across the room with a liquid grace a man shouldn't have, squeezing her shoulder as he walked by. With a sigh, she sat back down as he fixed himself a cup of coffee and lowered himself into the chair across from her.

Robin didn't think she'd ever get used to looking at him. She thought after seeing him every single day for a week that she might possibly become immune to his looks, but his handsome face made her heart skip a beat every time. Because of her nonstop work schedule, they could not enjoy an actual evening out. Instead, he showed up in the parking lot of Benedict's every afternoon at three. He had something new and fun to do every day. Movies, picnics on the floor of a limo, rowing, video arcades.

He had never approached her at the restaurant during working hours before. He'd made plans for that afternoon, but Robin had begged off, exhausted from the double shift she'd worked at Benedicts. She wondered if cancelling their date is what prompted this impromptu meeting.

"Tell me something," he said, reaching under the table and pulling her feet into his lap. Before she could protest, he had slipped off her shoes and his fingers and thumbs were suddenly doing the most delicious things to her arches.

"Hmmm?" Unable to stop herself, she melted into the chair and leaned her head back, closing her eyes.

"I've been paying attention to that little tip jar you have on the bar, not to mention the credit card tips and the cash the customers hand you personally."

She opened an eye and looked at him from under her lashes. "So?"

"So, between Benedict's and here, six days a week for both of them, you make a tidy sum."

Robin could barely concentrate on his words. His hands felt so powerful and so tender all at once. She didn't have the energy to do anything more than enjoy the foot rub. Last night she'd gotten exactly four point two hours of sleep. As she sat there, she had a minimum of eight hours in front of her. "What about it?"

"Are you on drugs?"

She opened one eye. "Don't irritate me when you're doing that with your hands." His fingers inched up her calves now, kneading and soothing. Robin had no idea how much her calf muscles ached until he rubbed the ache right out of them.

"I was just wondering why someone who makes what you make in tips in a single day, combined with what Maxine would have started making at the barest minimum, why you would live in the apartment you live in, and drive around in that hunk of junk you drive that isn't going to start one night out here at one o'clock in the morning." His voice became steely, but his hands stayed soothing, gentle with just the right amount of pressure.

She spoke without thinking about it. "Tuition."

For the first time since he started talking, his hands paused. "What tuition?"

She opened her eyes, slowly sat up and drew her feet from his lap. "Sarah's." Under the table, her feet sought out her shoes and wiggled back into them.

He stared at her. "The numbers don't add up, Robin. Maxine easily makes – "

"Stay out of it, Tony. It's truly none of your business."

His eyes flashed while his jaw tightened. "I'm making it my business."

She stood and pulled her peppermints out of her pocket. "Not until I do." He opened his mouth to speak, but she held a hand up to halt him. "No. Not everyone can wake up with the luxury of knowing they have enough money in the bank to never go hungry, to never be cold, to never have to worry about transportation for the rest of their lives." She stood and downed the remaining coffee in one swallow and popped a mint into her mouth.

"You think I don't know that?" He sat back a bit and crossed his arms across his thick chest.

"I think you have it so good that it's easy to wake up in your penthouse apartment and forget that there are mortals down below you who have to struggle while you send your blessings up to a god who lets children starve." She slapped both palms on the table and leaned forward. "I vowed that I would get my sisters through school. Me. Not with anyone's help, not even from them. They would have the chance at a life that our mother wasn't going to allow. I put Maxi through, and I'm putting Sarah through, and forget anyone who says I shouldn't or I can't or I look piqued when I do."

He stood as well and leaned forward until they stood nearly nose-to-nose. "Don't try to place me in a category, Robin. I won't fit."

She snorted and straightened. "Careful, Antonio Viscolli. You'll choke on your silver spoon."

For a split second, the heat in his eyes made her feel a little bit frightened, then he muttered something in Italian under his breath and came over the table to her side and grabbed her arm. "Come with me."

She struggled to free herself, but it was no use. "What are you doing?" she sputtered, clawing at his hand. "Let me go!"

"I'd rather not make a scene," he explained through gritted teeth while he eyed the suddenly still kitchen. He slammed open the back door and pulled her outside. A waiter crouched against a crate, book in one hand and cup of coffee in the other. His expression remained pleasant when he looked up at them. "Take over the bar for this shift, will you, Rob?"

The man stood up straight. "Sure. Sure, Mr. V."

Robin sputtered. "No way. Get your hands off me." Tony's stride never broke and he continued to haul her across the parking lot. "I'm not going anywhere with you. Do you hear me?" Nothing. "I'll scream for help."

He stopped so suddenly that she ran into his back. He turned her until she faced him, and he gripped both of her arms. "Do it."

She heard the very real threat in his voice. Not wanting to risk it, she clamped her lips together and stiffly shook her head. "Good. Now, get in the car."

Keeping a grip on one of her arms, he opened the door and waited. "No."

His voice was dangerously quiet. "Do you want to test whether or not I can bodily put you in there?"

She tried to stare him down, but eventually lost the battle, and with half a growl, she threw herself into the seat. Seconds later, Tony sat beside her, starting the powerful engine of the little sports car, and tearing out of the parking lot.

"Where are we going?"

"I have something to show you."

"I hope you realize that you just hauled your best bartender out of your bar on the busiest night of the week." She crossed her arms over her chest and glared out the window.

"Hank's isn't going to collapse because Robin Bartlett isn't manning the bar for one Saturday night. As a matter of fact, it would still be there without a bar." He took a corner fast enough to make her shoulder lean on the door.

"I'm losing tips."

"I'll give you a raise."

"I don't want a raise."

"But you deserve a raise. You're my best bartender."

In a rage now, she slapped the dashboard. "You can't just drag someone around like that and force them to do your bidding. I don't care who you are or how much money you ... "

"Robin," he said very quietly, but with enough ice to halt her screaming sentence, "I'm warning you, now, to just clam it."

She decided to save it until they got to wherever he was taking them. The longer she remained quiet, the more calmly he drove. In the late afternoon light, Robin recognized landmarks and realized they had traveled into a pretty rough section of town. She remembered, all too vividly, living as a child and a young teenager in many of the apartment buildings they passed. Deep into one of the worst neighborhoods she knew of, he casually pulled into the parking lot of a large church. Robin knew the church. It took up two full blocks with all of its buildings and schools. For her, as a little girl, she had always used it as a major landmark.

"Why are we here?" she asked, trying not to let her apprehension creep into her voice.

For several moments, Tony didn't speak. Finally, he said, "I apologize, sincerely, for losing my temper." He turned off the car and got out, moving slower than usual as he came around to her side to open her door. As soon as she was out of the car, he took her hand in his. "My feelings for you tend to override a lot of things. Please accept my apology."

His feelings for her? Reeling over the last several minutes, Robin could do nothing but nod and stammer, "Okay."

His smile did not quite reach his eyes. "Let's walk."

Robin looked all around her. "Uh, Tony, this isn't really the best neighborhood -"

Tony clinched his jaw. "Robin, *mi amante*, not everything in life is a debate. Could you, just once today, stop arguing with me? If it wouldn't be too much trouble?"

Robin closed her mouth. Whatever retort she had prepared vanished in a heartbeat. She sensed that he intended to share something important with her. She suddenly wanted to know what that important thing might be.

He led them away from the church. "Let me tell you a story."

"Really, that isn't – "

"Once upon a time, there was a young sixteen year old girl who fell in love with a fisherman in Florence, Italy. He was much older than her, and well below her station, but she didn't care. Thumbing her nose at her parents, she married him, anyway. They told her to never come back and disowned her." Tony steered her around the legs of a snoring man who sat against a building, empty bottle gripped in his dirty hands, and continued his story.

"Well, for about a year, life was bliss. Until the day a storm hit right off the coast and took the fisherman with it. She was young, devastated, alone, and pregnant. Not to mention poor. She tried to go to her parents for help, but they were true to their word and wouldn't even open the door to her. Now, her husband didn't have any family in Italy, but he spoke often of his Aunt Rosa in America. See, that was his dream. To eventually raise enough money to take his family away from the poverty that had trapped him in Italy and bring them to America."

Robin scooted closer to Tony as they passed a hooker with mean eyes. He squeezed her hand and kept talking. "So, she wrote Rosa, sold everything she could to raise enough money to get here, and came on her way. She had expected the grand American life, and was crushed when she learned that Rosa was actually even more poor than she was, and lived in an apartment that didn't even have a working heater half the time. She was miserable, very pregnant, and sleeping on a sofa in a cold two-room apartment. And Rosa was old. She was actually her husband's great aunt.

"Neither women spoke English, and she had a hard time finding a job. Now, in this neighborhood, there were several things a woman could do to earn money, few of which are legal, and she went that route, falling victim to a few vices along the way. Her son stayed with Rosa while she went about her life, popping in and out every so often. Then she'd leave and do whatever it was that she did to support her heroin addiction."

Robin knew, without a doubt, that the little boy in the story was Antonio Viscolli. Shamed at the way she'd spoken to him, at what she said, she suddenly didn't want to hear the rest of the story. "Tony ... "

The look in his eyes and his single raised finger stilled her. "Wait. I'm almost to the punch line. Anyway, Rosa died when the boy was ten. He was in school, but only in the second grade, because he was having to learn

English as he went. His mother showed up to claim the apartment, and having a young son did nothing to hamper her lifestyle. Life was hell for him, but he managed to make it on his own. Of course, rent had to be paid and food had to be bought, so, following the path of his mother, he hit the streets. He wasn't very big and could get in and out of an apartment quickly. He made some pretty good contacts, and could fence a television for a good price. He even hit the business section a few times, got caught by the police twice picking pockets, and was pretty much headed toward becoming a hoodlum."

She couldn't imagine Tony doing any of that. Looking at him, dressed to the nines in his suit, his shirt perfectly starched and gleaming white, his tie straight, the diamond on his pinkie catching the glow of the afternoon sun – he looked every single bit of the rich business man. No way could she picture him worming his way out of a window carrying a pilfered radio.

They stopped now, next to a dilapidated old building with boarded up windows. Tony turned to face her. The smooth cultured look vanished in a breath. His eyes had hardened. His mouth pulled into a thin line. Even his voice had changed. It sounded harsher, carried an accent that was a mix of Italian, South Boston, and insolence. "He found his mother dead when he was seventeen. She'd overdosed on her favorite drug. The needle was still sticking out of her arm." He stepped away from her and looked over her shoulder down the street. "The landlord had already taped the eviction notice on the door, so without a backward look, he left.

"He was just out of juvie, so none of his so-called friends trusted him. Too many came out narks at first, so he had no place to stay." He came toward her again and put an arm over her shoulder, turning her so that she was facing the building. He pointed toward the doorway. "That was a good place to sleep. It has a deep recess and a stoop. It blocked the wind, which was good, because January is bitter cold."

Robin's stomach muscles shivered, as if she personally felt that cold. Her voice quivered and her throat ached with unshed tears. "That's enough."

"No. It isn't." He turned her until they were looking down the street. "There's an Italian restaurant down that way. They make good calzones. The wife used to make all the pasta by hand. And the guy, he'd throw enough food away at night so that anyone hungry enough, right after he went inside, could hit the Dumpster and fight off the cats and rats and get himself something to eat."

"Stop!" She put a hand over her mouth and stared at him.

"I laid there in that doorway one night. It couldn't have been more than twenty degrees. I was cold, starving, exhausted, and I swore that I would die before I suffered through one more night. I swore that would be the very last night. And, miracle of miracles, it was." He turned them back the way they came and they headed back toward the tall steeples of the church. "The next night, I went into the church. I decided I'd case the place, see what I could get for what I could get. There was some service going on in there. I walked in right at the end of the singing and right before the preaching.

"Robin, I cannot put into human words what happened to me when I heard that pastor's message of salvation. It was like a dam burst and a floodgate of love poured into and out of my heart. The message that God loved me, that I wasn't alone, that no matter how cold I got or how hungry I got, He would provide a way for me. I'd been alone my entire life and suddenly, someone loved me. Me. A bad kid with a chip on his shoulder the size of the bay. A low life thief."

One of his eyebrows raised to emphasize his next words. "A liar." He paused as if to let that sink in; as if lying were worse than stealing or thuggery.

"And I learned the most important thing of all, that no matter what I did up until that moment, I was forgiven. The almighty, all powerful, all knowing God who created the universe and time knew everything I had ever done, every thought I ever had, and He still loved me and forgave me. As if I had never done any of it, as if I had never thought any of it. He forgave ME and he loved ME."

He put his hands on her shoulders. "It's hard for those of us who never had any good parenting models to grasp, but we are His children and He loves each one of us so much that He sent His own Son to die for us. And, Robin, He loves you as much as He loves me."

Chapter 9

ROBIN felt a tingling in the back of her chest, near her stomach. She took a deep breath hoping the cool evening air would still whatever strange sensation flooded her body. It didn't. Hearing that God, a being whom she didn't even know whether she believed existed, loved her made her want to cry and beg, but she didn't know why she should cry or for what she should beg. So, instead, she ignored the intensity of the feeling and refocused on Tony's story. "What happened?"

Tony saw her fight the battle inside herself, the battle between flesh and spirit, and witnessed her flesh win. He knew Robin didn't win though. Fighting back against the knocking of the Holy Spirit did nothing but place her on the losing side. He fervently prayed while he gently put a hand on her elbow and continued walking.

Robin could sense Tony's disappointment, but it confused her. She thought maybe he regretted telling her the story. She had never told anyone, ever, how she had lived, what she had endured. As far as it concerned her, nothing that happened to her before today had anything to do with anyone else. She wanted to rub his arm and tell him that she could forget everything he said and they could go back to the lighthearted fun they'd had all week.

They reached the church again but instead of taking her back to the car, he steered them onto a tree-lined residential street. The street didn't fit in the neighborhood. The freshly painted houses sported cute little lawns and picket fences. Kids' toys and bicycles sat propped against trees and chalk drawings decorated the sidewalks.

Rather than tell her what happened next, Tony decided to let her experience a small taste of it. He gestured. "The church owns this street. The staff lives here. Surprisingly, the crime in this neighborhood has never made its way down this row. I think the church does so much that no one wants to hurt the people who help." He winked at her, "Or there's an angel guarding the entrance. It could go either way."

Dusk settled around them and porch lights carved through the twilight. They walked about halfway down the street and Tony stopped Robin and unlatched a picket gate. How many times over the years had he reached down and lifted that latch? Thousands? When he felt overwhelmed, he came home to this place. When he felt frustrated, he lifted that little latch and walked down the little stone path. When the darts and arrows of the world overcame him, he would find solace and comfort beyond the picket fence. He suddenly realized that never, in all of his years, had he brought a female guest with him. Especially a female for whom he had such strong feelings. He realized that they would see it right away, and he grinned at the thought.

He led the way down the little path to the front door. Instead of opening it with the key in his pocket, he rang the doorbell and stepped back. The sounds from inside made him smile. Every single thing in his life might change, but everything here would always remain the same.

As he rang the bell, Robin could hear laughter, loud voices, running feet. A woman opened the door. Tendrils of hair escaped her ponytail and tickled the large freckles scattered across her cheeks, forehead, and nose. She had her long dress covered by an apron and fuzzy pink bunny house slippers on her feet. She looked maybe ten years older than Tony.

"*Buona sera*," Tony said.

"What in the world are you doing ringing the doorbell?" She asked, her eyes skimming over Tony then resting on Robin. "Ah. I see." She put her hands on her hips and smiled at Tony while she tried to act stern. "I don't see you or hear from you all week and you show up when I have on bunny slippers and no makeup!"

Tony smiled. "You're beautiful, *amico*."

She blushed and laughed before opening the door wider. "Please come in."

He stepped aside and put a hand on the small of Robin's back, steering her in front of him. "This is Robin Bartlett. Robin, allow me to introduce Caroline O'Farrell."

Caroline held her hand out in a very welcoming manner. Robin couldn't help feeling that she genuinely liked meeting her. "Pleasure to meet you, Robin." She looked wryly over Robin's head toward Tony. "Tony's never brought a girl home before."

Robin didn't know what to say and tried to resist Tony's pressure on her back to step forward. She lost that momentary battle and finally took her offered hand and allowed herself to be pulled into the house. "It's nice to meet you, Caroline. Sorry to pop in without calling first."

"Don't be silly. Don't need to announce Tony. He's one of us." They went from the small entryway into a good-sized living room. Books and puzzles spilled out of a bookshelf onto the carpeted floor. Framed pictures of children in various ages and ethnicities and general kiddish cuteness covered the walls. A white teenage boy and a younger black teenage girl sprawled on a sofa in front of a television. A little boy with tawny hair and round glasses carried plates to the table that filled the other half of the room. A little girl of Oriental descent came darting from the open kitchen door screaming, "Uncle Tony! Uncle Tony!"

He grinned as he bent to pick her up, swinging her around and kissing both cheeks. "Little Angel Dove. How are you?"

"I have a loose tooth," she said, then promptly bared her teeth and pushed her front tooth forward with her tongue. "I'll get a dollar when it comes out!"

Tony showed exactly the right amount of interest. "A whole dollar?"

"Yep!"

"What will you do with a whole dollar?"

"Well," she said, rolling her eyes to look at Caroline, "mom says that a whole dime of it has to go to church. But that will leave enough for at least a pack of gum, she said."

"At least." He kissed her temple before setting her down. "Haven't I taught you the art of negotiation?"

Caroline laughed. "We started at fifty cents."

Smiling, Tony patted Angel's head. "That's my girl."

A tall thin man with salt-and-pepper hair and black framed glasses came out of the kitchen and walked straight toward them with a smile on his face. His white apron sported giant red lips and the words "KISS THE COOK". In one hand he held grilling tongs and the other a bottle of barbeque sauce. He set them both on the table as he passed by it and had his arms out before he even reached them.

"Tony, my brother!" he said with great enthusiasm.

"Peter, *mi fratello*, it's great to see you," Tony said. He stepped forward. With interest, Robin watched the two men embrace and pound each other on the back as they broke contact. The smile on Tony's face removed the last of the traces of harshness the neighborhood had brought earlier. "I'd like you to meet someone," Tony said, turning to bring Robin into their fold. "Robin Bartlett, this is my good friend and brother, Peter O'Farrell. Peter, this is Robin."

Behind the black rimmed glasses, Peter's brow lifted with a keen interest but he didn't say anything except, "It's a pleasure to meet you, my dear. You two will be staying for dinner, then." He didn't ask, merely stated, and despite the fact that she had just recently inhaled a bread bowl filled with chili and half a slice of pecan pie, Robin found herself following the adults into the kitchen and out the back door to a little patio looking out over a back yard strewn with balls and bikes. On the small concrete slab, a large charcoal grill smoked away.

This yard wasn't fenced like the front yard. Similar patios stretched out on either side, and in the fading light, Robin could see church buildings in front of her. Between the church and the rows of houses, she could make out a large children's playground and a volleyball net. Well tended and somewhat worn bricked pathways led from the church buildings to the playground.

Peter had collected his supplies on their way out of the house. He lifted the lid on the grill and used a set of tongs to poke at some chicken thighs that lay spread out on the hot rack. As he fussed with the meat, he spoke to Tony. "Haven't heard from you all week. Figured you'd headed south a bit early."

Tony offered Robin a plastic chair. As she and Caroline sat next to each other, he made his way to Peter's side. "I've been otherwise occupied," he said smiling.

Peter glanced around Tony to Robin. "With work?"

"Not exactly." Tony put a hand on Robin's shoulder. She didn't realize how tense she felt until his touch drew it out of her. She slowly relaxed. "How was the conference?"

Caroline answered. "Antonio, it was wonderful! The more we can get the word out there, the better it will be for all of the children."

Tony caught Robin's eye and explained, "Peter and Caroline, on top of all of their other duties at the church, run a non profit corporation that helps people financially with adoption."

"What do you do at the church?" Robin asked.

"I teach the youth," Peter said.

Caroline snorted. "Don't let him be modest with you. He runs the youth department. He has about 900 children."

Robin's eyes grew wide. "Wow. What do you do?"

"As our department has grown, I have less time for a lot of hands-on and spend most of my time in administration, managing the pastors and teachers of the kids," he said, poking at a thigh. "Back when I first met Tony, we had about a third of the numbers we have now, and I actually taught down in the trenches."

Tony interjected. "Peter and I met the night I was saved; the night I was just telling you about. He took me to the gymnasium, let me grab a shower and gave me a change of clothes."

Peter laughed and interrupted. "That's because you smelled so bad."

Tony laughed and continued, "And then brought me here. Caroline fed me..."

This time Caroline interrupted. "Corned beef and cabbage. Food fit for a man." She looked at Robin with a wink. "About the only thing I can cook and not burn."

"...then they gave me a bedroom."

Robin looked up at Tony, who still had a hand on her shoulder. "Just like that?"

Caroline answered again. "When we're Spirit led, it's often just like that."

"Spirit led?"

Caroline's questioning eyes shot toward Tony, who ignored her. "Peter got me a job as a janitor at the church. I lived here and worked for a year."

This time Peter interrupted. "I appointed him as a custodial engineer. And when he wasn't working, he was in the church library reading. I think he only came here to sleep."

Tony smiled. "And eat."

"As only a teen aged boy can," Caroline said with a laugh.

"What did you read?" Robin could not help feeling intrigued by Tony's past, by his path.

"Anything and everything. I read the Bible three times that year. I read every word I could get my hands on to explain what I'd read. I watched every documentary they had on the shelves and went to every service I could go to."

"Hungry boy," Caroline said.

Peter finally finished prodding and started turning the meat over. "He saved every dime he made, too. Wore clothes out of the clothes closet so that he wouldn't have to buy any, even."

Tony remembered. Ill fitting pants and baggy shirts on his skinny frame. "My eighteenth birthday was fast approaching. I had to save."

"How did you…" Robin stopped short of asking, but Tony knew what she wanted to ask. How did he go from skinny waif to healthy and muscular, wealthy and successful, polished and proper?

"He took everything he made," Peter started, but his wife interrupted him.

"Prayed over it," she said.

Peter continued, "then put it all into a computer company on the stock market."

"You made your money in the stock market?"

Tony moved until he stood in front of her so that she wouldn't have to crane her neck to see him. "No. I made quite a bit of money off of my investment and then used that to buy a book store. The store was floundering, badly, and I got it for a fraction of its worth. Very quickly, I turned it around and used the profits from there to buy a bankrupt auto parts store. Very soon, I could buy a franchise of a fast food restaurant and…"

Caroline stood. "Everything that man touched turned to gold. Before a decade passed, he probably couldn't even tell you all of the different companies and corporations and franchises he owned."

Tony cut his eyes to her. "Sure I could." He looked back at Robin. "I stayed faithful to God, and He stayed faithful to me. I tithed with passion, studied the Bible with passion, prayed over every business venture I made, and God continued to bless me."

Robin opened her mouth to speak, but Tony didn't let her ask the "why" question he could tell was on her lips. "He continued to bless me because there's work to be done. Unfortunately, in order to work, you need to have money. He must have trusted me not to make an idol of money, and to pour forth as much as I could back into work for His kingdom."

He could tell she didn't understand. "My objective has never been to be rich and powerful. It has merely been to never be cold and hungry again. God took my drive and my faithfulness and used both to help others through me. To fiscally help this church and a dozen others like it, to donate to charities, to get kids off of the streets and into proper homes." Forgetting his friends, he knelt next to her chair. "If only you and I had ever had access to what my foundation does today, how different would our lives have been, eh?"

Robin felt that swirling, tingling feeling in her stomach again. She didn't know if it was Tony sitting so close to her or this deity to whom they all referred and appeared to revere. "But then, if you'd had access, you wouldn't have drive and we wouldn't be here today, would we?"

Caroline slapped her knee as she stood up. "Ha! That is a good point, there." She went to her husband and slipped an arm around his waist. "Need a platter for the bird, love?"

"That would be wonderful. Thank you."

Before long, Robin found herself sitting at a table with the entire family. She learned that Caroline and Peter adopted all but the oldest boy. After the entire table held hands and Peter said a long prayer over their food, they ate the chicken with potato salad and baked beans that came from a grocery store deli. Despite the size of the meal she'd had at Hank's, Robin found herself enjoying this one immensely. She had no experience with interacting in this setting of family dynamics, but she enjoyed observing them.

The biggest mystery she kept coming back to, though, was that Tony fit in with them. Never in a million years would she have guessed that he came from such humble roots. Never would she have thought that he spent Sunday afternoons after church in this living room with this family. She had always imagined him wining and dining in penthouse apartments or yachts on the Bay or mansions on the hill. But here, in this little home with the picket fence out front, here is where he fit – perfectly fit – his hand tailored shirt and twenty-four karat cuff links not withstanding.

After the meal and after children were dispatched to the kitchen to tackle the dishes, the adults moved to the living room with cake and coffee and talked. Robin enjoyed while Caroline and Peter bombarded her with stories of young Tony. She watched him interact with them, watched him completely relax as he leaned against the cushions and smiled at some story about him trying to learn Greek so that he could read the Bible in Greek.

"Turns out, I'm more inclined toward Latin," he punned.

She sat next to him and he turned his head slightly, looking away from Peter and toward her. As their eyes met, his smile slowly and gradually left his face. He looked very solemn, very serious. Robin felt pulled into his stare until even Peter's voice came from far away. Tony gently ran a finger down her cheek then took her hand in his. Robin felt a flutter in her heart. As soon as Tony broke eye contact with her and laughed at something Caroline said, the room came back into focus. She tried to pick up in her mind where the conversation left off, tried to pull her fingers out from his grasp, but he just entwined their fingers and squeezed.

It felt right to sit with him like this so she settled back into the couch and enjoyed the stories, and the company, and the ... love ... that just flowed all around her.

SAPPHIRE ICE - CHAPTER 10

ROBIN found herself very restless on Sunday. She'd hoped she would spend the day with Tony, but after leaving the O'Farrell's with him Saturday night and getting dropped off at her apartment door with nothing more than a smile and an invitation to attend church the next day – which she declined – she didn't hear from him.

She paced her apartment, cleaned out her closet, worried about doing laundry and missing his call, paced some more, and as the sun faded in the sky she found herself sitting on her couch staring mindlessly at some nature documentary and feeling a little blue. With Maxine on a date and Sarah at her parents' house, she found herself feeling lonely, too. With her schedule, living with her two sisters, and constantly having to interact with people, she had always enjoyed solitude.

Had she done or said something to offend Tony? Did he not like the way she reacted to his story? Did he regret introducing her to his friends?

Turning the television off in disgust, she surged to her feet. She would not be reduced to this emotional state of neediness by a man. She had survived twenty-six years without Antonio Viscolli, and she'd go on surviving without him.

Working herself into a good angry fit, she decided she would go ahead and do laundry, whether that meant that she'd miss his phone call or not. Not that she expected him to call this late, anyway. While she sorted her laundry and shoved it all into a bag, she muttered to herself all of the reasons why she'd spent so many years avoiding a relationship with anyone.

As she walked down to the laundry room and, with way more force than the chore required, shoved her clothes into the available washers, she built herself back up, reminding her inner self that she had tuition to pay, rent coming due, a car about to die on her. A man, or a relationship with a man, or a non-relationship with a man, did not fit into her schedule in any way at the moment.

With three machines loudly chugging away at her clothes, she left the laundry room with much less furor than she had entered it. She slowly walked up the flights of stairs to her apartment and let herself back in. As she contemplated maybe fixing something to eat, she noticed the red light blinking on the answering machine, signaling an incoming message.

Her heart skipped a beat before it started pounding. She rushed to push the button, and felt an immediate deflation of emotion as she heard Hank's gravely voice.

"Robin, Hank. I need to talk with you before your Benedicts shift tomorrow. Ten is a good time. If you have to work breakfast first, try to just make it as soon as you can. No need to call me back unless it's to tell me a better time. Thanks. Have a good night."

Never, in all of the years that she'd worked for him, had Hank ever called her in to meet with her. Frowning at the answering machine, Robin replayed the message, trying to glean some hint as to what he could possibly want to talk about with her. He'd pulled her into his office too many times to count for various reasons over the years – checking on her, she knew. Making sure she was emotionally handling everything in her life to his satisfaction. She allowed it because she loved him. But never had he called her at home, nor asked her to come in for a scheduled meeting while off shift.

After a night spent tossing and turning and tossing some more, worrying about Hank's call and fretting over the lack of a call from Tony, she finally quit trying to sleep and got up early. She braided her long hair, dressed herself in the first uniform of the week, her Benedict's lunch uniform, and headed to Hank's.

Hank's did not open until four on Mondays. Instead of a lunch shift, the kitchen staff received orders, stocked shelves, freezers, and refrigerators, and planned specials for the week. As Robin came in through the kitchen door, she had to twist aside to avoid colliding with a harried produce salesman who stamped quickly away from Casey's rage over, she assumed, the asparagus he clutched in both hands and held above his head.

Instead of exchanging their standard greeting, she avoided becoming Casey's target in the absence of the salesman and headed straight to Hank's office. She rapped her knuckles on the closed door in quick succession, waited for the bark of command to enter, and opened the door. As she opened the door, she had to step aside as two men in paint splattered coveralls left the room. When Robin entered, she stopped short to find Tony seated behind the desk and Hank in one of the chairs before it. The bare walls no longer sported photos of Hank in the Navy, plaques, awards, or posters. Instead, fresh white paint glared back and made the room seem smaller. The standard piles and stacks of papers and books no longer cluttered the top of the desk. The bookshelf had all personal knicknacks and Tom Clancy novels removed and in their place sat books whose spines bragged of financial or management success.

She took all of this in as she came farther into the room, but it confused her. Her understanding was that Hank would stay for a few years. "What's up?" she said. She looked at Hank first, then Tony, then back to Hank.

Hank spoke. "Jessica, my youngest daughter, fell down the stairs Saturday night and broke her femur."

Robin gasped and took the chair next to him. "Oh no."

"Marjorie's already there. She needed to go down and take care of the baby."

"Of course."

"I called Tony on Sunday and we've been here since five this morning working everything out."

Robin shifted her attention from Hank to Tony. "What everything?"

Tony didn't look like he'd been at the office since five. His shirt looked crisp, freshly starched, and his blue tie speckled with tiny gold icthuses looked sharp against the whiteness of the shirt. "Hank is declining the five year management position. He's decided to go ahead and leave."

Robin saw little bright lights in front of her eyes as a little swirl of panic start spinning in her chest. "I – ah …"

Hank reached over and engulfed her hand in his. "Marjorie didn't like that clause, and she and I have been trying to come to a compromise about it. When the contracts to sell the restaurant were signed, we kept it open. Jessica is going to be down and out for a long time. With her husband's ship deployed, there's nothing else we can do but go be there for her and help her."

Little beads of moisture formed on her upper lip. "But -"

Tony leaned back in his chair. His fingers fidgeted with the gold pen that lay on the clean white blotter in front of him. "Hank and I have spent the last few weeks immersed in personnel and personalities and positions. He and I are both in agreement."

"Agreement?" Did she miss a chunk of the conversation?

"Effective today, the bar is closed." As if on cue, Robin heard the sound of a saw fire up from somewhere in the restaurant. "We're tearing it out and opening up more seating in its place."

A little tinge of irritation helped slow down the spiral of panic. "Great." She'd known it was coming, though. The news didn't surprise her. Only, she still hadn't figured out what she'd do instead. "I guess I have the evening free, then."

Tony smiled. "As nice as that prospect is, I'm afraid that you're going to be a little busier than normal."

"Oh? Why is that?"

"I need to go out to California. I have a venture there that's still on shaky ground, and there's a hotel in Manhattan that I'm in the preliminary negotiations with that's going to start taking up a lot of my personal time." He spun the gold pen between his fingers like a tiny baton while he studied her face.

With shaking hands, Robin pulled her tin of mints out of her pocket and popped one in her mouth. "Look – you don't need to explain."

He tilted his head and gave her a confused look. "No. Let me finish." He hooked a foot over his knee. "Here's the problem. Hank's leaving about a month earlier than anticipated. We tried to look at resumes for a manager but neither of us were pleased with what we've seen out there. None of them have what I'm looking for."

She felt the frown crease her brow. "What's that?"

His eyes were intense, serious, while he looked at her. "Your experience. Your love of this place. Your drive."

She blinked. "Excuse me?"

"I talked it over with Hank. He's in complete agreement."

Hank squeezed her hand and released her. "Absolutely."

"Complete agreement about what?"

Tony quit spinning the pen and smiled a very charming smile. "About you."

A kind of fearful excitement tried to course through her veins, but she stamped it down. "What are you getting at?"

"I want you to run Hank's for me. I want to hire you on as the manager so that I don't have to worry about losing what it is that makes it Hank's."

She snorted. "Yeah, right."

"I'm absolutely serious."

She looked in his eyes and saw that he was. "Look, Tony. I'm just a barmaid, a waitress, and a high school dropout. You don't want me running this place for you."

"What does any of that have to do with anything? A person with your experience?" He felt the anger and only partially tried to keep it in check. "I didn't ask you about your educational background."

"Well, it's a good thing you didn't. I've never even gotten my GED."

"So?"

Now she laughed. "So, hire some guy who has a bunch of education and is trained for the position. A Viscolli company doesn't need some two-bit bartender running anything for it."

Tony's temperature rose a few degrees. He felt as if, in insulting her, she had personally insulted him. No one talked about Robin that way. "You think that I give 'two bits' about diplomas and accolades? If I wanted that, I could have had my pick all week. I want you."

Robin looked from one man to the other and felt heat flood her cheeks, trying to find the right words. "Look, Tony. If you're doing this just because we – "

He cut her off. "Robin, one of the reasons I'm what I am is because I don't mix my business and personal life. It will cut you off at the knees every time."

"You'll be laughed out of the Chamber of Commerce if you hire me."

"You think?" Taking a different approach, he slowly stood. "Do you think I'm qualified to run my company?"

Obviously not liking his advantage, she stood as well. "Obviously."

"I used to Dumpster dive to eat my one meal a day," he chided. Instead of continuing on, he took a deep breath and closed his eyes, praying to find the right words. "My point, *mi amante*, is that if the Chamber of Commerce were going to find something to laugh at me about, it wouldn't be because I picked the best, most qualified person in this entire city to run my newly acquired restaurant."

His words, the naked sincerity that weighed them down, penetrated Robin's very blood and beat through her veins in a rush. Robin had needed the reminder. Wow! She thought she hadn't forgotten, really, what he had disclosed about his past on Saturday. Somehow, though, she could barely reconcile those facts with this Tony; smooth, cultured, in charge. He commanded the room even over Hank.

When Tony talked about having to go to California and New York, she thought he'd been in the midst of firing her and ending their relationship. Now she had an opportunity to work even closer with him. That prospect alone promised some really unexplainable appeal for her.

Could she let herself harbor some tiny hope that even she could rise above her own personal birthright? Could someone one day meet her and not believe how she had lived her whole life? Would she one day find herself transformed as completely as a caterpillar to a butterfly? As completely changed as Tony had changed? Could she become a brand new creature?

She sat, looked between the two men again. "What now?"

Tony admired his own personal restraint that kept him from throwing back his head and laughing with glee. "Now, you look over my offer, the contract, haggle over the salary, get at least fifteen percent more, then you go to dinner with me tonight to celebrate your new promotion at work."

Hank's laugh reminded her of his presence. "I will take that as my leave to go. I have a lot of packing to do. Tony," he held his hand out and Tony leaned over the desk to shake it. "It has been an absolute joy to work with you."

"And you, sir. May God bless you and keep you."

He looked at Robin as he sat back down. "You still look a little dazed."

I'm going to give you a draft of the contract and let you read over it. I need you to put in your notice at Benedicts. This is more than a full time job."

"I can't afford -"

Tony felt the smile on his face, excited for her, anticipating her surprise over the salary offered. He had left the contract writing up to Barry, so even though he'd have personally padded it just because he loved her, Barry didn't and nothing was nonstandard. Even so, he had a feeling that the number hovering just under six figures would more than satisfy her current living situation, tuition notwithstanding.

"Just take this and read it. If you have any questions, I'll be happy to answer them." He held out the eight-page contract and waited for her to reach out and take it.

She stood as she did and said, "Okay. Thank you." She turned to leave, as if dismissed or dismissing him. He wanted her to stay with him and chat some more. He wanted to spend a portion of this insane morning with the soothing calm of her presence.

"How was your day off?" he asked.

Robin spun around. Her eyes flashed anger, which confused him a little bit, but her voice remained calm. "Fine."

"What did you do with your time?"

"Nothing," she said, rolling up the bound pages in her hand. "Absolutely nothing."

Tony raised an eyebrow, thinking that he'd discovered the root of the anger. "Is there something specifically wrong that you'd like to talk about?"

Robin advanced on him, waving the rolled up contract in front of her like a rapier. "You take me out every single day for a week. I work two jobs and in the brief hours each day I normally have to decompress and refocus my energies, I ended up with you. Suddenly, on the one day off I have for the entire week, I don't hear a word."

Ah. Clarity. "I asked if you wanted to come to church with me."

"So because I declined coming to church with you, you blow me off for the entire day?"

"Of course not. I don't just put on a tie and spend an hour in a building, Robin. My entire Sunday is spent in holy communion with God. There are two services on Sundays, and as the treasurer of the church board, I had a presentation to give to the church body regarding some land acquisitions, so I stayed for both services. I also teach a Sunday School class. By the time I leave the church building, it's late afternoon and I typically end up in the home of one of the staff members, enjoy a light lunch and some low key fellowship, then head back into the church building for evening worship."

As he spoke he watched her face fuse with color. Tony stood and moved quickly around the desk so that he could reach out and touch her, take her hand in his and look into her eyes as he spoke. "I wanted to spend the day with you. I thought about you all day long. I wished you'd been there to hear the music, to listen to the amazing sermon that I heard twice, to have lunch with me and my friends."

Robin felt her hand momentarily tremble in his. The back of her throat burned and she had no idea why. She cleared her throat and pulled her hand away. "Okay. I'm sorry that I was so upset."

Before she could turn back around, he grabbed her hand again. "You're still a little upset. I'm sorry that you didn't understand what my Sunday is like. I should have been more clear. While I enjoy thinking about you wanting to hear from me, I don't enjoy having unintentionally let you down or hurt you in any way."

Robin looked into his eyes and saw the sincerity and – something else. Something warm, wonderful, inviting. She saw safety, security, peace. Her heart started pounding. Blood roared in her ears. She wondered how he couldn't hear it, it sounded so loud.

He stood close enough that she could feel the heat of his body. Even so, she wanted to be closer to him still. She stepped forward until the tips of their shoes touched. Not knowing which one of them made the move to close the last of the gap, she found herself wrapped in his arms, his mouth on hers.

The initial punch in his gut from finally holding her and touching her spread until his whole body fairly tingled with want to get closer to her. Her cool lips almost immediately warmed under his, softened for him. He forcefully pushed back his desire and instead just reveled in the amazing feel of her lips, of her hands on his back, of her scent that surrounded him.

She was tired, worn out, still disturbed by the unfamiliar emotions she'd had assault her for a steady week. That was the reason her head started spinning, why her limbs trembled. His mouth felt hot, demanding. Wonderful.

His teeth nipped and she gasped. Taking advantage of her open mouth, his tongue swept inside. A feeling she didn't recognize streaked straight to her stomach and her knees buckled. But he was there, his arm caught her weight, pulled her closer until they were practically one.

He pulled away when she whimpered. The sound was so small, so desperate, that he sensed enough was enough. While he was willing to release her mouth, he wasn't quite ready to release her all together. He pressed his lips to her forehead, then pulled her face to his chest.

His heart pounded under her ear. She should have felt embarrassed, now that the room had stopped tilting. Instead, she was in awe over the fact that simply kissing her had caused such a reaction in him. His arms were strong and secure around her, and for just a moment, she let herself seep into him, let herself lean into his strength.

Then reality came flooding back.

He sensed it the instant before her body tensed. With great reluctance, he relaxed his arms and stepped back.

"I'm sorry," she said, stepping backward until there was at least two feet between them.

Tony laughed. "I'm not. I've been wanting to do that since we met."

Her lips felt a little numb and a lot tingly. She resisted the urge to touch them. "I need to go to work now."

Tony bent and picked up the forgotten contract. "Please accept my offer and put in your notice today."

How could he jump back to business as usual just like that? She had no cognitive thinking happening right now. Nothing inside of her jumbled up mind made any sense. "I need to go."

She spun and almost ran, throwing open the office door and pushing her way around construction workers and delivery personnel and sous chefs. Her hands shook so badly that she could barely get her car door unlocked, but finally threw it open and slid onto the seat. She tossed the contract onto the seat next to her and rested her forehead against the steering wheel. Finally, she allowed herself to give into the impulse and put three shaking fingers against her trembling lips.

TONY arrived at Robin's apartment at seven o'clock on the dot. A kind of nervous little excitement about a real dinner date with Robin made his smile stick and added a lightness to his step. He wanted to shower her with pretty things. She had so little pretty in her life. He ran his hand down the outside of his suit pocket and felt the bulge of Robin's promotion present. She would resist this gift, he knew, but he also knew she would eventually accept it.

He could hear loud music coming through the door. He paused to make sure he hadn't gone up an extra floor perhaps to stand at the wrong apartment door before rapping his knuckles hard on the door. No answer. He recognized the song and realized it neared the end so he waited. As soon as he heard a lull in the music between that song and the next, he knocked hard again. He heard "Come in!" just before he heard the beginning strands of the next song.

As he opened the door, the strong smell of oil paint assailed his nostrils. With the couch and chair pushed out of the way, Maxine had a painter's canvas set up in front of the television. Music blared out of speakers from somewhere in the room. She wore a pair of torn jeans, a half-cropped T-shirt, and had her hair bundled on top of her head. In one hand she held a palette of paints, in the other, her paintbrush.

"Hi Tony," Maxine said. She waved her brush like a wand, gesturing with it while she spoke.

Tony walked in until he stood behind her. On the canvas in front of him lay an almost complete bird's eye view of Boston Harbor as one would suppose it looked about two hundred years ago, every detail as perfect as he could imagine it. Majestic ships filled the harbor, horses and carriages lined the docks. Amazed, he watched as she dipped the brush in some blue and touched up the water.

The door opened and closed behind him. He could barely tear his eyes away from the perfection of the painting to see Sarah come into the apartment. She rolled her eyes and went to the stereo system and turned the volume way down. She paused next to Tony and looked at the painting. "Are you in love again?"

"Deeply." Maxine answered without hesitation. She arched her neck until their heads touched before she went back to work. "Can you fix me a drink?"

"Sure. What do you want?"

"Something cold."

Sarah had to climb over the couch to get to the kitchen, and Tony smiled while he continued to watch Maxine paint. Her brush moved with absolute confidence as she touched up here and there, fixing things he didn't realize were imperfect until she perfected them. Finally, she set the palette and brush down and stepped back to stand next to him. "What do you think?"

"I think you're a genius."

She laughed as she took a paint splattered rag and started rubbing at her stained fingers. "I've liked you from the first, Tony."

"Have you ever had a showing?"

"Nah. I don't do it for that. I just do it." She grinned up at him. "In my heart, I'm an advertiser. This is just dabbling. A hobby, really."

"This is the best dabbling I've ever seen. If you change your mind, let me know. I own a couple of studios around the country."

She shrugged and rushed over to get the drinks from Sarah's hands so that she could climb back over the couch.

"I'm serious, Maxine."

"I can tell," she said, "but I have no desire to make this my profession. I already have a profession."

He stared at the canvas again. The colors, the details, looked so perfect that the painting immediately swept him back in time. He could almost taste the salt air and hear the sounds from the dock. "No reason why you can't do both."

She handed him a glass of ice water. He accepted the drink and Maxine said, "Dozens of reasons, actually. But let's just leave it alone for now. You can bring it up again when I've not just come out of a massive all-night painting session."

Sarah sat down in the chair sideways, leaning against one arm and throwing her legs over the other. "So, who is it? Donald?"

Maxine started packing her paints. "Donald? Who?" Then she stopped and threw her head back, laughing hard. "No, honey, Dwayne."

At Tony's confused look, Sarah grinned. "Maxine only paints when she's in love."

She snapped the case shut with a click. "He proposed to me last night."

Sarah raised an eyebrow. "Are you getting married?"

"Of course not. But it was fun to get asked."

Tony said, "If you're in love, why say no?"

She reached up and released the clip securing her hair, shaking the black tendrils loose from their confinement. "Because, this is only fun love. It will fade." She stared at him, her green eyes serious. "I'm waiting for the big one. The real deal."

Sarah rolled her eyes and stood. "The big one?"

Maxine stared at Tony while she spoke, understanding the warmth in his eyes that was for her older sister alone. "The real one. The one that is destined. The one that will last forever."

"And how will you know the difference?" Sarah chided.

Though her sister spoke, she never took her eyes off Tony. "Oh, some people just know. Others need to be shown. Right, Tony?"

His nod was barely perceptible. But his smile stretched wide and real across his face.

Maxine climbed onto the couch and drew her legs up to her chin. "Where are you going tonight?" Maxine asked.

"Harbor House," Tony confided.

"Wow." She pushed herself up. "Hey Robin!" She yelled, angling her head toward the hallway. "Scratch that black dress and get the blue one out of my closet. With the scarf."

Robin's voice came from behind a closed door. "What blue dress with the scarf?"

"It's in a bag in the closet." Maxine crossed her hands behind her head. "Don't forget the shoes," she said loudly. "They're in the Piedmont's box."

She turned her head to grin at Tony before she closed her eyes and smiled. "I have this big salary and nothing to spend it on, so I'm afraid that I've become a clothes hound."

"Why don't you guys move into a bigger apartment?"

"Sure, as soon as you convince my darling sister that I'm done having things and I am perfectly capable of contributing to the household."

"What do you mean?"

"She wants me to move, but she won't move with me. I deserve nice things, she says." She threw her arm over her eyes, burnt out from painting. "Makes me angry. That girl saved me, literally and figuratively. Saved my life from any number of horrors and repeats of horrors, and she expects me just to leave her in this rat hole and move because I make a good salary." She moved her arm and raised her head to look at him. "But, in two more years, Sarah gets out of school. Maybe I can get her to relax a little then."

"How many dresses in bags do you have?" Robin's voice was muffled, but irritated just the same. "Geeze, Maxi!"

Maxine sighed then pushed herself to her feet. "I'll go rescue my wardrobe." She jumped over the couch. "Make yourself at home. I have to talk her into the shoes, too."

Tony chuckled. "Take your time."

He made a quick phone call and pushed his reservation back by thirty minutes. He stood in the cramped living room, touched his fingers to his tie to make sure the knot was still in place, and felt the present in his pocket again.

In his peripheral vision, he saw Sarah stand and sling her backpack over her shoulder. He turned to fully face her.

"I have to get to my parents' house. We're having a planning meeting tonight for our church's fall festival."

Tony's interested was peaked. "What church?"

"Crescent Christian in Framingham."

Mentally shifting through names and faces and people and places, he finally identified Crescent. "I know that church. Isn't Dr. Skinner the senior pastor there?"

"He is now, but he's retiring soon. There is already some uproar about staffing and such going on."

Tony nodded. "People don't like change." He slipped his hands in his pockets and his fingertips ran over Robin's gift. "Tell me about this festival."

"We have games and candy and blow up toys where kids can bounce and play. We serve hot dogs and chili and popcorn. It's a lot of fun. Tons of kids from the neighborhood come who would never have come to the church for another reason."

"We do something very similar. I go to Boston Central Christian. I've never served on the planning committee, but I'm often approached about donations and sponsorships. Let me know if there's anything you need in the way of anything like that." Out of a pocket he pulled a business card. From his shirt pocket, he extracted a gold pen and wrote on the back of the card. "This is my secretary's name and direct extension. She knows your name. Just let her know anything you need. Any gaps we can fill."

Sarah took the card, feeling a little intimidated and overwhelmed at the same time. "Your secretary knows my name?"

Tony smiled and shrugged. "Sure. You're Robin's sister."

They struggled every year to put on the festival. To think that this year the financial burden could be lifted brought hot tears to her eyes. She felt her face flood with heat. "I don't know what to say."

Tony smiled, trying to put her at ease. "There's no reason to say anything. We're all working for one goal, are we not?"

Sarah sniffled. "I wish everyone I had to work with thought the same way you do." She shifted her glasses on her face and hoped he couldn't see the tears swimming through her eyes. "How does Robin handle your faith?"

His laugh barked through the room. "With blinders. If she doesn't mention it, then it doesn't affect her, I think." His face turned serious. "But I pray for her, constantly."

Sarah opened her mouth then closed it. She closed her eyes, huffed out a breath, and decided to surge forward. "Listen, I've known her for a long time. She isn't open to the Word."

"She wouldn't be from you."

Her eyes widened. "Why not?"

"Because in her mind, she is responsible for you. She is the eldest, the protector, the provider." He smiled just to soften the next sentence, for him and for her. "She's already been in hell, so what can you possibly teach her?"

Leaning against the arm of the couch, Sarah shrugged and nodded again. "I know. Even Christ was rejected by his own people. But I've at least tried to serve as a silent witness for Robin and Maxi. I don't think I've ever done any good."

"While on this earth, we'll never see all of the fruits of our labors. You've planted seeds. And between your seed and my ..." He almost said his love for her sister, but stopped short. When he confessed his love for Robin, it would be while looking into her amazing sapphire eyes, not talking to her little sister in a cramped living room. "... and my not so silent witness, we can only pray that those seeds will grow and root and bloom and eventually thrive."

Sarah's pocket buzzed and she pulled out a phone, quickly scanning the text message that had just come in. "I'm going to be late. I enjoyed talking to you, Tony. I hope we get a chance to talk when we don't each already have other plans."

He smiled, wanting to hug her. His brotherly feelings for her didn't surprise him in the slightest. "I look forward to it."

After Sarah left, he turned back to the painting to study it further, in awe of the detail and the beauty. Maxine had surprised him, and he enjoyed that. He took in the painting and searched it with a sense of discovery and near excitement. So very often, Tony felt at least one step ahead of everyone all the time. Tony endured – and invented new ways to cope with – the boredom suffered by the brilliant every single day. He found most of life, and most people he encountered, extremely predictable. Maxine proved unpredictable. He liked that.

Time passed, but he didn't mind the wait. There was no reason to hurry. He sipped his water and considered the painting, trying to see all of the hidden elements.

"Hi."

He turned, stopping short when he saw Robin.

"Wow." He managed.

Her dress – a long blue sheath that fell tightly from her breasts to the floor – had a slit on one leg that reached to her knee and two thin spaghetti straps at the shoulders. It molded her curves beautifully, showed the faintest hint of cleavage, and accented the flare of her hips. For once, she hadn't put her hair up and it cascaded halfway down her back.

"You look amazing." Tony expressed sincerely after a thorough appraisal.

Her cheeks fused with color. "Thank you." She held up the thin wisp of material that served as the scarf. "What do I do with this?"

"Well," he said, reaching into his pocket with one hand while he took the scarf from her and stepped behind her. "What some do is drape it around their necks and let the ends trail behind them." He pulled the necklace out of his pocket and slipped it around her neck before she knew what he was doing. "But when you wear jewelry, it's fine just to drape it over one arm."

She gasped as her hand flew up to her neck. "What did – " Her fingers traced the sapphires, feeling the shape of the dripping gems, brushing over the rough diamonds, feeling the weight of actual stones against her skin. She didn't turn around, instead she skipped to the mirror hanging next to the door and gasped again at the sight. "Tony, I don't want – "

He followed her until he stood behind her and tenderly laid his fingertips on her bare shoulders. His eyes met hers in the mirror. "Sshh. It's perfect for the dress."

She stared at him, feeling a mixture of excitement and anger. Her hand never left the necklace. "I don't want jewelry from you, Tony. That's not why I'm with you."

"I believe you. I remember how you returned my tip." He grinned in genuine pleasure and his eyes twinkled with mischief. "And, ironically, it only makes me even more inclined to give you expensive gifts." His fingers moved softly up and down her arms. "I bought it a few days ago because the blue sapphires were a near perfect match with your eyes."

His fingers sent shivers through her whole body, but she slowly shook her head. "No. I'm not the type to shower with expensive gifts. Please, I don't want – "

He turned her around so that he could look directly at her. He slid an arm around her lower back, pulling her gently to him. "Just for tonight." His lips gently brushed hers. "We're celebrating in style because you deserve it."

Robin's lips tingled and she wanted to step forward and ask him to kiss her again. Kiss her deeper, longer. This close to him, feeling the heat from his body and smelling the amazing tang of his aftershave, she felt safe, secure, important. The warmth of his eyes beckoned her to let him give her this necklace, and she relented because, for some reason, pleasing him was important to her.

"Okay." She ran her hands over the length of it, until she felt the clasp in the back, terrified it wasn't secured properly and she'd lose what surely cost a few semesters worth of medical books. "Okay, but just this one time."

Tony ran a hand down her arm until he could clasp her fingers with his and bring her hand up to his mouth. He brushed his lips over her knuckles. "Thank you, *cara*. You make that necklace look beautiful. Shall we go?"

YOU know, I applied here before Benedict's." Robin took a sip of her water then propped her chin in her hand. "Almost got the job, too." In the dim light of the restaurant, with the candlelight flickering on their table, she felt very alone with him. In the intimate setting, other couples at other tables seemed to feel it, too, because people spoke quietly, almost in hushed tones, keeping up the secluded facade.

"Oh? What happened?"

"The manager objected to the fact that I wouldn't sleep with him."

"Really?" His voice was very calm, very cool, and his eyes were very hard. "And which manager was that?"

She felt a chill run up her back, glad that she wasn't the object of his anger. "Umm, his name was Brad, I think. No. No, wait, it was Brian."

He relaxed almost visibly. "I see. I fired him years ago."

"You?" She laughed. Not because he fired someone. She often feared losing one or both of her jobs and being left with nothing. She laughed because of the casual way he just dismissed it. "Of course. Why wouldn't I think that you owned this, too?"

His smile was quick and his eyes looked almost warm again. "I own a lot of things." He quickly reached out and took her hand. "I'm very happy that you're going to take the job."

She decided to be straightforward with him again. There was no sense in pretenses. "What happens when we – " she let the sentence hang in the air, confident that he would know what she asked.

He laced their fingers and looked at their joined hands. He liked the contrasts. Her hand light, his dark. Hers small and delicate, his bigger and stronger. "What happens when we break up and have all of this anger and angst and you still work for me?"

She couldn't help smiling at his choice of wording. "Yeah. Something like that."

"I don't know. I have zero experience with this. All I know is that I want to spend time with you. I want you to want to spend time with me. And you're the perfect person to manage Hanks. There has to be a way to do it all."

Robin shook her head. "I haven't signed the contract yet. Maybe -"

Tony squeezed her hand. "Listen. I really like you, and I respect you so much for everything you've done in your life. Whether or not we're involved romantically isn't going to change that."

She sat back while the waiter arrived with their first course. As he set the bowls of French onion soup in front of them, Robin watched Tony. He was sincere, she thought. He wasn't the type to play games. She picked up her spoon as the waiter departed, and felt excitement building. She hoped that they could work together once they were apart. All she knew right now was that she wanted to spend this time with Tony and she really wanted to manage Hanks.

"Besides," Tony said, "I believe God brought us together for a purpose. I don't see anger and angst involved in fulfilling God's desires.' He winked and held out his hand. "Shall we bless our meal?"

Robin set her spoon back down and took his hand.

Chapter 12

FOR weeks, rain pummeled the city, a cold rain that drove people indoors and off the streets while autumn surrendered to winter. Thanksgiving passed and the rain turned into sleet, which then turned into ice and snow.

The city buildings looked even more gray, morphing to match the dirty slush lining the roads. Even though the sun hadn't shown in weeks and the cold gray world remained perpetually wet, Robin's spirits remained high.

She understood now, what Maxine had meant when she said that she'd simply felt happier and not happy. For the first time in her life, Robin looked forward to the next new day. She looked forward to it with a smile and a sense of anticipation.

After giving Benedicts notice, Robin took over for Hank as if the place belonged to her. The staff never felt the bump in the transition, and never once challenged her authority. She had worked as a bartender and a waitress for years. Despite the grueling aspect of maintaining two physically stressful jobs, neither one of them challenged her. Managing Hank's challenged every part of her – intellectually, emotionally, physically – and she woke each morning anticipating what new challenges would face her that day.

Viscolli Enterprises sent in a tutor to teach her the fundamentals of accounting. She fell in love with perfect columns of numbers on a spreadsheet, with balance sheets and figures and projections. She spent hours after hours working with the accounting team to streamline the archaic records keeping of Hanks from handwritten ledgers to a state-of-the-art computer system that linked her to the Viscolli empire. As she worked, she learned. And learned. And soaked up everything that she could from the team of accountants and computer experts.

Hank's wife had served as his assistant manager, so she had a hole to fill with both of them suddenly leaving. After learning how to read a resume, then reading what felt like an endless stream of resumes, she finally settled on the current head hostess, Kelly Addison. Robin felt like, most importantly, that she could trust Kelly and that they could work together. The thirty-seven-year-old Navy wife and mother of three teenagers had not applied for the position but readily, and tearfully, accepted the offer. Then it was back to the resumes to find a new host or hostess.

Every turn in the bed, every new hour of every single day, brought something new and exciting to her life, and she realized that she loved her job.

Her little office in the back of the restaurant gradually became "hers" and not "Hank's". She no longer paused at the door with a hand raised to knock, and instead went through the threshold to her own inner sanctuary. Thanks to Maxine, photographs of her sisters showed up in pretty frames around the previously Spartan room. Then, thanks to Sarah, plants filled empty spots on shelves and the small window ledge. Her contributions included tins of peppermints, books on management and accounting, scattered coffee cups. Inside the walls of the little room, she could breathe, take a moment before charging back out into the challenge that was Hanks.

Robin also discovered sleep. What a phenomenon. She slept six or even eight hours a night, now. Between two full time jobs and the nightmares, good, restful sleep had become something of a luxury. Now, she left work as the restaurant closed, slept until late morning, and returned again as the lunch hour started.

Per company policy, she took two days off a week. Managers could work as many hours as required five days a week, but Viscolli Enterprises demanded without exception that, in addition to not working Sunday, another day off be taken. She resisted. Tony threatened to fire her. She'd already quit Benedict's. She capitulated.

She went to work early Mondays to do paperwork and place orders in the silence of the closed restaurant and worked until closing. Mondays had become her favorite day of the week. Typically, she took Wednesdays off. Wednesdays tended to be the slowest days of the week. She had always enjoyed having Sundays off, but adding an extra day of rest to her schedule threw her for a loop. She probably would have found herself climbing the walls of her apartment had it not been for Tony.

Despite the fact that he constantly worked out of town, acquiring this or merging that, Tony called her every morning. She found that she looked forward to his calls, anticipated them. She would lie in bed, relaxed, rested, half a smile on her face and wait for the phone to ring.

He almost always showed up on Wednesday to spend the day with her. He would call the office on Tuesday afternoon and confirm plans for this movie or that museum or this lunch. They started holding hands as they walked. He would put his arm around her at the movie. He would kiss her, oh how he would kiss her, hello and good-bye and times and times in between.

The more time they spent together, the more relaxed he became about touching her. He would brush her hair from her face, run a hand down her arm, rub her neck. However, despite her request that night so many weeks ago in that dirty laundry room, Tony never took anything any further than casual touching, warm hugs, or tender kisses. Robin thought that maybe, instinctively, she could feel him holding something back. It confused her to think that as warm and – loving – as he was, he wasn't really giving her everything. Thinking that maybe his faith had something to do with it, she wondered why he agreed to her request the night of his birthday in the first place. Regardless, she didn't feel like she could approach the subject with anything less than mortification, so she left it alone and decided to wait and see what came next.

No longer did she anticipate him using her – or her using him – and then discarding her. She began to feel very special. She felt very important to him. Treasured. She thought of him now as her "boyfriend" and smiled the first time she used that term.

Lying in bed early Monday morning after Thanksgiving, exhausted, sore, worn out from the last few weeks preparing for the holiday season, waiting for the phone to ring, she smiled. Contentment, happiness, and anticipation all waged a happy war inside of her. As she investigated these feelings, she detected a small frown mar her brow. Inside her heart, she felt like something – she didn't know what, but something – was missing.

She pondered that for a moment. Monday mornings were typically reflective, because Sunday was the one day she didn't get to spend with Tony or speak with Tony. Typically, church took up his entire day. If finally occurred to her that she missed him.

The more time she spent with him, the more she wanted to spend all of her free time with him. The thought of sitting next to him on a church pew, eating lunch after church with him and his friends, spending the entire day with him on the day he assigned such importance, held tremendous appeal to her. She decided that this coming Wednesday, she would go to his evening worship with him. He asked her every Wednesday and every Sunday if she wanted to go, and she always turned him down. Thinking about how much it would please him when she finally agreed to accompany him made her happy.

The phone interrupted her reverie. She snatched it up very quickly, not wanting it to wake her sisters. The caller ID confirmed Tony as the caller, so she simply said, "Good morning," with a smile on her face.

"Good morning, *cara*. How did you sleep?"

"Deeply. It's been an exhausting week."

"I imagine. It will stay that way until after New Year's."

"I know. Just working with the books I could see the massive incline for December."

Tony paused before continuing. "I know you're tired, and since it's Monday you likely plan on getting to work early, but I was wondering if you could meet me for breakfast."

Excited little butterflies started dancing in her stomach as they always did in anticipation of seeing Tony. "Sure. Where?"

"I've had a couple of overseas phone calls this morning, so I'm already at my office. Do you mind coming here? We could have the hotel restaurant bring something up."

Considering the time, she made some mental calculations. "I'll probably take the Charlie. I imagine traffic is a chore right now. Give me about an hour and I should be there."

"*Aspetto*. I look forward to it. I can send a car, if you wish."

"No. Don't be silly. Then we'd have to battle traffic both ways."

She could hear someone murmuring to him, but couldn't make out anything specific. "I have to go *cara*. I'll see you when you get here."

Robin threw the covers off of the bed and dashed to the closet to dress quickly so that she could get to the train.

TONY waited for Robin with a nervous anticipation he hadn't felt in a while. He couldn't predict the outcome of this conversation, and he didn't like that. His entire future stood in anticipation of how Robin would react.

As he ordered breakfast and waited for her, he thought back to the conversation he and Barry had the Wednesday before Thanksgiving...

"Did you lose track of time or something?"

Tony glanced up from his computer monitor and watched Barry saunter into the room. "Not lately." He saved his work and leaned his chair back. "Why do you ask?"

Barry sprawled into a chair across from the desk. "It's just odd that the high today is going to be a shivering twenty-nine, Christmas is just a month away, and no major deals that you're working on have crossed my desk. Despite all that, your plane hasn't left for Florida yet this year." He examined his nails.

"Really?"

"I also keep hearing rumors that the completely social Tony Viscolli has suddenly dropped from sight, which you only do when you're working on something major."

Tony leaned back in his chair. "Is that so?"

"Either you've suddenly decided you prefer the solitary life and you don't mind the cold so much, or you have a new lawyer and haven't told me. If you have a new lawyer, Tony, that would – you know – hurt my feelings."

"Well, I haven't found a new lawyer. No one submits billable hours like you do, Bear."

Barry laughed through his nose and half smiled. "So you decided to live a life of solitude, then?"

Tony raised an eyebrow. "There's another possibility that might be keeping me here."

"Nothing has ever kept you here when the temperature drops below fifty."

He opened his top drawer and pulled out the jewelry box, and without a word, tossed it to Barry. The former NFL star caught it with one massive hand and flipped open the lid with his thumb, exposing the ring with the square cut sapphire surrounded by diamonds. He shut the lid with a little pop, then opened it again for a closer look, his eyebrows knitting.

"Tony, this looks an awful lot like an engagement ring."

"Is that what it looks like?" Tony put his hands behind his head and leaned his chair even farther back. He felt a silly grin spread across his face.

"I don't know what to say. I mean, I know we've been friends for a long time, but this is just so sudden and unexpected." He started laughing. Without warning, he flipped the lid shut and tossed it back to Tony. "Can I have some time to think about it? And what will my wife say?"

"Ha ha. Oh, so funny." He caught the box with one hand and tossed it on the top of his desk.

"That's pretty serious, man. I'm assuming you're still seeing Robin? That this ring is intended for her?"

"*Esatto.* Yes."

"Let me get this straight." He hooked his leg over his knee. "You're going to ask a girl to marry you who you didn't even meet until September? This past September. Barely three months ago."

"That's the plan." Tony could practically see the gears shifting in Barry's mind.

"I don't like it."

He smiled. "Jealousy doesn't suit you, Bartholomew."

Barry dropped the whole relaxed façade and leaned forward. "No, listen to me, Tony. It doesn't make sense. How do you know she's sincere? I mean, come on, what are you worth?"

Tony laughed. "You'd have to know Robin to know how absurd that sounds."

"That's the point, man. I'm your best friend and I have never interacted with her. Ever. Is she keeping you from your friends so that she can fully sink in the hooks?"

Tony's smile faded. "No, actually, I've been all over the map lately, and only manage to see her one day a week. I took her by the church and we had dinner with Peter and Caroline. Other than that, I've been keeping her from my friends so I don't have to share."

Barry nodded faintly. "That just adds to it. You've declined every holiday party you've been invited to, and I am fully aware of how much business you actually manage to conduct at those parties."

Tony sighed and rubbed his eyes. "Barry, how long have we known each other?"

Barry chuckled and fed Tony his own words from a few months ago. "Too long for you to even ask that question."

"You ever know me to make a bad decision? Have you ever known me to go into any situation without prayer and petition?"

Barry shrugged, "Not when it comes to business. This is not business."

Tony nodded and then pursed his lips. Diplomatically, Tony said, "I appreciate your concern as a friend, then. I honestly do."

"Is she saved?"

Tony froze and slowly stretched his hand to the gold pen lying on the blotter. He gently started to spin it. "Why?"

"Should I take that as a no, or continue to press for the answer?"

Closing his eyes, he felt a weariness settle on his shoulders that he hadn't felt in a couple of decades. "I pray for her every single day. Every minute of every day. It's the one reason that ring is in that box instead of on her finger." He opened his eyes again and stared hard at his friend.

Barry folded his hands together and laid them on the desk. "Tony..."

"There isn't a single thing you can say to me that I don't already know. I know that God doesn't desire for us to be unevenly yoked. I know that my feelings for her can be a tool Satan can use against me. I know that every time I'm alone with her I face temptation that I don't know if I can fight another day without her prayer and consideration. I know all of that."

Tony started spinning the pen again. "But I also know that the moment that I saw her, I felt drawn to her. I know that every moment in her presence fills me with encouragement, unfathomable joy, delight. I knew – I KNEW – that I was in love with her within a matter of days. Maybe I've known it my whole life. And I believe, strongly, that she will love the Lord as much as I do. All I can do is stay faithful, pray for her, and just continue to be me."

Barry sat back again. Silence hung in the air for ten seconds, then for twenty. Finally he said, "And how does she feel about you?"

Tony rubbed both of his eyes and leaned back in his chair. "I don't know." He smiled and the seriousness left his face. "Well, actually, I know that she's in love with me. She just doesn't know that she knows it yet."

"Tony." The word was said on a sigh, and nothing else followed.

"I know that God is in control, *mi amico*. I trust Him. And I know you're afraid that I'm moving too fast, but I will not take this relationship any further as long as she is unsaved. I think there are few books I've read more in the last four months than the second book of Corinthians. In the sixth chapter, God is quite clear in this specific matter of the heart."

Barry sighed a deep rumbling sigh. He closed his eyes, took a couple of deep breaths, then opened them again. "I'd like to pray for you right now."

Tony coughed and cleared his throat against the emotions that flooded him. "I'd appreciate that very much." He stood and moved around the desk so that he could sit in the chair flanking Barry's. They turned their chairs facing each other and clasped hands and bowed their heads.

They had prayed for each other, jointly petitioning God for guidance and strength, and Tony felt his heart both lifted and burdened. The brotherly love that Barry displayed for him, the solidarity of his spiritual brother's love for him lifted and strengthened him in a way he hadn't realized he needed until the heaviness and imagined loneliness vanished before they said "Amen." But the burden he felt to bring Robin to an acceptance of the truth sharpened in those whispered moments and became a near physical ache.

Tony had thought about that conversation and those shared moments of fellowship for the last few days. When he had invited Robin to attend services with him Sunday, he had prayed for God to convict her of the sincerity of the invitation. He had prayed that God could fill him with a visible light that would shine brightly through him and cover her. And he had prayed for revelation as he studied God's holy word.

All of it had culminated in his telephone call early this Monday morning. He didn't look forward to the conversation he knew he would need to have with Robin this morning, but he knew that he had to say what needed saying and he could not let it go unsaid even one more day.

His secretary announced Robin's arrival and it brought Tony fully back to the present. He took a deep calming breath and smiled as the door to his office opened. He strode forward, his hands outstretched, to greet her.

After a lingering welcoming kiss, Tony led Robin to the conference table and held the chair out for her. He had the conference table in his office set beautifully. A vase full of flowers matched the linen, china plates with the gold scrolling "V" logo of Viscolli Enterprises sat perfectly centered on linen place mats, a silver pot of coffee gleamed under the lights, and a frosty carafe of orange juice sweated in the warmth of the room. A room service cart sat next to the table supporting an array of silver-dome covered dishes.

She took the proffered chair and he poured them both coffee. Then he lifted the dome lids on the room service cart, revealing muffins, bagels, corned beef, scrambled eggs, and a bowl of fresh fruit. Robin chose a bagel and some strawberries and couldn't help noticing that Tony took nothing for himself.

"You're not hungry?" She asked as she spread cream cheese on her whole wheat bagel.

"I've been up for several hours and have already eaten." He waved his hand dismissively. "Enjoy. I'll just have coffee."

Robin tried to engage him in general idle talk while she ate, but he was mostly unresponsive, his thoughts clearly elsewhere. Finally, she brushed the crumbs off of her fingertips and picked up her coffee cup. "So, what's up? Why the impromptu meeting?"

Tony always seemed so sure of himself. In the time that she'd known him, he never missed a beat. He always appeared to know what to say, how to say it, what to do and how to do it. She watched as he lifted his cup and set it down, as he rubbed a finger across his eye as if to ward off a headache, how he drummed his fingers on the table and realized he didn't know what to say or how to say it. She began to feel the beginnings of some pretty serious nerves dance along the back of her spine.

She cleared her throat. "I've always preferred a direct approach myself."

His eyes flashed surprised before he half grinned. "I appreciate you, Robin." As his fingers toyed with the knot on his tie, the diamond on his pinkie winked in the light. "I missed you yesterday. A lot." She opened her mouth to agree with him, but he held a finger up. "My worship is a huge part of my life. It encourages me, inspires me, rejuvenates me, and feeds my spirit. I cannot imagine getting through the kind of weeks I have without devoting an entire day to God and discovering the accompanying peace and solace I find in Him. But I also find myself distracted by missing you. Frankly, it's getting to be a problem for me, and it's interfering with my worship."

"Tony, that's something I've been wanting to talk with you about as well."

Thrown off of his prepared speech, he cocked his head. "Oh?"

She smiled. "There's this strange appeal to the thought of experiencing your church with you. I don't know why, but I do want to go. I'd already decided that on Wednesday when you ask me to go, I would say yes."

Tony closed his eyes, relief flooding from his heart through his soul and whispered a thank you to God, "*La ringrazio, Dio.*" He opened them again, and reached for her hand, cupping it with both of his. "I am so very happy to hear that." He smiled, and the smile warmed his eyes, giving her heart a little extra beat to it. "I planned on giving you an ultimatum."

Robin's eyes widened. "Wow. Good timing on my part."

Tony brought her hand to his lips and kissed the knuckles. "I don't know if I was going to be able to go through with it, but yes, *cara*. Excellent timing. Thank you so much for preempting what might have been a bad move on my part."

This time, Robin sat forward and used her other hand to cup one of his. "I am a straight forward kind of girl, Tony. I don't pick up on a lot of hints or subtleties, and I'll drive myself crazy wondering what you mean or what you feel if you don't come out and tell me."

Tony wondered if she realized how much she had changed over the last few months. She had completely blossomed with confidence and strength that he was certain she doubted ever even existed in her. "So you're saying just be blunt and straightforward?" Oh the things he wished he could tell her. How much he loved her, how much he desired for her to be his wife, how he longed for her soul to be saved, for her to give her life to Christ. Despite what she said, though, he knew she wasn't ready to hear it.

"Yes. Please just tell me what's up. I work much better that way."

He leaned forward and brushed his lips over hers. How much longer must he contain this amazing joy he had in the love he felt for her? "*Cara*, there is a time for everything under heaven. I hope to tell you everything in time. And I assure you I will try to be blunt and straightforward when the time comes."

Chapter 13

ROBIN watched the clock all day. She was a little nervous about going to church that night with Tony. What did one do at church? How weird were the people going to be? She hoped she didn't embarrass herself, or worse yet, embarrass Tony.

These thoughts plagued her off and on all day, so she went to work to try to take her mind off of it. It didn't help. The unknown kept distracting her from her job. She tried to work accounting, but couldn't focus. She tried to get with Casey about orders, but he was in a rare form and couldn't be bothered. So, she decided to just walk through the front of the house, check on customers, check on the hostess and the wait staff.

When she met Peter and Caroline, Robin thought that their loving acceptance of her fell well outside of the norm, an exception to every rule of life and living she had ever learned. Never before had anyone treated her so kindly, so naturally, without any expectations. When she walked into the doorway of the main church building of Boston Central Christian Church on that Wednesday night, though, she felt like she'd walked into the open arms of long lost family.

They came together and sang songs. A guitarist and someone playing a tambourine provided the only accompaniment, and the lyrics appeared on a big screen behind them. Robin enjoyed the songs, enjoyed the emotion and the passion behind them. She enjoyed hearing Tony's voice as he sang next to her. She found herself clapping along or smiling or doing both at the same time.

After songs and prayer, they broke away into smaller groups. Robin found herself in a classroom sitting on a folding metal chair, a Styrofoam cup of coffee in one hand a work sheet in the other, and the Bible Tony had given to her as a gift after they pulled into the church parking lot that evening sitting on her lap crisp and new. While holding the work sheet, she laid her hand on top of the Bible so that the back of her hand lay against the dark blue leather, enjoying the cool feel of it against her skin and instinctively knowing that this gift meant more to Tony than the dark blue sapphire necklace ever could.

As Tony took the seat next to her, he spoke softly to her, "There are several classes we could attend. This one is studying the book of Daniel. The teacher used to be a rabbi before he came to know Christ, and his Old Testament insight is amazing."

None of that meant anything to Robin. She didn't know what the book of Daniel was. She didn't know what the phrase "came to know Christ" meant, though she thought perhaps it had something to do with the conversation Tony had with her about getting off of the street, and she had absolutely no idea what Old Testament meant. The teacher started speaking, though, so she didn't ask for clarification.

Everyone in the class showed genuine pleasure at meeting Robin. She felt so loved and accepted that she hoped the class would never end. The teaching mostly went over her head, because she had zero background in anything to do with the Bible or church and with the way the discussions moved, she assumed this was an advanced class. She didn't mind, and was almost sorry when it ended.

People bombarded Tony as they left the class and made their way out of the church. She quit counting how many people asked to meet with him for this or that, how many wanted this lunch appointment or that coffee date. So many came to just meet her with kindness in their eyes and a hug or a warm handshake to hand out.

After church services she found herself back down that row of little houses with the picket fences and inside a different house – this time, the home of the former rabbi, Abram Rabinovich. He was probably about fifty, several inches shorter than her, with almost no hair. His wife was stunning, tall and thin with a beautiful face and strong Eastern European features.

"Sofia's family came from the Ukraine in the early seventies," Abram said as Sofia set a coffee tray on the low table in front of them then perched on the arm of his chair. "We met as children at synagogue so long ago that to find the exact date you might have to cut us in half and count the rings to be sure."

Sofia smiled as she draped her arm across her husband's shoulders and spoke with a slight accent. "We were married when we were seventeen. Twenty-nine beautiful years."

He laid a hand on her knee. "Not all of them so beautiful." He looked at Robin and Tony. "When Sofia came to know Christ, I'm afraid I didn't take it so well."

"Of course you didn't," Sofia said. "You had worked for fifteen years to get to where you were and were being offered that job at Brandeis University." She winked at Robin. "But you came around."

"Kicking and screaming," Abram said with a smile.

Robin shook her head. "I don't understand. If you were a rabbi, didn't you already 'know the Lord'?" She purposefully made air quotes so that he would know the clarification she sought.

Abram sat forward slightly and made a tent with his fingers. "I did not know Christ Jesus, God's only Son, to be my personal Lord and Savior. I studied God, but had no relationship with Christ."

"What's the difference?"

Abram pulled a pair of reading glasses out of his shirt pocket and held out his hand. "May I see your Bible?" As Robin handed it to him, he thanked her and flipped through a few pages. "This is a great version, and it has a comprehensive study guide. You are a smart girl. I can see that in your eyes. My suggestion to you is to read this book. When you read it, you'll understand the difference. He handed it back to her still open. She saw the words "The Gospel of Mark" in bold print across the top of the page.

"Start near the end?"

Sofia chuckled warmly. "No, darling. The Bible is not one book. It's like a library of books that are sorted by type. You have the law, which is in the front. You have prophets, poems, wisdom, eyewitnesses to Christ Jesus, letters, what our future will bring. You can read any book in any order you want. Start with Mark, it's a quick read and he talks all about what Jesus did. Then go to John. He was with Jesus, and saw the same things Mark spoke of, but used more words to describe them and focused a lot more on what Jesus said."

Robin nodded and thanked them. She looked over at Tony who sat next to her on the couch. "I imagine you've read this," she said with a smile.

He grinned and moved his hand from her shoulder to cup the back of her neck and squeeze. "A few times and in a couple different languages."

Sofia set her coffee cup on the table and stood. "Anyone interested in some cake? I don't cook, but I shop at wonderful bakeries."

They enjoyed the time at the Rabinovich's. Robin enjoyed watching them together. The love they had for each other shone through every gesture, every word, every touch. She liked watching their interactions and found herself scooting closer to Tony on the couch, and ended up cradled in his arm, holding his hand that draped over her shoulder, her arm resting against his leg. It felt comfortable and right to sit like this with him.

She wanted to freeze time and stay in that room in that little house for hours and hours more, but the clock ticked on and they had to leave. As Tony took her to her door that night, she wrapped her arms around his waist and hugged him to her, inhaling the smell of his cologne, enjoying the feel of the heat of his skin through his shirt. She didn't know how long they stood there, but when she finally broke the hug and stepped back slightly, he cradled her face in his hands and kissed her so sweetly, so gently that emotion flooded her system and clogged her throat. She had to blink tears away.

When he broke the kiss, she laid her head on his shoulder and stood there in the comfort of his arms. "Thank you for my Bible," she finally said, her lips nearly grazing the skin of his neck as she spoke.

"I'm glad you liked it. Did you enjoy church?" He asked.

"I did. I'm so glad I went." She sighed knowing that the night had to end. Straightening, she pulled her door key out of her purse. "I hope you'll be back from wherever in time to go again Sunday."

"If I was on the moon this week, I'd be back to take you to church on Sunday," he said. He pulled her close again and gave her one more long, lingering kiss.

Her arms slipped up around his neck and she kissed him back, feeling a flood of different emotions this time, less tender and sweet and more wanting, perhaps needing something – needing more. When he raised his head, he closed his eyes and rested his forehead against hers. "As it is," he said, his voice rough and low, "I'll be in town for the rest of the week. I'm really, really looking forward to church with you on Sunday."

"I am, too," she said. "Come inside."

She felt him tense as the words sank in, felt the muscles knot beneath her fingertips. She liked the feel of his strength. His voice sounded like a low growl as he asked, "Are your sisters home?"

She kissed his neck and felt his heat beneath her lips. Against his skin she answered, "No."

He felt tight like a bowstring, tight like a fist, tight like a clenched jaw. She felt his pulse race in his neck and heard him take in a massive breath before he said, "Then, let me just say no to your kind request. But understand that I genuinely appreciate the invitation. I hope you extend it again when the time is right."

"My sisters need to be home for you to come inside?"

"For now, yes." The way he said it was as if he were reminding himself.

"Is this a God thing?"

"It's about respecting you and respecting myself, *cara*. Respecting you as much as myself, actually. Kind of a golden rule thing."

It had never occurred to her that he respected her. What had she done to deserve his respect? He had slain dragons. She had simply scratched out a living for herself and her sisters. The mystery of being respected by this man would probably keep her puzzling for weeks.

Then he kissed her and her thoughts vanished. She had no idea how much time passed as they stood there in each other's arms, but eventually she found herself back in her apartment, alone, leaning against the door as she listened to the faint sound of his footsteps walking away. She could not hear the reluctance in his step, and had no idea of the real battle he waged with his flesh to make himself continue to put one foot in front of the other. She ran her fingertips lightly over her lips, feeling them tingle at the memory of his kiss.

Her work week went quickly. Sunday morning arrived and Robin woke up excited, anxious to see Tony and anxious for church. As she dressed in a baby blue cashmere sweater and a tan suede skirt with knee high boots, an outfit on loan to her from Maxine, she thought about the conversation with Abram and his talk about how knowing about God and a relationship with Jesus were two different things. She pondered the love and generosity that seemed to be the standard and which poured from all of the people she had met at the church, all of Tony's friends and employees with whom she had interacted.

As she brushed her hair, she stared at her own reflection and pondered. If something tangible, something attainable, was responsible for the happiness and contentment she found in the people in Tony's realm; responsible for the way they appeared to rise above the selfishness of human nature that Robin had always known to be the rule rather than the exception; then maybe she wanted to attain that tangible thing in her life, too. She wondered, though, how one went about acquiring this thing.

It seemed like it all centered around a personal relationship with Jesus Christ. Her entire experience with personal relationships existed in Maxine, Sarah, and now Tony. She had casual interactions with people at work, but casual was the key word. She had never scoured the personals and never joined a dating service and she never missed dating because you don't miss what you don't have. She spent too many years working too hard and too long to leave room for anyone else in her life, so she didn't go to happy hours or parties or movies or anything with co-workers that might end in uncomfortable entanglements. It worked out when she became manager, because no friendships got in the way of her doing her job, but it also meant that she had very little skill in acquiring a personal relationship with anyone, deity or not.

Tony's arrival at her door broke through her thoughts and she quickly put her brush away and moved through the apartment. She opened the door and grinned, so happy to see him and to get to spend the day with him that she just wanted to laugh with joy.

Tony always had to prepare himself to see Robin, to steel himself as he waited for her to open the door. Her physical beauty had a lot to do with it – her face and her eyes simply took his breath away. He loved the shape of her body, he loved her height and how the few times she'd worn heels she stood at least an inch taller than him which forced him to look up into her eyes. And, oh, how he loved the way she moved. But more than any of that, he simply longed for her, for so much from her, that he had to shore himself up when he saw her lest he cave in to those longings.

He longed to touch her and hold her and kiss her. He longed to tell her how deeply he felt for her, how much he loved her and desired to be with her for eternity. He longed to see her commit to Christ and to love the Lord their God with all of her heart and all of her soul. He longed for so much from her that, occasionally, he was happy that they couldn't see each other every single day or he feared he would eventually just give into the pressures of his flesh and of his heart.

When Robin opened the door, he almost had to take a step back. She grabbed her coat and her purse and stepped out of her apartment. The light blue sweater she wore made her eyes positively glow; the blue in them so vivid he thought he might drown in those sapphire pools. More than that, though, some thing about her had changed. She radiated some sort of positive energy that he could not quite define but that tugged at him. She had a smile on her face that lit up the dim hallway, and a laugh in her voice that struck musical tones.

Giving in, just for a moment, just for a small moment, he put his hand on the back of her neck and pulled her to him. His lips drank in the last of a laugh, and he felt it sparkle through his veins like a bubbly wine, leaving him drunk on her and wanting yet more. Rather than surrender all control and find himself just pushing her against the wall and ravishing her, he pulled back and away, putting his hands on her shoulders and physically taking a step back. He smiled at her, at the glow of joy on her face and the skirting of desire in her eyes. "You look beautiful, *cara. Bello.* I like the sweater."

Robin smiled. "Thank you. Maxine helped me."

"She has a good eye." He took her hand and held it as they walked down to his car.

Driving to the church, while they made small talk and enjoyed comfortable silences, she thought about that conversation she'd had with Tony in that dim laundry room those few months ago. How different things turned out than what she, without any thought about it at all, anticipated. She had expected sex, casual no-strings-attached sex, and then expected to be cast away when he had no further use for her. Never – with the way that she had felt about him at the time – never would she have expected to count the minutes until she could see him again, to enjoy sitting next to him, to reach for his hand and hold it with hers, or to attend church with him. Whatever she might have imagined, the reality was so much better, so amazing and wonderful that she wished she knew how to talk to God and thank Him properly for it.

As Tony pulled into the busy parking lot of the church, he felt Robin's hand clench in his and looked over at her. She looked so content, so happy that he wanted to ask her about her thoughts, about whatever it was that had changed inside of her. What he hoped was that she would realize it and initiate the conversation.

The air stung as they got out of the car and hurried into the church building. What Robin experienced Wednesday with the guitar and the tambourine did nothing to prepare her for Sunday morning and all its glory. A full orchestra had set up on the stage, hundreds of people milled about talking, laughing, looking for seats. Ushers ran back and forth, seating people, pushing wheelchairs, talking on radios. The big screen that had given the words to lyrics now flashed through announcements and news.

Robin and Tony found seats after speaking with dozens of people, some of whom she had met Wednesday. By the time they sat down, service began and, while she had enjoyed the music Wednesday night, Robin absolutely fell in love with the music Sunday morning. The orchestra played beautifully. The words all seemed to personally move her. The sound of almost a thousand voices raised in praise trembled through her soul.

After songs and songs and prayer and songs, the pastor approached the podium. He preached out of the book of John, a book that Robin had just started reading the morning before. He preached a sermon about love, redemption, and acceptance. He quoted the Bible and walked from one end of the platform to the other while energetically and passionately expressing how much God longed to have a personal relationship with each person in the building. For forty minutes he preached, and Robin felt every single word as if he spoke to her alone. As he stood there at the end of the platform and faced her section of the congregation, he raised his Bible in the air and said with such conviction that Robin felt the emotions closing up her throat, "God loves you and wants to know you. All you have to do," he paused and softened his voice and brought his hands to his chest, "all you have to do is let him. Just open the door to your heart and let Him in."

As he turned around, the choir stood and quietly started singing. Enthralled, Robin listened to the words as the pastor moved along the platform and continued to speak. The choir sang, "Softly and tenderly Jesus is calling, calling for you and for me."

The pastor spoke over the song, "He's calling for you to come to Him!"

The choir continued, "See on the portals he's waiting and watching, watching for you and for me."

The pastor's voice rose above the music again. "All you have to do to bring Jesus Christ into your heart is come forward. Come forward right now and accept that call from Jesus, that call to come home."

Robin felt an overwhelming emotion that took over every single cell in her body. It centered in her heart, over her chest, and spread out, magnifying by the second until she felt like something would physically burst out of her chest. She gripped the back of the chair in front of her and felt her knees start to tremble, and feared she'd fall.

The music grew a little louder and the choir sang a little stronger. "Come home, come home; ye who are weary come home."

"Are you weary?" The pastor was back and looking at her again.

The music poured through her very essence, the words wrote themselves on her heart. "Earnestly, tenderly, Jesus is calling, calling, O sinner, come home!"

"Come home." He held his hand out, as if he looked beyond the rows and rows of filled pews and spoke directly to Robin, personally. "Come home."

Not even certain that her legs would carry her, Robin stepped out in the aisle. She wasn't aware that Tony walked with her, his hand on the small of her back, but when she reached the front, an older woman with the most kind eyes she had ever encountered came forward to meet her.

She held both hands out and Robin placed hers in them. As soon as their skin touched, Robin fell to her knees, sobbing. "I'm so weary," she sobbed.

"I know." On her own knees, the woman put her arms around Robin's shoulders and wept with her. "I know, child."

With Tony kneeling beside her, his arm around her waist, Robin listened to the woman as she led her in prayer, taught her the words to say, how to say them, so that as she spoke the words, "Jesus, please forgive me of my sins and come into my heart," the pressure that had built and built inside of her chest during the sermon burst forth, like a million tiny sparks flooding from her chest through every vein in her body. It left her tingling, weak, and as it subsided, she felt strangely complete and fulfilled, and a peace settled over her shoulders like a mantle.

She didn't feel embarrassed about the storm of emotions that propelled her earlier as she thought she should. Instead she looked at Tony and saw the joy in his eyes and felt elated. He helped her to her feet and after they each hugged the woman, they held hands as they walked back up the aisle to their seats.

Robin lifted the damp hair off of her neck and took a few steadying breaths. She took the bulletin that she had placed inside of her Bible to mark the spot from where the pastor had preached and used it to fan her flushed face. Tony put his arm around her waist and pulled her into his side, cradling her next to him as they remained standing, singing the song that the choir had sung earlier, while more people flooded the front of the auditorium and sought their way home, too.

Chapter 14

ROBIN propped her elbow on the kitchen table and rested her forehead in her hand. She stared at the calendar in front of her, with horror. Somehow, the week snuck up on her and here she sat, the morning of the night of Tony's mega Viscolli Corporate Christmas party. "What am I supposed to wear to something like that?"

Maxine groaned and stretched, graceful as a jungle cat and with just as much pent up energy. "I wish you'd mentioned this before the actual day of."

"Honestly, I was hoping that something would happen that would keep me from having to go."

"Like what?"

"I don't know. Flood? Meteor? Locusts? Terrorist attack?"

"Okay. Let me think." Maxine rubbed her forehead, wishing the sinus headache would quit interfering with her thoughts. "Ugh, my brain is not functioning this morning."

"I knew that live Christmas tree you bought would mess with your allergies," Robin said with a touch of humor and a dose of concern.

"You enjoy saying, 'I told you so?'" She took a delicate sip of her orange juice. "It's in the back alley. Maybe a cat will use it as a scratching post. Or something more heinous."

"All I could find is Midol." Sarah came into the kitchen and set the bottle in front of Maxine, who sighed and popped open the tamper proof lid with one thumb.

"Well, my headache might not go away, but at least I won't have cramps."

"It has aspirin in it. Your headache will be taken care of."

"I was joking, Sarah. Sarcasm. Ever heard of it?"

"Only since I moved in here."

Robin groaned. "What is wrong with you two? You've been snapping at each other since yesterday morning."

Maxine stared at Sarah. "If you don't tell her, I will."

Sarah tore her eyes from Maxine's and stared at the table in front of her. "It's just that ... um, I mean ... well ... "

Maxine swallowed two of the pills with her juice and slammed the glass down, wincing at the sharp sound. "What little sis here is trying to get out is that she isn't going down to Florida with us for Christmas."

The words cut straight to her heart. Hoping she could keep her expression under control, she glanced at Sarah. "Oh? Did something come up?"

Her sister refused to meet her eyes. "Well, it's just that mom and dad have never had Christmas without me. I mean, I know I've never been with you, either, but – "

Maxine tossed her hair over her shoulder. "Her mommy started crying."

Sarah gasped and looked up. "You are horrible."

"No, you are. Robin works so hard, and you're constantly putting your parents in front of her. That was great when you were fifteen or even seventeen. We were happy you didn't have to live our lives, then, but you're an adult now, Sarah, and you need to learn that your mother manipulates you to keep you right there by her side."

"That's not true!"

Maxine raised her voice. "You want to bet? The woman cried when her nineteen year old said she had the opportunity to fly down to Florida in a private jet and spend three days in a mansion on the beach."

"No! She's just worried about who ..." Sarah gasped and jerked her eyes in Robin's direction.

The pain in her heart twisted like a knife. Oh, yes. What kind of element might the streetwise Robin and Maxine expose their precious Sarah to unchaperoned? The glow of a week of basking in the glory of God, in her newfound salvation, in her relationship with Tony started to dim. Robin put her hands over her ears. "Stop it! Both of you! I don't want to hear another word."

She stood slowly, feeling as if she were made of glass and if she moved too fast she might shatter. "Sarah, spend Christmas wherever you want. It won't be the same without you, but it wouldn't be for your parents, either." She looked at Maxine. "Do you have plans for today? I think I've decided to buy a dress instead of borrowing one of yours, but I'll probably need you to help me pick one out."

Maxine glared at Sarah one more time then looked at her watch. "No, I can't. I have to get some work done today."

"On Saturday?"

"Yeah, because I'm flying down to Florida with you, and the presentation is on the twenty-seventh."

"Okay." She started out of the room then stopped and turned. "You want to come, Sarah?"

Sarah pressed her lips tightly together and shook her head.

ROBIN hated shopping. She hated it with a passion. Her wardrobe had all the basics; jeans, sweatshirts, T-shirts. She could purchase them without much thought, and best of all, quickly. Christmas shopping was just as simple. Something silky or lacy for Maxine, something simple or cute for Sarah.

Some wicked part of her mind taunted her with the thought that she needed to update her wardrobe for church, church functions and such, but she tried to drown it out and focus instead on the task at hand. As much as she hated shopping, she found herself in a dress shop in the mall a week before Christmas. Oh, that's right. In a dress shop in the mall a week before Christmas Day buying a dress so she could attend a Christmas party and have everyone there wondering where they've seen her before, then realizing she was that waitress from Benedict's all "My Fair Ladied" up.

She audibly groaned when she realized that she hadn't even thought about buying Tony a Christmas present. Great. Now she not only had to buy a dress, she had to buy a present for a man. What did one buy for a man? Especially a man who seemed to own the whole world?

"May I help you?"

She turned around and saw a salesclerk with brown hair and a Santa cap perkily perched on the top of her head. "Frankly, I hope you can, or I'm in big trouble."

"Well, let's see what we can do. What are you looking for?"

"A dress for a Christmas party."

"No problem." She managed to make the word 'no' into a six syllable word. "Is it a formal party?"

Robin huffed out a breath. "I'm not positive, so my sister suggested I get a dress that could go either way."

The clerk looked her up and down. "Hmm. Let me think." Suddenly, her face lit up. "I've got it. Right this way. I think I have just the thing."

ROBIN had to dip into the savings account. Her rational mind wanted to feel guilty but her heart wouldn't let her. She figured once in her lifetime she could allow herself the luxury of spending a little too much money on a dress. And shoes. Robin flinched inwardly at the cost of the shoes. But she felt certain that Maxine didn't have a silver pair she could borrow.

It was her first Saturday off in ten years and she had to spend it at the stupid mall among throngs of holiday shoppers. She glanced at her watch, calculating that about five hours remained before she had to be ready for the party. Maybe she had enough time to figure out what to buy Tony for Christmas. At least she could have this trip serve a dual purpose.

Before she'd even completed the thought, she saw it sitting in the window of a gift shop. Robin stopped in her tracks quickly enough that the person behind her nearly bumped into her. It was a panther carved out of some sort of black stone, looking as though it was on the prowl. The way the muscles were bunched, the way the head was tilted down at a slight angle gave the impression that it was in motion, as if it had just spotted its prey and was moving closer for the kill.

It was absolutely perfect.

She dashed into the store, terrified that someone would buy it before she could get to it. The place was packed with people, and it took her a good ten minutes to find a clerk to take it off the display and package it for her.

As she left the store, she found herself cringing for the tenth time in the last five minutes. At least she no longer felt guilty about what she'd spent on the shoes. Robin quieted the numbers screaming in her mind. She forced herself not to care. She'd spent more money this afternoon on things other than necessities than she had spent in ten years, but it didn't matter. In her heart she knew that Tony was worth it.

For the second time that day, Robin stopped dead in her tracks in the middle of the crowded mall. When the realization came to her, came fully into focus in her conscious mind, it paralyzed her in the eye of a storm of conflicting thoughts and emotions such as she had never felt.

She was in love with Tony.

It felt right to think it, and terrifying. She felt like maybe she'd always been in love with him. Wow. What did that mean in the whole scheme of things?

God had worked so hard on her heart that she had focused only on that and those feelings for months. She spent almost her entire relationship with Tony running from the conviction of God that she had not even noticed how her heart had also turned toward Tony.

As tears fell from her eyes, she silently thanked God for the revelation. Now what? Did she rush to Tony's side and confess all of these feelings? What if he didn't feel the same way? Wait! Of course he felt the same way.

Think of the way he treats you, she thought. Think of the way that he talks to you, and smiles at you, and touches you.

Except that if he really did love her the way she loved him, why wouldn't he have told her by now? His confidence overwhelmed her sometimes.

As holiday shoppers thronged around her and brushed by her, she analyzed it. He must have been waiting for her to fall in love with God before he would allow himself to confess his love for her. She knew that there would be no future for them if she never became a Christian, if she hadn't accepted Christ. In the week that followed, he had allowed her the space to really soak in her newfound salvation and eternal security. He had spent their time together praying with her and teaching her and loving her the way that he always had.

She could not believe it, but could not longer deny it. She really was in love with him.

Her knees suddenly felt weak, and she looked around, spotting an unoccupied bench right beside her. She collapsed onto it before she draped the garment bag along the back of the bench and set the other bags at her feet. She'd just rest there for a minute. She needed to just rest.

What should she do now? Wait for him? Throw herself at him and confess her undying love? Even the thought of that made her giggle. She put her hands to her face and felt the silly grin and shook her head at herself. Giddy. Giddy in love. She wondered what would happen if she arrived at his office unannounced and suggested that he take her out to lunch. No, that was silly. The big company Christmas party was tonight and he was likely embroiled in all sorts of details about that. Managers and directors from all around the company were flying in and checking in to the hotel. She'd see him in a few hours. Maybe …

Just as she imagined how she would confess her love for Tony, someone sat next to her.

"Hiya, Robin."

She turned her head and managed a smile, though she sighed inwardly. "Hi, Sandy. Doing some Christmas shopping?"

She hadn't seen him since the week after the bar closed down at Hank's. It was odd seeing a bar patron in full light. The shadows in the dim bar always hid the flaws, and in Sandy's face, she could see the damage of years of alcoholism. The vessels on his face were broken, leaving little red marks. The skin around his eyes looked puffy and red and the whites of his eyes weren't quite white. She also noticed how much his hands shook.

"Actually, I was following you."

A touch of cautious fear twisted her stomach, but she kept her eyes steady and on his. She could handle Sandy. "Oh yeah? Why's that?"

He looked around him, his head moving in jerky movements. "Why don't we go somewhere more private?"

"No. I don't think so."

He leaned closer to her, and she had to hold her breath to keep from gagging on the stench of old beer that permeated the air around him. "You don't want to mess with me, little girl."

She rolled her eyes and chuckled while she adjusted her bags and stood. "What are you going to do to me, Sandy? Huh? Do us both a favor. Go home and sleep it off."

He stood with her, and for the first time, she realized how big he was. He was a good head taller than her, but he was also huge, bulky. He leaned down until his nose practically touched hers. "It's not what I can do to you, Robin, it's what my friends can do to your little sister. They're watching her right now, while she's at her parents' in Framingham. I just found out she's at the kitchen table, the one with the blue tablecloth, decorating Christmas cookies."

The finger of fear turned into a giant fist, tightening up and trembling in her gut. She believed him, and it terrified her. "Okay. Let's go somewhere more private."

He made a sweeping gesture with his arm, and she went ahead of him on stiff legs, through the mall, to the parking lot. Not knowing what else to do, she headed for her car. The whole time, he walked right behind her, half a step away, and her mind whirled while she tried to figure out what he wanted.

She stopped at her car and turned around, waiting for him to give her further direction. He did nothing but stuff his hands in the pockets of his worn coat and shiver against the bite in the air. Robin didn't even feel the cold.

"Do you know who I am?" he finally asked her.

She lifted her chin. "Should I?"

His eyes hardened. "I don't know why I thought that drunk slut would have told you anything about me." He huffed out a breath and rolled his eyes toward the gray sky. "I wouldn't have been caught if it hadn't been for her, anyway. I wouldn't have had to go to the pen for fifteen years if she hadn't screwed up the deal so bad. But still, not to tell a girl about her daddy, now that's just wrong."

Robin gasped and took a step backward. She opened her mouth, but no words came out. Then those watery eyes were back on hers. Eyes that would have been the same color as hers had they not been dulled by alcohol. He smiled, his teeth yellow against his pale skin. "Ah, you're quick. Just like your daddy. I had to be quick. It's what's kept me from being caught this whole time."

Somehow she knew the answer, but she asked the question anyway. "Caught for what?" she whispered.

He went on as if he hadn't heard her. "See, I called her when I got out, thinking we could start all over. Man, she was a looker. But what a nagging

—" He paused and shook his head. "I'd just scored big time, and we were going to hit it big. But she had that boyfriend she wanted to pull in on the deal. I didn't even know about him until we got back to the apartment. You can't even begin to imagine how angry that made me."

The air burned in her lungs. Suddenly, she could feel the cold and started shivering. She took another step away from him. "You killed them?"

He stepped forward. "He's the one who had the gun. He pulled it on me. But I knew how to move back then and got it from him. The first shot was an accident. I swear it was. But then I had to kill her, too. She knew who I was and I wasn't going back inside. No way was I going back."

He let out a shuddering breath. "But that's all water under the bridge. All in the past," he said in a calmer voice. "I wanted to talk to you about the present."

She dropped the packages on the ground, wondering if she could take him. Fear kept her frozen, and she knew she couldn't. She also knew she couldn't risk Sarah. "What about it?"

"See, here's the deal." He suddenly showed signs of nervousness, and that terrified her even more. "I really worked on going straight, you know? I wasn't ever even going to tell you who I was. I figured, you'd work the bar and I'd get to know you, and in the meantime I was doing whatever I could to keep it going, to have a roof over my head and still be able to pay my tab."

He calmed, grinned again. "But the problem is, the straight and narrow ain't never worked for me. I slipped here and there, nothing major, but a deal's a deal, you know?" He fished a pack of cigarettes out of his pocket, and his hands shook badly enough that she wanted to take it away from him and get the cigarette out for him. "Then the bar closed down and I had all this free time. So a few months ago, I got into something big. Only, I didn't know who I was dealing with, and they don't have a sense of humor about the money I skimmed off the top. I never touched the merchandise, never have. You gotta be stupid to touch the merchandise. But, I've always skimmed. Everybody does. You know, to cover expenses and what not."

He paused long enough to light the cigarette, then leaned against her car and hooked his thumb in the pocket of his dirty jeans as casually as if he were discussing last night's football game. "So, I'm finding myself in a bit of a jamb. I have to come up with the money, see, all of it."

She rubbed at throb that had suddenly appeared above her eye. "I don't have any money, Sandy."

He made a sound in the back of his throat like a strangled cough. "My name's Craig. Craig Bartlett."

She spoke with extreme patience, as one would to a child. "Okay, Craig. I don't have any money."

He laughed then bent over and coughed until his face turned beet red. He finally recovered and straightened. "I know you don't. But I also know that your boyfriend does."

Ice clawed through her stomach and began working through her veins. "What are you talking about?"

"Oh, come on. You can't lie to your old man. I know. I been watching." He straightened and flicked the cigarette away. "Here's how it's going to work. Either ask him for the money or pilfer something we can hock. I don't care which. But you do that, and you do it before Thursday. I have to pay these folks Friday morning. Got that? You got until Thursday."

"No way." She was mad now, and the heat of anger started to thaw the ice.

He grabbed her by her shirt front and dragged her toward him. "Ten thousand. I need ten large by Thursday, or I hurt your sisters. I don't care which one, either. Neither of them's mine." He pushed her away and she staggered into her car. "Thursday," he repeated, then stalked away, leaving her standing there in the cold.

Chapter 15

THE dress had the faintest of silver snowflakes sewn into icy blue satiny material. It had long tight sleeves hemmed at the wrist with silver thread and buttoned down the front with silver buttons in different snowflake shapes from the scooped neck down to where the dress stopped just below her knees. When she'd put it on in the store, she'd felt elegant and beautiful. Tonight she felt cheap and gaudy.

Robin managed to get her hair piled on top of her head and styled into a mass of curls secured by a silver clip on loan from Maxine. But when she tried to apply her makeup, tremors kept going through her hands and she had to wipe it off and start over again twice.

She added lipstick and stood back from the mirror. No one looking at her would know that it had taken a full half an hour to apply the makeup, and only the façade mattered, anyway. She took a deep breath and slowly released it before she reached for the necklace, another loan from Maxine. The latch wouldn't catch, so she took another breath to try and steel her nerves, then tried again. Still nothing.

It all started to overwhelm her, and suddenly her world began to gray and her heart started racing. Then she heard the knock on the door and let out a strangled cry.

Steeling herself, she met her own eyes in the mirror and tried to give herself a little boost. Tonight was a big deal for Tony, and she could pretend she felt perfectly fine and dandy until tomorrow.

Secure in her ability to control her emotions, but not sure how much time had passed since the knock, she quickly moved through the apartment and threw open the door. There stood Tony, clad in his tuxedo, looking gorgeous and strong. Her eyes met his, and some calm returned. Just remember the façade, she told herself. This night belonged to Tony.

"Wow," he said. "You look absolutely beautiful. More than beautiful. Amazing."

She smiled and fought back the sting of tears. "Thank you. I actually went shopping this morning."

"You have both beautiful eyes and a good eye, *cara*," he said with a smile. "Problem?" he asked, gesturing to the necklace she still had clutched in her hand.

"Yeah. The latch isn't working. Or my hands aren't. One of the two."

He picked the necklace up and made a show of inspecting the latch he'd personally had Maxine rig while her spicy perfume wafted up and assaulted every sense he had. His hands shook and he thought about them all alone in the apartment. Then he thought about the hundreds of people waiting for him at the hotel. So, he turned her toward the mirror by the door.

Behind her back, he switched necklaces, then put the new one around her neck. Maxine had done him the favor of calling him the very second Robin had returned with the dress, so he'd known exactly what to buy. It was a simple single strand choker of diamonds set in snowflake patterns in white gold that complemented the dress as if it had been made for it.

He watched the reflection of her face while he secured the ends of the chain. Her eyes were downcast, her expression serious, and he wondered what was going through her mind. He could almost see the waves of tension radiating from her.

"There," he said, "all fixed."

"Thanks, I don't know what was wrong with the stupid – " Her hand touched the choker as her eyes flew up to the mirror. She stared at her reflection with wide eyes before she slowly raised them to his. "Tony, I … you … I … "

Tony kissed the side of Robin's neck just below her ear and smiled. "It's perfect." He murmured. He turned her by her shoulders and tilted her chin up. "You're perfect."

He turned her gently, but firmly, and he deliberately took her mouth with his. The slow languid kiss made her sigh. The sound vibrated through him. She stepped closer and wound her arms around his neck. A spark of desire ignited and spread through his middle. He forced himself to break contact and stamp it down.

Robin closed her eyes and rested her forehead on his shoulder. "You need to quit giving me gifts like this."

He grinned and trailed a finger down her sleeve, over the pulse in her wrist and back up again. "Why?"

"Because I don't want you to think that I expect it." She raised her head and gripped the lapels of his coat and looked at him with eyes so intense they glittered. "That's not why I'm with you. I don't care about the jewelry or the money."

His eyes sobered as he tilted his head and looked at her. "I know that, Robin."

She jerked away and reached her hands behind her neck, fumbling with the clasp. "People will see me and they're going to think – "

"Stop!" He grabbed her wrists and jerked them down. "What does it matter? Huh?" He rolled his eyes over her head and muttered under his breath. "*Si un piccolo testardo.*"

She'd been working on learning Italian, and her eyes widened while she fought to keep up with the words as he rattled them out. "Did you just call me a little pig?"

"Pig headed. I called you pig headed, because I've already made it clear that I don't care what others think."

"People will – "

"So what?" He realized the level to which they'd raised their voices and took a deep steadying breath. "We know. You and I know. Us. God knows. That's all that counts."

She breathed in and out, concentrating on fighting off the panic. "Okay." Another breath, in and out. She nodded. "Okay, I'm sorry. I guess I'm just nervous."

He smiled and kissed her one more time. "Everyone will love you." Like I do, he silently added. "I have no doubt."

Wanting to lighten the mood, she pushed away and grabbed her clutch bag. She pulled out her lipstick tube, intending to repair the damage of his kisses. "Except those who call me a pig."

He laughed and kissed the top of her head before gathering her coat from the back of the couch. "The exact translation was you're a little pig headed fool."

She snorted while she laughed and tried to hold her arms steady through the gale while he helped her put on her coat.

BARRY watched them walk into the ballroom arm in arm – the tall, dark Italian with the cool, slim blonde. Even he, skeptic of their relationship, could see how well they looked together, and could see the way his friend practically hovered over her as they worked the room. His touches were casual but constant – a brush on her cheek here, a hand at the small of her back there, and Barry relaxed further when he saw how Robin responded, how she leaned into Tony or smiled a smile just for him. They communicated through touches as though they'd been married for years, and for the first time, Barry began to rethink his earlier opinion.

Deciding that he'd observed from a distance long enough, he headed in their direction. The party consisted of all of the people who ran the individual companies of Viscolli Enterprises across the country, and their spouses or companions. The gathering was mandatory without being called that, and airplane tickets and lodgings were part of the annual budget for this event. They all knew Barry and several accosted him with different legal questions. At one point, he lost sight of the couple while he talked to a manager and his deejay wife from a west coast radio station Tony owned. Finally, though, he managed to make it to them.

For the first time since they'd arrived, they stood in a corner alone. Barry watched Tony turn his head and whisper into her ear before he looked up and saw Barry's approach. He felt that conversation they'd had about Robin was the right conversation at the right time. Still felt that way. But he couldn't help feeling relieved when Tony's eyes warmed.

"Barry. I was wondering where you were." He looked over Barry's shoulder. "Where's Jacqueline?"

Barry looked at his watch. "She should be landing in Zurich within the hour."

Tony raised an eyebrow. "Christmas in the Alps this year?"

"Apparently." His lips formed a hard line. "My flight will leave Tuesday morning."

Catching Barry's tone and leaving the subject alone, Tony slipped an arm around Robin's back. "Robin, you haven't officially met Barry Anderson, Viscolli's lawyer and, I'm proud to say, a personal friend. My best friend, in fact."

Robin remembered the last time she'd seen the giant now standing in front of her. She'd been in Hank's kitchen and he had defended Tony when she claimed that Tony insinuated that she could be bought. Her cheeks flushed a little at the memory. "You're the Shirley Temple," she said with a big smile, hoping to cover some of her uneasiness.

Barry cleared his throat and squeezed her outstretched hand. "How can you even remember that?"

"It was just surprising that a guy who looked like a linebacker would order that drink. I guess it stood out." She noticed the same drink in his hand and laughed. "Anyway, it's nice to meet you. Tony speaks of you often."

Robin imagined he could look really mean if he gave it half an effort, but after so many years with Hank, his size did nothing to intimidate her. She could see the kindness in his eyes, and immediately liked him, though she couldn't help shifting under his appraisal.

"I wouldn't have recognized you if I hadn't known who you were," he said, finally releasing her hand.

She gestured at the dress. "Well, it's a far cry from a tuxedo shirt and slacks." She leaned closer to him. "But I'll confess that I'd be more comfortable." She shifted her feet in the silver heels. "Especially in those ugly shoes. I miss my ugly shoes."

The longer Barry spoke with her, the further Tony relaxed. He checked his watch. "It's about time for me to give my yearly pep talk." He glanced around the room until he made eye contact with someone and nodded. "Why don't you two go sit at the table and we'll get the party started."

Robin hooked her arm through Barry's. "How uncouth would it be for me to kick my shoes off at the table?"

"Your feet don't smell do they?"

"Of course not. My nose smells. My feet walk."

Barry patted her hand while Tony followed behind them. "In that case, anyone who wants to say anything will have to come through me."

She laughed and glanced back over her shoulder at Tony. He looked so relaxed, so at ease, and she vowed to keep the simulated smile solidly on her face, no matter what.

SILENCE cloaked the interior of the limo while Robin toyed with the choker around her neck and stared out of the window. Tony stayed quiet himself, choosing to just watch her while the car cut through the quiet streets. He'd known something had been bothering her earlier in the day and had assumed it was nerves from the party, but as the evening wore on, he watched her become more and more tense. He watched all night and whenever she wasn't actively engaged in speaking with someone or laughing just a second too long at something someone said, her face sobered up and a few times she seemed on the verge of tears.

Neither spoke when the car pulled up to her apartment building or when the driver let them out. They held hands as they climbed the stairs to her floor and walked, slowly, down the hallway to her door. She slipped one shoe off in the hall outside of her apartment, leaning into Tony when she wobbled on one foot and peeled the other shoe off, but still never spoke a word. Tony decided to be the one to break the silence. He took her key from her and unlocked the door but didn't open it.

"May I make an observation?" He asked, leaning against the wall by the door.

Robin raised her eyes from the ugly green and orange design in the carpet to look at him. "Sure."

"You wouldn't be able to play poker. Every single thought you have is written all over your face the very instant you think it."

Her head started spinning. She smiled a smile that hurt her face and stepped forward to run a finger over his bow-tie. "Then you know what I'm thinking right now," she said.

He covered her hand with one of his and waited until she raised her eyes to look at him. "Yes, I can tell what you're thinking now. I know you're trying to distract me, because something is seriously bothering you. And I know it's something important."

She raised an eyebrow. "Can you also tell that I don't want to talk about it?"

He closed his eyes and sighed before looking at her again. "I wish you would."

He didn't resist when she pulled her hands out from under his. Framing his face with her hands, she kissed his unyielding lips. "I don't know how." She tried to kiss him again but he didn't give in. Finally she stepped back. "I really wanted to wait until tomorrow. This was your big night." She opened the door and stepped into her apartment. "Can you please come in?"

After a moment of hesitation, he stepped inside. In the late hour, the apartment lay dark and silent. Robin knew her sisters lay sleeping in their shared room, so she kept her voice low as she and Tony sat on her love seat, their bodies turned toward each other. "Would you mind terribly if I said I didn't really want to go to Florida?"

Tony reached out and took her hand. Her fingers were like ice, so he sandwiched her hand between both of his, hoping to give her a little warmth. "Depends. Would you go if I said I had to go, regardless?"

She stared at his face, his handsome face, his beautiful face and thanked God for giving him to her. "I want to spend Christmas with you, but Sarah can't come."

He could hear the hurt in her voice, could see the sting of tears in her eyes. "I really need to go. I've been neglecting it, but it can wait until after the holiday, *mi amante*. I will spend Christmas wherever you are." The relief he saw flash in her eyes had nothing to do with her sister. He frowned at her. "What is wrong, *cara*?"

Robin felt tears flood her eyes and spill down her cheeks. She ripped her hand from his and scrubbed at both cheeks. "I'm afraid to talk about it." She sobbed.

He pulled her close. Almost immediately he could feel her tears soak through his shirt and he felt helpless. "I can't fix it if I don't know what it is."

Overwhelmed, Robin couldn't hear the love in his voice, didn't feel the security of his arms. All she could think was that he would regret starting this relationship with the daughter of a murdering extortionist. "You're going to hate me."

She felt his deep intake of breath and the slow release. "I can assure you that I will not hate you." He kissed the top of her head and pushed her back so that he could frame her face with his hands. She looked up at him, at his face, and could see the sincerity in his eyes. "Listen to me. Whatever it is, between me and God, we can fix it. You just have to talk to us. Trust Him and trust me. But don't despair."

Despair. How could he have worded it more perfectly? She pulled away from him and launched to her feet. Needing to move, she went into the little kitchenette and poured them each a glass of water. Glad to have something to do with her hands, she returned to the living room and set the glasses on the coffee table, but did not sit down.

She briefly left the living room and went to her room. The bags she'd brought in the previous afternoon still sat on her bed, a carnage of hangers and boxes and tissue paper left over from her getting ready for the party. She searched through them until she found the one from the gift shop. She wished, now, that she'd taken the clerk up on her offer to wrap the gift, but she'd wanted to do it herself. Now its package would have to be the bag.

When she returned to the living room, she found Tony standing by the couch. She set the bag on the coffee table and sat down.

"This is your Christmas present," she said, pushing it toward him. "I'd like for you to open it now."

She could sense his irritation and impatience. "Christmas is a week away."

She blinked and continued as if he hadn't spoken. "I was almost desperate. I mean, what do you get someone who has everything? I knew it had to be something special. Then I saw it."

He stared at the bag. She waited ten seconds, then thirty, then sixty, wanting to rip it open for him. Finally, with a lukewarm smile and leisurely movements, he sat back down on the couch and reached for and then opened the bag.

Tony lifted the panther out and tossed the bag somewhere behind him before gently setting the sleek black cat on the bar in front of him. He ran his hand along its back, tracing the line of muscles that looked ready to spring. When he finally looked back up at Robin, his eyes nearly matched the color of the stone, and she almost gasped.

He didn't speak, just looked back down at the statue. Then he took a sip of his water. She cleared her throat. "It reminded me of you." His eyes flew back up to hers and she hurried on to get out what she had to say. "Its strength is there, shimmering just under the surface, but it's contained – controlled. You're like that, you know? I can't really explain it. And those eyes – so intense they're nearly scary."

His hand ran along the back of the statue again. "Thank you, Robin."

On the bar between the living room and kitchen, she spotted one of her tins of peppermints. She moved over to the bar and opened it. "My father was put in prison for cocaine trafficking when my mother was pregnant with me."

She pulled a peppermint out of the tin and toyed with it before putting it in her mouth and sucking on it. "She was a horrible woman. I can't even begin to describe it to you."

When Robin looked up she found him watching her intently, staring. "Well, maybe I don't need to describe it to you. Maybe you already know." Nothing on his face changed, so she continued. "She was abusive, loud, harsh, neglectful. She used men and drugs. Men provided places to live, and income for drugs. She provided whatever it was they wanted in their sick minds. My earliest memories were hiding from her or the boyfriend of the week – and holding Maxi, then holding Maxi and Sarah. I remember cowering in this dark closet cradling Maxi to me, praying she wouldn't wake up and give away our hiding spot. I couldn't have been much more than three or four, and the noises coming from the outside of the closet –"

She cleared her throat and looked back down at the little metal tin. "When I was fifteen, my mother and her boyfriend were murdered." Finding some reserves of courage, she looked at him again. "He was a really bad guy. He …" She cleared her throat again and rolled the mint on her tongue. "He would come to my bed at night after mom passed out and …" her breath hitched and she stopped speaking.

For the first time since she started talking, Tony's eyes came to life, as if someone had flipped on a switch. Heat burned behind them and his jaw set like iron. In that heartbeat, she was sure that if he weren't already dead, Tony would have hunted him down. She didn't know how she felt about that so she didn't finish the sentence.

"We were all back in that closet. It wasn't the same closet, but they were all the same, really. Dark, smelly, sometimes there were things in there scurrying through the walls or on shelves above our heads. I'd taught Maxine and Sarah how to hide, how to get way back in the back against the back wall. Out of sight, out of mind, you know? He was trying to get me. My mother had left hours before, and by then he was good and drunk and he decided he wanted me to scratch an itch."

Robin spoke as if the events she related had happened to someone else. Occasionally, she sucked on her peppermint, letting the cooling mint soothe her taste buds, as if she wanted to cleanse her mouth of a bad taste left behind by speaking about these memories. "I managed to kick him in the groin, and ran to the closet. I hadn't been in there long when we heard our mother come back. She had another man with her. There was an argument, and then gunshots. Then it was so quiet. I felt like I couldn't breathe, and Maxi and Sarah were so strong and so good." Her voice hitched and for a moment, just a moment, she was fifteen again and trying her best to protect those two precious children. "When the police found us and pulled us out of the closet, we learned that our mother and her boyfriend had both been shot dead.

"Sarah got adopted. Maxi and I made it in the system. It was bad there." Another dark memory surged to the surface but she beat it back. It was a memory for another time. "Maxi and I were separated and I was put into a girls' home. I ran away when I turned eighteen. Hank gave me a job and he helped me get Maxine out, helped me keep her safe. Eventually, I got visitation with Sarah and for one hour a month, my family was together and I never really gave my mother much of another thought. I knew I would do anything in my power not to be like her, not to be used like her. All these years, and I never even cared who killed her." She sat again folded her hands in her lap. "Really, it was kind of a relief."

Tony reached forward and covered both of her hands with one of his. "Why haven't you ever told me this before?"

Her shrug was weak. "It's one thing to pull yourself off the streets and become what you've become. It's another to be a victim your entire life. That's why I did what I did, Tony. I got Maxi and I supported her, then I put her through college. I worked my tail off so she wouldn't ever have to be like our mother. She can count on me and she will never need a man to survive."

Robin watched Tony's eyebrows rise as he took in this concept, this motivation. "Then I talked Sarah's parents into letting me help her. It was hard, and exhausting, and there were times I just wanted to cry and cry because I was so tired and tuition and books cost so much and they needed to be secure."

"But you didn't cry."

She shook her head. "I couldn't. That would have been the ultimate feminine weakness. Cry when the chips get you down." She turned her hand and linked his fingers with hers.

He raised their joined hands and placed a kiss on the back of hers. Her heart did a flip-flop at the gesture. "What else? There's more."

"This afternoon at the mall, an old bar regular from Hank's approached me. He's a little annoying, but I never gave him too much of a thought. He paid his tab every night, and other than trying to hold my attention too much, he was nothing to me. A nobody." She pulled her hand from his and stood again, then started pacing. "He told me – " Her breath hitched and she spun around and looked at him. "He told me I had to go with him. He told me he had friends, that they were watching Sarah. He even described the room she was in."

Tony straightened. "Go on," he said in a tight voice.

"He took me out into the parking lot. He … he … "

In one move, Tony was up and in front of her, gripping her shoulders.

"What? What did he do?"

Robin looked at the intensity on his face, horrified at what would come next. "He told me he was my father. He told me that he killed my mother. He told me he would kill one of my sisters if I didn't give him ten thousand dollars by Thursday." She spoke as quickly as she could, never realizing that tears streamed down her face.

He gripped her shoulders hard enough to bruise but she didn't realize that either. "What did you say to him?"

"I ... I ... I t-t-told him I d-d-didn't have any money," she managed to get out.

"And?" He gave her a small shake. "And what, Robin?"

"He ... he ... he ... Oh dear God in heaven, you're going to hate me. I'm sorry. I'm so sorry."

"Robin, what else?"

She thought she was going to throw up. "He said you had money." She covered her face with her hands, and sobbed. "I don't know what to do, Tony." He pulled her to him and wrapped his arms around her. "I don't know what to do."

"Sshh. Shush, now, *cara*. Don't worry." For the first time since the day he gave his life over to Christ, Tony ceased the continual praying in his spirit. He shut it down as the all too human emotion of the need for retribution flooded through his heart. He felt his mouth thin as he refused to seek counsel from the Holy Spirit, knowing without asking that what he wanted to do would not be a recommended course of action. "I know exactly what to do."

Chapter 16

TONY sat in his apartment on his couch. He kept the shades drawn and all of the lights in the room extinguished, with the exception of the dimmed track lighting above the couch. Late morning had come and gone, but Tony did not feel fatigue yet. He sat back against the leather, staring at the panther on the table in front of him.

He had finally managed to soothe Robin out of the panic that caused her hysteria and calmed her down, assuring her that he did not hate her. After he persuaded her to go to bed, he let himself out of the apartment.

Tony made eye contact with the statue. Yes, he could see the similarities there, just as she'd seen. Only there was more that she hadn't touched on, perhaps because she didn't know. He also enjoyed the natural territorial instinct of the cat. He also commanded the ruthlessness that only true predators possessed, either when they hungered or when an intruder breached their territory.

She had thought that he would hate her because someone wanted to use her to get to him. He knew it had taken a lot for her to tell him. Robin wasn't the type of woman who would easily turn to someone, anyone, for help.

She had looked to him. That meant more to him coming from her than a declaration of love would ever mean. He would take care of it. He would take care of her. Just as the panther in front of him would handle any foe that foolishly encroached upon his territory. He leaned his head back and stared at the ceiling making plans, deciding on a course of action.

When he knew what he had to do and how to do it, he checked his watch and called Robin. She answered with a sleepy voice on the fourth ring, and he felt a pang of regret for waking her. "Hello, *cara*. I'm sorry I woke you."

"No. Don't be sorry." He could hear the shifting of the bedcovers and could picture her sitting up in the bed.

"I only wanted to ask if you could meet me at church. If not, I could send a car for you, but I have an errand to run and won't be able to get to your side of town."

"No, that's okay. I'll drive."

He smiled so that she would hear it in his voice. "Wonderful. I can't wait to see you."

They said their good-byes and he hung up the phone. With a last glance at the predatory cat on his coffee table, he stood and moved to his dressing room to prepare for the day.

TONY headed deep into his old neighborhood, driving slowly. As he passed the church, he noticed that the parking lot had a scattering of cars in it already. He knew he had another thirty minutes before he should be in his classroom, greeting students. At the moment, he couldn't even remember what he planned to teach that morning. Instead, he focused on the task at hand. He turned at the corner, drove another quarter of a mile, then turned down another street, relishing in the dark thoughts that surfaced as the memories assaulted him. He needed dark thoughts right now.

He pulled up to the curb in front of a dilapidated building. As soon as he stepped out of the car, a group of teenagers surrounded it. Cars like that, shiny black sports cars that cost more than ninety percent of the country could afford just didn't park in front of this building.

He picked the one with the meanest eyes and stabbed his gloved finger at him. "You." He pulled a bill out of his pocket. "You see this?" he asked. The kid sneered and nodded at the hundred dollar bill Tony held. "You get ten of these if this car is exactly the same when I come out."

"Why should I trust you?"

Tony shrugged. "The same reason I'm trusting you." He walked inside without a backward glance. He didn't even bother to lock the doors on the car.

It was eight forty-five on a Sunday morning, but it hardly mattered. Jake's Bar stayed open twenty-four hours a day, seven days a week, and Tony had a strong feeling that the person he sought would be here.

He removed his dark shades just as he walked inside to start the process of letting his eyes adjust to the murky darkness within. It took real effort to keep his nose from curling at the stench of a bar where spilled beer was rarely mopped up and most of the patrons didn't care whether they'd showered that week or not. His eyes scanned the room, noting the possible conflicts and searching for the familiar face. He found him at the far end of the bar with an unlit cigarette dangling out of his mouth and greasy hair falling into his eyes.

The bartender paused and watched him walk the length of the room, measuring him up. Tony met his eyes and finally recognition dawned on Jake's face. Once recognition hit, he grinned, choosing, Tony guessed, to ignore the fact that the last time he'd seen Tony he'd told him he'd kill him if he ever saw him near his joint again. Money and influence coaxed a lot of people into bouts of amnesia.

"Well, well, well," Jake said, "Look who decided to grace my doorway, again. What can I get you, Tony?"

"Whatever he's drinking," he said, gesturing at his target. He reached the end of the bar and leaned his hand on the grimy surface, trapping the weasel in front of him in the corner. "Hi, Billy. Remember me?"

Nervous eyes darted up and back down again. "Yeah. Sure. Who doesn't? You're a neighborhood legend." Billy's eyes darted around, perhaps looking to see if Tony had brought along any muscle. "What cha doin' here?"

"Who says I can't just drop by and catch up with old friends?" He ignored the glass that Jake slid toward him and leaned closer. "I never forget anyone who ripped me off, Billy. And I distinctly remember you ripping me off."

Billy's eyes skirted around, never resting on Tony. "What does it matter to you, anyway? You got out. You're living high and mighty now, right?"

He pulled out a fifty dollar bill. "Seems like you ripped me off for ten times this amount, didn't you, Billy boy?"

"Oh man!" He grabbed Tony's drink and downed it in one swallow. Tony looked up and nodded for Jake to pour another one. "Whatcha want, man? Just get to it without the games."

Tony leaned closer. "I need info. And I need someone to spread some info around."

"I don't know nothing."

"You owe me. Don't forget that." He reached into the pocket of his overcoat and pulled out a wad of fifties. "And I pay. Twice this much if you do it right."

Billy stared at the money, his eyes bugging like a strangled mouse. "Okay." He nodded, reminding Tony of a chicken. "Okay. Whatcha need to know?"

"I need to know who Craig Bartlett owes."

"What makes you think I know?"

"Billy, you know everything. Your slimy little ears are pressed to the ground more than anyone else's." He raised an eyebrow. "Unless you've lost your touch."

Billy stared at the bills and licked his lips. "Okay. Okay. Word is he owes Junior Mills."

"Who's Junior Mills?"

"God man, you've been gone too long." He took the fresh drink and swallowed it all. "Old man Jacob Mills bit the dust years ago. Apparently, some of the local bulls gave him a free stick therapy session and he saw the light long enough to recall the names of some southern gentlemen. After that, I hear his shoes got heavy and pulled him to the bottom of Boston harbor."

Tony felt a pang of the past. He had once worked for Jacob Mills, stole a few cars for him. Who could have foreseen that Jacob's untimely end would come at the hands of some South American drug lord?

Billy was still squealing. "Junior took over, and he's meaner than his daddy could ever have hoped to be. Can't stand a cop. Just as soon plug one as pay him off. Word is Bartlett skimmed the top of a deal and Junior blew him a kiss."

Tony shrugged. "Everybody skims. Cost of doing business."

Billy looked like he had no idea what to do with his hands. "I guess it depends on who ends up with the twenty and who ends up with the eighty."

"Eighty percent of the take? Jacob would have used the guy to fertilize his lawn."

"Yeah," Billy agreed sagely. "But Junior isn't as nice as his old man was."

Tony held up a finger signaling that Jake was to pour one more drink. Billy started feeling the confidence that only came with two straight shots spaced out over seconds. He sneered at Tony and nodded his head. "Looks like you have your ear in places, too."

"Nah. This is personal." He pushed the stack of money Billy's way and pulled an identical one out of his pocket. "You spread my message the way I tell you, and I'll see that you get this one, too."

The money in front of Billy disappeared faster than snow in Miami. "Hey, sure. Anything for you, old buddy."

"You tell anyone who will listen that Bartlett is talking big about skimming from Junior. You add that he said no one could have ever skimmed the old man. You got that?"

Billy snorted and laughed. "You want Bartlett killed or something?"

Tony stared at the little drunk. "Or something."

"Oh, Jeez." Billy breathed.

"Then you say how Bartlett knows that Junior has it out for him and he's thinking about going to the cops with it before the deadline." He looked up and nodded at Jake then leaned even closer to Billy. "You got it, Billy? Then you let Bartlett know he can find me at Hank's place, out by the college."

"Sure. When do I get the rest of my money?"

Tony straightened, pushed the fresh drink toward Billy, and tossed a bill for the tab toward Jake. "When I know the message has been sent."

Billy didn't drink the whole thing this time. He took a small sip and smiled up at Tony. "Hey man, sorry about whole thing from all those years ago. I'm glad it's forgotten."

"The only way we're square, Billy, is if you do what I asked you. Otherwise, I may start holding you in the same high regard I have for my good friend Bartlett." He pushed away from the bar.

"Sure, Tony, sure. I'll spread the word."

"Ciao." He slipped his glasses back on as he pushed his way outside.

HIS car was still there, and the kid with the mean eyes leaned against the hood. Two of his friends lay sprawled, unconscious, in uncomfortable looking positions on the street and sidewalk. He didn't see the other two. Tony looked the lad up and down, seeing a reflection of himself fifteen years earlier.

"Your friends look tired," Tony observed.

"They aren't my friends," the youth answered dryly.

Tony smiled, "What's your name?"

"Derrick. Derrick DiNunzio" He gestured at the unconscious pair. "I don't think these guys trusted you."

Tony looked around, up at the buildings, down the street. Something about this kid tugged at his heart. He tried to ignore it, but something deep inside wouldn't let him. "Do you have any friends around here, Derrick? Any family? Do you like living here?"

Derrick shrugged and stuffed his hands into the pockets of the old black leather jacket he wore. It had a hole in the right elbow. "Don't have a choice for now. But I ain't staying for long. I'm getting out." He looked at the car and back at Tony. "Just like you did. I'll go straight and narrow like you and make my break."

Tony liked the desire to go straight and narrow. He raised an eyebrow at the recognition. "How old are you?"

"Eighteen." Tony just stared. Derrick raised his chin defiantly. "Almost."

Tony pulled a business card out of his pocket. He scribbled a note on the back of it and set it atop the folded bills. "Come see me when it's a little more than almost. I may have something for you."

"You suddenly have a CIO position open up?"

Tony stopped short and barked a quick laugh.

"What would you want me doing for you, Mr. Tony Viscolli? Clean your toilets? Polish your silverware?"

Tony opened the car door and smiled. "Guess you'll just have to trust me."

He drove quickly, the desire to leave the stench of the past behind him helped him press the accelerator harder. He needed to get to church. He just wished he could shower beforehand.

Right before he turned the corner, he looked in his rearview mirror and saw Derrick still standing where he'd left him, the business card in one hand and the money in the other. The kid was staring at the card. Tony grinned, turned the heater up higher, and flipped the radio on, finding a good, loud jazz station.

TONY sat in Barry's weight room while his friend huffed his way through his last set of bench pressing one-hundred-twenty-pound weights. He had cancelled his Monday morning appointments and had come straight to Barry's house.

Barry had a weight room built into his house that rivaled any gymnasium around. Glass walls reflected state-of-the-art equipment. A large screen television hung on the wall in front of the treadmill, stationary bike, and rowing machine. At the moment, Mozart's Requiem pumped through the speakers, surrounding the room with the classical sounds.

Barry sat up and wiped his face with a towel. He looked at his friend closely. "What's wrong?"

Tony inspected his fingernails. "Why would you assume something is wrong?"

Barry laughed and tossed his towel around his neck. "You're wearing jeans and it's Monday. I'm trying to remember if I've ever personally seen you in jeans. Maybe, one time, when – no, wait, you wore Dockers."

Tony had a hard time seeing the humor. "What does that have to do with anything?"

"Nothing other than the fact that you always look like you're about to go for a cover shoot of GQ, no matter what, and you're sitting here on one of your busiest work days wearing blue jeans and you don't look like you've shaved. So, I'm assuming that something is wrong."

Tony pushed himself off of the weight bench and paced the room. The problem with this room, he decided, was that there was no escaping his reflection. Everywhere he looked, he could see himself. Of course, everywhere he saw himself, he saw a man filthy with sin.

He stopped in front of a wall and stared. His bloodshot eyes dimly glared back at him. The weight on his heart made it hard to stand up straight. He could not run from the conviction for another moment. "I've done something that cannot be undone."

Intrigued, Barry drained a bottle of water and tossed the empty plastic bottle into a trash can that stood next to the door to the rest room. "Nothing is undoable. Unless, of course, you murdered someone."

He said the last thing as a joke, but his friend's shoulders slumped forward slightly and he sighed heavily. Barry froze. No way. "Tony?"

Tony turned, moving like an old man. "I haven't murdered anyone yet, but I certainly signed his death warrant."

Barry cocked his head, trying to find another angle to look at his friend. His best friend. "I think you need to be a little more specific."

With his hands covering his face, Tony leaned against the mirrored wall and slid down until he sat on his heels. He rubbed his eyes, tired from two nights of no sleep, and finally lowered his hands. Barry sat next to him, waiting. Tony took a deep breath, and plunged forward, telling Barry about Robin's story and his own trip to the old neighborhood.

Barry sat quiet long after Tony finished speaking. He didn't look at him. Instead, he looked forward, staring at Tony's reflection in the opposite wall. Finally, he said, "Why did you do that?"

Tony wanted to shrug. He wanted to get angry and storm away from the judgement that he so rightfully felt directed his way. He wanted to do a lot of things. Instead, he leaned his head back and closed his eyes. "Because I was angry."

Barry nodded. "There are a lot of things I need to say to you right now. But, I think you know most of them. I think you know that this relationship you had with Robin wasn't good for you in a lot of ways. I am very happy she's accepted Christ now and can start growing in the Lord, but until she did that, there wasn't anything good about being with her. I think that because you determined to be the one responsible for her eternal destiny, that you almost created an idol of your feelings for her. And because of that, it opened a place in your heart where the enemy could worm his way in and break you."

Tony felt every single word as if Barry stabbed his heart with an ice pick at every syllable. He spoke the truth, and Tony knew it. Barry continued. "You are a powerful force in God's kingdom, Tony. You have money, influence, prestige, and you pour it back to God without hesitation. You know as well as I know that you are a constant target, and for some reason when this woman came into your life, you seemed to forget that."

Tony rolled his head until he looked at Barry directly. Barry's mouth thinned in a disapproving line, then relaxed again. His next words surprised

Tony. "The awesome thing about God is that He is a forgiving God. And, if you repent, your slate will once again be wiped clean."

Emotions clutched Tony's throat and he felt his eyes burn. He shoved the heels of his hands against his eyes. "That doesn't change this."

"No. It doesn't change this."

They sat in silence for a long time. Tony's emotions slowly overwhelmed him until he rocked forward and landed on his knees, then continued forward until he was bowed in humbled posture before God. He didn't realize he'd begun praying out loud until he felt Barry next to him praying along with him. He prayed for forgiveness first and foremost. Then he prayed for help. He begged God to help him figure out what to do next, how to fix it, how to set it right.

After a long time he simply fell silent in meditation and Barry left him alone so that he would have no distractions from hearing God's voice.

Chapter 17

ROBIN stood in her office and stared at a framed picture of her and her sisters. She didn't put it there, so one of them must have. A friend of Maxine's had snapped a picture of them at Maxi's college graduation party. Robin tilted her head and tried to look at it from maybe another angle, but it still looked the same. They looked like three perfectly normal women. They didn't look like the offspring of a murderer, a drug dealer, a prostitute. They just looked normal.

She turned back to face the room and saw Barry look at his watch. Tony sat in her chair behind her desk, where she had insisted that he sit, spinning his gold pen on her blotter. They had spent the last thirty minutes praying together – praying for help, wisdom, strength, courage. Since ending the prayer, though, no one had spoken. The silence in the room hovered heavy and thick, and she really couldn't stand it much longer.

"So, you're going to the Alps for Christmas?" she asked of Barry.

His head shot up and for a moment his eyes did not focus on her. When they did, he smiled slightly. "My wife enjoys travel. I guess the Alps are this year's hot spot for Christmas."

He said it with a twist to his lips. Years of public service had taught her well how to read people, and she thought better of pursuing the conversation. "Tony invited me and my sisters to the Keys with him this year, but we can't go."

"Yes you can," Tony said.

She looked at him and shook her head. "No. Remember? I told you that Sarah can't go."

He waved a hand. "She's going to come and then leave on Christmas Eve. It's already taken care of."

Robin ran her tongue over her upper lip. "That's an awful lot of flying for your pilot."

"He's a pilot. That's what he does. He's complained I haven't flown him as much as usual this year." His eyes warmed. "I've been sticking too close to Bean town." Robin flushed knowing that she was the reason he adjusted his schedule so much. Tony laughed. "Besides, he was already flying back because his family is here, so she's just catching a ride with him. We'll stay until the day after Christmas like we planned."

Barry surged to his feet. "How can you two just chit chat idly by when …?"

A knock at the door interrupted him. At Robin's beckoning, the hostess popped her head in. "There's someone out here asking for you, Robin."

Robin put her hand to her stomach and took a deep breath. "I'll be right out."

Barry moved with purpose to the door, closing the distance in two strides. "Let's get this over with." He held the door for Robin, then followed her out. Tony stayed. He murmured once they were in the hallway leading to the dining area. "You just look at me if you need help," he said, pausing by the huge Christmas tree that stood in the corner next to a grand piano.

Robin pressed her lips in a thin line and nodded stiffly. The hostess had seated Sandy – Craig – where she'd asked her to, and she had a clear view of him. He hadn't seen her yet. She watched as he drained his glass of ice water and looked behind him, then fidgeted with the glass and looked behind him again, then looked at his watch.

"You'd better get over there," Barry said.

"I hope this works," she said, and started walking. Until the moment Sandy saw her, she thought she might run away, but the second his watery blue eyes met hers, she relaxed. She felt God place a mantle of peace over her shoulders as if it had been a physical thing.

She pulled out the chair across from him and sat down. "Hi, Craig."

His knee started jerking up and down and his thumb tapped a rhythm on the tablecloth. "Remember when we used to play games? Like I give you the name of a drink and you give me what it's made out of?"

"Sure. Of course I remember."

"Good. I got one for you."

Confused, Robin tipped her head. "Okay."

"Dead Man Walking."

She gave a short shake of her head. "I'm afraid I don't know that one. I guess you finally stumped me"

"Dead Man Walking. That's me. The heat on the street is turned up. I need my ten large now."

Standing, Robin nodded. "Come on back to my office, Craig."

All of his nervous, jerky movement stopped. Suddenly. For a moment he sat completely still, then he smiled, showing a mouth full of yellow teeth. "You got it? That's my girl!"

As she led the way to her office, he babbled on behind her. "I wasn't sure you'd go for it, you know? You weren't exactly receptive to my offer the other day. But I knew you'd come through for your old man. I knew it!"

She opened the door and stepped aside, allowing him to precede her into the room. He stopped short the second that he saw Tony sitting at Robin's desk. "Hey now," he said. He turned to leave the room but found his exit blocked by Barry. "What's this?"

Tony stood and gestured to the chairs in front of the desk. "Mr. Bartlett, please sit down."

He balled his fists and his face turned bright red. "I ain't …"

Tony reached into the open desk drawer and pulled out a stack of money. Ten thousand dollars in one hundred dollar bills. Craig stopped, licked his lips, and sat in a chair.

Tony leaned back and the chair squeaked with his weight. "You obviously know that I've been seeing your daughter."

"Yeah. I been keepin' an eye on her. I know what's what."

"And you know who I am."

"Of course." Craig licked his lips and looked at the money again.

Tony reached out and laid his fingers on his pen, but kept it still. "I'm going to give you this money, but I'm going to do it on two conditions."

Craig's leg started moving up and down again in a fast, jerky rhythm. "Yeah. Sure. Whatever you want."

"Number one, you never, ever, ask for money again. If you ever do, then Robin or I will go to the police and file a complaint about extortion."

Robin watched as his leg paused momentarily before beating an even faster beat. "Yeah. Yeah. Okay. Thanks." He stood and reached for the money. Tony held up his hand and Craig slowly sat back down. "Right. Two conditions. Okay. What's numero two?"

Tony sat forward and laced his hands together. "That you allow me to pray for you right now."

Craig's entire body went still before he threw his head back and laughed. "What? What did you say?"

"I said that you can have this money if you never ask for money again and if you allow me to pray for you right here and right now."

Still laughing, Craig nodded. "Fine. Yeah, sure. Whatever. Go for it."

Robin stood next to Barry and watched as Tony got up from behind the desk and walked over to Craig. He stood next to him and placed a hand on his shoulder, then bowed his head. "Father God," he said, then began a beautiful prayer of petition to God for Craig's life, for sobriety, for the scales to be removed from his eyes, for discernment, for salvation, for grace – he prayed for twenty minutes and Robin watched in awe and wonder as Craig's fidgety body stilled. For a while he just sat there staring at the money, but eventually he closed his eyes and bowed his head.

When Tony was done, Craig surged to his feet. "You's guys, you're all crazy." He snatched up the money and shoved it in his pockets. He laughed a mean laugh. "But it was a pleasure doing business with ya."

As he left the office, he stopped in front of Robin. She didn't know what she expected to hear from her father's mouth, but what he said had her gasping in horror. "Tell that pretty little sister of yours I said hi."

He slammed the door behind him as he left. For a moment, the office was silent, then Barry let out a loud breath. "Well, next time he comes around let me know and we'll call the police."

"I can't believe you just let him take the money like that," Robin said.

Tony shrugged. "I made a deal with him, and he fulfilled as much of it as he could immediately. I'm like Barry, though. I expect him to be back." He straightened his tie. "Let's catch some dinner. What's the special here tonight, Robin?"

TWO hours later, Robin left Tony and Barry at the table to put out a personnel fire in the kitchen. After settling the argument between Casey and a sous chef and soothing the chef's hurt feelings, she went back to the dining room and stopped short, her heart in her throat, when she saw Craig standing next to Tony's table. The two men spoke briefly, then Tony nodded and stood. He gestured with his hand and they walked in the direction of Robin's office with Craig leading the way.

Robin rushed over to Barry. "What just happened?"

Barry looked as confused as Robin felt. "I have no idea. He just asked if he could talk with Tony alone."

They waited for Tony and Craig to emerge from the office. Customers came and went. Plates came out of the kitchen full and returned empty. The dining room gradually emptied and the staff gradually reset tables and pushed sweepers over the carpet. Still the two men stayed locked away. The kitchen quieted, the last dish was put away, the last knife re-sheathed, and the staff left. Robin and Barry waited.

Sitting in the hallway outside of the office, Robin and Barry played a game of Go-Fish while Robin asked Barry faith based questions, trying to learn as much as she could. Barry was really smart and knew a lot of information right off of the top of his head, and the more questions she asked, the more questions she had.

When the door to the office opened, they surged to their feet. What she saw next had her gaping with her mouth open in surprise. Tony walked out with his arm around Craig's shoulders. The older man's tearstained face practically glowed. She hardly recognized him as the same man.

Tony gestured at Barry. "He'll help you with everything from now on," Tony said.

Barry put his hands in his pockets and raised an eyebrow. "Oh? What's going on, brother?"

"It would seem," Tony said, "that Craig here suffered from some enormous conviction after leaving here. He took the money to Mr. Mills and on the way back to his apartment, he had a breakdown followed by an epiphany."

"I was a sinner," Craig said. "Tony here, he really knows how to pray, and I couldn't get his words out of my mind."

Confused, a little nervous, a little happy, Robin gave a small laugh. "Really?" She smiled at Tony. "I hadn't noticed."

"So Craig came back and asked to speak to me privately. When we got to your office, he wanted to know more about God and wanted to understand his conviction."

Tony moved until he could put an arm around Robin's shoulders. "We prayed for quite some time then Craig came to know Christ."

Robin gasped in surprise. "What? Seriously? That's wonderful!"

"The rest of the time was spent worrying about what to do next."

Tony looked at Craig, who nodded and sighed. "I need to turn myself in."

Robin gasped. "No!"

Craig nodded. "I do. I murdered two people, and I've done some things that I ain't proud of no more, but I need to pay for them."

Tony nodded to Barry. "Which is where you come in."

"Of course." The giant pulled a business card out of his pants pocket. "Just call me first thing in the morning. We'll meet and get some things straight before you turn yourself in." As Craig took the card, Barry gripped it a little tighter so that Craig met his eyes. "I mean it. Don't go in without me."

Craig nodded. "I understand." He pocketed the card and turned toward Robin. "I'm sorry. I'm sorry for everything."

Stunned, Robin nodded her head. "I appreciate that, but I really think I just going to have to digest all of this for now."

"That's fair, girl. I understand. I'm going to go stay at Tony's hotel tonight. He gave me a room so that I can stay safe until I meet with Mr. Andersen tomorrow."

"Barry."

Craig accepted the correction. "Until I meet with Barry tomorrow." He turned and hesitated before holding a hand out to Tony. "Thank you."

Tony took the hand to pull him to a hug. "My pleasure, brother. I will see you tomorrow."

After Craig left, Robin leaned against the hallway wall. "Wow."

Tony laughed. "Wow is a word for it, yes." He laughed some more. "Wow."

Chapter 18

ROBIN stood with the water lapping at her ankles while her feet slowly sank into the sand. The sun beat hot against her neck, and the wind blew her cotton skirt around her legs. She took the rubber band out of her braid and slowly loosened her hair, wanting to feel the strands blowing in the breeze.

She felt Tony approach before she heard him or saw him. Some radar inside of her perked up and she slowly turned, a smile on her face.

His heart lodged in his throat at the beautiful picture before him. He wanted to just stop and savor the view, to drink in Robin in such a happy, relaxed state, but her warm, welcoming smile beckoned him closer.

"I can't believe that it's Christmas Eve," she said. She ran her hands along her bare arms. Bare arms – in December! "Do we even know what the weather report for Boston is today?"

The second he stood close enough to touch, his arm snaked around her waist. He loved the feel of her against him. "I don't check the weather there until I have to go back. And I typically avoid it during the winter months."

Forgetting everything but the bliss surrounding her heart, Robin asked, "Why?"

Tony squeezed her close before releasing her. "I don't like to be cold." He gestured to the mammoth house behind him. "I'm like a bird. I fly south for the winter."

Robin heard a squealing sound of glee and shielded her eyes to look up at the house and see one of the O'Farrell children dive off of the high dive into the pool. They had come to spend Christmas with Tony, and from what Robin could understand, they came every year. An older laugh chased the squeal, and Robin saw Maxine go flying off of the high dive. Obviously, they were engaged in some sort of game of tag.

"It looks like you typically carry a flock with you."

Tony grinned, appreciating her subtle wit. He turned back to look out over the aquamarine water that stretched out beyond his private beach in the

Florida Keys. He pulled her closer so that she wrapped her arms around his waist and laid her head on his shoulder as they watched a sailboat meander along the horizon.

"Do you row here?"

"Only in my gym." He rested his head against hers and closed his eyes. "I windsurf here."

"That sounds like fun."

"I'll teach you how tomorrow." He squeezed her close then pulled away, running the tips of his fingers down her arm until their hands linked. "Want to take a walk?"

"Sure." She disengaged her feet from the sand and stepped in line with him. "I am so happy that you invited us here. I love it here."

"I do, too." He gestured at the water. "God's design is so perfect. It humbles me when I come here. It's a place for me to come when I start feeling a little too full of myself, a little too big man on the campus. I come here and I look at this expanse and the gloriousness of perfection and remember that it's all God, and it's all about God."

She stopped and smiled at him. "I love listening to you, especially when you're talking about God."

He turned slightly so that he faced her. "What do you like about me speaking?"

Looking at him in his cotton pants and white cotton short sleeved shirt, his skin dark in the sun, his eyes a rich chocolate brown, she felt her heartbeat pick up its rhythm. She suddenly wanted to kiss him, to keep kissing him, to never have to stop. She felt her tongue dart out, lick suddenly dry lips, as those images started popping up in her mind. "Well," she said, stepping forward so that she could feel the heat from his body. "I love your voice. And I love your passion. And," she said, feeling more bold than she had ever felt in her entire life, she reached up and put her hands on his shoulders, "I love the love in your voice when you talk about God."

He put his hands on her hips, feeling the effects of having her standing so close to him, the sunlight turning her hair to golden fire, her eyes bluer than the ocean behind him, wash over him in waves. "You like my voice, *cara*?"

Grinning she leaned forward and ran her lips along his cheek, feeling for the first time ever, a day's growth of stubble. "Especially when you say words like *cara*."

"Oh?" His mouth went a little dry and his heart's rhythm increased a bit in tempo. "You like Italian, eh?"

"Yes." She skimmed her lips over his cheek, down his chin, and along his other cheek. "Very much so."

He cupped her face in his hands and pulled her back just far enough to cover her lips with his own. He kissed her, drinking her in, tasting her, feeling her seep into his very soul. "How about this?" He said when he could finally bear to break the contact of their mouths. *"Te amo con tutto il cuore e con l'anima."*

Robin looked into his eyes and saw the seriousness of whatever he was saying. She tried to pick through the words, find something that sounded familiar so that she could translate it. Did he just ...? "Say it again," she demanded.

"Te amo con tutto il cuore e con l'anima." She started quaking inside of her stomach. His hands moved from her face down her neck until they rested on her shoulders. "I love you, Robin. With all of my heart and soul."

The quaking left her stomach and radiated out to her limbs. With shaking hands she cupped his cheeks. "Tony," she said, trying to talk around the huge smile on her face, around the nervous laughter bubbling up in her throat. "I realized I was in love with you the day of your party, but then Craig came and..." she stopped, not wanting to babble incessantly. "Let me try," she said.

He cupped her hands with his and pulled them off of his face. Keeping one hand gripped in his, he stepped back a bit while her inexperienced tongue fumbled on the words. *"Te amo, con tat,* no." she said, then gasped as he slipped the ring on her finger.

"Con tutto il cuore e con l'anima." He finished for her. Trapping her eyes with his, he slowly descended until one knee rested on the sandy beach. "Marry me, Robin. Make my life complete."

"I – I – " She couldn't tear her eyes off the sapphire.

Tony's face, always so stoic and guarded, could be read by anyone who saw it. He looked at her with naked need and tender hope. "I love you, *cara*. I don't think that there was a moment in my life that made me happier than the day that you came to know Christ, the day that you gave your life over to the Lord. If you would do me the honor of being my wife..." He stopped and closed his eyes. Holding her hand, he ran his thumb over the ring. "Let me love you in every way God commanded a man to love his wife. Let me treasure you, and abide in you, and protect you, and honor you."

The quaking subsided. Peace flooded her body, warmed her from the inside out. "Yes," she said through the tears that fell unencumbered down her cheeks. He stood and their eyes came back to even again. She laughed and grabbed him and hugged him. "Yes, of course. Of course I'll be your wife."

He wrapped both of his arms around her and hugged her tightly to him, lifting her up from the sand and spinning them both around until he felt the wet surf beneath his feet. As he gently returned her to earth, his lips found hers and they kissed, standing in the sand with the water swirling at their ankles.

THE END

READER'S GUIDE MENU

SUGGESTED luncheon menu for a group discussion about *Sapphire Ice*.

Those who follow my Hallee the Homemaker website know that one thing I am passionate about in life is selecting, cooking, and savoring good whole real food. A special luncheon just goes hand in hand with hospitality and ministry.

In case you're planning a discussion group surrounding this book, I offer some humble suggestions to help your special luncheon talk come off as a success. Quick as you like, you can whip up an appetizer, salad, entree and dessert that is sure to please and certain to enhance your discussion and time of friendship and fellowship.

The appetizer:

Benedicts' Parmesean Artichoke Dip

Readers ask about an artichoke dip tasty enough that Sarah's mother, Darlene Thomas, would request it for a party even if as a point of pride it arrives by way of her nemesis Robin Bartlett.

This recipe is *so* yummy, especially when the baguettes are still toasty warm. I pray it blesses you.

INGREDIENTS:

1 Baguette loaf

Extra virgin olive oil

2 garlic cloves

1 14-ounce can artichoke hearts in water

6 ounces cream cheese, softened

$1/4$ cup Greek yogurt

$1/4$ cup mayonnaise

$1/2$ cup grated fresh Parmesan cheese

$1/2$ teaspoon red pepper flakes

$1/4$ teaspoon salt

$1/4$ teaspoon garlic powder

PREPARATION:

Slice the Baguette into $1/2$ inch diagonal slices. Using a pastry brush, lightly brush olive oil on each slice.

Broil on the top rack of the oven until brown. Rub each toasted piece lightly with a garlic clove.

Preheat oven to 350° F (180° C).

Drain the artichoke hearts and roughly chop.

DIRECTIONS:

Beat the cream cheese until fluffy. Stir in the yogurt and mayonnaise. Stir in the cheese and spices. Mix with the artichoke hearts.

Pour into a pie plate and bake for 25-30 minutes, or until bubbly.

Let cool and serve with the Baguette toast.

The Salad:

Sarah's Strawberry Spinach Salad

Chef Casey at Hank's Place knows just how to please Sarah's vegetarian palate with this wonderful vegan friendly, Daniel fast friendly offering.

INGREDIENTS:

10 ounces fresh spinach leaves

1 quart strawberries

½ cup mandarin orange slices

½ cup pecan halves

1 TBS sunflower seeds

¼ cup balsamic vinegar

½ cup extra virgin olive oil

½ tsp salt (Kosher or sea salt is best)

¼ tsp fresh ground black pepper

PREPARATION:

Thoroughly wash and drain the spinach leaves. Tear into bite sized pieces.

Wash, hull, and halve the strawberries.

Roughly chop the pecans

DIRECTIONS:

Place the spinach in a large salad bowl. Top with the strawberries and orange slices. Sprinkle with the pecan halves and the sunflower seeds.

In a small bowl, whisk together the oil, vinegar, salt, and pepper until emulsified. Pour over the salad and lightly toss.

Serve immediately.

The Entrée:

Viscolli's Vermiccelli with Garden Vegetables

The Boston Viscolli Hotels are well known for 5-star international cuisine and the specialty is always, no surprise, Italian fare.

INGREDIENTS:

1 pound Vermicelli

1 TBS extra virgin olive oil

1 tsp salt (Kosher or sea salt is best)

1 TBS extra virgin olive oil

1 small onion

2 cloves garlic

1 large or 2 small carrot

1 zucchini

1 yellow squash

1 can diced tomatoes

1 tsp honey (local raw is best)

2 tsp dried oregano

2 tsp dried parsley

1 tsp dried basil

1 tsp salt (Kosher or sea salt is best)

$1/2$ tsp fresh ground pepper

PREPARATION:

Slice the onion.

Mince the garlic.

Thinly slice the carrot.

Slice the zucchini and squash

DIRECTIONS:

Bring a pot of pure water to boil. Add 1 TBS olive oil and 1 tsp salt. Add Vermicelli. If store bought, cook according to package directions.

Heat a large skillet over medium-high heat. Add 1 TBS extra virgin olive oil. Add the sliced onion. Cook about 5 minutes or until it starts to get tender.

Add the garlic and the carrots. Cook about 5 minutes.

Add the zucchini, squash, and canned tomatoes. Gently stir in the spices, salt, and pepper.

Bring to a gentle boil. Reduce heat and cover. Let cook for about 10 minutes.

Place the cooked pasta on a large platter. Top with the sauce. Serve with fresh ground parmesan cheese, if desired.

The Dessert:

Maxine's Marvelous Marble Cake

When Maxine invites Tony to stay and celebrate his birthday, she makes him Maxine's Marvelous Marble cake which brightens his day.

INGREDIENTS:

1 ½ cups butter, softened

1 ¾ cups granulated sugar

6 large eggs

Sapphire Ice

1 tsp vanilla extract

2 $\frac{2}{3}$ cup flour

4 tsp aluminum-free baking powder.

$\frac{1}{2}$ tsp salt (Kosher or sea salt is best)

$\frac{1}{2}$ cup whole milk

3 TBS baking cocoa powder

confectioner's sugar, for dusting.

PREPARATION:

Preheat the oven to 350° F (180° C). Butter and flour a Bundt pan. tapping out the excess flour.

Sift together the flour, baking powder, and salt. Set aside. Mix the milk and the vanilla. Set aside.

DIRECTIONS:

With an electric mixer, beat the butter and sugar on high for 3 minutes. Add the eggs one at a time, beating well after each addition.

Add about half of the dry mixture and beat on low speed. Add the milk mixture and beat on low speed until mixed. Add the remaining flour and beat until just mixed.

Spoon one-third of the batter into the pan. Transfer half the remaining batter into another bowl and sift in the cocoa powder. Mix well.

Spoon dallops of the chocolate batter into the pan. Top with the remaining plain batter. Use a knife to gently swirl the two batters together to create a marble pattern. Be careful not to mix it too much.

Bake for 45 minutes, or until a toothpick inserted into the center comes out clean.

Cool the cake for 10 minutes before removing from the pan. When cooled completely, dust with powdered sugar.

READER'S GUIDE DISCUSSION QUESTIONS

SUGGESTED group discussion questions for *Sapphire Ice*.

When asking ourselves how important the truth is to our Creator, we can look to the reason Jesus said he was born. In the book of John 18:37, Jesus explains that for this reason He was born and for this reason He came into the world. The reason? To testify to the truth.

In bringing those He ministered to into an understanding of the truth, Our Lord used fiction in the form of parables to illustrate very real truths. In the same way, we can minister to one another by the use of fictional characters and situations to help us to reach logical, valid, cogent, and very sound conclusions about our real lives here on earth.

While the characters and situations in **The Jewel Series** are fictional, I pray that these extended parables can help readers come to a better understanding of truth. Please prayerfully consider the questions that follow, consult scripture, and pray upon your conclusions. May the Lord of the universe richly bless you.

The sisters suffer a terrible childhood in an always unsafe environment. Too young, they know hunger, exposure, deprivation, and want. They know the dangers and evils of the world and are exposed to the very worst mankind has to offer. It is easy to pontificate that a loving God would not allow children to suffer like that, but the truth is that the very finest vessels are put through the fire several times.

1. To which sister do you most relate? What is it about her personality that makes you relate to her?

2. Is there something in your childhood you feel certain molded and shaped your adult world view especially with respect to relationships?

3. Do you think the sisters would be very different as adults if their childhood upbringing were positively different?

Barry cautioned Tony not to see Robin because she wasn't saved. Read 2 Corinthians 6:14 to see what the Bible says.

4. Are you in an evenly yoked relationship or are you spiritually on the same path? What are some evidences you can name?

Sarah has a burden lifted when Tony offers to fund her church's fall carnival. Many churches today could widen the outreach of their various ministries but they suffer from lack of funding.

5. Why do you believe churches have such a hard time finding funding for ministries? How can you help your church overcome such common issues?

Robin didn't believe in a just and loving God because she had seen and experienced the worst life has to offer.

6. How do you think desolation or tragedy relates to God?

7. Do you believe God wants us to lean on Him and look to Him in all things in life? How much of Robin's desire to "do it on her own" do you believe might have kept her separated from God?

Robin knew nothing about God and had a very low opinion of Christians in general. This despite the fact that she grew up in a neighborhood with a very large and very active church right in the middle of it. She later confesses that she remembers that church as one of her childhood landmarks.

>8. What can we do to better spread the word of God in a positive light among unbelievers?

Read Matthew 6:14 and Matthew 18:22. Put the meaning of these verses about forgiveness in your own words.

>9. What was your reaction to Tony and Robin's treatment of Craig at the end of Sapphire Ice?

>10. Are you currently coping with unforgiveness in your heart?

Greater Than Rubies

Book 1.5 of the Jewel Series

Includes Reader's Guide

Hallee Bridgeman

GREATER THAN RUBIES - COPYRIGHT NOTICE

Greater Than Rubies, a Novella

Book 1.5 of the Jewel Series

Second edition. Copyright © 2012 by Hallee Bridgeman. All rights reserved.

Original Cover Art and Graphics by Debi Warford (www.debiwarford.com)

Woburn Library (Winn Memorial Library) image used with permission. (Woburn Library located at 45 Pleasant Street, Woburn, MA 01801

Library Cataloging Data

Bridgeman, Hallee (Hallee A. Bridgeman) 1972-
   Greater Than Rubies; Jewel Series part 1.5 / Hallee Bridgeman
      p. 23cm x 15cm (9in x 6 in.)
   Summary: Robin Bartlett said yes. Soon, she will say I do. Or will she?
   ISBN: 978-1-939603-35-7 (trade perfect) ISBN-10: 1-939603-35-8
   ISBN: 978-1-939603-00-5 (ebook) ISBN: 978-1-301868-89-6 (text only)
1. Christian fiction 2. man-woman relationships 3. love stories 4. family relationships 5. wedding stories
   PS3568.B7534 G743 2012
   [Fic.] 813.6 (DDC 23)

GREATER THAN RUBIES - CHAPTER 1

ROBIN Bartlett walked into her church's main fellowship hall and surveyed the crowd. People young and old, fellow congregates, had gathered on that second Sunday afternoon in January to celebrate the engagement of Robin and Antonio "Tony" Viscolli. Everyone brought a covered dish to create a pot luck meal of such amazing amplitude that Robin wondered if the table would bow under the weight.

She could hear the clanging of dishes in the kitchen and started to step in that direction, but Tony slipped his hand into hers and halted her forward progress. She turned and looked at her handsome fiancé in his navy suit, white shirt, and red tie, looking every bit the Italian businessman. He stood barely an inch taller than her almost six feet. She knew she complemented him with her blonde hair and fair skin. This morning she wore a blue sweater dress the color of her eyes, belted at the waist with a silver belt that matched her shoes. No one meeting either one of them would know that they grew up on the streets in the same harsh Boston neighborhood around where this very church stood. "This is your party, *cara*. Let them bless you. Stay out here and socialize."

Leaning toward him so that only he could hear her, she whispered, "I'm not very good at that."

He smiled, a smile that made her heart pitter-patter in her chest and made her fall in love with him all over again. He raised her hand and kissed it just above the ridiculously large oval sapphire and diamond ring on her left hand. "You'll get better at it. You are positively beautiful and engaging. Everyone is looking forward to visiting with you."

She had started attending the church just a few months before, but Tony had attended for years. He had entered the church as a desperate, starving teen years before, looking for something to steal and fence. Instead he had heard the Gospel message and ended up dedicating his life to the Creator of the universe.

Tony knew so many people in that room, and Robin knew a select handful. Still, he looked so excited to introduce her around and let her meet the people who mattered the most in his life, she let go of her feelings of insecurity and walked from group to group, table to table, meeting friends and the family members of friends, watching her future husband talk to even the people he didn't know well with grace and with caring compassion. It was so easy to stand at his side and engage in conversation with everyone. Tony made it easy.

They worked their way through the room to the table of food and filled their plates. Tony, with his gold cufflinks and diamond pinkie ring looked out of place carrying a foam paper plate with a white plastic fork. Robin smiled as she sat in the metal folding chair next to him.

"There is so much food here," she observed, looking at her plate and thinking she might have overdone it on the *little bit here and little bit there* strategy. "Everything looks so amazing"

"I love potluck dinners," he said. "It's almost like a treasure hunt."

Robin laughed and laid her hand on top of his, gently squeezing. "That's a good way to look at it."

She dug into her food. She'd felt so nervous about today's party that she'd been unable to eat breakfast that morning. As she finished the impossibly full plate, she eyed the crowded dessert table and wondered if she dared.

Tony saw her glance and winked. "I'll go get you something. Chocolate?"

Robin leaned back in her chair and sighed. "I shouldn't but, yes. Definitely."

As he walked away, someone gripped her shoulders from behind. Robin turned and found herself in the presence of both of her younger half-sisters, Maxine and Sarah. Maxine had glided up behind her.

"I'm so sorry we're late," Maxine said, setting her purse on the seat next to Robin's. "Sarah's church service ran way over."

At twenty-six, blonde-haired, blue-eyed Robin was the oldest of the three half-sisters. Her father had spent her childhood in prison for trafficking cocaine.

Green-eyed Maxine was three years younger than Robin. Her nameless father had been a warm bed on a drunken night for their addicted mother. Only Maxine's Native American features and straight black hair gave evidence to which of the many one-night-stands had fathered her. Maxine was currently a junior associate at a Boston advertising agency.

Petite Sarah had honey-colored eyes and wild curly auburn hair. Her father had committed suicide when she was just a baby. Robin remembered him as one of the only nice men who had ever come into her childhood life. Now twenty-years-old, Sarah was in her third year of college and her first year of nursing school.

After a horrible night when their mother and the latest boyfriend had fallen victim to murder, a family had adopted Sarah while Robin and Maxine landed in the foster system. The older sisters had no contact with Sarah until her fifteenth birthday. She now lived with Robin and Maxine while her older sister paid for her college education.

Robin eyed her watch. "That's okay," she said, "I'm so happy you could make it."

"I tried to tell her to skip her parents' church this morning and just come here, but she had a thing."

Sarah rolled her eyes and pushed her glasses further up her tiny nose. "I teach a Sunday school class, Maxi. I can't very well just skip that."

Robin interjected, trying to stop the bickering before it unfolded into a full-blown argument. "It's cool. You didn't miss anything important. I'm just so happy you're here." She waved a hand in the general direction of the heavy-laden table. "Help yourself to food."

Maxine pushed away from the table and went behind Robin's chair, slipping her arms around her older sister's neck and hugging her. "I'm so excited for you. I just love Tony."

Robin grinned. "Yeah? Me, too."

As soon as Maxine let her go, Sarah hugged her. "Me, three. And, I'm thankful that you're back in my life. I was thinking about it this morning, about all those years I didn't even know you existed. I wish I'd grown up with you like Maxi did. You are amazing and I just love you so much."

Robin had never heard anything like that from Sarah before. Emotion, raw and real, swamped her and her eyes burned with tears. She pushed away from the table and pulled Sarah into her arms. "I'm glad you don't remember," she said, resting her cheek on top of her youngest sister's head. "I'm glad you're saved from that, and I'm so happy you live with me now. It helps make up for lost time."

As Sarah followed Maxine to the buffet tables, Tony returned with a too-large slice of chocolate cake. "Your cake, my love," he announced with flare.

He looked at her face and a frown immediately appeared between his brows. "Why are you crying?"

Robin took his face in her hands. "Because God has blessed me with such love in abundance. I don't even know how to begin to thank Him."

Tony put a hand on top of hers. "We'll work together for Him and serve Him. That's how."

Not caring how many hundreds of eyes might be watching, Robin leaned forward and kissed him, just a quick brush of her lips on his. "I'm looking forward to it."

Maxine returned with a plate piled high with food, followed by Sarah who had a bit of salad and some steamed broccoli on her plate. As Sarah sat down, she said, "Not many options for the herbivores among us," she said with a smile. "Pot luck suppers at churches are always full of meat and cheese."

Maxine took a bite of a chicken leg. "Ah. That's the good stuff," she said with a smile. She pointed the leg at Robin and Tony, who sat back down across from them. "Have you two set a date in stone yet?"

Robin grinned the silly grin that kept spreading across her face ever since Tony put the ring on her finger. "April twenty-first is about the soonest it can possibly be."

Tony rubbed the back of her neck. "Robin suggested we just elope, but I convinced her that I was worth a church wedding."

With a fork laden with potato salad, Maxine said, "You don't want to elope. There's no fun in that. I know I'll never elope."

"Oh, I don't know." Wiggling his eyebrows, Tony said, "It could be fun."

Sarah swallowed a laugh and covered her mouth. "Tony!"

Barry Anderson, former professional football player turned corporate lawyer, walked up to Tony, wool ski cap covering his ears and leather gloves on his large hands. He slapped Tony on the back. "My friend, congratulations."

Tony smiled and stood, shamelessly hugging Barry. "Barry, *mi fratello!*" He turned and faced the table. "Barry, my dearest brother, I would like to introduce you to Maxine Bartlett and Sarah Thomas, Robin's sisters." The two best friends could not have more different appearances. Barry stood a few inches shy of seven feet with icy blue eyes, blond hair, a thin blond goatee, and a body that gave evidence to his extensive workout regimen compared to Tony who stood at just six feet with dark coloring and a strong lean body strengthened by rowing. And yet they considered themselves brothers as if they'd been born to the same parents.

Sarah was closest, and reached forward to shake Barry's hand. He slipped the glove off of his right hand and gripped her petite hand, swamping it. Maxine, her eyes uncharacteristically wide, made no move to rise or shake his hand. She just said, "Nice to meet you."

"I should have realized Robin's sisters would be just as lovely and beautiful as Robin. It is very much my honor to finally meet you both." Barry nodded to each of them and looked them straight in the eye as he greeted them. Then he turned back to Tony. "Sorry I'm late. The flight out was delayed almost two hours."

"That big storm?" Tony inquired.

"Yeah. The snow has really been picking up. We passed 12 or 15 foot

Greater Than Rubies

drifts on the way to the airport. I guess it's a good thing we made it out at all."

Tony nodded. "How was Christmas in the Alps?"

Barry's lips thinned. "Same thing every year."

"You should really think about Florida next year." Tony chided. "You could water ski off the Keys instead of making snow angels."

Barry kept his face blank. "Maybe next year." He pulled his ski cap off and gestured to the buffet table. "I'm going to get something to eat. That little plate they give you on the airline is never enough for me."

As he walked away, Maxine leaned in to Robin and said in a low voice, "Do you know who that is? That is *the* Barry Anderson."

"Yeah, that's Barry. I told you about him helping my dad."

Maxine lightly thumped her sister on the forehead with her flat open palm. "No. That is Barry 'The Bear' Anderson. Like, that is really, really him. Don't you remember him playing? Remember the Super Bowl that year? Are you really that out of it?"

"Yes. And I remember telling you that he used to play sports and he's a lawyer, now." Robin said, feeling a little confused.

Maxine grinned. "Play sports. You are so cute. You said he was a big guy and a lawyer and drank Shirley Temples. I was imagining fat Elvis meets Perry Mason meets Freddie Mercury. You never said anything about him being *that* Barry Anderson. You know I had the biggest crush on him when he was in the League. And he is still the most gorgeous man I've ever seen in my life." She put her hand on her chest. "Oh my gosh. I can barely breathe."

Robin's eyes widened and she laughed a shocked laugh. "You are incorrigible."

Maxine winked and went back to her plate.

Tony's lips thinned as he stood again. "Good afternoon, Jacqui."

A tall redhead with porcelain smooth skin sailed toward their table, draped in a full length mink coat. "Antonio, what a pleasure to see you," she said, air kissing within inches of both of his cheeks.

"Ladies, I'd like you to meet Barry's wife, Jacqueline Anderson. Jacqui, this is Sarah Thomas, Maxine Bartlett, and my beautiful bride to be, Robin Bartlett."

She waved a hand toward Robin. "You are *such* a darling. Bartlett. Bartlett? Now, are your people any relation to the Chesapeake Bartletts?"

Maxine dryly interjected, "I seriously doubt it."

Jacqueline took that in. "Hmm. Well, it is just so very nice to meet you in person." Robin stood next to Tony and held her hand out. Jacqueline slipped off her gloves. Robin thought her long manicured nails made her hands look like she'd never worked a day in her life. The women briefly squeezed hands and Tony gestured to the buffet line. "Barry's fixing himself a plate. Would you care to eat?"

A quick look of disgust crossed her face as she surveyed either her husband or the selections on his plate. "Ugh. Church food. Not the slightest bit interested." She put a hand on Tony's shoulder. "I'm afraid I can't stay, Antonio. I just had to pop in and say 'hi.' My curiosity was positively killing me as to who finally landed the most eligible bachelor I know and snagged you right out from under the noses of Boston society!"

At the conclusion of this announcement, Jacqueline Anderson actually looked Robin up and down from head to toe as if inspecting a Dickensian orphan or a horse of questionable pedigree. "I'm so looking forward to the wedding. The papers are already talking about how it's going to be the event of the year." She nodded toward Barry, who had stopped on his way back to the table to talk to Peter O'Farrell. "Be a dear and tell Barry I'll see him later. I simply must go, now."

She swirled away, leaving the cloying smell of expensive French perfume in her wake. Robin slowly sat as she watched her mink clad departure for a second, then her eyes skimmed over Barry, who'd barely glanced at his wife's retreating back before continuing his conversation with Peter. She looked at Tony. "What was that?"

Tony lifted his red plastic cup. "That, *cara*, was Jacqui Anderson, in all her glory, being just as nice as she is humanly able."

With an astonished tone, she asked, "And – Antonio?"

Tony actually grit his teeth. "It doesn't bother me, but that fact doesn't seem to stop her from trying to make it bother me."

Maxine set her fork down. "Wow."

Tony patted the back of Robin's hand. "She will be extremely helpful in the wedding planning. She is a master at events. Just ... don't let her bully you."

Maxine wasn't done. "You know what? I'll say that backwards. Wow. There."

Robin took a bite of her cake, letting the chocolate frosting sing in her mouth before slowly chewing it and swallowing. She washed down that bite with a sip from a cup of really bad coffee in a white Styrofoam cup. "What did she mean by 'the event of the year?' She made this sound like it was going to be the next Royal Wedding."

Tony waved his hand in a dismissive manner as Barry set his plate next to him. "Don't let that bother you, *cara*."

"I think the event of the year is exactly what it should be," Sarah said dreamily. "Imagine what we could do!"

Maxine leaned forward and put her hand on top of Robin's. "It's okay, Robin. We'll help you. We'll get a really good wedding planner and it'll be a breeze. I even have an old design instructor from college who opened her business last year. I helped her with some initial advertising. I'll call her and see if we can meet."

Suddenly nervous, Robin licked her lips. "I'm not sure. Why can't we just elope?"

Tony laughed. "Because, *cara*, I want to show you off to the world." He turned to Barry. "You free in the morning? I have some things to go over with you."

Barry nodded around a mouth full of cauliflower casserole. "I have you blocked off until noon. After that, you're buying me lunch. I've been out of the office for two weeks. I'll go in at seven and make sure I don't have any major fires to put out before I come over."

Tony nodded as he looked at his watch. "Nine is good." He snapped his fingers and turned to Robin. "I know what I forgot to tell you."

"What?"

"You need to go ahead and get your passport application turned in. It takes several weeks, and I don't want to delay our honeymoon."

Her mouth felt a little dry as she contemplated, suddenly, all of the details she'd need to handle in the next four months. She barely heard him. "Passport?"

"Yes. To go to Italy. Remember?"

Mind whirling, wishing she had a pencil and a paper to take notes, she nodded. "Right, Italy."

He frowned. "You okay?"

She shook her head and nodded. "Just a little overwhelmed. I need to remember where my birth certificate is, too."

Tony took her hand and kissed the back of it. "Relax, my love. All will be fine. I promise."

GREATER THAN RUBIES - CHAPTER 2

TONY paused in working his way through the stack of end-of-the-year and fourth quarter revenue reports when his secretary, Margaret, buzzed through on the intercom. "Mr. Viscolli, there's a young man coming up who has a business card with a handwritten note from you on the back of it."

A happy relief flooded his chest. "Yes, Derrick. I remember him. Please have the chef send up some hearty hot food and some hot tea. Maybe hot chocolate, too. He's going to be cold and hungry."

He felt relieved to have a break. For the first time in nearly three years, Tony faced the unappealing prospect of having to instigate some layoffs. One of his West Coast endeavors was still infuriatingly and stubbornly unprofitable. The problem was that the project was currently overstaffed. But Tony had a stubborn streak of his own. From a public image perspective, he couldn't lay his reputation on the line and layoff nearly 200 workers right before Christmas then turn around and employ at least that number of staff to pull off his wedding and reception a few months down the road. From another perspective, he realized that his employees had families and financial obligations and depended on his company to meet their needs.

But for the last two years, he had been throwing money at that company with no tangible profitable return. Half a year ago, the tax write off and depreciation options had stopped being very much fun. The bottom line was that it would have to turn around before the end of first quarter next year, or else he would have to write it off as a complete loss. Since that wasn't an option, he had to get creative. He was going to have to pray long and hard about the problem.

Tony had time to file the reports away and make sure nothing pressing waited for him on his desk. Closing his eyes, he uttered a brief prayer, "Please God, help me focus on this meeting and let me make a difference in this young man's life."

As he raised his head, a knock sounded on his door. Margaret opened it without waiting for him to bid entrance, and in walked Derrick DiNunzio.

He had lost weight in the weeks since Tony first met him outside of a dirty bar in the absolutely wrong neighborhood. Tony had looked at the teenage boy with bloody knuckles and dirt on his face and seen a reflection of himself not long before. Then something, the Holy Spirit he supposed, pressed him to help this young man. He told Derrick to come see him when he turned eighteen. Now Derrick stood before him, right there in the same black leather jacket with the hole in the elbow, dirty jeans, worn out boots, and red-rimmed eyes. He had a scruffy beard and chapped lips.

"Derrick DiNunzio," Tony said, stepping forward with his hand out. Derrick looked at it and hesitantly shook it. Tony gripped Derrick's hand with his other hand, trying to convey friendship and warmth. "I'm pleased you decided to take me up on my offer and come see me."

Derrick shrugged and tried to act tough, but he kept looking around at the very large and well appointed office. "Yeah, well you said maybe you had a job for me, Mr. Viscolli, and I could really use the work, so I came."

Tony looked at Margaret over Derrick's shoulder. "Just go ahead and bring in the food when it arrives if you could, Margaret."

"Yes, sir," she said, closing the door behind her.

Tony gestured to the brown leather couch and chairs that formed a sitting area near a lit fireplace. "Please, sit down, Derrick."

Derrick shoved his hands in his pockets and slouched toward the couch. "What kind of job you need me to do, Mr. Viscolli?"

Tony ignored the question and sat in a chair facing Derrick. "*Lei parla Italiano?*"

The youth shook his head. "Nah. My mom, she didn't speak English and she wanted to learn. By the time I was old enough to talk, she refused to teach me any except when she was cussing me out."

"Well, cussing does sound more sincere in Italian, doesn't it?"

"I never questioned her sincerity, Mr. Viscolli."

Tony chuckled. "That's too bad. I was hoping to knock some of the rust off my Italian while we talked. I guess it will have to wait until my honeymoon." He sat back and hooked his foot on his knee, brushing an imaginary piece of lint off of the gray silk pants leg.

"Yeah, I saw in the Globe about you getting married. No disrespect. She looks smokin' hot. Like, smokin'. Congrats."

Once more it struck Tony just how much this young man reflected a younger version of himself. He vividly remembered – not so very long ago – having a very similar outlook and nearly identical priorities. What he couldn't have realized is how much better his life could be when he stopped trying to run it himself and instead gave his life up to Christ.

With a little smile, Tony said, "None taken. And I agree. She is the most beautiful woman I've ever seen. So, you have a mother. Who else is in your family?"

"Just me." Derrick's eyes narrowed. "Why ya asking?"

"I am a curious man. My mother was alone when she came to Boston, pregnant with me. Her family had disowned her in Florence and my father had a great aunt here so she came to America. To say she was disappointed in our neighborhood is not an exaggeration."

Derrick cocked his head. "My mom was from Naples."

"Ah. *Napoli*." Tony did a quick calculation. "Navy brat?"

"Air Force." Derrick crossed his arms and leaned back. "Knocked her up, brought her here, then dumped her. She didn't know anything about getting the military to track him down or nothing. Found out too late. He's dead, now. I never met him."

"In our neighborhood, that is nothing new."

"You say 'our' like you're still there. But, you're not. You got out."

Tony shrugged. "Not entirely. I still go to church near there, and I do a lot of community work there. But, you're right, I no longer live there."

"Again, no disrespect, Mr. Viscolli, but you don't even sound like you ever lived in Southie."

With a wave of his hand, Tony dismissed that remark. "That just takes hard work. I hired someone to teach me how to speak properly."

Derrick gestured with his chin. "And the suits."

"Right. That, too." He tapped a finger on the arm of his chair. "I have to maintain a certain look in order to do good business. That may or may not be 'right' on some fundamental level, but it is the way the world works. I recognized that and conformed." He thought back to his teenage years. It might as well have been him sitting in that chair instead of young Derrick DiNunzio. God had given him a chance, and he would do the same for this young man. "My last winter on the streets, I slept in the doorway of that old brick building near that pasta place, Buenos. You know where I'm talking about?"

Derrick uncrossed his arms. "Slept? Yeah, I know the spot. There's an old dude who sleeps there, named – "

"Georgio," Tony interrupted. "Yes. He gave me tips for surviving the winter. Glad to hear he's still alive. One of his tips was to go into churches during services to get warm. A lot of churches serve coffee and pastries afterward, too. I went into Boston Central Bible Church one cold night and it changed my life forever."

Margaret entered, pushing a service cart. Tony stood and thanked her, taking the cart from her and rolling it to where Derrick sat. He lifted the silver dome off a plate and found roast beef with mashed potatoes and green peas. Bless Margaret, he thought, who knew, despite the early hour, to bring something other than croissants and fruit. He set the plate in front of

Derrick. He watched the boy's hungry face light up and heard the audible sound of his stomach growling. He quickly poured him a cup of hot tea and sat down. "Let me bless this food before you eat," he said, not handing over the silverware wrapped in a cloth napkin just yet. He bowed his head and said, very quickly so that he did not torture the boy, "Father God, thank You for working in our lives and bringing Derrick and me together. I pray You bless this food to the nourishment of our bodies. In Your holy name we pray, Amen."

He handed Derrick the bundle of utensils and sat back with his own cup of tea while the young man attacked the plate of food. When it was empty, he lifted the dome on another identical plate and set that in front of him as well. This time, he ate more slowly.

"What do you mean, it changed your life?" Derrick asked with his mouth full.

"What?"

"The church. How did church do anything for you? Never did nothin' for me I tell ya that."

"Ah." Tony smiled and poured more tea for both of them. "Let me tell you a story about forgiveness and redemption."

ROBIN'S worn out car shuddered to a stop about 12 feet shy of the valet stand in front of the Boston Viscolli Hotel. She opened the door before the valet could get to her. "I'm so sorry, Ryan," she said, her cheeks burning with embarrassment. "I hope you can get it started."

"No problem, Miss Bartlett," he said smoothly. "We'll take care of it for you. Please don't concern yourself."

Rushing, she opened the back door and grabbed her purse and notepad, then slammed it shut and hit it with her hip to make sure it latched. She knew she was going to have to replace this car, and soon. The cold winter seemed to bring out the worst in the machine. Since her promotion from head bartender to restaurant manager at Hank's Place, she finally had the extra money to put away and had been saving for a more reliable used car, but she didn't have enough put aside yet. She had to limp the thing along for just another couple of months.

The frigid Boston wind bit at her cheeks and she rushed into the warm lobby of the hotel. Most people working there knew her by now. Tony's executive offices were on the top floor of the hotel, and she had been there several times in the last few months. She thought back to the first time she'd come there, how angry she'd been at Tony, how offended by him. Now she came in smiling, walking on air, coming to meet Maxine and a wedding planner, saying, "Hi," to the people she knew personally and basking in their smiles and returned greetings.

Green marble, shiny brass, brown leather, thick oriental rugs – it all worked together to create an atmosphere of luxury and style. As many times as she'd come through those doors, she still didn't stop from marveling at the ambiance. It was so beautiful and so rich feeling. Furniture was arranged in different seating areas around the lobby, and Robin wove her way through to the fireplace, where she'd arranged to meet the wedding planner.

A tall woman in a red suit with silver hair in a tight bun stood next to the hearth. Robin went straight for her. "Stephanie?" she said, holding out her hand, "I'm Robin. I'm so sorry I'm late."

If Maxine were already there, Robin imagined her sister would offer something very droll along the lines of, "Car trouble?"

Stephanie looked her up and down, from the toes of her brown boots, past her jeans and Harvard sweatshirt, to the top of her head, where she had her long blonde hair pulled back in a pony tail. "Robin Bartlett?" Stephanie asked. "I never would have guessed you were Maxine's sister."

Used to such confusion about their looks, Robin said, "I look like our mom. She looks like her dad." She waved at her outfit. "Sorry I'm so dressed down. I've been in the freezer of my restaurant since four this morning trying to organize a meat delivery." She pushed her coat off of her shoulders as a uniformed concierge approached. She held it out to him with a smile and continued speaking. "We were up to our eyeballs in Angus steaks and I didn't hear the alarm on my phone going off reminding me of this breakfast."

Stephanie smiled, but Robin could read the hesitation on her face. Then she asked, "Are they going to let you in? Isn't there a dress code in the restaurant?"

"It's not a problem." She gestured toward the restaurant. "Maxine will be here shortly. She got tied up in traffic. Cassandra texted me that she had a table waiting for us in the restaurant. Maxine will just meet us there."

"I've worked with Cassandra here before," Stephanie said as they approached the hostess stand. "She is one of the most helpful entertainment coordinators in any hotel around Boston."

"I know. Tony can't say enough about her."

Stephanie put a hand on Robin's arm. "Wait, Tony?"

Robin raised an eyebrow as the hostess approached. "Yeah, Tony. Tony Viscolli. My fiancé."

"*You* are Tony Viscolli's fiancée? How did I miss that?"

With a shrug, Robin laughed. "You never asked." She turned to the hostess. "Hi, Amy."

"Hi, Robin. Cassandra is already waiting for you. Right this way, please."

Cassandra smiled and held out her hand as Robin approached. "Hi, Robin. It's nice to meet you in person."

"Likewise," she said as she shook the brunette's hand. Cassandra had a round face with dimples that lit her face up when she smiled. Robin gestured at Stephanie. "You've met Stephanie Giordano. She's still reeling over the fact that she's going to be working on the Viscolli wedding."

"The Bartlett-Viscolli wedding," Cassandra enthused.

Stephanie sat across from Cassandra. "I guess I'd read your name in the paper, but never associated it with Maxine. When she called, she wasn't specific." She asked for a diet soda from the waitress and continued. "I am so honored to be asked to do this."

Maxine breezed toward their table, well over six-feet-tall in her three-inch boots, suede skirt, and silk blouse. "Sorry! There was a tow truck – oh, never mind." She said as she took the chair across from Robin. "It's good to see you all." She looked at the waitress who had finished taking drink orders. "Coffee please, black."

Stephanie pulled out her tablet and set it on the table in front of her, wiping some lint from the screen before waking it up. "April 21st?"

Robin nodded. "Yes. We're thinking late afternoon with a reception early evening."

"How many guests?" Stephanie asked while nodding and typing.

Robin deferred to Cassandra. "How many can we accommodate here?"

"We're going to use the Grand Ball Room. I can fit up to seven-fifty and maintain fire-code. We can also open the doors and use the patio area. And, we can bring in heated tents if we need to."

Stephanie paused, fingers on the screen. "Seven hundred and fifty?" She repeated in a near whisper.

Maxine laughed. "Think of the Viscolli wedding on your company's resume."

"Bartlett-Viscolli wedding," Cassandra corrected automatically.

Robin felt her heart skitter. Her mouth went dry and she suddenly felt overwhelmed by the concept. Trying to clear her head, she gave it a short shake. "Seven hundred and fifty people? Seriously?"

Maxine reached over and took her hand. "Easily. Just think of the church congregates alone. Tony's managers and supervisors, their spouses or guests, all of his ministries, his business contacts. I bet we reach a thousand before it's all done."

Cassandra opened her notebook. "We need to set a number now, if it's possible. I need to make sure I can accommodate with table settings and staff."

Robin held up a hand. "Let's limit it to what will fit inside. That will keep it simple."

"Okay, seven-fifty. Easily done." Cassandra wrote on a legal pad with a fine-tip pen while Stephanie typed.

"We need a guest list soon," Stephanie said. "That's a lot of envelopes to address. I will likely hire that out."

"Tony's secretary is already working on it," Cassandra said. "Her name is Margaret. I'll get you her contact info."

Stephanie jumped. "Oh, right. Here's my card."

Cassandra nodded. "And here's mine."

The women handed out business cards all around then Stephanie turned back to Robin. "Give me some ideas of what you're thinking about in terms of style or theme."

Robin raised an eyebrow. "Style?"

Maxine interjected, "She wants simple but elegant. Nothing ostentatious but nothing flashy, either. No swans or doves. Like they say in showbiz, never follow children or animals. And no elaborate foods, just tasteful simple fare."

Stephanie nodded and typed. Cassandra asked, "Are you going to do sit-down dinner?"

Finally, something to which she could speak with authority due to her years as a waitress. "Yes. But, I don't want to have too many choices for people. I want to do a small red meat, like maybe lamb, and a small poultry portion on the same plate with two simple sides. That will save the chefs a lot of headache and ensure that meals are set out hot. I do want to accommodate vegetarians if we need to, and make sure the vegetarian plates are fully organic, only fruits and vegetables with whole grains. Nothing processed at all, especially soy. Oh, maybe a nice tomato soup or consommé. My sister, Sarah, will thank us."

While Cassandra made notes, the waitress arrived with drinks and took their breakfast orders. As they waited for meals to arrive, Robin and Maxine – mainly Maxine – answered questions and let Stephanie and Cassandra work between them to get the initial outline of their planning started. Robin pondered just how quickly four short months could pass. How would they ever get it all done on time?

ROBIN hugged Maxine good-bye and watched her get into her little green sports car. After three hours of meeting with such competent women who seemed to know exactly what to say and do, she felt a little less overwhelmed by the process, but still a little anxious about the timing. Maybe Tony would consider pushing the wedding back to June. Or maybe next January. That would be even better. Or maybe they could just go to a Justice of the Peace and that would be that. Better still.

Shaking her head, knowing he wanted to get married as soon as possible and in their church, she waited for the valet, who pulled up in a sleek and shiny royal blue sedan. He walked toward her. "Hi, Ryan. Did you get it started?"

"Mr. V. took care of it, Robin."

She waited, but he didn't move. After several heartbeats, she said, "I don't understand."

He pointed with his thumb over his shoulder. "That's yours, now, ma'am."

His thumb loosely pointed at a brand new four dour sedan that looked like it had just rolled off of a high end showroom. Robin shook her head. "No, it's not."

"Yes, ma'am. Your other car was towed away and this one was brought in. The stuff that was in your trunk and back seat has already been transferred." He held out brand new shiny car keys that were absolutely not hers hanging on her key chain beside her apartment key and the keys to Hank's place.

She suddenly remembered Maxine mentioning a tow truck. Nice of her sister not to mention that her car was strapped to it. Without another word, Robin pivoted on her heel with military precision and marched back into the hotel. She stalked to the elevators and hit the top floor button harder than she should have. Thankfully, she had no wait and the elevator shot up twenty stories with efficient speed, but the ride seemed interminable to her.

The receptionist sitting behind a large half-moon desk saw her and smiled. "Good afternoon, Miss Bartlett," she greeted.

Robin nodded but did not speak. Instead, she stormed off the elevator and into the lobby of the office floor. She barely realized that her feet sank into the lush carpet nor did she pay any attention to the leather furniture and black granite tables.

Her eyes caught the scrolling brass on the wall behind the desk that read: *He has showed you, O man, what is good. And what does the Lord require of you? To act justly and to love mercy and to walk humbly with your God. Micah 6:8.*

She proceeded down the corridor and entered Tony's outer office. His secretary sat poised with hands on her keyboard but looked up when Robin entered. "Hello, Robin," Margaret said with a smile. "Mr. Viscolli will certainly be happy to see you."

"I doubt it," she said through gritted teeth. "Is he available?"

"He is in this morning, but he has someone in there. Let me call him out." She stood and walked around her desk, stopping at the large double oak doors. With a quick tap, she opened the door a crack and stuck her head in, speaking in a low tone. As she finished speaking, she stepped back and the doors opened wider.

Tony came out, looking like he had just stepped out of a shoot for the cover of a fashion magazine in his gray silk suit and dark green tie. He grinned and held his hands out to her. "*Cara*, my love. What a wonderful surprise."

Robin held her hands up to ward him off. "Where did you take my car?"

Tony stopped and raised his eyebrows, slipping his hands into his pockets. "Ah, so it's like that is it?" His smile grew infuriatingly broad. "I seem to remember the first time you ever came to this office. You threw a fist full of money at my chest like throwing a stone. Are we to metaphorically commemorate that act? Is today an anniversary or something?"

"Tony, where is my car?"

He gestured toward some double doors on the other side of the room. "Let's take this conversation into my conference room."

Robin stormed behind him and waited to speak until he had shut the door. "Answer me. Right now. Where is my car?"

"You mean where is that rusty junk heap that refused to start and had to be towed away?"

"Yeah, I mean *my* rusty junk heap that you had towed without my permission."

"I stand corrected. *Your* rusty, unreliable, and unsafe junk heap is at a mechanic's shop. I had a feeling you wouldn't approve of the new car, so I'm getting the old one fixed until I can charm you into accepting the gift of your new car." He smiled an endearing smile that started to melt her anger.

"Charm me?" She shook her head. "I don't want cars from you, Tony."

"I know that, Robin. I also don't care," He held up a hand, palm facing her, at her gasp. "Understand that my wife, when she becomes my wife, will drive a safe and reliable car that will not break down on her. Ever. Because, you see, I will take my God ordained responsibilities to my wife very seriously. My wife will be protected and provided for in a way that glorifies our Creator's design for husbands and wives. And as for giving you gifts, I cannot imagine a time when that will ever stop. You are the love of my life and I would give you the moon and stars."

Robin took a deep breath and released it. She rubbed her forehead. "Can we just wait to do things like buy me expensive new cars and such until after we're married? We aren't married yet, and I really, really don't feel right about this."

Tony stepped forward and put his hands on her shoulders. "We are married in my heart. The rest is just ceremony and tradition. But, yes, of course. We can wait. Your car should be back soon. Apparently, it only needs the engine and transmission replaced. And new tires, of course." She stepped forward and let him wrap her up in his arms. He smelled so good, and she buried her face in his neck and just breathed. "And brakes. And that back door and window fixed. Just a few details like that."

"Tony ..." she warned.

Tony cleared his throat. "*Cara*, I need to talk to you about something. A bit more serious than your inexplicable anger that I took care of your car for you, if I may."

She lifted her head, but before she could step back, he framed her face with his hands and leaned forward and kissed her. She wondered if there would ever come a day that the feel of his lips didn't warm her body all the way to her soul. Would her heart ever not pause between beats in her chest just long enough to trip forward at an impossible rate? Would her skin ever not tingle for want of his touch? As she stepped closer and deepened the kiss, her arms slipped around his neck and she sighed.

Tony lifted his head and looked at her, his eyes so dark they looked nearly black. He stared at her for a long time before giving her another quick kiss and stepping away.

Robin smiled. "You need to talk to me about something?"

"Yes." He pulled out a chair at the conference table and gestured toward it. Robin sat down and he sat next to her. "Last month, when I was in my old neighborhood, I met a boy. A young man, that is."

Robin grimaced, knowing exactly why he'd been in that neighborhood. "Go on."

"The Holy Spirit spoke to me, almost audibly, and told me to reach out to him. I gave him my card and told him to come see me when he turned eighteen. His birthday was yesterday."

Robin cocked her head, a little confused. "Did he come see you?"

"Yes. He's been here since about eight-thirty."

"And?"

Tony reached for her hand. She placed it in his. He ran his thumb over the sapphire. "And, I'm going to bring him home with me tonight. I've been gutting the apartment rooms, prepping for you and your sisters. Maxine let me know at church Sunday that she will not be moving in with us because she's purchasing that place on Newbury Street. Since I'd already started the work on a suite of rooms for her, I have the space nearly ready. I'm going to offer him a job and a home."

She felt her eyes widen. "Wow." Knowing people, and the neighborhood where Tony met this boy, she leaned forward. "Is this wise?"

Tony smiled and ran a finger down her cheek. "Is it wise to listen to the counsel of the Holy Spirit? I feel good saying yes to that."

Robin sandwiched his hand with both of hers. "Then I trust you, and Him." She smiled. "You are a good man, and I love your heart. I can't wait to marry you."

Tony brought her hands up to his mouth and kissed each one. "Thank you, *cara*. You do my heart good."

She stood. "I'll let you get back to him. What is his name?"

"Derrick." He stood with her. "Derrick DiNunzio. If you can meet us at the apartment in a couple of hours, that would be wonderful. My interior designer is there with a few contractors working as quickly as possible to get a room ready for him. I'm sure she'd appreciate some authoritative direction."

She mentally rearranged her day. "Okay. I'll go by there."

"Can you enlist Maxine? He'll need clothes. She might enjoy taking him shopping with my credit card."

"I'll call her as soon as I get to the car." She put a hand on his cheek and leaned forward, pressing her lips to his. "Don't forget that I want my old car back."

Tony sighed. "I haven't forgotten. I'll wait to have it crushed until the day after we get married."

She laughed as she put her purse over her shoulder. "Don't say that too loud before the wedding or she might not start anymore." She headed toward the door and paused. "Oh, before I forget, you're limited to 750 wedding guests."

"Oh? Just 750 couples? That should be fine."

"No, Tony, 750 total guests."

With a raised eyebrow, he said, "*Non possibile*."

"Well, you're just going to have to make it possible, mister."

Tony's laugh barked around the room. "Very well. I shall limit it. Let Margaret know. She'll have to start cutting down the invite list."

GREATER THAN RUBIES - CHAPTER 3

ROBIN and Maxine stepped off the elevator and into Tony's apartment. It took up the entire top floor of the building – space equal to four luxurious penthouse apartments. They stepped down from the entrance into a huge great room with a glass wall that looked out over the city. A large circular sectional couch and a low square coffee table created a sitting area. Double doors on one end of the room led through the dining room into the kitchen, and a wide hall on the other end led to four bedroom and bathroom suites.

Maxine looked right, then left, then up. "I should reconsider and move in here. Is it too late? It's too late, isn't it?"

Robin walked in the middle of the room and turned in a circle. This was only her second visit to Tony's apartment. A middle aged woman wearing designer jeans and a plaid flannel shirt with white hair falling out of a sloppy bun on the top of her head came out of the hallway and rushed into the room.

"Robin? Hello, I'm Betty." She went straight for Robin, with her hand extended. Then she looked at Maxine. "You must be the sister. Maxine, right? So pleased to meet you both." When her hand was free, she gestured toward the hallway. "If you'll follow me, I'll show you what we're doing."

Betty stopped at the first door on the left. She opened it, revealing a sitting area with a white couch and matching wing backed chair. By the far window sat a desk with a laptop, still in its box. A bookshelf was lined with medical books and titles about Christian living.

"This will be your sister, Sarah's room," she said, walking through the room and opening the far door. Maxine and Robin looked past her to see a four poster bed with plastic wrapped mattresses, two wing back chairs sitting in the middle of the room, and a carpet rolled up, propped against a wall. A fireplace with a white marble mantle occupied the center of the farthest wall from the door. "She has an appointment with me after classes tomorrow to finalize colors," she said, shutting the door and gesturing with her hand. "That door leads to the bathroom, and that one to the dressing room." They left the room and crossed the hall." This is Tony's office," she said. "I'm to redesign it and rearrange it to accommodate another desk, and make the decor a little more feminine."

Robin poked her head into the office and saw a huge oak desk with just a black blotter on top of it. A wooden filing cabinet sat behind the desk. A dark brown leather couch sat in the center of the room, and floor to ceiling bookshelves lined every wall. The single room was easily bigger than Robin's entire apartment.

Betty gestured down the hall. "I'll show you Derrick's room now. I've had painters here since Tony called me at ten this morning. I'm so thankful we were able to get someone in with absolutely no notice on a Thursday afternoon."

She took Robin and Maxine back into the hall to another room. This one had an open door. As soon as they got close to the door, the smell of fresh interior latex paint immediately wafted out. Robin could see through the open doorway beyond the sitting room. Plastic drop cloths covered the carpet and two men in coveralls rolled navy colored paint onto the trimmed walls with professional precision.

"Do you have furniture coming?" Maxine asked.

Betty answered. "Yes. At four today. I have a black leather couch coming for this room, and an oak desk and bookshelf. The bedroom is going to be white and with navy trim. I would have dearly loved to have done a wash but there really isn't time."

"That sounds great," Maxine said. "What are these walls going to be below the chair rail?"

"I'm thinking gray, with nautical paintings above and a matching gray mat inside oak frames."

Maxine nodded. "I can supply the artwork if you can get it framed and matted."

"She absolutely can," Robin said. Maxine's artistic eye that helped her excel in the advertising industry had also developed her into a stellar painter in her own right. "Wait until you see her work."

Betty raised an eyebrow. "Indeed. Tony had mentioned the same but I didn't want to presume. In fact, he wants me to commission you first for any of his contracts."

The three women discussed furniture, colors, and what needed to be bought until Robin's cell phone rang. She saw Tony's number and answered with a smile. "Hi, you."

"Hello, *cara*. I saw your new car in the garage and wanted to let you know we are on our way up."

Robin felt so excited at meeting Derrick she decided not to chide him about the car any more today. "I'll see you in a second." She walked through the apartment, so inspired to see the love that Tony had put into these rooms. She stepped down into the living room and crossed over to greet the elevator just as it arrived.

A young man hesitated before he stepped off, eyeing her with cautious curiosity. He wore dirty jeans and a black leather jacket with a hole in the elbow. His face was chapped red beneath scruffy, unshaven cheeks. He had black hair that was almost curly, brown eyes the color of dark caramel and pale olive skin. He looked wafer thin, nearly gaunt with sallow cheeks, as if he hadn't had many good meals in the last several weeks. Robin immediately fell in love with him. She held both of her hands out. "You must be Derrick," she said with a smile. "I'm Robin. It's so nice to meet you."

He stared at her hands before taking them. She squeezed his chapped and calloused fingers and released him just as Maxine came into the room, laughing. "This is my sister, Maxine," she said.

Maxine raised a hand in a greeting. "Hello, Derrick. It's wonderful to meet you." She fastened her jacket. "Are you ready?"

Derrick shoved his hands into his jacket pockets. "Ready for what?"

Maxine pulled her car keys out of her pocket and jingled them. "Shopping! Tony tells me you need new clothes. And, I'm just sure I need new shoes. You know the old saying about two birds?"

Robin said, "Maxi and I were just here supervising the decorator for your bedroom. Hopefully, we covered everything." She turned to Tony who followed Derrick out of the elevator. He reached into the inside pocket of his coat and pulled out a thin wallet. He handed a black credit card to Maxine and said, "I assume you will make it up to me in paintings very soon?"

Maxine looked at the credit card and asked, "Seriously?"

Tony answered, "If you are concerned or have any issues, call my cell. I have already spoken to the bank so you should have no problems anywhere you go."

He put a hand on Derrick's elbow. With a straight face, he said, "Derrick, you are about to go shopping for clothes, shoes, other apparel, and accessories in the company of a beautiful, smart, and talented woman who has just been given a credit limit that approaches infinity. Consider this a rare opportunity – and take advantage of it – but carry everything she hands you. For the next few hours, you are basically a pack mule."

At Derrick's puzzled look, Maxine released a joyful laugh. "Let's go. I can't wait to get to know more about you."

Robin looked at her watch. "I have to run, too. I have some paperwork to do then I have to meet Craig. I'll see you tomorrow?"

He took her hand and kissed the knuckles. "Count on it, my love."

ROBIN sat at the small, shabby, round table in her worn kitchen. She could reach and open the refrigerator with one hand, and reach and touch the wall opposite the refrigerator with the other. A Formica covered breakfast bar separated the kitchen from the 'living room,' a space squeezed tight with a couch, a chair, and an old television. Down a narrow hallway were two small bedrooms, one hers and one shared by Maxine and Sarah, and a bathroom that was barely big enough for the shower stall and toilet.

She had worked two jobs for years to provide a home and an education for her sisters. She'd vowed to herself that she would do it, without help from anyone, even them, and give them the opportunity to have the kind of life that their addiction-driven mother never offered them. She would give them careers that would allow them to live independently from ever needing anything provided to them by anyone else.

Thinking back, she pulled a tin of mints out from under a stack of mail and popped one in her mouth, sucking on it as she thought of the woman who had given birth to her. Their mother had been driven by her addictions – mastered by them really, enslaved to them – and never seemed to care one way or the other what that meant to her three daughters. Robin had cared for her younger sisters as well as possible, protecting them, doing her best to handle daily needs. But their lives had been the stuff of nightmares filled with hunger, fear, pain, and desperation.

The murder of their mother and her last boyfriend had released the girls from one nightmare, only to introduce the older two to another. From the time she could walk, it felt like Robin had scraped and scratched for survival and she so desperately wanted to make sure her sisters had a solid base to break the cycle.

It felt strange, now, to think that she no longer worked alone. There was a time when she wouldn't accept help from Tony, out of stubborn pride. Then she learned that he expressed love by doing and giving, and had gradually started to accept that.

The idea that Tony would soon be her partner in life gave her a bit of pause. Especially now that planning for the wedding was suddenly upon her, she honestly didn't know what she was doing. Who was she to think she could marry a man who had to whittle the invitation list to his wedding down from over fifteen hundred people and considered doing so a hardship? Whether Tony knew it or acknowledged it or not, he was entirely ten levels above her league.

The door opened and Maxine breezed into the apartment. "That boy is going to break some hearts now that I've had my way with him," she said,

Greater Than Rubies

shedding her coat. She threw it over the back of the couch and set her purse on the counter. "He has a natural sense of style, too. Once I explained to him the process, he took right to it. I even took him by my salon. Instead of balking at being at a women's salon, he sat there in his new clothes and just charmed Francine."

"I really like him. I can see why Tony was so drawn to him. Something about him – "

Maxine raised an eyebrow. "Okay. What's wrong?"

Robin's stared for a moment at Maxine before laughing and shaking her head. "Goodness, Maxi. I can't hide anything from you, can I?"

"What, Robin? What happened?"

"Nothing –" She looked at her phone again. "It's just that a homemaking magazine just called me for an interview. That makes three magazines and four newspapers since Monday."

"So give the interviews." Maxine set a shopping bag full of shoes on the floor by the couch. "I think it's awesome. Oh! Do them at Hank's Place! Get that name recognition out there."

"I don't know how to give an interview. I've never given an interview in my life."

"Then call Tony. I'm sure he has some PR department to handle this kind of thing. He is very careful with his public image."

"Maxi." Her breath came out in a sigh. She slowly stood from the table. "What am I doing? I feel like I'm playing a game and any minute now someone is going to unmask me and everyone will know how I am absolutely the wrong woman to be marrying that man."

Maxine came toward her and put her hands on her shoulders. "Listen to me. You will never find anyone who loves you as much as that man does. You have a jewel in him. You are blessed. Don't foolishly toss it aside because you can't see beyond his material possessions."

"Can anyone see past his material possessions?" She looked at her watch. "I have to run. I'm meeting Craig at the restaurant."

"Hey," Maxine said as Robin started to dash down the hallway. "Be careful with that."

Robin smiled and dismissively waved her hand. "It's fine."

CHEF Casey stood behind the big stainless steel island next to a nervous assistant who deftly cut carrots into julienne strips. He looked up as Robin walked into the room. He gave her the grimace that passed for his smile, making his uneven teeth flash startling white against his ebony face. "Hiya.

Robin smiled back, "Hiya yourself." She stepped aside and encouraged Craig Bartlett to step forward.

Casey looked with curiosity at Robin's guest, but continued their ritual greeting with, "All right, then."

"Casey, I'd like you to meet my father, Craig Bartlett." Robin still felt strange saying that. Craig's feet shuffled and he nervously nodded at Casey, but he did not speak. He stood well over six feet tall, with dirty blond hair and pale blue eyes. His plaid shirt stretched tight over a broad chest and large stomach.

The old chef left his assistant and came around the table. When he reached Craig, he held out his hand. "Pleasure," he said.

Craig took the thin chef's offered hand and shook it with a mumbled, "Nice to meet you."

Casey squinted his eyes. "Seen you around here. Recognize the face. Used to stay here late nights Robin tended bar."

It was nearly the longest speech Robin had ever heard Casey utter. And it told her that Casey knew that Craig was a recovering alcoholic. She had no idea what else he might already know.

The men shook hands and Robin spoke, "I told Craig you might be able to put him to work."

"That right? What can ya do, Craig?" The much shorter and bonier old man asked, his voice skeptical yet open.

Craig ran his finger under the collar of his new shirt. "The truth is I ain't never worked an honest day in my life. So, I don't know. I'll do whatever you tell me to do."

"Eh?" Casey's eyes shifted to Robin.

Knowing her friend's protective feelings toward her, Robin put her hand on her father's arm to convey her support of him. "Craig just came out of rehab. He has a court date in five months, after which he'll very probably go back to prison. In the meantime, he needs some kind of work."

"I can wash dishes, if you want." Craig offered, looking at the industrial washing station.

Casey stepped back and looked him up and down. "You's big. Look strong. You'll do." Robin smiled, relieved. Casey continued. "Need to get you into a uniform. For now, fetch one o' them aprons over there. But listen up. This is my kitchen. Do what I say how I say when I say or you's out. Don't care if your little girl is the boss. Nobody messes in my kitchen. Clear?"

Craig nodded. "Much obliged. I understand."

Robin left the men and moved through the kitchen and down the hall to her office. She opened it and slipped in, shutting it behind her and leaning against it. Her hands shook and she pressed them to her eyes.

She didn't know why she suddenly felt so overwhelmed. Six months ago, she was exhausted physically, and shut down emotionally. Working six days a week, she bartended at one job and waited tables at another. All that mattered to her then was getting Sarah through college and making sure both of her sisters had the means to support themselves so that they would never have to rely on anyone else for anything.

She didn't know God, then. She didn't know Tony, then. She had no idea that she served drinks to her own father every single night when she worked at the bar – a father who now faced sentencing in just a few short months for a fifteen year old manslaughter charge from when, years ago, he stepped out of prison, dug up his pistol, and shot and killed Robin's mother and her mother's male companion.

Now her mind reeled on how different things were, how much better. She slid down the door and wrapped her arms around her legs, whispering a tearful prayer of thanks to God for not turning His back on her, even when she didn't know He existed. While she had His attention, she put in a plea, begging him to help her with this looming fear of not being the right Mrs. Viscolli for Tony.

Chapter 4

TONY sat on the worn plaid couch in the living room of Peter and Caroline O'Farrell. Peter, Tony's mentor and dear friend, headed up the extensive children and youth department at Boston Central Bible Church. Next to Tony on the couch sat a little girl of Chinese descent with straight black hair and a crooked smile. Angel Dove, as Caroline named her, had no idea how she got there or where she came from.

Caroline had first found her digging through the church's soup kitchen Dumpster after lunch was served one afternoon two years ago. The doctor guessed her age at the time at about six. Angel Dove, currently the youngest child in the O'Farrell home, was at the time directing Tony which color of crayon to shade the puff of smoke coming off of the cartoon train in the coloring book in his lap.

Derrick and Peter had braved the winter storm to walk to the corner store so they could replenish the spent supply of milk the children would need with dinner. Robin and Caroline busied themselves in the kitchen. That meant that Tony and Angel Dove had a few moments of quiet time.

Looking at her sent Tony back a number of years in his memory. He remembered the first time Peter brought him here to this house, the very night he'd given his life to Christ. Peter's wife, Caroline, had greeted him warmly, with the first hug he'd had in his life. He remembered nearly being brought to tears by that embrace.

Like Angel Dove, the O'Farrell's had taken Tony in and fostered him, teaching him about life and God the Father, Jesus the Son, and the Holy Spirit. He had learned, grown, and learned some more. He cherished his relationship with these two amazing people. While Peter and Caroline taught him the love of a family, he used the extensive library at the huge inner city church to feed his hungry soul with the Word of God.

By the end of the year, he had saved every dime he earned as one of the church's janitorial crew and invested it. With the profit from his initial investment, he made another one, and another one. Now he was what the press labeled "Boston royalty," an entrepreneur who dabbled in just about anything, all the while pouring money into church ministries and local charities.

Never having children of their own, the O'Farrells fostered dozens over the years. Caroline never turned a child away, even if she had to make a pallet on the floor of a bedroom while she found a better home. Tony shared a room with three other boys the year he lived with them. Today, he financed a network of children's homes throughout the country.

"I have sandwiches," Caroline said, bringing Tony back to the present. She set a huge platter of peanut butter and jelly sandwiches next to two bowls of potato chips. Bright red tendrils of hair escaped the pony tail on the top of her head.

Tony glanced up to find Robin strolling out of the kitchen carrying a pitcher of lemonade. She gave him a warm smile that thrilled him. He so enjoyed seeing how well his bride to be fit so perfectly into his life and felt so comfortable with the people who meant the most to him.

"Yummy!" Angel said as she hopped off the couch and ran to the table.

Caroline smiled and put her hand on the head of her daughter. As they stood to go to the table, Tony slipped an arm around Robin's waist and said, "We are so honored that you and Peter are going to stand up with us at our wedding. We were hoping that Angel Dove could serve as our flower girl."

"Oh, I bet she would love it," Caroline said, walking forward to hug Robin first, then Tony.

In what seemed like incredible timing, the second youngest child and youngest boy in the O'Farrell home appeared from the kitchen carrying a stack of plates to the table. Little did he know he was about to become the topic of conversation.

"There's more," Robin said. "We would also be honored if Isaac would be our ring bearer. I know he's a little old, but – "

"What do you say, lad? Do you want to be in Uncle Tony's wedding?"

The little tawny haired boy with the round glasses scrunched his eight-year-old face up. "Do I have to dress up in a monkey suit?"

Caroline's laughter rang out through the room. "Aye, you do. And you'll look sharp in it, too. Like James Bond." She waved at the table. "Now, eat. Get as much as you want. I can make more."

The back door opened and Peter and Derrick came in, stomping the snow off their feet. Peter pulled his glasses from his face when they steamed up in the heat and Derrick shed his new ski coat. "It is really coming down out there." Peter set a gallon of milk on the table. "There's your milk, my dear."

"Thank you, love," Caroline said, taking the milk into the kitchen.

"Temperature is dropping," Derrick said. He grabbed half a sandwich from the platter and ate it in two bites. Caroline came back into the room carrying a glass of milk which she handed Derrick.

"We should probably go, then," Tony said. He grabbed Robin's coat that she'd hung on the back of a chair and held it out for her to slip her arms into it. "I still need to get Robin home."

"Can I drive?" Derrick asked. He drained the milk in a few long swallows and grabbed another sandwich.

"If the weather wasn't so nasty, I'd say yes."

"I have to learn how to drive in the snow sometime," Derrick said.

"He has a point," Peter said, pulling the ski cap off of his salt and pepper hair.

Tony nodded. "You're right. After we drop Robin off, maybe I'll let you drive. Let me see how bad the roads are.

Derrick let out a loud, "Whoop," and went rushing outside, yelling good-bye to Caroline as he went.

Caroline laughed and put her hand to her chest. "You make me proud, Tony," she said. "What you're doing for that young man is a good thing."

Tony nodded, looking at the door from which Derrick had gone out. "He seems like a fine boy. Ever since he came to me last Wednesday, he's just gratefully accepted what I've offered. I don't know if he's waiting for a catch, casing me, or just plain happy to be out."

Peter put his glasses back on. "I'm guessing the last," he said. "I've met a lot of lost boys. You can tell when they're sincere and when they're just biding their time. He will be a great man one day, if he lets God use him."

"I agree." Tony buttoned his coat. "Ready to traverse the roads, *cara*?"

"I guess," she said. "We probably should leave before it gets worse." She stepped forward and hugged Caroline. "Thank you. I enjoyed the movie and time with you."

"I enjoyed it as well, love. I shall see you at church tomorrow."

Tony stepped outside and the wind immediately drove snow into his face. He held up his arm to block the icy blast and took Robin's arm in his other hand. "Be careful," he yelled against the wind. "The walk will be slippery."

He walked carefully along the sidewalk to the gate. The latch was frozen shut. Derrick kicked it with a booted foot and it shook loose so that Tony could open it. They reached his car, parked on the curb, and piled in, Robin in the front seat next to Tony, Derrick in the back.

Tony started the car and cold air blasted out from the vents. "It will warm up in a sec," he said when Robin shivered. As he spoke, the air started to feel warmer.

He put the car in drive and realized after just a few yards that he would not be able to see in the driving snow. He stopped at an intersection. "We're going to have to take the Charlie," he said. "I can't drive in this."

Robin shivered and looked at her feet. She'd worn canvass shoes, not knowing that the weather would turn. "I don't have a Charlie stop close to me," she said.

"Well ..." He thought about the available options. "You'll just have to stay at my place. I have a stop right near me."

Just then, Robin's phone rang. Tony saw Sarah's picture on the screen as Robin answered it. "Hey, Sarah," she said. Tony inched the car forward carefully. "Slow down," Robin said. "I can't understand you."

Tony turned off of the street that housed the pastors of Boston Central Bible and pulled into the church parking lot, driving through the empty lot to the end. He parked in a spot closest to the entrance to the subway system, but did not turn the car off yet.

"Well, that's okay," she said. "I'm stuck, too, and am just going to go to Tony's. Take the Charlie to Tony's apartment. The two of us can just stay in your room tonight. Your bed's set up, and you have a couch in there, too." Tony nodded and Robin finished the call. "You know which stop to take? Oh, that's right. You met the decorator there. Okay. Good. I'll see you as soon as you get there." She hung up and turned her head to him. "She's been working at the hospital. There's no way she can drive home, either."

"It's just two stops up from my place," he said. "I'll call the guard in case she beats us there." While he placed the call, he realized that ninety percent of him was thankful Sarah would be spending the night as well. But he also admitted that there was that ten percent that fought the constant temptation of knowing that Robin would certainly be his wife, so why continue to deny themselves the fulfillment of pushing their physical relationship forward? Knowing she was sleeping in his apartment, he didn't know if he had the strength to battle that. Sarah's arrival was certainly an answer to prayer.

"This," he said before turning off the car and waving at the falling driven snow outside, "is why I live in Florida in the winter."

He looked over his shoulder at Derrick, who was adjusting his hat. "That's a good idea, man. Let's go to Florida."

Tony laughed. "I think we will. We can leave Tuesday. I think a week or two will warm our bones nicely."

Derrick stopped moving. "Seriously?"

"Of course. I have a ton of work waiting for me down there, so it will be good to go. You'll like my house there. It's right on the beach with a pool. You can vacation before starting your new job at the hotel."

Robin glared at him before her face cracked a smile and laughter bubbled past the feigned seriousness. "You're just mean."

"One day soon, *cara*, you will be free to come and go with me as well. I look forward to it." He put his hand on the door handle. "Ready?"

ROBIN met the elevator, relieved to see Sarah step off. "I've been worried!" She said, hugging her sister.

"I missed the train and had to wait for the next one," Sarah said, pulling her coat off and hanging it on the stand next to the door. She held up her overnight bag. "It was a long wait and my phone died right when we hung up. I'd planned on going to mom and dad's tonight, thankfully, so I have a bag packed."

"Did you find someone to take your Sunday School class?"

"Yep. All set. I'll just go with you in the morning since we can ride the train."

Robin's phone rang in her hand. "Hey Maxi. She just got here." Sarah rolled her eyes at her older sister's display of what she considered over-protectiveness. She made a drinking motion with her hand and headed toward the kitchen

On the other end, Maxine said. "Okay, good. Glad you're all safe. If the roads are clear, I'll bring you clothes in the morning. If not, I'll see you at church."

Robin disconnected the call and stepped down into the living room. She gestured at the doorway toward the kitchen. "I guess I should have warned her Derrick was in there."

"I guess she'll find out soon enough," Tony said, typing on his phone. "Did you get settled into Sarah's room okay?"

Robin curled up on the couch next to him. "I did. I'm so glad you're not thousands of miles away and that we were together tonight. She would have been stuck."

Tony put his arm around her and kissed her forehead. "This will be her home, too. You two will soon think of it that way. You could have come here whether I was home or not."

Robin linked her fingers with his, pulling his arm closer around her. "We could go ahead and skip this whole event of the year, thing, and just get married. Then I could move in now."

"You're not getting out of it that easy," he said, setting his phone on the couch next to him. "But, nice try, to tempt me like that."

She smiled up at him and stared into his eyes. "Tempted, eh?"

His smile faded and his eyes grew serious. Robin felt her heart rate accelerate. "Like you wouldn't believe," he admitted softly, running a finger down her cheek.

"Disgusting!" Sarah said, storming into the room.

Tony frowned and lifted his head. Robin settled more comfortably against him. "I beg your pardon?" she asked.

Sarah pointed in the general direction of the kitchen. "That boy in there is disgusting. And crude."

The dining room door swung open, and Derrick came through, wearing cotton pajama pants and a white T-shirt, holding a large tuna fish sandwich in one hand and a big glass of chocolate milk in the other. "You want to watch the game?" He asked Tony as he sat on the couch next to Robin.

"Sure," Tony said. He gestured at the coffee table. "The television remote is the black one."

"Seriously?" Sarah said, crossing her arms. "You're just going to let him eat that in here?"

"I wasn't rude. I offered her some," Derrick said around a bite of tuna. He chewed and swallowed. "But she *certainly* did *not* want any." He emphasized certainly and not to sound haughty.

Robin giggled and Sarah rolled her eyes. "I'm going to bed. I've had a long day. Goodnight."

ROBIN opened the door to Sarah's room and stopped short when she found her on the couch, reading a book. "Hey," she said, coming all the way into the room and sitting next to her, setting the T-shirt and shorts Tony had loaned her on the cushion next to her. "I thought you were tired an hour ago."

"I wasn't, but I just didn't want to stay in there with him and watch that silly basketball show."

Robin raised an eyebrow. "With Tony?"

Sarah sighed. "Of course not. I love Tony."

"So, Derrick then?"

"Yeah. Something about him irritates me. Maybe it's just the smell of that canned fish he's devouring." Sarah's eyebrows scrunched down behind her glasses, clearly perturbed.

"You must have just gotten off on the wrong foot. He's really nice."

Sarah put her book down and took off her glasses, then stretched. "I'll take your word for it." She looked around at the big, nicely furnished room. "It's crazy to think that this will be our home soon, isn't it?"

Robin nodded. "I'm having a hard time coming to grips with it myself. I don't know how it happened."

Sarah leaned over and hugged her. "Because you're wonderful and you deserve happiness a thousand times over."

"I don't deserve anything more than anyone else." Robin put her hands on the side of her head. "Look at this place. Your bedroom suite is the size of our entire apartment. How do I be a wife in this home?"

"You just learn how." Sarah frowned. "I'm not sure what you mean."

"It feels so right with Tony when we're at the O'Farrell's house or our apartment. Nothing seems out of place." Robin waved her hand. "It's okay. I'm just stressing out loud. Don't worry about it."

"If you're sure. I know that weddings are extremely stressful, even when you're not marrying Boston royalty. It will get better, I just know it. You and Tony were meant to be." Sarah stood. "I'm going to go to bed for real this time. Are you sleeping out here or in there with me?"

"With you, if you don't mind."

"Of course I don't mind."

Robin felt a pang of remembrance. "You used to sleep with me all the time," she said, running her hand over her sister's curly hair. "I was six when you came home from the hospital. But, you didn't have a bed, so Maxi slept on the floor and you slept next to me. Your dad would always kiss you on the forehead. I remember him. I remember he was really nice. He was just kind of, you know, not very smart I guess. I remember I'd get up at night and feed you and he would come in and sing heavy metal songs like lullabies."

Sarah's eyes filled with tears. "I wish I could remember."

Robin felt a cold shudder go through her. "No, you don't. You don't ever want to remember."

GREATER THAN RUBIES - CHAPTER 5

MAXINE opened the double door refrigerator and found the platter of sandwiches Tony said she would find there. Underneath, she found a container of potato salad and another one of cole slaw.

"Did you find everything, Maxi?" Robin asked, coming in behind her.

"I think so. If you'll put the coffee on, I'll set this out on the table."

Maxine carried the large platter through the kitchen door and into the dining room. She arranged the platter on the end of the long, long table but left the plastic wrap on it. When she went back into the kitchen, Robin was just pressing the button to start the coffee machine.

"I'm going to go ask Tony where to find plates and such," Robin said. "I don't know if he wanted to use real things or if he had paper plates somewhere."

"I'll get these salads into something other than deli containers." Maxine started opening cupboard doors. "Assuming I don't get lost in this massive edifice searching for bowls."

The door shut on Robin's laugh. Maxine kept searching. She finally opened a door and found a walk-in supply closet filled with serving platters, serving dishes, and serving bowls. Drawers revealed silverware – real silver – with a "V" engraved on the handles. On the shelf, she discovered two small glass bowls that would perfectly present the deli salads.

When Maxine went back into the kitchen, she stopped short upon seeing Barry at the sink, filling a cup with hot water. "Hi there, big guy," she greeted, hoping her lipstick was still on straight. She hadn't checked it since she left for church that morning.

"Hi, yourself," Barry said, giving her a quick glance. "Glad to see you in church this morning. I was worried the weather would keep everyone away."

She wore a plum colored knee-length skirt that perfectly matched her three-inch plum colored heels. She liked the fact that she still had to look up at him even with her three-inch boost. At her height, she considered it a rare treat to stand shorter than a man. "The streets were clear by the time I headed out. I brought Robin's new car. This way, I can take Sarah back to her car at the hospital and drive Robin home."

Barry nodded. "Sounds like a good plan. Is there anything I can help you with in here, Maxine?"

She raised an eyebrow. "Oh, no. I think I got it under control. And, it's Maxi, please. I've always hated Maxine. Thankfully, only Robin still sometimes calls me that." Although, she really liked hearing Barry "The Bear" say it.

Barry raised an eyebrow in his incredibly handsome face and what she could only call a teasing and somewhat mischievous grin appeared there. "Why have you always hated your name, Maxine?"

"It just doesn't suit me. I look more like a 'Stands with a Fist' than a Maxine."

Barry didn't even grin at her teasing tone. He opened a tea bag, steeped it into hot water, and set his cup out on the counter. Then put his hands in his pockets and leaned against the sink. Using a tone that teachers use when they are hopeful their students already know the answer, he asked, "You know where the name Maxine comes from?"

"Of course," Maxi nodded. "My drug addicted mother's addled brain."

Barry shook his head. "Emperor Maximus ..."

"Ooh." Maxi interrupted. "Emperor! So feminine!"

Barry smiled a little bit at her silliness. "He stood over eight feet tall. It's from his name that we get the word maximum. And the term maximal. And the name Maxine." With a half grin and a teasing tone meant to hook her heart, he announced, "Your name basically means you're ... the most."

Maxine cocked her head and slitted her eyes. "Really? No kidding?"

With an exaggerated motion that really turned out to look quite large considering his stature, Barry crossed his heart with his finger. For the moment, she managed to ignore the wedding ring on his left hand. "Hope to die if it's a lie."

She looked at him as if she remained unconvinced. "How did you know that?"

Barry's grin transformed into a smug smile, "I went to law school, Maxine. I know things."

She threw her head back and laughed. "I see. Apparently they taught you humility, there, too."

"Humility? Oh, absolutely." Barry nodded and sipped his tea.

The door opened and Robin came in. "Hi, Barry," she said, going to the refrigerator. "I didn't see Jacqui this morning."

His lips thinned. "She is not really a regular church attendee. She usually has other plans."

Robin's hands paused. "Oh. Okay. Sorry to bring it up."

"No need to apologize. It is what it is." He lifted his cup as if in a toast. "Ladies. Thank you for putting out lunch. Tony said he wants to make this a regular Sunday thing now that he will have a family here."

"I think that's awesome," Maxine said, "provided he allows me to find a television with a game on it."

Barry put his hand to his heart. "I will ensure that I, I mean you, have access to televised sporting events." He laughed. "See what I must sacrifice for my friends?"

Robin looked between the two of them. "I'm sure Tony won't mind you turning on the television. I bet Derrick would join you in watching, too."

"I'll go see what I can do." Barry left the room and Maxine went back to scooping potato salad into a bowl.

"What's going on, Maxine?" Robin grabbed a spoon and emptied the cole slaw into the bowl.

"What do you mean?"

"Don't be coy. I know you."

Maxine tossed the empty container into the sink. "I'm not meaning to flirt. He's just so handsome and so –"

"Married?"

Maxine sighed. "You're right." She picked up her bowl. "I know you're right. I'll let up."

Robin put a hand on Maxine's arm, "Was he flirting back?"

Maxine looked as if she could answer differently. Instead, she answered honestly. "Not even a little bit."

Before Robin could chide her any further, Maxine pushed through the kitchen door and set the salad next to the tray of sandwiches.

ROBIN spun around and Maxine catcalled at her. "Gorgeous, sister."

Sarah sat on her knees backwards on the couch, propping her elbow on the back of the couch and resting her chin in her hand. "You look wonderful!"

Robin ran her hand down the side of the red dress. It crisscrossed over the front and tied together at the hip. It fell to her knees, and she wore a pair of two-inch red heels Maxine had talked her into buying. She had to keep herself from tugging at the bodice, worried that the dress's design revealed too much cleavage.

"I don't know. Maybe it's too much," she said, turning to go back to her room. "I have a sweater dress I bought for Sundays."

A knock sounded at the door and Maxine rushed to answer it. "Don't you dare," she said. "You leave that on. Besides, he's here, now."

Robin heard Tony speak. "Hello, Maxine. *Buon san Valentino.*"

Maxine laughed and opened the door wider. "If you just said Happy Valentine's Day, then the same to you. Welcome back from the sunshine state."

Tony stepped into view. "Thank you. I thought I would have to drag Derrick back –" He stopped speaking when he saw Robin. His eyes widened and his mouth gaped open.

Robin took a step back and tugged at the dress. "I should probably put on a different dress," she said nervously.

"No!" All three people said at the same time.

The look on Tony's face made Robin's breath catch. She wasn't sure he was even breathing. She could see the pulse racing at his neck. He looked nearly angry, but that wasn't right. Just really intense. Very, very intense. After a heartbeat or two, Tony stepped toward her and took her hand. "No, please." he said more gently. "You look amazing. *Magnifico*. I am so proud that you will be my wife." He brushed at his black sleeve. "I am also glad I told Maxine I was wearing a tuxedo so that she would know how to advise you to dress."

Robin laughed and gathered her black shawl. "You know us too well."

Maxine held up her hand. "Have fun kids. Don't do anything I wouldn't do."

The door shut on Sarah saying, "Maxi!"

"I missed you. I'm glad you're home." Robin hooked her arm through Tony's. "I've never been out on Valentine's Day before, though I've worked plenty."

Tony put his hand on top of hers on his arm as they walked down the stairs to the parking lot. His limousine driver stood ready and opened the door as they approached, closing it quickly behind them. Robin settled back next to Tony against the soft leather seats. He rarely used the limo, and she was curious about what the evening would bring.

"Margaret got the final list of guests' names to Stephanie yesterday," Tony said as the car pulled into the late afternoon traffic.

"I know. They have both been texting me like mad. I have an appointment with Stephanie a week from Wednesday to look at flowers and place settings for the tables."

Tony linked his fingers with hers. "Have you selected your wedding dress yet?"

Robin sighed, mind whirling with details. "That's next Tuesday. I looked through magazines with Maxi and Sarah for hours and hours. We found four possibilities and sent them to the dress shop. I go try them on in a week. Whenever we get that dress figured out, Maxi said we'll be able to get their dresses. I guess there's something stylistic about that. Or something."

Tony laughed and brought her hand up to his lips, kissing the back of it. "Is it so terrible?"

She leaned forward and put her hand on his cheek. "No. Knowing how much you'll love it is making it bearable. But it's new territory and I'm well beyond out of my comfort zone."

"Just think about how easy planning a dinner party will be after this," he said. She opened her mouth to protest, but he covered her mouth with his own, drowning out the sound. Robin quit thinking about wedding colors and details and design and styles and just lost herself in the feel of him, the smell, the taste. Her head spun and her heart beat a frantic rhythm as the car shot through the streets of the city.

She barely felt them slowing down and stopping until Tony lifted his head. The inside of the car felt hot, and she fanned her face as she put a hand to the intricate "updo" Maxine had twisted out of her hair, making sure all strands were in place. The car started forward again, and she looked out the window and saw that they'd pulled into a small airport not far from Logan.

The car stopped next to Tony's Gulfstream. A pilot stood next to the open door and waved as they got out of the car. Tony took Robin's hand and walked toward the stairs leading into the jet. "Good afternoon, Jeremy," he said, shaking the pilot's hand.

"Mr. Viscolli. Happy Valentine's Day, Miss Bartlett. We have clear skies all night long."

"Wonderful." Tony gestured to the stairs. "After you, *cara*."

Curious now about where they might be going, Robin precariously climbed the stairs in her high heels. She ducked her head as she entered the cabin, remembering the white leather couch, white leather chairs, and the shiny mahogany tables from her trip to Florida at Christmas.

Choosing a chair next to a window for takeoff, she sat and buckled up. The only other time she'd flown anywhere in her life had been her recent trip to and from Florida in this same aircraft. Knowing how much Tony traveled, she knew she had better get used to it. But the thought of the little jet thousands of feet in the air made her stomach do a small flip.

Tony sat next to her and put a hand on her knee. "Relax," he said, "Jeremy is the best there is."

"You would have the best," she smiled, trying and failing to relax. "Are you going to tell me where we're going?"

He raised an eyebrow. "I told you. Dinner."

"Dinner requires an airplane?"

"For Valentine's Day? I should think so." He reached a hand into his jacket pocket as the plane taxied away, pulling out a long thin box wrapped in a red ribbon. "For you, my love. Because you have stolen my heart."

"Tony" Robin said, pleased and annoyed at the same time. She took the box and slipped off the ribbon. When she opened the lid, she gasped. Suspended from a silver chain was a heart framed out in diamonds. That heart was stacked on top of and slightly over top of a heart crusted with about a hundred small perfectly cut rubies. As she lifted it out of the box, she saw a card inside with a Bible verse written on it. It said: *Who can find a virtuous wife? For her worth is far above rubies. The heart of her husband safely trusts her; so he will have no lack of gain."* Proverbs 31:10-11

"Do you like it?" Tony asked, taking the necklace from her to slip it around her neck, reaching around her to fasten it. "I think it's perfect for this dress."

Robin brushed her fingers over the hearts. "I don't ... "

Tony sighed. "I know. You don't want jewelry from me. Etcetera. Do you like it, *cara*?"

With a smile, Robin leaned forward and kissed him. "Yes. Very much. Thank you."

"*Bene.*" He kissed her again as the plane's wheels left the ground.

ROBIN recognized the New York City skyline. She grinned and she clutched Tony's hand as the jet landed on a small airstrip just across the river. They stepped off the plane and were ushered to a waiting helicopter. Robin could not believe the thrill she felt as the helicopter took off and flew over the Hudson toward the city.

Tony put his arm around her and in the light of the setting sun pointed out land marks and places of interest. She didn't think she quit smiling the entire flight.

It felt like no sooner had they lifted off than the helicopter landed on the roof of a building. In just minutes she had seen the mighty Hudson River, the Statue of Liberty, and a collection of some of the tallest buildings in the world. It felt exhilarating. Robin thought she could have easily spent the entire evening just sightseeing the city from on high. But her stomach growled as they walked across the roof.

As the helicopter lifted away, it became just the two of them again. Robin wrapped her shawl tighter around her shoulders and kept her hand securely in Tony's. A uniformed guard met them at the door of the roof and opened it for them. Robin recognized the scrolling 'V' of the Viscolli emblem on his emerald green jacket.

As they entered the warm interior, she inquired, "Where are we?"

"A little restaurant I own," Tony answered with a smile. "I hope you're hungry. The chef here is the best in this amazing city. People have reservations for tonight going back to last year."

Another uniformed employee met them at the elevator. "Mr. Viscolli," he said in a smooth and cultured voice. "How was your trip?"

"We had a nice flight, Zach." Tony gestured and had Robin precede him into the elevator.

They rode the elevator down one flight. It opened onto the reception area of the restaurant. Robin stepped out and felt her feet sink into plush carpet. Emerald green, shiny brass, black marble – the entrance was absolutely beautiful. A hostess in a classy Viscolli uniform walked toward them through the crowd of hopeful patrons patiently waiting for their tables. "Mr. Viscolli," she greeted, her white teeth shining against her dark face, "it is such an honor to have you here with us tonight. Miss Bartlett, I'm so pleased you could join us. If you'll follow me, your table is ready."

They left the waiting area and entered the dining room. Robin avoided fiddling with the necklace while they approached a table for two nestled beside the huge window overlooking the amazing city. The table was covered with a cream colored cloth and in the center sat a gold vase with a single red rose. Robin sat in a plush chair with gold and cream brocade fabric.

As they took their seats, the hostess said, "This is Luke. He will be serving you tonight." She gestured at a waiter who approached just as Tony sat.

"Mr. Viscolli, it is an honor to serve you. "The young man looked to be about Sarah's age. He was short, thin, with dark black hair and a long nose.

"Drew the short straw, did you Luke?" Tony teased.

Luke directed his attention to Tony and, perfectly poised with a sincere smile, answered, "Hardly, sir. I've looked forward to this since you made your reservation and I will give you my very best. Would you care to see the menu, or do you know what you'd like to order this evening?"

Tony held his palm up in a questioning manner to Robin, who knew what he asked by the gesture. "Go ahead," she said, "you know what I like."

She barely listened to Tony order as she watched the sun set and the lights come on in the buildings around them. The Empire State building several blocks away suddenly lit up the inside windows in the shape of a gigantic heart. When the waiter left, she leaned forward and took his hand. "This is magical. Thank you."

Tony ran his thumb over the sapphire on her finger. "I am glad you are pleased. I have been looking forward to this date. I planned it while Derrick and I were in Florida."

"How's it going with Derrick?"

"It's going well. I think getting away with him and removing him from the city for a couple of weeks was the best thing to do. He was trying very hard to hide it, but he was going through withdrawal."

"I'm sure the sun and surf helped with that."

"More than you or I know. We also had a lot of down time to talk. I shared the Gospel with him, and my testimony. He is starting to trust me a little more. I don't think he believes we're quite for real yet, though."

"He starts work at the hotel tomorrow, right?"

"Yes. And night school next week." Tony released her hand and straightened as Luke arrived with their drinks and the hors d'oeuvre of bruschetta topped with tomatoes and Italian herbs as the first course of the seven courses he'd ordered. As soon as they were both served, Tony took her hand again. "Let us give thanks for this meal and the traveling mercies with which God has blessed us."

GREATER THAN RUBIES - CHAPTER 6

THE meal would go down as one of the finest she had ever eaten and she felt warm and full. After dessert and coffee, Robin followed Tony through the halls of the restaurant, passing by the huge kitchen, and into a small office. It was very similar to her office at Hank's Place. A tall man with a white chef's hat and a chocolate stained apron waited there for them. He had black hair and a close cropped black goatee. Every aspect of his uniform looked professional from his hat to his pants except that he wore a pair of purple high top sneakers with electric orange laces.

"Robin, I'd like to introduce to you Marcus Williams. Marcus is the head pastry chef here at the Viscolli New York, and the supervising pastry chef for all of the Viscolli restaurants around the world."

Marcus humbly shook her hand. "It is such a pleasure, Miss Bartlett."

It suddenly struck her. "I've seen your name on e-mails at Hank's Place."

Marcus smiled, "Chef Casey is a man after my own heart. I'm trying to get free to make a visit and see if I can assist with menu updates."

"I can't wait," Robin enthused. "That mousse I just had was probably the most amazing thing I've ever tasted."

He put a hand to his heart. "You encourage me greatly."

Tony interjected, quietly saying as if in an aside, "Marcus has gallantly volunteered to take on the very daunting task of creating our wedding cake. He has already come up with some preliminary plans. I will give you the drawings, but I wanted you two to meet in person."

Robin was very interested. "Thank you. I cannot wait to see what you came up with. How long will it take?"

"My team will arrive the first of April. The Boston hotel kitchen will accommodate us for the cake baking and decorating. Not having to transport everything to the site will make it much easier. We will do all of the flowers, gum paste, and sugar sculptures immediately and let them begin to set."

Eyes wide, she said, "It will take you three weeks to do the cake?"

"Oh yes. I would prefer five, but I have other commitments, unfortunately."

Tony made a clicking sound with his tongue, "The Camp David thing in March."

Marcus nodded exactly once. "Don't worry, sir. I'll be done with that in plenty of time."

Tony half grinned. "I'm not worried. You'll make us proud."

And it struck Robin, in that heart beat, that "the Camp David thing" when translated into English meant, "That cake Marcus Williams must set before the President of these United States, the First Lady, and, no doubt, select dignitaries." This man put a higher priority on *her* wedding cake than on preparing a dessert for the leader of the free world.

Marcus looked at his watch. "I must return to the kitchen. I look forward to working with you, Miss Bartlett. Mr. Viscolli knows how to contact me if you have any specific requests or instructions."

Marcus left them alone in the office and Robin spun in a circle. "Okay, I have to ask."

Tony cut her off, "What's with the shoes?"

"What's with the shoes?" She confirmed.

"I should have told you about that in advance. I apologize." Tony put his hand in the small of her back and his voice became almost solemn. "Some time ago, Marcus had a first cousin named Nick Williams. They were very close. Nick, fresh out of high school, joined the armed forces shortly after this great city fell under attack. Unfortunately, Nick was killed in action a few years later. There's a much longer story about the style and choice of colors, but the bottom line is that Marcus wears those shoes to honor Nick and the men with whom he served."

Suddenly, the purple and orange sneakers no longer struck her as funny. "And the Camp David thing?"

Tony shook his head, "Unrelated, but interesting that Marcus was handpicked, no? He probably doesn't even prioritize it as very important. I sponsor a special youth camp each year in support of children and families of our fallen heroes. Marcus runs the kitchen for that camp every summer. I think that is where his heart really is, with those children."

"You are an amazing man, Tony Viscolli. I love you more with every waking moment."

"You are an amazing and beautiful woman, Robin Bartlett. And I can hardly wait to change your name."

Feeling a little overwhelmed, Robin decided to change the subject, "I cannot believe we will be married in two months."

Tony ran his hand down her arm. "Sixty-six days and a wake-up."

She put her hands on her cheeks. "Sixty-six days," she said. "I don't even know what to do next."

Tony pulled her into his arms. "You pick out your dress, select table settings and flowers, and keep counting down the days with me. I love you, *cara*, and our wedding will be beautiful, whatever the arrangements."

ROBIN nervously fiddled with her ring while she waited for the *Inside Boston* magazine reporter to arrive. She sat in the conference room adjacent to the office of Tony's public relations manager, Linda Cross. She still wore the clothes and makeup from the photo shoot that had taken place in a room just down the hall. She'd hoped Tony could be there for the photos, but the magazine had specifically requested only her.

The door opened and Robin's heart lurched, but Linda entered alone. She was short and stocky, with a thick waist and jet black hair. Thick glasses with square black frames dominated her face. "Don will be in momentarily," she said. "He's signing some papers for me right now." She raised an eyebrow behind her glasses. "No worries, Miss Bartlett. I'll be here the whole time."

"I've just never done this before." She licked her lips.

"A year from now, it will be old hat," Linda assured. Robin wondered if she meant that to intimidate her or make her feel more at ease, because, honestly, she wasn't feeling better in the wake of that remark.

A tap at the door preceded the entrance of Don Roberts. He was younger than Robin, tall, boy-next-door good looking with straight brown hair and a fake tan. Nothing about him made her feel at ease about this interview.

He shook her hand – again – then sat in the chair adjacent to her. He took a phone out of his pocket, pressed a series of buttons on it, then set it on the table in front of her. She could only assume he'd activated some sort of recording device. "Miss Bartlett, Robin, thank you for giving me this opportunity."

"It's my pleasure," she said around a suddenly too-dry mouth.

"Let's go ahead and cover the basics. Tell us how you met Tony."

This was the first person outside of church to address Tony as Tony and not Mr. Viscolli. It intrigued Robin. "He, ah, bought a restaurant where I worked." She cleared her throat. "We met then."

"When was that?"

"Last fall."

"And, to add a spice of romance to our story, how did he propose?"

Robin smiled and relaxed, thinking back. "Christmas Eve, on the beach in the Florida Keys."

"That's really nice," Don said. He smiled. "Tony Viscolli is a powerful force in the business world, and not just in the Boston area. He has businesses all over the country and thousands of employees. What do you think drew him to you in particular?"

Uncomfortable, Robin shrugged. "I really couldn't tell you. You'd have to ask him."

"But we can probably guess what drew you to him, right?"

Robin put her hands in her lap and laced her fingers, squeezing them tightly. "If you knew his heart, or anything about him personally, you'd not have to ask that question. He is amazing and generous and loving, and I feel so incredibly blessed."

"Is he?"

"I beg your pardon?"

"Is he really all those things? Or simply uninformed?"

Robin felt her eyebrows crease under the thick makeup from the photo shoot. "What?"

"Does he know all there is to know about you?"

Robin shifted her eyes to Linda, who frowned but did not speak. "I beg your pardon?"

Don sat forward and tapped the top of the table with every question. He looked like an anaconda eyeing a mouse. "He knows you were a waitress moonlighting as a bartender. Does he know your father went to prison for drug smuggling and now faces double murder charges? Does he know your mother was an addict who was murdered in a drug deal? Does he know you, yourself, stabbed your foster parent in the back with a buck knife? Does he know you were a fugitive until you turned eighteen and your juvenile crimes were sealed? Does he know about the improprietary manner in which you had your former employer pull strings with city hall to clear your record so you could obtain custody of one of your sisters? How did you convince that retired sailor to help you pull those strings, Miss Bartlett?"

Panic swirled in her brain, freezing her ability to form cohesive thoughts. "I don't – what are you –?" Robin gasped and looked from Don to Linda. Her heart pounded and she felt sweat break out on her forehead.

Linda pressed a button on the table next to her before standing. "Mr. Roberts? This interview is over. Our attorneys at the Anderson firm will be in contact with your editor in light of the NDA you signed and this particular line of questioning."

"You can't hide her. Believe me if I know, the tabloids know, too. This is the kind of rags to riches story that everyone will be clamoring after. You need to let her – "

As he spoke the door opened and two uniformed security officers marched into the room. They walked straight up to Don. "You need to come with us, sir," one of them said.

"Now." The other one said, picking up the reporter's phone from the table.

"Hey! You can't have that!"

"We'll return your property when you're safely outside the building, sir." The guard stepped aside, placing his body between Roberts and the two women, and gestured with his hand. "Right this way, sir."

Roberts stood but quickly bent around the guard toward Robin. "You might as well figure out the best thing to do is embrace your story and tell it, or else others will do it with their own spin and you won't be able to influence what they say."

The second guard grabbed his arm at the elbow and said, "You've already outstayed your welcome, sir. Time to go."

Roberts jerked himself free. "Don't touch me. I'm leaving."

"Leave now," the guard warned, "Without another word, or I will use force." His finger stabbed in the direction of the door.

Robin stared at the closed door long after it shut behind them. Linda sat where Don had been and touched her hand. "I'm so sorry. All of his credentials checked out."

With a shaking hand, Robin brushed the hair off of her forehead. "I'm not doing something like this again."

Linda nodded. "I understand." She pressed some buttons on her phone. "Margaret? I need to talk to Mr. V. This isn't good."

Without waiting for Linda to hang up the phone or Tony to come gallantly into the room, Robin gathered her bag and her coat and left. Linda tried to call her back, but she was stuck on hold with Tony's office. Escape. Flee. Hide.

The elevator arrived. Thankful to find it empty, she slipped inside and pressed the lobby button, then the door close button in rapid succession. As soon as it started moving, she went to the back corner of the elevator and pressed back against the wall. She used to be good at hiding. Hide way in the back of the closet. Protect her sisters. Make the monsters forget you're there.

But she couldn't hide from her past, could she? What did she think she was doing, becoming Mrs. Antonio Viscolli? Inadequate didn't begin to describe her. Her cell phone started ringing, but she turned it off as she stepped off of the elevator and into the lobby of the hotel. As she walked out of the doors, the valet lifted his hand in greeting, grabbed her keys, and rushed to get her car. With no choice but to wait, she slipped her coat on and shoved her hands into the pockets, lifting her shoulders against the wind. Before her car arrived, she felt Tony at her elbow.

"I'm sorry."

"I'm not doing that again."

"It will never happen again."

Robin turned her head and looked him straight in the eye. "Oh, I know it won't."

Her car pulled up in front of them. Tony touched her elbow. "Robin, please."

"It's okay. I have to go now. But I'll see you when you get back from California." He looked so worried and a frown marred his forehead. Putting a hand on his cheek, loving him, needing him, she pressed her lips to his. "I love you. Have a safe trip."

GREATER THAN RUBIES - CHAPTER 7

MAXINE stood back and declared, "That one."

Robin stood on the platform staring at multiple reflections of herself wearing dress number nineteen thousand three hundred and two. Or maybe just the fifth one. Perhaps it just felt like nineteen thousand or so after all the pictures and websites and magazines and now the trying on. Perhaps she was just remembering the approximate price tag. The five dresses combined probably cost more than she paid for Maxine's first four semesters.

Sarah walked around the platform, surveying the ivory dress, running her fingers over the intricate beadwork on the long train. "Oh yes," she breathed. "This one."

Robin looked in the mirror directly in front of her. The sleeveless bodice almost formed a heart shape and cinched tight at her waist. The skirt flared out, split in the front to show an underskirt of the same material. The edges were scalloped, and tiny pearly beads were sewn into patterns and swirls all over the skirt and train. She felt amazing and beautiful in this dress.

"I don't know if I like the sleeveless," she said, touching her shoulders.

"You'll like it when you see the pictures," Maxine said. "Are you going to wear the necklace from Tony?"

Robin snorted. "Which one?" Maxine raised an eyebrow. "Of course, silly. The Valentine necklace. How could I not?"

"The way the bodice makes the heart shape will seriously make that necklace look like it was made for this dress." Sarah lifted her own curls. "And up. You need your hair up."

Maxine nodded. "Absolutely. My hairdresser is already arranged. You're meeting her next week to discuss hairstyle."

Hairstyle? Robin almost groaned. "Isn't my hair going to be under a veil? What difference does it make how it's up or styled under a veil?"

"I'm going to pretend you didn't say that." Maxine hooked her arm over Sarah's shoulders. "Tony is going to flip."

Sarah nodded. "Kind of like he did with that red dress."

"Yeah. I don't mean to brag," Maxine bragged, "but that red dress was the best idea I've had in a long time."

"Amen, sister." Sarah pulled out her phone and checked an incoming text. "We have an appointment at the hotel tomorrow morning to look at flowers," she said as she replied to the text. "Don't forget."

Robin pulled her hair up and looked at the reflection from every angle. "How could I forget? I don't even remember what my office looks like anymore. All I know is this wedding."

"Poor, poor, Robin. Don't worry. In two months it will be over and we can quit hearing you gripe about the hardship of it." Maxine waved the sales clerk over and her tone grew a bit less sarcastic and a bit more scolding. "You're planning a wedding so you can marry a hard working and Godly man who has the means to fly you to New York City in his private jet for a Valentine's Day dinner. Most women would kill or die for that. You need to lighten up and stop being such a wet blanket. Let us enjoy it, at least."

Robin felt contrite. She thought about what being wife to that man meant and her mind went back to the horrible interview. She put a hand to her forehead as a headache suddenly sprang up and assaulted the area behind her eyes. She heard Maxine speak to the store clerk. "We have a winner. It's going to need some minor alterations."

"Excellent," the tailor said. "I'll tell you in confidence, of the five you selected, this one was my very favorite. I'll just get my tape and some pins."

AS they walked into Cassandra's office in the administrative area of the Viscolli Hotel, Stephanie said, "I took your idea for red roses. I think you'll be pleased."

Cassandra met them at the door. "Ladies, if you'll follow me, please. I have a room with the same carpet and wall colors as the Grand Ballroom where I've set three different tables. You can choose the table settings and flowers, mix and match, whatever you want to do."

Robin quickly chose the ivory colored gold rimmed china for the place settings. She and Maxine and Sarah moved flowers around and finally settled on an arrangement of ivory roses in the shape of a ball that sat in a tall stand. Cream colored table clothes with gold accent covers would look very elegant in the grand ballroom.

The bridal table would have an arrangement of red and ivory roses that would run the entire length of the long table.

"Your bouquet," Stephanie said, "will be red and white roses, similar to the bridal table."

"Are we overdoing the red?" Robin asked.

"Oh no. The room is huge with vaulted ceilings. I think the red will just compliment the gold and cream nicely," Cassandra said.

Stephanie opened a leather portfolio and pulled out a card stock. "Here is the invitation sample. I have a calligrapher coming tomorrow to start working on addressing the envelopes."

Robin took the invitation. On heavy off-white colored paper lined with gold ribbon were the words:

Miss Robin Bartlett
and
Mister Antonio Viscolli
request the honor of your presence
as they come together before family and friends
in the sight of God
to be joined together in Holy matrimony
Saturday, April 21st
at
four o'clock in the afternoon
Boston Central Bible Church
Boston, Massachusetts

Reception immediately to follow
at
the Viscolli Hotel, BostonO

"So they are no longer two, but one.
Therefore, what God has joined together, let man not separate."
Matthew 19:6

"These are absolutely beautiful," Robin said, running a finger over the gold ribbon. "I can't believe how nicely they turned out."

"I agree. They are lovely. They'll go out the first of March," Stephanie said.

"How many names did Tony whittle his list down to?" Maxine asked.

Cassandra laughed. "Eight hundred. But –" she said, holding up a hand to forestall Robin's protest, "not everyone will RSVP."

"Maybe not, but we have an open invite going to the church, too," Robin said.

"Oh, right," Cassandra said. "I'd forgotten that part." She made a notation in her book. "Well, if we have to, we'll open the doors and set up the tents. But, I'm sure we'll be fine."

Stephanie gestured to another table. "Here are some favor options I've worked on with Cassandra." On a tray lay strawberries dipped in white and dark chocolate that had been decorated to look like wedding dresses and tuxedos, handmade chocolates, and some wedding themed cookies. "My personal favorite is the strawberries."

"What are favors?" Robin asked.

Sarah said, "They're gifts you give the guests. It's just something fun." She pointed to the tray. 'Those strawberries are amazing."

Maxine looked over Sarah's shoulder. "They are. I'd go with the strawberries."

Robin worried she'd forget some other detail she didn't know anything about – like favors for guests. "Okay. We'll go with the strawberries."

A waiter wheeled in a service cart. Cassandra clapped her hands in glee. "Awesome. Thank you, Ben."

"My pleasure, Cassandra. Radio when you want me to clear." He left.

Cassandra put a gentle hand on Robin's forearm. "This is the tasting of the menu! These are some of my all time favorite sides."

Four covered dishes sat on the cart. Cassandra removed all of the covers. One plate held a sampling of hors d'œuvres and canapés from caviar topped crackers to smoked salmon bites. One plate held a small lamb chop sitting on a bed of chick peas next to roast quail with some spring greens. Asparagus draped over cauliflower mashed potatoes added more green to the plate. Another plate had the vegetarian sampler, with a falafel and some labneh yogurt sauce, polenta on a bed of greens, and some asparagus. Maxine and Robin grabbed forks and napkins and tasted the meats, leaving Sarah to sample the vegetarian plate.

"This is amazing," Robin said before swallowing a tender bite of lamb seasoned perfectly with rosemary and garlic.

"I love that you went with lamb instead of beef," Stephanie said. "It will be something different."

Sarah dipped another bite of falafel into the labneh. "Oh wow," she said, mouth full. "I can't believe how good this is."

Cassandra grinned. "We have a chef from Dubai. The things that he can create starting with dried garbanzos would make you cry."

"This quail is so moist," Maxine said. "It's always dry whenever I've eaten it before."

"That will certainly be the challenge for the chef. Poultry can dry quickly. As you can see, though, that is moist and wonderful, and was plated about ten minutes ago. I think we'll be okay."

Robin nodded after taking the offered bite from Maxine. "I agree." She wiped her fingers on a cloth napkin. "What's under those domes?" she asked.

Cassandra use exaggerated motions to lift the silver lid. "Cake!" She said, dimples appearing on her round cheeks. "We have French Vanilla with a Chocolate Mousse, Red Velvet with Infused Whipped Cream, and Chocolate Fudge with Peanut Butter Mousse."

Robin took a small bite of the chocolate with the peanut butter and thought her tongue was going to just start dancing inside her head. "Oh my," she said. "This is wonderful. But someone might have a peanut allergy."

"The servers will all have careful instructions. Not to worry."

Maxine tasted the red velvet. "Oh! Oh, man. Oh my stars. Robin? You have got to taste this," she said, holding the fork out to Robin. She looked at Sarah. "No cake for you?"

Sarah held up her hand, palm out. "No. None."

Robin snapped her fingers as she swallowed the most heavenly bite of red velvet she'd ever tasted. "Oh, right. Eggs and milk." She looked at Cassandra. "We'll need a vegan tier."

"No we don't," Sarah said.

Robin winked. "Yes, we do. My sister is having cake at my wedding." She waved a hand over the samples. "I say yes to them all. The cake is going to have eight tiers. It's not like there's not room for different flavors."

Cassandra laughed and made a notation while Stephanie said, "If all of my clients were as easy as you."

DERRICK DiNunzio waited in the reception area just outside of Tony Viscolli's office on the top floor of the Viscolli Hotel, Boston. He wore a long coat with tails and held a top-hat in his gloved hands. For the last few days, he had been learning how to be a doorman and greeter for the hotel.

Over two months had gone by since Derrick had shown up right here in this office. Tony had offered him a salaried position with full benefits. He laid out a plan for Derrick's life for the next 3 years. Tony had hired a private education center to determine Derrick's strengths and weaknesses. Almost immediately, he started working with them.

"I've already worked with these people," Tony had said. "You know Sarah. She's going to be a nurse and these folks are optimizing her time and classes so she can get intern hours under her belt for credits, too. I think they are good choice for what we will do with you."

Derrick went to the private education center every day for two weeks and sat for test after test after test. With his results in hand, the specialists at the center set about getting Derrick on track to obtain his General Education Degree, the equivalent of a High School Diploma. He needed it since he had dropped out of school a few years earlier.

Once he had his GED, he would attend online and on-site classes five days a week in order to sit for tests called CLEP tests. Passing these tests meant he would earn equivalent college credits in fundamental areas like mathematics and English without having to attend the actual classes. At the end of this road, Derrick had a full blown college education and a college degree waiting for him. And once he had that pigskin, Tony assured him that the sky was the limit.

When Derrick got back to the apartment one night, he tried to talk about it with the only person there, Sarah Thomas. After Robin and Tony married, Sarah would move in to the room down the hall from his. She had planted herself in Tony's apartment that afternoon after having met with her interior decorator. Sarah was a few years older than him but much shorter, and he felt like she was approachable like her sisters. They had gotten off on the wrong foot when they first met, but he knew he could correct that given time. Derrick started talking and she let him speak until he started feeling uncomfortable with her impenetrable silence and stoic expression.

When he finished, she had said, "Wow. You dropped out of high school? Color me surprised."

Derrick had stared at her, not fully believing the depth of her hostility. Then he had nodded and said, "Yeah. I figured I needed the extra time to work on my tattoos, sweetheart."

Derrick had taken Tony up on his offer. Perhaps ironically, he had taken to his new lifestyle as if born to middle class parents in the suburbs. Comparing himself to Tony Viscolli with his super sharp appearance, Derrick had made every effort to clean up his own personal grooming. Granted, some things took some getting used to for him.

Derrick no longer had to worry about where his next meal might come from. He hesitated for long minutes the first time he realized that he should just go ahead and dispose of the disposable razor that had shaved its last good shave. Now, a fresh razor and a hot shower were only ever a few minutes away. Fresh, clean, brand new clothes that fit him as if tailor made were his for the asking. And shoes – shoes that looked so very nice and felt so incredibly good on his feet – shoes that no foot but his own had ever worn before surrounded his feet in the company of thick, warm socks. For Derrick, these things alone amounted to luxuries of untold worth.

Tony's secretary answered a quick call in her headset then caught Derrick's eye. "He'll see you now, Mr. DiNunzio."

Mr. DiNunzio. Derrick had been called much, much worse in his lifetime. He felt unexpectedly nervous about seeing Tony in his office. He saw him every evening when Tony was in town, shared a meal with him if his shifts at the hotel allowed it. But they never talked business at home, always God or sports or something else.

He knew that he hadn't done anything wrong. Intellectually, he knew that Tony would not have Derrick "tuned up" as they said in his neighborhood, or worse. He could not identify the source of the butterflies in his stomach or the feeling of apprehension that kept him checking the corners of his eyesight.

He strode into the office and Tony rose with a smile and extended his hand. "Derrick, *figlio*. So good to see you. I must say that uniform seems to suit you. How is it going? Learning the ropes?"

Derrick took Tony's manicured hand in his own white gloved hand and they shook. "It's fine, sir. All the guests are nice, and often tip, and all the people manning the concierge station are helping me a lot."

Tony nodded. "Good. Good. I want you to do that for at least a few more weeks. Let me know when you are ready for a new challenge. I want you to work with the wait staff some more, too. Your speech lessons are really paying off. Your inflection is nearly perfect. Sit. Sit." He gestured toward the couch.

Derrick reached behind him and picked up his tails with one hand before taking a seat. "Is that what you wanted to see me about, Mr. Viscolli?"

Tony resumed his place behind his desk. "Not everything. There is some more. I wanted you to know that I heard from the ed center this morning. I wanted to be the first to congratulate you on earning your GED. It seems you were a good investment on my part. I'm very proud of you."

Derrick felt amazement and, as that feeling surfaced, a lot of his unexplained anxiety vanished. "Really? I thought we'd hear back next week."

Tony smiled, "They have your diploma ready. You can pick it up tonight when you go in for your first CLEP class."

"That's awesome, Mr. V. I don't know what to say. Thank you so much! Thank you. I never would have done anything like this without you."

Tony put his hand up in a calming gesture, "*Non ne parlano*. Just keep working hard."

"I will, Mr. V. I promise."

Tony nodded, then he grew solemn and said, "Derrick, that isn't the only reason I asked you to see me this morning. I need to ask you something very serious, now. And I want you to know that your answer can be 'no' and nothing will change. I want you to trust me when I say that."

The anxiety Derrick felt suddenly returned full force. He had been waiting and waiting here in Never-never-land for the other shoe to drop. Billionaires didn't just give people anything. They loaned. And loans came due – with interest. A good investment? Yeah. If Derrick had learned anything in his life on the streets it was that the reason rich people stayed rich is because they didn't give anything away. Ever.

So this was when Tony would ask him to go do something that he, himself, could not be party to for risk of getting his squeaky-clean filthy-rich hands dirty. This was payback time. This was when Tony asked Derrick to beat someone up, or threaten someone, or courier some merchandise, or even kill someone. Derrick had dreaded this moment but he braced himself for what was to come. Because Derrick had no illusions about judging a book by its cover. One could never tell what the book said inside but one could always tell what the book was going to cost. He knew how much this deal could cost him when he accepted the terms weeks before. And Derrick had never, ever welshed on a deal.

His voice came out ragged and scratchy and he asked, "What is it, Tony?"

Tony grinned, "Tony, now, is it? That's fine but not in front of any of your coworkers. Only in private. I have a public image, after all."

"Sorry." Derrick quickly said. He imagined that Tony Viscolli did have quite a public image to maintain. He braced himself to play his part in maintaining that public image. No one would ever know what he did to repay this man's patronage.

Tony shook his head. "Don't be sorry, *figlio*. You and I are like brothers. It is right that my brother address me in that way. But not so when I am the boss. Regardless, this is my question. As my brother, I am requesting that you stand beside me on the most important day of my life. You would deeply honor me if you could act as one of my groomsmen. Please set aside anything else, and just consider it."

Of all the things in the world that Tony could have asked him to do, this was as far away from any possibility he could have predicted as the east is from the west. Derrick had no idea how long he sat there with a dumb look on his face before he blurted, "You can't know how much it means to me that you asked me, Tony. I can't believe it. Of course. Of course I will."

Tony felt one corner of his mouth creep up. "Ah, well, I think you might have agreed too soon. I had not yet informed you that you will have to walk down the aisle beside Sarah."

And so the other shoe finally dropped. Derrick nearly laughed.

GREATER THAN RUBIES - CHAPTER 8

ROBIN rubbed her hands together then gripped her coffee cup in both hands, trying to warm them. From the window of the little cafe, she could see the river. It looked exactly as cold outside as it felt. Chunks of ice still floated near the shore of the Charles River, but the trees had started budding as spring desperately tried to beat back winter.

Tony carried two fresh steaming cups of coffee to the table and took his seat across from her. "This is a neat place," Robin said, admiring the comfortable interior with hard wood floors, couches, leather chairs, and bookshelves lined with eclectic reading selections.

Tony nodded. "The church runs it. It's a nonprofit so all receipts and tips support overseas ministries. We have a lot of handmade art and jewelry that are made by girls in a pregnancy crisis center in Africa. Those are sold here, too."

Robin looked closer at the decor and noticed the price tags. "Wow. This is incredible."

"Coffee houses are in vogue. We're just leveraging that popularity until it stops meeting with success. It's all about the right marketing at the right time to the right audience." He took a sip of his coffee. "Plus, they make excellent coffee and scones."

She took a sip of the coffee and nodded. "That is good."

"I come here after rowing. I keep my scull in the boat house next door."

"It won't be long until you can be out there."

"I think I have another trip to Florida and some more wind surfing to do while that ice out there keeps melting." He lifted his cup as if in a toast and she laughed.

She set her cup back down in front of her. "How did the meeting with Derrick go?"

"It went well. I have a feeling that he thought I was about to hand him a bill for services rendered and was about to ask him to do something terrible. As soon as he realized nothing has changed, he relaxed so much. I hope he trusts me one day."

"He comes from a world where you don't get something for nothing."

"It isn't for nothing. I expect him to work hard and aim for success."

Robin laughed. "Tony, you know what I meant."

He leaned back as the waitress brought their scones. Steam piped up from them and Robin's mouth watered at the smell of fresh baked yumminess. "Of course I know what you meant," he said, breaking the blueberry scone in half and moving half to his plate, then breaking the cranberry scone in half and moving half to her plate.

"You don't mind, do you, that I asked him to move into our apartment? I know we'll be newlyweds."

Robin shrugged as she took her first heavenly bite of light, flaky, blueberry flavored scone. She washed it down with the amazing coffee and just let the flavors mingle on her tongue for a moment before answering. "I don't mind. I guess we could have gotten him some apartment somewhere and done the same for Sarah, but I don't feel right about doing that. I think we need to just live together, the four of us. Derrick needs the family structure, and I want to get to know Sarah better now that I'm not juggling two jobs and scraping a living."

Tony finished off the half of cranberry scone then set his fork down. "I want to talk to you about something."

"Okay." Robin set her own fork down and picked up her cup, sitting back in the chair.

"About the interview – "

With a sigh, Robin rubbed her temple with one hand. "You've managed to avoid talking to me about that. I was hoping it would go away."

"That's what I wanted to talk about." He placed his palm flat on the table in front of him. "People dig things up on me. It is inevitable. Who is this man slowly growing this fortune in this city with some of the biggest power players in the world? But, there was nothing to find out. I have no record, I have no paper trail. The best someone could do was to find my birth certificate, and that didn't tell them anything." He gestured at her with his palm. "You are a different story. You were in the system, so to speak. Your mother died as a tragic statistic. You were arrested after stabbing a foster father."

Robin snorted. "Yeah, and he – "

With a small smile, Tony said, "Yes. I know. The point is, people are going to dig, discover, and it's going to get out. The reporter was correct. I think you should be open about your past. Do another interview with him. We'll give it on the condition that we get to read the final product before publication. Stop the fire before it becomes a storm, so to speak."

Embarrassment, horror, fear, all sprang up in her chest, drowning her. "Wait. You can't be serious."

"I am completely serious." He reached for her hand and took it with both of his. "I can't stop this from happening. We can just try to control it."

Terrified that she would just burst into tears sitting right there, Robin closed her eyes and pulled her hand away. "Please," she whispered.

"My love, you have nothing for which you need be ashamed. You were a child and your story is a remarkable tale of endurance and sacrifice. You made it. Look at the woman you became."

He was right. They would never stop. The best defense was a good offense. She took deep long breaths. In and out. Inhale, exhale. Finally in control, she opened her eyes and looked at her fiancé. "If you think I need to, then I will. But I wish you didn't think I needed to."

"Robin, *cara*, I am sorry that it came to this, and I'm even sorrier that I didn't foresee it. Please forgive me."

This time, she reached forward and took his hand. "Tony, this isn't your fault. It's just life. And for whatever reason, people care about stuff like that. It's never been important to me, other peoples' stories. But I guess this is considered news. I trust your judgment in handling it, and I know you wouldn't put me in a position that would hurt me."

His eyes grew intense and Robin's heart skipped a beat. "Never," he said. "I promise you that."

"I just wish – "

Tony waited, but she didn't finish the sentence. Finally, he asked, "What, *cara*? What do you wish?"

Robin picked her fork back up again and cut a piece of scone. "I just sometimes wish you weren't richer than dirt. Then I wouldn't have to worry about people questioning how genuine my love for you is or what my motivations might be for marrying you."

ROBIN leaned back against the booth as the waitress placed a salad in front of her. Craig sat across from her and fidgeted as the waitress gave him his soup. He picked up his spoon but set it back down again. "Can we bless this?"

"Absolutely," Robin said, lacing her fingers in her lap and bowing her head.

Craig cleared his throat and said, "Dear God, thank You for this food. And thank You for my daughter and for her birthday. I know my future is not bright, what with the prison sentence in front of me, but I'm glad to at least get this one with her. Amen."

Robin smiled and put a hand to her chest. "What a beautiful prayer.

Thank you."

He shrugged, clearly uncomfortable. "This is all new to me. I don't always know what to say or how to act."

"Likewise."

With a nod, he picked up his spoon again. "That's right. It's new to you, too. You make it look easy."

"I have a good teacher," she said, looking at the ring on her finger. "Tony has been great."

"You got yerself a good man, there, girl. You keep him." He looked around the steak house. Loud country music blared from the speakers and peanut shells littered the floor. Robin loved the nostalgic post WWII decor and the relaxed atmosphere. "Pretty nice place, huh?"

"I think it's wonderful. Thank you for inviting me." She chewed on some iceberg lettuce and swallowed. "Can I ask you for a favor?"

"Sure." Craig took another sip of soup, then pushed his bowl aside.

"Well, two things, really." She was still trying to learn how to relate to her only living parent.

"Anything." His fingers tapped on the top of the table. Robin had noticed that he never sat still anymore. She remembered all the years serving him at Hank's and could always tell when he had reached his drink tolerance, because his fidgety body would slowly slow down.

"I have four months left on my lease and don't really want to break it. Maxine's apartment is ready for her to start moving into it. I know the halfway house is pushing you to get out."

Craig nodded. "Now that I have a job, they need to free up the bed. It's been hard to find something temporary, knowing what May will bring."

"Well, Maxine has offered to let Sarah and I stay with her, if you would be willing to take over my lease. I know it's two bedrooms, instead of one, but I can pay half of the rent if you need me to."

Craig nodded. "What's your rent there?" She told him. He frowned. "I might could swing it. I think Casey's being a little more generous with my pay because I'm the boss' dad." He grinned. "I'm okay with that, though, 'cause I won't be here for too long."

In a spontaneous movement, she reached forward and took his hand. "I'm really proud of you. You going forward to the police and turning yourself in is amazing."

With a shrug, he said, "I can't run anymore."

She squeezed his hand and went back to her salad. "You're doing the right thing. But it must be intimidating."

"Well, I don't know. I been inside more of my adult life than out. So, it's not like an unknown. Would be better if I knew how long they's going to give me. Barry doesn't seem to think it will be more than ten years,

Greater Than Rubies

seein's how I turned myself in and it's manslaughter. But, we'll see. What is going to be hard is to start a ministry inside. Abram and Tony, they're helping me and teaching me. I go to class every Wednesday to learn how."

Robin grinned. "I know. It's so exciting."

Craig shook his head and smiled at the same time. "So strange this turn in my life. But you know, we were praying about it and, this is going to sound funny."

Robin waited. When he didn't speak anymore, just kept his lips tight and his eyebrows knotted up, she prompted, "Go ahead."

He took a breath and raised one shoulder in a half shrug, "Well, it was like I heard someone talking to me inside my head. Like I heard an actual voice. It was telling me that I had already been to prison for a reason. That I already knew the system inside for a reason. That everything had already been planned ahead of time to bring me to this place and time that is coming. I can't get my head around it. I took two lives. It makes no sense to me. And since then, I find myself feeling excited about the idea of going back in. Imagine being excited about going back to prison."

"I know what you mean." Robin took a drink of her soda and pushed her plate aside just as the waitress arrived carrying platters of steak and potatoes. Her mouth watered at the tantalizing aromas wafting her way.

After she cut into her steak and chewed the first bite, she said," I was also wondering if you wouldn't mind giving me away at my wedding. I'd contemplated asking Hank, but – "

He shook his head. "I ain't been much of a father to you. Hank did so much more."

"But you are my father. I'm incredibly proud of you and want to show you off. But also, I was praying about you or Hank and I kept hearing my voice saying I must honor you because you are my father." She watched as he tugged at his collar and nervously took a sip of his iced tea. "I spent so many years feeling like I was alone. In the last few months, I've gained Tony and his friends and now I've found my dad. I want you to be the one to give me away."

Craig's eyes blinked rapidly and he cleared his throat a few times before speaking. "I'd be honored," he whispered, then furiously cut into his steak.

TONY rose from the couch as Robin came into her apartment. "Hi. How did the dinner with Craig go?"

"Hi." Robin shed her coat and put her purse and keys on the bar dividing the kitchen and living room. "It was really nice. My steak was great."

"Is he going to give you away?" Robin walked toward him and put her arms around him, resting her head on his shoulder. She loved the way it felt when he put his arms around her, and for a moment, she just breathed in the smell and feel of him.

"Yes," she said, pulling back and kissing him. "He thought Hank should do it, but I convinced him. He's also going to take over my lease."

Tony frowned. "Your lease?"

Robin shrugged and waved her hand in a dismissive gesture. "Instead of breaking my lease at the end of April, I'd rather give the apartment to Craig. Sarah and I are going to go stay with Maxine."

"Why didn't you come to me? I could have helped work this out. I could have gotten Craig a place, or you a hotel room or something."

"I don't know. Maybe because it doesn't have anything to do with you, and it was easy to work out?"

"*Cara*, everything pertaining to you pertains to me."

Robin sat down on the couch and raised an eyebrow. "Oh? Do you want to give me the specifics of your day and all of your wheeling and dealing, or do you plan to just gloss it over with your smooth voice and romantically tell me how the day stretched on and on in front of you until the moment you could see me again?"

Tony stared at her for a moment before throwing his head back and laughing. "Touché," he said. "Point made and point taken." He sat next to her and pulled a box out of his jacket pocket. "Happy Birthday, my beautiful bride-to-be."

Her knee-jerk was to complain about yet another expensive gift, but since it was her birthday, she grinned and took the box from him. Inside, nestled in tissue paper, was a business card. "What is this?"

"That is an all-inclusive spa weekend for you and your sisters to be taken at some point before the wedding. It includes – for each of you – a 90 minute full body massage, masks, hair and nail stuff – all that spa things that I am told women most enjoy. This place is supposed to be the spot to go to in Boston."

Robin read the business card. "So I just call the number."

"*Si*. The reservation for the three of you is under your name."

She put her arms around his neck and said, "Thank you, for my present."

"You are most welcome. I confess, I find that I am curious to see how much more relaxed you feel after enjoying your spa day with your sisters."

ROBIN sat in Stephanie Giordano's cute little office. All around her were pictures of weddings, parties, even elaborate birthday parties for children. Material lay draped over a couch in a corner and boxes of stuff from a company with the tag line "Your entertainment headquarters" were stacked in a corner.

Stephanie used a key to unlock a filing cabinet drawer, and pulled out four jewelry boxes. "I love that you used the necklace Tony gave you for Valentine's Day to design your bridesmaid gifts," she said. "My jeweler really enjoyed doing this."

"I'm so glad. The necklace is so pretty, and the dress I picked out just fits it so well that I wanted to keep the look flowing," Robin said, reaching for one of the boxes. She opened the top and smiled. An outline of a heart made out of alternating diamonds and rubies hung suspended from a silver chain. It was exactly the size and shape of the diamond heart on Robin's ruby and diamond necklace. "This is perfect!" she said.

"I think it will go nicely with the dresses you picked out for the girls, too," Stephanie said. "Here is the locket for the flower girl." Robin had also commissioned a silver locket for Angel Dove that contained a photo of Peter and Caroline. She opened the locket and smiled. "It's a little large for such a small girl, but I'm sure it will be something she treasures as she gets older."

"I love it," Robin said. "It was exactly what I had in mind."

Stephanie opened a file folder. "Tony's office sent me the order of ceremonies. Here is a sample of the printed program." She handed Robin a heavy card stock folded in half the color of rich rubies.

In formal white scrolling letters on the front it read, "The Wedding of Robin Bartlett and Antonio Viscolli," listing the names and addresses of the church and the hotel. Inside on the left, it listed the wedding party, and on the right it gave an order of service, from the invocation through the solos and message, to the vows, more singing, and the presentation of the bride and groom.

"I love this paper," Robin said. "I'm surprised it doesn't feel like too much red."

"I think red ink on white paper would have felt like too much red. This feels very elegant." Stephanie handed her another sheet of paper. "These are the shots the photographer is going to want before the ceremony. We'll take all the photos of you with or without your party that will not have Tony in them before the ceremony, so we don't tie up the time before the reception taking pictures."

"This is all very real," Robin said. "I can't believe we're just a month out."

"Oh, speaking of, I wanted to let you know that we are definitely going to have to put out heated tents at the hotel. RSVP's are coming in and we're pushing close to the limit of the capacity for the room, and that doesn't include the open invite to the church."

Robin nodded. "I had a feeling Tony wouldn't be able to streamline his list enough." She settled back in the chair. "He likes hosting parties far too much."

Stephanie laughed. "You know, you have been a joy to work with on this. I was so worried it would be a bear and my business would be ruined."

"Well, I don't know what I'm doing. I've never even been to a wedding. So, it's easy to concede to your judgment, since this is what you do for a living." Robin made a note in her notebook. "I still need to get with Tony about our vows. And, on the checklist you gave me, it said something about toasts?"

"You and Tony need to decide who is going to give toasts, and make sure they know it. Traditionally, it's the best man. It can also be your father, your maid of honor, whomever. You just need to make sure that is all arranged ahead of time."

As Robin put the jewelry boxes in her purse and stood to go, Stephanie snapped her fingers. "One other thing. Are you free on the second of April at two?"

Robin checked her phone. "I can be free," she said. "The restaurant is closed Mondays."

"Okay, good. Can you meet here at two to talk to your hair stylist again and meet your makeup artist?"

With a shrug, Robin made the notation in her phone. "I can be here."

"I should have your veil then. We can show it to the hair stylist and let her work your hair around the veil."

Robin put a hand to her hair. "It seems silly to focus so much on hair that will be covered the whole time."

Stephanie laughed. "It does. But you won't be wearing your veil for some of the pictures, and you won't be wearing it at the reception."

"I guess. And Maxine said something about nails?"

"Yes. The makeup artist will talk with you about that in some detail." Stephanie made a notation in her pad. "I will be with you for the conversation with them, so they'll know exactly what you want."

Robin laughed. "You mean, you'll tell me exactly what I want."

"Only because you have given me permission to do so." She walked around her desk. "Thank you for giving me this opportunity."

Robin gladly took the older woman's hand. "Thank you for taking such good care of me."

She left the building and slid onto the electronically warmed leather seat of her luxury sedan. It occurred to her that it had been well over a month since her car broke down. She loved her sleek little sapphire blue sedan as much as Tony likely knew she'd love it, and couldn't stand the idea of going back to her rusty old trouble making car. With a sigh and a smile, she figured Tony likely knew that, too. She bet that if she asked him, her car had already been repaired and was sitting in some parking lot somewhere just waiting for word from him to bring it to her or take it away forever. In the space of a heartbeat, she decided she'd tell him just to take it away forever.

She drove home in her new, safe, reliable car enjoying the brightness of the afternoon sun. She hoped to take the bright day as a sign that spring would come early. Then the weather would be so nice for the wedding that it somehow wouldn't matter that a few hundred guests would find themselves seated in tents.

After she arrived home, she went into her bedroom and stashed the jewelry boxes in her underwear drawer next to the jewels Tony had given her. She shut the drawer and worried, like always, that someone in her less than ideal neighborhood would realize they were in there and steal them. She was looking forward to being able to utilize Tony's security as a way for her to store her jewelry.

Chapter 9

BARRY shifted the end of the trunk in his hand and said, "Wait a second. Okay. Go." At the other end of the trunk, Derrick grunted and the two men slowly maneuvered out of the apartment.

"What is in this thing?" Derrick panted.

Sarah frowned at him. "Just books. Be careful with the trunk. It was a gift."

"We're being careful, sweetheart." Derrick carefully eased the trunk through the doorway. "We're being careful."

"I'm not your sweetheart." Sarah rolled her eyes at his back and turned to Robin. "I hate leaving with this much chaos going on."

Robin dismissed her with the wave of a hand. "You have a big test coming up. Go and study. I'll see you tonight."

Sarah hugged her quickly. "Okay. How about I bring dinner with me?"

"Yes. Do. Oh, from that sushi place you love so much," Robin encouraged, waving as Sarah left. She put her hands on the small of her back and stretched. As soon as she removed her hands, she felt Tony put his fingers on her hips and use his thumbs to knead the aching muscles in the small of her back. Robin turned her head and smiled. "I'll give you about an hour to quit doing that," she said.

He smiled and pulled her back against him to kiss the back of her neck. "You should have let me hire movers."

"Too chaotic. Something would get messed up. Maxine going one way, Sarah and me going to Maxi's then to your apartment. Craig moving in. Easier if we just do it." She unbuttoned her blue flannel shirt and slipped it off her shoulders, leaving her wearing a gray T-shirt with her jeans. "But, my back does hurt. That ninety minute massage is looking really good right now."

Craig came in, carrying two big boxes. With a heave, he set them on the floor by the couch.

"Craig, do you want me to leave any furniture?" Robin asked.

"Sure. Whatever you don't want to move."

"Tony's place is fully furnished, and Maxine has been buying new things for her apartment, so I think if you want it, it can stay."

"Sure, yeah. Then, you know, whatever."

Robin grinned. "All-righty."

Tony put a hand on the back of her neck and squeezed. "I'm heading to the apartment. Do you want me to hand-carry anything that is going there instead of Maxine's?"

Robin snapped her fingers then took him by the hand. "Actually, yes. Come on back and I'll get them for you."

"What?"

She led Tony down the hall to her room, furnished with a single bed on a metal frame and a worn-out dresser she bought at a thrift store. She opened the top drawer of her dresser and reached in but felt nothing. "Wait," she said.

"What?" Tony looked over her shoulder.

Frantic, Robin shifted underwear and socks around, but still felt nothing. "My necklaces," she said. "The ones you gave me, the gifts for the wedding party, your wedding ring, my passport –" Taking a deep breath and fighting back tears, she started pulling one piece of clothing out at a time. "I put them all here."

"Maybe you moved them." Tony started helping her, looking through the piles of clothes.

"No. I've been putting them here since you've been giving me gifts. I don't have anywhere else to put them."

"Maybe someone else removed them?"

Robin stepped back and put her hands on her hips. "No one knew they were there." She put her hands on the sides of her head. "Tony ... "

"It's okay, *cara*. No reason to panic. We have a full three weeks before the wedding. That's plenty of time to replace anything." He put his hands on her shoulders and squeezed.

"That doesn't change the fact that they were here and now they're gone."

Barry popped his head around the corner of the door. He started to speak but looked at Robin's face. "Something wrong?"

"All my jewelry is missing."

Barry looked behind him and stepped into the room, shutting the door to a crack behind him. His presence seemed to occupy a third of the room. "Where was it?"

"In this drawer," Robin said, looking into it again as if the jewelry would somehow magically appear. "Always in this drawer."

"Could someone else have packed it up?"

"No one knew it was here."

"Okay. It's just things," Tony said. "Unimportant in the long run."

"Things worth several thousand dollars, I imagine," Barry said. "Diamonds, sapphires, rubies … things that would be tempting for someone to take."

Robin narrowed her eyes. "What are you saying?"

"I'm saying that there have been a couple of people in and out of here that we don't know for certain we can trust just yet." Barry crossed his arms over his massive chest.

"A couple of people?" Tony asked.

Barry shrugged. "Sure. Craig, Derrick – I like them both and if they're sincere, they'll really do great things. But, what if they're not so sincere? What if the temptation of such a huge payday was too much to resist?"

Tony shook his head. "I trust Derrick implicitly – that is to say, as much as I trust you, Barry." He cocked his head. "And you and I both know how much I value and trust you."

Robin nodded. "I agree. There's no way Derrick would do that. I also think that if Craig – if my dad – were to take something like that, he wouldn't have stuck around for the theft to be discovered. He'd already be gone. So, I trust it wasn't him." Her phone vibrated in her pocket. She pulled it out and saw Sarah's face on the screen. "Hey, Sarah." she said as she answered it.

"Hey. I'm so sorry. I feel so stupid. I forgot to tell you that I packed your jewelry and passport up in my leather chest and locked it. The key is taped under the ice tray in the freezer. I just knew that boy Derrick was all over the apartment this morning and I just didn't trust him not to take them."

Robin felt her jaw clench. "I wish you would have told me before now," she said. "I have been in a panic looking for them."

"I'm so sorry. This test is really messing with my brain. There's my train. I love you. See you soon!" Sarah disconnected the call.

Robin put the phone back in her pocket. "Sarah packed them in that trunk you guys just took down," she said. "I knew no one would have taken them. At least, none of us would have."

"So did I," Tony agreed.

Barry gave a brief nod of his head. "I'm glad. Glad you found them."

ROBIN tossed her chopsticks into the empty carton of noodles and leaned back against the cushion on the floor. Sarah looked at another California roll and Robin watched her debate before she finally picked it up and ate it. Maxine took a sip of her water and leaned against the wall.

"This apartment is fantastic," Sarah said.

"It was a steal of a find," Maxine agreed. "I am so excited about furnishing it and painting it. That wall over there," she said, pointing to the main interior wall of the living room, "is going to be red brick. I have a friend, well, a guy I dated once. He's a demolition guy for a construction company. I called him and he has a pile of bricks I can buy off of him from an old building on this street."

Robin said, "What about the other apartment, the one that you put the air mattress in for me?"

"I'm going to knock out some walls that join the two apartments, then make that one into an art studio." Maxine stood and started collecting empty boxes and cartons.

"This is like a dream for you, Maxi," Sarah said. "Everything about it, from Newbury Street, to your plans for a brick wall, everything is just so totally you."

Maxine grinned. "I know, right?"

She left the room with the empty containers and returned empty handed. Sarah stood and walked to a window, looking out at the pedestrian traffic. "Just think about how different things are now than just a year ago." She wrapped her arms around herself and turned to face her sisters. "I just want to say out loud, how much I needed you in my life, even when I didn't know it. I didn't know how to take it, that day you showed up. I didn't know how to relate to you when I started living with you. But the longer I am around you, the more I love and admire both of you." She gestured with her hand. "Maxi, I absolutely cannot wait to see what you do with this place."

"Thank you." Maxine went to her and hugged her tight. "I love you, too. You completed our family. I missed you so much when we were apart."

Robin pushed herself to her feet and joined her sisters at the window. "You two have been my life for so long that I don't know how to shift that focus to a husband."

Sarah reached out and tucked a strand of Robin's hair behind her ear. "The first thing you need to do is to quit resisting it. God brought you and Tony together with a very obvious purpose. Let Him work. Quit worrying about the little things."

"Like reporters who ambush me with questions they shouldn't ask?" Robin felt her breath hitch with the memory.

"It doesn't matter. Just cling to Tony, and you two will weather anything." Maxine slipped an arm around Robin's waist and Sarah's waist.

IF Don Roberts felt contrite in any way, his contrition did not manifest in his outward appearance. He looked calm and collected as he waited in the reception area in front of Margaret's desk, eager for a second chance to interview the future Mrs. Viscolli. He didn't greet Robin as she walked through and entered Tony's office, seemingly entirely focused on his legal pad and his phone. Robin found it a bit amusing that Margaret occasionally eyed him as if he were an unruly child whose parents had momentarily stepped away leaving him to create mischief.

Robin tapped on the door and entered in the same heartbeat and immediately felt more at ease when not only Tony greeted her, but Barry Anderson as well. Barry nodded his blond head and greeted her with a warm smile and a simple, "Robin."

She had no idea if she would make it through the next hour, but she had endured coaching and prompting for three hours yesterday at the hands of Linda Cross. Linda had instructed her in a process by which if Robin detected any emotional response to a question, she had to first silently deal with her emotions then, secondly, restate or rephrase the question for the sake of clarity. Only when she fully understood the question being asked was she to take the most important step. The most important thing she had to do was silently ask herself, "Do you feel comfortable answering this question?" Only if she felt comfortable answering did she even need to do so because if she wasn't comfortable answering a question, she could very easily refuse.

Robin had also learned the very valuable meaning behind the interrogative phrase, "Is this off the record?" They had practiced scenarios and Linda had coached her in many practical ways. To be fair, Robin felt considerably more prepared for this interview. However, none of that set her nervousness aside.

Tony took her hands in his own and guided Robin to his very own chair behind his very own desk. Robin took her seat and nervously fiddled with her ring as she placed her hands in her lap, until she remembered that she was simply playing a part and folded her hands neatly in her lap. She adjusted her posture, squaring her shoulders and breathing deep to relax her diaphragm. Tony gave her a confident wink. "Are you ready my darling?"

"I'm still very nervous." Robin confessed.

Tony shook his head, "You'll do fine. I know it."

The phone buzzed and Margaret announced, "Linda is on 3, sir."

Tony answered, "We're ready. Put her on speaker." There was a click and Tony asked, "Linda?"

Linda answered, "I'm ready."

Tony smiled, "All right. Let's pray." He gently retrieved Robin's hand before he closed his eyes and bowed his head. As he began to pray, Robin followed suit. "God in heaven, we petition You that all of our speech and actions during this interview glorify and bring honor to Your holy name. We pray in one voice that You remove any fear, any doubt, any anxiety and we also pray for Don Roberts that he will see and hear only Your mighty voice. Father, we have petitioned You and we are faithful that You hear this prayer and that You will use us to work for Your kingdom in a glorious and miraculous way because we love You so and we ask these things in Your holy name, in the name of the Holy Spirit, and in the name of Jesus Christ. Amen."

With his concluding word, Robin suddenly realized that all of her butterflies were gone. She opened her eyes and realized that Barry had moved to take Tony's other hand. She had not heard him even move which, for a man of his size, could be disconcerting. They released hands and her fingers didn't tremble. Robin literally could not have been more ready for this interview and she said as much. "I didn't realize you were going to pray, Tony. I should have realized it. I'm ready, now."

Tony announced to the speakerphone, "Linda? Go ahead and bring Don in when you come up."

Before she disconnected, Linda acknowledged, "Yes, sir, Mr. V."

The office door opened and Robin calmly observed Don Roberts precede Linda Cross as they entered the space. Her thick square glasses turned toward Robin and she gestured Don to the chair in front of the desk but Barry intercepted him.

"Mr. Roberts. My name is Barry Anderson. I am the corporate attorney for Viscolli Enterprises." Don Roberts naively took Barry's offered handshake, a tactical error the journalist would regret over the course of the next several minutes.

Barry kept his voice even and emotionless as he gripped the man's hand. "As you know, I've already spoken with your editor and he assured me that he has already spoken with you as well."

The color began to drain from Don Robert's face when he suddenly realized that he had inserted his right hand into an inescapable vice. Barry didn't even increase his grip because that would have likely broken bones, but his grasp left no doubt as to who was in charge of the conversation.

"Miss Bartlett is prepared to answer every civil question you have for her today ... provided they are questions ..." When Barry paused for effect, Don's knuckles turned bright red, his fingertips turned a funny shade of purple, and his fingers themselves turned chalk white. "... and civil."

Don Roberts nodded his head energetically, clearly wishing he had not taken the giant's hand in the first place.

Barry cocked his head and asked, "Must I elaborate, Mr. Roberts, or have you a sufficient understanding of what will occur should this interview take an unexpected turn?"

Clearly trying not to let his discomfort seep into his voice, Don assured, "I'm good."

Barry grinned and released the smaller man's hand, admiring the newshound's mettle despite himself. "Then we should probably get started."

Linda walked around the desk and flanked Robin's left. Standing to her right, Tony casually placed a hand on the back of her chair. Barry waited until Don had seated himself before likewise taking his seat.

As Don set his phone out, he said, "Miss Bartlett, we obviously got off on the wrong foot last time. I want to apologize for that. I also want to thank you for asking me back today. I want you to know that I really do have your best interest at heart. I am not an unethical man."

After a few heartbeats, Robin licked her lips and said, "Okay."

Don fiddled with his phone and set it down then consulted his legal pad. Robin assumed that he had once more set his phone to record the interview. "So do you go by Robin or does Tony have a nickname for you, Miss Bartlett?"

Robin said, "Tony calls me *cara*. But Robin is fine."

Don jotted something then asked, "Robin, our readers will certainly want to know how the two of you met."

Robin spent a minute processing the essay question. "The first time we were formally introduced I was waiting on his table at a Chamber of Commerce breakfast that he sponsored. We had actually met the night before when he came to Hank's Place where I tended bar at the time."

"And that was last fall?" Don prompted.

"Yes, last fall."

"Then, he proposed on Christmas Eve while the two of you were vacationing in the Florida Keys?"

Robin said, "No."

Don looked up from his legal pad, "No?"

"The two of us weren't vacationing. Tony sponsors a trip to the Florida Keys for several foster children every year. This past Christmas season, he invited my sisters and me to join him on that trip. Since all of us came from a similar background as those kids, we took him up on his generous offer."

Don scribbled out something and said, "Oh, I see. So it wasn't just the two of you."

Barry shifted in his chair, crossing one giant leg over the other. Tony's face remained impassive. Robin didn't say another word.

"That's really nice," Don smiled. "Could you tell me more about the foster children?"

Robin processed the question and realized that the Holy Spirit was guiding her answers, "One of the things I admire about Tony is his heart for children. He supports hundreds of homes like the one here at Boston Bible that give children like my sisters and I once were a clean, safe, loving environment. I can't wait to support him in those ministries as his wife."

"Do you think the fact that you and Tony share such similar childhood experiences helped draw the two of you together?"

Robin tilted her head slightly and considered the question, "Are you asking if the fact that Tony and I both came from poverty is part of the attraction we feel for each other?"

Don nodded, his pencil poised. Robin said, "It certainly doesn't hurt."

Don asked, "So, if that's part of it, what's the rest? What do you think is his most attractive quality?" If he felt any discomfiture at posing the question with Tony Viscolli standing to her immediate right hand side, he showed none of it in his tone or expression.

Robin took a deep breath and decided to tell the truth. "Believe it or not, I didn't think I really found him that attractive at first. In hindsight, I realize that what I found most attractive – and still do to this very day – is his faith."

"His faith in you?"

Robin nearly laughed, "Certainly not, Mr. Roberts. His faith in God, specifically Yahweh, Jehovah, the creator of all things seen and unseen. His abiding and unshakable faith and his faithfulness to God is certainly the most attractive thing about my fiancée. Now that we share that faith, our lives can only get better."

Don sat back and lifted his pencil. "Well, I can't tell our readers that."

Robin considered that reply, then said, "I see. Naturally, that is entirely up to you, Mr. Roberts. Of course, it is my answer – and it also happens to be entirely true."

Don considered that and said, "So are you guys Catholic or Protestant or what?"

Robin smiled and said, "If forced to answer I would have to say we are 'or what' since those kind of labels largely mean divisions and divisions usually mean disunity in the body of Christ. We're Christians."

The reporter consulted his notes, clearly having gone into an area he didn't want to explore further. "So you guys have set the date for April. Where are you registered?"

Robin smiled, "I can put you in touch with our wedding coordinator for all of your questions about those kinds of details. She's the best and I really can't imagine we'd be ready by April without all her hard work."

Don didn't even jot a note down. "Robin, our readers are going to want to know about your father. Anything you want to tell me about that?"

Robin pursed her lips. "Just that I'm proud of him."

Don sat up a bit straighter, "You're proud of him?"

Robin said, "Absolutely."

"Robin, your father was in prison for most of your childhood and has since confessed to the slaying of your mother and another man when you were fifteen. Can you tell me what you're proud of?"

Robin said, "Sure. The Craig Bartlett of my childhood was a thug. He was an addict and a very, very violent man. I never even really knew him as a child because when he wasn't in jail he was never a part of our lives. If he were still a violent addict, there would be almost nothing about him I could find honorable. The Craig Bartlett of today, the man I know, is not the man in the tabloid stories. My father turned himself in and confessed to all of his crimes without even trying to strike a deal. He is doing what he can to make restitution for his past wrongs. The way he has turned his life around despite his past, I have to say I'm proud of him. And I pray for him every day."

"Your parents were both addicts, Robin. Have you ever used drugs?"

Without hesitation, Robin answered, "Thankfully, I have not. I think the fact that most of the adults in my childhood succumbed to addiction is one of the big reasons I never wanted to experiment."

"But you were a bartender. Alcoholism is a much larger social problem than drug addiction in this country."

"You know, after Tony bought Hank's Place where I tended bar, one of the changes he made that really made me angry was he demolished the bar." Robin admitted. "At the time I didn't understand. All I saw was the loss of potential income from the higher tips a bartender can get. Now I understand, and I am so happy to have learned. I'm proud to manage Hank's Place without the bar."

"Have you decided who's going to take over at Hank's Place after the wedding?"

The question surprised Robin. "I'll still run Hank's. Why wouldn't I?"

The journalist looked skeptical. "So, you're like those lottery winners that swear up and down they won't quit their jobs?"

Robin grinned, "I don't play the lottery, Mr. Roberts. But I love Hank's Place. I can't imagine any good reason to ever quit."

"Robin, what can you tell our readers about stabbing your foster father in the back?"

Barry sat forward, "Don't answer that, Robin."

Robin said, "It's okay … "

Barry held up a massive hand, "No, it isn't okay. Mr. Roberts, if you want to discuss this topic, you had better go off the record. Otherwise, you may have to explain to a Superior Court Judge how you apparently committed or were complicitous in felonious access to sealed juvenile records."

Roberts glanced back at Robin and asked, "Off the record okay?"

Robin nodded, "It's fine."

Barry sat back but his eyes never left Roberts. Robin explained, "At the age of 15, there was a set of very specific circumstances that led to that act of self-defense. I really don't care to elaborate on the details of those circumstances, but I can tell you that if I had it to do over again with the same outcome, I would do it again."

"Why run from the law? If stabbing a person in the back could possibly be self defense, why not press charges?"

"Because I was a child, Mr. Roberts. A little girl. The only thing anyone had ever taught me about conflict by age 15 was to fight, hide, or run. And one thing I learned about fighting is never to get into a fight I might lose. So I ran and I hid."

Don retrieved his legal pad and pencil. "Can we go on record about how your former employer pulled strings with city hall to get you custody of your sister Maxine?"

Barry kept his tone droll, "You mean about her then minor child sister Maxine? That one?"

Don looked at Barry, his eyes not giving anything away, "It isn't like that."

Robin interjected, "Off the record, Mr. Roberts. I wanted custody of Maxine to get her out of those circumstances." Robin felt her eyes begin to tear up and she took a slow deep breath. "Off the record, Mr. Roberts. You wouldn't want anyone to live in those circumstances. The thing is, the vast majority of foster parents and adoptive parents are loving, giving, and caring people. They are skilled and they are, well, parents for lack of a better word. My youngest sister, Sarah, was adopted by a wonderful, caring, loving couple who couldn't have children of their own.

"But, Mr. Roberts, for all the good people in the system, there is a minority of foster parents who are not all of those things. Not at all. The fact is that my sister Maxine and I just happened to fall into one of those rare bad situations."

Robin felt Tony's hand on her shoulder, his fingers gently squeezing, reassuring. "Maybe it had something to do with the fact that the police recovered my sisters and me from a very bad neighborhood. We were in the back of a dark, moldy closet in a condemned shack strewn with cigarettes and drugs and booze – oh, and two dead bodies. Maybe that's why. Maybe not. Who can say? The fact is, we ended up going from an unbelievably horrible situation to one that was merely intolerable. And Mr. Roberts, I don't regret doing what I had to do to get myself and my sister out. And I owe Hank so much for his help. For the record, the greatest thing I've done in my life so far was getting custody of my sister, Maxine."

The journalist took his pencil and very obviously lined out through three lines of his notes. He poised his finger above his phone and asked, "For the record, Robin, when did you know your life was going to change?"

Robin sat back and nodded. Don hit the button on his phone to start recording again. Tony subtly removed his hand and Robin somehow knew that he had rested it back atop the chair, just inches away, ready to intervene and reassure her once more if she needed his touch. "Well, Mr. Roberts, the first inkling I had that my life was about to change forever was on Tony's birthday. My sister, Maxine, had invited him to stay and celebrate and she even baked him a cake."

GREATER THAN RUBIES - CHAPTER 10

ROBIN drove to the church, but it was entirely under protest. Maxine and Sarah had shown up at Hank's at five and insisted that she eat dinner with them. All she longed to do was go home and hide, to mull over that morning's interview until she dissected all of the things she probably said the wrong way. But, she couldn't go home, could she? She didn't even have a home anymore. She had an air mattress in what would be Maxine's art studio.

Sarah slid out of the back seat of the car and looked at her watch. "What time does your church start?"

Maxine got out of the passenger's seat. "Seven on Wednesdays."

"It's five after."

Robin laid her head on the steering wheel. "I have a headache. Why don't you two go on. I'll come back and get you."

"No you don't," Maxine said, opening the door. "There's headache pills in the glove box. Let's go in. You'll be glad you did."

Robin covered her eyes with the palms of her hands. "I don't think so."

"For days now you've been completely down," Maxine said. "Let's go inside. You'll feel a lot better when you do."

Sarah wrapped her scarf tighter around her neck. "Come on, Robin, it's cold out here."

Robin glared at Maxine. "No. I'm going home and going to bed. I'll be back to get you."

Maxine leaned forward and put her forehead on Robin's. "You have a church full of girlfriends throwing you a surprise bridal shower. You need to swallow some aspirin, slap on a smile, and come in like you've never been so surprised in your life."

Tears burned in Robin's throat. "I don't want to have a wedding shower," she said in a near whisper. "Why would you do this to me?"

"Because, sister, this is what brides let their Maids of Honor do. They get showers thrown in their honor, and they enjoy them." Maxine knelt at

Robin's open door. "What is wrong with you? Don't you want to marry Tony?"

"Of course I do," Robin whispered. A tear slid down her cheek. "I just don't know if I can be Mrs. Tony Viscolli. Does that make sense?"

Maxine took her gloved hand. "I doubt Tony would have thought he could be Mr. Tony Viscolli, Captain of Industry, as few as just ten years ago. But, he is. Look at how well he handles it. You can do this. You're so smart, and so charming. And those people in there," she said, pointing to the church, "love you. Let them shower you with gifts that show you that love."

Robin scrubbed at her cheek and pushed herself out of the car. "Okay. I'm sorry I'm not as excited about all this as you think I should be. It's so much, and so daunting."

"But you're not alone," Sarah said, slipping an arm around her waist.

"No, you're not alone." Maxine put her arm around her waist on the other side of her, and the two of them hugged Robin close. She felt safe and secure in that moment.

They walked toward the building, arms entwined just like that, until they reached the door. Maxine opened it and let Robin precede her into the room. After a brief pause, forty women yelled, "Surprise!"

Robin laughed and acted properly surprised. She greeted and hugged her friends and acquaintances, working her way around the room. She finally sat next to her friend Sofia Rabinovich. "How are you doing, Robin?" Sofia asked.

"I'm exhausted and on the border of intimidated by the concept of my future," she said with a smile. "But this party has set everything to right again."

Sofia had brown hair lightly streaked with gray, a beautiful long face, and bright green eyes. Her husband, Abram, on staff at the church had mentored Tony in Old Testament studies and would be presiding over the marriage ceremony for them. "If you need someone to talk to, I'm here," Sofia said. "You know that Abram and I have been married for many years. I can talk or listen, whatever you need."

Robin took her hand and laid her head on her friend's shoulder. "Thank you," she said. "I don't know what I would do without you guys in my life."

Sofia patted her hand. "Likewise, my beautiful young friend."

The time came when the last hors d'ouvrés had been served and everyone was in a joyful mood. Jacqueline Anderson had arrived perhaps 20 minutes late hauling three pink shirt boxes wrapped with cheetah print ribbons and bows. Jacqueline had once more introduced herself to Maxine, apparently not having remembered they had met at the potluck in this very same gymnasium a little over a month before. Jacqueline then attempted to sequester Robin and monopolize her time.

"Why roses?" Jacqueline asked. "It's not like you're on some strict budget or something. Who is your wedding planner? Seriously?"

At Maxine's less than subtle urgings, Sarah interrupted and engaged Jacqueline in one of the games. As soon as the game ended, Jacqueline marched straight back up to Robin to continue the interrogation.

"I know you'll honeymoon in Italy, but where do you think you'll vacation? Aspen? Rio? The South of France?"

"Florida," Robin answered.

Jacqueline let her look of disgust turn to one of just appalled. "Florida? What, exactly, is good about Florida? It's all New York snow birds and tourists."

"Tony proposed to me in Florida."

Jacqueline shook her head. "Thank goodness you have such a big heart to accept that kind of treatment. I would have insisted on proposing to me somewhere nice, at least. Listen, darling, when Better Homes does the photo shoot of the apartment next June, have you given any thought to the appointments and accessories? I only ask because you really want the space to reflect your more feminine tastes instead of Tony's more masculine decor. Trust me, they have enough of that from all the shoots of his office. Who's your decorator? Don't tell me you don't already have a decorator."

"We're using Tony's decorator." Robin answered sounding a bit puzzled.

"Betty?" Jacqueline quizzed. "You're using Betty Lamordio? She's a dinosaur. I can recommend someone if you like."

"What photo shoot in June?" Robin asked.

"Oh, Barry told me all about it. He had to handle all the releases. Something about a human interest piece on the lifestyles of the rich and famous. Anyway – "

Maxine interrupted and asked Jacqueline if she couldn't be a dear and help her set up for the next party game. Jacqueline smiled a smile that never touched her eyes and oh-so-graciously agreed. The game was hosted by Caroline O'Farrell who asked Robin a series of questions about her betrothed. Whenever she got a question wrong, Robin had to stuff a grape into her cheek but not eat it. Whenever she got one right, she could make anyone else in the room hold a grape in her mouth. The winner was determined when either all the questions had been asked or someone couldn't fit another grape inside her mouth.

The softballs came out early. "On what day month and year was Tony born? What kind of car does Tony drive? What is his favorite sport? What is his favorite meal?"

By the end of the softballs, Jacqueline was holding six grapes in her mouth and her eyes smoldered. Then the questions got harder. "Okay, Robin, what was the name of Tony's very first company?"

Robin didn't know the answer. She stuffed a grape into her mouth.

"What part of Italy did Tony's mother originally come from?"

Grape.

"How many companies does Tony presently own and operate?"

Robin spoke around cheeks stuffed with grapes. "Fifty-six."

"Oh, no, honey. He owns 71 firms."

"What?"

"Yes, yes. Unless he bought something new or sold something since yesterday. Okay, got the grape in there? Okay, next is what is the symbol for Viscolli Enterprises on the New York Stock Exchange?"

After fourteen questions, Robin realized two things. She could fit no more than 11 grapes inside her mouth and she knew far less about the man she was going to marry in a few short weeks than she previously assumed. As soon as the game ended, and Robin and Jacqueline spit out their grapes, Jacqueline picked up exactly where they had left off with a kind of obsessiveness that infuriated Maxine.

"You simply must tell me some way I can be in your wedding party. What with my husband acting as the Best Man, it's only proper that I at least be a bride's maid. Although you really should consider how nice it would look to have you and Tony center stage reciting your vows flanked by my husband as his Best Man and me as your Matron of Honor. The brand new couple flanked by the old married couple. Can you imagine how nice that would look in the press releases?"

"Maxine is my maid of honor." Robin said.

"Who is Maxine?" Jacqueline asked in a distracted way.

At that point, Maxine handed Sarah a pad and pen with probably a little more force than she meant to use and walked between the two women. "I'm so sorry. I have to borrow my sister."

She escorted Robin back to the middle of the group which formed a rough circle and spoke over the dozens of conversations in the room. "All right everyone, it's time to open presents."

Robin tried to put Jacqueline Anderson out of her mind and focus on the fun of opening presents. Sarah sat next to her and wrote down who gave her what, and she unwrapped and unbagged item after item of fun presents: a heart-shaped photo frame, a wedding memories book, an awful clock that she just didn't know what to do with.

Maxine handed her a large flat pink box with a cheetah print ribbon, and she laughed at something Caroline O'Farrell said as she opened it. She brushed aside the tissue paper, and her face immediately fused with heat when she saw the white silk and lace. She quickly closed the top.

"What was that?" Sarah asked, pen ready.

"I don't – "

Maxine took it from her and opened the lid. A murmur of excitement and appreciation went through the ladies who saw her hold up a spaghetti strap on a pinafore before quickly putting it back in the box.

"I guessed on sizes," Jacqueline said from her vantage point behind Maxine. She did not sit in the circle with the other ladies. "I'm confident I guessed properly."

Maxine nodded. "I'm sure you did. You seem to be able to size people up rather well." She stacked the opened box on top of the two unopened and set them over with the already opened gifts table.

Robin cleared her throat. "What's next?" she asked, forcing a smile. Maxine met her eyes, conveying understanding and knowing, as she handed her a bag containing personalized stationary with the letter "V" and asked for another present, trying to put out of her mind the negligee sets and everything that they implied.

IN the nightmare, Robin fingered the satin spaghetti strap of the white silk gown she wore. Her finger ran over the frilly lace that barely covered the rise of her breasts. The stale smell of cigarette smoke and spilled cheap alcohol burned her nose. Confused, she looked around. Gin bottles, discarded needle, rubber hosing, an overflowing ashtray, a blackened spoon, and a yellow disposable lighter lay on top of the burned and scarred coffee table. A big rip on the brown plaid couch allowed stuffing to come out of the cushion.

Panicked, she started toward the kitchen, needing to get a garbage bag to clean up the mess before one of the little kids got to it. What if Maxine or Sarah pricked their skin on the needle? No telling how sick it could make them.

"Where you going, little girl?"

At the sound of that voice, she froze. Her heart stopped beating and her hands went ice cold. She wanted to run, she wanted to hide, but before she could force her feet to move, a strong calloused hand seized her upper arm with nicotine stained fingers in a mean, bruising grip. "I said where ya goin' little girl?"

He spun her around and red-rimmed yellow eyes looked her up and down, from her bare shoulders, down the skimpy white silk that brushed the top of her knees, to her bare feet. "Not so little though, are ya?"

His broken teeth were brown and yellow. A blistered tongue, burned from too many tries on an empty glass pipe, shot out to lick cracked lips. His foul breath reeked of cheap cigarettes and cheaper beer. Bitter bile rose up in the back of her throat and she tried to turn her head to get away from the smell.

"No, you're a woman. Or you will be, soon as I'm done with you." A hand gripped her breast, squeezed and twisted it until the pain made her vision gray. She realized that her nightgown had vanished. She screamed, but the sound was muffled by his hand.

Vomit clawed at her throat. She couldn't find her knife, the knife she had palmed in the garage that time. No matter how she resisted, she wasn't strong enough. She was never strong enough. A single tear rolled out of the corner of her eye while his gloating laughter echoed in her ears.

Suddenly, the ramshackle apartment vanished, replaced by the banks of the Charles River in the summertime. The warm sun shone down from a bright blue sky, and the softly blowing breeze caught the hem of her dress, slowly moving it around her bare legs.

Then his eyes changed. They turned from light blue, glassy, red-rimmed to chocolate dark. The putrid odor of his breath changed to faint peppermint. In the kind of transition that only makes sense in a dream, he wore white trousers and a white top, making his skin seem darker, his teeth whiter. Abruptly, his laughter no longer fell on her ears sounding sinister and selfish, but rather joyous and selfless. They laughed and danced on the grass while butterflies fluttered around them.

The river became the warm Atlantic Ocean and sea water surrounded her feet, making her toes sink into the warm sand. Tony's eyes grew serious and his lips touched hers. The weight of the engagement ring felt like a kettle bell on her finger.

Lost in each other, they fell onto the blanket that suddenly appeared on the sand at their feet. His mouth felt gentle, loving, glorious. Her hands moved in lazy patterns across his back, feeling the hard muscles, loving his strength. He raised his head and smiled down at her, and she saw the need inside her reflected in his eyes.

"You know what I want, Robin." Tony said.

"Tony, I can't," She whispered.

Tony stared at her, his jaw set. "You named your price and I paid it. You know what I want."

"Tony," she begged. "Tony, no."

"I always get what I want."

Robin clawed her way out of the nightmare, bolting into a sitting position on the bed. Her whole body quaked in the aftermath. Her hands trembled and her breath came in quick shaky gasps. Sweat poured over her body, and she lifted the damp tendrils of her bangs to wipe her forehead.

She drew her legs up and rested her forehead against her knees. Her breathing slowly returned to normal. Her hands slowly stopped shaking, and the sweat cooled on her body. She stayed where she sat, waiting for the effects of the dream to fade away. She didn't want to carry the cobwebs of the nightmare out of the room with her and into the presence of her sisters.

Chapter 11

ROBIN clutched the bag in her hand a little tighter as the elevator came to a stop. She stepped out into the lobby of Tony's executive offices. The receptionist was speaking into her headset, so she just lifted her hand in a greeting and walked to Tony's office.

Her stomach twisted itself into painful knots, and she could barely breathe. As she got closer to the double doors leading to his outer office, she felt like they lay suddenly farther away. A cold sweat broke out on her upper lip.

She'd dressed carefully this morning, choosing a long navy blue pencil skirt and gray cashmere sweater. Now she wished she'd worn something cooler, or maybe layers so she could shed some heat. Thankfully, she'd thought to pin her hair up, so at least that wasn't suffocating her.

She noticed the tremble in her hand as she opened the door and stepped into Margaret's office.

Margaret stood as Robin entered." Hello, Robin. Mr. Viscolli will be happy to see you," she said, moving around her desk to open the large door leading to Tony's inner sanctuary.

Not for long, she thought, but merely smiled and put a shaking hand to her stomach.

Tony stood next to his desk, sorting papers. His suit jacket was draped on the chair behind him. He wore a white shirt with a blue and black striped tie. When he looked up, he had a distracted frown on his face, but when his eyes met Robin's, his features immediately relaxed and he smiled.

"*Cara mia*," he said, setting the stack of papers down and coming around his desk. "What an unexpected pleasure. Nothing could have surprised or pleased me more."

Robin did not hear Margaret shut the door behind her. Her heart started pounding and nausea churned in her gut. As Tony walked forward, she had to resist the urge to step backward. When he was just a few feet away from her, he did not step any closer, nor did he reach out to her.

"What happened?" he asked, his eyes searching her face.

Robin gripped the twine handle of the bag so tightly that she was surprised it didn't cut her skin. "Can we sit?" She gestured at the leather sofa.

"Yes. Of course. Are you ill? What's wrong?" Tony put a hand on her elbow as they moved to the sitting area. Robin fought the urge to lean into him and let him make everything okay. When she was with him, it seemed like it would definitely always be okay. But in her heart, she knew that was a false sense of security.

He sat on the couch, and she perched on the edge of the couch, turning her body toward him. With a shaking hand, she wiped the sweat off of her lip. "I –" Her breath hiccupped, but she forced forward and refused to give in to tears. If she cried, he would put his arms around her, and she would lose all strength to go forward with this.

He reached for her hand, sandwiching it between both of his. "Your hands are freezing," he said, concerned.

"Tony," she whispered, "I can't marry you."

She kept eye contact, despite a desire to look away. She watched the emotions play across his face, watched as concern mixed with confusion and a little bit of panic. "I don't understand. What are you saying?"

"I've been so stressed about it. I can't be Mrs. Viscolli. I can't do the cars and the trips and the jewelry. I can't plan a wedding that has a governor and three senators attending. I can't be that person. It's not me. I'm just a bartender who didn't even graduate from high school." She could hear the frantic tone of her own voice. "That reporter, he knew the truth about me. Everyone will know the truth about who I really am."

Understanding replaced the panic in his eyes. "Robin, if we go into this together, we can do or be anything. They are just people, just names. God loves them equally to the beggar on the street."

"They expect a certain class, certain knowledge and understanding. I don't have that. Your world has rules and expectations I don't even know about. I can't – "

"I love you. God made me for you and you for me. Nothing else should matter."

Swallowing the tears that burned the back of her eyes she said, "I love you, too. Passionately and forever. But that doesn't fix it. I know I will be inadequate as your wife. You deserve someone better suited to that role. You deserve the best."

He lifted her hands and pressed a kiss against her wrist. She knew he could feel the skittering of her pulse. "You are one of the smartest people I've ever met. You can learn, just like I learned, how to maneuver through certain crowds, how to handle yourself."

"I don't want to learn," she said, barely above a whisper.

He released her hand and framed her face, tilting her head toward his and searching her eyes. "What else? Something else. What is it?"

Panic crowded her brain, cutting off her breathing, taking away her ability to think straight. Heart pounding, she pushed his hands away and stood, rubbing her palms on her hips. "I don't – "

Tony stood with her. Despite the heels on her boots, he felt taller than her. "*Spiegare*," he said, anger seeping into his voice. "Don't just flip some excuse at me and expect me to fall for it. You explain. Whatever it is, I can fix it. We can fix it. You must tell me what it is."

Wrapping her arms around herself, she cleared her throat. "I had a bridal shower last night."

Tony gave a barely imperceptible nod. "I know."

"I got this set of –" Robin waved her hand in the air. "– wedding night … things. Silk, lace."

He slipped his hands into his pockets, but she saw him ball them into fists. "Go on."

"It suddenly occurred to me what marrying you would mean. I mean, it's not like I didn't intellectually know before. But it never really hit me before."

"What it would mean?" He frowned. "You mean sex?"

"The thought –" Defeated, she slumped down into a chair, gripping her hands in her lap. "My mom had some boyfriends who – "

Tony knelt at her feet and put his hands on top of hers. "You told me that before, remember?"

"I hinted, I know. But I haven't told you. I haven't told you about the horror, the pain, the disgusting –" she swallowed, trying to keep from getting sick. "The humiliation. You can't know what it was like. Not being strong enough, not being smart enough. Just enduring."

She ripped her hands away from his and pushed to her feet. The bag sat on the table in front of the couch. "I can't marry you. I can't be some billionaire's wife, and I can't be who you need me to be in the bedroom. Marrying me, despite how much I long to be yours forever, would be horribly unfair for you." She pointed at the bag. "That has the jewels you've given me, the sapphire necklace and the ruby heart. It also has the car keys in it." Slipping off her sapphire engagement ring, she set it on the table next to the bag. "I wish I were different. I wish I could wipe my memory like Sarah and just not remember anything. But, I can't. I'm not going to tie you to me. You deserve so much better than a broken bride."

He hadn't moved from his spot on the floor next to the chair. He did not reach out to her nor try to stop her as she walked across the office and out the door. No tears fell as she waved good-bye to Margaret.

The ride down the elevator took just as long as the ride up but felt like decades. She halfway expected security to meet her at the bottom and escort her back to Tony's office, but she reached the lobby without incident and walked through, not even seeing the people whom she knew who greeted her.

She held the tears in check until she found herself seated in the subway and, as the train pulled away, the first sob nearly ripped her in two.

TONY felt trapped. He didn't know how long he knelt next to that chair. He didn't know how long it took for him to start breathing again, for the fist that clutched his chest so painfully to release its grip long enough to let him inhale and exhale.

He leaned forward and rested his forehead against the chair. He intended to pray, but no words came. Instead, he closed his eyes and just tried to stop the onrush of maddening thoughts – tried to still his racing mind.

How could he fix this? What could he do? He couldn't go back in time. The man who raped her was already dead. There was no closure there. He couldn't change that situation. How to fix this?

Powerless. Helpless. Impotent.

After an endless time of being unable to even talk to God, he shakily stood to his feet. Feeling like he was suffocating, he loosened his tie and unbuttoned the top button of his shirt. He paced to his window that overlooked Boston's business district. All the power and influence that money could buy lay at his fingertips, and everything he'd worked for and accumulated for so long, laying one brick atop another day after day, was the wall that separated him from his happiness. His wealth and her past conspired to keep Robin from wanting to be with him.

A swift knock on his door interrupted his thoughts simultaneously with the sound of his intercom buzzing. Impatient, resentful at the intrusion, he turned around as Barry Anderson and Abram Rabinovich entered his office.

He rubbed his eyes with one hand then pinched the bridge of his nose. "Not now," he said.

"Ah, but we have an appointment," Abram said, smiling around his bearded face. "We are meeting for lunch to discuss building a new playground at the low income daycare."

"Just build it. Build whatever you want," he said, turning back to look out the window. Through gritted teeth he murmured, "Send me the bill."

"Hey. What's wrong?" Barry asked, setting his briefcase on the chair in front of Tony's desk. "What happened?"

Tony shoved his hands into his pockets. "My beloved fiancée has just called off our wedding a mere two weeks before the happy day," he said, strangling around the words.

"What?" Abram put a hand on Tony's shoulder. "Did something happen?"

Tony gave a harsh laugh. "Yeah, I'm worth a fortune. And I'm a man. Apparently, those two things are working against me."

Barry slapped a hand on his other shoulder almost knocking Tony off balance and squeezed. They stayed like that for a while and Barry asked, "How do you feel about it?"

Tony reached up and squeezed the bridge of his nose, shutting his eyes tight. With a deep breath, he said, "I feel like a failure. A complete failure."

Barry said, "Let's talk it out, brother. Listen, it's possible she did you a favor. Better to know now than when it's too late, right?" Tony whipped his head around and glared at Barry. But the giant did not even flinch. "Come on, Tony. Don't look at me like you have no idea what I'm talking about. You're my best friend, so you never bring it up, but you know."

Abram put his arm all the way over Tony's shoulder, subtly yet not so subtly knocking Barry's hand off. "My friend, I know you're a prayerful person and Robin has been the center of your prayer life for many months, now. If the Holy Spirit is commanding you and directing you to make her your wife, who are you to ignore those commands?"

"I'm not the one ignoring anything. She came to me. She said she couldn't be Mrs. Viscolli. She said she couldn't interact with the people in my circles, that they'd see through to her background and she'd never measure up."

Abram nodded. "She likely has a point. Imagine how intimidating all this is to her. You're asking her to sacrifice everything she knows – her entire life. She has to change everything from her address to her name. Marriage is supposed to mirror our relationship with Christ." He led Tony across the large expanse of the room to the couch and guided him to sit down. "When I became a believer, I was disowned by my family. My father can barely even look at me, and to this day, I have a sister who refuses to acknowledge that I exist. And I lost everything. Everything. But, for Christ, I gave it all up."

Abram stopped speaking and just stared passively into Tony's eyes, as if waiting for Tony to say something, except Tony had no idea what to say. He didn't want to be rude and ask his mentor, "What's your point?" So he just nodded.

Abram shook his head, knowing that Tony had missed the point. "Tony, what is God calling you to sacrifice?"

Tony considered that. His default was to try to figure out what he should do, not what he should let go. What had he sacrificed? Had he sacrificed anything since he had met Robin? What was he willing to sacrifice to show her that he knew they belonged together? In the middle of his thoughts, his intercom buzzed. "Mr. Viscolli, Miss Maxine Bartlett is on the phone for you. You said to interrupt if she called today."

He cleared his throat before answering. "*Si. Grazie.*" He pushed off of the couch and crossed over to his desk. "Maxi. Hello."

"Tony," she said in a rush, "I'm so sorry to bother you. I just met with the contractor at my new place, and I was hoping I could come by and show you what he showed me. I want to make sure it's all on the up and up."

His mind rejected the idea of helping Maxine, but he had committed to her that he would help her in any way. She obviously did not know Robin's plans that morning, or she surely would not have even called him. Perhaps he could glean some insight into Robin's change of heart if he had a chance to talk with Maxine. "Please, come by," he said.

Tony buttoned his top button and straightened his tie. He held out his hand to Abram. "My brother, thank you. Your wisdom is a blessing to me."

"Call me if you need me."

Tony took a deep breath and released it. "Maybe ask Sofia – if she felt it was appropriate – for her to intervene on my behalf?"

"I will be happy to ask." Abram assured.

"Thank you."

He hugged Barry. "Thank you for your honesty."

Barry picked up his briefcase. "You know where to find me if you want to talk more. I'll be praying for you, brother."

MAXINE juggled a rolled up set of plans and a notebook as she entered Tony's office. He met her at the door and gestured at the conference table "I know you're busy. Are you sure you don't mind me barging in like this?" She placed the paperwork on top of the table and turned and looked him in the face. Red rimmed eyes stared at the door behind her. "Wait. What's wrong?"

Tony took a step backward. "I – "

The look of panic gave away more than his lack of warmth and lack of greeting combined. "No. Something's wrong. What's wrong?"

Tony rubbed the back of his neck. "Robin –" His voice hitched.

"Robin what?" Nervous, panicked butterflies leapt to life in her stomach.

"She broke off the engagement this morning."

Shocked, Maxine felt her mouth drop open. She felt her spine straighten and she asked, "What did she say?"

Tony's face hardened so that his eyes conveyed absolutely no emotion. It surprised her when she looked at him in that moment. She barely recognized him. He raised an eyebrow. "She tried to play it off that it's about the money –" he said, but Maxine interrupted him.

"Actually, that's been a big deal for her this entire time. She's seriously struggling with it."

For a moment, his mask slipped and she could see the pain in his eyes before he snapped it back into place. "Right," he said, clearing his throat, "and she's scared about our wedding night."

"Your wedding night?"

His cheeks tinged pink and he rocked on his heels. "Sex," he said in a low voice.

Memories assaulted her, making her involuntarily flinch and back up a step. She ended up with her back against the wall. Tony stepped forward, hand up, as if to help her, but she put up her own hand. "No, don't touch me," she said, putting a hand on her heart. "Just give me a second."

"Maxi," Tony said, stepping a little closer to her than she could stand. The desolation in his voice, the unshed tears in his eyes, almost made her want to hug him and comfort him. "Help me to help her."

"I don't know if you can," she said, emotions swirling, requiring pencil and paper or paint for their release. She struggled with what – with how much – to say. "I don't know if he was the first, but as far as I know, he was the last. And, she fought him every single time. She never made it easy for him, and he'd punch her or hurt her until she was subdued and he could –" She put her hands on her cheeks. "– for months and months. Our mom knew and hated Robin for it. She'd hit her, scream at her, threaten to sell her to the highest bidder. It was hell. We lived in hell." She sighed. "I don't know how you can help her."

Tony cleared his throat and closed his eyes. A single tear escaped and slid down his cheek and he took an angry swipe at it and cleared his throat again. "Okay. Thank you," he whispered. He took a step back and opened his eyes. "Can we talk about this another time?" he asked, gesturing at his conference table.

"Oh, what, this? Yeah, sure. I'll go. I'm so sorry, Tony." Mind whirling, she gathered her purse from under a notebook.

"*Grazie.*"

She turned to leave, but turned back. He was already headed back toward his desk. "Tony?" He paused but did not turn. She could see his shoulders shaking with the emotion he contained. "I love you. You are an amazing man and I'm thankful you're in our lives. But, I love her more."

Tony's shoulders suddenly slumped. Maxine went on, "I can't see her get hurt. I'll back whatever play she feels like she needs to make. If that means things have to change between you and me right now, then I understand."

His nod was very brief, but she saw it. She turned and left the office, desperate to go find her sister.

ROBIN sat on the front row of the small chapel affiliated with her church. She'd gone in here because she didn't want to walk into the main building and encounter anyone she knew. This chapel was a one-room structure used for small weddings and small funerals. She had come to pray, but she didn't know what to say, so she just poured her heart out to God with sobs while her mind swirled with thoughts of Tony, the love he'd shown her, the patience and understanding he'd given her. She thought of the joy in his eyes whenever he'd give her some stupidly expensive gift. Her heart ached at the thought of not being with him anymore.

She couldn't get over the look on Tony's face, the absolute helplessness. She wanted to go to him and take it all back and let him put the ring back on her finger, but she couldn't. The thought of conceding and what that meant she'd have to face – she just couldn't do it.

"Please God," she said, "help me. Guide me in this."

She heard the door open and she turned her head, startled. It partially surprised her and partially annoyed her when Sofia and Caroline came through the door.

The two pastors' wives could not look more different – Sofia in her trim camel colored suit perfectly coifed, Caroline in her blue jeans and flannel shirt with her red hair sticking out everywhere. Robin could not love either woman more but she felt she needed solitude and privacy just now. They marched right up to her and then sat on each side of her making it clear they were here to stay. Caroline took her hand and Sofia put her arm over her shoulders.

Giving in, Robin rested her head on Sofia's shoulder and sobbed. "I – "

"Hush, love," Caroline said, "just let it out." She handed Robin a cotton handkerchief, and Robin sobbed into it until it was soaked with sweat and tears. When she finally felt like she could cry no more, she closed her eyes and willed the headache to fade away.

"I called Stephanie Giordano," Sofia said. "She had not heard from you yesterday or today. That tells me you didn't cancel plans, and *that*, my very young child, tells me that you do not *want* to cancel plans."

Robin's sigh shuddered out of her body. "Of course I don't want to cancel any plans. In the midst of destroying the most amazing man on the planet, I simply forgot to call my wedding planner. I'll get on it right away."

Caroline ran her hand over Robin's hair. "Do you know why I don't have any children of my own?" she asked, her Irish voice lyrical and overwhelmingly comforting. Robin shook her head. "Because a man hurt me when I was far too young. It was actually a miracle I even lived. But I did, though the doctors in Dublin told my mother that I'd likely never have children. Turns out they were right."

Robin felt the air leave her body. "I'm so sorry," she whispered.

"I have had decades to heal," she said, "and the love of a good man. It wasn't easy trusting him, but I'm so very, very glad I did. I may never have known the special and private beauty God, in His incredible wisdom, has given husbands and wives."

"God created a perfect planet," Sofia said. "Then Eve took of the fruit, Adam took the fruit from her, and it broke the perfection. The world is groaning from the weight of sin. What God originally designed is not what is today." She hugged Robin. "God's nature is contrary to the violence that you, and so many others, have experienced."

Caroline interjected. "Tony's past is filled with women who abandoned him. Women who were supposed to take care of him, and love him, and nurture him, and protect him. Instead, at too young of an age, he had to take up for himself. His past is riddled with drugs and abuse, and the only love he could find was the momentary kind that he occasionally paid for, much to his present shame."

"God has given you to Tony as much as He has given Tony to you. You two can heal each other and become one together. Not just physically, but spiritually as well," Sofia said.

"I don't know how –" Robin said, her voice hitching.

Caroline interrupted. "As comfortable as you are with Tony, just holding hands, talking, laughing, kissing, a physical relationship beyond that will be just as loving and fulfilling." She put a hand on Robin's wet cheek. "I know this, love. I live it. You can't imagine it because you've never known it. But I tell you, child, I mourn for your loss if you never know it."

Robin put her elbows on her knees and laced her fingers, resting her forehead against her hands. "What if it's not?"

Sofia ran a hand over her hair. "It will be. But if there is a problem, you simply pray together. Everything will work out. God brought the two of you together, and He will work it out."

"Let's pray together now," Caroline said. "We'll pray for you to have wisdom and we'll pray that your heart not be troubled and be strengthened for the path ahead."

GREATER THAN RUBIES - CHAPTER 12

DERRICK DeNunzio sat outside Tony Viscolli's office wearing black slacks, a white button down shirt, and a waiter's vest. He was proud of his clean, crisp uniform.

He tried to start seeing himself through Tony's eyes. Tony had seen something in Derrick from the first time they met. Derrick had run out of options in his old life. He was miles underwater and drowning before Tony had thrown him a lifeline. Derrick had grabbed it and was hanging on by his fingernails and toes. He determined that he would work hard for Tony, show the man what he could do.

Derrick discovered that, for maybe the first time in his life, he was actually applying himself very tactically to a present path of work and personal sacrifice in order to strategically accomplish future goals in a committed way. That commitment and that personal hard work and sacrifice made him realize something even more shocking. He figured out that this new feeling he had been feeling since he decided to follow this path was a feeling he had never before had any reason to feel. He felt proud of himself and he felt valued and valuable.

But in the last few weeks, something had been on his mind more and more. Something he couldn't wrap his head around – or his heart. Or maybe his soul, he wasn't sure. It was something and he didn't really have anyone else he could talk to about it so he had made a breakfast appointment with Tony.

Tony arrived at 8:15 and Derrick found himself standing, unconsciously balancing his weight on the balls of his feet out of years of pure habit. He nodded a greeting to Derrick and said, "Margaret, could you please have the kitchen send up something hot for the two of us. Maybe some hot bagels and some cream cheese, too. No hurry."

Tony turned back to Derrick and gestured that the younger man should precede him into his office. Having worked the nightshift and not having seen Tony for a few days despite living in his apartment, Derrick said, "Good morning, sir."

"Just getting off?" Tony asked.

"Yes. It's a long shift until eight." Derrick's muscles felt slightly fatigued just from battling his body's desire to sleep.

They settled down on the couches as they had the very first time Derrick had ever come to this office. Tony remained silent, letting the young man collect his thoughts, lost in his own. Four days had gone by since Robin had visited him, and he felt like he was trapped in a swirling abyss. He simply did not know what to do next. The only thing, and it was truly the only thing, that kept him moving forward day after day was the fact that everyone in his employ involved in this wedding still thought Robin was going through with it. Robin hadn't canceled anything yet. He still had hope.

It almost took them both by surprise when, after a few minutes of silence, the breakfast arrived. Tony let Derrick pour them coffee, noticing the ear marks of Derrick's waiter training as the young man set the cups 'just so' and arranged the silverware to the Viscolli Boston standard on the cloth napkins to the right of each plate.

When Derrick didn't touch his food or drink, Tony finally spoke again. "Why don't I bless this meal and then you tell me why you called this meeting, Derrick." It wasn't a question.

Derrick nodded. Tony blessed their meal and sipped his coffee as Derrick began to speak. Tony pushed aside all thoughts of Robin, knowing he needed to be all there for Derrick.

"Mr. Viscolli, I have to tell you something. The other day when we was, I mean, when we were helping Robin and her sisters move, you were telling Robin and them that you knew I didn't steal anything. You know, those jewels. Her jewelry. I don't know if you know, but I heard you. I was just outside her bedroom door, in the hallway, and I heard you."

Tony pursed his lips. "That's fine, Derrick. I didn't say anything I wouldn't have said in front of you."

"I know, Mr. Viscolli. I just ..." His voice suddenly stopped working. Derrick found himself in a surprisingly awkward and precarious state. There was a giant lump in his throat that his words couldn't get around and he couldn't breathe past it either. He felt tears welling up in his eyes and he suddenly hung his head in shame when he realized that he was about to break down and cry in front of this man.

As unmanly and silent tears streamed down his face, he felt a strong hand grip his shoulder. "What is it, *figlio*? Tell me what is bothering you so." Tony urged.

Derrick gasped a baritone sob and heard silverware tumble as he grabbed his cloth napkin and covered his nose and mouth. Tony just kneaded the younger man's shoulder and somehow, someway, Derrick knew that the older man had started praying for him in that second.

After perhaps half a minute, Derrick's thick voice found its way out again. "No one has ever spoken up for me like that before. No one. Not even my mama." His voice vanished into three breathy, strangled sobs. Through gritted teeth, he said, "You have everything and I can't do anything for you. I looked around my room and realized something last night. I got almost nothing you didn't give me. Even the room you gave me. And I got nothing worth anything that you didn't. I don't understand this. I don't understand you. Why would you take up for me like that with them? How did you know I didn't steal that stuff?"

"Ahh." Tony clapped his hand on Derrick's shoulder. "Okay. I understand. I've been waiting for this, actually."

Tony walked over to the bookshelf behind his desk. He opened a file cabinet drawer and pulled out a miniature board game. It was a travel sized edition of the game of *Monopoly* and Derrick had a serious moment of doubt, wondering what a multi-billionaire was doing with a kid's game in his desk drawer.

"You know how to play this game?" He asked casually.

"I played a few times as a kid."

Tony met his eyes, "Ever win?"

Derrick shrugged. "I dunno. Maybe."

"Well, tell me this, how do you win this game?"

Derrick sat up. "I buy some properties and charge rent when you land on my property."

Tony nodded. "While that is a stunning display of your economic grasp of *lassais faire* capitalism, charging rent doesn't mean you win. What if I charge you higher rent when it's my turn? That's just how you play, right? Not how you win."

"Well, I can use the rent you pay me to build houses and then I collect higher rent. Then I can buy hotels."

Tony held up a little red hotel and then put it down on New York Avenue. "You mean a hotel like this one?" Somehow Derrick understood that Tony wasn't talking about the little plastic hotel game piece, but maybe he was actually referring to a hotel like the one in which they presently found themselves, or the Viscolli Hotel in Manhattan, or Atlanta, or Dallas, or Seattle, or Los Angeles. "Then you win?"

"No, it's a really long game. I would have to build houses and lots of hotels and eventually force you to sell and mortgage all your houses and hotels and properties and then I would have to buy them from you." Derrick said. "Then I would have to charge you rent until I took your very last dollar. Then I win. I win when you are flat broke."

Tony nodded and moved all the little dollar bills from his side of the board over to Derrick's side. Then he picked up the little hotel and set it on top of the pile of toy money. "Then you win."

Derrick nodded.

"So you are saying that now, when everyone else but you is flat broke, this is the end of the game. Okay. What did you learn? What did the game teach you? You own all the properties and railroads and houses and hotels and you even have yourself a get out of jail free card, maybe. So what did you learn in your rush to acquire absolutely everything and take away my very last dollar?"

Derrick sat back and looked at all the play money and the little red hotel sitting on his side of the board. "That if I work really hard, I can succeed?"

Tony nodded and stacked his empty dishes back on the rolling cart beside him. "What you say is true, Derrick, but it is not the most valuable lesson this game can teach you. I think I will give you one more try and then I will just tell you the answer."

Derrick searched his mind before he said, "I'm sorry. I don't know."

"I will tell you. The most important thing to learn is that now, it all goes back in the box." As he returned the items to the box, Tony continued. "See, you thought you owned all the properties and railroads and houses and hotels and your get out of jail free card. But now they go back in the box. Maybe you start to realize they were never even yours in the first place. They were there in the box long before you had them. Someone else owned them all before you did. And pretty soon, maybe someone else will come along and play with them after you're gone. All those houses you were so proud of. All the utility companies and rail lines. And all the wonderful, wonderful money. It all goes back in the box."

Tony put the lid on the box and said, "Now look around you. Tell me something. When you realize that the game isn't over when you have everything, when you realize the game isn't even over when you put everything back in the box – when you realize that – answer this question: what is *really* important?"

Tony stood and began to pace. He spoke low and deep, his voice quiet so that Derrick strained to hear his every word. "Maybe you get out the box again and you get all those properties and hotels and all that wonderful money back. Maybe. Or maybe you leave it all in the box and you realize what is really, really important in this life are not the things in there. What matters in this life is, in fact, much bigger than anything inside the box."

Tony stopped pacing and turned, his eyes boring into Derrick's eyes. "Because ultimately, everything you see and touch and consume in this world, all of it … even your own body … all of it goes back in the box one day."

Derrick sat back, his mind racing.

"Listen to me very carefully and I'll tell you about a gift that isn't inside the box. From this moment on, if you choose to accept this gift, your entire life will be very, very different. Do you want this gift? Because I am going to tell you something. Derrick, one day you will die. Everyone will. I will. You will. Your mother will. Everyone will. You are going to live and then you are going to die. And you are going to be dead a lot longer than you ever lived. That is the way it is. It is just that black and white. Now, when your life ends, when everything you owned in life gets put back in the box, you will suddenly find yourself on the outside of the box standing in front of that very same God who made you, and you will have to explain the choices you made while you played the game.

"See outside of this little game is you and me. Just like outside of here is the whole universe – and it is all just a box, Derrick. Outside of that box, my very young friend, is what is really, really important. Outside of all that is your Creator, God, Jehovah, A'doni, who is what He is, the great I AM.

"The truth is, you could have spent your life the way you had been living. You could have wasted your life away with drugs, pornography, gambling, thuggery, and spent your precious few remaining days and nights in the company of evil men and women – then died. But you knew that wasn't what you wanted. You didn't know this, but I was praying for you. I prayed for you every day. And then on the day after your birthday, you came to me and accepted the earthly gifts I had to offer. But your life still isn't what it could be, is it? Do you want it to be? Do you want to reach your full potential even if it means you will radically change?"

Derrick didn't realize that he was even speaking until the sound of his voice echoed in his own ears, "Yes."

Tony turned and said, "Good. Now I think you're ready for that gift I promised you." He knelt in front of Derrick. Derrick suddenly realized that his cheeks were wet with silent tears. "Do you believe in God, Derrick?"

Derrick barely recognized his own voice, "Yes."

Tony nodded, both of his hands holding Derrick's right hand. "And do you know what's important to that very same God you confess you believe in?"

Derrick shook his head.

"What's important to Him, more than anything else, is you. You, Derrick DiNunzio. You are the most precious thing in the universe to the Creator of the universe. You feel overwhelmed by the fact that I, a man, love you enough to stand up for you the way I did? That notion reduces you to tears? That I love you enough to take you in and feed you when you are hungry, clothe you when you are cold and exposed, pray for you when you are struggling with addiction and a life of crime? You feel overwhelmed by one man's love for you? Imagine how much God loves you.

"He loves you so much that He would actually lay down his very life for you and die for you. In fact, He already did. He sent His only begotten son, Yeshua, called Jesus of Nazareth, as a living sacrifice in atonement for everything you have ever done wrong in this life. Do you believe that Derrick? Do you believe in Jesus Christ, that He was born of a virgin, lived a life that was pure, suffered under Pilate, and died for you? That on the third day He rose from the dead, conquering the grave, in testimony to the truth of his godhead?"

"Yes." Derrick whispered.

Tony said, "Then all you have to do now is accept that gift. You have so many things in your heart and mind that make you feel unworthy of love, but Derrick, you are worthy. You are worthy, Derrick. You are not here by accident. God created you on purpose. He knew you before He knitted you in your mother's womb. He loved you even then. The reason I wanted you to come to church with me was to educate you about God's love, about what the real love offered by the Creator of the universe can do. God loves you so much that His love can move mountains. And God tells me that I have to love you just as much. *Capisc*e?

"So what you must do is just let go. Let go of your game. Open your hands. Let Jesus Christ rule your life. Bow down before him and accept the gift of His atoning blood that wipes the slate clean. Give up the stranglehold you have on your personal selfish hopes and desires, and turn your life over to a life of service in His name. Commit that you will stand for him even if you stand alone. Open your grasping hands and arms wide, as Christ did on the cross, and He will fill your empty arms with purpose and love and abundant life."

In the very next heartbeat, in the privacy of that very well appointed office, in the company of Tony Viscolli, the most unlikely event took place. Derrick finally understood the overwhelming truth. In the space of a heartbeat, all of the puzzles and riddles that had plagued him for weeks clicked into place. When the weight of his past life fell from his heart, for the first time his life opened up. Where he had existed in constant agonizing torture inside an emotional iron maiden, he suddenly knew freedom. Where he had lived a life of simple survival in unbearable pain and darkness, he suddenly saw light and hope. In his heart of hearts, he heard a voice, his own voice it seemed, assuring him that everything would be all right. Yes, he would face struggles and adversity, but it would all work out fine. And Derrick, for the first time ever, believed it.

In the space of that heartbeat, the dying creature the world knew as Derrick DiNunzio went ahead and died and a brand new living creature named Derrick DiNunzio rose in its place. From that very next heartbeat, the Holy Spirit would guide the new Derrick not to see himself as others did, but rather as God saw him. The scales fell from his eyes. He would no longer judge the unimportant things in life as overly relevant, but rather see what really mattered and fight to make a difference. And he would love his neighbor the way God loved him.

GREATER THAN RUBIES - CHAPTER 13

ROBIN nearly felt her heart explode when she saw her photograph on the cover of *Inside Boston* magazine. A messenger had delivered this advance copy just before noon. The magazine would hit newsstands all over the city tomorrow morning. Not only had they given her the entire cover, they had selected what looked like a candid shot of Robin wearing a knee length skirt and matching jacket with a light blue blouse. In the picture, her unsmiling face looked speculative, confident, wise, and secure – pretty much the opposite of how she actually felt. Her crossed arms framed the engagement ring perfectly against the navy sleeve of her jacket. The headline read, *Millionaire Marries Manager*.

In the time since she had last seen Tony, Robin had neglected a few things. For example, she had neglected to inform another living soul that she would not, in fact, be marrying Tony Viscolli. She could not imagine how calling off the wedding would hurt Tony's public image. If she let herself think about it too much, she might burst into tears again so she stopped her racing thoughts in their tracks and opened the magazine.

> *Inside Boston's* intrepid reporter Don Roberts had the rare opportunity to sit down with Robin Bartlett. Robin manages Hank's Place restaurant which recently became one of Viscolli Enterprises newest acquisitions. It's unlikely that Tony Viscolli knew when he purchased the local eatery that the love of his life would come with the deal.
>
> While Tony Viscolli is as well known for his clout in the boardroom as his beneficence to Boston's less fortunate and his generosity to so many worthy charitable causes, Robin is very far from the blue blood debutante many might expect. In fact, just like her future husband, Robin came from humble beginnings right here in Boston. Despite her untraditional childhood, Robin Bartlett is sweet and

smart, the kind of "girl next door" every Boston boy hopes to bring home to meet mom and dad one day. We asked Robin some questions about the upcoming wedding and her expectations for married life as the wife of one of Boston's royal family.

She skimmed the article down to the interview questions. Some of the information she skimmed came straight out of Stephanie's press release with dates, places, names of designers and dress makers, jewelers, entrées and dinner courses, hors d' oeuvres and desserts, and even florists. Her canceled wedding was laid bare on the pages for the world to see in every excruciating detail except for the one minor detail: that it would never happen.

She skimmed down to the interview questions.

IB: You two come from opposite ends of the financial spectrum. How do you feel about marrying one of the wealthiest bachelors in Boston?

Robin: He is amazing and generous and loving, and I feel so incredibly blessed.

She remembered saying those words during the first interview, the one that concluded with security guards turkey trotting Don Roberts from the building. She skimmed further down.

IB: Robin, so many things about your childhood would astonish our readers. From what you've shared with us, it was pretty rough. Your father was in prison. Your mother died of gunshot wounds. For part of your childhood, you were in the foster system. Anything you want to share with our readers about that?

Robin: One of the things I admire about Tony is his heart for children. He supports hundreds of homes like the one here at Boston Bible that give children like my sisters and I once were a clean, safe, loving environment. I can't wait to support him in those ministries as his wife.

He had taken her answer out of context but somehow it fit perfectly. She spotted her father's name and read carefully.

IB: Your father, Craig Bartlett, has been the topic of a number of news stories in recent months. What can you tell our readers about your dad?

Robin: The Craig Bartlett of today, the man I know is not the man in the tabloid stories. My father turned himself in and confessed to all of his crimes without even trying to strike a deal. He is doing what he can to make restitution for his past wrongs. The way he has turned his life around despite his past, I have to say I'm proud of him. I pray for him every day.

It was a direct quote, what she had said word for word, but again out of context. Is this how interviews were supposed to be written?

IB: Robin, in your opinion, what is the most attractive thing about Tony Viscolli?

Robin: His abiding and unshakable faith in God and his faithfulness to Him is certainly the most attractive thing about my fiancée.

IB: Your faith is important to you and your future husband. How would you characterize your beliefs?

Robin: We're Christians.

She remembered how negatively Don Roberts had treated anything she had said about faith. Yet here, he highlighted their faith in the way that she wanted it seen by the world.

IB: What do you think is your greatest accomplishment in life, Robin?

Robin: The greatest thing I've done in my life so far was getting custody of my sister, Maxine.

IB: Any plans for after the wedding? Plan on doing a lot of shopping?

Robin: I'll still run Hank's.

She read through all of the questions twice. The way that Don Roberts had combined answers from their initial and second interview into a cohesive article revealed every fact she had shared, but also put Robin Bartlett and Tony Viscolli in the best possible light.

When she turned the final page, she found a handwritten sticky note Don had left for her. In really minuscule print, he had written, "Robin, I realize Tony is a billionaire, not a millionaire, but it didn't have the same alliterative ring to it for the headline. You should know that I'm also a believer. I admire what the two of you are doing. The truth is you gave me a lot to think about, a lot to admire, and a lot to pray about. I wanted you to know that I am going to stop hiding my light under a bushel so much and let it shine a little more often. I pray I did you justice with this piece. Thanks for witnessing to me. Yours in Christ, DR."

The woman this *Inside Boston* article portrayed, from the photographs to the out of context quotations, was not the woman holding and reading the magazine. The woman within these pages was confident, competent, and capable. Magazine article Robin was accomplished, witty, polished, and professional. That Robin would certainly make a fine match for Tony Viscolli. She would love him and support him and make him happy throughout his lifetime.

By contrast, the very real Robin Bartlett had brought nothing but conflict, heartache, and shame to Tony Viscolli since the very day he had first laid eyes on her. Everything about her spelled trouble from her heritage, her violent past, her lack of education, to her ignorance of the day to day politics of the high society world in which he lived. She wondered how Don Roberts would handle the fact that the woman who had witnessed to him so profoundly was less than two weeks away from leaving Tony Viscolli at the altar.

This magazine would hit newsstands tomorrow. She could not fight that. She could not run from that. She could not hide from that. She envisioned her life spinning away and out of control, down into a bottomless vortex like a fast sinking ship. She envisioned taking Tony and dozens of others down along with her.

TONY stood in Barry's office, hands in his pockets, looking out at the courthouse. A copy of the most recent *Inside Boston* lay atop Barry's desk but both men had studiously ignored its presence there. Although neither mentioned it, both of them occasionally let their eyes stray back to glance at Robin Bartlett's photo on the cover.

"You're right. It isn't unethical or illegal. It's just completely unheard of." Barry ran his massive hand through his straw blond hair. "Tony, I can't do this."

"You must. I'm ordering you to," Tony said with a half grin that had nothing to do with humor.

Barry shook his head. "You must be of sound mind and body to execute legal instruments of this nature. And clearly, you're just a little bit out of your mind right now," his friend observed.

"No, I'm not." Or, maybe Barry was right. Maybe Tony had lost his senses. Could it be that he was getting in the way of God's will for his life right now? Was he allowing greed, or pride, or anger to dictate or manipulate his actions? He really didn't think so. This felt exactly right. He had a lot of fear and he felt very angry that he could still feel fear, but outside of that was nothing except a sense of peace. "I'm really not crazy. I know what I'm doing."

Tony turned to look at his attorney and very best friend in the entire world and Barry shook his head again. "Do you have any idea what this will mean?"

"We can work it out to make it as simple as possible. But I'm serious about my timeline."

Barry sighed. "I don't think I can do this for you. Tony, I'm your lawyer but you and I are best friends. If you go through with this, what will happen to our friendship? You're the only person I can really even talk to anymore. I can't – "

Tony stepped forward and held up a finger. His voice became hard, like steel, and cold. He spoke as if to a subordinate, ensuring that Barry knew that friendship was on the line already. "You will do it, Barry, or else I'll find someone who will. Again, I'm not asking your opinion or your advice in this matter. I am simply hiring you to do a job and you will be paid very well to accomplish it."

Tony watched Barry's eyes flash, but felt no remorse at standing up to his best friend. "Fine," Barry bit. Then with practiced cordiality, "Please have a seat, Mr. Viscolli. Make yourself comfortable. Pardon my unprofessional outburst. I can ask Elizabeth to order up some lunch, if you like. We have quite a number of details to cover and this will take some time."

ROBIN tried to pay attention to whatever show Sarah had put on the television for them, but honestly, she couldn't focus. Tomorrow would be Tuesday, which means she destroyed her life and the life of the most amazing man on the planet just five short days ago. Since the day their relationship started, she hadn't ever gone so long without talking with him, without seeing him. Sunday she'd skipped church, afraid to go and be seen by him, or be seen with him. She could barely breathe. She felt lost, floundering, sinking, and had no idea what to do next.

She still hadn't told Maxine or Sarah. All evening, Sarah had excitedly talked about the shoes Maxine had found for them to wear with their bridesmaid dresses. How could she tell them? What could she say?

Now she sat limp on the edge of the couch staring at the television screen. She didn't even know what they were watching.

She heard Maxine's keys in the door. She barely looked up when her sister stormed into the apartment.

"All right. I've had enough. I've kept my mouth shut for nearly a week, waiting for you to come to me, and I'm tired of it." Maxine announced as she tossed her keys on a little table by the door. Sarah used the remote to pause the movie and looked between Robin and Maxine. "Are you planning to mention it to us?"

Robin glared at Maxine. She'd cried until she honestly didn't think she could cry anymore. Today she'd been kind of a zombie, stumbling around, not sure about what she should do, what she should wear, what she should eat. It took a moment to understand what Maxine was talking about. "No."

Maxine slammed the door, making Sarah jump. "What's going on?" the youngest sister asked.

"Robin here," Maxine said, "broke it off with Tony."

Sarah looked as confused as if Maxine had just announced that pigeons no longer flew, preferring instead to swim. "What?"

"Last Thursday."

"What?!" Sarah's head whirled around. "Robin? Why didn't you say something?"

Robin stood. "Because I don't want you two cooing over Tony and telling me how great he is, how great it is that I'm going to be his wife."

Sarah blinked. "But – "

Maxine stepped forward. "No, we won't. We are here to tell you we love you, and whatever you need from us, you'll get." She grabbed Robin and hugged her. "I understand." She pulled back and looked into Robin's eyes. Robin saw all of the pain and fear that she felt reflected back from her sister's emerald pools. "You know I understand. Whatever you need."

Tears fell from burning dry eyes literally worn out from crying. "Thank you," Robin whispered.

Sarah got up and hugged both Robin and Maxine. "Honey, I'm so sorry," she said. "What can I do?"

Robin closed her eyes, resetting back to last summer, to the way she thought, to her motivations then. "Graduate with honors and get a good job," she said. "That's all I've ever wanted from you."

Sarah reached out and put a tentative light hand on Robin's shoulder. "Did he, you know, did he do something?"

Robin shook her head slowly. "No." She sobbed as she said, "He didn't do anything. He didn't do anything at all. He is absolutely as wonderful as ever."

TONY shifted his portfolio in his hand and opened the door to Robin's office. For the briefest second, he had a chance to observe her working, head down, scribbling on a scheduling sheet in front of her. Then she looked up, and the distracted concentrated look abandoned her face, replaced with hesitation and apprehension. He prayed, as he had been praying all morning, that this went smoothly. Because, he honestly never wanted to see that look on her face when she looked at him ever again.

He stepped into the office and shut the door, reaching behind him to lock it. Robin leaned back in her chair and raised an eyebrow. "Is that to keep me in or others out?"

"*Qualunque*," he said with a shrug. At her blank look, he said, "Whichever."

Her eyes flashed and he watched her look at the door then at him. "I see."

He walked to her desk and set the portfolio on top of it. "I had Margaret call Stephanie today about RSVP's and just to – well, in general – to make small talk. Apparently, the wedding is still on."

Robin's cheeks turned red and she looked at the blotter in front of her. "I guess I should call and cancel. But – "

"But that seems final and extreme," he finished for her. "And very, very real." He pulled a piece of paper out of the portfolio.

Robin's eyes swam with tears. "I don't want this." Her voice sounded raw. She ripped open the desk drawer and pulled out her tin of mints. Her hands trembled and it took her a second to open it and pop one into her mouth.

"But you want this?" he asked, tossing her two-week resignation notice onto the desk in front of her.

"Of course not," she said, pushing the paper toward him. "But I can't keep working for you, either."

"Why not?"

"Because I love you too much to constantly see you and talk to you, to work as your subordinate when I want nothing more than to be by your side."

Tony's heart skipped a furious beat in his chest. He took a deep breath and sat down. "I've never had a restaurant run with such love as what you give this place. I am here to ask you to reconsider quitting."

"I'm afraid that's out of the question." She leaned back in her chair and rested her elbows on the arm, clutching her pen with both hands. "I can't do it. It will hurt too much."

Tony pulled a stack of papers out of the case. "You won't need to worry about that," he said. He tossed them in front of her.

"What are these?" She leaned forward and picked up a packet, recognizing the layout of a legal court document.

"These," he said as he sat in the chair across from her, "are the documents to legally dissolve my stakes in all of my companies. I will sell shares, give some away, and hand over corporate responsibilities to someone else, depending on the company. Metaphorically, I'm putting this game back in the box. When these documents are executed I will be penniless and, in a few short months, homeless, too." He straightened his tie. "I started with nothing. I can certainly start over."

He said it all very matter-of-factly while his insides turned to a boiling mass of fear and emotion. "But I can only face something like that with you by my side, *cara*."

"What?" Robin furiously flipped through a packet of paper. "What are you talking about?"

"Well," Tony said, "you have an issue with my money and my status. So, I'll make those things a non-issue."

"What about your employees?"

"Obviously, some of them will need new employers."

Robin tossed the packet on top of her desk. "Is this some kind of joke?"

He narrowed his eyes and very dangerously said, "Why in the name of the most holy God would you think anything about this is a joke?"

"Because you sound very casual about something that should be much more important to you."

He was around the desk, gripping the arms of her chair with both hands and leaning down so that his face was close to hers before he even realized he was in motion. "This is one of the most important things in my life, I can assure you. But, as important as it is, you are a million times more important. Do you understand that?" He shook the chair so that it rattled. "Do you get that I would do anything for you? Sell off everything, become a penniless pauper, have a celibate marriage – anything I need to have you by my side."

Robin's breath hitched and she put her hand on her chest. "How do I – ?"

Kneeling to take her hands with his, he gentled his voice. "My darling love, you tell me what to do. You tell me how to fix it so that you are willing to be with me. I don't need companies or money or things. But I need you."

Tears slid down her cheeks, breaking him into a million pieces. "You can't disband Viscolli Enterprises," she said. "God uses it for too much good."

"Robin, that is exactly wrong. God does not need me. I need Him. And I assure you, He will find other ways to use us."

"No." Shredded pieces of Tony's heart landed at her feet at the finality of the tone in her voice. "No. You can't do that. There are ministries, shelters, orphanages. I can't be responsible for that." Tony bowed his head and closed his eyes. He rested his forehead on their joined hands, broken. "If you will make me a couple of promises, then maybe I can marry you."

It took a second for her words to penetrate the mist of desolation in his brain. As soon as he understood her, he looked up. "What promises?"

Robin took a deep shaky breath and brushed the hair on his forehead. He felt the tingle from the touch of her fingertips go down the nape of his neck. "I can't jump right in to your world. I need to gradually get my feet wet. Keep our social engagements to a bare minimum for at least a year."

"Done."

"Don't leave my side during a function and leave me floundering without you."

"*Cara*, I would not want to leave your side for any reason."

"I don't want to talk to any reporters without you."

"Already done."

As her eyes welled with fresh tears, she put a shaking hand on his cheek. "I'm so afraid of our wedding night. I can't even think straight. How will I get through the ceremony in front of all those people? How will I ever handle the reception and the small talk and hours of socializing knowing what waits for me?"

Tony reached forward and cupped her cheeks with his hands. "My darling, what horror of horrors waits for you is me. Robin, my beloved, I will never hurt you. You don't need to be afraid of me. But, I promise you, that everything will go at your pace and any time you want to stop, I will stop. Every time. As for the other, I have an idea."

AT two p.m., Barry's phone chimed and he distractedly said, "Yes, Elizabeth?"

"Sir, Tony Viscolli is here to see you."

Intrigued, Barry slipped off his reading glasses and shut the lid of his laptop. "Send him in."

Tony never came to visit him. Barry always went to him. It didn't bother him because, after all, Tony was the client. In their personal meetings, they typically met outside of their individual offices. But their last meeting two days ago had taken place in this very office and ended with each of them feeling extremely tense. Barry wasn't even certain exactly where their friendship stood right now.

He pushed back from his desk and stood, slipping on his suit jacket as Tony came through the door. Tony carried a leather portfolio, but was dressed down in khaki slacks and a black cotton sweater. Barry could see the wet cuffs of his pants and knew Tony had spent the morning out on the water, rowing. He knew that was what Tony did to get completely away from all distractions and to think while his body worked the boat through the water. He also knew Tony chose that sport above all others because it was the sport of choice for the blue-bloods of this part of the country.

As Barry rounded his desk, his friend spoke first. "I owe you an apology for the way I spoke to you the last time we were together," he said.

Barry paused in the buttoning of his coat. He raised an eyebrow, but did not reply. Tony continued speaking. "I was extremely emotional at the moment and not quite acting myself."

Barry nodded. "Hence the whole 'are you sure you want to do this' question from me and the observation regarding your mental state."

"I understand. I needed to do it, but I understand why you questioned it and what you said." He opened the portfolio and pulled out a stack of papers. "Robin and I have reconciled." He set the papers on the conference table near him. "You can destroy these documents."

Barry waged an internal debate for about ten seconds before finally stepping forward. "Can we talk?"

"Of course," Tony said. He pulled out a leather chair from the table and sat, crossing his legs and brushing at his knee.

Barry sat next to him and said, "Tony, if there is even the most remote possibility of any issues with this marriage, I'm asking you as your best friend and your Best Man to reconsider it."

Tony raised an eyebrow. "Oh?"

Barry sighed. "We never really talk about this so I'm not sure how I should approach it. I'll just get this out of the way. Are you aware that my wife is often unfaithful? Are you aware that, as far as I know, she hasn't been faithful to me for at least the last six years?"

Tony kept his face perfectly schooled and nodded once, holding Barry's eyes with his own. He did not speak.

Barry seemed to relax a little bit, his enormous shoulders lowering as some tension left them. "For the longest time, I focused on the book of Hosea. I really am trying to do God's will in my marriage, Tony. The fact is, I love my wife and I intend to keep my vows even if she doesn't. But there is nothing worse than waking up in the morning, alone in my bed, knowing how much my wife despises me, and knowing there is absolutely nothing I can do about it because I've tried everything already."

Tony closed his eyes and took a deep breath, running a finger over his forehead. When he opened them again, Barry could read love, friendship, and sadness in them. "I don't know how you do it, Barry. But know that if there is anything at all I can do to help you, I wouldn't hesitate."

"I know," Barry said impatiently. "I've never doubted that. I just want to make sure you don't end up in a similar position as that in which I find myself. I thought I was marrying a princess who would be my queen. Instead I married a diva."

"Thank you for being candid." Tony sat forward. "Robin is coming from a background of abuse – mental, physical, and sexual – she's a poster child. It's incredible she survived her childhood. Her issues stem directly from that, not from – and understand I mean no disrespect to you in saying this – not from being an overindulged self-important diva."

Barry snorted and thought that it would be wrong to laugh. But he wanted to. "Okay. I think you should know that I really like Robin. I'm sorry that I might have ever given you any other impression. It's just that I don't want to end up seeing you hurt."

"Barry, thank you. For everything."

Barry grinned and teased, "Don't worry. I'll bill you for the hour."

Tony laughed. "Of that I have no doubt."

Barry schooled his features and said, "My prayer is that the two of you will be happy for the rest of your lives."

Tony stood and slapped his hand on Barry's shoulder. "That is my prayer for you as well, my friend."

JACQUELINE Anderson took a moment to lecture, "The purpose of the trousseau is to start your marriage off with a bunch of amazing clothes that you feel absolutely beautiful wearing."

She stood in the middle of the carpeted floor of the high end boutique on Newbury Street, just a short distance from Maxine's new apartment. She wore a royal blue pantsuit with a yellow and blue scarf and yellow high heeled shoes. Robin felt rather underdressed beside Barry's wife wearing her black slacks and a pink sweater with comfortable walking shoes. "If you feel beautiful in your clothes, you will naturally project beauty," Jacqueline said.

Robin nodded, understanding what the red head said. She currently felt frumpy and unattractive next to the stylish beauty.

"So, we need to see what styles work for you, then we'll pick out some outfits from there."

Jacqueline lifted her hand and the sales clerk came forward. "Mrs. Anderson, are we ready?"

"We are. Miss Bartlett, who will very soon be Mrs. Viscolli, needs to get an idea of what you offer, then we'll make some selections."

"Wonderful!" The clerk led them to some comfortable chairs. "Please have a seat here." She raised her voice slightly and said, "Ladies?"

From the back, a train of models walked through the small area in front of Robin and Jacqueline. Mirrors all around them showed the clothes they wore from all angles. Robin murmured to Jacqueline what she liked or didn't like about outfits, shoes, and accessories. When the show was over, Jacqueline took the lead and let the clerk know what else they wanted to see.

Two hours later, the clerk rang up the incomprehensibly expensive bill and Robin used the credit card Tony had given her that morning to satisfy the tab. She signed the receipt, arranged for the packages to be delivered to Tony's apartment, and assumed they were all done for the day. Until Jacqueline spoke and said, "Now, let's go two doors down. They have a fabulous new line."

"More?" Robin asked.

"Of course! We're starting with nothing. You have a whole month in front of you in Italy, darling. Six outfits from one store does not a full trousseau make!"

At the next shop, Jacqueline already had an idea of what Robin liked, so they didn't have to go through that learning experience again. Instead, they just shopped, bought, and shopped some more. Four stores and more money than Robin used to earn in a year later, they found themselves sitting across from one another in a trendy little cafe.

"That was an absolute blast," Jacqueline said, taking a delicate sip of her tea. "I haven't shopped on that scale in ages. Far too long, in fact."

Robin wished she could prop her feet up somewhere. "I can't believe we just spent that much money on clothes," she said, picking up her coffee.

"You need a base. Your sister, what's her name? The one that's obviously mixed blood."

"Maxine." Robin tried not to feel resentment over the mixed blood remark. After all, it was true.

"Right. Maxine. She has great taste. I'm surprised she hasn't handled this for you."

Robin smiled. "Well, she would have loved to, but I wanted a chance to spend some time with you, too. After all, your husband and my soon-to-be husband are like brothers."

"Indeed," Jacqueline said, her mouth twisting in distaste.

"I assume we will spend a lot more time together."

"Honey, something about me and Bartholomew you should know is that we spend as little time together as possible. He and Antonio do all their stuff without me."

Robin frowned. "Why?"

"We just prefer it that way." She waved a dismissive hand. "But that doesn't mean we can't be friends, right? Mrs. Viscolli needs to know there are people she can count on to be her friends regardless of what her last name once was."

Robin pondered whether Jacqueline Anderson would even give her the time of day if she didn't currently sport an engagement ring from Tony Viscolli, but dismissed the negative thought. Whatever Jacqueline's motivations, Robin wanted to stay on friendly terms with her. She would hate having any bad feelings between the two of them as often as Tony and Barry were together.

GREATER THAN RUBIES - CHAPTER 15

ROBIN poured herself onto the couch. "Oh my heavens, I don't think I've ever felt so relaxed."

Maxine slouched into a chair and Sarah took the big cushion on the floor. "Who knew a ninety minute massage, manicure, pedicure, and facial could just suck the life right out of you?" Sarah said.

"I think I'm going to arrange to have this done monthly," Maxine said.

"Wouldn't you worry your bones would turn to Jell-O?" Robin asked. A rubbery arm covered her eyes, blocking out the track lighting.

"At this point, I don't think I'd care." Maxine closed her eyes. "I'm hungry, but I honestly don't want to move."

Sarah rose on her elbow. "How are you feeling about tomorrow, Robin? We haven't had a lot of time to talk about how you and Tony got back together."

Robin rolled her head and looked at her youngest sister. "I am not as nervous as I was. Tony has been praying with me daily about my fears. I've talked to Sofia and Caroline a couple of times. Somehow, the wedding night thing doesn't horrify me as much as it did."

Maxine shuddered. "I don't think I can ever get married."

With a snort, Sarah stretched. "You fall in and out of love daily, Maxi. How could you ever commit to one man and marriage?"

Only Robin saw the hurt cross Maxine's face before she blithely answered, "Hence my point."

Robin sat up, slowly. "I would have said six months ago that I'd never even date, much less marry. Obviously, God's plans for us aren't always what we have in mind, for which I am infinitely thankful." She groaned and pushed her loose body to her feet. "Rehearsal is at seven, dinner at Barry's immediately after. I have some errands to run. Don't be late."

ROBIN put her hands in the pockets of her trench coat and waited for Peter to unlock the back door of the church. "I'm hoping for warmer weather tomorrow afternoon," she said with a smile.

"Supposed to be lovely tomorrow. With everything else, you should not stress about that," Caroline said, hugging her close. Their five foster kids played a game of chase on the lawn next to the building.

Peter finally got the door unlocked and opened it wide, letting Robin and Caroline precede him. "Lads and lasses," Caroline sing-songed with a clap of her hands, and all five children never broke stride. They just pivoted on their feet and dashed into the open church.

The women slipped inside and Caroline went to a far wall, throwing switches to light up the room. They crossed the hall, passing administrative offices, and went through the door leading to the main sanctuary through the choir loft. Caroline threw some more switches, and the sanctuary lit up.

"Oh Robin, how beautiful!" she exclaimed. Then, her voice took on a warning note. "Kids, don't touch a thing. Absolutely nothing."

Huge bouquets of white roses, freesia, and lisianthus stood in tall pedestals at the end of the aisle near the main doors, and white cloth draped from the pedestals and swooping from pew to pew, closing off the main aisle. Where the cloth attached to the pew, red and white roses in bouquets held together with white satin ribbon were attached. At the front of the church, identical pillars of flowers flanked the pulpit next to large candelabras.

"Thank you. I think the decorators did a tremendous job," Robin said, turning when the door behind her opened. In walked Maxine and Sarah. "Hi you two," she said with a grin. Nervous excitement fluttered in her chest.

"Hello, bride," Maxine said, hugging Robin. She stepped back and took off her coat. "Do you want me to hang up your coat, too?"

Robin shook her head, "No. I'll leave it on for now."

The door opened again and the photographer, Gerald Parr, came in. "Gerald," she said, walking forward with her hand extended. "Welcome to Boston Bible."

"Thank you," he said as he shook her hand. "This architecture is amazing. I may take some time in the morning and just snap photos of the building."

"Peter here is one of the pastors. I'm sure he could speak for the church and say they didn't mind."

"Absolutely," Peter said.

The door opened again and Tony, Barry, and Derrick came in. Tony went straight to Robin. "*Cara*, my bride to be." He gave her a gentle kiss, then hugged her tight, giving her a reassuring squeeze. "Are you ready?"

With a nervous laugh, she said, "We're still missing a few people."

As if on cue, the Rabonovich's came in followed by Stephanie Giordano. Sofia Rabonovich set down the box she carried and went to Robin, putting her hands on her shoulders, kissing both of her cheeks. "My dear, how incredibly exciting."

Robin nodded and whispered, "No one knows."

Craig came in while Tony and Abram were shaking hands. "I'm not late, am I?"

"Not at all," Tony said, walking to his future father-in-law with his hand extended. "We are so honored that you're giving Robin away."

"I'm thanking God for the chance to be doing things right for once," Craig said, cheeks fusing bright pink with color.

The far door opened, and two high school boys from the youth group came in together. Peter held up a hand in greeting. "Good to see you boys. Thank you for arriving very nearly on time."

The only redhead in the group said, "My mom said to tell you again how much she appreciates you asking us to do this, Mr. V.," he said.

Tony smiled. "I'm sure you'll do a great job ushering. There are twenty of you all together, and I know Stephanie has you meeting her for instruction and training in the morning, but you two will be part of the ceremony, so I wanted you to be here tonight.

"And now," Tony said, putting an arm around Robin's shoulders. "We have a surprise for you all."

Robin's fingers shook slightly, not from nerves but just from general excitement, as she worked the belt loose on her coat. As soon as it was loose, she shrugged out of it, revealing a white satin tea-length dress with short capped sleeves and a scrolling pattern of pearls sewn into the skirt.

Maxine gasped. "Seriously?" she asked, laughing. "I love it!"

"What's going on?" Sarah asked.

"We decided instead of the big hoopla tomorrow, we wanted to experience our most special day with the people closest to us rather than share it with another thousand people," Robin said.

Sarah's eyes narrowed. "What am I not understanding?"

Maxine put her hand on her hip. "They're actually going to get married tonight. This isn't practice – it's for real."

Caroline clapped her hands and threw her head back and laughed. "Fantastic!"

"Wait," Derrick said. "What about tomorrow? Did you cancel everyone coming?"

"Not at all," Tony said. "We'll still go through all the motions. But Robin thought, and I agreed, that she would enjoy the day much more if the added stress of getting married wasn't weighing down on her."

Barry frowned. "Isn't that the point of tomorrow? The stress of getting married?"

Robin walked up to him and slipped her arm around his waist, hugging him to her. "I've been trying to get him to elope with me since he proposed. Don't stop this now, Barry."

He laughed and squeezed her then released her. "I'm glad you didn't elope. Well, until now. Tony enjoys the hoopla too much."

With a sigh Robin said, "I know. God help me, I know."

Stephanie smiled and said, "She told me about it last week, and I have been absolutely bursting with it. What a fun and clever idea!"

Sophia opened the box she carried in and handed simple bouquets of white roses and fresh greenery to Maxine, Sarah, and Caroline.

"You want me to go ahead and walk you down the aisle now," Craig asked, "or wait for tomorrow?"

"We still need to practice for tomorrow, so we're going to go through all of the motions. But, the ceremony will be real and we'll say our vows," Robin said.

The door opened again and the church's organist and sound manager came in together. They stopped briefly to confer with Abram and Stephanie before she went to the huge pipe organ and flipped switches to get it turned on and the sound manager went back out the door to go up to the sound booth in the balcony.

Abram clapped his hands. "Is everyone ready?"

Robin, her sisters, and Caroline, with Angel Dove and Isaac, all went to the back of the church with Craig while Tony, Barry, Derrick, and Peter went out the side doors at the front of the church. They left the doors propped open so that they could hear Stephanie's directions.

Sarah fiddled with the ribbon on her bouquet. "I wish you'd told us. We could have been prepared."

Robin put an arm around her shoulders. "We intentionally didn't tell anyone but Stephanie, who needed to make flower and dress arrangements for me, and Abram, who will be officiating. We wanted it to be a surprise."

Sarah looked at Maxine. "You didn't know?"

With a shake of her head, Maxine confirmed it. "No. This is a huge surprise for me. I'm thrilled though." She turned to Robin. "What are you guys doing tonight?"

Robin felt her cheeks heat. "We will still have dinner as planned, catered at Barry's house. Only afterward, instead of going back to the hotel, Derrick will take my room and I'll go home with, ah, my husband."

Her upper lip dotted with sweat. Maxine ran a hand over her arm. "You okay with that?"

Robin nodded. "Way more than I would be if it were tomorrow. I can't even handle the thought of dealing with all those eyes and all those people –

the small talk and networking – along with the wedding night stress. It was just too much. Tony came up with this idea. I just hope …" She trailed off, not really sure what she meant to say.

Maxine hugged her. "Everything will be magical," she said in Robin's ear. "I believe that."

Robin fanned her face and turned to Craig. "Ready, dad?"

"Kinda glad to be getting a practice in before the real thing, that's for sure," he said, offering his arm. Gerald came down the aisle and snapped a photo just as Robin put her hand on his arm.

From the front of the church, Stephanie held a microphone and tapped it to make sure it was on. "Okay, here's the order of services. Before any of the wedding party come out, there's a soloist. She's going to come and take microphone B and move to here," Stephanie said, walking to the left side of the stage. "She'll sing, and when she finishes, Tony, you, Abram, and your party will come through the doors together and take your places." She paused. "You can come now."

The men came together and Stephanie directed them where to stand. "Okay," she said, "once they're in place, then the two ushers will take the cords on the runner that's back there and walk forward, together pulling it open." The two youth rushed to take the cords and started walking. As the runner opened, Robin could see the beautiful scrolling "V" and the intricate artwork around it. "Come all the way to the front and it should run out just –" the roll ended and they were left holding the cords and an empty holder right in front of Tony and Abram. "Perfect!"

Stephanie continued, "Now the organist will be playing some music the whole time. As soon as they finish the roll, Angel Dove and Isaac will walk together." She looked at Tony but continued to speak into the mike. "Is he still going to carry the rings?"

Tony nodded. "We'll exchange rings again tomorrow. No one need know our practice was the real thing but us."

"So, Angel Dove and Isaac will come down the aisle, followed by the bridal party with Caroline first, then Sarah, and finally Maxi." Stephanie looked at notes as she spoke. Isaac held his sister's hand as they walked with some trepidation, down the long aisle. Eyes wide behind the round glasses, he kept his face focused on his father's, who waited for him at the end.

As soon as they were four rows into the march, Stephanie said, "Okay, now Caroline." She directed Sarah and Maxine at the same time. As they came up front, she told each of them where to stand and how to face the audience. When Maxine was in place, the organist paused for one heart beat, then two, and then played the beginning chords of the wedding march.

Robin looked at Craig. "You ready?"

"As ever," he said, patting her hand that gripped his other arm. While the familiar music played, Robin and Craig slowly walked down the aisle, and she looked at Tony and smiled. His face was serious, almost intense, but when she smiled, he relaxed and smiled back.

It seemed to take forever to reach the front. She and Craig stopped in front of Tony and Abram.

"Who gives this bride to this groom?" Abram asked.

Craig cleared his throat twice before he spoke, "I do." His voice rang clearly through the church.

Stephanie said, "Craig, at this point, you'll raise her veil."

Craig mocked raising her veil. He looked so uncomfortable, that Robin hugged him. Blinking back tears, she stepped forward and took Tony's hand. Holding her hand, he turned and faced Abram.

In a strong and rich voice, Abram said, "It really is a joy to be here tonight, gathered with you, Tony and Robin, and surrounded here by friends. It is such a privilege to officiate this celebration. You two are very special to my Sofia and me, and I thank you for inviting me to be a part of it."

Robin thought about the first time she met Abram. While she and Tony had sat in the Rabonovich's home and had after-church cake and coffee, he had very kindly and lovingly instructed her on how to start reading her Bible.

"After the ceremony today, I will sign the marriage certificate. Everyone who has been married in recent years has a piece of paper that certifies that they had a wedding. Some folks have it in a nice frame, up on the wall somewhere in their house. Some might have it in a lock box with other important documents in order to keep it safe. Regardless of what you do with this piece of paper, I want to tell something I hope you never forget – it's just a piece of paper. Really. That's all. A piece of paper is not a marriage. In fact, everything we are doing today is not a marriage."

Robin looked at Tony. He must have felt her glance, because he shifted his eyes from Abram and looked over at her. They had conspired to get married tonight instead of tomorrow so that this moment, this ceremony, could be something just them and the people closest to them could share. She grinned a secret grin meant for Tony alone. Despite nearly bursting with the desire to share the plan with her sisters, she didn't spoil the surprise. That made this all the more fun, she thought.

"Don't get me wrong, this is a great day – a beautiful day. It is wonderful to be here in this place, with all these friends, witnessing your vows to one another in this historic building where thousands of others through four generations have said their own vows. But as good as it is to be here, we should all remember that this is a wedding, not a marriage. What makes a marriage is what comes next."

It was hard not to lean over and kiss Tony. He had looked so intense, his dark eyes so serious. But when she gave him that secret grin, everything about him softened and he smiled and winked at her.

"What makes a marriage is what you do tomorrow, and the next day, and the following weeks and months and years and decades to come ... growing older and weaker in the flesh and wiser and stronger in love. There is a verse of scripture that claims, 'No one has greater love than this, to lay down one's life for one's friends.' Chances are that you will never be asked to give up your life for your spouse. But, you will have to give up yourself for your spouse every day from now on. Marriage is not a piece of paper."

Since Abram was speaking directly to them, Robin looked back at their friend. She thought forward to the coming night and realized that anticipation had replaced the trepidation. Excitement had replaced the fear. Once she acknowledged what had eaten at her for weeks, once she knew where all of her hesitation in marrying Tony lay, it gave her a target, a focus, and she started fighting it back.

"Marriage is a gift. Marriage is a choice. Marriage is sacrifice. And marriage is when two become one. Robin, today you will give yourself entirely to Tony. And Tony, today you will give yourself entirely to Robin. In a moment, those are exactly the words that we will use to begin this ceremony: Tony, will you give yourself to Robin? Robin, will you give yourself to Tony?

"Marriage is a gift, the gift of yourself, your heart, your thoughts, and your hopes and dreams ... Marriage is the gift of your life. And it is not just today."

It amazed Robin that what she had discovered through Tony's willingness to sacrifice his entire life in order to be with her, that he needed her as much as she needed him. How had she missed that in this courtship? He seemed so strong, confident, and so self assured that she didn't think he needed anyone. She never truly understood the depths of his feelings for her.

"Every day from here forward, you must continue to give yourselves to one another. Today you will state a public vow and commit yourselves to each other. Every morning after this one, you will have to wake up and choose to recommit yourselves to each other. Marriage is a choice. Marriage means letting go of petty fights about who's right and wrong. It means putting your spouse's interests, wants and desires, and happiness ahead of your own. It means, Tony, that after today Robin's happiness is more important than yours. And it means, Robin, that after today Tony's happiness is more important than yours."

Out of the corner of her eye, she saw Tony's head turn, so she looked at him. At Abram's words about his happiness, Tony raised an eyebrow and with a teasing glint in his eye, he winked at her. Robin had to swallow a laugh.

"Marriage is sacrificing for each other and acting as one. That is what it means to become one flesh, forever joined together ... Cleaved unto each other. You are each your wedding gift to one another. Your wedding day is the symbol of your marriage to each other. And your marriage is the gift of continuing to give the gift of yourselves to each other. And with that gift to each other, with that shared love, I know that you will have a marriage that will last through the ages, and stand as a witness to all of the love of God. God bless you."

They both looked back at Abram, who looked each one of them in the eye and smiled at them. "But that is enough of me because today is about the two of you. Tony and Robin, I invite you to come and begin the adventure of your marriage by declaring your vows to one another here in this place."

He gestured with his hands, telling Tony and Robin to turn and face each other. Stephanie said, "Robin, at this point, hand your bouquet to Maxine. Maxine, be prepared, because her bouquet is heavy, so you might want to prep and hand yours to Sarah."

The bouquet that Robin held tonight was very small and very simple. She handed it to Maxine and turned back to Tony, letting him take both of her hands. She looked into the eyes of the man with whom she was about to vow to become one, and felt excitement, peace, love. Gone was apprehension, gone was fear. She whispered a "thank you" to God for answering her prayers.

Abram smiled and nodded. "I am going to pray. Please bow your heads." As everyone complied, he spoke into the silent, reverent room. "Jehovah God, we thank You for the way that You work in our lives. We know You brought Tony and Robin together with a purpose, and I am praying that You bless this union, strengthen their bond, and let them work for You in a powerful way in your ministry. Guide their future, convict their hearts, and touch the lives of their future children. We are so honored to be in front of You today, and we thank You for giving us this opportunity. Amen."

Abram looked at Stephanie. "It is my understanding that they have their own vows?"

"We worked on them together. Here they are," Tony said pulling a piece of paper out of his jacket pocket.

"Okay," Abram said, waving a hand toward them. "This is where you say your vows. Let me see." He cleared his throat and started reading.

Chapter 16

ROBIN and Tony held hands as they walked up the walk to Barry's home. Just as they reached the door, Barry threw it open. "I thought you might have gotten lost," he joked.

"The photographer wanted a few more shots of us before we left," Robin said. She gestured behind her. "I hope you don't mind that he's here, too."

"Of course not," Barry said, stepping aside so they could come in. "The more the merrier."

As they entered the large front room, Jacqueline came toward them wearing a tight black dress and three-inch red heels. "Antonio, Robin, darlings, you're here." She air kissed both of their cheeks and stepped back, leaving a cloying smell of perfume behind her. "The caterers had to hold dinner from being served waiting on you."

The tone of disapproval did little to damper Robin's spirits. "We missed you at the rehearsal," Robin said. She slipped off her coat and Jacqueline's eyebrow rose.

"I had to handle the caterers," she said distracted as she looked Robin's dress up and down. Her face became frozen solid as she pointedly looked at their left hands and noted the band of diamonds on Robin's and the large gold bad on Tony's. "Apparently, I missed something."

Tony comfortably slipped his arm over Robin's shoulders. "We surprised everyone and had the official wedding ceremony tonight," he said. "It's too bad you couldn't delegate the dinner and join us."

"Someone should have mentioned it," Jacqueline said through gritted teeth. She turned her head and looked at her husband.

"He was just as surprised as everyone else, Jacqui. Sheathe your claws," Tony said in a warning. "You will not make a scene or you will not be welcome tomorrow, and we both know you will be looking just stunning for as many publicity shots as possible tomorrow."

Jacqueline stepped backward and took a deep breath, then lifted one of her red curls before she patted her hair to make sure everything stayed smooth. "No worries, Antonio. No scenes. Don't be ridiculous." She looked at Robin from head to toe. "Cute dress. Very retro. Nice choice."

Robin smoothed the skirt. "Thank you." Needing to not be at odds with her husband's best friend, she stepped forward and linked her arm with Jacqueline's, steering her away from Tony. "I had a great time shopping with you last week. This is all very new to me, and I learned so much from you. Can we make plans again soon?"

"Of course, darling," Jacqueline said, shooting Tony a parting glance. "When you get back from your honeymoon, we'll need to get your summer wardrobe built. We'll make plans to go."

"I'd like that very much, thank you." Having successfully steered her away from Tony, Robin disengaged her arm. "And thank you again for hosting the dinner tonight. I know the groom's family is supposed to be the host for the rehearsal dinner."

"Well, Antonio has always considered my husband as a brother, for whatever reason." She gestured toward one of the O'Farrell kids. "I need to go rescue my Italian leather furniture from those … children," she said the last word like it stuck in her mouth.

Robin looked as one of the older O'Farrell's sat down on the white leather sofa and brought his knees up, resting his boots on the seat of the couch. Caroline and Jacqueline both made a beeline for him at the same time.

"Nice place," Maxine said, coming up to Robin and handing her a glass of water. She gestured at the sweeping stairway that led to the rooms upstairs. An open balcony showed several closed doors. "I like the open second floor."

"It makes the room feel huge," Robin said. "Jacqui told me about some photo shoot that some home magazine is coming to do at Tony's apartment. This world is so different from anything we've known."

"You'll fit in. You served most of these people at Benedict's over the years. You know how they think, act, interact. And, you can remember names. That's a huge deal."

Robin nodded and took a long pull of her water. She didn't realize how thirsty she was until she started drinking. "It's less and less intimidating as the days go by."

She felt Tony's hand on her waist and turned her head to smile at him. "You handled that with expertise," he said, referring to Jacqueline.

"Well, all those years as a waitress and bartender have taught me the fine art of soothing angry souls," Robin said with a smile.

"Color me impressed. She is often difficult to get along with."

"Nah," Robin said, shaking her head. "She is afraid of not being accepted, so she goes overboard to make sure she is. I feel kind of bad for her."

Tony brought her hand up to his lips and kissed it. "I love your heart," he said.

"And I love you."

"I wasn't finished." Tony said, "I love your heart but please don't fall for Jacqui's tricks. Trust me when I tell you she is not someone anyone needs to feel sorry for. In fact, she is a hungry lion roaming the earth seeking whom she may devour. She has teeth and claws and very often malevolent intent. Know that going into any conversation and guard your heart my beloved bride."

"Tony, you aren't really describing the woman I spent an entire day shopping with."

Tony nodded. "I understand that."

"I guess I'm just surprised to hear you say these things. I mean, look at this party she's hosting."

Tony grinned. "You are so generous with your love, my darling. Listen, Barry is hosting this party. And believe me when I tell you that Jacqui has given him no end of grief over it among many other things. Do me a favor and just watch her when she is around Barry tonight. I trust your instincts and so should you."

Something about Maxine's stance and demeanor changed as Tony spoke. When he concluded his last request, Maxine interrupted. "Hey, I'm starving. Let's make sure they know everyone is here so they can start serving."

ROBIN stood in the middle of the living room and held her hands out, whirling in a circle. She laughed, and the sound filled and satisfied Tony's soul. He smiled, delighting in her.

"We are married," she said with a grin, kicking her shoes off.

"Till death," Tony smiled walking toward her until he could hook her waist with his arm. "Or until I get tired of you," he said.

With a snort, Robin grabbed his tie. "You won't get rid of me that easy."

"God, I hope not," he said, putting a hand on her cheek. "You are amazing and beautiful. I think what we did tonight was a great idea. Now you can enjoy tomorrow without the added stress of getting married."

Robin slipped her arms around his neck. "I love you, Antonio Viscolli. I am eternally grateful for the day God placed you in my life."

"And I you, *mia moglie*." He smiled and looked into her sapphire blue eyes. "I like that, calling you 'my wife'. I look forward to doing that for many years." He brought his lips down to hers, feeling his breath sweep away at the mere brush of her skin on his. The blood roared in his ears as he deepened the kiss, and he fought for control even as he pulled her tighter to him.

He kissed her and kissed her, drinking her in. Ripping his mouth away, he ran his lips along her jaw to the nape of her neck, inhaling the scent of her perfume, feeling all cognitive thinking sweep away. He felt Robin's hands slide up his head and grip his hair as he kissed the sensitive skin under her ear. Her gasp, the clutch of her hands, the way her body moved against his almost made him lose control, but he clawed for it and grasped it back.

He ripped his head up and tried to take a breath that wasn't consumed with her taste or smell. She placed her lips on his neck, almost mimicking his kiss. "Wait," he panted. His skin burned under her touch.

"Wait for what?" Robin purred, kissing his jaw, placing her lips at the corner of his mouth.

"You need – "

Robin silenced him with her kiss, wrapping her arms around his neck and standing on tiptoe as if she wanted to devour him. When she finally broke her mouth away, she said, "I need you." Framing his face with her hands, she stared into his eyes and he started to drown. "I need you, *mio marito*."

Hearing her call him her husband in his native tongue broke the last thread of control he clumsily held. Sweeping her into his arms he cradled her to him as he kissed her and carried her into his – into their – bedroom.

Chapter 17

ROBIN opened her eyes, momentarily panicked by the unfamiliar surroundings. Then memories of the night before came flooding back and she slowly sat up, pulling the sheet up with her. She surveyed the room around her with interest, recognizing her bath robe hanging on the back of the open closet door next to his. Boxes lay stacked in a corner labeled "bedroom," obviously waiting for her to fully move in.

She sat up against a mahogany headboard. A heavy cream-colored cover trimmed in brown lay folded at the foot of the bed. A huge Oriental rug covered the floor. Against one wall, a fireplace had wood stacked next to it ready to be lit. In front of it two leather chairs flanked a large chess set. On the walls hung paintings of Boston, various locations at various times of the year.

Tony came into the room wearing khaki pants and a white shirt open at the neck. He carried a steaming mug of coffee. Her heart immediately started racing at the sight of him. She wondered if seeing him in the morning would do that for the rest of her life.

"Good morning, *cara*," he said. He set the mug on the night stand next to the bed and sat on the edge of the bed by her hip. Putting a hand on either side of her, he leaned forward and brushed her lips with his own. She sighed and tried to deepen the kiss, but he chuckled and pulled back. "As much as spending the day with you in bed really appeals to me, we're running late as it is. Much to do today," he said. "We have to get married, after all."

He presented her with the coffee and she took the first heavenly sip. As the caffeine worked its way through her body, she pulled her knees up and wrapped her free arm around her legs. "We're already married. Can't we just skip to the cake?"

Tony laughed. "Cake will come soon enough." He kissed her again and stood. "And then the honeymoon." He wiggled his eyebrows. "Which means all day in bed if we want."

Robin grinned and put her arms over her head, stretching. When the sheet fell, she watched Tony's eyes darken. "Oh, I want," she said giggling.

She pulled the sheet back up. "Where are my clothes?"

Tony cleared his throat and sweat popped out on his forehead. He took a step backward and gestured at the closet. "There's new and old in there. The clothes you purchased with Jacqui are all put away. If I were you, I'd wear something from there. Our friends in the press are going to be everywhere today."

"Press?"

He shrugged. "You'll be fine." He smiled and bent to kiss her one more time. "Get dressed before I make us late to our own wedding." He started from the room, but paused and snapped is fingers. "I have a car arriving in thirty minutes to take you to the hotel. Your sisters and Caroline are already there. I have to run."

"Where will you be?" Robin asked.

"The groom isn't supposed to see the bride before the wedding, remember? The next time I see you, you'll be walking down the aisle toward me."

SARAH stepped into the massive Grand Ballroom of the Viscolli hotel. The sight that greeted her nearly took her breath away. Hundreds of tables covered in ivory and gold, formally set with gold-rimmed china and crystal filled the room. Each table had a beautiful centerpiece of a round ball of ivory roses sitting on a tall pillar. The chairs at the tables were covered with ivory brocade and tied at the top of the chair with a large red ribbon that formed a bow on the back of the chair.

At the far end of the room, massive doors opened to the tent area, but the carpet and ceiling matched so well that Sarah could barely tell where the ballroom ended and the tent began. Waiters and bus boys worked inside the tent, covering chairs, setting tables, and placing centerpieces.

The long head table spanned the front of the room with a gorgeous red and ivory rose centerpiece that ran along its entire length. The chairs for Tony and Robin, at the middle of the table, looked like thrones fit for a king and queen. And, honestly, as far as Sarah could tell, Tony seemed like royalty. This wedding certainly felt like the royal wedding, Sarah thought, especially with the mob of reporters camped outside the hotel and roving the hotel lobby. She imagined the church would be just as chaotic.

Sarah really liked Tony. Having been raised in the church and taught to work and give to God, she loved that he dedicated his entire life and fortune to ministry. She knew he would do anything for anyone if he could. He had certainly proven it by opening his home to Derrick.

Thinking of that boy set her teeth on edge. Tony met him outside of a seedy bar in the very worst neighborhood possible, and a month later the boy was living with him? She wouldn't care, it would be just fine, except that Robin and Sarah were going to be living there, too.

Not wanting thoughts of him to ruin this day, because certainly his presence during the ceremony would be enough, Sarah shook her head and walked over to the far end of the ballroom, away from the open doors and the tent area, to where the cake table was set up.

The massive, amazing structure was simply stunning. Eight tiers rose up in ivory colored buttercream. Beautifully hand crafted sugar flowers of roses, lilies, hydrangea, ranunculus, and orchids created an amazing waterfall of flowers spilling from the top on down the tiers, widening as it reached the huge bottom tier.

Sarah shifted her overnight bag on her shoulder and turned, looking at the room from this angle. Robin had absolutely outdone herself. Well, Robin with the help and guidance of Stephanie and Maxine. Without them, Robin had joked that they'd have had a backyard wedding in blue jeans with chocolate cake.

Sarah thought back to the first time she met Robin. She had no memory of her life before waking up in her then foster parents' home. In an effort to protect and shield her, they'd made no mention of sisters or a murdered mother or the life from which she'd come to them. They just told her that God gave her to them, and shushed any possible questions until she just learned not to ask them.

But on the morning of her fifteenth birthday, Robin and Maxine sat at the kitchen table at her parents' house, not knowing she didn't know them. Robin had been fighting in the court system for visitation rights, and finally won the right to visit Sarah for an hour each week. Sarah fell in love with her sisters, though they intimidated her. They were hard, with hard eyes and air of desperation about them that Sarah thought needed to be avoided. But she waited all week for the time to arrive when she could see them again, and gradually got to know them.

When her high school graduation loomed in front of her, her parents broke the news - they would not be able to afford college on any level. Because they did not believe in borrowing money, and because Sarah had been taught at a very young age not to borrow money, the idea of a student loan repelled her. Struggling to find a way to afford to go to college, Robin's suggestion that she pay for it was a welcome option. The only condition was that Sarah live with her and Maxine while she went to school. Sarah was thrilled. Not only would she get to actually go to school, but she would get to know these beautiful and brilliant sisters of hers.

Her parents had objected, but they relented knowing that it was the only way Sarah could go.

She didn't fit in with the two of them. She ate differently - from her earliest memory, the smell and taste of meat made her physically ill, so she ate a completely vegan diet - no meat and no meat products. And, she had dedicated her life to Christ. Robin and Maxine, though they intellectually knew that about her, didn't understand it so therefore didn't bring it up. Growing up in a Christian home with a loving family left her with absolutely nothing in common with her sisters.

For two years, she watched Robin work herself into the ground. The first year was the hardest, because Sarah and Maxine were both in school at the same time. At just 24 years of age, Robin worked two jobs six-days-a-week to pay for tuition and books for both sisters. Maxine constantly tried to get a job to help out, and Sarah offered as well, but Robin adamantly insisted that she be the one to do this for them.

After Tony came into her life, Sarah saw her sister gradually relax. The desperation on her face slid away and became peace. She watched Robin give her life to Christ, and sat in Tony's big downtown church to see her oldest sister baptized.

As soon as Robin became saved, Sarah felt like they had something in common, and suddenly, they started talking – full blown conversations that Sarah actually enjoyed. It was such a relief to actually feel a part of Robin's life instead of another burden on her shoulders, and a part of her that she constantly held back softened and she grew to love both of her sisters like she didn't even know was possible.

And now, Tony was giving Robin a royal wedding. Sarah knew, because she knew Tony, that a desire to show Robin how much he valued her motivated him – which was why he never gave in to Robin wanting to elope. He wanted this pomp and circumstance so that he could show Robin off to the watching world. Sarah believed, with all of her heart, that there wasn't another person on earth who deserved this kind of pampering more than Robin.

She put her hands to her mouth and blinked back tears of joy at the beauty and style that the day would bring. Excited, honored to be a part of it, she said a quick prayer of thanksgiving to God for giving Robin the steadfastness to battle her parents for visitation, or Sarah might have gone her whole life never meeting her two wonderful sisters.

Her phone buzzed in her pocket, breaking her reverie. She pulled it out and scanned the text from Maxine, asking her location. "BALLROOM" she wrote back, and slipped the phone back into her pocket.

By the time she crossed the room, Maxine entered wearing dark sunglasses, black yoga pants, and a tight-fitting fleece. "Holy cow, it's like a zoo out there. Did you see the news vans?"

"I did. It's hysterical. How do you look so fashionable dressed like that?" Sarah asked. "I don't think I'll look that good in our dresses tonight."

Maxine slipped off her glasses and hugged her sister. "Don't be silly. You are gorgeous." She spun in a circle. "Look at this place! Amazing!"

"I know. You and Stephanie really helped Robin. I am stunned."

"We actually just guided her in the beginning. Once she got her feet wet, I was able to pull back a bit. She just didn't know she could do it until she did it." Maxine put her hand into the pocket of her fleece and pulled out a keycard. "Suite 1914. It has a couple of bedrooms, a full living room and dining room, and a fully stocked kitchen. Should be perfect for our little hair and makeup party today."

Sarah looked at her watch. "What time will everyone be here?"

"Caroline is bringing Angel Dove with her at ten. The stylist and her assistants will be here at nine, but we need to get Robin's hair rolled before they do anything else. I have makeup coming at one."

"What about Robin?"

They left the ballroom. "Tony texted me twenty minutes ago and said she'd be here by nine."

"We have time to grab breakfast then," Sarah said, putting an arm around Maxine's waist.

"Already ordered, sister of mine. Hopefully, room service will beat us to our room."

ROBIN sat back in the chair, eyes closed while a woman coated color on her eyelid and another pinned yet even more babies breath into the intricate structure of curls and twists of her hair. She could hear Caroline's lyrical voice as she read a book to Angel Dove and smiled at the sound.

"Open," the makeup artist said. Robin opened her eyes and the woman took her chin, tilting her head this way and that before nodding and stepping back. "All done. I know it feels like a lot, but when you see pictures, you'll be pleased."

"Thank you," Robin said.

The hair stylist stepped away as well. "Ready for the veil," she said.

"Go on into the bedroom and get your dress on," Caroline said. "Maxine? Go help her."

Robin's head felt heavy with the weight of the pins and flowers. She wanted to put her hand up and feel and fuss, but as many hours as she sat while they worked it into place, she was afraid to mess it up.

Maxine followed her into the bedroom. She already had on her dress - a strapless red gown that shimmered when she moved. It fell just below her knees in the front and dropped nearly to the floor in the back. She wore red heels the color of the dress. It looked stunning on all three of the bridesmaids, which was a feat considering the differences in age and body style. Maxine's hair was twisted into an intricate knot on the base of her skull, with tendrils of hair left flowing down along her temples.

Robin unbuttoned her blouse and slipped out of it, then slipped off her sweat pants. She already had on her white silk stockings.

Maxine carefully pulled her dress off of the hanger and unsnapped, unzipped, and unhooked it to allow Robin to step into it, then she slid it up and zipped, snapped, and hooked it into place.

"Wow," Maxine said, stepping back. "That looks even a million times more fabulous than it did when you tried it on without the makeup and the hair."

A wide full-length mirror had been installed in the room for her and she walked to it. When she saw her reflection, she was speechless. She wore heart-shaped ruby earrings that Caroline had loaned her. "A Valentine's Day gift from last year," she'd said. "A treasure of mine." On her wrist, she wore the antique gold bracelets that Maxine and Sarah had given her as a wedding present. On her neck, she wore the new ruby and diamond necklace Tony gave her, and on her finger, she wore the blue sapphire engagement ring.

Maxine held up a mirror so she could see the back of her hair. A wide, flat braid started at the crown of her head and snaked around and formed into a bun. The stylist had pulled the strands of the braid and pinned them back so that the bun looked like an open rose. Baby's breath was dotted all through the braid.

"Wow," Robin said. As much as the makeup artist had worked on her face, Robin had felt certain she'd end up looking like a clown. Instead, the makeup, while heavy, looked so subtle and exceptionally worked with Robin's face. "I look like a princess," she whispered.

Sarah came in and stopped short. "Robin," she said on a breath, "wow."

Maxine laughed. "I know! It's here. It's finally here."

Sarah clapped her hands. "I can't believe it's finally time. Are you nervous?"

Robin shook her head. "Strangely, no. I think what we did yesterday took away all the nerves. I'm just ready for cake."

Sarah laughed. "Now shoes!" She went to the bed and grabbed the small shoebox. It contained a pair of simple white heels with a sparkling red ribbon woven through the top of them to a bow on the back. Robin lifted the skirt of her dress and slipped them on.

"Gerald!" Maxine said. The door immediately opened and Gerald came in with two cameras with different lenses hanging by straps around his neck.

"We're ready for the veil."

Robin carefully perched on a sitting stool while Maxine and Sarah pinned the veil onto her head and Gerald took a dozen pictures. When they were finished, all three women were crying and hugged each other tightly in a group hug.

GREATER THAN RUBIES - CHAPTER 18

ROBIN followed the security guard through the hotel lobby. She wanted to duck and hide from the whirring sounds of cameras, but she didn't. She held her shoulders back and walked next to her sisters through the crowd and into the waiting limo.

They all piled in … Robin, Maxine, Sarah, Caroline, and Angel Dove. Gerald sat in front with the driver.

"Well, that was sure a circus," Caroline said. She put a hand to her temple. Somehow, the hairstylist had managed to contain her wild red hair and keep it contained. Robin had never seen her look so beautiful before.

"Tony called and said it was worse at the church."

"Is everyone there?" Caroline asked.

"He said the guys all got there about two."

Sarah brushed at the skirt of her dress. "Oh to be a man at times like this."

"But then you wouldn't look as pretty," Angel Dove said, pushing away from Caroline and climbing into Sarah's lap. She wore a dress with a white sleeveless top made out of shiny satin and a pattern of red heart-shaped crystals sewn into the neckline. The skirt was long and shiny red satin trimmed in white. On her feet, she wore white socks with red hearts and white patent leather shoes. A crown of baby red roses and white baby's breath would go on her head before she walked down the aisle.

"And I wouldn't have had the chance to spend the day with you," Sarah said, putting her cheek on the top of Angel Dove's head.

Robin felt the burn of tears watching Sarah warm to her friends. She looked at Caroline and smiled. "I can't wait to see if Isaac actually put the tux on."

"He better, and he knows it."

"He also knows you're all bluster."

Caroline laughed as the limo slowed and came to a stop. "True."

"Wow," Maxine said, looking out the window. "This is outrageous."

A security team kept the crowds behind a barricade. As soon as the driver had the door open, Robin could hear the noise of the crowd. It drowned out every sound around them. Her stomach dropped at the sight of everyone yelling and taking pictures and she felt nerves dance up into her chest. She wanted to duck her head and run inside, but instead she waved at the crowd then stepped back and waited for everyone to get out of the car.

They walked calmly together through the double doors of the church, which shut behind them, cutting off the noise.

"What in the world?" Caroline said.

"Tony's guest list brought the crowds," Barry said approaching them. "Celebrities, politicians, religious leaders … I'm glad he thought ahead to security."

"There you are," Stephanie said, rushing toward them. She wore a stunning rose colored suit that went well with her silver hair. Her heels clicked rapidly on the tile floor. "Oh Robin, girls, you all look amazing."

Robin put a hand over her necklace. She could feel the furious pounding of her heart. "I'm suddenly very nervous."

"I'm sure. Me too!" She gestured toward the sanctuary. "Let's get some pictures made before your guests arrive. We have an hour tops."

For the next forty-five minutes, Robin sat, stood, and posed for more pictures than she could possibly count. Alone, with bridesmaids, with sisters, with Abram, with groomsmen, she smiled and smiled and smiled until her face hurt. Then she drank some water and smiled some more.

Her makeup artist came at one point and refreshed lipstick and powdered her nose, and then she sat for a dozen more poses.

"Enough," she said, holding up her hand. "We have enough pictures."

Stephanie looked at her watch. "That's good, because we need to go ahead and sequester you, anyway."

She followed Stephanie through the church and into a small room off of the narthex. Through the door, she could hear the noise of the crowds every time the main doors opened and closed, and could hear the conversations of the ushers and guests in the lobby.

She sat on a small stool and waited. "This is where it's hard," she said. "Staying hidden instead of just getting it over with."

"There are a lot of people to seat," Sarah said. "I'm surprised you went with youth boys for ushers. I'm sure you could have hired trained staff."

"If you expect big things out of youth, they'll do big things," Robin said. "So says Tony, anyway."

Maxine came closer and spoke softly. "You okay. I mean, about, uh, last night?"

Robin felt the heat on her cheeks but took Maxine's hand. "Oh yes. Unimaginably okay."

Maxine squeezed her hand. "Good. What a relief. When you didn't say anything all day, I worried."

Robin cleared her throat. "It's not exactly a conversation starter."

Sarah laughed. "No doubt."

Robin felt her whole face flush and fanned herself with her hands. "Girls!"

Stephanie came in by a back door. "Your dad is outside. Can he come in?"

Robin stood. "Of course."

Stephanie stuck her head out the door and then opened it wide enough to allow Craig to come in. He crossed the room and stood in front of her, tugging on his collar. He looked great in his black tuxedo, white shirt, and black bow tie. "Someone lady in a pink dress said to come in here and get a flower."

Maxine went to the boxes of flowers on a far table and found the white rose boutonniere that had a tag on it with Craig's name. She walked back toward them and handed it to Robin to pin on him. "You look so nice, dad," Robin said. "You clean up good."

He stepped back and raised his hand in her direction. "Look who's talking. You look like a princess. Hard to believe that you are mine."

"I think it just goes to show you that any of us can clean up good if we want." In a spontaneous motion, she kissed his cheek. "I'm so proud of you and so happy you've come to know the Lord. Thank you for agreeing to give me away."

With a large hand, he clumsily patted her shoulder and swallowed tears. "You do an old man proud," he whispered, then pivoted and exited the room. Robin smiled at his retreating back, and said a silent prayer of thanks to God for this time she's had with Craig. She worried a little that he would be put back in prison by the time she got home from her honeymoon.

"That was incredibly sweet," Sarah said. "There's nothing like a dad. I'm so thankful that mine has always been such a good friend to me."

"You're very lucky," Maxine said, her mouth in a thin line. Someone rapped sharply on the door. After a few heartbeats, Barry stuck his head inside.

"We're getting ready to get into our positions," he said. He looked around the room and gave a low whistle. "You ladies all look absolutely beautiful."

"Thank you, Barry," Robin said, walking up to him. He came further into the room and she brushed at the jacket on his shoulder. "Can you find Stephanie? I still seem to have boutonnieres for the guys."

As she spoke, Stephanie rushed in. "Boutonnieres," she said. "How could I have forgotten?"

"They're right there," Maxine said with a laugh. Stephanie grabbed the long flat box and rushed out of the room with it. Maxine looked at Barry. "Guess you should follow her."

He smiled. "Guess I should. See you guys at the end of the aisle!"

He shut the door behind him. Robin felt her whole body start quaking. She put a hand on her chest and sat back on the stool. "I – don't – know – I – can – do – this." She felt like she couldn't take a deep enough breath.

Caroline rushed over and put her hands on Robin's bare shoulders. "Just breathe, lass. Nice and easy. Slowly in and slowly out."

Robin's vision started to gray. "Can I have some water?" she whispered.

Sarah rushed to hand her a bottle of water.

"Thank you." Robin took a sip of the water, then tilted it back and drained the whole bottle. She gently patted her mouth, worried about messing up lipstick if she wiped against it. "That's better."

Maxine knelt next to her chair. "You got this," she said. "The part in front of the crowd will be over in no time."

"Then the best part starts," Sarah said.

Robin closed her eyes and concentrated on Tony's face, thought about worshipping with him in the sanctuary at this very church and felt calmer. They were just people – a thousand people – but just people.

She stood, feeling better. As she stood, she heard the sound of Nat King Cole's "When I Fall in Love" and the sweet melodious voice of a friend from church start singing the song.

"I think that's our cue, friends." She brushed at her skirt. "Caroline, can you distribute our bouquets?"

"First," Caroline said, "we are going to pray." She held out her hands, and Maxine, Sarah, Angel Dove, and Robin all joined hands, forming a circle. "Dear God, I pray you give Robin a calming strength to get through the next few hours. Give her physical strength, ease her pain in those shoes, and let her just enjoy herself and all of the hard work she put into it."

Robin hugged her when she finished praying. "Thank you, my friend. You are a blessing to me."

"Likewise, love."

Stephanie came rushing in. "This is it," she said, all grins. "I can't wait to see their faces when they see how beautiful you are, Robin." She went to the table with the bouquets. She handed each of the bridesmaids their bouquets of white roses, and then handed Robin the long flowing bouquet of red and white roses.

"Wow," Robin said, lifting it up and down. "You weren't kidding about the weight."

"Okay, Angel Dove. Let's go find your brother." At Caroline's nod,

Angel Dove took Stephanie's hand.

They walked out. Caroline followed in her turn, then Sarah, and Maxine. In the lobby of the church, ten of the twenty ushers milled around, looking smart in their black tuxes. Robin hugged the closest one. "Was it hard organizing everyone?"

"You have a packed house, Robin. I don't think I've ever seen the church this full. We had to have people shift and move to get everyone seats." He tugged at his jacket. "I met Senator Carson. He was really nice. My dad always likes him."

Robin grinned. "That's so exciting."

She heard the last notes of the song play. Everyone lined up at the door, and Craig came to stand by her. Stephanie unhooked her train from the hook on her waist and spread it out behind her while she whispered directions to the two teens tasked with rolling out the runner. The crowd murmured in anticipation during the silence of this act. As the organist began to play, Angel Dove and Isaac, in his tuxedo, entered through the double doors. Robin watched Caroline's head as she kept time with their steps and the organist's rhythm. When it was time, she put her shoulders back, smiled, and stepped into the church.

Sarah looked over her shoulder at Robin. "Yay," she silently cheered. When it was time for her to go, she walked forward.

Maxine grinned and winked at Robin. "You're gorgeous," she said, "Tony's going to fall over." She looked forward, smiled, and started walking.

Robin wanted to go to the doors and peek in, but Stephanie had told her not to because everyone would be craning trying to look at her. Instead, she pulled her veil down and she and Craig waited for Stephanie's signal. When she gestured with her hands, they walked and stood at the entrance.

Robin could see Tony down at the front of the church. The aisle seemed so much longer than it had the night before. When the organist began the wedding march, all of the audience stood to their feet and Robin and Craig started walking down the white runner.

She smiled and made eye contact with friends, church friends, and business friends. When she got closer to the front, she looked right at Tony, and the look of awe and wonder on his face made her realize that every single step in this four-month process had been worth it.

After what seemed like a mile, they reached the end of the aisle. Abram stood in full vestments, looking very handsome and regal. He gestured with his hands and the audience sat down. It took several seconds for everyone to sit and get settled and get quiet.

"Who gives this bride to be married?" he asked.

Craig said in a loud and confident voice, "I do."

Abram nodded, and Craig turned and lifted Robin's veil, smoothly guiding it over her head. Robin held her bouquet with one hand and hugged Craig's neck tight with the other. He cleared his throat and blinked overly wet eyes as he placed Robin's hand in Tony's. As they turned to face Abram, and listened to him talk in beautiful ways about what it meant to be married, Robin whispered to Tony, "I can't believe how much longer that aisle is today than yesterday."

He gave her hand a gentle squeeze. "I didn't think you'd ever make it to me."

She smiled and looked at him. "You look very nice in your Zoot suit."

"Yeah? If you knew how amazing you looked, you'd just be sitting in front of a mirror all day." He lifted her hand and kissed it. "You are the most beautiful woman I have ever laid eyes on."

Robin's heart fluttered at his words. "It was hard to see through this veil."

"I bet."

Abram said, "But that's enough of me because today is about the two of you. Tony and Robin, I invite you to come and begin the adventure of your marriage by declaring your vows to one another here in this place."

She turned and handed Maxine her bouquet. Then she fully faced her husband, placing both of her hands in his. The look in his eyes took her breath away.

"Let everyone hear these words. Tony has proposed matrimony and Robin has graciously accepted. Should there be anyone here who has an objection to the marriage of these two, let that person speak now or forevermore be silent."

Abram waited just a small heartbeat in the silence before continuing. "In the absence of an objection, we will now proceed. Please bow your heads and pray with me."

She bowed her head and listened to the prayer Abram prayed over their future, their lives, and their ministries. While he spoke, Robin prayed that God would bless them and use them in mighty ways, that He would give them wisdom and strength to face adversaries and attacks. And, at the end, she prayed, for the thousandth time, a prayer of thanksgiving for giving her Tony.

As the congregation said, "Amen," in chorus with Abram, they raised their heads and he looked at Robin. "Will you, Robin, take this man, Tony, to be your beloved bridegroom? Will you respect and honor him, comfort and keep him, in good times and in bad, in times of failure and in times of triumph, for better or for worse, for richer, for poorer, in sickness and in health, and – forsaking all others – remain true and faithful to him for as long as you both shall live?"

Robin smiled. "I will."

Abram nodded. "Then in the presence of God and all those gathered here, repeat this solemn vow which you will uphold from this day forward. I, Robin, promise you, Tony, that I will give you my heart and my life."

Robin repeated the words with a strong and clear voice, making sure she conveyed just how much she meant them.

"I will stand by your side in sorrow or in joy."

"I will comfort and encourage you."

"I will support you in all that you do."

"I will laugh with you and cry with you."

"Above all, I will honor and respect you as your loving wife until death us do part."

"This is my solemn vow."

Abram smiled so big Robin wondered if his face would crack. He turned to Tony. "Will you, Antonio, take this woman, Robin, to be your beloved bride? Will you love and cherish her, protect and provide for her, in good times and in bad, in times of failure and in times of triumph, for better or for worse, for richer, for poorer, in sickness and in health, and – forsaking all others – remain true and faithful to her for as long as you both shall live?"

Tony squeezed Robin's hand. "I will."

"Then in the presence of God and all those gathered here, repeat this solemn vow which you will uphold from this day forward," Abram said. "I, Tony, promise you, Robin, that I will give you my heart and my life."

Tony spoke the words clearly, his strong voice ringing through the church. As he repeated the vows he had written for her and with her, she felt tears burning her eyes and furiously blinked them back afraid makeup would run if she let them fall. Every sentence he spoke, she fell more and more in love with him."

"I will stand by your side in sorrow or in joy."

"I will care for you and protect you."

"I will support you in all that you do."

"I will laugh with you and cry with you."

"Above all, I will love and cherish you as your adoring husband until death us do part."

"This is my solemn vow."

The look on his face was intense, making her believe him, telling her that he would treasure her love.

Abram said, "May I have the rings?"

Barry and Maxine both stepped forward to release the rings off of Isaac's pillow. She handed Abram Robin's ring, and Barry handed Abram

Tony's ring. As soon as he was released from ring duty, Isaac dropped his pillow and ran to the front row where his oldest brother sat. Robin could see Peter roll his eyes as a thousand people chuckled.

Abram laughed and then said, "Robin, place the ring upon Tony's finger and repeat after me."

Robin took the ring from Abram and mimicking her moves from the night before, placed it on Tony's finger and said, "With this ring I thee wed."

Abram nodded and said, "Tony, place the ring upon Robin's finger and repeat after me."

Tony gently held her hand and slid the band of sapphires and diamonds onto her left finger. He looked into her eyes and said, "With this ring I thee wed." Just for her benefit, he whispered, "Again."

Robin laughed. Abram paused and nodded, and a man and woman took the stage, getting the microphones from the appropriate place and moving to stand in front of the audience. When they started singing, "When God Made You," Tony and Robin walked hand in hand to a table that had two lit candles and a third unlit. They each took a candle, and together lit the third one, then extinguished the original two, symbolizing the coming together as one.

They moved back to their positions in front of Abram. As the song ended, he said, "By the power vested in me by the Creator of marriage and the church of God, and in accordance with the laws of the state of Massachusetts and these United States, I now pronounce you husband and wife. What God has joined together, let no one put asunder. You may now kiss your bride."

Tony stepped closer and put his hands on her shoulders. When his lips met hers, the audience around them faded away and she felt a warmth flood her body straight through her heart. She put a hand on the back of his neck and willed him closer even as he pulled back. He smiled and lifted her left hand, kissing her knuckles right above her rings. She reached for her bouquet from Maxine, then she and Tony turned around, hand in hand, and faced the congregation. For the first time, Robin looked around and saw every seat full, even in the upper balcony. She squeezed Tony's hand harder, and he laced her fingers with his.

Abram said, "Ladies and gentlemen, allow me to introduce to you for the first time ever, Mr. and Mrs. Antonio Viscolli."

THE END

READER'S GUIDE MENU

SUGGESTED luncheon menu for a group discussion about *Greater Than Rubies*.

Those who follow my Hallee the Homemaker website know that one thing I am passionate about in life is selecting, cooking, and savoring good whole real food. A special luncheon just goes hand in hand with hospitality and ministry.

For those planning a discussion group surrounding these books, I offer some humble suggestions to help your special luncheon talk come off as a success. Quick as you like, you can whip up an appetizer, salad, entree and dessert that is sure to please and certain to enhance your discussion and time of friendship and fellowship.

The Appetizer:

Sarah's Choice Falafel

As a vegan, Sarah's choices at a wedding may sometimes be limited. But, Robin knows what her sister will and won't eat, and this Falafel prepared by Viscolli's chef is a perfect appetizer.

INGREDIENTS:

FOR THE FALAFEL:

1 pound (about 2 cups) dry chickpeas/garbanzo beans
1 small onion, roughly chopped
¼ cup chopped fresh parsley
4 cloves garlic
1 ½ tbsp flour
1 ¾ tsp salt
2 tsp cumin
1 tsp ground coriander
¼ tsp black pepper
¼ tsp cayenne pepper
Pinch of ground cardamom
Grapeseed oil for frying

FOR THE YOGURT SAUCE:

1 cup plain Greek yogurt
½ TBS lemon zest
1 TBS freshly squeezed lemon juice
1 TBS chopped cilantro leaves
2 tsp chopped parsley leaves
½ teaspoon ground cumin
salt, as needed (Kosher or sea salt is best)

PREPARATION:

Cover the chick peas with cold water and let them soak overnight. They will double in size to about 4-5 cups of beans.

Chop the onion.

Chop the parsley (divided) and cilantro

Zest and squeeze the lemon.

DIRECTIONS:

Mix the ingredients for the yogurt sauce and refrigerate.

Drain and rinse the garbanzo beans well. Pour them into a food processor along with the chopped onion, garlic cloves, parsley, flour, salt, cumin, ground coriander, black pepper, cayenne pepper, and cardamom.

Pulse all ingredients together until a rough, coarse meal forms. Scrape the sides of the processor periodically and push the mixture down the sides. Process till the mixture is still textured but going toward a paste. (You don't want to over mix).

Transfer to a bowl. Cover and refrigerate for 2 hours.

Fill a deep skillet with $1 \frac{1}{2}$ inches grapeseed oil. Heat over medium heat. While the oil heats, take 2 TBS of the falafel mixture and form it into a slightly squished ball. (The balls may not stick perfectly together as you're forming them, but they will bind together once you start frying.)

Gently place the balls into the oil, a few at a time, and fry for 3 minutes. Using a slotted spoon, gently turn them over and fry for another 3 minutes. Remove from oil and drain on a paper towel.

Serve with the yogurt sauce.

The Vegetable:

Cauliflower Mashed Potatoes with Asparagus

Nothing beats a creamy cauliflower mashed potato, and the steamed asparagus pair perfectly with the Rosemary Garlic Lamb served at Robin and Tony's wedding.

INGREDIENTS:

15 red skinned potatoes
1 large cauliflower head
¼ cup butter
¼ cup half and half
1 ½ tsp salt (divided) (Kosher or sea salt is best)
¼ tsp fresh ground black pepper
2 asparagus stems per person

PREPARATION:

Scrub the potatoes. Cut into chunks.

Break the cauliflower into small chunks

DIRECTIONS:

Place the potatoes in a pot of cold water. Add 1 tsp salt. Bring to a boil.

Place the cauliflower in a steamer basket and place into the pot with the potatoes so that it can steam while the potatoes cook.

Cook the potatoes until a fork inserts into them easily.

Drain and transfer the potatoes and cauliflower to a bowl and mash (or us a potato ricer). Stir in the butter, cream, salt, and pepper.

While you're mashing the potatoes and cauliflower, steam the asparagus for 5 minutes.

Serve the cauliflower mashed potatoes with two pieces of asparagus draped over them.

The Entree:

Rosemary Garlic Lamb Chops

The Boston Viscolli Hotel is well known for 5-star international cuisine. Robin went with one of their specialties, rosemary garlic lamb, for her wedding banquet.

INGREDIENTS:

Lamb Loin Chops – 2 per person

extra virgin olive oil – about 1 TBS chops

1 clove of garlic per 2 chops

1 sprig of rosemary per 2 chops

salt to taste (Kosher or sea salt is best)

fresh ground pepper to taste

PREPARATION:

Mince the garlic.

Remove the rosemary leaves from the stems and chop the leaves.

DIRECTIONS:

Lightly spray or using your finger, wipe, olive oil on the chops.

Rub the garlic and rosemary onto the lamb. Salt and pepper to taste.

Cover and refrigerate for several hours.

Cook on a hot grill or a hot skillet for about 10 minutes per side for medium to medium rare lamb. If you want it done a little more, cook it to your taste.

The Dessert:

Heavenly Chocolate Covered Strawberries

Robin and Tony give their wedding guests the gift of chocolate covered strawberries decorated to look like wedding gowns and tuxedos.

INGREDIENTS:

1 pound ripe, organic strawberries with stems

6 ounces dark chocolate

3 ounces white chocolate

PREPARATION:

Chop the dark chocolate and the white chocolate separately.

DIRECTIONS:

Melt both the dark and the white chocolate (separately) completely in a double broiler.d

Dip the strawberries into the dark chocolate. Lift and twist, letting the excess chocolate drip off. Carefully set on parchment paper.

Dip a fork into the white chocolate and drizzle the dark chocolate covered strawberries.

Let chocolate set for about 30 minutes.

Hallee Bridgeman

READER'S GUIDE DISCUSSION QUESTIONS

SUGGESTED luncheon discussion group questions for *Greater Than Rubies*.

When asking ourselves how important the truth is to our Creator, we can look to the reason Jesus said he was born. In the book of John 18:37, Jesus explains that for this reason He was born and for this reason He came into the world. The reason? To testify to the truth.

In bringing those He ministered to into an understanding of the truth, Our Lord used fiction in the form of parables to illustrate very real truths. In the same way, we can minister to one another by the use of fictional characters and situations to help us to reach logical, valid, cogent, and very sound conclusions about our real lives here on earth.

While the characters and situations in *The Jewel Series* are fictional, I pray that these extended parables can help readers come to a better understanding of truth. Please prayerfully consider the questions that follow, consult scripture, and pray upon your conclusions. May the Lord of the universe richly bless you.

Tony felt led by the Holy Spirit to help Derrick DiNunzio. He followed through with that guidance and opened his home up to him.

1. What was your reaction to Tony's willingness to heed the call of the Holy Spirit?

2. How often do we as Christians ignore the need of at risk youth in our cities?

3. What can we as Christians do to help *more* at risk youth?

Jacqueline Anderson took Robin shopping to teach her how to adorn herself "more suitably" as Tony Viscolli's wife.

> 4. Do you agree that appearance is important? How important or unimportant is one's appearance when you are evaluating his or her character or intentions? How do you think your appearance may influence those around you positively or negatively?

Tony uses a board game as an allegory for life on this earth when he witnesses to Derrick.

> 5. Did Tony's illustration with the Monopoly board in any way change your perception of material possessions?

Tony is willing to get rid of his vast fortune in order to keep Robin by his side. Read Luke 18:18-23.

> 6. Do you think Tony would have really given up "everything" to be with Robin?

> 7. Christ has likened His relationship with the church as a marriage. What would you be willing to give up to follow Christ?

Read Abram Rabinovich's sermon during Robin and Tony's wedding ceremony.

> 8. Do you agree with Abram's definition of marriage?

> 9. What do you think it means to "give up oneself" for your spouse?

Book 2 of the Jewel Series

Includes Reader's Guide

Inspirational Novel of the Year

EMERALD Fire

HALLEE BRIDGEMAN

Hallee Bridgeman

EMERALD FIRE - COPYRIGHT NOTICE

EMERALD Fire

Emerald Fire, Book 2 of the Jewel Series

Fourth Edition. Copyright © 2012 by Hallee Bridgeman. All rights reserved.

Original Cover Art and Graphics by Debi Warford (www.debiwarford.com)

Boston photo by Robert Lowe (username rmlowe on Flickr) licensed under Creative Commons (CC) license

---

Library Cataloging Data

Bridgeman, Hallee (Hallee A. Bridgeman) 1972-
  Emerald Fire; Jewel Series part 2 / Hallee Bridgeman
    p. 23cm x 15cm (9in x 6 in.)
Summary: Beautiful, vivacious Maxine Bartlett finally finds a love that releases her from the prison of her terrifying past.
  ISBN: 978-1-939603-34-0 (trade perfect) ISBN-10: 1-939603-34-X
ISBN: 978-1-452449-71-5 (ebook) ISBN: 978-1-476194-91-2 (text only)
1. Christian fiction 2. man-woman relationships 3. love stories 4. family relationships

  PS3568.B7534 E447 2012
  [Fic.] 813.6 (DDC 23)

EMERALD FIRE - PROLOGUE

THAT afternoon, Maxine Bartlett had watched two policemen drag her sister, Robin, kicking and screaming, away. Maxine could remember with perfect clarity Robin's blood soaked clothes, the blood on her hands, the ferocious look on her face, her blonde curls damp with sweat born of fury, one shoe kicked off in her struggle with the police. They'd separated the girls, bundling Robin into the back of a police car and Maxine into the back of an ambulance. For the first time in her fourteen year long life, Maxine no longer had Robin beside her. She felt completely alone.

And absolutely terrified.

Maxine clutched the broken strap of her backpack tightly while she stared down at the hole in the toe of her sneakers. She let her straight black hair dangle down in front of her face while she kept her head bowed, effectively shielding her from the outside world. Despite her many questions, no one would tell her anything.

The visit to the county hospital in the heart of Boston had humiliated her. A rushed female doctor poked and prodded and scraped and assured that "this won't hurt a bit" right before hurting Maxine quite a bit. The whole while, a female nurse with bored and somewhat distracted eyes and an absent touch chaperoned the ordeal, snapping occasional Polariods each time the doctor requested one. Someone brought her some new underwear and a pair of scrubs that hung loosely on her long skinny body. The clean scrubs looked starkly bright against Maxine's darker skin and straight black hair.

Five long hours later, a harried social worker arrived and collected Maxine. She introduced herself politely and Maxine instantly forgot the woman's name.

So here she stood – her fourth foster home in just under two years. She could hear other kids playing somewhere out of sight. She wondered, briefly, if anyone her age lived here. She took time to wonder, yet again, where Robin was and what was happening with her – or to her.

She zoned in on the conversation the nameless social worker was having with foster mother number four, catching the last part of the sentence.

"...watch her closely for any kind of symptoms, since she refused any prophylactic measures. She has two sisters, and is looking for information on them. I'll see what I can find out."

Maxine flinched and shifted away as the foster mother tried to lay a hand on her shoulder. She felt heat flush her cheeks when she realized what she'd done and tried to relax. The woman didn't reach out again. Fine by Maxine.

"... any other injuries? Does she have stitches or anything that will require special care?"

"Just bruises. No broken bones or open wounds, thank goodness. I'd say she's lucky except, of course, he hurt her in other ways..."

Maxine wished she could drown out their voices. She missed her music, her earphones. She wondered if her Walkman made it into her backpack or if it got left behind. She'd investigate what got packed later.

"Do I need to worry about the other children?" foster mother number four asked.

The social worker flipped through the file in her hand. Maxine knew it was all about her and felt the flush on her cheeks spread to her ears and down her neck. "There's no telling, honestly. Her mother died violently, her sister obviously displays violent tendencies, her last home environment was less than ideal..."

Maxine lowered her head and let the curtain of hair encase her in solitude once more. She kept her head bowed and tried to make her hair completely hide her strongly native American features.

She let her thoughts drift away again, not wanting to hear them talk about her anymore. She imagined herself on the docks listening to the sound of the water slap against the side of the boats harbored there. In her imagination, seagulls squawked overhead, flying against the bright blue sky. She could smell fish and wet wood and salt water and felt the bright spring sun shining down on her black hair.

Her second grade class had gone to a seaport museum once. Maxine fell in love with the docks then and used those few hours she spent there years ago as her refuge – her solace against the horrible outside world.

In her mind's eye, she imagined that her sisters Robin and Sarah stood on either side of her, each holding her hands, as they looked out over the expanse of the sea. The breeze blew Sarah's little curls against her pale cheek. Maxine wondered if Sarah was still really tiny or if finding a good foster home had helped her put on some weight. Almost two years had gone by since that fateful night, and she'd looked like a six year old instead of a nine year old. None of them had ever really eaten well, and Sarah's body just couldn't handle the lack of nutrition.

Robin stood strong and tall against the wind, a force to be reckoned with at the ripe old age of seventeen. She acted as Maxine and Sarah's protector, their defender, and their caregiver. Without her, Maxine didn't know what would have happened to them.

All of a sudden, Robin's face started to lose detail. Then she faded away altogether. Where was Robin? What would happen to her, now? Would Robin vanish just as Sarah had vanished from her life?

If she could find the right song, if she could figure out the right music to pump into her ears, it would make all the bad thoughts go away. She wanted her earphones. She wanted the bad thoughts to go away.

Their mother had used a lot of drugs, which really meant she had used a lot of men to get drugs. When she tired of them or they tired of her, she'd move on to the next man, dragging her daughters along in tow. Robin knew of the dangers, through experiences she would not talk about, and taught her sisters how to hide in closets, how to be quiet as mice, how to go unnoticed in a room filled with used syringes and empty gin bottles, smelling so much like old copper and cheap pine cleaner.

Robin would put her arms around her sisters in the dark and sing under her breath, sometimes. She didn't like music so much but it soothed her younger siblings. What did Robin used to sing when things got really bad? She couldn't remember.

The sisters survived it. Their mother didn't. While the sisters hid in the closet and their mother argued with the man who would be the last in a long line of boyfriends, an unseen killer burst into the apartment and murdered them both. When the police came, they took Sarah to a good home and took Robin and Maxine to the first of several foster homes. The two older sisters clung to each other and vowed to get Sarah back one day so that they could stay together and face the world as one.

Now they were all separated. Maxine didn't know what to do without Robin there to guide her, so she clung to Robin's hand on that imaginary dock. She breathed in the scent of the ocean. They continued to talk very loudly about exactly what had happened to her just as if she weren't standing right there next to them. She tried to hum really loudly to drown out the noise of what's-her-name the social worker and newest foster mother four million miles away from the place in her thoughts.

"Maxine?"

Startled, Maxine returned to the little house in the suburbs of Boston and realized that the social worker had departed. Maxine stood alone in the foyer with new – newest – foster mother. She brushed her hair out of her eyes and blinked. "Yes?"

"Maxine, I'm Juliette. Do you like to be called Maxine?"

Maxine shook her head.

"Well, I have to call you something. What do you like to be called, sweetie?" Juliette asked.

"Max. Or Maxi." The words came out slowly, as if she had to form them out of a sticky dough and let the dough rise first.

"Max it is, then. You can call me Juliette or Jules. My husband, Steven, will be home from work soon. You'll meet him then."

Maxine nodded and tried to swallow around the fist of fear that had closed on her throat. What would Steven be like?

"Max, Steve is a very good man. He was named for the disciple, Stephen, in the Bible. Do you know that story?" Maxine shook her head. "Well, that's okay. I'll tell you the story later if you like. Or maybe he can tell you."

Maxine could feel her lip quivering and she tried to make it stop. She didn't want to show any weakness or uncertainty. She couldn't afford it. She had to remain strong until she could find Robin. She made herself a promise that she could endure anything that happened until she found Robin again.

"There are four other children here. Three girls and a boy. I expect you will get along fine with my girls. But you know, little boys are different. He's going to be sad that you aren't a boy. When we got the call this morning, he was hopeful." Juliette smiled, but Maxine was still thinking about the husband, Steve, Stephen, from the Bible, who was due home any second. "They're in the play room, for now. I thought maybe you'd like to help out for a little while instead of meeting them just yet."

Maxine tried to keep her face composed, and forced a whisper out. "Help you do what?"

"I have a studio in the garage. I'm cleaning out some of my old paintings so I'll have room to store my new ones. Why don't you give me a hand and we'll talk and get to know each other better."

The idea of paintings caught Maxine's attention. She loved paintings and loved to draw. She felt the fingers of apprehension loosen their grip around her gut and shifted her backpack to her other hand. "Sure."

Juliette smiled and gestured grandly. "This way to the garage," she said. "We'll keep the scrubs on you for now, because there are some dusty corners in there. I have my husband stopping at the store on his way home to get you some decent clothes. Just enough until you and I can go to the store tomorrow morning. As soon as he gets here, you can go take a long bath and stay in the tub just as long as you want. Just for tonight, it's okay."

Maxine slowly nodded her understanding.

Jules put a hand on Maxine's shoulder and searched her eyes. "You wash every single inch and scrub really good. And when you get out of the tub, you put on your fresh new clothes, and then I am going to give you a manicure and a pedicure. Do you know what that is?"

Maxine guessed she was just keeping her away from the other kids because of her "less than ideal" previous home, but she was okay with that.

She wasn't quite ready to face other kids without Robin by her side, anyway.

"You want to do my nails?"

Juliette smiled. "The girls will help. We can all get to know you and you can get to know us a little better. And tomorrow, you will wake up feeling fresh and clean and you can start a brand new day in your new home."

They walked toward the garage and Maxine knew home was with Robin, not here with Juliette and Steven. But she wondered what waking up feeling fresh and clean would really feel like.

EMERALD FIRE - CHAPTER 1

MAXINE rolled over in the bed. As the blankets slipped off, she felt cool air on her shoulders. While her partially asleep brain pondered that, she tugged the sheets back up to cover herself and her ring caught a thread on the blanket.

Her ring?

Maxine's eyes flew open as memories of the night before flooded her mind. She whipped her head around and stared at the empty space in the bed next to her, the pillow indented from where her husband's head had lain.

Her husband!

Alone in the bedroom, she lifted her left hand and stared. There sat the ridiculously enormous, preposterously expensive platinum ring, encrusted with emeralds and diamonds, that the man with whom she had been engaged for less than two hours before their wedding ceremony had picked out for her. When he slipped it onto her finger, he'd said something about the color of her eyes. Seconds later, he'd kissed her.

After a cursory glance around the room to be certain she was actually alone and the bedroom door was shut, she threw off the covers and rushed to the closet, looking for anything at all to wear. She grabbed a pair of jeans and a sweater and dashed to the bathroom, shutting and locking the door behind her. She leaned against the closed door for a moment while her heart raced and her mind reeled.

What in the name of all things holy had they done? Rather, what had she done?

With a few flicks of her wrist, she turned the water on for a shower and stopped to look at herself in the mirror. She lifted her fingers to her mouth and traced lips swollen from his kisses. Her green eyes sparkled like the stones on her hand. She normally had straight black hair and olive skin, both traits inherited from her father, a nameless one-night stand her mother would only ever crudely and often drunkenly refer to as Crazy Horse. But this morning her hair was mussed all around her head and her cheeks looked rosy, flushed. She felt warm inside despite the morning chill.

In her entire adult life, no other man had ever even so much as kissed her. Not once. Many men had tried to taste her mouth, but whenever they'd gotten close enough, panic would rise up and make her push them away. That typically ended the relationship. The ones who suffered that humiliation soon learned that it wasn't a one-time thing and very quickly gave up trying. As she stepped under the warm spray of water, she thought back to the night before and to her complete lack of fear.

Her husband of less than twelve hours – her husband didn't frighten her at all. When he kissed her, it occurred to her that she felt absolutely none of her normal panic. Instead, what she felt was warmth, excitement, attraction. He made her feel safe. He made her feel ... loved.

"Husband and wife," the Elvis impersonating officiator had proclaimed with a shimmy and a shake. Then her husband had slowly leaned in, leaned close, and taken her lips with his strong, masculine mouth as if her lips were the most delicate rose petals. Her knees had vanished and she felt his arm around her waist holding her up, lifting her, supporting her as she kissed his heavenly mouth.

Then, here, in this hotel suite last night, her husband had carefully led the way. It was as if he sensed that she needed to be able to control the pace of the activity. She never had to say anything to him or explain her fear. He just accepted her hesitations or kissed her through them. He slowly coaxed and guided and offered until she accepted. It had been so wonderful, so beautiful, that he had held her to him with her head cradled against his broad, thick chest and his strong arms around her while she wept at the beauty of it.

Her sister, Robin, was going to kill her. Reflecting on that for a moment, Maxine realized she didn't much care. She was excited, thrilled. Married!

She quickly finished showering and got dressed. After brushing her teeth and running a comb through her hair, she left the bathroom, again comforted by the solitude. Little nervous butterflies woke up in her stomach while she slipped into her shoes, the sight of the enormous ring on her finger distracting her with every motion of her hand.

Stalling, she straightened the bed. As she pulled the coverlet up, her ring caught the light. Running her hand over his pillow, she smiled and felt a warm rush of love flow through her heart, quelling the nervous butterflies.

When she could think of nothing else to do, she opened the bedroom door and stepped out into the living room. Seeing him standing there staring out into the sunrise brought back visions of every time she had seen his face in the last three years. She thought of every time she had sketched his face. She could not believe how much had happened in the last three weeks.

The thought stopped her. Three weeks? Had it only been that long since they put her brand new husband's first wife in the ground?

He turned as soon as she opened the door and their eyes met across the room. Maxine's smile froze at the stoic look on his face. "Hi." His voice sounded low, scratchy, thick. She wondered if he had slept at all.

"Hi." She smiled. She noticed the cup in his hand. "Is there coffee, too, or just tea?"

Using the cup, he gestured at the room service cart sitting next to the table and chairs. "I didn't know how to make the coffee, so I just ordered you some instead."

Warmth flooded her heart at his thoughtfulness. "Thank you." She crossed the room and poured herself a cup. Her hand shook a little bit. What did they do now? What did they talk about? How did she handle this first full day of being a wife? His wife? More than anything at all, she wanted to please him.

When she turned back around, she saw that he had silently moved and now stood next to the couch.

"Obviously, we need to talk."

She didn't like the sound of his voice. No warmth, nothing she had felt from him the night before existed in his tone. She gripped the cup so hard she was surprised it didn't break. "Yeah." Needing to ease her own tension, she teased, "Kind of a little late for that, isn't it?"

SIX WEEKS EARLIER...

BARRY Anderson sat on the bench behind the little kitchen table in the alcove of his kitchen. His former linebacker physique made the bench look like an ottoman and the table look like an end table. He stared at his reflection in the huge bay window that looked out into his back yard without really seeing his reflected piercing blue eyes, close cropped blonde hair, or stony expression.

A closed Bible sat next to a steaming cup of tea and his mobile phone kept buzzing with incoming texts. As recently as a few months ago, Barry would have pored over the scriptures for up to an hour before leaving for the office. His morning habit would have had him meditating and praying over the space of his commute. This morning, Barry ignored the Bible, the tea, and the phone as he had for weeks.

Instead, he let his mind wander.

Had someone pulled him aside twenty years ago and asked his twenty-year-old self what he thought marriage would be like, never in a million years would he have answered that marriage resembled his present reality. He could never have imagined he'd be living in separate bedrooms from a woman who treated him like something she wanted to clean off the bottom of her shoe.

He remembered when they had met their Freshman year of college. He had worked hard for a football scholarship, and she had made the cheerleading squad. They were wed eighteen years ago, the day after graduation, with all their friends and family still in town. He couldn't imagine a more beautiful woman to be his wife. According to those present, they were a match made in heaven.

That heaven only lasted about five years. Now, six or seven months out of the year, Jacqueline barely uttered two words to him while coming and going at her leisure; taking summer trips with "friends," or enjoying extended vacations away from Boston – and away from Barry. Lately, Barry practically enjoyed the solitude during her absences and generally managed to ignore the special circumstances.

He threw himself into work and church activities and watched the occasional game with his best friend, Tony Viscolli, or Tony's sister-in-law, Maxine. Maxine knew more about football than most of his former coaches and was as passionate about the game as Barry himself.

So for about half the year, Barry coped with unwanted solitude and earnestly prayed that God would soften Jacqueline's heart and bring her back to him as his wife. However, when the leaves started turning, that time of year the couple typically established an informal truce. Football season for a former professional athlete was a very social time. The early winter holidays brought parties and more social occasions. Former college cheerleader, Jacqueline, craved that lifestyle. Since Barry required either a hostess or a date, and Jacqueline lived for the social lifestyle, it worked out for both of them.

Fall and winter fed her need for attention and fed him hope. Hope that this year, during their annual armistice, she would let herself love him again, or at least respect him, if even just a little.

In his memory, he replayed the last meaningful encounter he had with his wife which had taken place just over a month ago. Football season had just started, and the New England Patriots had a home game that week. Barry and Jacqueline had maintained season tickets ever since Barry retired from professional football years ago, and they almost never missed a home game.

That September morning, his Bible sat open before him and he had occasionally taken of sip of his steaming hot tea while he refreshed his knowledge of Paul's letter to the church at Ephesus. A landscaper with a backpack blower had walked along the edge of the covered pool blowing leaves off the stretched canvas. Another worked in the far corner of the yard using a different machine to mulch a pile of leaves. The noise and the activity hadn't stolen Barry's attention from God's word.

He'd heard Jacqueline come into the kitchen and glanced at his watch. It was still early. Jacqueline never made an appearance before eleven, so a nine-thirty emergence threw him off his game.

With some concern, he had noted that she looked sick. Her normally immaculately coifed deep red hair lay stringy and flat against her head. Her pale face accented the deep circles she'd had under her eyes. With shaking hands, she pushed her hair out of her face.

"Good morning," he'd offered.

"Barry," was her rejoinder. Jacqueline had retrieved a bottle of water from the refrigerator then surprised him by coming to the table and sitting down next to him. She'd pushed his Bible toward the center of the table and out of her way, propped her elbows on the table and cupped her chin in her palms, then announced, "We need to talk."

"Oh?" A million things they needed to talk about had cascaded through his mind like a waterfall of thought. They could rationally discuss the way their marriage had started crumbling the instant he turned down a new football contract and decided to practice law instead. They could discuss the emotional distance between them that stretched wider each day like a bottomless chasm. They could discuss the fact that she had flatly and repeatedly refused to join him in visiting a Christian marriage counselor.

"This doesn't have to be a fight," she'd snarled.

Keeping his voice calm, even soothing, he'd rhetorically asked, "Who's fighting?"

He'd watched her face relax from the snarl. "You're right." Then, unbelievably, she whispered, "I'm sorry."

I'm sorry. Barry had let the words sink in and started silently praying. *God, if she's finally coming to me to start to set this right, please keep me from messing it up.*

He'd turned on the bench to directly face her. "Okay. What do you think we need to talk about, Jacqui?"

As Jacqueline had taken a sip of her water, her hand shook so badly that some of it splashed out of the top of the bottle. She'd wiped her chin and tears filled her eyes. "I don't know where to start." Giant tears fell from her lashes and slid down her face.

Barry's heart had tightened in his chest and he reached for her. "Jacqui, baby, come here." When she'd slipped her arms around his neck and sat on his lap, he'd felt like he was transported back twenty years, to a time of love, life, happiness. He'd pulled her close in that moment.

Her tears had soaked the shoulder of his shirt. For a long time, he had just been content to hold his wife. *Please, God, soothe my wife. Soften her heart toward me. Let her hear your voice. Stir the waters in her heart and let her know that she needs You in her life. Let her know that I can help her come to You.*

"What is it, Jax?" He'd asked, using a private pet name he hadn't uttered in more than a decade. "What's wrong?"

Jacqueline had sat back and looked up at him. She'd looked absolutely exhausted and deathly pale. "I'm sorry," she'd said, pushing all the way away and standing up. "I don't know what came over me. I'm so emotional right now."

Barry had taken her hand. It always looked like a child's toy in his enormous grasp. "It's okay."

"No." With her other hand, she'd covered his, sandwiching his massive hand between her two small palms. "Barry, I'm pregnant."

For a heartbeat, his world had frozen. Even the buzzing sound of the leaf blower outside vanished from his senses. Barry had felt his heart stop, heard a roaring in his ears, and all at once, what she said struck him. Hard. "Is that a fact." It wasn't a question.

She'd nodded and then smiled. She'd smiled. She'd smiled just like she felt really happy. Like she had a right to be happy. Like ripping his heart to shreds gave her the right to be happy.

"We haven't –"

"I know, silly. Why do you have to act so dense all the time?"

Barry stood, then. Something about his movement made her eyes widen. At six-nine, he easily towered over his wife. "Silly? Dense?"

For the first time in their marriage, he'd felt like lashing out in anger. Physically lashing out. Recognizing that, realizing that, he had crossed the room to put space between them. Jacqueline, apparently unaware of how close she had come to being knocked unconscious in her own kitchen, had followed him. She'd reached out and reclaimed his hand once more. He'd stared down their joined fingers, noting her long red nails and the giant diamond ring on her left hand. How could someone so small make him wish he were dead?

"Barry, I don't know what to do. Charles –" Her breath had hitched and she'd squeezed her hands together almost painfully gripping his. "He's married and he is really angry with me right now."

The roaring in his ears had distracted him. He'd had a hard time understanding what she was babbling about. "So you know who the father is, at least."

"Don't be nasty."

He had simply raised an eyebrow. "Asking kind of a lot right this second, aren't you, darling?"

"I said I was sorry, Barry."

She's sorry. That makes everything better. His voice had sounded icy even in his own ears. "And the father of your only begotten soon to arrive bundle of joy is angry, apparently."

Good thing someone's allowed to be angry, he thought.

Jacqueline had nodded. "Yeah. He thinks I should get rid of it. He won't have anything to do with me until I do. I just don't know what to do." She then stepped forward and put her hand on his cheek. "Can you help me?"

He'd thought, Help her? HELP her? Is this God's sick way of saving my marriage?

Barry had cleared his throat and stared down at his wife of eighteen years. His wife. His responsibility. Was God punishing him for not covering her? Not husbanding her? Leading her? Anger, betrayal, hurt, and deep humiliation warred with duty, honor, forgiveness, and love. He'd managed to strangle out, "Exactly how is it that you want me to help you, Mrs. Anderson?"

"Couldn't we just, I don't know, go back to the way it was?"

"The way it was?" he'd prompted.

"You know. Before we started fighting all the time."

"You mean like that time when we vowed in front of God and a church full of witnesses that we would love, honor, and cherish each other until death us do part?" He'd pushed her away. "Is that how far back you want to go?"

Jacqueline had buried her face in her hands and sobbed. "You're right," she'd wailed. "I've been awful. But can't we just put all that behind us for the sake of the baby?"

For the sake of the baby. Of another man's child. A married man, at that.

"I'm just not sure –"

Jacqueline then fell to her knees in front of him and grabbed the hem of his shirt. "Please, Barry. Please don't abandon me. Please. You've always wanted this. You've always wanted me to love you again. I'll do anything. Just don't make me go through this alone."

She was right. He desperately wanted nothing more than to have his wife back. But at this cost? At the cost of raising another man's child?

Maybe. With God's help, maybe he could.

"How long have you known?" His massive arms crossed across his broad chest. He'd felt his heart beating like a stampede beneath his forearm and he strained to keep his breathing even.

"I found out a week ago."

He'd snorted in disgust and wasn't even ashamed that he had audibly expressed his disdain. What frustrated him almost entirely was a very unexpected realization. Truth be told, no matter how bad things got, no matter how angry or ashamed or disappointed he felt, the ferocious and inescapable fact was that he loved his wife.

He'd felt the Holy Spirit telling him that he needed to keep her close, make her feel secure, help her feel safe. A tiny little part of him, a dark little part he wasn't exactly proud of, wanted to hurt her back and ignored the divine voice in his heart. She had pushed him away for a decade, belittled him, disrespected him, shunned him, and ultimately betrayed him. In the space of a heartbeat, Barry had surrendered to an overwhelming impulse to push her away and let her feel some of that same insecurity and uncertainty she had inflicted on him for years.

"Jacqueline, I need some time to think about all this." He'd tried to unclench his jaw and speak very calmly. He then bent down and helped her to her feet. "I need to process it. You've had a week. I need more than a few minutes. How about you go somewhere else. Give me some space so I can think about all this."

So it came down to trust. If she was sincere about a fresh start, she would have to prove it to him. He was going to give her a week or two of insecurity and see if she ran back to her married boyfriend or came back to her husband.

"Barry, I ..."

At the sound of her voice, the fear and desperation, he'd taken a little bit of pity on her. "I'm done talking for now. I'll call you when I'm ready to talk again. Don't be here when I get home. I will call you, Jacqui." With that little bit of hope for reconciliation stated aloud, he'd turned and left the room, leaving his pregnant wife, his tea, and his Bible behind.

He had hoped and he had prayed for the last month and a half. The result? This morning, he set his tea cup atop the Bible he hadn't opened in weeks, snatched up his mobile phone, and headed to the office leaving his empty house behind.

Chapter 2

THE Grand Ballroom of the Viscolli hotel in downtown Boston stood empty, a clean slate ready for whatever the half-sisters, Maxine Bartlett and Sarah Thomas, could throw at it. They stood together in the center of the room, one of many huge chandeliers directly above them. Maxine idly tapped a fingernail against her lips as she spun in a circle.

Sarah, a fresh *cum laude* nursing school graduate and the newest member of the obstetrics team at St. Catherine's hospital, wore her surgical scrubs and clasped hairpins in her teeth while she twisted her mass of strawberry blonde curls into some semblance of order.

Maxine stood next to her clad in a camel colored suede suit, the long skirt falling just to her calves and brushing against the tops of her brown leather boots. With the heels on the boots, Sarah barely came up to Maxine's shoulder.

"You know," Sarah said as she pinned the last pin, "most people do the planning before the day of the event." In twelve short hours, the room would fill with hundreds of people, friends and acquaintances of their elder sister, Robin Viscolli, and her husband Tony, all in celebration of the impending birth of the couple's first child. Tony, a self-made entrepreneur, owned this hotel along with many other businesses in Boston and beyond.

"I selected and ordered all the food and flowers, I just never worked it all into the room." Maxine glanced at her watch. She couldn't believe it was already seven in the morning. "I think the day snuck up on me. I'm going to blame Cassandra. She's the event coordinator here."

"Hard for her to sneak anything by Tony in his own hotel. Besides, the last time she tried to help you, you shot her down. I bet she figured you'd let her know what you needed."

"What makes you say that?"

Maxine turned to look at Sarah, who smiled a very sarcastic, sweet smile. "Because that's what I do."

"Yeah? What have you done for this party?" Maxine teased, knowing exactly how hard Sarah had worked.

"I mailed 500 invitations and logged RSVP's. Quite a bit more labor intensive than deciding between yellow roses or Gerbera daisies for the centerpieces."

Ignoring Sarah's sarcastic jab, Maxine checked her phone. "I still haven't heard from Jacqui."

Sarah frowned. "How are we going to run the games if she isn't here?"

"Maybe we just won't have games," Maxine said. "How were we going to do it with 500 people, anyway?"

"We ordered the supplies she needed, and we have the game instructions, so we'll just have to do it for her," Sarah said. "It's a baby shower. You have to have games. That's what you do."

Maxine spotted Derrick DiNunzio coming through the far door. "Derrick!" she called, waving her hand.

She crossed the carpeted floor with long, graceful strides. Sarah followed, almost at a run compared to Maxine's fast walk. Derrick nodded and lifted his hand in greeting. By the time they reached him, Maxine felt a huge grin on her face. She loved Derrick and had since the first day she met him.

Three years ago, Derrick had shown up at Tony's office with a worn business card in hand, following up on an employment promise Tony had made him. As good as his word, Tony took Derrick in and made him his protégé. At present, Derrick was finishing up college. Surrounded by the luxury of the Viscolli ballroom, wearing a thick cream colored sweater and navy slacks as easily as he wore a quiet inner strength and outer confidence, Maxine could not pick out anything about Derrick, his demeanor, his accent, or his countenance, that suggested he hadn't grown up surrounded by anything other than love and riches.

Though Derrick made eye contact with Maxine first, and though Maxine reached him first, it was Sarah to whom he first spoke with an ironic lift of a single eyebrow and an undeniable teasing tone in his voice. "Hiya, sweetheart."

After Robin and Tony's wedding, Sarah and Derrick had lived under the same roof with Tony and Robin for a full year while Sarah finished nursing school. Even so, instead of treating each other like acquaintances, they barely tolerated each other. Maxine watched in fascination as her younger sister's lip curled in unfeigned loathing, astonished by the force of her sister's reaction this morning. Sarah's increasing vehemence toward Derrick never ceased to amaze Maxine. The way Derrick invited it – nicknaming her petite half sister "sweetheart" for example – also presented a perpetual puzzle.

"I told you not to call me that." Sarah's voice came out low and laced with loathing.

Derrick appeared utterly oblivious to Sarah's venom. "Whatever you say, sweetheart." Before Maxine could give much more thought to the interplay between them, Derrick's grin grew wide and his eyes danced with genuine mirth as he took in the sight of her. "Maxi! You look like a hundred bucks."

Maxine laughed at his teasing and explained, "I've only had one cup of coffee so far."

Derrick's eyebrow quirked and he said, "We'll have to fix that."

Maxine opened her mouth to enthusiastically agree when Sarah unexpectedly piped up, "As if you could fix anything. Where's Cassandra?" Sarah crossed her arms and glared at Derrick from beneath her strawberry curls. Rather than making her appear threatening, her stance comically transformed her into a Little Orphan Annie double.

Instead of reacting, Derrick insinuatingly winked at Sarah before turning his attention back to Maxine. "I have an army of help ready to place tables and chairs where they need to go. I also have confirmation of a flower delivery at noon, and Chef Armand called up from the pastry kitchen to let you know that the cake is ready for you to view."

Maxine looked at her watch again and mentally structured her day. "Okay. I have a nine-thirty meeting in the restaurant here, so hopefully I can get everything organized and still be able to put in a couple of hours this afternoon at the office."

"My shift starts at eleven," Sarah said, pulling her phone out of her pocket to check the time. "So I can help until ten. My roommate is going to cover for me this afternoon, so I should be able to be back by four."

Derrick reached into the pocket of his slacks and pulled out several sheets of graph paper. "I knew you hadn't met with Cassandra yet, so I sketched a few possible ideas for layout of the room." As Maxine took the sheets from him, he looked at Sarah. "How many people RSVP'd?"

"Four eighty-six," she said, "but there was also an announcement made at church. I'd count on at least fifty more."

"Maybe we should plan for six hundred."

"Maybe we should plan for five-forty," Sarah sneered. "Otherwise, you're going to end up with a bunch of empty tables."

"I think you're going to get more than fifty from an open invitation at a church that size."

"Why? Because the Viscollis are so amazing?"

Maxine watched Derrick's eyes look Sarah's petite body up and down. "Someone certainly is," he observed.

Sarah gasped as Derrick turned his attention back to Maxine once again. "Well?"

"Let's split the difference," she said. "Five-seventy?"

Derrick nodded and pulled a two-way radio from a clip on his belt. "Rubert? Five-seventy, as we discussed yesterday."

"As you discussed?" Maxine laughed.

Derrick waited for the confirmation from the catering department's head sous chef before turning the volume down on the radio and re-clipping it. He shrugged. "I guessed."

"Hotel and restaurant management was a good major for you to pick, then."

"Speaking of which," Sarah interrupted, "why aren't you in class? Playing hooky?"

"It's seven in the morning, sweetheart. Even BU doesn't start before nine." As if on cue, the double doors leading to the kitchen hall opened and a uniformed waitress pushed a room service cart into the room.

"Breakfast, ladies?" He gestured to the cart, "I even accounted for the herbivore," he said to Sarah, "with a fruit platter and some dairy-free, egg-free muffins."

Despite herself, Maxine shook her head and giggled, overcome by Derrick's relentless wit at Sarah's expense. "I'm dieting, but if there's coffee on that cart, I'll love you forever."

Derrick covered his heart with his hand. "Another conquest. And so easily won."

Two more waiters brought in a table and chairs, and the trio sat down to breakfast and coffee while they planned, and bickered, over the layout of the room.

ON the commute into work, Barry pondered how badly things had deteriorated since that day six weeks ago. In the time since that morning conversation with his wife, a great deal had changed.

Barry stopped reading his Bible, though it remained a fixture on his breakfast table. He stopped attending worship services. He started dodging calls from friends and family, and avoided seeing them in person as often as possible.

An irrational part of him felt that the humiliation of his personal life could be plainly seen by those who knew him best. So he didn't go to any friends with his problem. It seemed too enormous. He figured he knew what they would say, anyway, so why bother? Maxine would advise him to just ditch Jacqueline and all of the evil and drama Jacqueline constantly introduced into his life. Tony would counsel him to pray and seek the will of the Holy Spirit.

Barry kept it all inside and, after a few weeks, he called Jacqueline. They met and he told her he was willing to forgive her, raise her child as his, and love them both. His condition was that they begin living together as husband and wife with the same bedroom, the same vacations, and the same social activities.

He also asked her to begin attending church together with him every Sunday and, after services, spending time in fellowship with friends. He said that if she didn't think she could do these few things, they likely would have no way of working things out.

After he finished speaking, she had stared at him for a very long time. For the life of him, he could not read her expression.

At last, she had said, "Barry, I appreciate all the thought you've put into this. But the fact is that I just don't love you anymore. I'll tell you the truth for once. I don't know if I ever really did. If I ever did, I certainly haven't for a very long time. I think I just want a divorce. The thought of us playing house again after all this time, honestly, is disgusting to me. Charles and I have been talking and he is going to leave his wife. We're going to get married and have our baby."

This morning, he reflected on the fact that he had no idea where Jacqueline even was. The next time they met, he would hand her the divorce papers he had quietly drawn up and he fully expected she would sign them.

That fact, that fact alone, paralyzed Barry. He would be a divorcé – a childless divorcé. After nearly twenty years of marriage to the same woman, he had nothing to show for it. The shame of that burned his mind like hot coals. Ultimately, after all of his successes, he had utterly failed in his marriage.

God, he silently prayed, *if You are the author of this situation, then You already have a plan to spare me from any shame. Please spare me from this shame.*

His entire life all he had ever wanted to be was the very best husband and father he could be. Since he had married Jacqueline, the only thing on this earth he craved – more than the adoration of 20,000 cheering fans and more than the grateful praise of any of his clients – was to be seen as a hero by his wife.

Why did she have to ruin everything? Was his enduring love for this woman, his wife, was that just God mocking him for a fool? Just ripping his heart and life to shreds even as God had allowed Job to suffer?

Was it something as common as pride that made him want to reconcile with his wife? Was it just that base and banal? Or did he really love her?

The shame of it alone would crush him. The weight of that shame loomed over his head like the sword of Damocles. For the first time in his Christian life, Barry felt a constant speck of mistrust in his relationship with the creator of the universe.

One thing was certain, Barry would never again let a woman undo him so completely.

Chapter 3

MAXINE unzipped her boots and slipped her feet out of them, thankful for the privacy of the hotel room that allowed her to grab a few hours of comfort before she had to put the boots back on.

Her meeting at nine-thirty ran over. It was originally intended to be an informal meeting. The client wasn't certain she wanted Maxine representing her as her advertiser for a local veterinary hospital, and Maxine wasn't really ready to put too much effort into a proposal that might or might not be selected. When the morning meeting turned into a lunch meeting, and they haggled over details and concepts and price, she left the meeting feeling like maybe she had won the client over.

After shooting a few e-mails from her phone to her secretary and adding another meeting later in the week with this almost-certain client, she secured a room at the Viscolli hotel to get back to party planning details.

She checked her watch then dialed Jacqueline Anderson's number. Up until a few weeks ago, she'd been actively involved with Maxine and Sarah with the party planning and insisted on running the games for them. But for the last two weeks, she'd not returned Maxine's calls. Maxine couldn't figure out what kind of game she was playing. Where was she?

As close-knit as Maxine and Robin were, Jacqueline's position – as the wife of her brother-in-law's best friend – forced Barry's wife into her life far more often than Maxine enjoyed. She found the woman plastic, stuck up, and rude.

Maxine loved it when Jacqueline was out of town because Barry seemed to be happier, more relaxed, less on guard. He always seemed more open to watching a football game or talking about basketball scores or anything. Though the second Jacqueline showed up, he turned reticent, withdrawn, noncommunicative, and obviously unhappy. Maxine couldn't figure out how they'd stayed married for almost twenty years.

Every Sunday after church, family and friends gathered for lunch at the Viscolli home. Tony and Robin would have a soup and sandwich bar and they would eat and fellowship and rest before evening services. In the three years since Robin married Tony, that tradition had been something that kept Maxine going to church even on her most "exhausted from the Saturday night before" Sunday mornings.

Tony and Robin had close friends at their church who joined them on a semi-regular basis, and almost always some pastor or visiting evangelist joined as well. In attendance without fail, in addition to Tony and Robin, one could nearly always count on: Derrick; Sarah and a few boyfriends here and there over the years; Barry, but rarely with Jacqueline; and an always unescorted Maxine.

In those three years of Sunday lunches, Maxine and Barry had become really good friends – great friends. They typically found a corner somewhere in the massive apartment and spent hours talking, laughing, planning lunches or, to Barry's dismay, golf outings. They both loved football and a few times when Jacqueline was on one of her regular out of town excursions, Maxine would head to Barry's house after Sunday evening services to watch the day's games that he'd recorded. He usually let her fast forward through the commercials and the endless game replays. She looked forward to that time with him and had really grown to count on his friendship.

Shaking her head at the train of her thoughts, she brought herself back to the present. Shooting Barry text number three of the day, worried about why he hadn't texted her back yet, asking him if he knew where Jacqueline was and how Maxine could reach her, she went ahead and placed a call to the kitchen and reconfirmed the schedule for the night ahead.

Checking her watch and calculating the time until the party, she determined she had about two hours to do some office work before she had to refocus on party work. She knew she owed the bulk of the party preparation credit to Derrick and the rest of Tony's staff. She wasn't even going to pretend that she could have done this without them.

Her phone rang, interrupting her thoughts. She caught a glimpse of the caller ID as she answered it. "Hey, Sarah."

"Hey. I got your text. Thanks for getting a room. My roommate is dropping my clothes off on her way in to cover for my shift."

"Awesome. I thought about what you said and I agree. I think it'll just be easier to have a command center here."

"Are you staying there tonight?"

Maxine looked around the luxury of the suite. "Probably. We'll be here rather late. What about you?"

"Definitely. It isn't every day I get to stay at the Viscolli." She laughed. "Any news from Jacqui?"

Maxine felt herself frown. "No. It's not like her not to be in the center of the party planning. I can't help but feel like something's wrong."

"It's possible she's just having too much fun to come back to town." Sarah answered drily.

"I can't even get Barry to return my calls," Maxine said.

"Well, the world must be coming to an end if Barry isn't calling you back," Sarah observed.

Maxine frowned. "I beg your pardon?"

"Nothing. Sorry. Did you read over the game instructions?"

Maxine sighed. "I did. They're easy and will be manageable with the size of crowd we have. Hopefully the wait staff will be available to help us."

"Since it's Tony's hotel and Tony's wife's baby shower, I'm sure the wait staff will be more than available," Sarah offered with a wry smile. "We can't spend a lot more time worrying about Jacqui." Maxine could hear noise happening around Sarah. "I have to run, Maxi. See you whenever Melissa gets here to relieve me. Love you!"

"Love you, too." Maxine hit the button to disconnect the call and frowned. Trying to ignore the sense of foreboding, she removed her laptop from her bag and turned it on, determined to get some work done before she had to go supervise the placement of the centerpieces.

BARRY didn't recognize the incoming number on his mobile phone's caller ID at 10:26 that morning. Since he was in the middle of a conference call with a client he ignored it and let it go to voice mail. Two minutes later at 10:28, he let the same number go to voice mail again.

A little over one minute later his secretary, Elizabeth, burst into his office. The look on her face alone silently informed him that he needed to end his conference call immediately. So he did.

As soon as his handset hit the receiver, he said, "My cell's been ringing constantly ..."

Elizabeth interrupted, "Please pick up on line two, Barry."

Barry noted that she did not address him as "Mr. Anderson," or "Sir." He noted that she cut him off and heard the hint of anxiety in her voice as if it were a scream.

"What is it?"

Elizabeth shook her head. "It's the hospital up by your ski resort in the Berkshires. They won't tell me anything."

A cold, sinking feeling hit Barry in the pit of his stomach as he punched the blinking button and brought the phone to his ear. He heard his own voice, sounding numb and distant in his ears, saying, "This is Barry Anderson."

The cold, sinking feeling turned to a frozen ball of iron when he heard a distracted voice answer, "This is the Trauma Center. Can you hold please, Mr. Anderson?"

"Yes, I can hold." Barry didn't even complete the sentence. He began listening to canned hold music before the first word completely left his lips.

A few more heartbeats passed after which a new voice came on the line and asked, "Is this Jacqueline Anderson's husband?"

Barry paused before affirming, "Yes, this is Mr. Anderson."

The voice went into a kind of rehearsed speech mode. "Mr. Anderson, there's been an accident. Your wife sustained very serious injuries and was rushed here less than an hour ago. We've been treating her to the extent that we can within the limits of the law."

Barry suddenly realized how serious this conversation was. Out of all the conversations of his life on earth, this one might end up ranking in the top two, second only to when he had asked Jesus Christ to become the Lord and Master of his life as a youth.

The hospital representative continued to explain, "Your friend, Charles Mason, is here but can't legally sign the consent forms."

Barry thought, *Charles Mason? As in the married man I strongly suspect impregnated my wife, Charles Mason? That Charles Mason? Why exactly would THAT Charles Mason be at the trauma center in the Berkshires?*

Then an absolutely terrifying thought struck him and he blurted, "Is the baby okay?" He ignored the widening of Elizabeth's eyes and the sound of her gasp.

The voice kept talking. "Mr. Anderson, you're an attorney. You know I can't speak to that on the phone. We need you to get here as soon as possible so we can advise you as to the prognosis. Could you please allow me to record the remainder of our conversation while you grant me verbal consent to continue treatment?"

Again he heard his own voice, but he had no idea how he was speaking. "Please proceed. Whatever you need."

With the receiver of his desk telephone pressed into his ear by his massive shoulder, he listened to the questions and answered them. He wished he were on his cell phone so that he could start moving right now. He stated his full name as "Bartholomew James Anderson," and said, "I'm her husband," then he impatiently said, "Yes, I agree," three times. He leaned down, and years of habit made him pack his laptop and some paperwork into his briefcase before he shouldered it. Before hanging up, he said, "I'm on my way."

He caught Elizabeth's eye as he stalked out of his office, headed toward the elevators that would take him to the parking garage. Over his shoulder, he ordered, "Cancel the rest of my week."

THEY sat amongst the debris of the party. A few members of the staff set about removing furnishings and cleaning the room. They studiously avoided the little group stubbornly claiming the head table because the owner of the Viscolli Boston, Tony Viscolli, had arrived to retrieve Robin, his wife.

He sat with her feet in his lap, gently rubbing her arches. Maxine had her head back, reclining as best she could in the cloth-covered banquet chair. Sarah sat next to her, phone in hand, texting someone.

"You two did an amazing job. What a wonderful gift," Robin said.

"Speaking of," Maxine said, rolling her head on her shoulders, "what do you want to do with the presents people brought despite our request not to?"

Robin sighed. "I guess we need to open them. There are just so many, though."

Maxine's phone vibrated next to her elbow. Recognizing Barry's number, she snatched up the phone. "Barry, hi. If you're looking for Jacqui, she isn't here. Did you get my texts?"

Barry was silent for a few breaths. "I know where she is, Maxi. Is Tony with you? I've been trying to get him for the last hour."

Something was wrong. She could hear it in his voice. Wanting to ask, but feeling it wasn't her place, she held the phone out to her brother-in-law. "Tony? It's Barry. He says he's been trying to reach you."

Tony patted his jacket then shook his head. "I left my phone in the car."

Robin smiled. "Miracle of miracles."

Picking up her hand, he gently kissed her knuckles. "I'm here with you, *cara*. What call would I want to take?" He smiled at her blush and took Maxine's phone. "Barry, *mi fratello*."

Maxine watched Tony's face fall as he sat straighter in his chair.

"*Come tragica*! Where are you right now?" Tony asked as he bolted to his feet. Maxine found herself standing with Tony. "I'll be there as soon as I can." He held the phone out to her and she saw his hand tremble as she retrieved it. "There's been an accident. Jacqui's dead."

Simultaneously, Maxine exclaimed, "What?" as Sarah repeated, "Dead?" and Robin gasped, "When?"

Tony leaned down and kissed Robin's forehead. "I don't have all the details and I don't know when I'll be home. I'll call you as soon as I get there."

"Don't worry about me." She looked at Maxine. "Can you take me home?"

"Of course." Maxine assured. "Or you can stay with me here. Sarah and I have a suite upstairs. I'll sleep on the couch and you can take one of the beds."

Derrick quietly asked, "Should I come, too?"

Tony considered, then said, "Better if it's just me for now. But I'll let him know you asked about him." By way of answer, Derrick offered a single nod of understanding.

A well of panic bubbled up in Maxine's chest as she watched Tony march away. "Tony, wait!" He stopped and pivoted on his heel, a questioning eyebrow raised at the distraction.

Maxine rushed toward him. "Tell Barry…" She paused and felt her throat burn with tears. "Tell him to call me if he needs anything."

Tony cocked his head and his brown eyes searched her face before he answered, "I'll be sure to tell him, Maxine."

"Thank you." Maxine felt her cheeks burn with unidentified embarrassment as she slowly turned back toward her group. "I left my room key with the front desk so that I wouldn't have to keep up with it all night. I'll go get it."

Robin maneuvered herself to a standing position, rubbing her large belly. "I hate that our evening ended with such tragic news."

Sarah put one arm around Robin's back and with her other hand, rubbed Robin's stomach. "You okay?"

"I'm fine. I have some time yet." She patted Sarah's arm. "Just us three girls. Kind of like old times, huh?"

Chapter 4

THE engine of the tiny green sports car hummed in perfect tune and all four tires left the pavement as it crested the hill. The tires chirped as the empty street, slick and glistening from a recent downpour, reached up and welcomed the vehicle back to earth. Maxine managed to continue accelerating, watching the speedometer climb as the clock on the dash remorselessly ticked away precious seconds.

The headlights cut through a sudden mist and spotlighted an unforeseen puddle less than a second before all four tires plowed through it, sending an almost artistic rooster-tail spray high into the air that Maxine could see in her rearview window. The engine whirred as she shifted gears and turned the wheels hard. A little bit of a fishtail sent her heart pounding. She regained control, straightened the car, and punched it.

Harsh music blared out of the speakers, a modern staccato rock beat with heavy emphasis on the bass. The music felt exciting, dangerous, thrilling. Maxine stabbed the knob to increase the volume even further as the swift car continued to whip down the interstate ramp. After what seemed like forever but was actually mere minutes, the suburban exit appeared. Maxine hit the blinker to announce her intention to take that exit, then whipped into the left lane to pass three more cars before careening back to the right, barely missing the bumper of the car she just cut off as she downshifted in an attempt to slow down the little green bullet.

Barely pausing at the red light at the end of the exit, she made a quick right, a succession of a few turns into the heart of suburbia, and finally wheeled onto the street where she would find the big white church with the tall black steeple.

She forced herself to slow down. Nothing could be gained by the sound of screeching tires penetrating the walls of the building. She parked her car, double-parked it, technically, at the end of the parking lot and grabbed her little black purse that perfectly matched her sedate and stylish black suit. A quick check of her lipstick and she could go.

Few women could get away with that shade of red lipstick. Maxine considered herself one of the lucky few. Her straight black hair and olive skin, both traits inherited from her father, made the lipstick a perfect shade for her. She bared her teeth to the mirror to make sure no lipstick marks marred the white surfaces, then slipped out of the car.

The two sets of double-doors at the top of the stone steps were shut tight and no one remained outside the church. The December sky, pregnant with ominous looking gray clouds, silently spit out a few flakes of snow and Maxine shivered. Before quietly shutting the car door with her hip, she bent and reached inside and grabbed her long black trench coat and threw it over her shoulders as she dashed up the stairs.

She silently opened the giant wooden church door just wide enough to squeeze inside, and found herself standing in a huge vestibule with ceilings at least three stories high. Corridors branched off in either direction, with rest rooms on either side of the massive lobby. A large tripod supporting a poster sized framed head-shot dominated the middle of the room. Maxine walked up to it and bit her lip to keep herself from snarling.

Jacqueline Mayfield Anderson's long, wavy red hair, her porcelain smooth skin, and her glowing blue eyes all mingled together to create a classically beautiful woman. The artist in Maxine allowed herself to admire Jacqueline's bone structure and cream cheese exterior.

Her personal knowledge of Jacqueline's character, however, identified a true wolf in sheep's clothing. Maxine hesitated to speak or even think uncharitably about the dead but she also considered herself a realist. Her own mother had been murdered when Maxine was very young, and Maxine never minced words about the kind of woman she had been in life.

In life, Maxine had never, ever liked Jacqueline. In fact, she sometimes imagined some kind of slimy wormlike alien had inhabited Jacqueline's insides, feeding itself on her rudeness, carnality, and avarice. So unlike, she thought, the Spirit whose fruits include such things as kindness and self control.

Now, the woman was dead and had to answer to her Maker. The fact was that Maxine wasn't here for Jacqueline. She was here for Barry. She started forward, stopped long enough to sign the registry, then quickly moved toward the usher who stood sentry by one of the several sets of massive double doors leading to the sanctuary of the church. Her heels made no sound on the carpeted floor.

The usher didn't return her smile, but opened the door for her. She slipped into the sanctuary and stopped.

Every seat appeared taken. She slipped back out again and spoke in low volumes to the usher, trying to determine if moving up to the balcony would prove worthwhile. In whispered tones, he informed her that she would find the balcony just as full as the main floor, so she slipped back into the room and stood against the back wall.

She could not see her family, but knew that the front rows on the left side were reserved for Barry's family. Tony would be seated as close to Barry's parents as possible since he was Barry's best friend. Maxine often felt the men acted like fraternal twin brothers. Tony considered Barry family in the same way he considered Robin's sisters family, and to him the differing last names meant absolutely nothing.

She decided to walk along the far left wall until she spotted them. She started to move to the far side of the room so that she could sneak along the wall but just as she took her first steps, Barry took the podium.

At six-nine and nearly three hundred pounds of muscle, Barry looked like the professional football player that the Super Bowl ring on his left hand proclaimed, but Maxine knew football had only been Barry's shortest path to his law degree, and he had never looked back or regretted retiring from the game. Fitness was center to his life, though, and he still kept in very good shape. She could not help admiring the way he filled out his dark charcoal suit from his broad shoulders to his thick limbs.

Not wanting to distract him by walking to the front while he was speaking, she resumed her position against the back wall just beside the door and watched her best friend eulogize his late wife. As he faced the crowd, Maxine realized he'd shaved off his goatee, and she wasn't certain if she liked the clean-shaven look or not.

She hadn't seen him in weeks. She tried to remember the last time she'd talked to him. Mid-September, maybe. She'd called to see if he had a ticket to an upcoming Patriots game.

"I have a client who would probably give me his first born if I could get him tickets," she said.

Barry had been very abrupt and distracted. "No. Someone else has my tickets this week. I can't help you. I have to go."

Despite her occasionally trying to get in touch with him since then, she hadn't heard from him.

She watched Barry pull a small sheet of paper out of his jacket pocket. On either side of the massive stage, large screens provided a close-up view, and the person manning the camera zoomed in on Barry's face. Maxine couldn't help but stare at the handsome man, his strong features hard as stone. He raised one of his massive hands and rubbed his forehead. Maxine noted the Super Bowl ring he sported on his left ring finger in lieu of a wedding band.

She watched him close his eyes and take a deep breath before opening them again, focusing on some point in the crowd near the front. She almost gasped out loud, nearly tried to take a step back, at the intensity of his stare – even from a distance she could see it.

He cleared his throat and put away the paper. "I had a nice speech prepared. Something impassioned and just the right amount of emotional, but it's all just a bunch of hogwash."

A murmur rippled through the crowd as hundreds of people bent their heads together and started whispering. Barry gripped the podium with both hands and leaned down toward the microphone. "I would probably have kept up whatever pretense I needed to keep up to save my parents and sisters any kind of embarrassment, but marrying Jacqui eighteen years ago was probably embarrassment enough so that anything that happens now probably won't even faze them."

The murmur changed to a full gasp, and now people sat forward, on the edges of their seats, ready for more. "The truth is, I always loved my wife. Even when she gave me absolutely every possible imaginable reason to stop, I still loved her. I always prayed that she would come to know Christ, that I could witness to her. But God chose not to answer that prayer. I don't understand why. So, in that mission, I failed. I have absolutely no doubt that I will answer for that one day."

Barry bowed his head. Maxine felt her heart hurting for him. She could almost see the emotions he struggled to hold in check.

The population of the church murmured continuously. It sounded like a constant quiet hum. Maxine wasn't sure how much time passed before Barry said, with his head still bowed, "As you all sit out there in your funeral best, let me go ahead and confirm whatever rumors I must to keep this town in gossip for a few days. Yes, Jacqui was pregnant when she died." Suddenly, the church turned so silent it was almost a roar. Barry continued, ruthlessly, his voice even, a monotone. "Of course, the baby wasn't mine."

Maxine felt her knees turn to water. *Oh, Barry. What are you doing, Barry? Please stop, Barry. Please don't.*

He continued, "Apparently, she was really in love this time. Our divorce was quietly in the works. I have absolutely no business eulogizing her today. So I won't stand before you and say anything I don't mean. I won't be joining you at the graveside. In fact, I have just enough self respect left in me to turn the podium over to Charles Mason, the father of that unborn child and Jacqueline's future husband. Charles? You have the floor."

No one murmured as Barry stormed off the stage. The mood of the entire room was that of complete shock. The giant flew down the stairs. His footsteps clapped like nearby thunder in the deafening silence.

Maxine slipped back out the very same door she had entered and moved very quickly across the outer narthex to the double doors leading to the outside. She stepped into the cold December air and made it halfway down the church steps when she heard one of the doors above her slam open hard enough to hit the outer wall.

She looked behind her but kept going down the steps just to keep her momentum going. "Hey, Barry," she said, holding up her car keys. "Need a getaway driver?"

He stopped – totally stopped – halfway down the stairs. She reached the bottom and turned fully around to look at him. "You probably have about three seconds left before my brother-in-law comes racing through those doors."

Barry glanced back, then took the last ten steps in three massive strides. "Let's go," he urged. They reached Maxine's car as the doors to the church flew open again. As Maxine buckled up, she heard Tony calling Barry's name.

She pealed away, tires chirping on the cold pavement. She looked over at Barry, who grabbed the seat belt behind him and clicked it shut just as she turned onto the main road and darted into traffic. "Where to, big guy?"

Barry rubbed his face with both hands. "I don't care." He sat quietly for a moment, staring out the car window, then pointed at a restaurant sign. "That's fine, there. I haven't eaten today. Pull in and park around back so they don't see your car."

MAXINE parked the car behind the restaurant and grabbed her purse as she slid out of the car. Barry put a hand on the small of her back to lead her to the door. Catching their reflection in the glass, she thought they looked like a very serious, very handsome couple. She, in her long black funeral suit, he in his charcoal suit with crisp white shirt and staid gray tie – they matched well.

Even with her six feet of height and additional three-inch heels, Barry towered over her by several inches. Barry leaned around her and grabbed the door handle, scanning the street behind him as he opened the door for her.

They didn't speak as the hostess seated them and handed them menus and the waitress brought them ice water and took an order for coffee. Maxine's eyes skimmed over everything on the vinyl coated menu within seconds and she folded it and set it aside. She ran her finger over the condensation on her water glass as she leaned back in the booth and looked at Barry. He looked very tired. His blue eyes seemed a little dull, his mouth a bit pinched, his color off.

"I've missed you the last few weeks," she murmured just to break the silence.

He peered at her over the rim of the menu before tossing it down. He propped his elbows on the table and rubbed his face then ran his hands through his close cropped blond hair. "It's been a difficult time."

Maxine nodded. "I gathered."

He leaned back against the booth and crossed his arms over his massive chest. He released a deep breath. "We'd been living separate lives for years; different bedrooms; different holiday plans ..."

Maxine raised an eyebrow. "Why?"

Barry shrugged. "I don't know. I needed a wife or a hostess sometimes. She needed money to support her lifestyle. She could throw a killer dinner party, and that kind of networking really helped my law firm." He sighed and threw an arm over the back of the booth. "It worked for us. When she told me she was pregnant, I just kind of shut off."

Maxine could hear the hurt in his voice. Deep hurt. Her heart twisted and she felt tears burn the back of her throat. Barry continued, "I realized that there'd been some small hope inside me – for years now – that if I lived a righteous enough life and if my righteous life witnessed to her, that one day she'd come to know the Lord and that would change things. We could really be married and start a family together."

She watched his finger tap to the beat of an unheard rhythm on the back of the booth. "At first, we tried to reconcile. For the sake of the baby, I was willing to forgive. I was making plans about how we could work it out. Then the baby's father decided he was really in love with her. He left his wife and Jacqui went running to him without looking back. He was there when she died."

The waitress started toward the table, but Maxine lifted a finger and gave a brief shake of her head to ward her off. Barry continued, "Probably once a year I would read the commands of God for husbands and realize that I wasn't where I should be, and I'd pray for help. But it seems like whenever I did that, she'd flaunt some lover in my face and I'd go right back to apathy."

Maxine tried to grasp the extent of what he was saying, but she couldn't. As deeply faithful to God as her sister and husband were, as deeply faithful as Barry had always been, Maxine simply didn't feel it. She liked church, she prayed at family meals, she attended church functions, but this abounding faith that those around her professed to have seemed to have missed the boat with her. Not knowing what else to say, she simply said, "I'm sorry."

"Yeah." He met her eyes and smiled. "Everyone's very sorry." His smiled turned into a wry smile. "I'll probably be sorrier when the impact of what I did today sets in."

Maxine sat back and gripped her hands in her lap, strangely wanting to reach out to him and comfort him with just a touch of her hand. "If you were trying to avoid gossip, you kind of managed the opposite of your intent."

"Everyone knew. Why keep up such an absurd pretense?" Barry looked over his shoulder and caught the waitress' eye. He waved her over. "I saw him sitting there and realized that he was the one really mourning. Apparently, they were really in love and all gaga over the baby."

"Does he have kids?" Maxine wondered.

Barry nodded. "I understand he has two but they are both teens. Still, makes you wonder."

Maxine had no idea what it was supposed to make her wonder about but she nodded in agreement anyway. The waitress approached, pad and pencil in hand. "What can I get you?"

Barry gestured with his hands. "I want a huge steak – the biggest you have. And some grilled vegetables. Do a double order if you need to. And an iced tea. No sweetener."

The waitress looked at Maxine who smiled. "Just a plain salad, no meat, with some oil and vinegar on the side."

When the waitress left, Barry raised an eyebrow. "What's with the rabbit food?"

Shrugging, Maxine took a sip of water. "I eat like a rabbit and workout five days a week and still seem to be losing a battle with something. Nature, I guess."

If she'd been standing, he would have looked her up and down. She could tell the way his eyes moved over her that he was processing her size and shape. "I'm sorry, Maxi, but I'm not seeing you losing a battle with anything."

She felt a flush of heat tinge the tops of her cheeks. "Well, working out helps."

"What kind of working out?"

Maxine knew Barry had a private gym in his home that could rival any fitness club's setup. "Twice a week, I go to a spinning class, and twice a week I do a cardio-kick class."

He snorted and smiled his first genuine smile since they sat down. "Cardio- kick?"

"Sure. It's like kick boxing and aerobics rolled into one."

He started laughing and repeated, "Cardio-kick?"

Maxine felt herself getting a little irritated at it. "Yeah. Why?"

He smiled as he spoke. "Nothing, I guess. If you want to prance around in a decorative leotard and look good for your trainer, then nothing."

"Prance around?" Thinking of the hours and hours of grueling sweaty kicking being called prancing around just made her anger rise. "What would you suggest?"

"I'd suggest working out."

"That's not working out?"

He snorted again. She thought if he did that one more time she'd have to throw her ice water right at his face. "No. It's not working out."

Running her tongue over her teeth, she raised an eyebrow. "You could teach me how?"

She could swear he looked her up and down again. "Oh yeah. You bet I could."

Ignoring the double entendre, she tapped the top of the table. "Then show me."

He paused and cocked his head. "Okay. Be at my house …"

This time Maxine laughed. "No way, big guy. Come to my gym and show me how to work out for real. Teach me how to properly work out on equipment I can access anytime."

He straightened and grabbed his napkin wrapped silverware as the waitress approached with a platter mounded with meat, squash, and carrots. "Sure. When?"

Maxine eyed the wilted iceberg lettuce and dried out carrots on her plate and resignedly reached for the oil and vinegar containers that the waitress set next to her plate. "Monday morning at six sound good?"

A look of surprise crossed Barry's face about two seconds after he agreed to meet her. Maxine was curious about the little flutter of excitement that began in the pit of her stomach at the confirmation of the – her mind purposefully skipped over the word date and replaced it with appointment.

Chapter 5

BARRY found himself sitting in his Jeep at five-fifteen on Newbury Street outside a designer gym four buildings down from Maxine's apartment Monday morning. Part of him wondered why. Another part knew exactly why.

He got out of his Jeep and snugged his ski cap down over his ears. The December air took his breath away. He reached into the back seat and grabbed a pair of wool gloves. Checking his watch to confirm his starting time, he set out in a slow jog. He would run four or five miles and arrive back in time to meet Maxine at six.

He kept his pace careful, not wanting to slip on any unseen ice. Another couple of weeks and he would be stuck running on a treadmill for the rest of the winter. He didn't enjoy that as much. It just didn't feel like a good run under the bright fluorescent lights while watching the morning news.

As he passed a restaurant, he saw the lights flicker on, flooding the sidewalk with their glow. The day was starting. He sighed inwardly. Today would prove to be a very tiresome day. After Maxine dropped him at a car rental place on Thursday, he rented a car and drove to the Cape, where he had hidden out in a no-tell-motel for three days. He'd left his cell and laptop in his Jeep at the church. No one could reach him and he didn't feel obligated to contact anyone. He wondered, briefly, how Maxine handled the family after acting as his accomplice in the getaway.

What he hoped would happen likely would not. It seemed hugely unlikely that everyone would ignore the whole thing and get on with their lives. He knew Tony too well. He knew his mother, too. And his sisters. No. No one would ignore anything.

After three days of solitude, Barry still didn't understand his motivations on Thursday. Why in the world had he done that? Maybe he couldn't bear the thought of one more pretense, one more lie, in a marriage that had been built on nothing but pretenses and lies.

It felt good, whatever the reason. Internally, the part of him that knew the sinfulness of his emotions recoiled from this newer, more dominant part of himself. His dark persona had put his wife away as soon as he realized that their marriage could never be saved. This alter ego had discovered that Jacqueline's lover had spent the past few months destroying his own wife with a divorce while wooing back the pregnant Mrs. Anderson.

Barry had changed so radically that just five short days after his wife broke her neck and died while skiing next to the father of her unborn child, he couldn't wait to see what kind of outfit Maxine wore to workout with him this morning. She always dressed perfectly to the nine's for any occasion, which told him he was in for a treat.

He knew that most people would think his thoughts weren't appropriate. As a rule, Barry had never cared overly much what most people thought, and this stood as no exception to the rule. He wondered, though, if Maxine would find his attraction improper. That thought gave him pause. He almost didn't recognize himself lately. Angry dark thoughts occupied his mind, and he found himself occasionally fighting feelings of despair. He was learning how to shut it out, to feel nothing, to function with total apathy.

Barry worked his way through the beautiful downtown area as the restaurants and flower shops turned on their lights and opened their doors, as delivery truck drivers cautiously guided their oversized vehicles through the mazes of the wet streets. He listened to the voices calling greetings and the hard clanging of loading dock doors, smelled the heavenly scents drifting out from bakeries. The sights, sounds, and smells struck him in stark contrast to his normal jog at this time of the morning in the total seclusion and near silence of suburbia.

He made it back to his Jeep with about five minutes to spare. He opened the back door and dug through the gym bag he'd packed last night, finding a clean towel and a bottle of water. A spicy, citrusy smell wafting on the breeze teased his nostrils, and he knew Maxine stood behind him as he closed the back door.

"Hey, big guy," she greeted as he turned to face her.

The first time Barry had ever seen Maxine, even before he grew to know and like and respect her, he thought that perhaps he had never met a more classically beautiful woman. Her oval face, full lips, and high cheekbones all formed this perfect, beautiful visage that framed almond shaped eyes the most striking color of green he had ever seen. She had long limbs and long straight black hair that reached her waist. He had always appreciated her beauty in a detached, faithfully married kind of way.

"Good morning," he said, eyeing her blue spandex pants and white sweatshirt. She wore designer tennis shoes the color of red hots and he realized that she'd pieced together the colors of their favorite football team.

"I wondered if you'd show."

He chugged half the water then tossed it in the bag he'd slung over his shoulder. "Why?"

"Because you weren't exactly in a normal frame of mind on Thursday. Then you pulled a Houdini." She reached up behind her head and gathered her long, long hair into her hand. She made a rubber band magically appear and expertly twisted the strands until she had completely contained them at the base of her neck. "Thanks for that, by the way. That was a lot of fun."

Barry winced. "Pretty bad, huh?"

They walked together to the door of the gym. Barry reached around her and grabbed the handle before she could. Opening the door, he let her precede him inside. Bright lights, shiny equipment, a local radio station morning show pumped through cheap speakers, a sweaty smell beneath some designer scent intended to cover it; the place was exactly what he'd expected.

At the desk, Maxine pulled a key chain out of another hidden pocket and scanned the key tag. To the ridiculously muscled attendant with the one size-too-small muscle tank top and the moussed-up hair, she announced, "He's my guest this morning."

The attendant sidled up to the desk and leaned in, angling his body to show just the right amount of chest and biceps. Barry laughed inwardly. Maxine, as usual, acted oblivious. He wondered if she could possibly always be that unaware to the way men reacted to her. "Sure thing, Miss Bartlett," he said. "I'll take care of it for you."

He said it like he was doing her a favor instead of his job, and Barry rolled his eyes at the ridiculousness of it. Maxine simply smiled in thanks and turned to Barry. "What first, big guy?"

He looked around before pointing to the corner. "First we stretch." He led the way to the far corner. He set his bag down and turned to her. "We're going to stretch, do some sit-ups, a few warm-up exercises, then we'll utilize some of the machines." While he explained the way she needed to stretch and the gradual escalation in the warm-up, she took off her sweatshirt, revealing a Patriots T-shirt ... a loose-fitting Patriots T-shirt. With a silent thank you for little blessings, Barry counted off to eight then started back again for the cycle to twenty reps of eight. "How bad?" he asked, continuing their conversation from earlier.

"Tony was cool," Maxine said, shifting her body as she stretched her hamstring. "Robin was mad. She couldn't believe that I helped you get away from everyone."

"I appreciated it."

"I'm just glad I was running late." She grinned as she shifted again. "I couldn't believe I was late for your wife's funeral. That's terrible."

"I doubt she minded," Barry observed dryly. When they finished that rep of twenty, they moved to the floor so he could hold her feet while she knocked out some sit-ups. "I'm sure they have a setup where you can do this alone," he said, "But I'm comfortable here." He glanced up, noticing how full the gym had become in the last twenty minutes. "Popular place."

Maxine effortlessly pulled her body up then lay back against the mat before pulling herself back up again. "Yeah. It seems like a good place."

"Lots of bells and whistles."

She grinned, making her eyes dance like jewels. "Women need bells." She huffed up and back down again. "And whistles."

"About your diet," he said. This time when her shoulders touched the mat, she didn't immediately pull herself back up. He watched her hesitate. "Come on, Maxi. Three more."

"What about my diet?" she asked, closing her eyes and drawing her body up then back down again.

"Rabbit food won't cut it."

With a grunt she finished the last two reps. "What else is there?"

He put a hand on the side of her bent knee and squeezed, signaling in silence the end of that exercise. He silently acknowledged how she tensed up then jerked away from the touch and mentally filed that away. He fished another bottle of water out of his bag and tossed it to her. "High protein, whole grains, eating small portions every couple of hours but eating the right foods." While she drank the water, he pulled a book out of the bag. "This book will tell you what to eat, how to eat it, and when. The guy who wrote it knows what he's talking about."

Maxine eyed the book suspiciously, but took it from him. "I'll give it a look."

"Do more than that. Get on this starting right now. You should see noticeable changes in your energy and concentration levels in about 10 days. It requires a lifestyle change in your eating habits. You need to approach it in a disciplined manner."

Maxine couldn't stop herself from grinning. "Yes, coach." She pushed herself to her feet. "What now?"

AN hour later, Maxine sat across from Barry in a little bakery next door to the gym. Her muscles felt rubbery and very tired. As she sat there, she could still feel her thighs burning from that one last repetition. She felt like she'd worked more muscles in her body in the forty-five minutes with Barry than in a week's worth of aerobic classes.

She took a sip of hazelnut flavored coffee and closed her eyes in ecstasy. "If coffee is disallowed by that diet book, I'm not reading it."

He wrinkled his nose and dunked his tea bag in the hot water in his cup. "It's allowed."

"Yet you obviously disapprove."

As he shrugged, she wondered if his huge frame would crush the little filigreed café chair in which he sat. "There are too many ways to naturally generate energy without requiring a drug."

"Man, you are still on that kick. There's a difference between God-given caffeine in coffee and laboratory made industrial grade steroids, you know." She sipped.

Barry shrugged again, this time as if to announce that nothing would change his mind in this conversation that was months old between them. "What those men did hurt more than the team. It hurt the League and it hurt every kid in the world who looked up to them as role-models."

Hoping the little plastic knife wouldn't break under the weight of the cream cheese, she carefully applied it to her whole grain bagel. "Coffee was put on this earth to provide pleasure and ecstasy, especially hazelnut flavored coffee on cold December mornings."

Barry reached into that never ending bottomless gym bag that hung on the back of the metal chair and pulled out a plastic drink container. When he opened the lid to take a sip, she caught a glimpse of something thick and gray. He took a long swallow then used a paper napkin to wipe the sludge off his lips. Maxine pushed back any curiosity as to what ingredients might possibly be found in nature to produce a concoction of that particular color for fear he would offer to share. Instead, she took a small bite of bagel and thought she much preferred this focus Barry had on protein, such as this cream cheese, over her usual breakfast of a banana.

Using his drink container, Barry gestured at her shirt. "Catch the game yesterday?"

"Not until I got home last night at seven. I don't know how I managed to get through the day without hearing anything about it, but I'm so glad I went into that third quarter completely ignorant of just what excitement awaited me." She took another bite and washed it down with coffee. "I imagined you couldn't even sit down."

"I had to pay for my room for Sunday night, too, so that I could stay and watch the game. Worth every single dime." Barry shook his head while he grinned. "It was crazy. I thought they'd kick me out of the hotel. I kept screaming at the television."

"It's really turning out to be a great season."

Barry took another long pull of the drink then put the lid back on and tossed it in his bag. He picked up his own bagel and ripped it in half, then bit into it and gestured with the remaining piece. "Hey. You want to go to the game with me this Sunday?"

Maxine raised an eyebrow and ran her tongue over her teeth. It took her about a second and a half to grin and agree. "Heck yeah, I want to go."

"Great." He glanced at the massive watch that he sported on his left wrist. Maxine couldn't help noticing that it didn't look too massive on his arm. It would swamp most men. "I have to go. I have to be at the courthouse at eight-thirty. I'll be outside the gym at six Wednesday morning if that works for you."

Maxine raised an eyebrow. "You will?"

"Of course." Barry stood with a grace a man his size shouldn't have. "You didn't think today was it, did you?"

She'd hoped not but didn't dare ask. "I didn't think about it, honestly."

His face became very intense as he put both of his massive hands on the little round table and leaned forward. "We just breached the bare surface. There are so many things that you could do that you don't, that you should do that you don't know about. First of all, start eating right today. Maxine, diet is 90 percent of the whole thing. If you're serious about wanting to get fit and healthy…"

Maxine nodded and interrupted. "Of course I'm serious."

Barry straightened and pulled a ski cap out of the pocket of his pants. "Then I'll see you at six on Wednesday." He slung the bag over his shoulder and started to leave the bakery but paused and turned around. "Thank you." With eyes turning very serious and very somber, he said it again. "Thank you for Thursday. I needed that."

Maxi tilted her head and gave a slight nod. "Glad I could help."

He paused for a long time, two heartbeats, then three, before pushing open the door and walking away. The bell on the door jingled as it shut behind him, sending a draft of cold air toward Maxine's table. She couldn't take a sip of her coffee until she quit smiling the ridiculous smile that had somehow taken occupancy on her lips, but she just honestly couldn't help it.

Chapter 6

A hard rock "hair band" from several decades earlier beat a frantic rhythm and exclaimed that it had been a long time since they'd rocked and rolled while Maxine played with the background color of the template she had designed on her computer. She lifted a finger to adjust the earbud of her MP3 player while she clicked between a violet and a blue-violet, trying to decide the best interior wall colors for a set for a bedroom furniture commercial that would shoot next month. The white headboard and bedding would really pop in front of purple walls.

She'd used the MP3 player since she'd worked in a cubicle as an intern and needed to isolate herself from the world. For the last year, she'd worked from the privacy of her own office complete with the services of a secretary she shared with three other associates. Even though she could shut the door and play music at a somewhat reasonable level, the habit of total isolation had long been established and she found she worked better with it.

As she reviewed her notes to make sure she had incorporated all of the elements in the original design, the song ended. Before the next one could shuffle forward, her door opened. Maxine popped the earbuds out of her ears before her rather eclectic secretary could wave her bejeweled arms to get her attention.

"Mike Robison is on six," she said, as the sound of a dozen bracelets clinking together preceded her handing Maxine a stack of messages. "You said to flag you when he called. And your meeting with the design department for that," she gestured to the computer, "has been pushed back an hour. The director is tied up somewhere else."

"Thanks, Julie." As her secretary turned to go, Maxine called her back. "Hey, Julie. Violet or blue violet?" she asked, pointing to the computer monitors on the credenza behind her.

Julie raised a hand to her bangs. "My hair? It's more like an eggplant, don't you think?"

With a chuckle, Maxine shook her head. "I like the eggplant. It works well. I'm talking about the walls of the bedroom."

Julie walked around the side of the desk to peer closer at the monitors. "I'm not seeing a difference," she said when she straightened.

Maxine laughed as she picked up the phone and hit the flashing light for line six. "No biggie. Thanks."

"Sure." With a swoosh of her long fuchsia skirts, Julie left the room.

"Mike," Maxine said, "thanks for calling me back."

She could hear the sound of the police station in the background of the phone. "Sure," he said. "We still on for tonight?"

Opening her desk drawer, she drew out a new pack of raw almonds, recommended by Barry's book as an in-between meals snack, and used her letter opener to break the seal on the package. "That's why I called. I have to cancel."

"Why?"

The incredulous tone had her frowning. She grabbed a handful of nuts and piled them on her desk before putting the package back in her drawer. "Something else came up."

"What could possibly come up instead of Monday night football at O-Leary's pub?"

Absolutely nothing could possibly come up. Even the atmosphere at O'Leary's didn't appeal to her if she had to go with Mike. She hadn't enjoyed spending time with him for the last few weeks, and decided that it was time to end it. After a few weeks, every man she'd ever dated wanted to take their relationship to the next level, to the physical level, and Maxine just didn't do physical. Ever.

She found it best to just end it instead of trying to explain that, *yes I like you*, and *thank you for dinner*, but, *no*, I'm not going to hold your hand or kiss you good night or sleep with you and thank you for *not touching me*. Even thinking about a man's touch made her stomach crawl and her blood run cold. The two times in her past when she'd actually tried to explain the why's just didn't go well, and were experiences she personally never wanted to relive.

Julie cracked open her office door and gestured at the phone, mouthing the word, "Robin," and held up four fingers. Maxine closed her eyes and sighed. "I have to go, Mike. Have fun tonight."

Without waiting for a response, she disconnected and hit the button for line four. "Hey."

Little fingers of anticipation danced up her spine, tightening the muscles on her neck. She wondered if Robin was still really mad at her. "Hey. Can we have lunch?"

"Of course," Maxine said in a rush, wishing she could read more into the tone. "Where?"

"Hank's if you can make it out here. If not, tell me where to meet you."

Closing her eyes and thanking God for the shift in the meeting with the set people, she agreed to meet at Hank's in an hour. With Monday traffic, Maxine decided she probably needed to start heading in that direction. Her sister's restaurant was well outside the city limits, closer to one of the colleges, and the spits of snow out there would make traffic beastly.

MAXINE tapped on the frosted glass of the door leading to Robin's office. With Hank's not open on Mondays, Robin would be in there doing whatever she did to manage one of the best family restaurants in the Boston area, if the food critics could be believed.

Robin's voice beckoned her inside. When she opened the door, she found her older sister standing by the tall bookshelf stretching her lower back, rubbing one hand over her incredibly pregnant belly. An open cardboard box lay at her feet, and a picture of her and Tony on their honeymoon in Italy lay on a piece of newspaper on the corner of her desk.

"Moving day?" Maxine asked.

"It is. Our new manager starts Wednesday. I needed to take a break from working on the computer and move around some." She gestured at her desk. "Casey made us some hamburgers."

"That's awesome. I'm starving." She couldn't understand why she was so hungry since she'd been eating every two hours following Barry's book, but the sight of the hamburger with melting Swiss cheese sitting on two sourdough buns made her mouth water and her stomach grumble with anticipation.

Robin met Tony when he bought Hank's place back when she worked there as a bartender. He promoted her to manager when they pulled the bar out and added more seating. Maxine knew that Robin didn't intend to work once the baby came.

Robin finished stretching and came forward the three steps to hug Maxine. As she released her and stepped back, Maxine put her hands on either side of her sister's swelling stomach, leaning her face close enough that her nose touched it. "Hello little niece or nephew." She smiled as she received a kick in the nose. "Hey, let's sit. You can put your feet in my lap."

Robin smiled as they took a seat at the desk. "I don't need to put my feet up, but thank you." She held her hand out and Maxine took it and bowed her head. Robin blessed the meal, thanking God for the food and for the relationship that only sisters could share.

Maxine felt the sting of tears in her throat when it was over. It wasn't until she chewed and swallowed the first heavenly bite that she asked,

"What did you want to talk about?"

Robin washed down her own bite of hamburger with a long pull of water before answering. "I want to start off by apologizing for getting so angry with you. That was wrong of me. Please forgive me."

Maxine cocked an eyebrow. "Sure."

Robin put a hand on the side of her stomach and shifted. "Secondly, I want to ask just what you're doing."

"I'm sharing lunch with my sister. What do you think I'm doing?"

"I don't know. I've never been a big fan of your closeness with Barry. He is ..." she paused and corrected herself, "... was married and you two spent an awful lot of time alone."

Maxine felt some heat creep into her cheeks. "Alone while his wife was ..."

"There's no reason that one person's wrong should justify another's."

"Barry and I were only friends. It never went further."

"I understand that. But you just used past tense, and now that there isn't a wife in the picture, will it stay that way?"

"How should I know the answer to that?" Maxine surged to her feet and grabbed an empty box. She snatched a picture frame off the desk and shoved it into the box.

"Maxi ..."

A paperweight and a stress ball followed. "No. I'm not listening to anymore. I admire Barry's ability to have worked at being faithful to that – that woman he was married to. I don't know what will happen in my future or his future. I just know that he is one of my best friends and I have always enjoyed spending time with him. I realize that you've never understood my relationship with men and that you condemn it in your mind, but I can watch a football game with a widower and not end up like our mother!"

Robin's eyes widened. "Is that what you think this is about?"

"What else is there?"

Robin teetered her way out of the chair and put a hand on her lower back. "Maxi, I'm concerned about you. Not because our mother was a drug addict who moved from dealer to pusher and hauled us with her. I'm concerned because Barry has been pulling away from God, and I'm worried about his anger right now."

All of the steam left Maxine and her hands stilled. "His anger?"

"His anger. He's spent weeks pushing everyone aside. He won't even talk with Tony or pray with Tony about it. He is full of anger about Jacqueline's pregnancy, his marriage, her death. I'm worried that he's going to go through some all out rebellion and take you with him." Her eyes filled with tears and she dashed them away with jerky movements.

Maxine rushed forward and took Robin's hand. "You don't have to worry about me."

"Maxi, I know you believe in God. But I also know that you go to church to please me and Sarah. I know that. I know you don't have the zest I have. But I also know that you will. One day, the Holy Spirit is going to knock you in the head with a two by four and you'll not be able to deny it. But starting a relationship with a man who is so angry will pull you away from God."

Maxine couldn't fathom why Robin was so upset. It didn't make sense to her. She put her hands on either side of Robin's belly. "You have so much going on right now that worrying about whether I will start a relationship with Barry Anderson should be at the bottom of the list." She pulled her close and hugged her. "I love you. And I so appreciate how much you love me. Did you know that?"

"I know you do." She pulled back and looked deeply into Maxine's eyes. "But, please. Keep this conversation in mind as you go forward from this day."

To make Robin feel better, she smiled. "Of course." Gesturing back to the desk, she said, "Let's get that meal eaten. I'd hate to face Casey's wrath if we sent back plates with just one bite out of each burger."

"After work tonight, can you help me run an errand?"

"Sure." Maxine sat back down in her chair and picked up her hamburger. "Where are we going?" She took a big bite of the delicious sandwich.

"I have a box of Bibles and hymnals I need to take to Craig at the prison. Tony usually goes with me, but he's not free tonight, and they need them for a worship service Craig's leading tomorrow."

Craig Bartlett was Robin's biological father who was currently serving the remainder of a 20 year sentence for a double homicide committed decades in the past. One of the lives he had taken had been their mother.

Maxine nodded and swallowed. "Glad to help," she said.

Robin put a hand on her shoulder and squeezed. "Thank you."

EMERALD FIRE - CHAPTER 7

Chapter 7

BARRY didn't know what to expect when he walked into his offices after court on Monday afternoon. He felt a very real uncertainty about how people would treat him. Almost all of the staff had attended the funeral, and those who hadn't attended had most certainly heard about his outburst by now. So if he felt a bit of trepidation as he stepped off the elevator, certainly some justification for that feeling existed.

The receptionist's face flushed and she stammered as she bid him good afternoon. He thought she would actually thank God outright when the phone interrupted them. As he walked through the outer area and past secretaries' cubicles and desks, a wake of first silence then murmuring and whispering followed. When he finally made it to his office area, his own secretary quickly hung up the phone and stood. "Mr. Anderson," she said, grabbing at a stack of messages. "I wasn't sure if you were going to be in or not today."

A war widow with two teenage sons, his secretary, Elizabeth, had worked for him since he opened his own practice. Her knowledge of the law often rivaled his junior associates, and he occasionally wondered why she didn't bite the bullet and take her husband's pension to attend law school herself. She typically dressed in conservative pantsuits and wore cross necklaces in all different styles and colors – whatever matched her suit of the day. She wore her hair in a long braid every day, and had never removed her wedding ring.

He paused beside her desk and set his briefcase on the floor by his feet and his travel mug of herbal tea on the corner of her desk so that he could thumb through the messages. "There's no reason for me not to work today," he said.

As he thumbed through the dozens of messages, she let out a breath. "I'm not quite sure what to say about that."

The wall of callous defense he'd shorn up before entering the building fell at the look on her face. He immediately felt like an inhuman heel. "I apologize. I think I was prepared for this to all be a bad experience. I was defensive before there was cause, and that made me rude."

"May I say something?"

"Of course." He gripped the messages and mug in one hand and bent to pick up his briefcase.

"I realize that your marriage to Mrs. Anderson has – had – been strained for sometime. But despite that, she was a human being whom you shared a house with, if not a portion of your life. If you don't allow some grieving, despite everything, you're going to regret it at some point."

"I appreciate that, Elizabeth. Thank you." He gave her a slight nod. "Now I have work piled up from the last week, I'm sure, and I need to get to it."

He left her standing there, gripping her necklace. He imagined her thinking about her late husband and wished that anything to do with his late wife wouldn't cause her any pain. Elizabeth didn't deserve any pain for anything.

Shutting the door behind him, a signal to everyone in his firm not to bother him, he entered his office. A decorator had taken the former football player persona to the extreme, but he'd never had it redone. People who came to see him because of his past life expected the decor to be what it was, so it did no harm. The dark green walls with stark white trim held shadow boxes of signed footballs, autographed photos, and Super Bowl posters. The hardwood floor had scattered rugs that mingled the colors of his former team with the colors of the wall, and flowers and knickknacks around the room drew it all together.

In one corner of the large expanse, a leather sofa and two leather wing-backed chairs formed a sitting area around a heavy wood coffee table. He often met with clients there. Removing the barrier of the desk lowered defenses and in many cases, fear. In the opposite corner and closest to the door, a conference table that comfortably seated eight crouched beneath a crystal chandelier. His huge desk, especially designed and customized to accommodate his large size, filled the other half of the room. It sat in front of a picture window that overlooked the water and the financial skyline. He purposefully picked the location of his offices for an easy walk to the courthouse. Credenzas on either side of his desk held the customary law journals and business books. He rarely opened them. He much preferred the ease of research using the slim laptop that he pulled out of his briefcase when he reached his desk.

Along with the half dozen messages she'd left on his cell phone and home phone voice mails, his mother had called here twice. He needed to go ahead and call her and get that out of the way. As he picked up the receiver of his phone, he sorted the messages between personal and business. The business stack was very small compared to the personal stack.

He quickly dialed his parents' home and his mother answered on the first ring. "Hi, mom," he said, sitting in his chair and swiveling it around to look out over the water.

"Barry." She made the word a whole sentence. "I'm glad you're okay."

"I'm just fine, mom."

From her end, a deep breath punctuated a long pause. "As long as you are. Do you need anything?"

Barry closed his eyes and felt an unfamiliar rush of emotion. He needed something. He needed to erase the last twenty years and hit restart. "I just want to get the next few days out of the way so that everyone and everything can go back to normal."

Another long pause. "Okay. Fair enough. Do you want to come to dinner Sunday?"

"I would, but I'm going to the game. How about Saturday?"

"Your sisters will be here."

With a short laugh, he thought of his three older sisters and shook his head. "Might as well get it all over with at one time."

He could hear the smile in her voice. "Saturday it is then. See you at six."

"Yes, ma'am," he agreed as he hung up the phone. He scribbled a note on the message slip which would later go into his laptop calendar just to ensure he would not forget. He knew that absolutely no excuse, no matter how grand, would allow him to duck out of that dinner.

Feeling a huge weight lifted by walking into his offices and then that simple phone call, he ignored the stack of personal calls and started making his way through the business calls. As he ended his third call, he pulled his laptop out of the briefcase and docked it, connecting it to its various plugs and ports, connecting the battery to power and the network card to hard wired connectivity. He didn't yet trust wireless networks to keep his client's information totally secure.

While concluding typing in the notes from the last call, his office door flew open and Tony Viscolli marched in. At his heels, Elizabeth looked surprised and a little bit angry. Tony turned around and gave her a smile. "Don't worry, Liz. He'll be fine with the interruption." He shut the door in her face and came all the way into the room.

Tony always looked like the cover model of a men's fashion magazine, whether he was going to a business meeting in some handmade Italian silk suit or sailing in the harbor in white Dockers and a cable knit sweater. This morning proved no exception. His gray suit, light blue shirt, and dark blue tie authoritatively announced confidence and business acumen. His dark hair and Sicilian features perfectly complemented the light fabric.

Barry didn't stand. Instead, he leaned back in his chair. "Good afternoon."

Tony sat in one of the chairs opposite Barry. "Is it?"

Barry rubbed his face with his hands and sat forward. "Not particularly."

"Didn't think so."

Tony rarely came to Barry's office. Barry typically went to Tony, which was fair since Tony paid him. He pretty much only came when there was a third party meeting on a legal level that required a neutral environment. "Are you here on business?" Barry asked hopefully.

"What gave you that idea?" Tony answered, leaning back in his chair.

Barry grinned. Anyone else, even a client as important as Tony Viscolli, he would have dismissed at that point. Of course they shared business interests. He and Tony, though, had a relationship much more like brothers than close business partners. Around his ironic grin, he asked, "Why are you here, then?"

Tony cocked an eyebrow and tilted his head as if to look at Barry from a different angle. "Because I love you."

Barry nodded. "So my not calling you back didn't tell you that what I really need is some time alone and some emotional space?"

"Well, you've been pulling away from me for weeks now. I think I've given you all of the space you can handle."

Barry felt a little tickle of annoyance. "What does that mean?"

Tony sat forward. "It means that when I gave you the space you so clearly projected you needed, I watched you withdraw from everything normal and become quite rude in the process." As Barry prepared a retort, Tony held up a finger. "Maybe rude is the wrong word. Abrupt? Terse? I think the stress Jacqueline constantly brought to your doorstep contributed to that. But you have also been pulling away from church and men's groups, and that greatly concerns me."

Barry started feeling a little antsy. He slowly drummed his fingers on his desk. "Why?"

"Because I wonder if you've pulled away from your relationship with God the same way you've pulled away from everything else."

Defensiveness surged through him in a hot, painful flicker of flame. He wanted this conversation over and he wanted Tony out of his office. "Is that any of your business?"

Tony's eyes hardened and his mouth firmed. "Barry. What is wrong? What happened?"

Pushing the negative feelings aside, Barry leaned back again in his seat and covered his eyes with the heels of his hands. "I don't know what happened, Tony. I spent two decades trying to do the right – the Christian thing – with Jacqui. I stayed faithful. I stayed loving. I prayed for her. I prayed a lot. You prayed with me on more than a few occasions. I never gave up on her."

"I know..."

Barry sat forward quickly and slammed a hand on the desk. "No you do not know, Tony. Don't even try to say you know. You don't know what it was like. You don't know what she was like. You don't know how I felt." He let out a breath and felt energy drain from his body. "Toward the end she didn't even pretend to hide her lovers anymore. Then she met this guy and was suddenly in love." He felt his lip curl. "As if that makes everything okay."

"Bear..."

Barry closed his eyes and massaged the bridge of his nose with his giant fingers. "I just wanted to do the right thing. I just wanted to get to heaven one day and have God say to me, 'Good game, Barry. You played well. Head to the locker room.'" He opened his eyes and looked at his best friend, someone from whom he'd shielded all of this misery. Or tried to, anyway. "Then she got pregnant."

Tony waited out the silence, then finally said, "Why did you never say anything?"

"What is there to say? You wouldn't understand it. You and Robin have this magical perfection, and here I am, married for eighteen years and my wife gets pregnant by one of her many lovers. How do I talk about that with you? How do I talk about that with anyone?"

"There's someone you could have talked to, who always understands."

Barry barked out a laugh. "God?" Unable to contain the energy anymore, Barry surged to his feet. He turned his back to Tony and looked out over the expanse of water below. His very view screamed success, but in his heart he knew he had no real accomplishment to stand upon. What would his legacy be? To whom could he leave it? He put both of his hands on the glass and pressed against it with his body. "You want to know what I said to God?"

"Yes, I do," Tony answered quietly.

"For years, I said to God, 'Please fix whatever's wrong with my wife. She's sadistic and evil.' Years and years went by. Then she came to me all weepy and pregnant asking me to help her. It took me a while to finally agree to it."

Tears burned his throat, but he would not give in to the emotion. Pushing it back, finding the balance of feeling absolutely nothing, he continued his story. "Then Jacqui didn't want that anymore. He'd left his wife, filed for divorce, and asked Jacqui to marry him. He asked *my* wife to marry him." Barry stared out the window, at the business of the street far below, at the people going through their lives like nothing different had happened in the world. "So then, I hit my knees and I said to God, 'Please, God. Spare me this embarrassment. Spare me the humiliation. Spare me from the world finding out she's pregnant by another man.'"

He heard Tony get out of his chair. He heard the tap of Tony's shoes on the wooden floor. He felt the comforting hand on his shoulder but he didn't turn his head to look at his best friend as he continued, "Last week, on a trip to celebrate her finally feeling better, their coming nuptials and baby, she tumbled down a slope in the Berkshires, and broke her neck."

"*Amico...*"

Barry formed both hands into fists and punched at the glass. The safety glass didn't break, but it shook with the force. "No! Don't even try to hand me platitudes. I'm quite over it. I don't know what I did. I don't know how I've gone into every single situation in my life, including my marriage to that woman, in prayer and supplication and still managed to have what I had. Then the only prayer in eighteen years about her that gets answered ends up killing her and taking an innocent life. Spare me whatever it is that you're about to say, Tony. I don't care about any of it."

He turned around and fully faced Tony. "I love you. You're my best friend, and my brother. But if you're going to tell me you're praying for me or God will fix it or whatever it is that you're about to tell me, please just don't."

Tony raised an eyebrow. "I was simply going to say, *mi amico*, that anything you need at all, you can call me. You need to vent, you need to play a game of chess, you need a boxing partner – just call me. Don't shut me out of your life, because I need you in mine. You are my best friend, and my brother, too."

Barry stared at Tony for several seconds then felt his hands unfist. He rubbed his face and nodded. "Okay. Thank you."

Tony looked at his watch. "Now I must go, Bear. Robin has an ultrasound this morning."

Clearing his throat, Barry shoved his hands in his pockets. "How's she feeling?"

"Very large." Tony smiled. "But anticipatory. She is ready for the next few weeks to come and go."

"And you?"

"I could not be better. God is awesome." Tony held up both hands in a defensive move. "And before you take me up on that boxing, I will leave."

"Hey." Tony paused with his hand on the doorknob and turned to look directly at Barry. "Thanks," Barry said, swallowing emotion.

"*Sei benvenuto.*" He started to leave, but stopped. "Robin will be occupied with her sisters tomorrow night. She is doing thank-you cards for her shower gifts. Do you want to get dinner?"

Barry paused, but then nodded. "That sounds great. Sure."

"One more thing, Barry. Think about this. You prayed for God to spare you from the world learning that your wife had been faithless, that she was carrying another man's child. You are angry that God answered your prayer. But Barry, everyone in your world knows. Did God really answer your prayer?" Tony held up a hand to forestall any answer. "Just think about it. I'll see you tomorrow."

Long after the door shut behind Tony, Barry stood at the window, looking out over the buildings in his field of view. He watched the birds swoop and dive over the water, watched snow spit in the rain. Finally, he shook his head as if to clear it and turned back to his desk, to his work, to the one area of success in his life. He opened his laptop and shot Elizabeth an instant message asking her to bring him water when she had a free minute. Then he pulled up a client file and reviewed some notes before he picked up the telephone again.

Chapter 8

"ARE you cold?" Barry yelled against Maxine's ear to be heard above the roar of the crowd. Maxine grinned and shook her head but didn't try to speak over the noise of the crowd. Seventy thousand fans cheered the Patriots down the field and she knew her voice would never make it to his ear.

When they sat back down and the noise returned to a better level, he leaned down again. "We can go into the deck if you want," he said.

She tore her eyes from the field as the teams broke away for a time-out. Looking Barry in the eye, she said, "Why in the world would I want to go into an isolated deck to watch the game? If I wanted to sip a drink from a real glass and eat finger sandwiches, I'd be watching the game from my living room couch." She narrowed her eyes. "And why are you so worried about me?"

Barry grinned. His face relaxed and he settled back comfortably in his seat. "I totally agree with you. I just wanted to make sure you didn't expect to go into the lounge and watch from the high life."

"Why would I want to do that?"

With a shrug he said, "I don't know. It's been a while since I took another girl to a game."

Maxine felt her eyes widen as she realized what he meant. "Don't worry about me, big guy. Whenever you wonder about what I'd prefer, just go with the opposite of what Jacqui would have preferred. That should cover all the bases."

For a moment, Maxine felt horror that she'd said that aloud. Then, when a slow smile gradually took over Barry's face before he threw his head back and laughed, she knew she hadn't crossed some invisible faux pas boundary.

After that, he relaxed. They shivered in their seats, never realizing they felt the cold, while their team stomped the other team into the ground. They yelled and cheered and talked back to the field until Maxine's scratchy throat sounded hoarse.

At the end of the game, she wrapped her Patriots scarf tight around her neck and pulled her Patriots hat low on her forehead and followed closely behind Barry, who muscled his way through the crowd. It took quite some time to reach Barry's Jeep, but they chatted the whole way and she didn't mind. The crowds and parking lot and traffic were part of the whole package.

When they finally left the stadium parking lot and turned onto a main road, Barry looked over at her. "Where to?"

Maxine had to clear her throat a couple of times to get any sound out at all. "Tony and Robin's, I guess. We missed lunch. Might as well go graze before church."

Barry tapped his finger on the clock on his dashboard. "Too late. They'd be gone by the time we got there."

"Well, hmm," Maxine said, pursing her lips and tapping her chin. "I guess we could go straight to church."

"Why don't we stop at this pub I know and grab a sandwich and watch one of the west coast games?"

It possibly ought to have taken her more than half a second to decide to agree to go. In that half second, she wondered, pondered, contemplated whether she should press the church issue. Her conversation with Robin crept into the front of her brain somehow, and she had a brief moment of worry about Barry's avoidance of all things normal and typical for him. However, despite Robin's fears that Barry would pull Maxine away from God with his anger, Maxine didn't find him angry. She found him happy, even relaxed. An element that always held him back no longer existed, and she'd enjoyed watching him start to unfurl his wings a little bit in the last week.

Barry and Maxine had worked out together four mornings in the last week, and shared breakfast after every muscle searing session. They hadn't yet found a conversation they didn't enjoy, and Maxine hated to see the clock strike eight those mornings. That's when Barry lifted his immense frame out of the little scrolly iron chair, pulled a ski cap down over his ears, and smiled at her as he told her good-bye. The smile always made her heart skip a little beat, and the good-bye made her wish the next twenty-two hours would go by really fast.

She had looked forward to Sunday all week, knowing that they'd get back into their football watching schedule that they'd shared for the last few years. When he pulled tickets out of his pocket Thursday morning, Maxine laughed with delight and snatched them from his hand. Friday morning, he had a breakfast meeting and couldn't work out with her. She didn't enjoy doing it alone, but the anticipation of Sunday made the time go by much quicker than usual.

They reached the little pub in short order. Once they left the football traffic behind them, they encountered very few cars. Set outside the city limits, more toward Barry's neighborhood, the little pub had a very full parking lot.

Barry held her door open as she got out of the Jeep and stepped into the cold air. Maxine shoved her hands into her pockets and rushed toward the door while the wind cut through her jacket and fleece pullover. Walking into the welcoming warmth of the building, she pushed her cap off her head and unwound her scarf. Barry stood above her, scanning the room, and nodded in the direction of a couple standing near a booth putting on their coats. "Let's grab that table," he said, putting a hand on the small of her back to guide her. Maxine inched forward as much as possible hoping to create a space between his hand and her back.

As they maneuvered their way through the full crowd, a cheer erupted around them. Maxine looked at one of the many wide-screened televisions that seemed to cover every spare inch of wall space and saw the game everyone else seemed to be watching. She noticed that the booth would offer no good view of that game, but it beat sitting at the bar.

Barry took her jacket from her before she slid into the booth, and he set their coats next to him as he sat across from her. They both gathered plates and glasses and stacked them at the end of the table. As Maxine used a paper napkin to wipe water rings from the table, the waitress approached. "What can I get you?"

Barry pointed at Maxine, who shrugged and said, "Anything seared meat."

He smiled and ordered. "Two Reubens, double meat. Instead of fries, we'll take carrot sticks and celery with some Ranch and Blue Cheese. And two waters, with lemon if you have it." The waitress jotted her shorthand quickly on her pad, then took as many of the dishes as she could. "I'll come back for the rest," she said.

Once she left, Maxine scanned the televisions in her view and decided that none of the games held her interest much. Instead, she focused on Barry. "Thank you for taking me to the game today."

He grinned. "Good game."

"Do you miss it?"

The shake of his head happened suddenly, like a reflex. "Never have. I didn't ever have a passion for it. I simply used it as a tool to get me through law school without having to pay back student loans for a decade." He fiddled with the Super Bowl ring on his hand. Maxine noticed that he'd moved it from his left ring finger to his right ring finger. She wondered when he did that. "I played third string – took a beating from the first and second string players at practice and hardly left the bench during the regular games."

The waitress rushed by their table and slid their waters toward them with barely a pause. She did reach into the small apron she wore on her hip and grabbed a handful of straws, two of which she tossed on their table, then grabbed the remaining dishes.

"What was playing in the Super Bowl like?"

The grin covered his face quickly. "Thrilling. More than I'd like to admit."

Her chuckle flowed over him, through him. "Why more? Isn't it every man's dream?"

He casually shrugged. "I'd just passed the bar and it was the end of my contract. I never had to put the uniform on again. But that game, we had three touchdowns the first quarter. By the third quarter, we were ahead by twenty points. Their offensive line decided that they needed to break down our defense. I was a defensive lineman, but our first string was the best in the country, which is why I rarely played."

"Did you get to play?"

With a smile, he twisted the ring on his finger. "Yeah. Four of our guys were on stretchers in the locker room at the half and two of them on the bench with ice packs or bandages by the fourth quarter. By then I was angry. They weren't playing football, they'd decided to go to war. They'd managed to push the score up to just a six-point spread and by then we were in the second half of the fourth quarter. The crowd was insane. It was cold and rainy, but I was so mad, I didn't even care. Without ever even speaking the words, we decided to give back. Only we didn't hit their offensive line. We went straight for the jugular."

Maxine turned her body so that her back was in the corner of the booth and she could stretch her long legs along the bench. She played with the straw in her water and enjoyed watching him talk. She could almost feel the cold, hear the roar of the crowd. "You went after the quarterback," she said with a smile.

"Yes. And he knew it. He started getting scared. They kept losing yardage, because he'd fall back so far, trying to get as far away from us as possible. But most of us on the line were fresh. We hadn't been playing for hours, and they'd hurt our guys, not just as part of the game, but intentionally tried to wreck a few careers, so we started playing for blood."

"What happened?"

"We sacked him three times in five minutes."

"You did that?"

He gave her a quick, heart stopping grin. "Once." His eyes shone with the memory he relived in his mind. "And as you know, we won. It was amazing. The crowd was so loud you could feel them inside of your chest."

She smiled. "Then what happened?"

His shrug wasn't as casual this time. "Then the season was over, I turned down another contract with a huge signing bonus, and Jacqueline never forgave me."

Maxine didn't want to breach Jacqueline territory just yet. "So what was next?"

"I took the money I earned from playing football and paid back my student loans. I had enough money left over to rent a little office in downtown Boston and hang a shingle on the door. Ten days later, this street-tough kid named Antonio Viscolli, barely twenty-one, walks into my office full of God and genius and says he needs a lawyer for a big business deal he was about to venture into."

Maxine straightened in her seat as the waitress came to their table with platters of food. "And history was made."

Barry helped the waitress set plates of food and bowls of dressings on the table then nodded his thanks. "No, that day it was just forged. One month later, the green attorney and the street rat bought a boat engine manufacturing plant for one quarter of its net worth."

"Ah," she said as she dipped a carrot stick in some Blue Cheese dressing and took a big bite. "That sealed it. That's awesome." She waited to see if he intended to pray over the meal, but he simply picked his sandwich up and started eating so she followed suit. It made her a little uncomfortable. She'd known Barry for a few years. While they hadn't been praying over coffee and tea and croissants, she'd never shared a real meal with him, other than the day of Jacqueline's funeral, when he also didn't ask God to bless the meal. Again, Robin's worries whispered through her subconscious but she shrugged it off. "I'm glad you still like to watch football, though."

He ripped a paper napkin out of the holder before responding. "Yeah? Why is that?"

She didn't realize she'd spoken out loud. Taking a pull of her water, she formed her response carefully. "Because it brought us together and made us friends when we first met."

Barry paused eating and stared at her for the space of several heartbeats. Maxine felt a rush from her heart spread through her veins and up her neck in a warm flush. He finally spoke. "Yeah." Maxine wondered if he meant as much in that one syllable word as she hoped he meant. He broke the stare and picked up a celery stick. "I love to watch. It's why I didn't mind sitting on the bench. I've always had the tickets I have. I rarely miss a home game. And some buddies of mine and I always pick a bowl game to go to every year. We take our wives and make a big weekend of it." He froze, obviously realizing what he'd said.

Maxine let it slide. You couldn't spend the better part of two decades of your life with someone and have them gone in an instant and not trip up occasionally. She wished he'd realize that. "Where are you going this year?"

"MAACO." He cleared his throat and relaxed again. "Christmas week in Las Vegas."

With a smile, Maxine took a small bite of her sandwich. "Talk about Christmas lights."

"It's going to be fantastic."

"You probably had to use every string you have to get those tickets."

"You know it." He smiled. "Want to come?"

As he asked, she swallowed, then promptly choked. Her eyes watered and she couldn't catch her breath. Finally, with the help of the water and God, she managed to get the little piece of corned beef dislodged from her windpipe and swallowed properly. She wiped her eyes with a fresh napkin and looked at him. "What?"

"Well," he drawled, "I have this extra ticket. I thought about asking my dad if he wanted to go, but I bet you'd get a kick out of it. Vegas at Christmas is a hard place to beat."

"I don't think …"

He leaned forward and reached for her hand. She saw him coming and put both of her hands in her lap, so instead he just rested his large palm on the table in front of her. "Come on, Maxi. I have a suite – two bedrooms and a living room. It would be perfectly respectable. And, it's MAACO. Don't tell me you've never wished you could go to one of those holiday bowl games."

With a grin, she picked up a carrot stick and nervously broke it into pieces. "You're right. I have wished I could go."

"But …?"

"But Robin …"

"Robin has Tony and Sarah. Sarah's a nurse. An OB nurse. There's nothing that you could do for her in the three days you'd be gone that one of them couldn't do."

As she wavered between really-really wanting to go and really-really knowing she shouldn't go at all, he pressed forward. "It will be so much fun. We'd fly out the day before and come back the day after. Tony's loaning us the Viscolli G-5 so we wouldn't even have to deal with the crazy holiday travel at the airport."

All of her instincts screamed in panic to turn him down. She didn't go on out of town trips with men. She didn't share hotel suites with men. She didn't do anything with a man that would lead him to think that she'd be willing to …

But this was Barry. He didn't buy the tickets or get the hotel room in order to set a scene with her. He didn't have any preconceived ideas of what the trip would bring.

Against her own will, her mouth formed the words, "Sure. That would be a lot of fun." To hide her nervousness over what she just said, she picked up her sandwich and took a bite.

He relaxed and leaned back in his seat. "Really? That's great. We're going to have such a great time."

She held up a hand. "As long as you get two hotel rooms. Suite or not, I want separate rooms."

Barry nodded. "I'll see what I can do."

Maxine just smiled and took another bite and wondered, really, what she'd just gotten herself into.

EMERALD FIRE - CHAPTER 9

STEVEN Tyler appealed to Maxine to dream on while her paintbrush maneuvered in time to the music, rapidly dotting the green landscape she had created with Scottish heather on the stretched canvas before her. Gray mountains rose in the distance and the gold of the rising sun reflected off the scabbard of the lone armor clad horseman riding wearily toward the keep.

One final stroke of her brush marked the end of the song and the completion of the painting. Maxine, barefoot in ripped jeans and a half-top, stepped back from the canvas and narrowed her eyes, seeking any flaw in the oils. As she shifted her eyes, the mirrored wall across from her caught her attention. Something about her stance made her look primitive, primal, elemental. She shook her head to clear the image of another painting as a mandolin heralded the next song, and Robert Plant began singing about the Queen of Light.

Satisfied, Maxine set her palette and brush down and rubbed the back of her neck with paint splotched fingertips. She felt drained, sucked dry, like she felt every time she finished a painting, but it was in no way a bad thing. In fact, she sought this feeling, this cleansing, perhaps, as her chief goal.

With natural grace, she slid across the hardwood floor of her studio and silenced the music. She rolled her head on her neck as she walked back into the main apartment.

Long before Tony entered their lives, Robin had worked two jobs to put Maxine and Sarah through college. Maxine lived with her even after college and after securing a good job with an advertising agency. While she tried to help Robin pay for tuition or living expenses or even food, Robin thwarted every attempt until Maxine just decided to start banking the money with the intent of handing Robin a paid tuition package the year after Sarah graduated. Before that could happen, Robin married Tony. So, Maxine had a large portfolio and no plans for it.

With Tony's sharp business mind, he took half of her savings and taught her how to invest it. With the other half, she purchased the top floor of a brownstone on Newbury Street. The two large apartments on that floor easily converted to one large apartment and one studio. With the help of a contracting company that Tony owned, she soundproofed the studio and installed a state-of-the art stereo system that played music with enough volume that she could feel the beat in her pulse, but kept the noise contained so as not to disturb everyone within a three-block radius.

She often found herself pulling all-nighters, rushing home from work, kicking off her heels, slipping out of the suit of the day, throwing on torn and tattered jeans and an old football jersey or sweatshirt from her college days and just painting and painting until the sun peaked through the blinds. Despite the artistic outlet her job afforded, she resented its intrusion on her purely creative side and often wondered, "when?"

When would she feel comfortable enough with her portfolio to quit that high paying job with the newly acquired office and shared secretary and just give in to her dreams of simply painting? Painting; the passion of her life; the succor her jaded soul required; the solace her troubled heart sought. When could she just paint?

Tony's guidance and mentorship had allowed her portfolio to grow and grow. Every quarter, Maxine watched the numbers and had almost reached her comfort level. She owned her apartment, she owned her car, and she owed no one anything. Maybe in another three months, she'd have the magic number savings that would allow her to quit her job and rely fully on her painting for the rest of her days. The very thought made fear and anxiety form into a tight little ball in her stomach. What if she couldn't succeed?

Maybe she needed to raise the number a little higher. Growing up the daughter of a drug addict who pimped herself out to whatever druggie boyfriend would take in her and her three girls made security extremely important to Maxine. So many nights she'd lay on her bare mattress or on dirty sheets next to one or both of her sisters and her stomach would growl with such intensity that the pain of hunger would claw through her body. The first twelve years of her life revolved around terror and hunger and pain. She needed that cushion of self-sufficiency to back her so that no matter what happened, no matter if she ended up completely alone and isolated from everyone she loved, she would still never be hungry again.

Maxine moved through her apartment. A brick wall on the far end made the room feel very "Newbury" Street to her. She loved it and had installed it, brick-by-brick, herself.

Her big red leather couch sat against that wall covered in bright pillows designed with stripes, polka-dots, zigzags – it didn't matter to Maxine. She sought a hodgepodge look with the patterns and kept a similar color scheme going. Angled with the couch sat a love seat in a red and blue with yellow floral design. Maxine found it at a flea market and fell in love with it so instantly that she sat on it while bargaining over the price because she worried someone else would come and take the treasure away before she could complete the deal. A large area rug with a large, modern floral design in muted reds and blues and soft yellows sat on the hardwood floor between the two couches. She covered the walls with her art, picking up little details from the furniture pillows or rugs or bright knickknacks and painting them to tie all of the room together.

Against the picture window looking out onto the street she dearly loved sat her Christmas tree. She surprised herself by going traditional with it – a green tree with reds and golds and silvers. She had it decorated with angels and stars. On the top of the tree sat a tacky plastic lit-up star covered in worn-out gold tinsel. Robin bought that to go on top of their very first Christmas tree when Maxine was sixteen. She'd been with Robin for just a few months, then, after being separated from her for two long years. As they put that cheap little star on the top of their sad little tree, they vowed that no matter what, they would win. They would win in this battle they called life – the pitiful hands they'd been dealt would win the house.

The first Christmas after Robin and Tony married, she and Maxine fought over who got to keep the star. They ended up drawing straws for it. Maxine won, and in the subsequent three Christmases, she had her sisters over for dinner and together the three of them decorated her tree and topped it with that star.

She moved past her living room and through her dining room with the stark black table and Amish backed-chairs. A flat gold bowl of red ornaments sat on the center of the table.

Maxine had remodeled the kitchen almost immediately upon completion of the studio. She loved to cook and loved to entertain, so she had a large island work station installed along with a commercial-grade stainless steel stove, double ovens in the wall, a massive refrigerator, and deep steel sinks. She could spend hours in the kitchen, preparing recipes, making big trays of perfect little hors d'oeuvres, applying frosting to a sister's birthday cake. She loved the whole art of preparing food and often hosted dinner parties with church friends or work colleagues.

She reached the sink and used the back of her hand to flip the handle to open up a stream of warm water. Before going to her studio to paint, she'd left a dish of olive oil by the sink. She dipped her hands in it and started scrubbing the paint off. The oil worked the oil paint off her hands in no time. Then she used a light soap to remove the oil.

Grabbing the towel she'd lain out for herself, she went back through the dining room and living room to enter her bedroom. This room she'd decorated in grays and turquoise. A thick gray rug covered the floor, a shade lighter than the walls. A turquoise spread covered the bed accented with dark and light gray pillows.

The open suitcase on the bed made her stop. Little butterflies of anticipation reawakened in her stomach and started fluttering around. Her heart beat a little bit faster and sweat beaded her upper lip. Why in the world had she agreed to go with Barry to Las Vegas?

Shopping bags covered the bed. For some reason, her extensive wardrobe didn't seem to suit for this trip. In a fit of nervous energy, she'd left work last night and gone straight to her favorite mall. New boots, new pants, new sweaters – Christmas and plain – new pajamas … they all lay on the bright spread while she put together outfits and tried to think of what else she'd need. Maxine knew they would be with friends, so she assumed there would be dinners out and such. That in mind, she tried to add some dressy and some casual until she just wanted to call him and cancel the whole thing.

Yet she knew, deep down, that clothes weren't the problem. The problem lay in the fact that she preferred to never be alone with a man, and somehow she'd managed to allow herself to agree to be alone with a man for several days, thousands of miles from home, and completely out of her element.

Maxine had always liked Barry. For some reason his immense size had never intimidated her. Now she realized that not only was he big, he was incredibly strong, and had spent a good portion of his life knocking down men at least as big and strong as him. If he wanted to …

The butterflies flew together and formed a ball of nausea. Maxine fisted her hand and pressed it against her stomach, pushing back old memories. Memories that had sent her racing to her studio to mindlessly paint for the last six hours. He wouldn't want to. He wouldn't force. He wouldn't do anything. Maxine could trust Barry. She had to make herself trust him.

Because if she couldn't trust him that would mean that she didn't win this hand she was dealt, no matter what.

The ringing of her phone brought her out of her little panicked moment. She snatched up the extension next to her bed. "Hello?"

Robin's voice answered. "Hi."

"Hey, sis. How's my niece?"

"Your nephew's still there. I think he's going to take up permanent residence."

Maxine chuckled as she opened her nightstand and pulled out a small pair of scissors. "You're not due for another two weeks."

"I know. I just kept hoping that maybe he or she would get tired of hanging out in my stomach and get ready to meet the world."

Maxine picked up a sweater and carefully cut off the tags. "As long as we aren't a Christmas baby, all will be good."

"I know. I've been dreading this week coming up." As Maxine folded the sweater and laid it in her suitcase, Robin continued. "I hear you're taking a couple of days off."

Maxine's busy hands stilled and she closed her eyes. "You heard about that, did you?"

"Can I ask you something?"

"Of course." Opening her eyes, she picked up the scissors again and methodically removed the tags. "As long as it's a question and not a lecture."

"No lecture. Question: Is there an end game in sight here?"

"How so?"

"Are you just going with the flow, or do you have an objective in mind?"

For the first time in her life, Maxine started to feel anger toward Robin. Robin, her sister, the one who saved her from unspeakable horror, the one who worked two jobs to put her through college – made her angry with this line of questioning. "I don't know what you think my objective might be."

She heard her sister sigh. "Listen. I just feel like you're getting involved in a situation that is going to get out of control."

"Oh, really? How?"

"Barry is really hurting right now. You are beautiful and wonderful and outgoing and nice. Most of all, you're nice. Kind of the antithesis of his late wife. I'm worried that he's going to rebound and end up getting hurt even more."

Anger spread across her shoulder blades and down her hands, where her palms started sweating. "I'm just a rebound, huh? Maxine, who bounces from man to man like a flighty little hummingbird. You think I'm not worthy of a real relationship because I don't ever have them? Is that it?"

Robin's response came very quickly, very hurriedly. "No. No, Maxi."

"So you're just saying that I am bound to hurt Barry?"

"No! That's not what I'm saying. I don't want either one of you to get hurt and I'm just worried that ..."

"You're worried that he'll rebound and fall madly in love with me and I'll dump him after a couple of weeks, as is my normal pattern, and then both of us will be depressed lumps that you'll then have to contend with."

"Maxi, please. I just ..."

"No. You listen. Barry and I are friends. Just friends. He had an extra ticket to this game because his wife will not be able to attend. And, despite MACCO and the holiday, he managed to swing getting an extra hotel room. You don't have to worry about Barry's virtue or his heart or anything. We've been friends for a long time and there's nothing wrong with that. Does it occur to anyone that Barry might need my friendship right now? That being able to count on it might help him through this season of his life?" She folded a pair of pants very precisely. When the seam wouldn't line up, she unfolded them and started over. "You know what? I have some packing to do. I love you. Have a great week and I'll see you Christmas Eve."

When she hung up the phone with shaking hands, she realized that wet tears streamed down her face. Beyond anger lay hurt; hurt feelings because Robin obviously thought so poorly of her. She went into her connecting bathroom and turned on the faucet. Looking in the mirror, she could see the fatigue from painting. Her eyes, normally a very bright green, stared dully back at her, wet with tears, rimmed in red. She broke eye contact with herself and leaned down to splash cold water on her face. As she dried her face with a soft towel the color of her bedroom rug, she went back to the bed and the suitcase and the clothes.

Fear didn't paralyze her from packing anymore. Instead, umbrage drove her to pack perfectly, completely, precisely – she went through her written list and managed to get it all packed in a short amount of time and all in one suitcase.

After changing into a soft flannel nightshirt, she brushed her teeth and left the list on her bathroom sink ready to pack the toiletries. It was late, almost midnight, and she had to meet Barry at the airport at nine. She set her alarm because she knew the traffic would be horrendous. She had no desire to keep Barry or his friends waiting in the morning.

The painting session, combined with the strong emotions, combined with the restless emotions of the last few days, lent to her exhaustion and she fell right to sleep.

EMERALD FIRE - CHAPTER 10

MAXINE enjoyed the plane ride. She got along well with Barry's friends and their wives. Dealing with clients on a regular basis made her feel at ease in social settings, and since this trip had the goal of attending a major football bowl game, she boarded the plane knowing she would enjoy the conversation with people whom she had at least that one thing in common.

When she first boarded, she met Bart and Melanie Jacobs. He was an attorney on the floor above Barry's. He had shocking red hair and pale blue eyes, and she had blonde frosted hair and green eyes. She immediately grabbed Maxine's arm and pulled her down onto the sofa next to her where she launched into a conversation about a little boutique on Newbury Street that Maxine knew well.

Right on their heels, Terrence and Kisha Lee boarded. He was a large man with skin the color of warm cocoa. From what Maxine knew from her conversation with Barry on their way to the airport, he had played with Barry for part of a season before an injury brought a promising career to a sudden halt. His wife spoke with a strong accent that Maxine identified as Haitian. Maxine soon found out that she owned a French restaurant in the art district and found herself as passionately engaged in conversation about cooking as she had been about shopping.

About two minutes before they would have to shut the door and leave them behind, Justin and Caitlyn Meyers rushed on board. Maxine knew that a decade earlier he had been a client of Barry's. He was tall and thin, his bald head shaved. She had curly strawberry-blonde hair and freckles. Caitlyn sat quietly until Maxine asked her what she did. When she found out that she was a homemaker with three kids, Maxine talked about Robin's impending birth and Sarah's occupation and discovered that Sarah had helped deliver Caitlyn's third baby.

Maxine didn't realize the level of apprehension she had over how they would treat her in Jacqueline's absence until it appeared that the apprehension had no place. All of Barry's friends treated her with warmth and courtesy and she immediately relaxed in their presence. The camaraderie of the men made the flight go quickly. They talked and laughed about old bowl games they'd seen, and in between her conversations with the wives, Maxine smiled and learned and enjoyed watching Barry interact with his friends.

She watched him talk, watched him gesture with his hands as he replayed some old college football play and felt her heart skip a beat. She wasn't there as his wife, but still felt strangely proud to be with him.

The plane ride ended quicker than she anticipated, and the cab ride from the airport to the hotel was incredible. Maxine had never been to Las Vegas before, and she couldn't look fast enough to see everything on The Vegas Strip that she'd like to see. Too quickly, they pulled up in front of the hotel.

The beautiful hotel had a spacious lobby that led to the entrance of the casino on one end and a line of restaurants and shops on the other. A massive Christmas tree dominated the center of the lobby and Maxine caught the wonderful smell of the pine sap as they went by it. The jingling sound of the slot machines interfered slightly with the Christmas music playing over the speaker system, but it made Maxine smile.

As they approached the desk, the concierge waved a hand and four bell hops appeared almost immediately, taking bags and suitcases up to the respective rooms. He greeted them all by name as he welcomed them to the hotel and handed the men gold keycards to the suites of rooms. All four couples shared an elevator to the top floor where they had five of the six suites on the floor. They agreed to freshen up and meet in one of the restaurants in an hour to get lunch.

Barry handed Maxine her own key card and pointed to her room. "I'm here," he said, tapping the door.

"I really appreciate you getting an extra room. I imagine between Christmas and the game, they've probably been booked since the game schedule was announced."

"It wasn't a problem. They had a last minute cancellation, so it worked out." Barry looked at his watch. "How long do you need to freshen up?"

"I just need to unpack. Is fifteen minutes okay with you?"

Barry shrugged. "No problem. I'll see you then."

Maxine went to her own room. She stepped into a small foyer with a low table against the wall that held a vase of fresh flowers in bright reds and soft creams. As she moved through the foyer into the living room, she smiled at the Christmas tree in the corner, decorated in a theme that matched the casino's. It even had some miniaturized house chips as ornaments. A bar separated a small kitchen from the room, and on either side of the room stood a door. The far wall had a glass door that opened up to a patio that overlooked the Vegas strip.

Maxine crossed the room and opened one of the doors. She saw a large four-poster bed and an adjoining bath. A quick rap on the door signaled the arrival of the luggage. While the twenty-something man in the cheap tuxedo carried her bags to the bedroom, she grabbed the purse she'd thrown on the couch and looked through it for a tip.

Once she was alone in the suite, she locked the door and slipped her shoes off. Maxine wandered around, examining the other bedroom – which was identical to the one she'd picked out – and the bathroom with the garden tub. She had a patio off her room, too, and stepped out into the cold, dry air to look down at the traffic below.

When she returned to her room she quickly unpacked just in time for the rap of knuckles on her door. She opened it to find Barry standing in the doorway. With a smile, she invited him in. "What shall we do first, big guy?"

He slipped his hands into his slacks and rocked back on his heels. "Want to go play some slots?"

Maxine shrugged. "Eh. I don't think I want to gamble."

Barry visibly relaxed. "I'm glad. I don't really want to gamble either. But that's what the rest of the gang is doing this afternoon. What else is there to do here?"

"Tons. I want to see a show, though you don't have to go with me if you don't want to. And I want to see the Hoover Dam." She laughed and looked at him to watch his reaction to her next list item. "And I really want to go see a wedding officiated by an Elvis impersonator."

Barry laughed. "What?"

"I really do. I think it would be as good as any of the billed shows. I wonder if you can just go sit and watch."

"What do you hope to see?"

Maxine sat and threw her arm over the back of the couch. "No idea. I just want to find out."

Barry nodded. "Well," he said, "we can probably go after the game tomorrow."

Maxine sat forward and grabbed his hand in excitement. "Really?"

With a shrug, he turned his hand so that he could grip hers. Maxine realized they held hands and slowly took hers back. She put it on her lap and gripped it with her other hand. Barry didn't seem to notice as he stood and went to the kitchen. "Sure. Why not?"

"That's awesome. What about a show?"

He came out of the kitchen with a bottle of water. "I'd been kind of hoping that Elvis would make you forget the show." He softened that with a smile, which she returned in the humor that he intended. "I'm sure the other wives already have the tickets secured to a show. This is all of our first trip to a bowl game in Vegas. They usually have a whole schedule mapped out to the minute. Let's join them for lunch and see if there's anything you'd want to do with them." Maxine wondered if he realized that he included her in with the wives when he said, "other wives."

She enjoyed lunch with their group. After lunch, she and Barry separated from the couples, leaving them at the entrance of the casino while the two of them worked with the concierge and discovered a helicopter tour of the Hoover Dam. He pulled some strings and got them tickets on a flight that would leave from their hotel roof. They only had about twenty minutes before the flight departed, so they went straight from the lobby to the roof where they found the helicopter and pilot waiting for them.

Within ten minutes, the other passengers had arrived and they loaded into the helicopter and followed the pilot's instructions for fastening seat belts and putting on helmets that had built in speakers to provide a way for the pilot to give them the verbal tour.

They flew over the Grand Canyon and circled back to the Hoover Dam. Maxine sat by the window and Barry sat to her right. To get a better view, he angled his body so that he was pressed up against her back, looking out the window over her shoulder. It bothered her at first. She didn't like to feel trapped, especially by another person. So she leaned forward until her helmet hit the glass in front of her, trying to distance herself from him.

Some bump in the air, some air pocket or crosswind shook the aircraft making the other passengers gasp or exclaim. Barry's right arm came around Maxine's waist and stayed there even after the pilot smoothed them out. She immediately put both of her hands over his arm with the intent of prying it from her, but didn't. She stopped. It was time for this stupid fear of being touched by anyone – by men – to go away.

So the fingers that gripped his massive forearm gradually relaxed. For the remainder of the three-hour flight, she slowly, inch by inch, relaxed against him, relinquishing the panic of being touched or held as she looked out the window first at the magnificence of God's creation as they flew down into the Grand Canyon, then at the brilliance of man's creation as they flew close to America's largest dam.

BARRY sat in the helicopter with his arm around Maxine, breathing in the scent of her hair, feeling the press of her warm, lithe body against his, and had to close his eyes to battle for focus.

To say that he had never acknowledged Maxine's attractiveness would quite simply be a lie. Even married, when he struggled with the pain of his wife's betrayal and wanting to keep everything right with God so that his prayers about his wife would be answered, he could not help but acknowledge Maxine's loveliness. Calling her beautiful would be an understatement. When she walked into a room, every man and many women would simply stop and look at her. Her physical beauty surpassed anything he could have ever imagined in a woman.

Except, beauty fades, and Barry knew it meant little. Once he learned how to redirect that initial punch of attraction every time he saw her, he almost got used to the way she looked. Then he got to know her spirit.

He had never met anyone so colorful in his life. She took life head-on, with a smile and a laugh. She took delight in little things like the wonderful taste of an appetizer at a social function, and took delight in fun things like getting tickets to a Celtics game. She was fun, and vivacious, and relished life. On top of that, her loyalty to those she loved knew no bounds. He'd watched her for three years with her sisters, with Derrick, with Tony, and stood amazed at the generous spirit she had for her family.

Getting to know her through sports, as platonic as it could possibly be, worked for him. She was just a "buddy" and he felt like he wasn't doing anything wrong – and nearly convinced himself of that. Sitting here, now, on this helicopter with his arms around her and her body pressed close against him, as he closed his eyes and fought for some measure of control against his attraction, he knew he'd been lying to himself the entire time.

Over the years, the shared football games and basketball conversations, and lately the workout sessions, had been nothing more than a way to spend time with her, however he could, in any socially acceptable way. He knew that should he ever desire to reconcile with God again, that would definitely be something he would have to face.

He wondered what to do about it. They had two more days, here. Should he pursue it? Was a quick bowl game trip to Las Vegas the right place for this? Would his pursuit cheapen what could be? He considered the line of men in Maxine's social life over the years and wondered.

A vibration in his pocket stopped his train of thought. He reluctantly relinquished his hold on her. When she shifted her body slightly away from his, he knew that the invite to touch had passed and that they would not return to their previous position. Then he looked out the window and saw the roof of the hotel approaching.

He fished his phone out of his pocket and saw the text message from Justin:

LAST MINUTE DINNER THEATER. LIMO IN 5
OR ELSE C U AT BREAKFAST.

Their helicopter landed twenty minutes later, and they unstrapped and handed the helmets back over to the pilot. He showed his phone to Maxine.

She looked at him, her cheeks flushed and her eyes sparkling with the excitement of the flight. "Wasn't that amazing?"

Barry tried to remember seeing anything out of the window, but drew a blank. Instead, he remembered the feel of her and the scent of her hair. "Absolutely. Definitely worth the trip. I'd love to do it again."

She read the text message. "So it's just us for dinner, then. Did you want to go anywhere in particular?"

With a shrug, he opened the door to the roof stairwell. "The steak place here in the hotel works for me."

THEY headed straight to the restaurant without stopping at their rooms first. They flashed their gold key cards and found themselves seated almost instantly. While they waited for their meals, Barry studied Maxine's face. She had pulled out her phone, verified the local time in Boston, and called to check on Robin. He watched her eyes in the glow of the candlelight, watched them light up while she talked with her sister about the baby and how Robin was feeling. When she hung up her phone, she grinned at Barry.

"I don't think it will be much longer. Sarah's been working the night shift lately, so she's been staying over there while Tony works during the day."

Barry laughed. "I'm surprised Tony hasn't opened a remote office out of his apartment."

"If there was room, I bet he would have by now."

"It's a good thing they haven't moved out to the coast, yet."

"He probably would have just hired a full time OB staff if they had," Maxine said, smiling as she put her napkin in her lap and leaned back in her chair to give the waiter space to set her salad in front of her.

Barry followed suit and took his spoon to his soup while they chatted about Tony and Robin. Their conversation moved from her family to football to working out to sports cars as they worked their way through soup and salad, thick T-bones, and a fruit and cheese plate.

As Barry signed the chit to have the meal billed to his room, Maxine suggested they walk the strip. "I know we saw it from the air this afternoon, but I'd love to see it up close at night."

"I think that's a great idea," Barry said. He helped her into her coat and slipped his on while they exited the hotel.

Maxine put her arms around herself. "Brr," she said. "I wouldn't have expected the desert to be this cold. I'm glad I thought to check the weather forecast before we left Boston."

Barry stepped closer intending to put his arm around her, hoping to help warm her, but she shifted away and pointed out some lighted sign. He watched her joy at all of the sights to see on their walk down the strip and enjoyed her much more than the man-made light show surrounding them.

Maxine surprised him when she took his hand. "Look!" She shouted. A woman in a wedding dress entered a building holding hands with a man in a tuxedo. Four girls in slinky red dresses and four men in tuxedos with matching red ties and cummerbunds followed. "Let's see if they're getting married," she said, pulling him forward.

She peered inside and laughed in delight. "Elvis is in there, all Blue Hawaii."

Barry looked over her head and grinned. "I can't see planning that."

She turned and looked up at him. He put a hand on either side of her head, boxing her in, and looked down at her. Her emerald eyes sparkled with joy and laughter, her cheeks and nose rosy with cold. "Planning what?" she asked with a smile.

"Planning to be joined together in holy matrimony by a 40-year-old man dressed like a dead rock star singing Blue Hawaii."

Maxine made a fist and playfully punched him in the stomach. "I think it would be fun as long as someone didn't try to take a pin and poke a hole in all the fun."

He slowly lowered his body so that he wasn't supported by his hands, but by his forearms, bringing him even closer to her. He could feel her body heat and only his knowledge of how she usually shied away from touch kept him from pressing all the way up against her. Instead he stared down at her as the lights and crowd and noise around him faded away.

Maxine stared up at him, and her smile slowly turned more serious as she looked away from his eyes and briefly to his mouth before looking back at his eyes. He desperately wanted to take that as an invitation to kiss her, but he had no desire to see her bolt. However, the temptation was too strong to ignore so he slowly, very slowly, just to give her time to get used to how close he was, to give him some signal that she would rather he not, he lowered his head until their breath mingled.

For the first time in her life, Maxine wanted — desperately wanted — to be kissed. The nerve endings in her lips came alive, aching, waiting, needing to feel Barry's pressed against hers. She held her breath, stared into his blue eyes, and noticed that they darkened when he watched the tip of her tongue dart out to lick her dry lips.

She wondered what to do from here. It seemed that if he wanted to kiss her, he would have already. A drive she didn't recognize compelled her to grab the lapels of his jacket and pull him closer. Just when she thought she would have to actually beg him to kiss her, he closed the distance and covered her mouth with his.

Maxine felt her breath shudder out of her body. No fear. She realized as her arm snaked around his neck and she raised herself up on her toes to get closer to him that she felt absolutely no fear.

How exhilarating!

He wrapped a strong arm around her waist and pulled her closer to him even as he stepped forward, pushing her further back against the window.

She wanted to feel him, touch him, caress him. A very base and visceral need rose up in her and made her head spin. Desperate to catch her breath, she ripped her mouth away and framed his face with her hands.

He pressed his forehead against hers and kept his eyes closed, breathing hard, gripping her hips with his hands. He smelled good. He felt good. She wanted to run her lips over his cheek, along his neck, feel his pulse under her lips.

He slowly raised his head and looked down at her while she leaned her head against the glass window behind her and solemnly returned his glance.

With achingly gentle movements, he brushed a strand of hair off of her face. Then he smiled, a smile that lit up his face and lightened his eyes. "Want to get married by an Elvis impersonator, Maxine?" he asked.

She somehow knew he was teasing, lightening the mood. But the answer popped out of her mouth as if from a wellspring deep inside of her. Before she knew what she was saying, the word was out.

"Yes."

EMERALD FIRE - CHAPTER 11

PRESENT DAY

AS soon as Maxine had fallen asleep, Barry spent long minutes just staring at her, marveling at her beauty. He felt a thrill in every cell of his body at the sheer perfection, the indescribable loveliness of his beautiful bride. She presented such a tough exterior to the world, so confident, so self-assured. In the hours since the wedding ceremony, he had learned about a different person completely. In reality, she was so vulnerable and so fragile.

Despite the fact that she had visibly forced herself to relax each and every time he touched her, the fact was that she tensed up first and without fail, each and every time. Laying next to him, asleep, he reached out and tenderly ran his fingers through her raven tresses eliciting a contented moan from her in her dreams. There was no tension in her sleep, no fear, no unreasonable terror at his tender touch.

He lifted the covers, threw on his jeans, and slipped outside. He strolled over to the patio and opened the door. The cold blast struck his bare chest and he thought better of it. He found her key, then, barefoot and shirtless, rushed to his room and threw on a cotton sweater. Looking at the time, he realized that the sun would soon rise over the desert.

Back in Maxine's room, Barry casually picked up the phone and dialed up room service. In a quiet voice, he ordered coffee, hot tea, and a continental breakfast and sides of breakfast steak and boiled eggs. He ordered pineapple juice, fresh cold milk, and four orders of yogurt. He asked that it be delivered in thirty minutes or so if possible.

Then he started to think. First, he reviewed the events of the previous evening. He had been engaged for less than two hours. During that time, he and Maxine got the paperwork handled and purchased the largest emerald encrusted diamond engagement ring this place had to offer. Then he had solemnly looked Elvis in the eye and answered, "I do."

Jacqueline had been dead and buried just over three weeks. Apparently, he chose to mourn his late wife by pursuing, marrying, and bedding the one woman whom he had found attractive since the very first time he had laid eyes on her. Any shred of self-respect he felt for himself after Jacqueline's betrayal vanished in a moment of self-loathing at his present low state.

The sick thing, the twisted thing, the awful thing that he could not have known until last night was that Maxine loved him. She loved him no matter how unworthy of accepting that love he felt. She loved him, she married him, and she surrendered to him. The look in her eyes when she said "I do," spoke volumes.

The terrible truth Barry wrestled with this morning, a truth that shook him to his core, was that he might not love Maxine in the same way. He felt like he had just stolen something he had no right to possess, like a low criminal. Like a deceitful thief. He felt dirty. He felt unworthy.

Room service quietly knocked and Barry bounded with surprising stealth and grace for a man of his bulk to catch the door before they knocked again. He handed the young man a huge tip, the crumpled cash in his right jeans pocket, and wheeled the cart inside himself. Peripherally, he heard the shower going in the next room. So, she was awake.

He poured himself a cup of hot tea and walked to the patio door. He held his cup in his right hand and leaned against the cool glass overlooking the rising sun, supporting his entire weight on his left hand.

He sipped the tea and contemplated how Maxine deserved so much better. She deserved so much more than he could offer. He would not run her home and introduce her to his family as the woman he had wedded and bedded in Las Vegas less than a month after his first wife died. He would not subject her to that kind of scrutiny. He would not subject himself to any backhanded whispered sneers. He refused to put them through that.

No. He would undo it. He would fix it. It was the least he could do for Maxine for the constant friendship and trust she had given him over the years. He resolved himself as the bedroom door opened behind him.

BARRY stood staring out through the patio door. He wore dark blue jeans and a cream colored sweater that stretched across his strong back. His feet were bare, and Maxine felt a little flutter of warmth at the intimacy of that. She thought back over the last several weeks, amazed at how the events transpired to bring them to this place, this here and now. Had it only been three weeks since Jacqueline's funeral? Since their shared dinner after fleeing from the church?

Barry turned as soon as she opened the door and their eyes met across the room. Maxine's smile froze at the stoic look on his face. "Hi." His voice sounded low, scratchy, thick. She wondered if he had slept at all.

"Hi." She smiled. She noticed the cup in his hand. "Is there coffee, too, or just tea?"

Using the cup, he gestured at the room service cart sitting next to the table and chairs. "I didn't know how to make the coffee, so I just ordered you some instead."

Warmth flooded her heart at his thoughtfulness. "Thank you." She crossed the room and poured herself a cup of coffee. Her hand shook a little bit. What did they do now? What did they talk about? How did she handle this first full day of being Mrs. Barry Anderson?

When she turned back around, she saw that he had silently moved and now stood next to the couch.

"Obviously, we need to talk."

She didn't like the sound of his voice. No warmth, nothing she had felt from him the night before existed in his tone. She gripped the cup so hard she was surprised it didn't shatter. "Yeah." Needing to ease her own tension, she teased, "Kind of a little late for that, isn't it?"

His bark of laughter signaled his agreement with her statement and she smiled a stiff smile as she crossed the room toward him. As soon as she sat on one end of the couch, with her back to the arm, he sat down, too, closer to the middle.

In a way, she was glad he didn't sit at the other end of the couch thus leaving a huge expanse of leather between them. In a way, she wished he had, so maybe she wouldn't actually feel the warmth of his body and want to scoot closer to him. He set his tea on the coffee table and turned his body toward her. "I don't know what came over us last night – what came over me."

Maxine tilted her head and looked closely at his face. He had circles under his eyes. It didn't look like he'd slept at all. She put her cup down next to his and slid forward, fighting down years of survival instinct to take his hand. She cared about this man. She had cared about him for a long time. He was a dear friend, and considering the things that he had experienced over the years, she hated to think that she had added to any pain in his life.

"Shh," she said. Heart pounding in fear of being the first to move toward any kind of intimacy, she knelt next to him, one knee on the couch cushion while she planted her other foot on the ground to brace herself. Placing a hand on his cheek, she leaned forward and rested her forehead against his. "Last night was wonderful."

Barry groaned and gripped her hips with his hands. He closed his eyes and sighed. "Getting married wasn't the right thing to do."

"It's done, though."

When he opened his eyes, she leaned back away from the resignation she saw there. "I can undo it."

She raised an eyebrow. "Can you? It's legal, binding, and consummated. What can you undo?"

He smiled for the first time since she came out of the bedroom. "I'm a lawyer, Maxi. I can undo it."

She wanted to scream, "No!" but instead started to shift back, to break the physical contact with him while she asked, "Do you really think we should?"

Before she could completely withdraw, he gripped her wrist to hold her still. "I value your friendship, Maxine. I've lost so much. I can't lose that, too."

Cupping his face with her hands, she gave him the gentlest whisper of kisses. "You haven't lost my friendship." She pushed away fully and straightened, pulling her wrist from his hand. She felt her pulse accelerate and her heart start to flutter. Panic made it hard to breathe, and she put a hand against her stomach. "What time do we need to leave for the game?"

Barry opened his mouth, then closed it again. He cocked his head and looked at her, then looked at his watch. "We have some time."

Maxine nodded. "Good." She rubbed her hands together, trying to stimulate some warmth. "Then let's eat, and I'll call one of the girls and see what everyone's plans are this morning." She froze when he reached out and gently took her left hand in his large grip. She looked down at him and saw him staring at her face. As soon as they made eye contact, he looked at her hand. "While you're out, I'll see about returning the ring."

How had she forgotten the ring? Wouldn't that have been the kicker? To go home with a wedding ring the size of Rhode Island on her finger? She felt a small tremble in her hands as she took the ring off and surrendered it to him. "Of course. I hope they'll take it back."

"I'll take care of it." His fingers closed around it and his hand formed into a fist. "Go ahead and make the phone call and I'll set out breakfast."

After breakfast, which ended up being the most tense, silent meal the two had ever shared, Barry went to his room. Maxine turned around in a circle in the middle of her huge suite, gripping the sides of her face, feeling as if the room would close in on her at any second. She wanted to scream and wail, but feared someone would hear, so she fell to her knees and sobbed, silently, heel of her hand pressed against her mouth to keep the sound down to low groans.

As soon as she felt like she could function, she rose to her feet and stumbled to her phone. Fingers quaking, she clumsily maneuvered the internet and worked the buttons until she found a flight out for Boston that morning. She called down to the front desk and requested a shuttle to McCarran, then very quickly packed.

She scanned the room for any rogue articles of clothing, and found Barry's shoes, socks, sweater, and jacket on the floor of the bedroom near the patio door. As much as she wished she could just sneak out without saying good bye, she knew that was the wrong thing to do.

After washing her face and carefully applying makeup, Maxine took his folded clothes and left the sanctuary of her suite. She went to his door and lightly tapped.

He answered very quickly, opening the door as if expecting her. She noticed he'd showered and changed clothes.

"I, uh, didn't want to bother you," she started to say, but he cut her off.

"You're not bothering me." He stood back and opened the door wider. "Come in."

No. No way. She couldn't go into his room. Chances are good she'd end up throwing herself at him, begging him to love her just a little bit, cherish her and protect her like Elvis had made him promise. Her heart stopped and she wondered where that thought had come from. "No thank you. I just wanted to bring you these things." She held out the neatly folded stack of clothes with his shoes carefully perched on top. "I decided to go on home. I'm not up for the game."

His eyes widened and he reflexively took the clothes from her. Before he could speak, Maxine pivoted and rushed back to her room.

"Maxi, wait!"

She turned as she unlocked her door and watched as he tossed the clothes into the room behind him before rushing toward her. "What, Barry?" Her voice sounded tired to her own ears.

"I'm going to get a flight out tonight right after the game. I'll bring paperwork by tomorrow or the next day. Hopefully tomorrow since Friday's Christmas Eve. I'm not positive what hours the clerks at the courthouse are working Friday."

She almost asked him what he meant then realized he was talking about the annulment. For some reason, that made sadness overwhelm her again. But she knew it had to happen. "Sounds good," she said. "I'll be at Robin's. I just got a text from Sarah. Tony has some fire somewhere he has to handle out of town and won't be back until Friday. So I'll just go straight there and stay through Christmas."

He nodded and she opened her door. He stood there, looking down at her. She waited several heartbeats before she spoke. "I had an amazing time, Barry. Thank you for inviting me."

Somberly, he nodded, his lips tight. "See you tomorrow, I guess."

She stepped into her room and shut the door in his face. The smile she'd forced faded away and her knees felt weak. Leaning against the door, she slid down until she sat with her back against the door and her face buried in her knees, silent sobs wracking her body.

EMERALD FIRE - CHAPTER 12

BARRY brushed ice and snow off his overcoat as he stepped into the lobby of Tony's apartment building. A security guard at the big circular desk looked up from his computer monitor and welcomed him by name. "Mr. Anderson, Mrs. V said to tell you that she and Miss Bartlett are running late, but to please go up and wait for them." He pushed a button on his console and an elevator door apart from the bank of elevators opened.

Barry nodded his thanks and shifted his briefcase to his other hand as he entered Tony's private elevator. It only went to the top floor, so the ride up twenty stories took no time.

He should have brought the annulment paperwork yesterday, but he got bogged down with work that accumulated during his brief absence. Since he couldn't ask his secretary or any of his paralegals to prepare the documents, he did it on his down time and didn't finish until late last night. Now here it was, not only Friday, but Christmas Eve. So even if she did sign tonight, they wouldn't be able to do anything with them until Monday.

What he ought to do, he thought, is just leave and make a lunch date with her for Monday so that she didn't have to associate Christmas Eve with annulment paperwork. Still, getting it done as quickly as possible seemed better for all parties involved.

The elevator door slid open into Tony and Robin's apartment. He stepped out of the elevator into a small entryway. A coat stand beckoned. Out of habit, he removed and draped his coat on a spare hook. He set his briefcase on the small bench next to it and then walked fully into the apartment.

Stepping down a step into the living area, his feet sank into the plush carpet. The smell of gingerbread spice from the flickering candles on the fireplace mantle warmed him, and the glow of the huge Christmas tree standing next to the far window gave the room a loving, intimate feel. He had always felt as "at home" in Tony's apartment as he had in his own home, sometimes more-so. When Robin moved in after marrying Tony, that feeling had only become more intimate.

A large circular black leather couch surrounded the living area. Barry sat down and closed his eyes, weary to his bones. He hadn't slept much the last few nights. He scooted down and propped his feet on the coffee table, intending to doze until Maxine came back. Something pushed against his back and he shifted again, trying to get comfortable.

He winced and reached behind him, pulling a sketch pad out of the cushions. He glared at it, as if it were the cause of all of his problems, and started to toss it to the table but paused.

After some hesitation, he opened it, feeling a little like a kid sneaking a look at Christmas presents, or the pesky brother reading big sister's diary. Without permission, it would be wrong to look at this, but Maxine was the only artist in the house and the temptation overwhelmed him. So, with an ear tuned for the sound of the elevator's hum, he started flipping through the pages.

He had very little actual exposure to any of Maxine's work. He had only ever seen the pieces Tony owned. Only what he saw in the sketch pad stunned him. He didn't know it was possible to create the details he saw with a mere pencil. He didn't know that moods and entire depths of emotion could be portrayed in plain black and white. Reaching over to the lamp next to him, he flipped it on for better light by which to see.

The first sketch portrayed Robin, laughing and grinning, holding a pair of baby booties behind her back while Tony tucked a strand of hair behind her ear, looking at her with such an expression of love that the page nearly sizzled with it. Barry smiled, remembering that was how Robin had told him she was pregnant, by handing him a pair of baby booties. Another one showed Sarah in her nursing uniform, her curly hair barely contained by the clips that secured it back, her eyes serious behind her trim glasses.

He flipped the page and paused, staring at his own face drawn four different times on one page, showing different angles and expressions. She captured the details of his face so perfectly that it was like looking in a mirror. The next three pages were of him, lifting weights at the gym, sitting in that impossibly little metal chair at their breakfast cafe, standing by his Jeep with his skull cap pulled low over his ears while he drank a bottle of water after a morning run. He smiled and turned another page.

His stomach turned while he stared at the drawing. It was a woman, an older version of Robin, with haggard lines on her face and dead eyes. Her stringy, dirty hair crawled up in greasy strands out of a rubber band behind her neck. She sat on a worn couch wearing a T-shirt and jeans, staring down at the inside of her arm while a man with dark hair and hard, mean eyes filled a syringe from a dirty spoon with confidence born of experience. Glasses and a bottle of gin, a few beer cans, and cigarette butts littered the table in front of them.

Barry knew Maxine's childhood story. He had defended Robin's father a few years ago against murder charges. He knew enough of the story to know that the woman in the sketch represented their mother and her boyfriend, the man and woman whom Robin's father had slain.

The next few pages showed more of Robin, Tony, and Sarah. Robin in varying stages of her pregnancy, Tony in different poses, Sarah in various moods.

Then he saw himself again, more close-ups of his face, one of him gesturing at a football game on television.

Eagerly, he turned to the next page. Sick fear churned inside his gut before a slow rage overtook the feeling. A man loomed over a girl on a bed, one hand covered her mouth, the other pawed at the waistband of her pants. He leered down at her, his eyes insane, mean, unspeakably selfish. His unbuttoned shirt revealed a tattoo of an eagle on his chest. Barry didn't like recognizing it, but the girl beneath him was a very young Maxine. Hatred and tears filled her terrified eyes while she clawed at the hand covering her mouth. She had her knees bent as she struggled against her molester.

He didn't want to look at the picture anymore, so he turned the page and noticed the tremor in his hand. It was the last page in the book, and it was of him again, but not in this apartment like the others. This was in Vegas, in Maxine's bed, her head on his shoulder, his arms around her, her hair spread over them like a blanket.

He flipped back to the previous page, then forward again to the last one. So many questions answered from a simple pencil sketch. He had known Maxine's story. He had known that her drug addict mother had moved her and her three daughters from man to man, pimp to drug dealer. He had known that Robin and Maxine and Sarah's early years had been the building blocks of nightmares.

After serving fifteen years for dealing cocaine, Robin's biological father had walked out of prison and promptly murdered Robin's mother along with her current sleazy boyfriend. That double murder had sent Robin and Maxine into the system and young Sarah to her adoptive parents. He'd known that as soon as Robin turned eighteen, she got a job at Hank's Place and, with the help of her employer, obtained legal counsel and gained custody of Maxine. When Maxine was fifteen, they'd finally lived together as a family.

He had intellectually known all of that, but somehow had never applied it to Maxine; not to the Maxine he knew. She was so happy, so vivacious, so full of life that it never occurred to him to equate her with the girl who cowered in a closet while she listened to the gunshots that took her mother's life, to the young teen who clawed at the hands of the man with the eagle tattoo on his chest.

Not ready to face her right now, Barry shoved the sketchbook back into the couch and sprang up. He hurried now, afraid that they'd step off the elevator any moment, worried that they'd cross paths in the lobby. He snatched up his coat and briefcase and left, pushing against the floor of the elevator with the bottom of his feet as if he could make it go faster. Thankful to find a lobby empty of anyone he knew, he mumbled some excuse to the guard and exited the warm building into the icy wet blast of the Boston Christmas Eve.

MAXINE laughed as she and Robin stepped off the elevator, bags in hand. "You shouldn't wait 'til Christmas Eve to go shopping, especially nine months pregnant," she said with a smile.

"I hate shopping." Robin set her many packages on the floor while she unbuttoned her coat and slipped it off her shoulders.

"Yes, I know, silly, but it still has to be done and waiting until Christmas Eve isn't going to make it any better."

"You're right. But it's done now."

"I just hope we can get them wrapped before Tony and Sarah get here."

Robin froze. Maxine had a moment of panic thinking she was about to say that the baby was coming. Instead she put her hands to her cheeks and said, "Wrapping paper!"

Maxine hugged Robin, love flooding her heart. "I brought some. I know you, you see."

"Ugh! I can't wait to have this baby! I can't think when I'm pregnant."

They set up a wrapping assembly line in the dining room, working quickly while they chatted. "You haven't told me much about your trip," Robin said, folding the corners of a box that contained an engraved stethoscope for Sarah.

Maxine felt her fingertips get cold. She paused cutting the paper around a new scarf for Tony. What should she say? Should she say anything at all? "It was cool. We took a helicopter tour."

"Yeah," Robin said dryly. "You've said all that."

The scissors fell out of her hand and clamored onto the table. Tears welled up in Maxine's throat then with a sob, poured out of her eyes. Robin immediately put down everything she was doing and wrapped Maxine into her arms, as she had when she was a little girl – when they were both little girls. "What's wrong?"

Maxine fought to control her voice long enough to blurt out, "Robin, I love Barry."

Robin had been rubbing her shoulder blades, but her hands froze. "What?"

Putting both heels of her hands against her eyes, attempting to stop the flow of tears, Maxine backed away. "I do. I love him. And I'm in love with him."

"Maxi." Robin said the word on a sigh and Maxine immediately felt defensive. She almost knew what her sister would say next. "You're in love all the time. Men come and go ..."

The tears dried as a touch of anger wormed through. "Stop." Robin stopped with her mouth open, obviously unaccustomed to Maxine's anger. Maxine continued, "Stop talking. I have never come to you crying over any man. I'd appreciate it if you would respect my feelings."

"I ..."

Maxine held up a hand. "No. I know you're opinion about my relationship with him. I've listened to every word you've said. You don't approve. I get it. You think I will chew him up and spit him out. He's been hurt. Blah blah whoopity blah. The fact of the matter is that I am the one crying. I am the one hurt. And what you're not going to do is try to make me into some frigid, man-eating black widow who just leaves remnants of past relationships in her wake."

Robin reached out and touched her shoulder. "Maxi, I don't think that about you. I love you and admire your spirit and your nature. I've never thought that about you. But you have regularly professed love for one man or another since you were in high school."

Maxine took her sister's hand and looked her in the eye. "I've always hoped that the next guy, the next relationship, would make me forget. But they never have." More tears filled her eyes, spilled down her cheeks. "I kept thinking that this one could hold my hand and I wouldn't feel terrified that he'd pull me down, or that one with his arm around me in a movie wouldn't make me feel like I was drowning in fear."

Robin cried now. Few could relate the way she could. "I understand."

"But with Barry it's different. This weekend I realized how much I care for him. And I realized I am in love with him."

Robin paused and tilted her head. "But?"

With a sigh, Maxine squeezed Robin's hand and let it go. She picked up the scissors again and went back to cutting. "But – his wife has been dead for less than a month. But – he's twelve years older than me. But – he's your husband's best friend. But – he's undergoing a spiritual crisis right now."

Maxine heard Robin clear her throat. "Speaking of that," she said, picking up the tape again. "You haven't been to church since Jacqueline's funeral."

With a sigh, Maxine finished cutting the paper and started folding it around the box. "I know. That's what I mean. Now isn't good for Barry."

"So what will you do?" Robin held a piece of tape out on the tip of her finger.

Maxine took the offered tape. "I don't know what to do. I've never been in love with a man before. I guess give him some room."

"Why don't you pray about it?"

Her fingers paused on the package and she looked at her sister. "I know you get something out of that, but honestly, Robin, I never have. I don't understand how you do it. I don't know what to say or how to hear an answer."

Robin tilted her head and looked at her very seriously. "Do you believe God answers?"

"I don't know." She quit messing with the package and pulled a chair out to sit down, suddenly feeling very tired. "I don't know."

Robin pulled the chair next to her out and sat down, angling so that their knees touched. She reached out and took Maxine's hands. "Matthew seven promises us that God will answer our prayers. What you need to do is relinquish that final hold you have on the control in your life to God, trust Him, and you will find an amazing whole new world out there with direction and purpose and security."

Maxine felt a longing in her heart, a physical tugging. Her breath caught so suddenly that she had to clear her throat. "I don't know how."

Robin smiled. "Let me pray for you. Just relax and close your eyes and let me pray." Robin bowed her head and after a moment, Maxine followed suit. Robin's voice very gently washed over her as she began praying. "God, thank You for my sister. Thank You for saving us, thank You for bringing us together all of those years ago. Thank You for Your son, Jesus."

Memories flooded Maxine's mind, of stench and drugs and screams and blood. She smelled gunpowder and felt hunger pains and fear. "Lord, I would like to pray for her right now. I'd like for You to guide her to You, to give to her what You have given to me; peace that passes all understanding, love beyond all measure, deep and abiding joy over anything else. Help her to trust You like she has never trusted another person. Teach her how to find in Your Word the direction she seeks, and answers to the questions that plague her."

The memories that assaulted Maxine faded into the background and a mantle fell over her, as if someone had laid a blanket over her shoulders. She felt her hands tremble in Robin's as a warmth flooded her body.

"If her love for Barry is what You would have, Lord, give her wisdom in how to handle the situation so that Barry returns to Your arms and they can worship You together. Thank You, God, for allowing us to come to You this way, for being our Father, for loving us so much. Thank You for the gift of your Son, and for our salvation. It is in Your Son's holy and precious name that I pray, Amen."

Sobs shook Maxine's shoulders as she fell out of her chair and onto her knees at her sister's feet. She lay her head in Robin's lap, against her sister's ample pregnant belly, and cried while Robin soothed her with hands running through her hair and her voice speaking calming, soothing words.

SUNDAY afternoon after Christmas, Maxine went back to her apartment to get ready for evening services at church. Weary, she got out of Derrick's primer gray Shelby Mustang and watched him squeal down her street. She had not come home in more than a week. First, on the Vegas trip with Barry, then spending the nights at Robin's house while Sarah worked the third shift and Tony worked out of town.

She spent Christmas Eve with Robin and Tony, Sarah, and Derrick and they all woke up Christmas morning to full stockings, compliments of Santa Tony, and a huge waffle breakfast, compliments of Chef Maxine.

Christmas evening, Derrick, Sarah, and Maxine went to the movies and back to Sarah's apartment for coffee and gingerbread cookies made by Sarah's adopted mom. By the time they finished their third round of Trivial Pursuit, during which Derrick and Sarah traded insults with alarming regularity, Maxine felt exhausted. Derrick offered to drive her home, but they quickly discovered that the rain which had started that evening had turned into an ice storm that trapped them. Sarah's roommate was stuck at the hospital working the third shift, so Maxine took her room. Derrick, who seemed uncharacteristically angry at the situation, took the couch.

All she wanted was her bathtub with the jets and whirlpools and some loud music drowning out any thoughts she might have the energy to think. As Maxine wearily climbed the steps to the entrance of her apartment, balancing boxes and bags of Christmas presents, an overnight bag slung over her shoulder, she saw a movement out of the corner of her eye. Startled, she turned and saw Barry walking toward her. He wore a heavy wool coat the color of burnt charcoal and a black ski cap pulled low over his ears. Her heart skipped a little beat at the sight of him. She hadn't seen him since the hallway of the hotel. "Barry. Hi."

He stopped at the base of her steps. From the middle step, she met him at eye level. "Where have you been?"

She frowned. "Been?"

"I've been trying to call you since last night."

"Oh. We got trapped by the ice."

"We?"

Maxine looked down the street where Derrick's car had disappeared and back to Barry's scowling face. "What's going on?"

"I'm a little curious about who just dropped you off."

Maxine felt her jaw clench in reaction to the supposition. "Oh. Well that would be that 'none of your business' person." She whirled around and reached into her pocket to grab her keys to the outer door of her building when she heard the sound of the throttle of the engine of the Mustang pause behind her and Derrick's voice call out to her.

"Maxi!"

Closing her eyes and taking a deep breath, she turned and smiled. "Did I forget something?"

"You might need these," he said as he held her keys out through the open window. "They must have fallen out of your coat. I found them on the front seat." He looked at Barry. "Hey man. Check out the Christmas present from Tony!" He grinned as he revved the engine.

Barry nodded back. "He told me he was on the lookout for one but never came back with whether he'd found it or not. It sounds fantastic."

"Needs a paint job and a little bit of work. She'll be a beaut' when she's done."

"Oh, yeah."

Looking at Barry with her lips tight, Maxine shoved her boxes and bags toward him. With surprise on his face, he grabbed them to keep them from falling to the snowy ground while she carefully stepped down from the steps and walked to the curb. "Thank you for turning around. It would have been a cold afternoon waiting for someone to bring me keys."

Derrick laughed. "I bet. Merry Christmas again, and thanks for the jacket."

"Bye."

She turned around and glared again at Barry. "What were you asking again?"

"Nothing." He cleared his throat while she unlocked her door. "Always good to see Derrick None of My Business DiNunzio."

Maxine glared at him and fumbled with her keys with gloved hands. Barry said, "Hey, I'm sorry. I just ..."

"Sorry? You just? What kind of girl do you think I am, exactly?" She pushed open the door and started up the staircase to her apartment. Her voice echoed against the blank walls. "Never mind. You don't need to answer that." She stopped outside of her apartment door and turned to look at him. "I'm sorry. I shouldn't have gotten angry. I'm just worn out." She took the strap of her overnight bag from his shoulder. Setting the bag at her feet, she reached for the boxes he held. "I'll take these."

Barry shifted so that she couldn't take anything from him. "I'll carry them inside."

With a shrug, Maxine opened the door. "How was your Christmas?"

"Christmas?" Barry followed her into her apartment. She led the way to the living room, where she tossed her keys and purse on the black coffee table and gestured toward the tree. "You can set those things there, if you want. I'll sort through it all later." While he completed that small task, she noticed the light blinking on her answering machine. "Did you leave me a message?"

Barry turned and took his cap off as he did so. "No. I called your cell. Several times."

Snapping her fingers as if she just remembered something, she took her cell phone out of her purse. "I turned it off at the movies yesterday and forgot to turn it back on." As she pressed the button to power up the phone, she went to her desk and hit the "play" button on her answering machine.

"Maxine. Hi. This is Henry. From the office." Maxine shook her head. As if she wouldn't recognize or place the team member from a huge project she's been working on. "Listen, our meeting with Crow has been moved up to Monday morning. Vic is counting on you to make story boards. Just go with the last good idea we had. Thanks. Nine a.m. Looking forward to it. Hope you have a good Christmas."

Maxine froze. The last good idea they had was to discard everything and start fresh Monday morning. She had missed a full week of work. She snatched the phone out of the cradle and checked recent calls. This message had been left Thursday evening – the day before Christmas Eve.

"Maxi ..."

Remembering Barry, she slowly turned. "Barry, I can't talk right now."

She couldn't avoid doing the presentation. Crow Chicken was the biggest client to cross her firm's threshold ever. Daniel Crow had searched the city high and low for an agency that could present him with fresh new ideas, and he had chewed up and spit out nearly everyone on the block. Mitchell & Associates had an opportunity to step up to the big leagues, here. She didn't think Crow would accept the excuse of a junior associate who ran off to Vegas to watch a football game as a good enough excuse to postpone this meeting.

The only problem was she had nothing. Her mind drew a blank on any good idea she might have. Knowing how many firms he'd dismissed made any idea she could come up with in those terrifying first few minutes seem tired, used, unsellable. The right presentation would land her the much sought after partnership. The wrong one, well ...

Her phone rang, startling her. Recognizing Sarah's number, she distractedly answered.

"Just checking to make sure you got home okay. Derrick drives like an idiot, and the roads are still so bad."

"I'm fine. Listen." Groaning out loud, she decided desperate times called for desperate measures. "Sarah, what's the first thing that comes to mind when you think of fried chicken?"

"The hapless genocidal slaughter of innocent hormone-fed fowl for the sake of human convenience and the almighty dollar. Oh! And greasy fried food clogging arteries and raising cholesterol leading to high-blood pressure, Type II Diabetes, and heart failure. Why do you ask?"

Realizing the folly of asking her vegan sister's opinion on the matter, she snapped back. "Oh, give me a break. You couldn't help me out just a little here, could you?"

"Sorry, sis. Best I can give you. Want to talk about spinach?"

"Gee, thanks." She rubbed a sudden ache in the center of her forehead. "My entire career may be at stake, and now the only thing in my head is a gruesome picture of chickens running in terror from carnage while innocent diners drop dead from coronaries. Really appreciate it."

"Just keep thinking of it the next time you're trying to decide between the Caesar salad and the chicken salad. Then I'll know I've accomplished something."

Maxine blinked. "Sarah, you wouldn't pick the Caesar salad, either, because it has cheese in it, and, horror of horrors, dressing made from dairy products and salty little fish."

Sarah chuckled. "Well, for you, being that you are an unrepentant carnivore, we're taking it slow. Baby steps, hon. Baby steps."

Maxine rolled her eyes and ended the call abruptly. "Never mind. I've got to go. I love you." She turned to Barry, who was unbuttoning his coat. "What about you?"

"Me?"

"What's the first thing you think of when you hear the words fried chicken?"

He responded without thinking. "Sunshine."

"Sunshine?" Her brow wrinkled in concentration. She still looked in his direction, but she didn't see him anymore. She saw sunshine. "Sunshine. Okay. What else?"

"Gingham checkered table cloth on lush green grass, blue skies, summertime, white dresses, potato salad." He shifted the coat from his shoulders and removed the envelope from the inner pocket.

The full power of her green eyes suddenly hit him once more, accompanied with a smile that warmed him more than that sunshine he'd just alluded to ever could. "Barry, you are wonderful. Absolutely wonderful."

She abruptly left the room, and he gave in to the impulse to follow her. "I think we need to talk, Maxine." He followed her through the apartment and through a door that led to her studio. He stopped suddenly, enveloped in a whole new world.

The studio was the size of an entire apartment. Bright light from the fluorescent lights she turned on lit the room with a white glow. Along one wall, supplies filled the shelves; paints and brushes and pencils and containers. A huge basket of clean rags sat on a shelf and a large basket of dirty rags overflowed below. One bookshelf held book after book after book of sketch pads. Against every wall, on every surface, she had stacked canvases; some empty, most completed.

Maxine went to a closet in the corner and opened it. Even more supplies lined the shelves in the closet. She drew out a stack of white drafting boards and shut the closet with her heel. "I know we need to talk, Barry. But I really need to work." She looked at him while she set the boards on her drafting table.

"Yes. But give me five minutes to show you this paperwork and we can meet for lunch tomorrow to go over it."

Maxine reached behind her head and started gathering up her long black tresses. Barry remembered the silky feel of her hair against his skin and suddenly and inexplicably missed it. "It will have to wait. I need to get this down before I lose it."

She grabbed a pencil from the holder in front of her and started sketching more quickly than he'd ever seen. It looked like her hand moved in double time.

Barry moved up behind her and watched a nearly identical scene to the one he had imagined unfold onto the blank space before her. A wrinkle of concentration appeared between her brow, and he found himself wanting to kiss it away. Within minutes she had the basic outline of people picnicking in a sunny field. The rough sketch looked perfect, and he watched as she set it aside and started working on a new scene on a fresh board.

"Snoop around all you want. I'll be done in a few minutes," Maxine said, her voice completely distracted, her mind elsewhere.

Curious, he moved toward a stack of canvases propped next to the window and began to inspect them. He started out just absently thumbing through the paintings, but ended up engrossed in them. They ranged in styles from abstract images, to portraits of photographic perfection, to landscapes. She had beautifully crafted each painting, filled them with detail, and imparted a range of strong emotions.

He moved to the shelf of sketch pads. Hundreds of them, he was sure it was hundreds, were stacked neatly and labeled with dates. Some ranged months at a time, some covered only a day. Deciding to fully accept her permission to snoop, Barry picked one out at random. The date on the spine went back five years, and he found sketch after sketch of Robin and Sarah. Another one chronicled Robin and Tony's wedding, detailing the elegance and grandness Tony had insisted upon. Book after book started giving Barry a view of her life from her eyes, something so few people could convey.

Three sketch pads were out of place under a box of paints. They were all over a decade old, and each had only one date on them. His hand trembled slightly as he opened the cover of the first one, instinctively suspecting the horror that would greet his eyes.

This drawing wasn't as – controlled – as the one he'd seen in Tony's apartment. The emotions of the artist poured out onto the page, making the lines almost jerky, the background details not as important. However, the details of the man were excruciatingly exact, down to a frayed buttonhole. The tattoo of the eagle on his chest was more exposed, and Barry saw that the tip of the wing headed toward the man's shoulder. His eyes moved lower on the page, but where Maxine should have been was just a shadow; no details at all.

He knelt on the floor next to the shelves and turned page after page as the image haunted him over and over again. Different rooms, different clothing, showing him that this wasn't a one time incident. On drawing after drawing, the girl remained shadowed.

"I used to have nightmares about it. I'd wake up and draw and draw until I couldn't even move my hand anymore." Her voice startled him. She stood directly behind him, her chin almost resting on his shoulder. "I burned most of the books, but eventually, I learned to keep them. I try to think of them as therapy. It was years before I could put myself in the picture."

Barry cleared his throat. "Who is he?"

"His name's Monty Jordan." She settled onto the floor next to him. "He was a foster parent when I was fourteen." She drew her legs up and rested her chin on her knees.

"Fourteen?" His voice came out sounding like a harsh whisper, almost pulled from him.

Maxine nodded. "Robin and I went there together. That was our fourth home in less than two years. He wasn't entirely fond of someone with mixed blood living under his roof and had all sorts of ways to show me."

"What happened?"

She smiled, still remembering absolute shock entering those evil eyes. "Robin caught him in the act one day and stabbed him with his own knife." Maxine shuddered. "I was covered in his blood when the cops got there. The paramedics took me, too, because I was so bloody and hysterical they couldn't figure out if I was hurt or not. Thankfully, the doctors examined me thoroughly and found enough physical evidence on me to put Monty in prison for a while." She tore her gaze from his and looked at the floor in front of her. "The hard part was getting separated from Robin after that. They sent her to a home for girls, and kept me in the foster system. It was a terrifying year before she was able to get out and several more months before she could get me."

Barry swallowed. Rage and pain boiled inside his chest, choking him. "Maxi ... "

She turned her head back around. "Hey, it's all a long time ago, now. I had an outlet for all of it. I never even dream about it anymore." She shook her head. "Well, sometimes I do. The other night I watched a bad scene in a movie at Robin's. So I did what I do. I drew it out, gave it its own life, and then let it die again."

"How can it be that easy?"

She laughed and turned to kneel, covering one of his hands with both of her own. "You think any of this was easy? This was twelve years ago. I still ...a man trying to touch me –" She paused and looked down, a flush covering her cheekbones. "Barry, you're the first man who has ever even kissed me." She shifted until she faced him, both of them kneeling on the wooden floor, the sketchbook the only thing separating them. Without thinking twice, she took it from his hands and tossed it on the floor next to her. "You're the only man who has never once made me feel terrified."

"There's no way for this to work, Maxine," he said as her arms went around his neck. She felt his pulse beneath her touch, his heart pounded so fast and hard she could almost hear it. Despite his words, his hands skimmed up her sides and hauled her closer to him.

"Shut up, Barry." Her legs hooked around his waist, her arms locked behind his thick neck, and she dragged his mouth to hers. For a moment, he remained completely still, fighting it with all of his will. It was a worthless battle and, with a groan of surrender, he wrapped his arms fully around her in return and kissed her back.

Maxine felt everything become right and perfect in the world the second his arms went around her. She sighed and hummed, feeling her love for Barry flow through every nerve ending in her body, making her head reel and her fingertips ache to touch his skin.

The second his lips softened against hers and he deepened the kiss, she heard her phone ringing. Maxine didn't move, didn't make a move to stop, so Barry ignored it too. Until his phone rang. From his pocket, the tones of a special ring broke through the fog that enveloped them. He lifted his head and shifted her away from him. "That's Tony."

Maxine shook her head as if to clear it and jumped up. "My phone's ringing, too." She dashed out of the room while he took the call. "Hey, brother."

Without preamble, Tony said, "It's time. St. Mary's."

Knowing without asking for clarification, Barry stood. "I'm close by. See you there."

Maxine came rushing back into the room. "That was Sarah. Robin's in labor."

"I know. I'll drive. My Jeep will do better on these roads." He held out a hand and she placed her slim one in his. "Let's go have a baby," he said, leading her from the room.

Chapter 14

AFTER waiting with nothing to do with her hands for nearly an hour, Maxine begged Derrick to run to her apartment and retrieve her boards and colored pencils. If the baby came between now and eight, she'd have to go to the meeting. If not, someone from her office would need to have them, anyway. She might as well get them ready.

Normally, she'd have everything scanned into the computer for an electronic presentation. Due to the rescheduling, there was no time for that, so they'd go the old fashioned route and present with just her boards. The hard part, getting her ideas down, had been accomplished. Coloring in was mindless, but it kept her hands busy and at least part of her mind occupied.

She sat with Barry and Derrick in the private waiting room connected to the room Robin occupied. Occasionally, Tony came in for a break, and twice Sarah stepped in to give them a brief update, only to go back into the room almost immediately.

Eventually, activity increased through that door, and every so often the sound of Robin's voice reached them. Sometimes she cried. Sometimes she screamed. Maxine's fingers gripped the pencil tighter and tighter as the hours passed.

She sat on the vinyl couch, supporting a large board on her thighs with her feet propped on the table in front of her. She glanced out of the corner of her eye as Derrick sat on the cushion next to her. "We never talked about it this weekend. How's school going, Derrick?"

He ran a hand through his hair. "Half of it is a complete waste of time. The other half is only mostly a waste of time. I guess it was my mistake telling Tony I wanted to manage hotels. I should have picked something that didn't require a degree."

"Nah. He would have sent you anyway. Besides, college was fun." She threw down the yellow pencil and selected the shade of red she wanted to use to color in the gingham cloth on the emerald green grass. Emerald green was her trademark color. All of her ads had it in there somewhere. "Sometimes, I wish I wasn't in the nine-to-five world and I still had Art 101 at ten."

"Hmm. Well, I happen to know that most of what they are teaching is obsolete and I already have practical experience with the few things they teach that are useful. Usually, I feel decades older than the other kids. And, there's the fact that my idea of a good time isn't going to O'Malley's Pub and getting falling down drunk three nights a week. That's a bit of a problem."

She laughed. "Yeah? What is your idea of a good time, Derrick?"

He shrugged, a habit brought from his life on the streets that he never shed. "A quiet evening, an intelligent woman, good food, stringed instruments."

"Well, there's that fiddle some nights at O'Malley's."

His smile looked strained. "How can you sit there and color like that?"

With a smile, she colored in the blue eyes of the little girl happily munching on a chicken leg. "You nervous, Derrick?"

"Honestly? I'm very nervous."

A piercing scream came through the door and the pencil Maxine held snapped in two. With a sigh, she set the board on the floor by her feet. "Yeah, me too."

"Why don't you go in there, Maxi?" Barry asked from the chair across from the couch. For the last hour, he'd pretended to find a two year old parenting magazine highly engrossing, but had actually surreptitiously studied Maxine, noticing how she gradually paled as the minutes stretched into hours, watched the lines around her lips slowly tighten.

She shuddered and shook her head. "No way."

Another scream came, peppered with some rather ingenious colorful language. Maxine ran her hands through her hair. "Aren't there drugs or something they can give her?"

"She didn't want anything. She wanted to do this all natural." Barry stretched in the little chair and contemplated going for a cup of tea from the coffee shop across the street.

Maxine surged to her feet and paced the small room, avoiding looking through the small window of the door separating her and the rest of her family. "How can you be so calm and collected? Can't you hear that?"

"I have three sisters, Maxi, with seven kids between them." His eyes followed her pacing around the room. "You'll feel better if you would go in."

She stopped in her tracks. "Um, no I won't. Trust me."

Barry laughed. "Why?"

"Because there's pain in there. And blood. And probably needles. No way. I'm not going. I'll just wait here until they get everything cleaned up and I'll never know how the whole process happened." She visibly jumped with another scream.

He grinned. "You don't like blood?"

"What a stupid question. How can anyone actually like blood?"

"I'll have to remember to tone down some of my football stories."

She heard Tony's voice this time, but he wasn't speaking English. She whirled around and looked at Derrick. "What did he say?"

"Maxine, I don't speak Italian."

She snapped at him. "Isn't your last name DiNunzio? How can you not speak Italian?"

Derrick shrugged again. Maxine snarled. Barry's chuckle distracted her from her retort. She whirled toward him. If he did that one more time she was going to hit him over the head with something.

"You don't plan on having children, Maxi?" Barry watched as she turned her back on him and paced the length of the room at nearly a jog. At the wall she stopped, tense and drawn. When she came to rest, she resembled still photographs of athletes taken the very instant before they spring into a sprint or set the world record for the longest jump. Her body nearly vibrated with restrained energy. She spun around and paced back to the table.

Barry's question confronted her. At the notion of children, all of the thoughts she had ever had about children over the course of her life including her own childhood experiences, tumbled through her head as she paced. Her face turned to study the sketches she had brought to life of imaginary families enjoying a summer picnic. She mentally overlaid their generic faces with her face, Barry's face, and the children became a blend of the two of them. His children. Her children. Their children. Children they would shelter and keep safe; children she could nurse, nurture, and feed; children he could teach, guide, and mentor. Children who would reach noble heights because, while they would understand the pain and horrors the world could bring to their doorstep, they would never personally experience it as long as blood beat through her veins.

Soundlessly, she studied Barry, and her possible future stretched out before her in the space of her glance. Then she remembered that Barry had some paperwork that would ensure none of those children would ever exist. Quietly, she said, "Maybe someday."

The moment broke when Robin's voice reached them again. Maxine began pacing again and offered, "But they have technology nowadays that makes all the pain just go away."

Twenty minutes later, the door opened and three sets of eyes flew to Sarah. The smile on her face helped them all relax just before she spoke. "We have a boy!" she said with a grin.

"A boy. Oh, how fun. Robin wanted a boy." Maxine rushed to her sister.

"What about Robin?"

Sarah laughed. "She's wonderful. A little hoarse, but fine." She opened the door again and looked over her shoulder. "In a few minutes it will be safe for you to come in, Maxi. Just let me get some of this cleaned up."

Maxine looked through the window and caught a glimpse of the baby as another nurse handed him to Robin. She felt a familiar hand on her neck and suddenly felt exhausted. Without a second thought, she leaned against Barry's side and smiled.

THE second she had her apartment door open, Maxine started moving. She whipped her shirt over her head on the way to her room, stopping only long enough to kick off her shoes. "Can you get those boards into my car?" she asked as she opened the door to her bedroom.

Barry heard his wife's words, but Maxine might as well have spoken them in some foreign tongue. The majority of his awareness was still trying to permanently burn the glimpse he'd gotten of her smooth brown back and the curves he had observed as she undressed mid-stride into his memory. She had been so casual about disrobing in his presence. He felt his pulse beating heavy in his fingertips and lips as memories of their wedding night flooded his mind.

"Barry?"

He cleared his head and her words all suddenly became clear in his understanding. Fit those boards into her tiny little sports car? "I doubt it."

"Argh!" Thirty seconds later, she stuck her head out of the doorway. This time, he caught sight of lace nearly identical to the color of her skin. His mouth went dry. "I don't have time to take the train. Maybe I'll call a cab?"

He shrugged. "I don't know if I'd trust a cab on this ice."

He could hear muttered words as she went back into her room.

Distracted by the thought of her dressing in the other room, he picked up the telephone and dialed his office. His secretary picked up on the first ring. "I'll be coming in late this morning. Send flowers to Robin Viscolli at St. Mary's. She had a little boy early this morning."

"Aww. Do you have the stats?"

"What stats? She had a baby. She didn't win the World Series."

"The baby's stats. Height, weight, all of that."

"What does that matter? The baby's healthy and Robin's doing fine."

"For heaven's sake, Barry, we've been through this seven times with your sisters. This is important information."

He sighed and rubbed his eyes, dimly remembering other conversations like this one. "Call Tony's secretary. She'll probably know."

"Okay. Do you at least have a name?"

"Antonio Frances Viscolli, Junior."

"Aww. What are they going to call him?"

He saw the envelope with the annulment papers in it. He reluctantly picked it up. "Am I supposed to know that, too?"

He heard a sigh in the receiver. "Never mind. I'll just call the Viscolli offices. What time can I expect you?"

He caught a whiff of perfume and glanced up as Maxine walked by him, wearing a bright yellow suit. The jacket fit snugly and the skirt barely brushed her knees, showing off her long legs. Her hands were up and behind her head while she whipped her hair around, twisting it into a fancy knot as easily as if she were putting it into a rubber band. As she turned her body to nudge the door to the dining room open with her hip, he noticed that she had hair pins clenched between her teeth.

Whether Elizabeth was still talking to him or not, he didn't know. "Listen, I'll be in later this morning, maybe. I'll call back later and let you know."

He hung up without waiting for confirmation and followed the trail of the spicy scent Maxine wore as if in a daze. He went through the dining room and into the kitchen, finding her biting into an apple.

"Did you call a cab?" she asked, catching a wandering drop of apple juice on her chin with her finger and gesturing at the phone in his hand.

The only thing he could think of was that she must be a witch who'd cast a spell on him. Otherwise, he wouldn't find a fully dressed woman eating an apple so completely tantalizing. "No. I'll just drive you."

Her expression didn't change as she eyed her husband's steady gaze. "What time is it?"

"Just after eight."

She nodded and brushed by him. "Okay. I can put makeup on during the ride."

He caught her arm and whirled her around. "Just a second."

"Wha..." Before the word was completely out, his mouth covered hers, sealing the question. The apple fell to the floor with a thump while Maxine smiled and stepped further into the circle of his arms.

MAXINE stepped out of the elevator and carried the boards through the hallway, already five minutes late. She didn't run, though, because she had the presentation to give, and she didn't want to show up out of breath. Peter Mitchell was already going to be rather peeved that he didn't get the quick rundown she'd promised him on the phone that morning, and she didn't want to add sloppy presentation skills to the strikes against her.

Still, as she nudged the door to the conference room open with her hip, she smiled to herself. The extra fifteen minutes she'd spent at home with her husband was worth all that trouble and more.

"Good morning everyone," she said, getting herself completely into the room. She headed straight for the head of the table, where the empty tripod awaited her boards. She spoke as she checked their order and neatened up the stack. "I'm so sorry I'm late. My sister had a baby boy this morning, and I'm afraid I didn't anticipate the traffic from the hospital." She turned and felt her smile freeze. Ten sets of eyes faced her, ten stony expressions. The only slightly pleasant face in the room was Pete's, and she could see through the slick expression down to the annoyance.

Four of the men allegedly were on her team, but they were the ones who dumped the entire project in her lap right before Christmas. She knew half of the reason they were angry was because Pete probably spent a good portion of the morning gouging them for doing just that. The other half was due to her coming in late with the boards because it showed the clients who among them had actually done the work. She gave all of them her sweetest smile. Only one, Henry Monroe, shifted in guilt.

The clients took up the other side of the table. Though she smiled and met each of their eyes individually, she received nothing in return. She sighed inwardly. This team had ripped through ten different agencies in a quarter, and she could already see Mitchell and Associates being added to the rejection pile.

"Before you begin," came a voice from the foot of the table, "and since you weren't a part of the initial consultations we've had with your firm, I'd like to make it clear that if you have anything even remotely similar to the ads that have been run in recent history for my company, my time is valuable and I don't want it wasted."

She focused on the source of the voice and could immediately see how this company had risen through the ranks of national fast food chains established decades in advance to become one of the fastest growing franchises in America. Power practically emanated from him as he sat there, sitting completely still wearing a spotless silk business suit. He was also incredibly handsome, obviously Native American, probably full blood, with his black hair tied in a ponytail on the back of his neck, and eyes dark enough to be nearly black.

Maxine had Tony Viscolli in her life for over three years. Dark, handsome men who radiated power no longer intimidated her. Rather, she found him endearing.

Added to that, she'd just spent fifteen minutes in Barry Anderson's arms, so she was completely unaffected by his otherwise devastating good looks. She was certain the ease with which she held herself as she responded surprised him. She knew that men in his position were used to some reverence from everyone. "You're right, Mr. Crow, I wasn't a part of the initial consultations. I apologize for going into this rather blindly, but I've seen the ads that have been produced for you in recent years, and to be honest, they did nothing to make me want to buy your chicken. Pop-culture hype may appeal to a younger audience, but it never appealed to me and I bet it didn't appeal to your primary demographic, your tried and true customer base, either."

Pete cleared his throat, and the other men shifted uncomfortably, but she ignored that when she saw the corner of Daniel Crow's mouth tilt up. That helped her relax almost completely. Not entirely. She still had to sell this. She cleared her throat.

"Again, I'll apologize ahead of time for the roughness of these boards. Half of them were done in the hospital waiting room, and part of them didn't get colored in so I'll ask you to use your imaginations."

She opened her mouth to speak but was interrupted again by Mr. Crow. "And was the rest of this group at the hospital working on this with you?"

She flashed him a brilliant smile. "No, I'm afraid not."

Crow glanced at the men sitting across from him at the table. "So, they gave you conceptual ideas and let you run with them?"

Still smiling, Maxine said, "No, the ideas you will see are entirely mine."

He nodded. "Then," he turned to Pete, "why is this crack team sitting in here this morning, Peter? Trying to learn something?"

Pete began with, "Mr. Crow, I assure you that…"

Crow held up a forestalling hand. He turned back to Maxine and nodded, and she took that as his permission to continue. "When I think of fried chicken, I don't think of a wild character screaming all over the screen with loud music playing. I think of summer afternoons, the deep south, sunshine, picnics." She removed the cover board that contained the logos of both companies and started going through the concept. Her words helped enhance what her drawings conveyed; a nearly dreamlike sequence with hazy light and a summer field, gentle music playing, views of a happy family picnicking among the flowers, children playing, the sun shining down, laughter, all while they ate fried chicken from a Crow's Chicken box.

"No spoken words. No written words. Just the visual images. Then we'll fade into your logo at the end. It gives you instant cross-cultural appeal when we market overseas because nothing gets lost in translation. Also, it makes your brand completely unique. While every other ad your demographic will experience will be screaming, thumping, flashing, loud, rushed, explosive conflict – your ads will be that momentary quiet, that peace. That comfort consumers are desperately seeking. That's what we sell. Nostalgia. Mom, apple pie, and Crow's Chicken."

She risked a glance at her so-called team and caught them glaring at her accusingly. She felt like sticking her tongue out at them. Pete looked from her to Daniel Crow, his head moving back and forth as if watching a tennis match. Crow's group gave absolutely nothing away. They stared at their leader with completely blank expressions. Maxine knew that Daniel Crow was the ultimate authority, probably the only authority, in this decision.

Crow sat staring at her, as if waiting for her to bring her attention back to him. The second she did, he nodded. "I like the concept." He pushed away from the table and stood. Almost comically, the rest of his crew stood with him. "I like it very much. I'll get back with you later today with my decision."

As soon as he was gone, she collapsed into the nearest chair. "I'm so glad that's over."

The head of the Crow account, and one of the partners, Victor Adams, turned on her the instant the door shut. "That was entirely uncalled for."

She sneered at him. "Oh? Well, Vic, the next time I'm given the task of single-handedly securing a national contract, are you saying I shouldn't try so hard?"

"That isn't what I'm talking about. I'm talking about making the rest of us look like cronies who did nothing more than show up this morning."

"I'm confused. Isn't that exactly what you did?"

"No. We spent hours on preliminary work."

She knew he was bloviating for Pete's benefit, but she refused to fall in line. "Last Friday, we all agreed that the preliminary work was no good, that we would go over other options in a meeting this morning for the presentation two days from now. *And*," she added emphatically, "I've been gone for a full week on vacation. What has the team accomplished in that week?"

He gestured at the last board, a rough sketch that had no color. "What we developed in prelim would have presented better than this. At least we would have come across as something other than some local, two-bit, fly-by-night company."

She rose to her feet. "Do I have to remind you that we're agency number eleven in ninety days, and he said he liked the idea. *My* idea."

His eyes skimmed her up and down. "I'm betting he just liked your skirt."

"That's quite enough, Vic," Pete said.

Maxine slapped her hands on the table and leaned forward into Vic's face. "You dumped this on me knowing I was out of town. You called my home and not my company provided cell, probably because you couldn't come up with anything on your own, and by giving it to me on my home answering machine you knew I wouldn't get the message until it was too late, probably hoping that the ultimate failure would be entirely mine. Well, Vic, looks like that backfired on you, because now the ultimate success is entirely mine, and you can eat your heart out."

She straightened and whirled toward Pete. "I have sick time and personal time up the whazoo. I'm taking the rest of the day off to go visit my new nephew."

He probably would have said something if she hadn't stormed out of the room. She was angry enough that it had been on the tip of her tongue to quit, which was why she was just going to leave and deal with it all tomorrow.

Her assistant jumped up from her cubicle as she headed toward her office door. "Maxi!"

"Not now, Tina" she said, pushing the door open and slamming it shut behind her. She was halfway across her office before she saw Daniel Crow standing at her window. She froze, barely stifling a scream, and took a deep breath, desperately trying to get a handle on her temper.

He turned at the loud crack of the door slamming. His hands were in the pockets of his pants and he gave her a slight nod of his head. "We haven't been formally introduced," he said by way of an opening.

No longer feeling like she was going to scream, she extended her hand and stepped forward. "Maxine Bartlett." In her heels, she met him at eye level.

Instead of shaking her hand, he took it in both of his and held it. "Bartlett. A white name. So your mother was Native American?"

Using more force than should have been necessary, she reclaimed her hand. "No, actually my father. But I never knew him and don't know anything about it."

"So you know nothing of your heritage?"

"Not really. It's not something I've ever bothered to research."

His eyes were dark, searching. "And why is that?"

"Let's assume I'm as interested in my father as he was in me," She took a step back. "Did you have questions about the presentation?"

"You wear jewelry but no wedding ring." His smile could barely be called a smile. "Can I assume this means you're not married?"

She sighed inwardly and took another step backward. "You know what, Mr. Crow? I've been awake since yesterday morning, and I was just getting ready to leave for the day. Why don't we arrange a meeting later in the week so I can answer any questions about my proposal?"

"I'll take that as a no." He glanced at his watch. "My mind is made up about whether to give your agency a pass. My marketing team can take it from here. I came to your office to see if you would like to have dinner with me tonight."

Her morning was steadily going downhill. "And if your pass at me doesn't go your way, will my reply affect your decision to 'take a pass' on my agency?"

He cocked his head and almost smiled again. "What if I said yes?"

With a bright smile, she said, "Then I'd have to ask you to find yourself another rep, sir. The sooner, the better."

It surprised her when he threw back his head and laughed. "Now, I am very intrigued." He stepped forward and took her hand again. She bit back panic, her heart racing. As much as she pulled, he wouldn't release her. She started feeling trapped. "No," He asserted. "Your response will in no way affect my business decision." His smile disappeared and his eyes grew serious. As he spoke, her office door opened. "Now, will you have dinner with me, lovely Maxine Bartlett?"

Maxine stared into his rich black eyes, eyes that stared at her like a starless night. His face was youthful and ancient at once, a perfect symmetry carved from the brown earth with lips that could be cruel or let slip ancient wisdom. She felt her hand relax, no longer struggling to pull her fingers from his grasp and thought of all of the different ways she could sketch this face.

Why couldn't Barry look at her like that? Why couldn't he hold her hand like that? She remembered how he had snatched her up this morning, claiming her mouth with his, conquering her hurried rush with his slow desire. She remembered the feel of his iron muscles wrapping her up, covering her like a warm blanket, shutting out everything save his touch and his mouth.

"Miss Bartlett. How nice." Barry observed from behind her. Barry. Her husband. Maxine closed her eyes and groaned.

Chapter 15

BY the time she disengaged her hand from Daniel Crow's, Maxine realized that Barry had already vanished. Daniel Crow smirked and asked, "Boyfriend?"

Maxine, deflated, answered, "No." She wearily walked to her desk. She slipped her black wool coat on over her yellow suit, wrapped her white scarf around her neck, and picked up the purse and briefcase she'd haphazardly tossed on top of her desk when she rushed into the office less than an hour ago.

Hopefully, Crow followed up with a raised eyebrow and an inquiring, "No?"

Maxine shook her head, her eyes level with her client. "That was my husband." It didn't feel wrong to say the word out loud, as it related to Barry. It felt very right.

Crow had the dignity to look surprised. He actually took a step backward, perhaps considering Barry's hulking size. "Oh."

"Mr. Crow, it was nice to meet you. I look forward to working with your team." She gestured toward the door. Maybe he didn't notice that she failed to offer her hand this time – maybe he did. She honestly didn't care.

"I'm sure we'll meet again. I'm sincerely sorry ..." he gestured vaguely, "for my part in any misunderstanding with your husband. I'm happy to do whatever it takes to clear it up."

Maxine didn't reply, but she nodded her head and followed him out. She stopped at Tina's desk and, as soon as she was sure he was out of hearing, said, "Don't allow clients into my office without me. There is proprietary information on other firms in there."

"I know," the eclectic woman before her said. She wore earrings in the shape of New Year party hats that moved and glittered. "He kind of strong armed his way inside. He's a little bit intimidating."

Maxine felt her lips thin. "Then you should have been standing in there with him until I arrived or else simply called security." She slipped her briefcase and purse straps over her shoulder and pulled black leather gloves out of her pocket. "I'm taking a personal day. No calls."

SINCE Barry brought her to the office, Maxine's car was still at her apartment. She took a cab to her church, the sprawling church in the very center of one of Boston's most troubled neighborhoods. The giant complex filled two city blocks with buildings and schools and chapels. The cab dropped her off in the main parking lot in front of the sanctuary building. As she stepped out of the taxi, she looked up at the huge steeple visible for blocks around. A weight settled over her heart, making her steps to the front door feel heavy laden.

The door opened without resistance, and she stepped into the huge entryway. It felt very quiet, very empty. She knew the staff was working, she saw their cars in the parking lot, but no one came to the vestibule to see why the door had opened and shut.

Why had she come here? "I don't know what to do," she whispered. In her mind she heard the word as if it had been spoken out loud. Pray.

She pushed the coat from her shoulders as she crossed the large lobby. Her heels clicked on the marble tile, echoing in the surrounding space. Doors to her left and right led to stairwells that went up to the balcony levels or down to classrooms and offices. Huge sets of doors in front of her led to the sanctuary, and that is where she headed.

The warm scent of lemon oil welcomed her as she entered the giant room. She could see the gleam of the old wooden pews and guessed that they had recently been polished. She had thought she would slide into the first pew she came to, but instead felt compelled to keep walking all the way down to the front where the altar was strategically lined with boxes of tissues and evenly placed on the floor next to where people knelt in prayer.

As she stepped, she stripped off her gloves, scarf, and coat. She laid them in a pile on the front pew, then fell to her knees and bowed her head, resting her arms on the prayer bench. For the first time in her life, she prayed out loud. "God, please help me."

Her voice sounded odd to her own ears, but she kept going, fervently appealing to God almighty to show her what to do. "Father, You know, even before I knew it, that I've loved Barry forever, even when I probably wasn't supposed to. You know that my heart is good where he is concerned. But I'm afraid that impulsiveness ruined what could be." She smiled. "I'd like to say that You led the two of us to get married, but I doubt either one of us were open to You at the time. But doesn't Your Word say that all things work together for good if I love You?" With tears choking her words, she said, "God I love You. I don't know that I knew before. I don't know if I was just going through the motions to please Robin or if I was really sincere, but right now I know I love You. I know I want to serve You. I know I want to live my life for You and give myself to You. And now I just need You to tell me what You want me to do."

For an hour she prayed on her knees. When her knees and back started to hurt, she shifted backward until she sat on the first pew, but she kept her head bowed and kept talking to God. Without actually ending the prayer, she eventually quit speaking and just sat there, letting her heart do the talking for her.

Eventually, she felt someone sit next to her. She raised her head and saw Abram Rabinovich, a very close friend of Tony's and a pastor at the church. Maxine had always liked him very much. He taught Old Testament classes at the school. As a former rabbi who had come to know Christ well into adulthood, he was very well versed in the Law of Moses.

"Want to talk about it?" he asked.

"I'm not sure," she said. Strangely, the surge of emotions she expected didn't happen. She felt wrung out, tired, but the weight on her heart had lifted sometime in the last hour and she felt lighter. "I think I just spent the last hour talking about it."

Abram chuckled. Maxine heard both compassion and wisdom in that soft laugh. He shifted in the pew until he could face her fully. "Excellent point."

"I'm just trying to figure out where to go from here."

"Did you find your answer?"

"How will I know?"

He put his hand out evenly and pursed his lips. "God speaks to us all in His own way, and to each of us as we need to hear His voice. But He does speak, Maxine. Sometimes, God says 'yes.' Sometimes, He says 'no.' Sometimes, it's 'wait.' If you don't know, then God hasn't answered yet. But He will, I promise you."

She could hear the assurance in his voice. He spoke of certainties. "What do I do now?"

Abram patted her on the shoulder before he stood. "Be still." He loosened his tie and looked up at the massive cross that towered behind the choir loft. "Christ Himself often sought solitude to talk to God and to listen to Him. Why don't you go somewhere quiet and just let Him speak to your heart?" He looked back at her and smiled. "And then do what He tells you, without question, and without hesitation. Stop trying to tell Him what to do. Put your life fully in His hands. Do it and know in your bones that He will work out the details."

He sat back down again. "When I came to know Christ, I was teaching in a Jewish Orthodox university, and quickly rising up through the ranks of rabbi. My entire family for thousands of years had worshipped Jehovah God a certain way, and I had to turn my back on all that. Doing so made me an outcast, a leper so to speak. It wasn't easy, but it was God's will and when I surrendered to His will, God opened doors all around me. I got this wonderful job here, my beautiful Sofia has brought her brother and her parents to know the Messiah, and I was blessed to see my mother accept Christ before she passed. Now, my father is starting to speak to me again. Even if it is only to debate with me, still we are talking again. And there is love there."

He stood again. "God will make the way clear when the choices you make are in accordance with His will and His purpose, when you listen to His desires for your life." Slipping his hand into his pocket, he pulled out his phone and read a text message. "Now I must meet my beauteous Sofia for lunch. Would you care to join us, child? Sofia would be happy to see you."

"No. Thank you."

He pulled a business card out of his front pocket. "I am available any time you need to talk. Please call me, if you have questions or just need an ear or a prayer."

"Thank you." She took the card and clutched it in her hand. When she heard the last of his steps echo up the aisle and the large door gently close behind him, she stood and picked up her coat and her purse. Dizzy, she realized how exhausted and hungry she felt. Putting the business card in her wallet, she called for a cab and decided that a large pepperoni pizza was her first order of business, and her warm bed second.

UPON returning home from the church, Maxine ordered delivery pizza. While she ate, she called Robin, promising a visit in the morning. After eating pizza and changing into a comfortable pair of sweatpants and a sweatshirt, she had collapsed in exhaustion on her bed. At midnight, she woke up and ate more pizza, set up the coffee maker, and sorted through the mail that had piled up in her absence. Restless, she had gone back to bed and only slept a couple more hours.

She woke at four-thirty in the morning. She tossed and turned for a few minutes before finally getting up and out of the bed. She went to her kitchen and bypassed the coffee maker's timer, ordering it to deliver a pot right away. While she waited for the invigorating brew, she went back into her studio.

She stood in the very middle of her studio floor, barefoot, her body aching with fatigue and stress. Nothing felt right. Her apartment felt too empty, too lifeless. Her bedroom felt cold, barren. This home that she had poured so much energy into every decorating detail felt wrong. And in here, in this room where no one other than she had ever stood – no, wait. Barry came in here with her just two days ago, just the day before yesterday. She told him about Monty Jordan. Had it only been two days? How had so much gone on inside of her, outside of her, in such a small span of time?

She felt … ready. But ready for what? What was God telling her to do? When would He tell her to do it? Abram had advised that she be still and listen. With her hands on either side of her head, she spun in a circle in the middle of her studio floor and wondered, prayed, begged God to be clear when He gave her the answer because she needed to know what to do.

MAXINE hung up the phone for the dozenth time that morning. She rolled her head around, trying to ease the muscles in her neck. Two weeks had gone by since the acquisition of the Crow Chicken campaign. Two weeks of Crow cronies calling every five minutes with instruction, guidance, counsel, advice – constant interruptions about the final written proposal, statement of work, and detailed scope that they wanted by five o'clock today. If they would simply stop interrupting her …

A rat-tat-tat on her office door seconds before it opened interrupted even that thought. Peter Mitchell opened the door without waiting for her to answer the knock. "Got a minute?"

Maxine's eyes shifted to the clock sitting on the corner of her desk. Twelve forty-five. "Only if you have food."

Peter grinned and walked fully into the office, holding up a paper bag that bore the logo of her favorite sandwich shop. "Julie ordered for us."

She waved him forward as she shifted papers in order to clear a spot in front of her. "I think I love you."

"I'll be sure to inform my wife."

"She'd understand." Maxine greedily removed the white butcher paper that accommodated her favorite turkey Reuben on rye. Around a mouthful she asked, "What's up?"

"I just wanted to tell you that the preliminary work I've seen on the Crow scope is nothing less than exemplary."

Maxine lifted an eyebrow as she took another bite. Her teeth crunched through the toasted marble rye and crisp sour kraut. "You didn't bring me a sandwich to tell me I do good work. I've been trying to get a meeting with you for over a week and I feel like you've been dodging me. All of a sudden you're in my office with a bag of buttered rye in hand. What's up, really?"

Peter did not take a bite of his own sandwich. Instead, he stood and wandered to Maxine's project bulletin board and looked at the various computer printouts and sketches and proposals for actors from agents for the Crow ad. "I'm not entirely positive that a partnership is going to open up."

Maxine sighed and put her sandwich down. She gingerly brushed the crumbs off her fingertips and thought very, very carefully about the words on the tip of her tongue. With a silent appeal to God to keep from letting emotion override common sense, she finally responded. "I have worked hard for you for over four years. Most weeks, I work six or seven days, sometimes pushing seventy or eighty hours. I do it without complaint because that's what it takes. And I single-handedly brought in the biggest client you have ever had." She stood only because she towered over him and wanted to have that slight advantage. "Single-handedly, Peter. Given that context, I need you to explain why you aren't entirely sure about a partnership offer."

He put his hands in his pockets and turned to face her. "I just don't know if it is the right decision. The timing ..."

"The right decision?" With a huff of breath, she closed her eyes and fought for control. She picked up her sandwich and threw it into the trash can. "Well, let me tell you something about timing. I have a meeting with Crow's people at five. They'll receive the written scope and go over it, I'm sure, with a fine toothed comb. I will give you one week of being completely available to them for questions and concerns, because I care about this company and the fact that we have this big contract. But I also have fifty-two days of accrued leave. Starting tomorrow, other than direct contact from anyone at Crow, I'm taking those fifty-two days. While I'm gone, why don't you consider the timing so you can be sure?" She leaned over the desk and picked up his sandwich and threw it into the trash can, too. "My lunch break is over. I have to finish what I'm doing to prepare for that meeting. Thank you for finally taking time to speak with me."

She dismissed him by sitting down and putting the earbuds of her MP3 player into her ears and cranking up Skillet singing about the monster in the closet. She turned to her computer and didn't watch her employer leave.

RATHER than battle the rush hour traffic that is nothing less than agonizing in downtown Boston on a Wednesday afternoon, Maxine chose to walk to Robin's apartment after work. Inside, she still seethed over the impromptu lunchtime meeting with Peter. While she honestly felt like she had handled it reasonably well, the end result was that she now had over two months in front of her and wasn't quite certain what to do with herself in all that time.

She spoke momentarily with the guard at the big circular desk then took the private elevator to the top floor of the building. Without knocking, knowing the guard would have announced her arrival, she pushed open the outer door and entered Tony and Robin's apartment.

Smiling, Robin rushed to greet her. Robin reached her and hugged her. "I'm so happy to see you. What a surprise!"

Maxine noted Sarah sitting on the big circular leather couch cradling Antonio Frances Viscolli, Junior – already nicknamed TJ – in her arms. Sarah looked up and grinned. "Are you here to cook us dinner?"

Maxine laughed and returned Robin's hug before she dashed to scoop the baby up from her little sister. "I can. What is mommy hungry for?"

With a smile, she handed Maxine a burp cloth. "I think that anything Aunt Maxi makes will be fantastic. I'm just not sure what's in there. I haven't been to the grocery in weeks."

"I'll dig around." Maxine put her lips on TJ's perfect little head and inhaled the fragrant baby smell. "I love him so much. How can I love him so much when I've only known him for two weeks?"

Sarah smiled. "I feel the same way. I feel like moving back in here. Maybe if I go to graduate school, Tony will let me have my old room back."

Robin snorted. "Talk to me at feeding time at three in the morning and see if you still want to live here." She looked at Maxine. "What's up, Maxi? Everything okay?"

TJ gave a little snort and started rooting at Maxine's neck. She handed him over to his mama and watched while her big sister settled into a chair and started nursing him. Maxine sat on the couch next to Sarah. "I, ah, need to talk to you two."

Sarah pushed her glasses up further on her nose and shifted until she faced Maxine and had her back to the arm of the couch. "What's wrong?"

Maxine ran her fingers over the naked ring finger of her left hand. She cleared her throat. "When I went to Vegas …" She paused and looked at Sarah then Robin then back to Sarah.

Sarah leaned forward and touched her hand. "Maxi?"

"Barry and I got married." She blurted it out then froze. Both sisters just stared at her for a moment, then simultaneously, the words sank in and their eyes widened. Sarah was the first to speak.

"You did what?"

"It was just this spontaneous thing." Maxine surged to her feet and paced around the circular room. "I didn't think about it. We have always been such good friends. I don't know. I'm pretty sure I've always loved him. Even when he was with her," she paused as memories of Barry's marriage to that awful woman played through her mind like a little movie. "And then we were at this wedding chapel watching this Elvis impersonator do a Blue Hawaii wedding and the next thing I know, I was saying, 'I do.'"

Another long silence stretched throughout the room. Maxine slowly walked back to the couch and sat down. This time, Robin spoke. "Well, that is some news."

"Indeed," Sarah said. "Vegas was before the new year. What about since you came home?"

Maxine shook her head. "I think he had divorce papers ready when I saw him the day TJ was born, but the baby coming and the big project at work has kept me distracted for the last two weeks." She let out another breath. "I also took a leave of absence from my job today."

Robin repeated, "Leave of absence?"

Maxine waved her hand. "Vacation, really. But I have months of vacation due so we'll call it a paid leave." She told them about the partnership and the work and the project. Oddly, she did not feel emotionally overwhelmed. She felt blank inside.

Sarah scooted over until she could put her arm around her older sister. "What now, honey?"

Maxine lowered her head. "I just don't know. I am just waiting for God to tell me what to do. The break from work felt like the right decision. I don't regret it. Now I just need to see what's next."

Robin shifted TJ to her shoulder and leaned forward to touch Maxine's knee. "We're here for you, whatever happens. And we'll be praying for you."

She leaned back and started burping TJ, but Sarah grabbed Maxine's hand and put another hand on Robin's thigh. "Let's pray right now." The three women bowed their heads and closed their eyes as Sarah prayed for Maxine.

Chapter 16

NEARLY a week later, Maxine sat at her drafting table in her studio, a blank sketch pad in front of her. For the first time in her life, she could not find the inspiration to draw out her feelings. For over a decade, she'd used her gift of art to purge the demons from her mind, a cleansing ritual that worked nearly every time. Now, though, the pencil lay still in her hand and the unblemished page stared back at her, a stark white, mocking blank space.

"Well, God," she muttered, "I'm here. And I'm trying to be still. But I honestly just don't know how." She grabbed her remote control and pushed the button for music. Instantly, the sound of the Newsboys filled her studio. The speakers lining the ceiling flooded the surround sound of a ticker tape parade falling like a million pieces. She had spent a good portion of the last week purging her secular music collection and trying on different bands and different sounds. She loved hard, thumping music, and found herself pleasantly surprised at the different Christian offerings.

A restless feeling had sent her into her studio this morning. This was day three that she had holed up in her apartment. By noon every day, after baking some amazing bread or dessert, or cooking some rich stew that she promptly froze because no one else was around to eat it, she wandered into her studio. Inspiration never came, though, so she found herself going through her paintings and drawings, cataloging them, remembering times she painted them, reminiscing over her life.

She knew one thing. She would not passively allow an annulment. She loved Barry, deeply, truly. She longed to be the wife he deserved, the wife he may not even know he desired. How to go about that, though?

Her mind wandered, and she thought of ways to communicate to him, writing him a letter, sending him an e-mail, showing up at his office. Nothing appealed to her, though. As she thought, her hand moved of its own accord and she very quickly recognized what she drew. Barry's house. She filled in the bricks, added the trim, drew his Jeep in the driveway. One word went through her mind as she worked. "Home."

THE next day, Maxine found herself back in the front pew where she had spent so many hours praying that day not too long ago. Today, she waited for her turn to join Robin and Tony on the chancel stage as they dedicated baby Tony to the Lord. She still found herself waiting for an answer from God about what she should do, but the more time she spent in solitude with Him on her knees in prayer, the more confident she felt that He would answer in His good time.

As pastor called the family, she and Sarah climbed the steps of the chancel stage. As she walked toward Robin and Tony, she was pleasantly surprised to see Derrick and Barry walking toward them from the other side of the chancel. Unlike Robin, Tony had no family. He treated Derrick and Barry like brothers as much as if they had been born to the same mother. The O'Farrell's, the youth minister of the church and his wife, also joined. They had fostered Tony through his early Christian life, rescuing him from the streets and providing a home for him.

Going through the dedication ceremony, Maxine could not help observing Barry. His face remained very stoic, and she silently prayed that God would take advantage of his presence for this ritual to convict him about his withdrawal from God's love. He seemed unaffected by any of it and refused even to meet her eyes. After the ceremony, after the family returned to their seats, she watched him leave the sanctuary. Unlike the day of his wife's funeral, she did not follow him. Instead, she listened to the sermon and felt a door in her heart open up. After the sermon, she found herself joining the wave of people going to the front of the church and fell to her knees before God and felt more doors open and His answer poured into her heart.

MAXINE rushed home from church, skipping the family lunch. She burst through the door of her apartment and tossed her purse and keys atop the desk next to her phone. Taking her Bible to the couch with her, she sat with her back against the arm and spoke to God. "I know what I think You want, but since I'm a little unschooled at listening to Your voice, I sure would like some confirmation. I hope I'm not doing something wrong by asking. Thank you for answering my prayer. Now, just to be sure, please help me confirm. Thank you."

She closed her eyes and opened her Bible, then opened her eyes and read at the first passage she saw. She read of Ruth, who mustered up her own courage and went to Boaz. In that moment, Maxine knew that what she felt stirring in her heart had come directly from God.

SIX o'clock Monday morning, Maxine rang Barry's doorbell. She waited a few moments and rang it again. And again. Finally, he answered. He wore jogging shorts and a sleeveless shirt. His muscles bulged against his sweaty skin and she knew she'd interrupted his morning workout.

"Hi," she greeted with a smile.

"Maxi," he said with a surprised look on his face. He looked past her, to her car in the driveway next to his Jeep, then back at her. "What are you doing here?"

"Freezing, for one." She stepped forward and he stepped backward until she crossed the threshold and shut the door behind her. "That's better." She peeled her red knit cap off and shoved it in the pocket of her gray wool coat. Her gloves followed, then she unbuttoned her coat and slipped it off her shoulders. "Did I interrupt you?"

He looked down at his attire then shrugged. "I was just finishing up." He turned and started walking away. "I'm not really set up for company right now, Maxi."

"I'm not exactly company, Barry."

He nodded with a half shrug. "Care for some tea?"

"I'd prefer coffee," she said, trailing behind him. She stepped into the large great room, with its huge stone fireplace and plush furniture. The stairwell leading upstairs flowed to her left, and the balcony above revealed three closed doors. Barry continued walking through the room and through a swinging door into the kitchen, and Maxine followed right behind him.

A breakfast nook overlooked a snowy backyard. Stone floors and three walls of windows made the room kind of chilly. The large granite island, the commercial sized gas stove, and the double ovens in the wall made Maxine want to get cooking.

Barry pulled a cup from the cupboard above and filled it with water hot from the kettle on the stove. "I don't have coffee," he said. "I have tea. If you want some I'll be glad to make you some."

Maxine waved her hand. "No thanks."

He added a tea bag to the cup and turned to face her fully. She slipped into a bar stool at the island and smiled at him. He stared at her for a moment then said, "Why are you here, Maxi?"

"Well," she began, excitement bubbling through her chest until she feared it would spill out of her and make her unable to form coherent words.

"I'm here because I'm your wife. And as your wife, I should be living with you."

He stared at her for five long seconds. Finally, he blinked and took a sip of tea. "Really?"

"Really."

"And what if I say I don't want you to live here?"

Maxine hopped off the bar stool and came around the island until she stood in front of him. "I'd say that if you didn't want me here, or anywhere else for that matter, that you'd have moved heaven and earth to get those papers to me to sign. I'd say that I know how I feel."

She put one hand over his heart, the other hand on his shoulder. She watched his eyes flare at her touch and could see the physical restraint he had to exercise over himself. "I'd say that I love you as a wife should love her husband. That I've missed you like you wouldn't believe these last three weeks, and that I prayed and prayed for God to tell me what to do, and every indication of an answer pointed me to this house and me coming to you. This is where I belong, Barry. Here. With you."

He put his hands on her shoulders, but didn't pull her close. Instead, he kept her from stepping any closer. "We can't be together, Maxine." he said, but she cut him off.

"We're already together. We're married. You haven't changed that. I don't want to change it. I want to live as your wife."

"People will say ..."

"People will always say, no matter what. Barry, listen to me." Despite his resistance, she stepped forward and wrapped her arms around his waist. She leaned forward until her head lay against his chest and she could hear his heart beat beneath her ear. "We are one. It's that simple."

He didn't wrap his arms around her. He didn't pull her closer. He didn't kiss her. He didn't sweep her away. All of those things she secretly wished he'd do. But he also didn't push her away, so she took that as a positive sign. She smiled as she stepped away from him. "I have movers coming this afternoon. They're bringing some things I want from my apartment. Obviously I don't need a lot of the furniture, but there are some pieces I plan to keep." He merely raised an eyebrow as he took another sip of his tea. "I'm going to need a key. If you don't have a spare, please let me borrow yours so I can get a copy made. I'll be here when you get home from work tonight, so you don't have to worry about that."

He stared at her for one heartbeat, then another, then pulled open a drawer. He rooted around until he found a key which he tossed on the counter. "That was Jacqueline's."

"Wonderful," Maxine said with a grin as she scooped up the key. "I assume that anything that was hers I can dispose of?" She held up the key hanging from the bejeweled key chain. "Aside from this, of course."

He offered a stiff nod just as the cell phone on the counter started vibrating. Without speaking to her, he picked it up and pressed a series of buttons, read either a text or an e-mail, then put it back on the counter. "I need to run."

After he left the kitchen, Maxine clasped her hands together in glee and gave a little spin. Then she rushed out of the kitchen and back through the large front room. No sign of Barry led her to believe he'd gone upstairs to get ready for work. She rushed outside, careful not to slip on the patches of ice that lined the driveway, and retrieved a tote bag from the backseat of her car.

She brought it back to the kitchen and unpacked the coffee maker and bag of coffee. She found the appliance a temporary home near the sink and determined that the first order of business for the day would be to scrub the kitchen. She wanted to learn where everything was and rearrange as needed to accommodate her left handed cooking methods.

EMERALD FIRE - CHAPTER 17

BARRY stood staring at his reflection until the hot water pouring out of the shower caused the mirror to fog up and obscure his view. Finally, he stripped and stepped under the hot spray and closed his eyes, letting the water beat down on his head.

When had he lost complete control of this situation with Maxine?

The crux of it was that he felt a small thrill at the thought of her living here, of her being here when he got home from work tonight. Another part of him could only see her fingers in the gentle embrace of that man in her office, and her face got replaced over and over again in his memory with the face of his dead adulterous wife.

Maxine was right, though. If he truly didn't want to be married to her anymore, he would have moved mountains to get those annulment papers signed and filed. So what had held him up? What kept him from doing it?

A skitter in his mind suggested that he pray about it, but he dismissed the thought. He prayed no more. Not since the answer to his prayer had been his wife's death had he gone to God about anything. He certainly wouldn't risk Maxine that way.

Robotically, he slapped shampoo onto his palm and scrubbed at his scalp, then went through the motions to finish showering. The e-mail he'd received from Tony took an hour away from his morning. He wondered if his best friend beckoning him to the top floor of the Viscolli hotel and to his corporate offices had to do with business or Maxine.

As he stepped out of the shower and dried off, Barry realized that he'd have to take this opportunity of an unplanned meeting to confess to Tony what he'd done. Maybe he wouldn't have to worry about how he'd handle coming home to Maxine. Maybe Tony would just kill him and all of his earthly problems would be over.

With a sigh, he moved into his bedroom and kicked a stack of dirty laundry farther into the corner and out of his path to the closet. He walked into the closet and moved toward the blue suits, mechanically matching shirt to tie to socks to belt to shoes. There would be no easy death to get him out of this. No. Tony would make him suffer.

He slipped a tie around his neck, tied his shoes, and headed back downstairs. No sign of Maxine in the living room meant that she either left – not likely – or was still in the kitchen. He pushed open the door with his shoulder while he tied his tie, and immediately smelled the rich brew of her coffee. For some reason, the smell soothed him. He found her at the kitchen table writing in a notebook, the snowy back yard at her back, a steaming cup of coffee at her elbow.

"I have a meeting with Tony in a few minutes," he said, retrieving his phone and keys from the countertop.

Maxine smiled. "You might want to talk to him. About us, I mean."

Barry sighed. "Have you talked to Tony about this?"

She smiled and shrugged. "No, but Robin knows we're married, so count on Tony knowing it too."

"Great." The knot complete, he tightened his tie and buttoned his jacket. "That's just great."

"It all had to come out, eventually." She rose from the table and approached him. He simultaneously wanted to run away and pull her close to him. So he did neither. She put a hand on either shoulder and stood on tiptoes to kiss his cheek. "I'll see you tonight. Please give me a call and let me know what time to expect you so that I can plan dinner accordingly."

She turned her back on him and went back to her list. Barry stared at her for a few seconds before leaving the kitchen and wondering, again, how he'd lost control of this situation.

WAITING in Tony's outer office, Barry checked his watch a second time. So far, Tony had kept him cooling his heels for fifteen minutes. He could not remember the last time Tony had kept him waiting. Barry had a feeling that the meeting this morning was not going to be about zoning problems for a Christian school gymnasium project.

When the phone issued a soft electronic tone, Tony's secretary, Margaret, nodded at Barry. He picked up his briefcase and walked through the double doors behind her desk.

Typically, at seven-thirty in the morning, Tony would have a breakfast spread laid out on his conference table. It would include such Barry-friendly items as yogurt, fresh fruit, his favorite brand of tea, perfectly brewed. And, typically, Tony would meet him at the door with a handshake and a "bro-hug" and the two would make their way over to the table as they chitchatted about life since last they saw each other.

Not this morning, though. This morning Tony sat behind his monstrous desk, signing papers. He gestured toward the chairs adjacent to him but did not speak, did not stand and offer his hand, and did not give any kind of verbal or nonverbal salutation.

As much as Barry knew this moment would eventually come, he would have much preferred it had been on his terms. He'd had time in the last few weeks to talk to Tony about it, so the fact that he was on Tony's playing field was his own fault, but that didn't make it any easier to bear. Since this would be a fight, though, he could certainly throw the first punch.

"Maxine moved in this morning." He set his briefcase down at his feet as he loosened his tie and kicked back informally in the chair. "She's at the house making lists as we speak."

Tony's hand stopped scribbling the pen. For a moment he sat completely frozen, then he tossed the pen aside and made eye contact with Barry. "We obviously have some catching up to do."

Barry shrugged. "I'd intended to save her the embarrassment and seek a silent annulment. Things just didn't happen that way."

"You shrug?" Tony leaned forward and pointed at Barry. "You mistreat my sister this way and then shrug at me? As if it were nothing?" Barry could barely understand Tony between the suddenly thick Italian accent and rich South Boston dialects. Tony's elocution abandoned him, and all of the years spent shedding the outward evidence of growing up on the streets vanished. In that glimpse Barry caught sight of a tough kid who would do whatever he needed to do in order to survive.

"Mistreat?" Despite knowing that on some level Tony's antagonism had some merit, Barry felt the anger bubble up inside of him. "I have not, nor would I ever, mistreat Maxi."

"You take her to Vegas on your little annual excursion, then you –"

Barry stood and slapped his hands on Tony's desk. "Then. I. Married. Her." He spoke each word as if it were a sentence of its own. "I didn't seduce her. I didn't take advantage of her. I asked her to marry me and she – willingly – said yes."

Tony picked up his previous train as if he'd never stopped speaking. "And then you discard her and leave her brokenhearted and lost for weeks."

Barry shook his head. "Is your problem with the getting married or the problem with the not intending to stay married?"

Tony leaned back in his chair and rubbed his face with his hands. Barry slowly resumed his seat. Tony sighed, reached forward, and spun the pen that sat on his desk. "Maxine has been in love with you forever. I doubt she has fully realized it yet, but it's what spurred her friendship with you; the late night Sunday football, the golf outings, the funeral getaway. I think those feelings for you are what kept her from really seeking out God.

Because she knew that you were married and finding ways to spend time with you, however she could, was quite sinful. But now she's come to Him. She has dedicated her life to Him, and is carving out a relationship with Him and it's beautiful to see. Yet all of this…" Tony's voice softened. "All of this is at a time when you have apparently turned your back on Him."

Barry gave a small shake of his head, very confused about the conversation. "I'm not understanding what you're upset about."

"She isn't strong enough in her faith yet to carry you both. If you can't find a way back to God, you're going to do nothing but hurt her in the end."

Barry felt a tug on his heart at Tony's words. However, he pushed it aside and stood. "My relationship with God is my own business. Maxine's feelings for me are her business. My marriage to her is our business. I don't need your counsel or your concern."

Tony raised an eyebrow. "And what about your feelings for her?"

The tug on his heart became quite painful. "What do you mean?"

"I mean, how do you feel about her, Bartholomew? Do you like her? Do you get a kick out of hanging out with her? Or do you *love* her? Do you love her with every molecule in your body and every waking thought? Do you put her needs ahead of your own? Ask yourself, would you die for her?"

The verse from Ephesians raced into Barry's memory, commanding husbands to love their wives even as Christ loved the church. It was a commandment without compromise, that husbands must love their wives sacrificially and more than their very own flesh. Emotion welled in Barry's throat, effectively cutting off anything he might have wanted to say or even could have said. He felt rebuked and suddenly ashamed. Instead of answering any of his best friend's questions, he glared at Tony, pivoted on his heel, and left the room, slamming the office door behind him.

Chapter 18

BARRY closed the file and moved it to the outbox on the corner of his desk. He turned to his laptop sitting on his credenza behind him and made a notation about a deposition on Monday next week, then wrote an instruction for Elizabeth on a sticky note. As he turned to stick it to the outside of the file, he saw Elizabeth standing in front of his desk. She normally knocked, and rarely interrupted his Monday post-lunch organizational time, so he frowned and slipped off his reading glasses.

"Yes, Elizabeth?"

Her lips thinned in apparent disapproval over something. "Is there something you'd like to tell me?"

With his focus on the file he'd just closed, he had absolutely no idea what she was talking about or why. "I don't think so."

"There's a woman," and she said the last two words as if they left a bad taste in her mouth, "on line four who claims that she is your wife."

Barry blinked and felt the tips of his ears grow hot. "Oh, yeah. That."

"Mmm hmm." She held up her fingers. "Line four."

She stood there, obviously intending to listen to the way he answered the phone. Barry cleared his throat and picked it up. "Maxi."

Elizabeth's eyes widened, then rolled up before she shook her head.

Maxine said, "Barry. Hi. I was just checking to see if you had any clear idea about what time you'll be home tonight."

He checked his watch. "Probably after six. Maybe pushing seven."

"Wonderful. Thank you so much. I'll see you then."

Barry carefully set the phone back in the cradle and looked at Elizabeth. She had her arms crossed and tapped a finger on her arm. "When did you get married?"

He sat his chair up and straightened an already perfectly straight stack of papers on his desk. "Yeah. About that."

While he searched for the words to say, she interrupted his thoughts. "I hate to say it, Mr. Anderson, but I mean, this seems kind of sudden. I hope that, you know, you know what you're doing. Because you've been in a pretty vulnerable spot. Trust me, I've been there. And I'd hate to think that you are being taken advantage of by someone."

Barry waved his hand in the air. "Stop. I appreciate your concern, but that's not your business."

Elizabeth froze mid-sentence. Without changing her facial expression even a fraction, she nodded her head exactly once and punctuated the gesture by answering with, "You're right." She pivoted on a heel and left his office without another word.

With a sigh, Barry stared at the closed door for several minutes before he picked up another file and opened it. For a while, he stared blankly at the page in front of him, then forced himself to focus and work on the task at hand.

MAXINE stood on the balcony of the second floor and looked down at the two men carrying the boxes of stereo equipment. "Just there, by the hearth, is fine," she said.

As she turned to go back into the master bedroom, the room in which Jacqueline had obviously resided, her phone rang. Glancing at the caller ID as she hit the button to accept the call she said, "Hi Robin."

"Hi. Just seeing how it went this morning."

"About like I expected. He didn't resist."

"What do you think that means?"

She moved the phone away from her mouth and spoke to the two men working in the huge walk-in closet. "Just box everything up. I don't want any of it."

She turned her attention back to her sister. "I hope it means that he'll fall madly in love with me and we'll have a beautiful marriage. If that isn't what it means, I'll know that I tried, if nothing else."

She could hear Robin sigh. "I hope you're doing the right thing."

Maxine grabbed the roll of packing tape and sealed the box of jewelry she had packed before the movers came. "I am doing what God told me to do. The rest is up to Barry." She marked the box. "Listen, I have boxes of jewelry and furs - real furs. Any idea what I should do with them?"

"I don't know. Did she have family?"

Maxine smiled. "I knew you were my sister for a reason. Brilliant girl. I'll find out her parents' address and get them delivered."

"Glad I could help. I love you."

"I love you, too. I'll talk to you later."

The bedroom was about the size of Maxine's living room. A small sitting area with two winged-back chairs facing a small round table sat next to a fireplace. Maxine ran her fingers over the table and thought a marble chess set would look perfect there. She went to the nightstand where she'd set her notebook and made some notes about decorating the mantle. A noise in the doorway broke her concentration and she looked up.

"We have boxes of clothes, ma'am," the supervisor from the moving company said. "We just need you to tell us where to put them."

Maxine huffed out a breath. "As soon as they're done cleaning out this closet, I want you to put them in here."

"When we've finished that, I think that will be all, ma'am, unless you had something else."

She glanced at her watch. They'd made great time that morning. "That will be it for today. Thank you for doing such a great job on such a short notice."

BARRY stood in the living room of his home – their home– the residence once central to the worst marriage on planet earth. Now he apparently shared that exact same domicile with another woman. A new wife.

The room glistened, sparkled, and smelled good. A new table stood by a different lamp. The couch sported brighter pillows and colorful throws. The intense stereo system sat unboxed next to the entertainment center. From the kitchen, the smell of roasted meat and baking bread warmed him and tempted him.

He set his briefcase near the stairs and moved through the room, letting the sound of thumping music lead him to the kitchen. Maxine stood at the sink, washing a large pot. He noticed the coffee pot almost right away and smiled for the first time that day. The red cloth covering the table warmed the snowscape beyond the windowed walls. Candles stood unlit and serving dishes sat covered, waiting.

While he felt comfort, warmth, and appreciation, nothing else stirred. He had shut his emotions off for so many years, he didn't even know what he was capable of feeling, much less his actual emotions. He felt irreparably damaged inside and wondered if Jacqueline might have broken him. He couldn't understand what Maxine saw in him, or why she intended to pursue this. He could certainly imagine loving her, if he understood the word. He had some affection for her and he really enjoyed her company, so he was willing to see what ended up coming of it.

"Hi."

She spun around, soap suds flying from her hands. When she saw him, she smiled. "Hi. You startled me."

He gestured at the radio on the counter. "The volume must have muffled my arrival."

As she approached him, he steeled himself for her wrapping her arms around him and hugging him. He didn't return the gesture of affection. But he did put his hands on her shoulders and smile down at her. "Smells good."

"Do you want to eat now?"

"I'm good." He looked at his watch. "I'm a little later than I said."

She waved a hand at him dismissively. "The meal is one that isn't time reliant. Roast beef is easy to keep warm. Go ahead and wash up and have a seat. I'm afraid the dining room is kind of a staging area for my stuff right now, so we'll have to eat in the kitchen."

"I've been eating standing beside the sink for years. It'll be a treat to sit down for dinner."

They chatted comfortably while they ate the amazing meal Maxine set out. After dinner, they washed the dishes together then went into the living room and enjoyed watching a basketball game. As the time passed, Barry grew more apprehensive about the coming end to the evening. Lending credence to his concerns, when the game ended Maxine rose and stood next to him, lightly placing a hand on his shoulder.

"I feel like there's a big wall between us right now," she said. He opened his mouth to speak, but really didn't know what he intended to say. He didn't have to worry about it for long, though, because she leaned her hip against the arm of the couch and leaned toward him, her arms slipping around his neck, her elbows resting on his shoulders. Were it not for the arm of the couch, she would be in his lap. "Shh. I know you feel all gallant and chivalrous. That's fine. I've moved into the master bedroom, because that's where we belong ... together. But I also found your room, where you obviously lived before. I understand your hesitancy. I'm okay with it. Just know that when you are ready, I love you, and I want you to join me in our room."

She framed his face with her hands. He closed his eyes and savored the feel for just a moment. The he opened them again in time to see her lower her head and brush his lips with hers. "Good night, Barry, my amazing husband."

He watched her walk from the room, up the stairs, and listened for the sound of the master bedroom door shutting, a sound he had heard most of the nights during his married life with Jacqueline, but the sound never came. After about twenty minutes, he rose and went up the stairs himself. As he reached the top landing, he saw the door standing wide open. Invitingly open. For the second time that day, a verse ran through his mind. "Knock, and the door shall be opened unto you."

He put his hand on the doorknob to his room, but it took several long heartbeats before he turned the handle to let himself in, and it was much, much longer before sleep finally found him.

Chapter 19

MAXINE drew in the warm spring air in one long, deep breath. Oh, how she loved springtime. While she couldn't possibly fool herself into thinking the warm weather that greeted her this first Saturday in March might stick around for even a few more weeks, she certainly intended to savor every single second of it while it lasted. The late morning sun warmed the skin of her arms beneath her short sleeved shirt. What a treat to wear a short sleeved shirt in March.

She carried a notebook filled with rough sketches. She used it to devise landscaping and planting ideas as she walked the perimeter of the property. As she plotted outdoor furniture, a patio kitchen with a grill, and dreamed of possibly inaugurating the first annual Anderson Fourth of July party, the back door opened and Barry joined her outside. With a grin, Maxine held out her arms and lifted her face. "Look!" she said, "The sun! It shines!"

Barry smiled in return. "About this time of year, I start doubting its return myself."

He wore khaki pants and a collared golf shirt that accentuated the shape of his broad chest. She gestured at the keys in his hand. "Do you have to work today?"

"I do, some, but I can do it from here." He rubbed the back of his neck. "I, ah, have a church budget committee meeting, though."

Maxine felt a little burst of excitement, but she tried not to show it. She had lived here for five weeks. For five weeks, she'd prayed alone before every meal. She'd come and gone to this church function or that church meeting alone. She'd hosted only one small Sunday School gathering. Barry knew everyone, seemed to enjoy the fellowship, but he didn't even talk about it afterward. He'd shown absolutely no interest in anything related to his walk with God or their church, so his announcement loomed tremendously in her heart.

"Oh?" She crossed the patio to him and slipped her arms around his waist. "I'm so happy you're getting back into it." She laid her head against his chest and breathed in the scent of his aftershave. Just as she started to pull away, his arms came around her. Another first.

Savoring that moment, she closed her eyes and just abided. She thought maybe she could stand like that all day. Smiling, she pulled her head back just enough to smile up at him. He used a hand to brush a wayward strand of hair from her forehead and, for a moment, Maxine was certain he was about to kiss her. Then the cell phone in his pocket vibrated and chirped.

A look of annoyance that mirrored how she felt flickered across his face. Maxine stepped back and let him dig the offending device out of his pocket and answer it in the middle of the fifth ring, seconds before the call would have forwarded to voice mail. She watched as he glanced at the caller id as he answered. "Good morning, mom."

Maxine stepped even farther back, smiling her understanding, and went back to her sketch pad. The first time she met Barry's mother and sisters had not gone well. Those women had come to the meeting hostile, having already made up their collective minds about the newest addition to the family long before anyone ever laid eyes on her.

Given their rather sudden nuptials, while considering how poorly his first wife had treated everyone, Maxine had known it wouldn't be easy to win over Barry's family, so she wasn't hurt or upset by the attitude. Instead, she made it her mission to have an intimate meeting with each of them. Lunch with his mother, brunch with a sister, shopping with another sister. Eventually, they each learned of her commitment to God, her long-standing friendship with and respect for Barry, and of her genuine empathy for Barry's previous relationship.

Asking Barry's accountant father to prepare her taxes also helped seal the deal on acceptance of Maxine into the fold. If they suspected that she might simply be interested in Barry's material wealth, then exposing her own surprisingly substantial personal portfolio in such a subtle way put an end to that notion rather quickly.

As the weeks went by, his family had warmed and opened up to her. She knew how much Barry loved his sisters and parents, and how important they were to him. Establishing relationships with them would make the rest of their life together much easier and happier.

Putting her mind back to her plans for the back yard, Maxine wandered away from her husband and inspected the fence line, thinking to herself that some flowering bushes in the far corner might look nice. As she scribbled in her notebook, Barry interrupted her.

"Mom said 'hi' and wanted me to remind you about dinner tonight?"

She slapped a hand to her forehead. "I'm glad she called. I forgot all about it. Honey?" She grinned. "We're supposed to have dinner with your parents tonight!"

"It's okay. I rescheduled. I told her I had other plans."

Frowning, Maxine looked up at him. "Other plans?"

He slipped an arm around her waist. "Yeah. I told her I had to take my beautiful bride out to dinner tonight."

Maxine's heart began to flutter. She felt emotion surge up and tighten her throat, threatening her eyes with tears. "I ..." Nothing would come out.

Barry shushed her and gently put his hands in her hair. As his lips met hers, the tears spilled from her eyes and flowed freely down her cheeks. She stood on her tiptoes and slipped her arms around his neck. The kiss was beautiful, amazing, left her aching and wanting. She needed more of his taste on her lips, needed to step even closer to him.

Just as he angled her head to deepen the kiss, the cell phone in his hand vibrated against her skull. Barry pulled back and looked at it, scrolling through a message. He cleared his throat as he took a step backward. "Apparently, your sister needs some sunshine on her skin. Her husband is requesting a foursome of 9-holes followed by lunch at the club."

"What about TJ?"

"Aunt Sarah's baby-sitting but will join us there, with him, at lunchtime."

Maxine glanced at her watch. "What about your committee meeting?"

"I can hit that first and catch up with you guys on the course." He pushed a series of buttons and slipped the phone into his pocket. "Do you want to do that or did you have other plans?"

As she shrugged, she smiled. "Sure. That would be fun. We should all enjoy this weather while we can before the dreary cold comes back next week." She shut her notebook and slipped the pen into the spiral top. "And dinner tonight?"

He put a hand on her shoulder and ran it up the side of her cheek, then gently squeezed the back of her neck. She leaned into his touch, enjoying it. "Dinner tonight will be a little more than lunch at the club. How does Benedicts sound?"

Maxine grinned. "Wonderful."

"Good." He fished some keys out of his pocket. "You have me blocked. Just take the Jeep. I'll load both sets of clubs before I go. I'll take your car and meet you all there."

"Oh, you'll just use any excuse to drive my sports car, won't you?"

He grinned then kissed her good-bye. Another first. As soon as he was out of sight, as soon as she heard the sound of the powerful little engine in her car fade, Maxine spread her arms out and lifted her face to the sky, praising God for the miracles of this morning.

Then she checked her watch and rushed back into the house to change into clothes appropriate for a morning of golf at Tony's club.

Barry had loaded the golf clubs as promised and, twenty minutes after confirming the plans, Maxine backed the Jeep out of the garage. It felt strange driving the cumbersome vehicle compared to her slick little machine. It didn't respond to her the same way her car did, and she found herself stalling out at the first stop sign.

Annoyed, she paid closer attention to the clutch and less attention to the warm sunshine. At the exit gates of her housing complex, she came to a full stop. Sitting at the stop sign, she faced a six lane highway. Traffic, heavy for a Saturday morning, whizzed by with barely an interval. Her road sat halfway down a large hill, and every time she thought she had a break in traffic, another three or four cars crested the top of the hill and raced down toward her. Just when she decided to simply turn right and make a U-turn a little farther up, a break in the traffic magically appeared. With an audible, "Thank you," she went for it.

Maxine lifted her foot off the clutch and the Jeep bucked and groaned, jerked once, then stalled out dead in the middle of the road. "No!" Maxine managed to get out while she pushed the clutch back in and turned the ignition.

She had the engine started and had begun to ease up on the clutch and press the accelerator as far down as it would go when she heard the blaring of a horn and the screeching of tires. She whipped her head to the left a split second before her field of vision filled entirely with a chrome grill. The world suddenly shrunk down to a pinpoint perfectly surrounded by pure pain.

Then the pinpoint vanished.

Chapter 20

BARRY jotted some notes in the yellow legal pad in front of him but, honestly, he struggled to keep his thoughts on the proposed budget for the church's soup kitchen. His thoughts remained on his wife. His wife. Could it be that this was the first time he had thought of Maxine as his wife in his mind?

He looked forward to spending the day with her, and with their family. Even more so, he looked forward to spending the evening with her. He let his mind play out the scene of the two of them walking into the dining room of Benedicts. He savored the idea of walking into a crowded restaurant with the most beautiful woman in the world on his arm. He imagined slipping the emerald encrusted diamond ring back onto her finger – the very same ring he had kept in his pocket since she the moment she handed it to him in the hotel room in Vegas. The very same ring he touched a hundred times a day, thinking of placing it on her finger, of kissing her and officially sealing their marriage, of their wedding night. The very same ring he had never returned to the casino shop, that he had never intended to return in the first place.

Perched next to the legal pad, his cell phone vibrated with an incoming call. He glanced at the display and, not recognizing the number, stabbed a button that sent the call to voice mail.

He tried to return his attention to the associate pastor who spoke at the head of the long conference table, but again his mind wandered away from the rising cost of bread flour to emerald green eyes framed by long dark lashes surrounded by an impossibly lovely face.

Absently, he answered direct questions, but he glanced at his watch three times in five minutes, wishing that the meeting would just end so he could join everyone on the golf course. He grinned a little grin at the thought because, truth be known, he didn't even really like golf.

His phone vibrated again and he saw Tony's number flash across the screen. Barry knew that the meeting hadn't run late yet, and Tony knew he was at the church. He decided that whatever it was could wait. If he interrupted the meeting for a phone call, the meeting would only last that much longer.

Not two minutes later, the door to the conference room flew open, flung wide by Caroline O'Farrell who nearly fell into the room, her hand over her chest, breathing hard. "Sorry ... to ... interrupt," she gasped between breaths. Her eyes found Barry. "Had to run here from the house."

Barry didn't know why, but flutters started low in his stomach and moved up to the back of his neck, tingling tenseness into the muscles there. The other men in the room sat silent, unmoving. It created a strange tableau, a portrait of tension and alert anticipation.

As Barry's phone vibrated again, Catherine nodded her head toward it. "Answer it, Barry," she whispered, as Barry scooped up the phone and hit the button to take the call.

"Barry ..." Tony's tone sounded impatient, worried, and uncertain.

Barry felt his heart stop. The tone of voice spoke volumes. After all, he'd taken just this kind of call before. *Mr. Anderson, there's been an accident. Your wife sustained very serious injuries and was rushed here less than an hour ago.*

He knew. He could tell. Still, he had to be sure. His voice came out in a scratchy whisper. "What happened?"

"It's Maxine."

The world around him started to gray as panic flooded his veins and color abandoned his face. "Tony, tell me what happened."

"There's been an accident." Tony said, "She was driving your Jeep and..."

"Where is she now?" Barry interrupted.

CAROLINE'S husband, Peter, drove. Barry sat in the passenger's seat of Maxine's sports car and pushed against the floorboard with his feet, willing the car to go faster. Begging the car to go faster. Peter drove the little green bullet with absolute precision, darting in and out of traffic, cutting off this car or shooting past that car, going through a few lights that were more red than yellow. Barry didn't care. He just counted off blocks then miles then blocks again as they raced to the hospital nearest to his home. Their home. His and Maxine's home.

He saw Tony's car skewed carelessly across the line into the "No Parking" zone and knew he'd beat them here. Peter barely had the car stopped before Barry had the door open and his feet on the asphalt of the parking lot, running – driving toward the emergency room doors. He turned sideways to slide between them because they opened too slowly. He barely noticed how people leaped out of his way as he dashed into the waiting area.

He scanned faces in the waiting room, taking in Robin's tears, Tony's stoicism. Sarah, who looked shell-shocked but calm. He picked Sarah as he rushed forward. Sarah the nurse. Sarah who would understand.

"What have they told you?"

Sarah reached under her glasses and rubbed her eyes. "Nothing. Absolutely nothing."

"Will they let you go back and see her?"

She pressed her lips together and shook her head. "I've tried twice in the last ten minutes. They won't let me."

Barry ran a hand through his hair, not surprised to find it shaking. "What does that mean? That can't be good, can it?"

She gave half a shake of her head before she stopped herself. "We don't know that. Better if we just wait and see."

"Oh, dear God," Robin breathed

Barry whirled around to see what had made Robin gasp that little prayer. A trauma team had thrown the emergency room doors open as they rolled a gurney through in a real hurry. A nurse crouched atop the bed straddling the patient, pressing up and down on her chest. Two nurses pushed the bed toward the elevator doors a third nurse held open. A female doctor at the side of the gurney squeezed a breathing bag every few seconds. Barry made out a strand of jet black hair against the bloodstained sheet seconds before the bed disappeared into the elevator.

EMERALD FIRE - CHAPTER 21

Chapter 21

THE wait was interminable. Sarah continued to try to get information – any information at all – but all she could get out of anyone was that Maxine was still in surgery. They wouldn't even tell her what was being operated on, they just directed them all to a waiting room on the surgical floor. The family moved up there to hold their vigil.

Barry signed form after form for the hospital. A police officer came to speak to Barry, and the group learned what had happened. Maxine apparently stalled out in the middle of the road and was t-boned by a driver of an SUV. Forensics verified that the driver had only been doing the speed limit of 45 miles per hour. The impact turned the Jeep around until it faced oncoming traffic, where it was hit head-on by a midsized Honda. Both the driver of the SUV and the driver of the Honda were saved from serious injuries by their air bags and were able to leave the hospital with little more than stitches. Both drivers confirmed what the crash site investigators predicted. Maxine had simply stalled out in the middle of the road.

"I don't understand. Maxine could out-drive any Formula One racer. She's the best driver I know." Robin said. "How could she stall out?"

Barry sat in the vinyl chair with his elbows on his knees and stared at the tiny black specs in the white tile floor. "The clutch has been sticking lately. I noticed it last week. It hadn't gotten too bad yet but I should have taken it in." Guilt clawed at his chest and tried to rip through his flesh.

Robin put a hand on his shoulder and squeezed, then shifted TJ from her breast to her shoulder. "There's no way you could have known."

He sighed and stared at the floor. "I should have taken it in."

The door flew open and Caroline O'Farrell hurried in, closing her cell phone. "I've updated the prayer chain." She looked at Robin. "If you're done nursing the lad, I'll take him home with me," she said. "I have three teenaged girls at home who can help me watch him."

Robin started to protest, "No, please don't worry about it."

Caroline put a hand over Robin's, stilling her patting on TJ's back. "You have to worry about the other men in your life right now. Let me take my first grandchild home with me. You can come nurse him in a few hours, or I'll bring him back here, whichever."

Tears spilled out of Robin's eyes and flooded her cheeks as she whispered, "Thank you."

Caroline gingerly took TJ from his mother's arms. "Come here sweet pumpkin. Come see your *Seanmháthair*." She patted the baby's diapered bottom as she rounded up the diaper bag and stroller. In a few moments, she departed with TJ and all his gear.

Barry watched the door shut behind them and sank further into himself, feeling the dark fist of despair clutch at his chest with jagged claws. The spots on the floor shimmered and shifted until he closed his eyes so that he wouldn't have to use the energy it took to focus.

If only. If only he had moved her car out of his way and driven his Jeep. He had been fighting the temperamental clutch all week and wouldn't have stalled it in the middle of the intersection, which meant that two cars wouldn't have plowed into his wife. Then Maxine wouldn't be lying on a table while doctors tried desperately to repair her shattered body.

The tendrils of fear sank deeper, blackening his thoughts, banishing any hope. He just realized how much he loved Maxine – how much he wanted to give it his all, and he realized that she may never hear the words pass his lips.

The door opened again, but he was afraid to look up, afraid to see compassion in some doctor's eyes when he told them how they had done everything they could, but that her injuries were too severe. How despite their best efforts, Maxine had died.

He braced himself to simply hear the words, nearly the same words he had heard once before. Before, his feelings were so confused. When he heard them today, his world would crash down around him and life would lose meaning. He braced, except he didn't hear a stranger's voice. He heard Derrick's.

"I just got your message. Do we know anything?"

"Nothing yet," was Tony's reply. "We're still just waiting."

He felt the brush of clothing as Derrick took the seat next to his. "What happened?" He talked to Tony over Barry's hunched form.

Sarah answered him. Sarah, the calming force for all of them that day, set aside her animosity and spoke kindly to Derrick. "She stalled out in the middle of the road. The other driver said it looked like she'd just got the car restarted before he hit her."

Because, Barry silently added, her husband left her with a broken vehicle to drive. Because he couldn't be bothered with something as mundane as swinging by an auto mechanic when he had obviously more pressing business at hand.

He couldn't take it any more. Barry lunged to his feet and ripped the door open, never looking behind him. Scanning the halls for the exit sign, the need to escape flooded him, panicked him. Then immediately departed. He found he didn't even have the strength to go back into the room. Leaning against the wall, he raised both hands and pressed them against his eyelids. All around him, he heard the sounds of a hospital, and wanted to scream and find out how people could be going on with their lives as if nothing had changed. As if the world wasn't teetering on its axis, ready to collapse in on itself.

Barry lowered his hands when he felt Tony take up the wall space next to him. They didn't immediately speak, because no words needed saying, but Barry was surprised when he realized just how much he required the company of his friend.

"She loves me," he said at one point.

"I know." Tony shifted and crossed his ankles in front of him. "I think she always has."

"It just dawned on me what I might lose."

Tony sighed and rubbed the back of his neck. "Bear, if Maxi doesn't make it, she gets to go home. One day, you get to go home and you'll see her again. But we're going to count on her pulling through this."

Barry took Tony's rebuke to heart with a single solemn nod. "My head is spinning."

Tony stood straight. "You'll go insane pondering the 'might have beens.' I have to believe, and Robin has to believe – and you have to believe – that she'll pull through. We have to have faith. If not, whoever walks through the door next will find a group of raving lunatics."

Barry leaned his head back against the cold wall – Why were hospitals always so cold?– and pressed the heels of his hands to his eyes again. "I know. I know. You're right." Pushing away from the wall, he looked down the hall to the set of doors that led to the operating rooms. There was no movement that he could see.

The cry in his heart that he had ignored all of these months suddenly became audible to him. The unexpected death of his first wife sent him careening away from God. The impending loss of his current wife, this beloved woman, almost sent him to his knees. He turned his head and looked at his best friend, at his brother, as tears burned the back of his throat. "Will you do me a favor?" he asked, his voice hoarse with emotion.

"Of course, *mi fratello*."

"Will you pray with me?"

Tony faced Barry and placed both hands on his shoulders. "It would be my honor."

IT was the darkest part of the night, the part of the night that hangs on just before dawn takes over. Peter had come and gone with TJ, bringing the baby to be fed, comforting both infant and mother. Derrick vanished and shortly returned with food that no one ate and strong coffee that everyone made disappear. Sarah went back and forth pestering the staff, finally finding someone that would tell her only that they were still working on Maxine and offered vagaries about internal bleeding. Mostly, they all sat silently, each numb from the worry and the fear, no longer even interested in the pretense of conversation. At last, the doctor finally arrived.

"Brian?" Barry stood as the doctor strode into the waiting room, his voice echoing his surprise to recognize a longtime friend of his father's.

"Glad I was on call tonight, Barry," Dr. Brian McDonald replied, extending his hand.

Dr. McDonald looked as ragged as they all felt. Barry searched his face, trying to read his eyes, but found only weariness. The doctor gestured for Barry to retake his seat before he slowly lowered himself into the chair beside Barry, turning to face him fully.

"Your wife is in recovery, now," he said by way of a preamble. A collective breath was released, and they all tried to release some of the fear and brace for her condition. "She's very weak, and I'll honestly tell you that for the next several hours it's still going to be touch and go."

"How is she?" Robin asked in a rush.

The doctor pursed his lips and looked into every face. "Her condition is critical. I have to tell you it isn't good. The entire left side of her body was basically crushed, and we had to get her put back together. We salvaged her spleen and her liver and that is very, very good, believe me. It does a lot to increase her chances. We're trying to save her kidney, too, but we really need to watch it closely. We might have to go back and take it. The next few hours will tell. We're watching her fluids very closely. She's a fighter. She tried to leave us a couple of times, but hung on in the end."

"What …" Barry cleared his throat, but the doctor seemed to know what he was asking.

Brian ran a hand through his hair. "There was a lot of internal bleeding because one of her ribs punctured her lung."

Barry's stomach churned and Robin gasped, covering her mouth with her hand. The doctor continued. "It's repaired, and we replaced several liters of blood. Somehow, that was the worst of the internal damage. She's not out of the woods but she's stable for now.

"Her left arm was broken in a couple of places. Her left hand and left leg got trapped when the door buckled in and ... both were crushed. We called in an orthopedic surgeon who worked on her leg and hand. He's the best and we were lucky he was in the hospital tonight. Without him, I'd have put her chances of ever walking again at zero. Even with him, we still debated the merits of radical amputation."

He put a hand up to forestall the protests and mitigate the indrawn breaths. "I'm just telling you it was considered. Instead, he did a superior job of reattachment and reconstruction. There's going to be more to do. It's going to take at least two more surgeries on her hand – probably more – and a lot of therapy. Still, and this is just a preliminary guess, but I think with some serious physical therapy, she has a chance of a meaningful recovery assuming she survives for the next few weeks."

Barry felt the room swirling around him, imagining it draining him into a dark abyss. "It's touch and go with her hand. If she doesn't sustain an infection, she should be able to keep it but she'll probably never have full use again. The bones were badly crushed. We'll really have to just wait and see how she heals. You should know that radical amputation of some of the digits is still on the table, especially if she starts getting septic. The bottom line is that her internal organs are too damaged to fight off a serious infection."

He paused for a moment. Sarah nodded her understanding, silently communicating that she could answer any questions her family might have about what he had said so far. The doctor continued.

"You should know that she appears mentally altered."

Sarah interrupted for the first time, "What was her...?"

The doctor forestalled the entire question when he held up three fingers by way of answer. Sarah's entire body tensed.

"Best we can guess, her head hit the steering wheel. It hit something solid and unforgiving, for sure. There's no fracture but there is major blunt force trauma and there's some swelling of the brain. There's some bruising, but that should slowly go back to normal over the next few weeks. Neuro's keeping a close watch. We want to make sure she doesn't hemorrhage or have an aneurysm. There is likely going to be some immediate effects from the head injuries when she regains consciousness, but hopefully they'll diminish over time. Try not to be concerned if she acts confused or forgetful for now."

He pushed himself out of the chair. "She needs to heal, and she needs to be still. If she were conscious and in this much pain, there's a risk of shock. We're going to keep her in a medically induced coma for the next twelve hours at least, maybe for a few days while we watch all of her vitals. As soon as she's out of recovery we'll move her down to intensive care. That's two floors down. Family can see her just one or two at a time, no longer than ten minutes every hour. You need to know that she's going to look pretty rough. Sarah can probably explain what all the tubes and hookups are there for. I'll be here ..." He rubbed his eyes and looked at his watch. After grinning a private, ironic grin he continued," ... later this afternoon if you have any questions or problems. Does anyone have any questions before I go?"

Barry found a thread of propriety and stood with the doctor. He held out his hand to shake Brian's. "Thank you"

Brian released the handshake and put a hand on Barry's shoulder. "She's tough. You can tell." He pulled him in for a quick, familiar hug. "Call me at home if you need to. Margie and I will be praying for you both."

"Thank you."

As soon as the door closed behind him, Robin started crying. Tony pulled her into his lap and tucked her head under his chin.

"It's silly to cry now," she said, brushing at the tears impatiently. "But all I can think about is her hand."

"Why?" Derrick asked.

Barry swallowed and forced words past a throat that hurt. "Because she's left-handed. A left handed artist with a crushed left hand."

He leaned his head back against the wall and closed his eyes, preparing his mind to wait another several hours before he could look in on her. He slid off the chair and turned so that his knees were on the ground. He clasped his hands, bowed his head, and began appealing to God with a desperate plea. He felt Tony kneel next to him on one side and Sarah kneel on the other.

BARRY had to stop for half a minute when he entered the room. He thought Sarah had prepared him for what Maxine would look like, but he wasn't prepared for the physical hurt that looking at her would cause. The bed seemed far too large for her thin frame, and tubes and lines ran from machines and bags, snaking under the blankets all around her. She lay completely still with her eyes taped closed.

A tube attached to a respirator was taped to her lips and presumably went all the way down her throat. A white bandage, that looked stark against the black of her hair, covered half of her forehead. Her left arm lay on top of the covers, a bandage covering the tips of her knuckles to the top of her shoulder. A chest tube went under the covers on the right side of her body, keeping her lung inflated. A monitor beeped the steady rhythm of her heart and the respirator made a rasping sound as it breathed air into her lungs.

Barry collapsed in the chair next to the bed and gingerly touched her right hand. His touch elicited no response. Not even the flicker of her eyelashes beneath the tape. He bowed his head, resting it on their joined hands. "I love you," he whispered. "Maxine, please stay with me."

THE only time he left her side was when the medical staffed forced the issue or one of the others came to visit. Sarah came before and after her shifts and Tony and Robin took turns with the baby and came in and out.

Once a day he left while Robin sat with her, to go to his house and shower and change clothes. He couldn't stand being away for long, and returned within the hour. They all took turns trying to persuade him to leave, to go home and sleep, but he wouldn't do it. Once he made it out to the parking deck before he turned around and went back inside. By Tuesday night, he felt tired enough that he thought he might sleep, so he stretched out on the master bed – the bed in which she slept but he had never shared with her – after his shower. Her scent overpowered him, seeped into his pores, tortured him until he knew he would find no rest.

And still there was no change.

Nurses removed the tape from her eyelids and they carefully cleaned her with cool, damp swabs. They tended to her, administering drugs, replacing full bags with empty bags and replacing empty bags with full bags depending upon protocol. Occasionally, Doctor McDonald would pop in and tell him how good her results were looking, or that he would be taking her out of the coma soon, or that he would continue to pray for healing. His grip on Barry's shoulder before departing always afforded Barry some comfort.

When they were alone, Barry talked to her, revealing everything inside him. He revealed regrets about the past and plans for their future. Peppered through it all, he lavished her with words of his love for her – the love he carried around inside for who knows how long, the love that had always been there. He prayed to God that he wasn't too late.

And still she didn't move. She didn't wake.

It terrified him.

On Wednesday, he reached his limit. He caught himself breathing in time with her ventilator, counting the breaths, and slowly let out a long breath, hoping it would relax him. He realized at that point how very close to the edge of collapse he was, but he didn't know what he could do about it.

He leaned forward, gripping her hand in one of his, laying his other one on the bed and resting his head on it. His hand swallowed hers like a whale swallows a shrimp. Confined to the sterile sheets of the hospital bed, she looked like a very small child resting next to a giant. He closed his eyes and willed her to wake up, willed her hand to squeeze his, willed her not to die. A wave of tiredness born of raw exhaustion and fear washed over him. Gripping her hand tightly, he let the wave take over and lull him into oblivion.

EMERALD FIRE - CHAPTER 22

MAXINE floated on a wave of nothingness, surrounded by a soothing, comforting void that cushioned her from something she didn't want to face. She remembered driving the Jeep, stalling out, then a very loud noise. She remembered every single vivid detail until the blackness took over after the impact. She couldn't remember exactly what happened next, but knew her last coherent thoughts had to do with fear and pain. So she enjoyed where she was, knowing on some instinctive level that when she finally woke, it would hurt more than she could imagine.

She had no sense of time. She could have existed in her void for five minutes or five years. Disjointed sentences from voices she recognized occasionally penetrated the darkness. She felt more aware when she heard them – aware of the weight that seemed to press down on the left side of her body, aware of a steady rhythmic beeping, aware of her hand being lifted or touched. She could hear the voices, but never comprehended the words. During those times, she felt comfort knowing that people she loved were nearby.

Eventually, she tired of the dark. She wanted her color back, her visible spectrum that gave the world its beauty. Somehow she knew that pain would exact a toll for the color, but she thought maybe she was ready, so she slowly pulled herself forward, toward the light, toward life.

Thirst was her first sensation. She felt thirstier than she had ever felt before. Thirst almost won out over the dull throb in her head, over the tight pain in her chest, over the weight on her left side. Almost, but not quite.

She wanted to move, to shift around a little and maybe help alleviate some of the discomfort, but found herself unable to do so. It was disconcerting to feel trapped, tied down, and she had to shake off the panic that lobbied to claw its way to the forefront of her thoughts. She pushed it firmly back because she sensed that panic would make it hurt worse.

She felt sort of light, as if ever since the impact that had crushed the Jeep, she'd accidentally tripped into an abyss. She felt as if she had simply fallen and fallen and fallen this entire time.

Suddenly, she realized that she had finally hit the solid ground at the bottom of that endless pit. She had come to earth and hit the ground with every single part of her body. Hard.

It all registered at once. She hurt. Lord in heaven, she hurt everywhere.

There was no more thought of shifting to ease discomfort. She didn't think she could move at all. The steady beeping noise she had been hearing suddenly sped up, went out of control, the weight on her own flesh felt like an elephant sitting on top of her, and something was choking her, blocking her throat making it so hard to breathe. She gagged, muscles tensing, and it felt as if her entire torso was on fire.

Her eyes flew open, and if she'd had the breath she would have screamed in agony. She tried to draw in another breath but couldn't and tried to lift her hand to claw at her throat, but it wouldn't move. The dim light above her wavered as tears filled her eyes. Oddly, she wondered how she could make tears when her throat felt as dry as a desert.

Lights glared bright, searing her eyes. Then a face filled her vision, blocking out everything else. She didn't recognize the face, a black woman with kind eyes and pearl earrings. She tried to focus, but her eyes swam with tears.

"Maxine, it's good to see you back with us," the woman said. Her voice was rhythmic, soothing, and Maxine clung to that. "You have a tube in your throat that's been helping you breathe. That's part of the reason you're panicking. I need you to relax so I can remove it. Blink if you can understand me." Desperate to have the thing removed, she blinked rapidly, ignoring the shooting pain through her temples that simply blinking caused. "Okay. Take a deep breath, as deep and big as you can. When you exhale, I'll take the tube out. Here we go."

The second it cleared her throat, Maxine felt herself starting to calm. Then the woman was back. "I'm Dr. Roxanne O'Neill. I know you're hurting, and the nurse is bringing something in right now to ease your discomfort. Just lie back and relax. You've been on quite a journey."

"I don't …" Maxine uttered, barely a weak whisper. She felt her hand being patted.

"I know. There's time for that later. Right now, just close your eyes."

"Thirsty," she said, complying.

The doctor chuckled. "I bet. When you wake up next time, we'll get you some ice chips."

Maxine heard some shuffling and something warm shot through her vein and up her arm. "Barry," she whispered. The warmth turned hot as it reached her chest. Oblivion beckoned from the next heartbeat.

Maxine heard a chuckle and some more shuffling. "Your husband's here, hon. He's right outside for now. He hasn't left your side this whole time. He'll be back the second we finish."

This whole time? How long had she been here? Where was Barry? Could he salvage the Jeep? Were his golf-clubs okay? Was the other driver okay? Why was she so cold? Were they keeping her in a freezer?

She let the darkness overtake her, seeking the bliss that shielded her from the pain.

MAXINE slowly opened her eyes. For the first time since the accident, she felt that the rational side of her brain had a little more control over the emotional. She didn't know how much time had transpired since the first time she woke up, but it was a haze of panic and pain, of different faces and different voices, all soothing and calm while they did whatever they did before giving her the escape of the drug. Sprinkled among all the fleeting memories was Barry. Sometimes someone else in her family, but always Barry. Someone was always there when she opened her eyes, always smiling down at her and holding her hand.

She was in a different room than she remembered. This one was brighter, more open, lacking the constant beep and surge of machines. The walls were wallpapered with a pink and green floral design on a cream background, creating a very calming pattern.

She smelled fresh flowers. Carefully, to test her ability to move at all, she turned her head, surprised that nothing screamed in protest. There was a large window looking out onto the lawn of the hospital, and on a table in front of the window – actually, on the table, under the table, and to the sides of the table – were baskets and vases and jars of flowers. Every type of flower she could think of was represented, along with stuffed animals, balloons, and potted plants. She tried to smile, but her dry lips cracked.

"We've eaten all the chocolate, of course." Robin appeared from behind her. The way she adjusted her shirt as she came into Maxine's line of sight told her that her sister had been breast feeding the infant who was now propped on a shoulder.

"Of course." Her voice sounded like nothing more than a harsh whisper. She tried to swallow, but her mouth felt like an arid desert complete with gritty hot sand.

"You couldn't have flowers when you were in ICU, and by the time they moved you, the florists had such a backlog of orders that they brought them in waves, new ones every few days."

"Who?" Maxine croaked out.

"I've saved the cards. Old clients, business whatever's with Tony,

Barry's clients, church." Robin hooked her foot on a chair and pulled it close to the bed while she patted TJ's tiny back to coax him to burp. "It's good to see your eyes focused."

"How long?"

"Yesterday made two weeks." Robin grinned and leaned forward to grip her hand. "I'm so excited. So glad you're actually lucid. I'll have to call Tony in a sec so he can come home and see you. He left for Florida when we knew you were out of the woods. He was supposed to be back any day, but once he hears you're awake, he'll come home immediately, I'm sure."

Robin propped her legs on the bottom of the bed and laid the baby's head near her knees, forming a natural cradle out of her long legs. "Sarah gets off at three. She's on the morning shift and hates it, so she'll have plenty to complain to you about while she's here. She had her lunch break at ten, so you missed her by an hour. Barry had court, and Derrick and I had to practically hold him at gunpoint to go. But I'm certain he'll be here mere minutes after it's done."

Maxine lifted her right hand, surprised at the effort it took. She waved toward Robin. Her hand fell limply back onto the bed and she stared at Robin. "How are you?"

Robin's eyes welled with tears as she smiled. "I'm strung out, emotionally spent, and physically exhausted." She leaned forward and lowered her voice. "But, I'm still better off than you, and I've found the sure fire cure for losing all the weight you gain with pregnancy. Your timing is and always has been perfect."

"Don't make me laugh." It was easier this time to lift her hand. "It will hurt."

"I know. Of all of us to get hurt, you have, by far, the lowest pain threshold. I'm sorry."

"Hey," she croaked, "at least I won't be scared to give birth now."

For just a second, Robin's face clouded. Maxine suddenly wondered just how extensive her injuries might be, and for the first time felt real fear start to creep up on her. She closed her eyes for a moment, tired from the effort to speak. "What happened?"

There was a pause and she opened her eyes to meet Robin's. "You don't remember?"

"No, not that. I remember the accident. What happened to me? How bad is it?"

"Maxi, maybe you should wait for the doctor … or Sarah. I don't know all the details about healing and therapy and recovery time and stuff."

"Tell me."

Robin blew out a breath and leaned back in the chair. "Your leg is broken in several places. I guess the door crushed it. You need another surgery on it. And your left arm snapped in two when your hand got caught between the door and the steering wheel."

Maxine looked down and stared at her hand, completely engulfed in bandages and a soft cast. Robin touched her arm. "The surgeon who worked on your arm and leg says you can heal. He says there's a really good chance you can walk again, sooner than you think." She squeezed Maxine's hand harder. "There was a moment when they wondered if you would be able to keep your hand or leg at all, so that's amazing progress. God is so good."

Maxine tried to raise her left arm but had no strength. "My hand?"

Robin's lips tightened and she gave a short shake of her head. "It isn't good. It was crushed. With extensive therapy, maybe you can draw again. Maybe. It will take time."

"How much time?" Maxine asked, trying to keep her voice calm and sound unconcerned.

"Maxi, I just don't know. Doc Rox, the orthopedic doctor, can give you better information. But you can get better. That's what matters. Who cares how long it takes?"

Maxine enveloped her fear of never crafting with a pencil again, never picking up a paintbrush again, and tucked it into a far corner of her mind. "My stomach hurts."

Robin took a deep breath. "A lot of your internal organs were bruised. You bled a lot into your abdomen. They tell me you're healing up well."

Maxine searched her sister's face. "What else?"

"A couple of broken ribs. They had to fix a hole in your lung." Her voice was mild, and Maxine wondered if she even knew about the tears streaming down her face. "And your head injury is over. The bruise is even nearly gone."

She let it all digest slowly, one thing at a time. "That all seems pretty workable."

Surprised, Robin looked at her before she nodded. "You're only saying that because you're on some pretty powerful drugs right now."

"Probably." She smiled and felt her lips crack. "Can you find out if I can drink something? My mouth is so dry!"

"I bet it feels like it was stuffed with cotton and blow-dried." She stood and shifted TJ to her shoulder and walked out of the room. The second she was gone, Maxine covered her eyes with her right hand, noticing how badly it shook. She squeezed her eyes shut and pushed back the tears, promising them they could come back out when she was alone. Robin put on a good front, but she looked as close as Maxine felt to a break down, and neither one of them needed that right now. Taking some very careful breaths, she realized it didn't hurt all that much, and slowly inhaled and exhaled until she had warded off the panic. She sniffed and wiped her right palm dry on the starchy cotton blanket.

"Okay, you can have ice chips. The nurse said that's all you get until the doctor says otherwise. But, she's on the phone with her now, so maybe she'll clear actual water or something." Robin scooped a piece of ice onto Maxine's tongue before she sat back down.

"Mmm," Maxine said, closing her eyes and enjoying the cool wet in her parched mouth. "No, this is fine. Manna."

"I'm going to try to get a message to Barry, but he's in court. His secretary will wait outside of the courtroom, I'm sure, and he'll get back here as soon as he can."

Maxine wanted to stay awake, but her eyelids grew heavy and she felt herself drift away.

Chapter 23

BARRY stole a glance at the watch he'd laid out on the table in front of him. Two minutes later than the last time he checked. Another hour and forty minutes until lunch. He didn't have the focus he needed to be in here today. His mind was across town, lying in a hospital bed for the fifteenth day in a row. Maxine was out of ICU, which left Barry with little to no excuses to keep from showing up for work. The world didn't stop just because his life had a massive and sudden trauma, followed by a spiritual awakening he could not even begin to explain.

One hour and thirty-eight minutes.

He wondered what the person on the witness stand was talking about. He looked down at his legal pad and realized that what was left of his rational brain was sending signals to the hand holding the pen and he was at least taking notes.

A prior downtown Boston restaurant manager threatened Mr. Tony Viscolli with a sexual harassment charge. Since the restaurant was owned and operated by Viscolli Enterprises, she thought she could extort the millionaire. Barry was still baffled as to how the case made it all the way to court. He wondered how opposing counsel, her attorney, could show such poor judgement.

He refocused on the witness, caught up with his notes, and took his turn questioning the human resources director of Viscolli Enterprises. When he finished he sat down and looked at his watch again. One hour, seven minutes.

AS the judge dismissed the court for lunch, he called counsel into his chambers to review the plaintiff's motion to suppress the video of the accuser in Tony's office, threatening him with a lawsuit if he didn't give her a raise. Barry pointed out the signs throughout the hotel where Tony had his corporate offices that clearly read security cameras were in use, and showed that such a sign hung in Tony's office. "This is a professional building, judge. It's ridiculous to suggest that there isn't any security."

The plaintiff's attorney tried to turn his nose down on Barry, but Barry had a good seven inches on him. "Your Honor, there was no reason for her to think that the office would be monitored during business hours. She had a reasonable expectation of privacy."

"There wasn't any sign that said that the monitoring only takes place during specific hours. No indication was given anywhere for that to be the case. Her assumption, in addition to being logically baseless, has no legal standing. Employees should have no reasonable expectation of privacy when standing in their employer's office."

The judge shifted some papers on his desk out of his way as his clerk brought him a sandwich. "He's right. Motion to suppress denied. Go eat lunch. I'll see you back in the court room in," he looked at his watch, "forty-seven minutes."

Barry went through the maze of courtroom hallways and went out a back door that he knew sidled next door to a deli. He ordered a roast beef on whole wheat to go, then reached into his pocket for his phone to check messages.

It wasn't there.

He patted his jacket pockets, his briefcase, re-checked his pants pockets … nothing.

He must have left it sitting on the table in the courtroom. Mentally rushing the deli clerk, he had a $10 bill sitting on the counter before she even finished wrapping his lunch in the white paper. As soon as the sack was out of her hands, Barry grabbed it. "Keep the change," he said, rushing out of the deli.

He had to go back through the front doors of the courthouse to clear security. Thankfully, the abnormally short line moved rather quickly and in no time he found himself in the inner sanctum of the courthouse. He took stairs instead of elevators and shimmied past groups of colleagues lining the halls until he made it back to his courtroom. As he walked to the front of the room, he recognized the back of his secretary's head. Elizabeth turned as soon as she heard the sound of the double doors swishing shut behind him.

"There you are," she said, holding up his phone. "I've been trying to reach you for an hour."

"What happened? Is everything okay?" Barry rushed forward.

"Robin called." Barry's heart nearly stopped as fear gripped it. "Your wife is awake, cognizant, and asking for you."

The air escaped his lungs in a rush. For a moment he just looked at her, then he gathered her into his arms and gave her a quick hug. "Thank God," he said, setting Elizabeth down gently.

"Ann Morganson is coming to take over for you."

Barry grabbed his phone and started scrolling through texts. "Good. We resume in twenty-two minutes. She needs to be here by then."

"She's in the building, so that shouldn't be a problem. I've talked to her myself."

He saw the text from Robin, and another one from Sarah. "Good. Good. I'll just go then." Distracted, he left Elizabeth at the table, walking slowly while he scrolled through a text. "Tell her the motion to suppress the video was denied, and that it's a cakewalk from here. She can read my notes." He paused and turned back, holding out his briefcase. "They're in here."

Elizabeth took the briefcase from him and shooed him with her hand. "Go. We got it. See you whenever I see you next."

Phone in pocket, keys in hand, he rushed out of the room. Elation, relief, joy ... intense emotions battled for priority in his heart as uncharacteristic tears threatened. Awake. Cognizant. Two weeks ago, there was some doubt either one would ever happen again. A week ago, there was hope that she would wake, but uncertainty as to what her mental status would be. Cognizant was good. Asking for him was far better.

He drove her little green sports car through the lunch traffic, trying not to break any traffic laws, trying not to endanger himself in the process. While he drove, he prayed. He prayed a prayer of thanksgiving, hope, thanksgiving, joy ... not even making a lot of sense to himself, but he knew God understood what he was saying.

As he entered the hospital, he nodded a hello to the volunteer behind the big circular desk. He wondered what they thought of the family members that they saw every day, week after week. Did they wonder? Did they know? Did they figure out who was visiting whom?

In the elevator, he happily bypassed the intensive care unit and made his way up to her floor. Nervous little jolts started zipping through his system. Excitement urged his feet to move faster down the hall. The wave of relief rushing through his system left his knees feeling shaky.

"MAXINE, you need the medicine." Sarah stood next to the bed with her hands on her hips, still wearing her nursing uniform, and staring down at her sister like a mother reprimanding a child. Meanwhile, Maxine couldn't help feeling like one. A nurse standing next to her held the syringe and an alcohol pad.

"I don't want it. I'd rather have some aspirin or something."

"You're only saying that because the last shot hasn't completely worn off yet."

Her voice was no longer a weak whisper, but it was still very scratchy. "I don't care, Sarah. The stupid shot hurts worse than anything on my body right now. At least let me see if I can manage the pain without it."

Sarah glared at her until a look of understanding popped into her eyes. Then she stepped closer to the bed and leaned down. "Maxine, please don't be stupid. You aren't going to become a drug addict because you received managed pain medication in the hospital after being in a car accident that nearly ripped you in half."

The only thing that kept her from rolling her eyes was the fact that they ached. She had honestly not thought about the fact that their mother had been a habitual IV drug user in years. "I'm not worried about becoming a drug addict. The shot hurts. Instead of my IV, they put it in my hip and it burned and ached forever after. I'd rather just try this without it."

"In about forty-five minutes, I promise you will regret this."

"I'll decide then, in that case."

Sarah sighed. "Listen, Maxi. I know you. You can't handle a nick on your finger when you're peeling potatoes. There's a lot of pain being shielded from your senses right now. Why suffer when you don't have to?"

"Because I don't like pain. Right now, my hip hurts worse than my arm, chest, or leg."

Sarah sneered. "You're not making any sense at all."

Barry stood in the doorway, so shocked he couldn't move. Twenty-four hours ago, Maxine had either been incoherent and delirious or completely still and asleep. Now she was arguing with her sister as if the last two weeks hadn't happened. He'd known that Doctor Roxanne had intentionally kept her heavily medicated to keep her movements to a minimum as well as combat the pain and shock of the trauma, and he'd known that they intended to change the dosage today, but he'd had no idea of the result.

Guilt immediately flooded his system, pushing away the elation and the joy. The first day he didn't keep a diligent post by her bedside and she was cognizant enough to win an argument with Sarah. Even the preparations for the court hearing today had been done in the chair next to her bed.

He suddenly realized how selfish he was being. Instead of feeling angry that he hadn't been present when she woke up, he should feel overjoyed. So he grinned and stepped all the way into the room.

"Welcome back," he said, moving around Sarah and the nurse to the other side of her bed.

Maxine rolled her head on the pillow. "Barry. Thank God. Will you please tell Sarah to leave me alone?"

When she spotted him at the door, his eyes had been swirling with emotion; relief, joy, anger, too many to count, really. By the time he'd made it to her side, his expression looked pleasant, his eyes nearly blank. He lowered his head and gave her the gentlest of kisses, barely touching her lips. She wanted to ask him about it, but she still had the syringe to contend with.

"Why would I want Sarah to leave you alone?" he asked, lowering his bulk into a chair.

"Because she wants her friend to stick a needle into my rear end."

Sarah sighed dramatically. "Barry, she's never going to be able to handle it when the pain medication wears off entirely."

He shrugged. "Then wait it out. Tell her you told her so when she admits she was wrong. I don't see the point in getting her riled up now." He shifted his eyes to Maxine. "Why don't you want it?"

"Because it hurts."

He stared at her blankly then blinked. "That doesn't make sense."

"It does to me."

"That's because you've had a rather serious head injury. You're confused," Sarah said with her hands on her hips.

Maxine sneered. "This from the woman who denies herself the basic pleasure of ice cream because it has mammal's milk and bird eggs in it. Don't talk to me about confusion."

Sarah turned to the other nurse. "Forget it. If she asks for this in an hour, I'd find ten other patients to see to first if I were you."

The nurse chuckled and recapped the syringe. "Just buzz me if you need to, Mrs. Anderson."

"Thank you."

Sarah leaned over and kissed Maxine's cheek. "I'm glad you're alive. I'm glad you're back to being my annoying big sister. I'll see you in the morning."

"Okay." She let out a breath and closed her eyes for a moment. Arguing with Sarah was easy, but this time it took a lot out of her. Feeling like she'd recouped some of her strength, she turned her head toward Barry again. "Did you win today?"

His head was still reeling from seeing her so awake and … alive. "Win what?"

"Whatever you did in court."

"Oh." He shrugged. "Probably. They didn't have much of a case."

"What was it?"

He caught himself staring into her eyes, green pools that captured him and held him. Once dazed with drugs, her eyes now looked clear and sharp. "What was what?"

"The court thing."

"Sexual harassment."

The pull was immediately broken when she closed her eyes for a moment. He shook his head to clear it and rubbed his own eyes. He must be more exhausted than he realized. "Who were you harassing?"

"It wasn't me. It was Tony."

She smiled. "I'd laugh but I'd end up needing that shot if I did."

He smiled. "I know. I think she thought we'd settle out of court instead of going all the way with it. But she rather irritated your brother-in-law with the whole thing, and he refused to settle anything."

Her eyes were closed and she grew quiet, so he settled back in his chair. The relief at seeing her like this lifted such a huge load, one he'd gotten used to carrying over the last two weeks. As soon as it was gone he felt all the nervous energy he'd been riding on leave him behind. His eyes burned and his arms felt heavy.

Her voice startled him, and he realized he'd nearly dozed off. "I want to talk to you, but I'm so tired."

He gingerly lifted her hand and gave her the lightest of kisses on her knuckles. "Shush. Rest. We have later. We have the rest of our lives."

BY the end of the first week of consciousness, Maxine thought she was going to go out of her mind. She'd managed to avoid taking the shot for the pain, though there were two nights when she thought her resolve might vanish. It was silly, she knew, to manage the pain of a broken body to avoid the pain of the shot. Illogical, actually, but a phobia was a phobia. She couldn't grasp the concept of willingly subjecting herself to the shot regardless of the bliss it would have provided.

Robin came daily for short bursts of time because of the baby. Tony saw her twice in between court and traveling to one of his businesses in Utah, and Sarah stopped by for a few minutes before and after her shifts and on her lunches.

Every morning before work, Barry came to see her. Every evening, he would come in after work. Most nights he slept in the chair next to her bed, but occasionally he went home only to return within just a few hours. He would come in, brush a feather light kiss on her lips, then sit and talk. Many of their conversations were lighthearted, as if they were seated across the table from each other at dinner. Sometimes he prayed with her, sometimes he talked about work, sometimes he told her football stories, sometimes he talked about his family.

He was driving her up a wall.

If he touched her, he always seemed surprised. When he kissed her, it was so light she wondered if there was actual contact. He treated her emotionally, mentally, and physically as if she were made of glass, until she wanted to scream at him that she was still Maxine, broken bones or no broken bones. But while she couldn't remember the events leading up to the last week, her brokenness, her touch and go status, she knew that he could remember. He remembered vividly. Robin had finally broken down and told her what it was like. She guessed he just needed some adjusting time.

As frustrating as it was, she willed herself to wait until he figured out that he could at least give her a real kiss and she wouldn't shatter.

BARRY leaned back in his chair and closed his eyes. The state of weary had been a constant companion for weeks now, and he felt like he might be coming to the end of his rope. He needed to get some real rest soon. Except he didn't know how to turn it all off and rest.

He heard his office door open, but it took a moment for him to feel willing to open his eyes. Instead of Elizabeth, he saw his best friend.

"What's up, brother?" He asked as he straightened his chair and lowered his feet to the floor.

Tony smiled. "Robin said that they're releasing Maxi."

Barry felt a twinge in his heart. "To a nursing home."

The smile faded from Tony's face. Barry knew it had more to do with his tone rather than the information. His lips pursed and he offered, "I thought it was a long term care facility."

"It's a nursing home, Tony."

Tony held out an open hand and asked, "Problem?"

"Yeah. She needs to come home. She'll get better faster at home."

"Okay." Tony sat back and Barry could see the wheels turning in his mind. "What will that take?"

With a gesture, Barry drew his attention to the stacks of folders and brochures that littered his desk. "Hospital bed, doors wide enough for a wheelchair, ramps, renovation on the bathroom to handle her needs, a physical therapist, some specialized equipment for therapy…"

"You have everything you need?"

Barry cocked his head and stared at his amazing, God given friend. He knew the question Tony was actually asking. Could he afford it? Did he need financial assistance or strings pulled? "I do. But I love you and appreciate you."

"Good. Let me know if that changes because I want to help any way I can."

"I know," Barry confirmed, nearly choked up on some unexpected emotion.

Tony cleared his throat. "I am here on a mission."

"Oh?"

"Yes. My wife sent me, so there is no arguing."

Despite it all, Barry laughed. "Okay."

"I am to take you to your favorite restaurant and buy you a thick steak. Then I am to take you to church tonight and attend the Wednesday night prayer meeting, where we'll pray over you. Then I am to take you home and watch whatever sporting event you pick from what you have saved in your recorder to watch until you want to go to bed. Then I'm to sit sentry in your home while you sleep tonight, knowing your sisters-in-law, your mother, and your sisters, will be with your wife."

That sounded ... wonderful. "I ..."

"No arguing." Tony stood. "Do you need to take any of that stuff with you?"

Barry shook his head. "I've called someone to handle the details for me."

"Good. Delegation. I do that all the time. In fact, Derrick is surprisingly good at project management. Maybe have your guy call him. He has spring break starting soon. He'll enjoy the project."

"Maybe I will." Barry stood and grabbed his jacket from the back of his chair. "Benedict's steaks?"

Tony pulled his keys from his pocket. "Wonderful choice."

EMERALD FIRE - CHAPTER 24

BARRY let himself into the house quietly, not wanting to disturb Maxine. He wasn't quite sure what his reasons were, but he wasn't sure of a lot of things about himself when it came to his wife.

His love for her was absolute, he knew that, but her feelings for him after the accident remained a mystery. Her spark was gone, which was understandable considering what she was going through. She found little joy in anything anymore, and the times she appeared to be enjoying herself seemed contrived. Toward him, she gradually became cool and detached, and the flicker of annoyance in her eyes as he bent to kiss her each night tore his heart a fraction at a time. Soon, she would be able to get up and walk away. Part of him wished she never could, and he hated himself for it.

He slipped his keys into his pocket and moved silently through the house. He'd converted the dining room to create a bedroom for her, and the glow of a full moon lighted the room through the thin curtains enough to see her perfectly.

Before the accident, she took over any bed, buried under covers, on her stomach, her head under the pillow. The hindrance of the cast on her leg had retrained her to lie perfectly still on her back. He wondered if she would ever get her vibrancy back, either asleep or awake.

Worried he would disturb her slumber, he stood in the doorway and looked in on her, but didn't enter the room. Instead, he moved silently through the house and up the stairs to his room. The master bedroom. Their room. He wondered if she would ever join him there, or if he was facing the end of their unconventional marriage. The last surgery on her leg was the last surgery the doctors would perform. They removed the cast tomorrow. Maybe another surgery would have to be performed on her hand, but that was inconsequential to the scheme of her freedom outside of this house. Their house. Their home.

Weary, he shed his clothes on his way to the shower. Every step toward healing was a step away from him, he feared. He didn't know how to bring it up to her.

"GIVE me two more, Maxine."

"You're out of your mind."

"Just two more and that will be it for the day."

Maxine closed her eyes and concentrated on lifting the weights. Her leg objected to the movement, tried to refuse to obey the command of her mind. After two more surgeries and three months of confinement in a hard cast, the muscles screamed in protest.

Sweat poured off her face, mixing with tears, but the weights lifted and fell again.

"Okay, once more."

She opened her eyes and glared at Muriel Harrison. For the first few days after her release from the hospital, Muriel had been her near constant companion, acting as nurse and physical therapist. Once the cast had come off her arm and her muscles started working again, she no longer spent the night, but came for several hours a day to torture Maxine. She stood tall for her lean frame, with dark straight hair she kept cut nearly to her chin, and light, light blue eyes. She'd been so kind and patient as a nurse, but the second Maxine's arm had been freed, she became a sadistic drill sergeant, pushing and pushing until Maxine knew she couldn't take anymore, then pushing her one more time.

"I hate you," she spat as her leg trembled from the force of the weights.

Muriel smiled and crossed her arms over her thin chest. "I know."

Maxine looked down at her leg as she lifted the weights and it became fully extended. Well, what was left of her leg, anyway. It was pale, skinny, and crisscrossed with scars from her surgeries. The scars would fade and the color would return to normal, but she didn't know if she had the strength any longer to build the muscle back up.

Slowly, she let the weights come back down, then leaned back against the seat of the machine and caught the towel Muriel tossed at her. She wiped her face and leg before she reached for the leg brace to strap it back on.

"You look tired, Maxi. Are you hurting too much at night? Do you need me to call your doctor to give you something to help you sleep?" Muriel moved to the weight bench across from her and gracefully sat down.

"No." She tossed the towel on the floor. "I'm just having nightmares."

Muriel's eyes were direct, unwavering. "Why don't you draw them out onto paper? It's good therapy."

Maxine stole a surreptitious glance at her mangled left hand and shrugged. "It'll pass."

The therapist stared for several more seconds before she nodded and stood. "Okay. You need a shower, I'll make us lunch, then I want to show you some exercises you need to do before bed every night."

Maxine nodded and inched forward on the seat while Muriel walked behind her. When she came back into view, Maxine's eyes widened. "Where's my chair?"

Muriel pushed a walker toward her. "No more wheelchair. It's time for you to be back on your feet."

She shook her head, as much to protest as to beat back the tension that mounted toward her neck. "No. I'm not ready."

"Maxine, your arm is strong, now. You need to start teaching your leg to work again."

She stared at the walker, her vision closing in until that was all she could see. "I could fall. You're not here all the time. I could fall and break my arm and I wouldn't be able to get back up again."

Muriel's expression never changed. "I'll go make lunch. If you want to eat, then I suggest you take a shower and walk into the kitchen."

Hot tears of rage quickly sprang to her eyes. "Why are you doing this?"

Muriel smiled. "Because someone has to. Lunch in twenty minutes."

Maxine stared at the door, enraged that Muriel actually left, but not surprised. That was how she did things. A command, unrelenting, and then she'd leave, fully expecting Maxine to comply. Her eyes moved back to the walker.

She snarled at it. Then her stomach growled at her. Muriel would leave her there until the next full moon. Or until Barry came home, which would be hours yet. He would pick her up and carry her around if she asked.

Knowing that, she gripped the handles of the walker and pushed herself into a standing position. Barry would carry her around, coddle her, and then talk to her with that infuriatingly pleasant look on his face. Then he would tuck her into her bed downstairs, brush one of those whispers of a kiss on her forehead, and make his escape upstairs.

She'd get strong and walk again, if for no other reason than to follow him up and demand that he start acting like Barry again. A good rousing argument would be nice. A real kiss would be wonderful. Just seeing genuine emotion in his eyes would work for her.

Before she knew it, she had crossed half the room. It was slow, but the brace kept her leg from collapsing. It hurt a little. She knew enough about pain by now to know it was a good hurt – a muscles working kind of hurt. Her arms were strong, easily taking her weight while she compensated for the leg.

By the time she made it to the bathroom she was a little tired, but energized at the same time. She'd just crossed the entire house, and it felt great. She sat on the lid of the toilet to get undressed, then used the bars that had been installed to help her maneuver into the tub. A chair had been installed inside the bathtub, and she smiled as she sat under the warm spray. Soon she would be able to stand under it.

Her workout clothes were gone and a towel and fresh clothes waited for her when she finished her shower. She was tired now, but it would do no good to call for Muriel. She'd said she would be in the kitchen, and that's where Maxine would find her, no doubt.

She slipped on a long, loose dress, her standard outfit since her release from the hospital, dried her hair with the towel, strapped the brace back on, and gripped the handle of the walker again. Her leg trembled a little, and acted like it wanted to cramp up, but she adjusted the way she put pressure on it and it felt better. Her left hand ached. As she walked into the kitchen, Muriel was setting plates on the table.

"Do you still think you're going to fall?"

"Not if I don't overdo it." She laughed as she lowered herself into a chair, sighing at sitting on something that wasn't her wheelchair. "And you were right, as always."

"Every patient thinks they're the only one who has ever been through it." She set glasses of tea in front of the plates before she sat down.

Maxine raised an eyebrow. "To us, we are."

Muriel paused before she nodded. "You're right. But I still have to push. Family won't."

Thoughts of Robin and Barry fluttered through her mind. "No, they wouldn't. I have the benefit of Sarah, though."

"Even Sarah wouldn't have left you alone with it. She would have hovered over you, worried you might fall. I knew you wouldn't."

"And if I had?"

Muriel snickered. "Then I would have been wrong. Very rare." She speared a piece of pasta from her salad with her fork. "I need a favor."

"Sure."

"My mother's birthday is next week. I was wondering ... "

"You need some time off?"

She shook her head. "No. That wasn't what I was going to ask you. I was wondering if you would do a portrait of me. Not a painting, just a drawing."

Maxine's hand trembled and she set her fork down. "I'm sorry, but no."

"Why?"

"I'm not ready."

Muriel leaned forward. "Not ready for what?"

She hadn't voiced it, and her voice wanted to close in on the words. Tears quickly filled her eyes, and she bit her lip to fight them back. "Not ready to find out that I can't." Despite her efforts, the tears spilled over, rolled down her cheeks. "I'm afraid to try."

"You'll never know if you don't pick up a pencil and just draw."

She gripped her left hand with her right and held it up for Muriel to see the scars, the gouges of skin that used to be smooth. "Look at this. Nothing is like it was. My hand was literally put back together. I don't have the same grip. I won't have the same stamina ... "

"I don't care. You'll try."

"I don't want to."

"I dare you."

Maxine snarled. "In three months you've never listened to me."

Muriel smiled. "I don't get paid to listen to you."

"I'm not ready," she whispered.

The doorbell rang, interrupting them. Muriel just raised her eyebrow when Maxine stared at her. "I don't live here," she said, making no move to get up.

Maxine grabbed her walker and glared at Muriel. "I swear I want to fire you," she said, moving as quickly as she could, balking at her slowness and weakness.

"You aren't the first and I doubt you'll be the last."

She slowly, frustratingly slowly, made her way to the front door. When she opened it, she was surprised to see her boss, Peter Mitchell, standing there with a large manila envelope in his hand.

"Peter," she said, a little breathless. "Come in. What's going on?"

"Hi Maxine," he said, shifting his eyes from her face to the walker. "I didn't expect you to answer the door. I was just going to leave this with you."

"What is it?" He held out the envelope and she automatically reached for it.

"Just your paperwork for termination. Retirement accounts and such."

"Termination?"

"We can't just have you hanging on. Work continues. We still need product. Your office, your secretary, your clients are all just hanging."

"We never discussed whether or not I would come back, and we never discussed the timing of anything," Maxine said. Her arm muscles were quivering, but she didn't want to show weakness so she kept standing.

"You said fifty days. It's been fifty plus three months. I think that has been enough time for you to consider whether you're willing to come back or not. From what I understand, you can't even grip a pencil anymore, much less do what we do. I cannot hold your position indefinitely."

Fear, failure, insecurity clawed at her throat. She wanted to walk away from Mitchell and Associates of her own accord, not because she got into a stupid wreck and couldn't perform anymore.

She would not cry in front of him. Exhaustion, muscle fatigue, emotions, fear – sadness choked her throat but tears would not escape. "I'll look over these papers and let you know."

"The decision has all but been made."

Maxine opened the envelope and pulled the papers out. A quick glance confirmed her suspicions. "These say I'm leaving of my own accord. These say I'm quitting. Unless you come up with the gumption to fire me right now, then I will look over these papers and let you know what I decide."

Peter opened and closed his mouth, much like a fish trying to breathe the crisp air next to a mountain stream. He finally nodded and stepped outside. "I'll give you to close of business tomorrow."

Maxine sneered. "Fine."

She slammed the door in his face, then, exhausted, lowered herself onto the little table in the foyer. When she looked up, Muriel was leaning against the wall, her arms crossed over her chest and grinning.

"Looks to me like you're ready for about anything," she said.

Maxine started crying, but it quickly turned to laughter that had tears falling out of her eyes and rolling down her cheeks. "You're right. Bring me my pad and a pencil."

BARRY rolled his head on his neck as he shut the door behind him. It was late, later than he'd anticipated. His meeting with the church board over zoning laws had gone much longer than he planned, which put him behind at the office and had him working too late. Of course, he had to admit to himself that a lot of the work he'd finished that night could have waited until morning, but it seemed easier coming home after Maxine went to bed.

He silently made his way through the house and, as he did every night for three months, stopped at Maxine's door. Clouds obscured the moon tonight, making it impossible to see any distinguishable shapes, but as he stood there and stared, he was certain that there was no form in her bed. Reaching behind him, he flicked on the hall light, bathing her room in a faint glow, and realized he was right. Her bed hadn't even been slept in. Her wheelchair sat in the corner, away from the bed.

He crossed the room, thinking maybe she had fallen and was on the other side of the bed, but found nothing.

Worried, closing in on panic, he pushed open the door to the kitchen. Could one of her sisters or one of his sisters taken her home with them? No. Someone would have called him. He stepped into the kitchen and spotted her.

She sat at the table with her back to him. Her left leg was kicked out to the side, covered with the brace that stopped at the hem of an oversized T-shirt. Her hair was piled on top of her head, tendrils escaping from the loose knot to tease the back of her neck. Whatever she was doing, she was engrossed in it, because she never looked up as he walked toward her.

He came around the table until he was facing her and realized what she was doing. "You're drawing," he said, frozen with surprise.

Her hand paused on the pencil and she glanced up at him through her bangs. There was no welcoming smile, no light in her eyes when she spotted him. "Yes. And walking."

"Walking?"

She went back to drawing. "Yep."

He opened his mouth to speak, but her pencil fell from her hand and she cried out, clutching her hand. He was at her side immediately. "What happened?"

"Cramp," she panted. He was close enough to see the sweat that formed on her brow.

Taking her hand in his, he started rubbing the muscles, coaxing them out of the claw position they'd taken in the spasm. "Maybe you're doing this too soon."

Her hand slowly relaxed and he watched her color return. "I'm not doing anything too soon. I've just been at it on and off all evening. This used to happen even before it was held together with paper clips and sheet-metal screws."

The muscles under his finger were completely relaxed now, but he didn't stop in his ministrations. Instead, he rested his hips against the table as his hands slowly traveled up over her wrist, to her arm, lightly kneading the muscles, gently touching her smooth skin. She closed her eyes and sighed, leaning farther back in the chair.

This close he could see that all she wore was the T-shirt. The hem stopped somewhere at mid-thigh, and the entire length of her good leg was there to torment him. It made him wonder what was or wasn't under the shirt.

Feeling the slight tremor go through his own hands at the thought, he slowly released hers and straightened. "You should go to bed. You've done a lot today."

Her eyes flew open, the green sparking as they came to life. She kept her voice very calm. "Let me tell you something. Never in all the years I've been alive have I pined for my father or wished I had an older brother. I'm not looking for either one of them now."

He took a step back. "I don't know what you're talking about."

"Don't you?" She braced her hands on the table and pushed herself to a standing position, holding her hand up to ward him off as he started toward her. "I can do it. All by myself." She stood next to the table, facing him. "That's the first time that you've touched me for real since the day of the accident. You've been treating me like some porcelain doll, or your little sister or something, and, quite frankly, I'm sick of it."

"What was I supposed to do, maul you in the hospital bed?"

"You could have at least let me know you wanted to."

He stared at her, not seeing her standing there now, but seeing her as she had been that first day. "You were so hurt. You were so hurt and it was my fault."

Maxine blinked, trying to comprehend what he'd just said. "What?"

"If I had fixed my Jeep. If I had taken care of the clutch. If I ... "

"Are you serious?" Using the table as a brace, she walked toward him. "You are serious. My heavens, Barry, you could go through dozens of scenarios of 'what if' and nothing would change. The first time I stalled out, I should have realized something was wrong. I'm of at least average intelligence myself, you know."

"You nearly died."

She finally reached him and put a hand on his chest. "But I didn't."

"And every time I come near you, it's like you're annoyed that I'm there."

"I have been annoyed." She let go of the table and put her other hand on his chest. She could feel his heart under her hand, felt it speed up. "I've been thoroughly annoyed with the fact that you don't want me anymore."

He tentatively cupped her cheek with his hand. "That's not it."

She turned her head and kissed his palm. "Prove it."

He slowly lowered his head and paused a breath away from her lips. He stared into her eyes, watched the emerald pools flare and burn, and with a groan, closed the distance. She sighed and slipped her arms around his neck, opening her mouth under his. Six months of ignoring wants and desire flooded through him as he hooked his arm around her waist and pulled her closer to him.

She gripped his hair with her hands and completely gave herself to the kiss. When he tried to gentle it, she nipped his lips with her teeth and forced him back. She wasn't in the mood for gentle. She'd had months of gentle and tender. Now she needed to know her husband wanted her; that he needed her.

He lifted her in his arms and carried her out of the kitchen, passing her temporary bedroom, and strolled through the living room to the staircase, kissing her all the while.

"I missed you." Maxine's voice was muffled against his chest. She lay on top of him, her legs trapped between his. She didn't even know how long they had been lying there.

Barry didn't speak, but he let go of the hair he'd been playing with and wrapped his arms tightly around her and kissed the top of her head. She could hear his heart speed up.

She lifted her head and kissed his chin. "I have to move. This position is really uncomfortable."

He immediately rolled her over and propped himself up on his elbow, resting his head in his hand. She tried to read his expression, but his face remained solemn, his eyes guarded. He lifted a finger and traced the puckered scar that crossed her abdomen.

"That will fade," she whispered.

"Will it?" He ran his finger back up it, then traced the line of her face before he brushed some hair off her forehead. "Does it matter to you that much?"

"I don't have to look at it."

For a second his guard went down and she could see the anger flash in his eyes. It told her what she wanted to know, and she didn't even need to hear his next words. "Do you really think I'm that shallow?"

She shrugged. "People never know for sure what will bother them."

He put the tip of his finger back on the edge of the scar. "A doctor cut from here," he said, drawing his finger downwards, "to here. Then he repaired damaged organs and saved your life." Her eyes welled with tears, and he used the same finger to brush one away. "Did you believe that the evidence left behind as proof that I nearly lost you, as a reminder of the day I realized how much I loved you, how thankful I was to God for bringing us together, would turn me off for some reason?"

Her breath hitched and she realized that she didn't know what to say. "I ... I ..."

He cut her off as he cupped her cheek and closed his mouth over hers. The sweetness of it, the depth of the emotion that was conveyed through his lips made her throat tighten, made the tears in her eyes cascade down, soaking her hair and the pillow under her. He raised his head again and she was surprised to see the shine of tears in his eyes. His finger traced the scar on her forehead. "It's true. I sat in that chair next to your bed, and I held your hand and begged you not to die because I hadn't told you how much I love you. I told you over and over again, but you couldn't hear me and my biggest fear was that you were going to die never knowing."

Her heart started beating so fast it surprised her that it didn't beat right out of her chest and fly away on hummingbird wings. She wrapped her arms around his neck and hugged him tight. "I didn't think my feelings for you could ever get any stronger," she said, using his neck as leverage to raise herself up and kiss him. "I like being wrong."

He kept his weight off her, supporting himself on his elbows. "I am thankful for every breath you take. I want to spend the rest of my life never forgetting the blessings God has given us in our love. I want to serve Him with you. I want to make our lives – make His giving you back to me – I want all that for His glory."

Maxine scrubbed at the tears on her cheeks as she sat up, taking one of Barry's massive hands and sandwiching it between hers. She brought it to her lips and kissed the palm, then pressed it against her cheek.

Barry continued, "I want us to be man and wife, as God intended. I desperately want you to be the mother of my children," he said. "Your patience when you first moved in, the love you showed me, the depth of love that you gave me – I want you to teach that to me. I want to love you and honor you and worship God with you."

She was dizzy with joy and closed her eyes. "Thank you, God," she whispered.

She felt the bed shift and opened her eyes to see Barry digging through the pocket of his pants. He let them fall back to the floor then turned back to her and opened his palm. In the center of his huge hand lay the platinum, diamond, and emerald ring he had first placed on her finger months before in a little chapel in front of an Elvis impersonator.

"My ring!" She said.

"I never could return it. I tried, but I didn't want to." Barry took her left hand and slipped the ring on her finger. "I should have known then that we were meant to be together."

Maxine cupped his cheek with her palm. "Forever," she said with a smile.

"And ever," he said, kissing her again.

THE END

READER'S GUIDE LUNCHEON MENU

SUGGESTED luncheon menu for a group discussion about *Emerald Fire*.

Those who follow my Hallee the Homemaker website know that one thing I am passionate about in life is selecting, cooking, and savoring good whole real food. A special luncheon just goes hand in hand with hospitality and ministry.

For those planning a discussion group surrounding these books, I offer some humble suggestions to help your special luncheon talk come off as a success.

Quick as you like, you can whip up an appetizer, salad, entree and dessert that is sure to please and certain to enhance your discussion and time of friendship and fellowship.

The Appetizer:

Heathy Protein Packed Hummus

Barry's focus with food is good ingredients, high protein, careful sugars. This hummus is just what the lawyer ordered.

Serve it with triangles of toasted whole wheat pita bread or as a dip with a vegetable tray.

INGREDIENTS:

1 cup dried chickpeas (garbonzo beans) or 2 cups cooked chickpeas

juice of 2 lemons

2/3 cup Tahini Paste

2 garlic cloves

1 lemon

1/2 tsp salt (Kosher or sea salt is best)

2 tablespoons of extra virgin olive oil

1 tsp paprika

1 TBS fresh parsley

PREPARATION:

If using dried chickpes: Soak the chickpeas overnight – OR – cover with 2 inches of water and bring to a boil. Boil for 2 minutes, place the cover on the pan, and let sit for one hour.

Drain soaked chickpeas and cover with water. Bring to a boil. Reduce to a simmer. Cover the pot and cook for 1½ hours or until very tender.

Juice the lemon.

Chop the parsley.

DIRECTIONS:

Put chickpeas, tahini paste, lemon juice, garlic, and salt in food processor. Process until smooth. If it's too thick, you can add a little olive oil or water until it's the consistency you want. The result should be a smooth, slightly granular paste.

Put in serving dish. Mix the olive oil and the paprika. Drizzle over the top. Sprinkle with chopped parsley.

The Salad:

"Rabbit Food" Chopped Salad

What could be better than a one-bit appetizer that satisfies all of the tastebuds in your mouth. Here is a dish that is offered in Viscolli hotels worldwide.

INGREDIENTS:

1 cup feta cheese
½ cup extra virgin olive oil
3 TBS lemon juice
3 TBS water
3 TBS dill
3 small garlic cloves
3 Romaine Hearts
1 large cucumber
4 celery stalks
2 large carrots
1 large tomato
6 radishes
1 cup frozen peas
2 cans chick peas
fresh ground pepper to taste
salt to taste (Kosher or sea salt is best)

PREPARATION:

Grate the garlic clove. Chop the romaine. Slice the cucumber, celery, carrots, tomato, radishes. Rinse the peas. Drain and rinse the chick peas.

DIRECTIONS:

Place the cheese, oil, lemon juice, water, dill, garlic, salt, and pepper in a food processor. Blend.

Mix all of the chopped vegetables. Toss with the dressing.

Serves 6.

The Entree:

Succulent Roast Beef

The first meal Maxine prepares Barry in their home is roast beef. This recipe doesn't use a lot of spices - it lets the meat and vegetables do all the talking.

INGREDIENTS:

1 3-pound Bottom Round Beef Roast
2 TBS flour
2 tsp salt (Kosher or sea salt works best)
$1/2$ tsp fresh ground pepper
1 TBS extra virgin olive oil
2 large onions
6 large carrots
2 lbs. small red potatoes
8 oz baby portabella mushrooms

PREPARATION:

Preheat the oven to 350° F (180° C).

Salt and pepper all sides of the roast. Rub with flour.

Quarter the onions. Peel & slice the carrots into 2-inch chunks. Slice the mushrooms. Wash the potatoes. Halve the larger ones, but the smaller ones you can keep whole.

DIRECTIONS:

In a skillet large enough for the roast, heat the extra virgin olive oil. Place the roast in the oil and brown each side just until browned. Remove and place in roasting pan. Add about $1/2$ cup water.

Surround the roast with the vegetables, letting the onions touch the meat. Cover loosely with aluminum foil. Bake at 350° F (180° C) for 2 $1/2$ to 3 hours.

Remove from oven and let cool. Serve.

The Dessert:

Simple Fruit and Cheese Plate

Barry is very conscious about his diet. Instead of reaching for sugar as a dessert, he is prone to a simple fruit and cheese plate.

INGREDIENTS:

6 ounces Brie Cheese
6 ounces Stilton Cheese
6 ounces Gouda Cheese
1 large bunch purple grapes
1 lb. Ripe organic strawberries
4 Bartlett pears
Half of a ripe honeydew melon, sliced thin
Package of "Entertainment" Crackers (variety)

PREPARATION:

Slice the melon thin.

DIRECTIONS:

Artfully arrange the crackers, fruit, and cheese on different platters. Let guests mix and match to their individual tastes.

Hallee Bridgeman

READER'S GUIDE DISCUSSION QUESTIONS

SUGGESTED luncheon group discussion questions about *Emerald Fire*.

When asking ourselves how important the truth is to our Creator, we can look to the reason Jesus said he was born. In the book of John 18:37, Jesus explains that for this reason He was born and for this reason He came into the world. The reason? To testify to the truth.

In bringing those He ministered to into an understanding of the truth, Our Lord used fiction in the form of parables to illustrate very real truths. In the same way, we can minister to one another by the use of fictional characters and situations to help us to reach logical, valid, cogent, and very sound conclusions about our real lives here on earth.

While the characters and situations in **The Jewel Series** are fictional, I pray that these extended parables can help readers come to a better understanding of truth. Please prayerfully consider the questions that follow, consult scripture, and pray upon your conclusions. May the Lord of the universe richly bless you.

Maxine goes from a horrible foster home environment to one that is obviously very loving and Christ-centered.

1. Do you believe the church, as a whole, does enough to help the "widows and orphans?"

Barry suffered for many years with an unfaithful wife, determined that he could be holy enough for both of them and that one day she would come to God.

> 2. When should we, as Christians, give up on those we love. Should we ever?

Maxine disregards her sister's cautions about deepening her relationship with Barry because he was currently suffering a crisis of faith. Maxine disregards the conversation and jumps in with both feet.

> 3. Do you think we should avoid pursuing relationships with people who aren't spiritually steady?

> 4. 2 Corinthians 6:14 warns us not to become unequally yoked with non-believers, but Barry wasn't a non-believer. He was just struggling. When one person in the relationship is struggling with God, do you think it will typically have an adverse effect on the other person's relationship with God?

Maxine didn't feel the deep conviction Robin felt about God. She was just "doing church" to please the people in her life whom she loved.

> 5. Take some time to examine your heart. Are you on fire for God, or do you need an influx of the Holy Spirit?

Maxine moves in with Barry, determined to live with him and love him as a wife loves a husband.

6. What was your reaction when she did this?

7. Why do you think it took Maxine's accident to bring Barry back to God?

Book 3 of the Jewel Series

Includes Reader's Guide

Inspirational Novel of the Year

Topaz Heat

Hallee Bridgeman

Hallee Bridgeman

TOPAZ HEAT - COPYRIGHT NOTICE

Topaz Heat, Book 3 of the Jewel Series

Third edition. Copyright © 2012 by Hallee Bridgeman. All rights reserved.

Original cover Art by Debi Warford (www.debiwarford.com)

Boston Public Garden photo by Andrew Nash (username andynash on flickr, licensed under Creative Commons CC)

Library Cataloging Data

Bridgeman, Hallee (Hallee A. Bridgeman) 1972-
 Topaz Heat; Jewel Series part 3 / Hallee Bridgeman
 p. 23cm x 15cm (9in x 6 in.)
Summary: Can Sarah finally set aside her decade old prejudices and open her heart to Derrick's true love?
 ISBN: 978-1-939603-36-4 (trade perfect) ISBN-10: 1-939603-36-6
 ISBN: 978-1-452471-60-0 (ebook) ISBN: 978-1-476232-46-1 (text only)
1. Christian fiction 2. man-woman relationships 3. love stories 4. family relationships

 PS3568.B7534 T673 2012
 [Fic.] 813.6 (DDC 23)

TOPAZ HEAT - PROLOGUE

THE little girl stood next to the bed, her feet encased in warm slippers that peeked out from beneath the hem of a long nightgown. She couldn't make out anything in the room except for the bed. Everything else looked blurry and shadowed. She squinted, but it did little to help bring things into focus.

For the dozenth time that morning, she ran her hands over her sides, feeling the fabric of the nightgown. It felt wonderful. Then she pulled her hair forward until she could bury her nose in the unruly curls and inhale, breathing in the wonderful clean strawberry smell.

She couldn't see anything. Where was she? She couldn't remember anything. Nothing around her seemed familiar. The clothes felt unusual. Her hair smelling clean seemed odd.

Her heart started racing at the sound of footsteps outside her door. She put a hand on the bed, clutching the cover, wondering where she should hide. Hiding is what they did, right? You hide, way in the back.

Hide? From what? She couldn't remember.

A shadowy figure appeared in the door and Sarah took a step back, her hip hitting the table by the bed.

"Good morning, honey. I'm glad you're awake."

The gentle voice of the woman sounded unusual to her. She didn't recognize it, couldn't place a name or face with it. The woman came closer and details on her face became clearer. She had blonde hair, graying temples, and remarkably kind eyes. Her skirt came to her knees, and she wore a sweater over her shirt. She knelt next to her.

"Where am I?" the little girl asked.

"You're home." The woman knelt next to her and reached a hand out. The little girl felt trapped by the table and the bed and flinched from the hand but could not move.

The woman frowned but still touched the girl's hair, running a soothing hand over it. "You got here late last night. My name is Darlene Thomas, but I hope that you'll just call me mom."

Looking down at the toe of her slipper, she felt a burn of tears. "What ... what's my name?"

Darlene's breath caught and the girl saw the shine of tears in her eyes. "Your name is Sarah." A tear slipped down Darlene's cheek. "You're nine years old and this is your new home." She reached into the pocket of her skirt. "The police found these at your house. They look about your size, so we thought they might be yours. We've taped them until we can get you to the eye doctor today."

Sarah looked at the bent and broken glasses in Darlene's hand. She tentatively reached for them, running her finger over the frame. Somewhere in her memory, a scene played out of angry male hands ripping them from her face and smashing them, then the sound of harsh male laughter. The memory fled as quickly as it had come.

She brushed her curly red hair from her ears then took the glasses and carefully perched them on her nose. The room came into sharp focus. She saw bright sunlight streaming through crisp white curtains. A dresser against the wall propped up a bouquet of fresh daisies in an ornate vase. A little television sat in front of a child's sized couch in the corner next to a bookshelf. Dozens of books lined the shelf, their pretty colors and bindings made Sarah feel happy.

"Is this my room?" Sarah asked, feeling awe but not understanding it.

Darlene smiled and stood. "Yes. It is."

"Just mine? No one else's?"

Darlene's lips pursed. "Whose else would it be?" She smiled again. "Now, it's time for breakfast. I've made bacon and pancakes. I hope you're hungry."

As they walked down the hall, Sarah could smell glorious smells coming out of the kitchen. Her stomach gnawed at her from the inside. Her mouth watered. Her arms suddenly felt very weak.

She followed Darlene into the little kitchen but stopped short when she saw a man sitting at the table. He stopped reading the paper and set it down, turning in his chair to face her. Sarah's heart started pounding and she felt the urge to run. "Hi there," he said. "You sure are a tiny little thing what for being a big nine-year-old."

He stood, and Sarah backed toward the door. Darlene held her hand up to ward him off. "She apparently can't remember coming in last night." She put an arm around Sarah's shoulders. "It's okay, Sarah. Charles is your new dad. He won't hurt you."

"Of course I won't hurt you." He walked toward her slowly. She stood with her back against the door, looking around, wondering where she could run, where she could hide. Darlene's arm tightened over her shoulders, trapping her. He knelt in front of her just as Darlene had and his face filled her vision.

He smelled good; spicy and soapy and not at all like beer or cigarettes. His gray eyes behind his thin framed glasses looked so nice. The more she stared into his eyes, the more she relaxed. "I'm so happy God brought you to us. We've been praying for you before we even knew who you were." He held out a hand.

Sarah stared at it for several seconds before placing her shaking hand in his. "God brought me here?" She asked, unsure of what he meant.

"Oh yes." His eyes filled with unshed tears. "Most definitely."

He tenderly placed his other hand on top of hers and pushed his hands together, completely engulfing her little hand with both of his. She didn't feel trapped or scared by his touch. She felt … safe.

"Are you hungry?" he asked.

Sarah nodded and Charles Thomas stood. He set her at the table and gave her a plate with a blueberry pancake and two slices of bacon on it. The sight of the meat gave her stomach a sick little pain, but she picked up her fork and dug into the pancake.

Darlene set a little glass of orange juice next to her plate. As she swallowed another heavenly bite, Sarah reached for the glass, but the skewed eyeglasses made her vision a little wobbly and she knocked it over.

Terror immediately struck her. As Charles stood quickly and reached for the glass, Sarah flinched back, bracing for the painful slap he would deliver. Only he didn't. Nothing bad happened. No harsh words. No recriminations. Darlene actually comforted her and assured her that everything was all right while Charles took a kitchen towel and mopped up the juice.

Chapter 1

BLOODY claw marks left smears of scarlet along Sarah Thomas' forearm and all over her shirt and pants. Using a cotton pad, she gingerly dabbed at the scratches, thinking maybe she should have taken the doctor up on his offer to clean them for her. Sarah winced as the antiseptic came in contact with the open wounds. She slowly moved her jaw from side to side, wondering if the left cross to her right cheek would leave a bruise. It certainly felt sore.

"Nothing like a full moon on a Thursday night," Melissa Potts said with a wry smile and an always surprising British accent.

Sarah snorted at her roommate's observation. "At least it's Friday morning now."

Melissa leaned against the doorway to the nurse's station. As she crossed her arms, she gestured with her head toward Sarah. "Story?"

As she wrapped a clean cotton bandage around her arm, Sarah answered her friend. "Addict. Delivered a two-pound, four-ounce baby girl. Wasn't too happy about the whole labor part interfering with her evening cocktail hour."

Clicking her tongue with her teeth, Melissa came all the way into the room and gently prodded Sarah's jaw line. "She got you good."

"She was trying to get out of the bed to go find another fix," Sarah said, flinching when Melissa pushed against the main point of injury. "Let's just say she didn't take kindly to us restraining her."

"Poor girl," Melissa murmured. Sarah didn't know if by "girl," Melissa referred to the mother, the baby, or to Sarah. With Melissa, it could be any of those.

"I tried to pray with her." Sarah stated matter-of-factly.

"Before or after she treated you like a punching bag?" Melissa asked with an ironic little grin.

Sarah looked up at her roommate and rubbed the darkening bruise along her jaw as she frowned in puzzlement. "Both," She answered.

Melissa slowly shook her head and the little grin turned into a genuine and warm smile that silently communicated just how very much the taller, more tan, and far more exotic looking woman admired her short dynamo of a friend. "Well, you're off now, right?"

"I am. I intend to go home, take a long bubble bath, read a Jane Austen novel until I go to bed, then sleep all day." Sarah stood. At her full height of five-foot, half an inch, she barely reached Melissa's shoulder.

"Sorry, love," Melissa said in her cultured British voice, pulling her stethoscope out of her bag and hooking it around her neck. "Painters are coming today." She reached into the pocket of her nurse's scrubs and pulled out a roll of medical tape.

Sarah sighed and closed her eyes. "I forgot." She held her arm out and let her friend tape the bandage. "I guess I'll go home and cover my dresser and bed with drop cloths, then go to one of my sisters' houses."

"You could probably squeeze the bubble bath into the schedule."

"True, but Robin has a hot tub. That will be even better."

Melissa laughed as she finished taping the bandage. "See you in twelve hours?"

Releasing the clip that contained her unruly curls, Sarah shook her head. "Nope. I'll be back at three. Darla is sick and I need the overtime."

"Well, I hope you get some rest between now and three."

"Have a good shift."

Sarah slung her bag over her shoulder and left the nurse's station. Hospital personnel maneuvered through the sometimes crowded maze of hallways of one of the largest medical centers in downtown Boston, Massachusetts. Employees filled the halls at shift change. Sarah loved every single bit of the organized chaos.

While she could pull in a higher wage in a smaller, private hospital, she loved her job and her department too much to leave it behind. She considered her career there a ministry, a place where she could touch people from all walks of life, regardless of income or social standing. A different hospital might mean more money, but she would lose the ability to act as a positive force amongst so much negativity. She would lose the ability to meet people in such need and then pray for them regularly. She would lose the ability to see lives changed, to touch lives, to encourage and support people who might otherwise never know another human being who offered encouragement or support.

As she wiggled her jaw again, she acknowledged that it came at a cost, but she could take the stripes.

Stepping outside, she squinted in the warm sun. In mid-October, cold rain should have been heralding a winter of wet snow, but instead people walked around in shirtsleeves and drank cool drinks to battle the extended summer.

Moving through the crowded sidewalk, Sarah rushed to the subway entrance and pulled her Charlie Card from the outside pocket of her backpack. She swiped it along the reader in a fluid movement as she approached the gate.

She had a car at her house, but preferred not to battle the city traffic and city parking. With a metro station near her brownstone and another one right by the hospital, she enjoyed the stress-free twenty minute commute versus the bumper to bumper, fighting cabs for holes in traffic nightmare.

In the afternoons, she could sit back and read a book. This time of the morning, though, she had to squeeze herself in between two businessmen commuting to their offices. She found a spare pole and stood, shoulder against the pole, and just let her thoughts drift while she let the conductor do the driving for her.

She'd forgotten about the painters or else she would have arranged things ahead of time. On impulse, she pulled out her phone and shot her sister Robin a quick text, asking if she was free for breakfast. Sarah knew she could stay with her sister and family at their house on the coast. She knew that Robin and Tony would be more than happy to have her. For that matter, Maxine lived even closer. Maxine would welcome Sarah just as happily and lovingly. Except that, because Sarah had to be back at work this afternoon, she thought she'd just see whether she could stay in Tony's old apartment.

Sarah thought back to the morning of her fifteenth birthday and the introduction of those two beautiful women into her life. She often wondered how deeply all the wounds of the past continued to affect her even today. Their youth had hardened the eldest sister, Robin, and made her cold as a young adult. Driven by their childhood, Robin determined to give her younger sisters the opportunities that they might not have found otherwise and sacrificed a significant part of her own life for many years to provide just that.

At nearly thirty, Sarah still encountered a big black spot of nothing whenever she tried to remember the first ten years of her life. Robin and Maxine had never elaborated on details and Sarah had never really investigated too deeply into it. In a way, she rather feared what she might remember if she started trying.

Her phone vibrated in her hand, pulling her out of her reminiscence. She read the reply from Robin, asking her to meet her at one of Tony's restaurants. Sarah shot a quick text off, telling her what time she'd be able to make it there, then thought about what she needed to pack and what she might already have at the penthouse.

As the train left the business section of downtown and got closer to her neighborhood of brownstones, the passenger load got a little lighter. By the time she got off at her station, she barely had to shoulder her way through the crowd.

DERRICK DiNunzio felt the car slow and glanced up from the file he had been studying during the ten-minute ride from Logan airport. He snapped it closed and slid it into his briefcase as the car pulled up to the curb and came to a stop. He finished off his orange juice in a few swallows. By the time he set his glass down and secured his briefcase, the driver had opened his door.

Mid October welcomed him to the grand city of Boston, but summer stubbornly refused to hand the reins over to autumn. Though the trees had started to turn colors and line the street in the garnet and gold magnificence of God's beauty, the sky still insisted on painting itself a very clear bright blue, and the temperature remained warm enough that several people walking by outside wore shorts.

He buttoned the jacket of his suit, acknowledging that part of him wanted to be a passerby, dressed down and ready to do something – anything – outside. Long weeks had passed since he'd taken even a few hours off, and the summer had ended up leaving him behind. That happened easily with city dwellers, especially New York City where he had lived for the last six years. One could miss the seasons with their different nuances that provided their own recreation and relaxation. However long he ended up in Boston, he determined that he would find a way to enjoy at least part of the autumn. Perhaps he would find a way to take in some hiking, definitely do some rock climbing, maybe even some rowing – all the things he used to do in the city he called home.

First, though, he had to find out what brought him here. The e-mail from his once rescuer and now employer, Tony Viscolli, simply instructed him to arrive this morning and plan on staying awhile.

"Where shall I take your luggage, Mr. DiNunzio?"

"Pull over to Valet, Howard. Wait there and I'll let you know as soon as I know."

"Right away, sir." Howard answered with a little nod. Though his face hid his reaction well, it still unnerved Derrick that nearly everyone in the Viscolli empire addressed him as "sir."

Derrick turned and lifted his head. His eyes automatically skimmed up the building taking in the complicated masonry design; the ornate balconies carved out of living stone. All of it looked reminiscent of the feel of the old town. He loved this hotel. The New York Viscolli where he worked was bigger, grander, a different style of luxury, but the Boston Hotel would always have his heart.

He remembered the first time he really saw this hotel. His eighteenth birthday, on a bitter cold January morning, he'd stood in this very spot and stared up at the massive stone structure, gripping a business card in his hand, fighting an internal battle. To trust or to run?

Born and raised in Boston – south Boston, specifically – Derrick came from a poor family. His mother was an immigrant Italian woman who never learned to speak English and never had anymore children after his American father, who he didn't remember, abandoned them once Derrick was born. Like nearly every other teenager in his tough neighborhood, he had taken to the streets where he stole, fought, and scraped to survive until a few weeks before his eighteenth birthday, when he had a chance encounter with Antonio "Tony" Viscolli on the street in front of a seedy bar in his neighborhood.

Tony had seen something in him – what the man had seen, God alone knew. They came from the same place, more than a decade apart, and Derrick told Tony he would get out just like the older man had. For some reason, Tony had handed Derrick a business card, a note scrawled on the back that said, "Let him see me – no appointment required." He told Derrick to come find him after he turned eighteen.

Pulling himself back to the present, he stepped through the brass and glass revolving door etched with the intricate golden V emblematic of all the Viscolli companies and stepped into a life of opulence. His heels clicked on highly polished alabaster and deep emerald marble floors. Luxurious goat skin leather couches appointed all the sitting areas. They were set out in circular arrangements, perched atop Cardassian silk Persian rugs that warmed the rich marble floors. On one side, doors led to the shops and amenities offered by the hotel. On the other side, doors led to the restaurant. The same V crest, trimmed with brass – hand polished to a golden gleam – adorned the black marble front desk. On the wall behind the desk, gold letters formed the words, *"Whatever you do, work at it with all your heart, as working for the Lord, not for men. Colossians 3:23"* Derrick had long ago hidden those words away in his heart, repeating them to himself often.

Employees wearing distinctive uniforms moved invisibly through the throng of customers and clients, making sure they met needs and answered questions all quite quickly, professionally, and discreetly. The guests stood out of this crowd – tailored, accessorized, groomed, and coifed to perfection.

Ten years ago, the warmth of the lobby had been his first sensation. The luxury seemed surreal. He'd felt out of place. He'd stolen the Charlie tokens to get there and his stomach growled. He hadn't eaten in two days and hadn't bathed in longer than that. The desk clerk had read the note on the card and directed him to the elevators with a friendly smile.

Now, ten years later, he returned the greetings of those who recognized him, both clientele and employees, as he made his way to the bank of elevators. While he waited, he spoke with a Baron and Baroness, visiting from Great Britain, who had spent a stint in the New York Viscolli the previous week. He felt at ease with the conversation, one of the talents required to interact with so many different people on a daily basis. He could switch gears in conversations, remember names and little details, and still pay attention to everything going on around him, a necessity for his job.

He left the Baron and his wife on the sixth floor and continued his journey upward, beyond the hotel proper and on into the business offices that formed the heart of Viscolli Enterprises.

The receptionist sat behind a large half-mooned desk. Scrolling brass letters on the wall behind the desk read, *"He has showed you, O man, what is good. And what does the Lord require of you? To act justly and to love mercy and to walk humbly with your God. Micah 6:8"*

She smiled warmly and directed him to go through the frosted panes of the double doors. He stepped through into the outer office and found Tony's secretary, Margaret, at her desk.

A decade before, she'd stood when he entered and greeted him by name. "Derrick, it's nice to finally meet you. Mr. Viscolli told me to expect you."

He hadn't understood her cordiality and had no idea how to respond in kind. Inside the imposing office, Tony had greeted him genuinely and with warmth. Derrick didn't understand him, either. Tony had a roast beef dinner and hot tea brought up to his office and talked to Derrick for hours, asking him questions about his family, the neighborhood, his schooling, his thoughts about God. At the end of the meal and conversation, he offered Derrick a job.

And a home.

Bringing himself out of nostalgia and back to the present, he gave her his most charming smile. "Margaret," he said, "I have missed you."

She laughed and stood. "Always a charmer, you," she said, then opened one of the heavy oak doors leading into Tony's office.

"Would you care for something to drink, Derrick?"

Finally, someone who didn't cow-tow and call him Mister. He remembered back to his early college days when Margaret had given him a very thorough tongue-lashing for using a foul word in her office. "Ginger ale would be great," he said as he walked past her and fully into Tony's office.

Tony quickly ended his conversation and hung up the telephone as Derrick entered. Then he stood and walked around his desk.

Derrick could see Tony summing him up as he crossed the room. He wondered if the older man still saw the skinny, dirty kid he'd brought home out of a life on the streets ten years earlier. He had grown a little taller than Tony and filled out a lot. Like his mentor, his Italian heritage was very much a part of his appearance. His hair was jet black, his skin olive tan, and his rich eyes chocolate brown, all set in a lean face with sharp angles and an aristocratic nose.

Despite his upbringing, Derrick very purposefully proclaimed class. He had paid attention, soaked in the details, until he'd cleaned the streets and the hard living of his childhood completely off his persona.

No one meeting him for the first time would think for a second that he hadn't been born in a stately mansion, eating from silver spoons and riding in long cars that someone else drove. They could never even imagine that perhaps, as a child, he had eaten sometimes only because he'd stolen a couple of those spoons or cars from time to time. Instead, they saw the quality Derrick nearly exuded. They saw youthful good looks, and clothes that were always the epitome of style that Derrick wore as if born in them. They heard the upper crust accent in his voice that he had perfected after long practice. Not a trace of South Boston ever spilled from his well-trained lips.

"My brother," Tony said warmly, arms outstretched for a warm hug. "Welcome home." He embraced Derrick then gestured to his sitting area.

Derrick lowered himself into one of the chairs. "How's the lovely Robin faring these days?"

"Pitiful," Tony said, his eyes softening at the thought of his wife. "TJ started second grade last week, and Madeline started kindergarten. Robin's been randomly bursting into tears for the last week. I finally convinced her this morning to go to Hank's Place and work on new menus."

"I'll have to swing by while I'm in town, give her someone to mother for a couple of hours."

"You should. She will be so thrilled to see you. She's at Hank's all day today. That may be just what she needs." He leaned back in his chair and his face lost its softness. Derrick knew that personal time was over and it was time for business. "We have a problem."

"Which 'we'?"

"The 'we' that is Hotel Viscolli – Boston."

"And what might our problem be?"

"It might be any number of things." He sighed. "What it actually is, however, is that our manager and assistant manager have run off together."

Derrick raised an eyebrow. "Bill Matheson and Adrienne Christopher?"

Tony nodded. "It has been terrible. Apparently, they have been involved for some time. Bill's wife called me about it last night. It was already too late. They left work together yesterday afternoon and are currently on some tropical island somewhere."

"Wow," Derrick said. "I find that astonishing." He really did. Derrick could not imagine a more unlikely pair of employees in a more unlikely place under more unlikely circumstances.

They were interrupted when Margaret brought in Derrick's drink. Derrick thanked her then took a long pull of the ginger ale and waited. Tony finally spoke again. "So what do you say?"

"What do I say about what?"

"Do you want it?"

"Do I want what?"

"Viscolli – Boston."

The ginger ale he'd just swallowed caught in the back of his throat and choked him. He coughed and fought to get a breath, finally sitting back up and wiping the tears from his eyes. "You aren't serious."

"Always."

Years ago, Tony had told Derrick that he reminded him of a nineteen year old version of himself. Derrick didn't know why, because by the time Tony was nineteen, he was well on his way to becoming the tycoon everyone knew today.

Like Tony, Derrick had wanted out. Out of the poverty, off the streets, away from the fast money he could make if only he could sell his soul. So, over his mother's very vocal objections, he took the job Tony offered all those years ago, accepted the education Tony paid for, and replaced the faceless father in his dreams with Tony Viscolli. If his mother thought that made him wrong, then he could do nothing to change that – because nothing would ever make him go back to the life he'd fled.

While he had attended college, he worked as Tony's assistant doing whatever needed doing -- from carrying his luggage to caddying for him on the golf course, from touring potential companies to offering his ground floor opinion on their merit should Tony wish to purchase them. In the process, Tony opened his home and his family, giving Derrick a place of welcome where he had never felt welcome before.

The first time he'd walked into the Viscolli hotel in downtown Boston and seen the grand luxury, seen the faces of the elite as they moved through the lobby, watched the competence of the staff as they served the clients, he knew what he wanted to do for a living. He chose to study hotel management in school, and graduated within three years.

He had worked in this very hotel, first as a bellboy, then as kitchen help, and finally on the front desk and concierge station. He agreed with Tony, believing that as a future manager, he should experience as many of the positions within the hotel as he could. In the process, he had watched Bill

Matheson run the place, creating a well-oiled machine that gave the clientele what they had come to expect from a Viscolli company – sleek luxury without a bump in the ride.

"Tony, I'm still just an assistant manager. I'm not qualified to manage yet. And this is your flagship."

"Nonsense. You're fully qualified."

"I don't have the experience –"

"Enough." He sat forward and put his elbows on his knees. "You learned the technical stuff in college. You learned all the jobs here. You learned management in New York. You're a natural with people, and you're ready. None of those are questions."

Derrick tried to cut him off, but Tony held up a finger to forestall the protest. "You also love this hotel. I could hire hundreds of people with more experience, but none of them would genuinely love this place like you do." He sat back again. "My mind's made up. I only hope I can afford the extortionist salary you are shortly to command."

Derrick let out a breath to keep from shouting his excitement. When he was sure his voice would be smooth, he nodded. "Few know better than I about trying to argue with you when your mind is made up."

Tony grinned. "I always said you were smart." He rose. "Arrangements have already been made. My apartment in town is free. You may live there as long as you like until you find a place of your own."

He set the glass on the table next to him and stood. "That's a rather large place for a bachelor."

Tony laughed. "No one knows that more than I. It's large and lonely. It may encourage you to find me a sister-in-law to love and provide you a means to fill those rooms."

Derrick shook his head. "You sound like your wife."

"Don't tell her that." He pulled a set of keys out of his pocket. "You'll need a car, here. Your Mustang is in the hotel garage."

His Mustang – his 1967 Mustang GT fastback – his Shelby. A Christmas present from Tony and Robin. He'd spent two wonderful years restoring her. Leaving her behind when he left for New York had broken his heart. He plucked the keys from Tony's hand, immediately recognizing their weight.

"I took the liberty of having her detailed. If you need to go back to New York and tie up any loose ends, I can spare you for the weekend, but I would need you to start not later than Monday morning."

"I appreciate that. I'll head back right now, since it's Friday. Give me the rest of the day to do business. Then I'm going to take the weekend all the way off." He looked at his watch. It was only eight in the morning. He had read the e-mail from Tony a short thirteen hours ago. "I'm nearing burnout, and need to get outside for a while."

Tony nodded. "Absolutely. I need you clearheaded."

The phone on his desk sounded a tone. "Mr. V, your wife is on your private line."

He held his hand out, and Derrick shook it. "Hey, don't let Robin know I'm here. I'll head on out to Hank's Place right now and surprise her. Give me an excuse to drive, too. I'll go to the airport after seeing her."

Tony grinned as he walked to his desk. "She'll like that. I'll let the pilot know to be on standby and I'll see you Monday morning." He picked up the telephone and accessed his line. As he walked out, Derrick heard, "Hello, *cara*, how is the menu planning going?"

Margaret spoke into the telephone while typing something on her computer, so Derrick just winked good-bye in her direction as he left the office.

Chapter 2

"I can't believe my husband didn't tell me you were coming back to town," Robin said, leaning across the table to squeeze his hand again. Papers and notebooks and menus covered the table.

"I didn't know until about nine last night." He added some honey to his coffee. "So, big surprise for all of us."

"How long are you here for?"

"I hope forever, but we'll see how it goes." He took a long look at her. She hadn't changed much in ten years. A small part of him would always carry the crush he'd had on her when he first met her. She wasn't as thin as she had been then, but she'd needed the weight she'd gained. "You look really good, Robin. Life suits you."

"That's because I'm happy." She stacked menus together and moved them to the table next to them to make room for the tray of pastries the waitress carried to them. "What about you? Are you bringing a girl home for my approval?"

A tug on his heart made him force a smile on his face, fearful she'd read the wistfulness he felt. "Not yet. One day, I hope."

She nodded thanks to the waitress and selected something with raspberry and cream cheese. "Derrick, I have a feeling that when you fall, you're going to fall hard."

A face flitted through his mind. Wanting a different subject, Derrick said, "How's Maxi?"

"She's great. The twins keep her really busy, but she has someone come in a few times a week so she can get to her studio and paint."

He leaned back where he sat, a look on his face that said he was accessing a decade worth of memories. "I saw them in New York when they were there for her show at the beginning of summer. How old are they now, four?"

"Yep. They just turned four."

He shook his head, wanting to disbelieve the fact that four years had vanished in a breath. Then he asked the question he'd been waiting to ask, struggling to sound utterly disinterested in the potential answer. "What about Sarah? Married yet?"

"Don't you think you would have gotten a wedding invitation?" Her cell phone vibrated next to a notebook. She pressed a series of buttons and returned her attention to him. "She's okay. She moved out of her parents' house when her mom put her dad in the home two years ago. I think she was really angry that her mom wouldn't let her take care of him."

"Why didn't she?"

"His Alzheimer's got worse, and Sarah was having to miss shifts at work. It was just a bad scene all around. Sarah's had a hard time with it. So now she's living with another nurse in a brownstone by the hospital. Nice girl."

She fielded another text message so Derrick finished his coffee and stood. "You're busy. I have a flight at noon back to New York anyway, and need to call ahead and have some things done and waiting on me."

Robin waved her hand at her phone. "I'm sorry. Tony has me working on menus for about twenty restaurants right now." She stood and hugged him. "Come by the house and have dinner."

"I will. My return flight won't get me home until after eleven tonight. But maybe tomorrow night."

She started to speak, but her phone rang and interrupted her. As she answered it, she said, "I'm glad you're back, Derrick."

"Me, too."

He squeezed her shoulder and turned to go.

SARAH slowed the car as she came upon the sharp curve just before the entrance to Hank's Place. Just as she rounded the turn, she heard the squeal of tires and automatically cut her wheel to the right seconds before a silver car with black racing stripes flashed by heading in the other direction.

"Idiot," she muttered, watching it disappear in her rearview mirror. Derrick DiNunzio had a car like that, and drove his car like that, and she always thought it was the dumbest thing in the world. Life was too precious to risk it with some hopped up car that went way too fast and was far too powerful for human reflexes to control. It wasn't just the driver in the car who was at risk, but anyone else on the road.

She had her heart rate back under control by the time she pulled into the parking lot and shut off her engine. Dismissing the speeding car from her mind, she strode into Hank's Place.

Memories of her first two years with Robin and Maxine assailed her as she walked through the front door and immersed herself in the familiar smells and decor. Robin quit working at Hank's after the birth of her first son. Had Sarah really never come back to this place since then?

She entered the dining area and immediately saw her oldest sister surrounded by stacks of menus and notebooks. "Hey."

Robin grinned and jumped up to offer Sarah a hug. "Hey yourself! What a treat!" She gestured at the opposite chair and sat down again. "You'll never guess who was just in here."

The anticipation on Robin's face coupled with the car she'd seen gave her all the hints she needed. She crossed her arms and offered, "Derrick DiNunzio?"

Robin's jaw dropped. "How did you know that?"

"He left some slime here on the table."

Robin grinned, shaking her head. "That's not nice. Shame on you. And Derrick isn't slime. How did you really know he was here?"

"There aren't many silver Shelby's out on the road, nor are there many drivers quite like Double D. He nearly ran me off the road."

Robin laughed. "He's here for good, he says. It's so exciting. Kind of like a child coming home."

Derrick wasn't her favorite topic of conversation, so she changed the subject. "What's Casey's special today? I just came off shift and could use something other than the banana I ate coming over here."

"Mmm, beef stew. It's really good. Want some?"

She suppressed the shudder at the thought of consuming meat. "No. Just a salad, with vinegar dressing and no cheese."

Robin waved a waitress over. "Pitiful." Directing her attention to the waitress, she said, "Ask Casey if he'll make Sarah a salad. He'll know how." Looking back to her sister, she said, "So, what's up?"

"They're painting my apartment today. Do you think I could stay at your penthouse tonight?"

Robin shrugged. "Of course. You know you don't have to ask."

"I wouldn't feel right not asking. It's not my place anymore."

"Why don't you come stay out at the house?"

She toyed with the straw in her water. "Same reason I'm not going out to mom's or Maxi's. I just came off the night shift, and have to be back to work three to eleven tonight. I don't have the energy for the commute."

"No problem. You're welcome any time."

"Thanks." She glanced at her watch. If she hurried with the salad, she could get in a good nap before her shift.

DERRICK leaned wearily against the wall of the elevator. He watched the numbers light up as the elevator climbed. He had certainly had a day of it. The early morning flight in the private jet to Boston then the commercial flight back to New York led to a few very quick hours of details, delegation, decisions, and finally a return flight back to Boston that arrived at Logan just before midnight. Quite a few hours logged in the air, not to mention everything that he'd had to accomplish in the day.

He didn't know why he hadn't just spent the weekend in New York and wrapped everything up, but he just really felt a pull to be home. As the elevator chime dinged, announcing his arrival at the requested floor, and he sensed the slight feeling of vertigo as the elevator came to a stop, he felt an overwhelming nostalgia wash over him.

Home.

He couldn't help thinking about the first time he ever rode in this very same elevator. Tony had spent the morning with him at his office, feeding him good food, talking to him about hopes, dreams, life, and God. Then he brought him here.

Derrick didn't trust him. In the pocket of his dirty, torn leather coat, he had a long switchblade and his sweaty, nervous hand gripped the handle. Rich men just didn't pick dirty street boys like him up and offer them jobs and a home without something being required in return. As for Derrick, no matter how cold or hungry he might have felt when he walked into Tony's life on that January day, he just didn't play that way.

He figured he could roll the guy. Maybe get something good out of these "fancy-schmancy" digs. Then he'd high tail it back where he belonged.

He extinguished the glimmer of hope that kept trying to light itself inside of his chest. This was the real world. No one saved you but number one.

The surprise he felt when Robin met the elevator threw him for a loop. Beautiful, clean, wonderful Robin. Tony's fiancée. She had smiled and held out her hand to warmly shake his. "It's so wonderful to meet you, Derrick."

Maxine came out of a back room then. Derrick had been temporarily struck dumb by her beauty. She had laughed at something, and the sound of her joy sang through the room.

Robin had said, "Maxi and I were just here supervising the decorator for your bedroom. Hopefully, we covered everything." She had turned to Tony. "I'll see you tomorrow?"

He'd taken her hand and kissed the knuckles. "Count on it, my love."

That flame of hope wouldn't be extinguished. It burned brighter every minute that passed. Tony had shown him to the kitchen and had opened the refrigerator. "Help yourself," he said. "Nothing is off limits."

When Tony had turned, Derrick took a reflexive step backward. "What do you want?" he'd asked out loud.

Tony had held his hands up. "I don't want anything from you. I felt led by God to help you and I typically do what He says." Derrick didn't know how to trust him. He had continued speaking. "Just a couple of rules."

This was it, Derrick thought. Now the hand would be played. He felt his shoulders tense up defensively, but Tony surprised him. "If you live here, you can't break the law – that includes illegal drugs and underage drinking. As long as you stay straight, you can stay."

Derrick shrugged and stuck out his chin defensively. "Yeah? What else?"

"You go to church with me every time I go."

He could probably manage that, maybe. "And?"

It was Tony's turn to shrug. "And nothing. *Semplici*."

What Tony had casually brushed off as "simple" was the world to Derrick. Slowly, daily, gradually, his trust built. That flame of hope never flickered again. It grew, burned, and filled him with passion for his new life, his new family, his new relationship with Jesus Christ. Now, when he stepped off the elevator and into the living room, one word echoed through his mind.

Home.

SARAH stared dumbly at the dashboard of her car. Not knowing what else to do, she turned the key again. Nothing. None of the little warning lights on the dash even lit. She leaned forward and rested her head on the steering wheel. Not tonight. She didn't have it in her tonight. She hadn't been able to nap and instead decided to go visit her dad. The visit took a lot longer than she thought it might which is how she happened to have her car in the hospital parking garage. Then she'd gotten caught up in a difficult delivery and ended up working well past her eleven o'clock end of shift. At this point, she hadn't slept in more than a day.

Accepting that the car simply wasn't going to start, she determined that she'd have to walk. It would take longer to get seated on a train than it would to just walk to the apartment.

While she had worked the weather had turned and a light but very cold rain served as the harbinger of the harsh winter to come. With a sigh she grabbed her purse and umbrella, deciding to leave everything else there, then locked the car. The apartment was just around the corner. Her feet ached, but walking would be better than waiting for a taxi in the light rain.

By the time a taxi got there, she'd already be in a warm robe, sipping on a cup of tea.

On Friday nights, even this far into Saturday mornings, the downtown streets were far from quiet. The air felt a little cool, but the jacket of her nursing uniform shielded her arms, and after being in the controlled air of the hospital for nine hours it came as a welcome relief.

It never crossed her mind to worry about walking downtown after midnight. Of course, if she mentioned it to her mother, she'd hear every unpleasant possibility in a seemingly endless litany. She grinned as she rounded the corner. Her mother was a melodramatic worry-over-every-nuance kind of person. It helped when abstract details needed deliberation, but it grew tiresome when one was a daughter discussing a date or a social function. Thinking of the date as an ax-murderer could be hilarious in hindsight, but beforehand could put a damper on dinner plans.

Sarah reached the building and pushed into the lobby. She wanted to groan out loud when she recognized the guard working the security desk. Brian was nice, but extremely talkative. It was late, she was on the edge of exhaustion, and she just wasn't in the mood.

"Miss Sarah," he said with a surprised look on his face. "I didn't know you were expected tonight."

She didn't pause at the desk, but kept walking toward the elevator. She pulled her keys out of her pocket so she wouldn't have to wait on him to quit talking long enough to access the elevator for her. "Hi, Brian. Good to see you."

She slid the key into the lock and gave it half a turn. The doors immediately opened.

"Miss Sarah, wait!"

"No time, Brian. Sorry!" She hit the button and waved as the doors slid shut. She leaned against the side of the elevator as she felt the lift slide upward. Whew. Missed being trapped in a conversation for half an hour. Normally she didn't really mind, and she didn't want to be unkind, but fatigue weighed her down.

She was stepping down into the living room before she realized that something was wrong. The lights shouldn't be on full – they should be on dim. She froze at the bottom of the step. The television definitely shouldn't be blaring out an old black and white John Wayne movie. The clang of something hitting something metal in the kitchen made her heart pause, stop, then race.

Obviously, someone else was in the apartment.

Chapter 3

SARAH heard another clang. She quietly set her purse down but held onto the umbrella, holding it just above the handle like a baseball bat. Running lightly on her toes, she crossed the room quickly and stood by the door of the dining room. There were a few more sounds, then the sound of a man whistling that got louder as he got closer.

Taking a deep breath, she raised the umbrella over her head and waited, focused on the door. She let it swing open, watched the figure of the man come out of the dining room, and brought the umbrella down. Hard.

He must have sensed the movement because he ducked and the umbrella hit him across the back of his shoulders. "Ow! Hey!"

In the next second and utterly without warning, he rolled to the floor and used one of his legs to sweep hers out from under her. She flailed her arms as she landed on her backside, finding herself under his weight. She started struggling, but he threw one of his legs over hers and grabbed her arms in a bone-lock, pinning them up by her head.

"Sarah?"

She realized her eyes were closed and at the sound of his voice, they flew open. Immediate recognition prefaced the heat that rushed her face from total embarrassment. "Derrick? What are you doing here?"

"I was about to ask you the same question."

She hadn't seen him in at least five years. No, it was six. He left town right after his mother's funeral. He'd not been back. She got updates from Maxine or Robin each time they'd seen him in New York. She hadn't seen him at all in that space of time. He'd filled out, she thought. His face looked more mature, almost tougher, his shoulders wider.

Meanwhile, Sarah hadn't changed at all. She still looked like a teenager. She still had the spray of freckles across her nose. Behind her glasses, her eyes were still the color of richest amber topaz. Her hair had come out of the clip and lay spread out around her head on the carpet, the curly red highlights reflecting the dim light.

Realizing he was staring, Derrick released her instantly, pushed away, and sat next to her. "What in the world did you hit me with?" He reached back and gingerly touched his shoulder, wincing when his hand came away smeared in blood.

The only thing he wore was a pair of sweat pants. "My, um, umbrella."

He saw it next to her and grabbed it. It was snapped in half. Irritated anger burned through him. "This? You suspect there's an intruder and this is what you use to defend yourself?"

She ripped it out of his hands and stood. "It was all I had."

"It never occurred to you to call security?"

Sarah's cheeks flushed bright red. She waved her hand as if to dismiss his last statement. "Let me see it," she said, moving behind him.

He jerked to his feet. "No thank you. Don't touch it."

"Don't be such a baby. Let me see."

He held a hand up to ward her off. "Really. Don't worry about it."

"I promise not to hurt you, Derrick. I won't even touch it." She put her hands on her hips. "I *am* a nurse, you know."

She almost withdrew the offer. But then he glared at her before moving to one of the oversized chairs, sitting sideways so she could see his back. The space across his shoulders was already starting to purple with a bruise, and it looked like something had caught the skin and ripped it. He had a gash about three inches long diagonally across his right shoulder. "Ouch, Derrick. Sorry about that."

Over his left shoulder, just shy of the bruise, was a tattoo of a dragon, done in brilliant colors – turquoise, fuchsia, purple, bright green. She was surprised it was there; intrigued even. He had done everything to get rid of his past and she wondered why he kept the tattoo. Before she realized it, her fingers hovered above it, about to touch it.

He eyed her over his shoulder and glared at her. She bit her lip and redirected her fingers to gingerly touch the bruise. "You'll want to put some ice on it and you should let me clean and dress the cut."

She turned to leave. "What are you doing?" he asked.

She was halfway down the hallway before she answered him. "I'll be right back." Moving quickly, she went to the master bathroom and pulled open the medicine cabinet, finding the supplies she needed. She slipped the roll of tape and the package of bandages into her scrubs pocket, then pulled a washcloth out of the linen closet and dampened it beneath the faucet.

When she returned to the front room, he stared suspiciously at the brown bottle in her hand. "What's that?"

"Hydrogen peroxide."

"Uh huh. And what do you think you're going to do with it?"

With a sigh, she poured some on the cloth and stepped closer. "I'm going to clean the cut."

"What happened to you not touching it?" He hissed the breath between his teeth and cringed away as the cloth came in contact with his skin. "Ouch. That hurts."

"Good Lord, Derrick, quit being such a baby."

He clenched his teeth and swallowed a retort. Then he felt her warm breath gently blowing on the wound. He imagined her puckered lips as her breath caressed his fevered skin.

"There. Is that better?"

"It's great. Thank you."

He heard her moving behind him, heard the sound of the cap going back on the bottle. He felt her fingers graze his skin as she placed a bandage over the cut and taped it to his skin. He tried, desperately, not to react to her touch in any way, to pretend she was some platonic stranger tending his wound. "You need to ice it. I'll go get some."

While she was gone, he closed his eyes and took a deep breath, seeking some inner steadiness. Why was she here? She quickly returned and gently set a plastic bag filled with ice across his shoulders, then perched herself on the couch that angled with the chair so that she faced him.

"You never answered my question," he said, staring at her with those brown eyes that always made her feel uncomfortable. "What are you doing here?"

"They're painting my brownstone today and tomorrow. My furniture is under sheets in the middle of the rooms. Robin didn't mention you were going to be here." She looked down at her shoes. "I'm really sorry, Derrick."

"I guess I forgot to tell her where I was staying. I thought Tony might've let her know." He reached behind him and shifted the bag of ice. "Didn't you see my car? You'd have had to park next to it in the parking garage."

"I walked."

His eyes narrowed. "From where?"

She gestured at her pastel pink pants, the matching top, and the white jacket with the pastel slashes of color. "Hello? From the hospital."

"Are you out of your mind?" She opened her mouth to argue with him, but he cut her off. "That's easily four or five blocks. Downtown. On a Friday night."

"It's not like the streets were deserted, Derrick."

"What possessed you to walk?"

She bared her teeth. "It might have something to do with the fact that my car wouldn't start."

"Why didn't you call someone?"

She'd had enough. She felt sorry that she'd whacked him with her umbrella, but the truth was she really couldn't stand the man and never really had enjoyed his presence. "I've been an adult for a long time, Derrick, and I don't answer to anyone, most especially you. If you'll excuse me, I've had a really long day and I'm going to bed."

"Sarah ..."

She stood. "No. I'm done. Good night."

As she brushed by him, his hand came out of nowhere and grabbed her forearm. She froze, stared down at him, waiting. "I apologize," he offered with his most velvet voice.

"I'm not going to fall for the smooth charm, Derrick. Now let me go. I'm tired."

His jaw clenched as he released her. When he heard the click of her bedroom door shutting, he ripped the ice pack off his back and threw it across the room. He turned and carefully leaned backward until his back touched the chair. Then he closed his eyes and sighed.

Six years later. Six years and he was still completely in love with her.

He'd hoped it had been a crush, kind of like what he had for Robin, even a touch for Maxine. The sisters had charmed him the second he laid eyes on them, and he loved them for their beauty and their love of life. But it was more – much more – with Sarah.

And she couldn't stand him.

She would never look at him and see anything but the teenager in the ripped leather jacket with the "I dare you" scowl. He'd changed, though, in every way he possibly could. He had cleaned his clothes, cleaned his act, found Christ and followed God. Like his water baptism cleansed his soul and made him a new person, he shed his past and created a new person. It didn't matter. She still looked down her perky little befreckled nose at him.

He rubbed his face with his hands and surged to his feet. He thought about her traipsing through the heart of the city alone at this hour with only a purse and an umbrella and thought about all the terrible things that could have been waiting for her during that five block walk. He whispered a prayer of thanksgiving for God's protection over her in those early morning hours, and retired to his own bedroom, sorry that their reunion had not gone well at all.

Any secret, unacknowledged hope he had of winning her over with a smoothly executed reunion meeting was now shed forever.

SARAH got out of the shower, still angry. Seething, really. She ripped a towel off its holder and wrapped up in it, unlocking the bathroom door and walking into her old bedroom.

No one could make her as angry as Derrick DiNunzio. After almost any contact with him, she found herself grinding her teeth in frustration or anger, though she had absolutely no idea why.

At first she thought it was because of the neighborhood he came from, because of the past he carried with him. But Tony had a similar background, and she loved the man. So she knew it wasn't that.

For a while, she thought it was the way he stared at her with those eyes; a lazy, sultry stare that made her think of steamy southern summers. It was a look that peeled away her glasses and shook out her hair and blanketed her with warmth. That look made her uncomfortable until she wanted to just squirm. But he didn't always look at her like that; it was actually rare that she caught him doing it.

She thought maybe it was because he was using Tony as his step up from the street life. He had housing, clothes, food, education, all because someone else was paying for it. But then, so did she, even if the someone else were her parents and her sister, then her sister's husband. That would have been rather hypocritical, if accepting generosity born of love made her angry with him. And, she had to admit, he wasn't ungrateful. He worked hard – harder than anyone she'd ever known.

She finally settled on the fact that she just plain didn't like him. She was allowed to simply not like someone, even a brother in Christ. Right? And after six years, if the sight of him still made her teeth clench in anger, then obviously that must be what it was about.

Sarah threw a long shirt over her head, glad she still kept some clothes here, and ripped the covers of the bed down. She listened, but couldn't hear anything coming from the main room. Silly to even listen. The apartment was built so well that it would be hard to hear even the stereo with the door shut.

But he was out there, and she knew it. He was right out there with his jet black hair and his chocolate eyes and his colorful tattoos and his perfectly muscled chest and washboard stomach. And really! Why not put a shirt on for goodness sakes?

With a frustrated sigh she flipped off the light and crawled into bed. Her eyes burned and twitched. Her head spun with exhaustion but her brain simply would not shut down. Worry for her car, worry for her dad, sorrow at the relationship with her mother, and anger at Derrick all swirled in her thoughts.

She finally rolled out of bed and found herself on her knees, elbows in the mattress, praying to God in the same position she used when she was just a little girl.

AT four-thirty in the morning, Sarah gave up trying to fall asleep. She slipped out of bed and dug through the dressers, finally locating a pair of running shoes and some shorts. A sweatshirt from her college days was on the top shelf of her closet, and she was just able to spring high enough to snag the sleeve and pull it down. She slipped it over the night shirt she wore and opened her bedroom door.

The apartment was dark, quiet. She guessed that Derrick was in one of the bedrooms.

Normally, she spent Saturdays on a long bike ride, but she didn't have a bike here, so she settled for a jog.

She tried to do different forms of exercise all week. She had aerobics classes she frequented once or twice a week, she had her bike, and she loved to run. Then there were the days she ended up at Maxine's house, working out with Barry, learning more about muscle toning in an afternoon than she could have over the course of a month in a gym. She enjoyed keeping fit, enjoyed taking care of her body, and it gave her the energy and strength she needed most days for her job or her father.

The tug on her heart when she thought about her dad was a common occurrence now, and barely made her pause as she leaned against the back of the couch to stretch her legs. He didn't even know her. Three days ago, he didn't know anything. It was getting worse, and all her training meant nothing, because she couldn't help him. He was the love of her life and there was nothing she could do to help him.

Sarah was barely civil with her mother these days. Not only had she snuck around and had her father placed in a home, mom never went to see him. As far as her mother was concerned, he was already dead. It wasn't easy, talking to a man you've loved most of your life, having him either stare at you blankly or ask your name. She knew that from experience. And last month when she finally convinced her mom to go visit him, even Sarah knew it had been a really bad day. He was in a rage and finally had to be sedated. But if she would have just gone more often, she would have known that it was just a bad day, and every once in a while, there was maybe a flicker of recognition in his eyes. Sarah believed that. She had to believe that.

She finished stretching and rubbed her face with her hands. She must be more tired than she thought to be thinking about this right now. Normally she was able to push it into the farthest corners of her mind.

Huffing out a breath, she pulled a band from her pocket and did her best to secure her hair back, while she waited for the elevator. Maybe she'd call her mom today and see if she would go with her this time.

Deciding that's what she'd do, she stepped into the elevator and raised her arms to stretch her lower back.

THERE were times when Sarah had no idea she was tense until exercise loosened her up. She felt really good by the time she got back to the apartment. Her legs felt weak – rubbery. Her face was flushed. Her soaking wet hair stuck to her skin. She felt fantastic.

As she stepped down into the living room, she peeled the sweatshirt over her head and froze. Derrick was on the floor in front of the couch, doing push-ups. She yanked the sweatshirt back down.

He hadn't shaved, and he looked dark, dangerous, all the class and charm hidden for now. He wore a sweatshirt that had the sleeves cut off at the shoulder and a pair of spandex shorts, showing his long legs, well defined with muscle, covered with fine dark hair. His arms were lean and strong, the muscles bulged as he pushed himself up and down, and she noticed another tattoo on the top of one arm at the base of his shoulder, a rough homemade tattoo that looked like someone had carved his initials and just smeared them with ink. His other arm sported an elaborate eagle that went from his shoulder almost to his elbow.

She realized he wasn't moving anymore. He was still in the push-up position, supported by his arms, and staring up at her. He didn't move or speak, just stared at her with those eyes, trapping her. A bead of sweat trickling down his forehead seemed to break the spell he put on her, and she tore her eyes away and ran to her room.

TOPAZ HEAT - CHAPTER 4

SARAH dialed the phone while she dug through the pantry looking for an extra container of rice milk. No one else in the family drank it but her, and she knew she had extras from the last time she stayed here.

She located it on the back corner of the top shelf as the phone on the other end was answered. "Mary, this is Sarah. Is Dennis still there?" She dragged a step-stool into the pantry while she listened to the recorded message give the benefits of Community Hospital over any others. She was teetering on the top step when the voice was interrupted. "Dr. Benson."

"Hi, Dennis."

"Sarah. What's wrong?"

"My car is in the parking garage there. It wouldn't start last night." Just when she thought she would fall over, she was able to grab the carton and step back down.

"I see. Why?"

She left the pantry and cradled the phone to her ear with her shoulder while she pulled the plastic tab on the top of the carton. "I don't know. It was completely dead. No lights or buzzers or anything."

"Have you contacted a mechanic?"

The tab was stuck, so she pulled harder. It ripped off, but the container remained unopened. "No, I didn't call a mechanic. I'm calling my boyfriend."

She moved to the butcher block counter and grabbed a small knife out of the holder. "What is it exactly that you think I should do about it?"

Her hand made a fist around the knife and she stabbed it into the top of the carton, sending milk flying everywhere. "Ugh!"

"Excuse me?"

"Nothing. I just spilled some milk." She ripped open a drawer and whipped out a dish towel. "Listen. Never mind. Do you get off at seven?"

"Yes."

"Okay, well have a good rest this morning."

"I will. Thank you." The telephone clicked in her ear, and she stared at it before hitting the button to disconnect it.

"Problem?"

She whirled around and spotted Derrick leaning against the kitchen door. He'd showered, shaved, and changed into slacks and a button down shirt. He was back to looking like a back page ad in GQ, and she felt her balance around him return. "No. No problem."

"Your boyfriend helped, then?"

Her smile made her face feel like it was going to crack. "Absolutely. He recommended a good mechanic," she said, lying through her teeth.

Derrick raised an eyebrow. "For a dead battery?"

"A dead battery?"

"You said no lights or buzzers. Did the engine make any sound when you tried the ignition?"

Her eyebrows came together in a frown. "The first time. Very weakly."

"And this boyfriend recommended a mechanic?"

The frown remained in place. "Like you would recommend something different?"

He crossed his arms over his chest. "Yes, sweetheart, as a matter of fact I would. But I am – what's the word – competent."

"I'm not your sweetheart."

His chin gestured at the phone. "No, you're right. You're his sweetheart. I apologize."

"I'm not anyone's sweetheart."

He smiled. "Ah, that's too bad."

Sarah closed her eyes and rubbed between them. "Derrick." Her voice sounded tired to her own ears.

"Okay, sorry. I couldn't help it." He straightened and came all the way into the room. "Yes, I would recommend something different. I would suggest going to an auto parts store, purchasing a battery, and installing it."

Very carefully, because she felt like throwing it across the room, she picked up the milk and poured it over her cereal. "Thank you. As soon as I finish eating, I'll call Tony or Barry and ask one of them to help me."

"No need. I'll take care of it." He spotted the mug sitting beside the teapot and poured the rich brew into it before setting it in front of her and getting his own cup.

"I don't want to get in the way of your plans for the day."

He added a little bit of honey to his tea and took a sip. "I have no concrete plans."

Well, why not? She was desperate, after all. She had to be at work at seven that night and needed her car so that she could go to her mom's and sleep. She certainly wasn't going to stay here another night. "If you're sure."

SARAH watched Derrick wield the tools with confidence as he replaced the alternator under her hood with a new one. They had already made two trips to the auto parts store, and she fervently hoped it would be the last. He drove like the gates of hell were opening behind him. She didn't think she could stomach riding with him for another trip.

"How did you learn so much about cars, anyway?" she asked. "I'm pretty sure BU doesn't offer mechanics courses."

"I stole enough of them in my desperate youth," he answered, trying to sound like he was kidding. He'd changed into worn jeans and a black T-shirt, and when he turned his head to grin at her from under the car, her heart did a little flip-flop. She rationalized once more that she really needed to get some sleep today.

"Stole what? Cars?" She glared at him. "You're serious."

His face sobered before he went back to fiddling with whatever it was he was fiddling with under the hood. "Hunger and survival can drive people to do a lot of regrettable things. Thankfully, we have salvation by grace or I'd be in some real trouble."

"They have programs for families in need, Derrick. Crime isn't the answer."

"Sure they do," he said, straightening and wiping his hands on a towel, "if you're legal."

"You're saying you're an illegal alien?"

"No. I was born here. But my father never bothered to marry my mother, just carted her here when his tour in Italy was over and then left her when the Air Force sent him somewhere else, so she never was legal."

His logic didn't make sense to her. "Still, once you were old enough to legally drive, you were old enough to get a job, right?"

His eyes were blank when they looked at her. "Once you're in, sweetheart, you're in. And there isn't a thing you can do about it until someone bigger and stronger than them gets you out. Tony is way bigger and way stronger."

"Well, Derrick. All this time I thought you were once just a petty thief. I didn't realize you had graduated to grand theft auto. Still, there are all sorts of things ..."

She broke off when he stepped forward and laid his index finger over her lips, effectively silencing her. He moved fast, faster than she could imagine, and his touch for such violent speed was incongruously gentle. His movement literally shocked her into silence.

He stood close enough to her that the toes of their shoes touched. Her vision became his chocolate brown eyes. Through clenched teeth, he spoke, "Listen to me, you spoiled little brat. There's a whole world out there you don't remember or understand. As far as I'm concerned, you're from the little blue house with the white picket fence and you don't know anything about anything beyond that or Tony's penthouse and private jet. If you ever want to know, without spouting one of your little self-important ignorant lectures, come talk to me like a person. Until then, kindly consider the subject closed."

She glared at him, laying her hand on his wrist until he removed his finger from her lips. With a tone that rang self-righteously even in her own ears, she pronounced, "I know a lot more than you could ever understand."

"Right," he sneered sarcastically, his tone telling her just how judged he felt.

"Have you ever held a crack baby, Derrick? Or a heroin baby? Or seen a baby born dead because he had a heart attack and his mother was too stoned out and drunk to know she was even in labor? Because I have.

"I know all about that world out there, and I know and have heard every excuse for that kind of life that's ever been told. If you want to justify your actions, fine, but don't try it on me. You want to tell me you like the danger or the thrill, go ahead, but don't give me puissant excuses about hunger and fear and a bad childhood. Pure rationalization. I don't buy it."

His upper lip twitched. "I bet it's easy to sit back with a full stomach, clothes on your back, and heat in February and judge."

She pointed at the tattoo creeping out from under his shirt sleeve. "I'll admit I'm spoiled. But I don't try to be something I'm not, either."

His eyes narrowed and she reflexively took a step back. "What's that supposed to mean?"

"Why do you still have those tatoos, Derrick? Proud of your past?"

She knew she had gone too far when she saw the complete hurt in his eyes. She opened her mouth to apologize but he turned his back on her while muttering, "Some of us can't forget our past, Sarah. No matter how much I want to, I can't forget. I'm not like you. I wish I could just erase it all."

"Is there a problem here, Sarah?"

Both of them whipped their heads around at the same time.

"Dennis," Sarah said as her face turned bright red. "What are you doing here?"

"I'm on call all day." He looked Derrick up and down, but didn't offer his hand. "I appreciate you coming out on a Saturday."

The man looked like he'd stepped off the set of a cheesy hospital soap opera. His hair was artificially blonde, his skin was artificially tanned to a golden brown, and his teeth were artificially pearly white. He stood about eye level with Derrick and wore a spotless white jacket over his suit shirt and pants. Derrick recognized him, but wasn't surprised that the recollection wasn't returned. Obviously, he thought Derrick was some mechanic on call. "Not a problem, doc," he answered with a service station attendant smile.

Dennis looked at the open hood of the car and back at Sarah. "Don't let him overcharge you." He looked at his watch. "Well, if it's all under control, I'll go inside and see what the big emergency was."

Sarah smiled brightly. "Thanks."

"Of course. Anything to help." He turned on his polished wing-tips and walked toward the doors of the hospital. The second he was out of earshot, Derrick couldn't help himself.

"That's Dennis?"

She jutted her chin out. "So?"

"So? So did you know he's married?"

Her eyes flared and her face fused with color again. "Yes, but he's separated from his wife. They're trying to work through the divorce right now."

"Then he's playing you for a fool, sweetheart, because he's not separated from anyone." Derrick snatched his wrench off the top of the battery, scanned the space under the hood to ensure he hadn't missed anything, and slammed the hood shut.

She put her hands on her hips. "How would you presume to know that? You just met the man and you haven't even been here for six years."

"That isn't the first time I've met him." He slid behind the wheel and turned the ignition switch, smiling when her car started without even a cough. As he got out of the driver's seat, he examined the grease beneath his fingernails. It was going to be a chore to get them clean. Maybe he'd go somewhere for a manicure. "I've been in New York, managing a hotel. Just last weekend, Mr. Golden Boy there and a little slinky redhead with a rock the size of Venus on her finger enjoyed a weekend getaway designed to help spice up their marriage. We call it our Second Honeymoon package."

She gasped and a vein started hammering in her forehead. "You're obviously mistaken. Dennis was at a seminar in New Jersey last weekend."

"Nope. I never forget a face or a name. He clearly doesn't share the same power of recall, considering the fact that it's been a mere seven days since I last saw him, but, I can't blame him. He was distracted by your helpless heroine routine after all. The batting eyelashes were a nice touch, by the way."

He acknowledged that he should have felt a little sorry for her, but really, he didn't. He was enjoying her look of discomfort far too much to feel any real pity.

Her face wasn't flushed any longer. It was pale, the freckles across her nose and cheeks standing out as if someone had darkened them with a marker. "You must be mistaken," she repeated with a whisper.

"Oh, I'm not mistaken. He registered under his own name. Doctor Dennis ..." He cocked his head, studying her reaction as he pronounced the man's last name. "... Benson. Wife, Jennifer. Lovely woman, really. Collects spoons. Honestly, if you're going to date married men, maybe you should tell them they shouldn't stay in your brother-in-law's hotels when they sneak away with their wives for a special weekend."

"You know something Derrick DiNunzio?" She made sure he was looking in her eyes. "I *hate* you," she whispered as she pushed by him and got in her car.

"Oh, you're welcome. Glad I could help!" He shouted, his voice on the edge of laughter. He stood there as he watched her car scream out of the parking garage, and felt a sudden and terrible conviction of guilt. He flung the rag down and raked his hands through his hair.

TOPAZ HEAT - CHAPTER 5

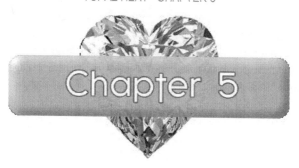

SARAH'S Sunday School class consisted of eighteen college-aged girls who ranged in age from seventeen to twenty-three. Sarah had started teaching the class two years ago and grew to love these girls more and more every year.

Currently, they had completed a little more than half of a book about modern secular culture versus Biblical womanhood, concentrating on one chapter each week. The discussions the book sparked turned livelier each Sunday – especially from a group of women attending colleges, thinking of careers, and finding themselves with each foot in almost two entirely different worlds. Needless to say, the lessons meandered from loquacious to lively.

She glanced at the clock on the wall and cringed. They had already gone five minutes over time. "I am loving this discussion this morning, but if we want to make it in time for the service, we need to wrap up, now."

"We really need more than forty-five minutes once a week with this," Jane Hampton, a pre-law student, said.

Her best friend, Miriam Wright, laughed. "I think we could all talk for forty-five hours on each chapter."

An amused murmur of agreement went around the room.

Sarah smiled. "I know what you mean. Next week, chapter four. And, did we want to try to do something together next weekend?"

They spent five more minutes arranging plans to meet for dinner on Friday night. Sarah made the notation in her phone then finished packing up her materials. She waved good-bye to a couple girls leaving and turned to erase the prayer requests off the white board.

"Sarah?"

She looked over her shoulder. "Yes, Lisa?"

The young brunette's eyes filled with tears. "Do you have a minute?"

Sarah dropped everything and turned fully around, putting an arm around Lisa's thin shoulders. "Of course." She led them to a table and pulled a chair out, guiding the marketing student into a chair. "What's wrong?"

Lisa toyed with the ring on her right finger, spinning the diamond around and around while she struggled to speak. "I'm so confused."

Sarah leaned forward and put a hand on Lisa's knee. "About what?"

Lisa swallowed. "When I was home this summer, my parents had a big Fourth of July party, and there in front of everyone, my boyfriend proposed to me."

Sarah smiled. "I noticed the ring, but you wear it on your right hand and you hadn't said anything."

A tear spilled out of Lisa's eye and ran down her cheek. "My parents love him. He graduates from college this year and will start law school. He'll go work in his father's firm when he's out of school."

"So what's confusing you?"

Lisa took a deep shuddering breath. "He's not a Christian." She pushed away from the table and stood. With long, nervous strides, she crossed the room and looked out the window, down to the parking lot a floor below. "My parents aren't, either, for that matter. I was saved last year when Miriam brought me to church with her. Everything inside of me was screaming to tell him, 'No', but our families were all there and I felt pressured into saying, 'Yes.'"

Sarah followed her, looking down and seeing the cars coming into the parking lot in a steady stream. "Have you talked to him about God?"

"Some." She shrugged. "Not a lot. He becomes kind of patronizing about it. Like this is a phase I'll get over when I finish school."

Sarah nodded. "I see. Have you prayed about it?"

Lisa wrapped her arms around herself. "I have. If we'd been alone, I would have told him that I couldn't marry him unless he came to know Christ. I know that the right thing to do is to end the engagement. I wear the ring only because I'm terrified something will happen to it before I can return it. I want to do it in person instead of over the phone or mail. I'm just counting down the days until Thanksgiving break until I can get this burden off my shoulders."

Sarah felt her eyebrows wrinkle. "So why are you confused?"

"There's this guy," Lisa started, then stopped. Sarah felt her heart tug, felt a little panicky about the way the conversation was going. What did she know about men? Her boyfriend was apparently still married.

"What guy?" Sarah said.

"He's in the choir with me. He's so nice, and he loves God so much. He's a seminary student."

Sarah ran through the faces in the choir and decided she knew the man to whom Lisa was referring. "And?"

"And he wants to take me out. Only, my parents would totally not approve. He's not..."

The flush on Lisa's cheek and the way she left the sentence hanging gave Sarah all the clues she needed. "He's not a future attorney whose daddy is paying his way through law school?"

"Exactly. He's a seminary student on scholarship who bags groceries six days a week so that he can eat. And before that, he had a really hard time in high school and ended up quitting school. He was in a grunge rock band for a few years before he came to know Christ. Now he's turned his life around and wants to preach."

Sarah thought that maybe Lisa needed to do some reflection. "What are you afraid of?"

Lisa shrugged. "I'm not sure."

"Well, it's obviously something. So, let's talk about it. Why have you not gone on a date with this man yet?"

Lisa walked back to the table and sat down again, immediately beginning to toy with the ring again. "Because there's a man back in Wisconsin who thinks that we're engaged to be married."

Sarah nodded. "So, the right thing to do would be to make sure he doesn't think that anymore, right?"

Lisa slowly nodded her head. "Right."

"And as for this new man, if he's right for you, he'll wait. God will speak to him. In the meantime, consider this." She sat down and took Lisa's hands in hers. The young girl met her eyes. "God doesn't care about where we came from." She thought about the descriptions of her childhood her sisters had given her – drugs and men and horrible living conditions. "God only cares who we are now. That's what you need to look at."

Lisa licked her lips as the tears welled out of her eyes. "I know. I know you're right." She sniffed and scrubbed her cheeks. "I'll try to get home next weekend and talk to him, give him his ring back." She leaned forward and hugged Sarah. "Thank you for listening. I haven't talked about it with anyone."

Sarah hugged her back. "I'm glad you talked to me. Do it any time. You have my number."

DERRICK sat in the back of the huge sanctuary and watched the activity spread out below him. Early service had just ended. The next service wouldn't start for about thirty minutes. In the meantime, somewhere in this old stone and mortar building, and spread out throughout the vast downtown campus, thousands of people attended Sunday morning classes, learning about everything from Biblical marriage to the plans, specifications, and magnitude of Noah's ark.

In the foyer of this building, a staff member of the church worked the information center, giving guests and members alike the summaries of the classes offered. Volunteers stood by, ready to lead and guide people to the appropriate building and classroom. Derrick, however, just wanted to sit back and watch, remember.

He'd come into this church for the first time on a freezing January Sunday morning. Walking in with Tony and Robin had somehow validated him, and everyone stopped to talk to Tony, which made Tony introduce him to about forty different people. For the first time in his entire life, he'd felt like he was a respected member of society, someone people enjoyed meeting rather than someone people mistrusted on sight. Men held their hands out to him to shake. Women hugged him. It made him feel good, strong, worthy.

He'd like to say that he immediately felt the call of Christ in his life. But, he didn't. Instead, he asked Tony a dozen questions after the service, and then he read the books Tony gave him to read and asked a hundred more questions. As winter raged around them and Tony and Robin planned their spring wedding, Derrick got to know God. Early summer, when the happy newlyweds returned from their honeymoon, Derrick was officially baptized.

He looked at the baptismal behind the massive choir loft. He remembered rising out of the water and looking at the throngs of people who cheered and applauded the symbolic washing away of his old life and his rebirth into the family of Christ.

As he smiled and remembered, he felt someone take the seat next to him. He turned his head and saw seven-year-old Tony, Jr., legs swinging because he was still a little too short to touch the ground while in the stadium style seat. "Hey, bro," Derrick said, holding his hand out, palm up.

TJ slapped the palm. "Hi Uncle D."

"What's happening?" He looked down into the dark brown eyes of his best friend's son.

"Papa said to sit next to you and not get into anything. He had to go talk to Pastor Peter."

"Ah." Derrick looked up and saw Tony halfway down the aisle speaking to the head of youth ministries, Peter O'Farrell. He raised a hand in greeting, and Derrick smiled and returned the gesture. "Where's your sister?"

"She went to Aunt Maxi's house last night. They'll be here next service." The intelligent little eyes searched his face. "Papa says you're here for good now."

"I am. I've moved into your old apartment."

"Can I come visit you there?"

"Absolutely. Say the word, and ask your mom, and I'll even take you rock climbing this summer."

TJ's serious little face burst into a huge smile. "That would be so awesome. She'll just have to say yes."

"Say yes about what?" Tony sat in a seat in front of Derrick and turned his body toward them.

"Rock climbing with Uncle D."

Tony leaned over and patted his son's knee. "I'm sure she'll say yes. You couldn't be in safer hands." He directed his attention to Derrick. "I was surprised to see you. I figured you'd still be in New York."

"I came back on the ten o'clock flight Friday night."

Tony raised an eyebrow. "Oh?"

Derrick shrugged, because he couldn't explain it himself. "It worked out. Sarah's car needed a new alternator, so at least I was around."

Tony stared at him for several seconds before he slowly pursed his lips. "So, you were there in the apartment on Friday night with Sarah and fixed her car Saturday morning?"

Clearing his throat, Derrick nodded. "Yeah. I guess you and Robin didn't communicate my return to her."

"Robin didn't know you were at the apartment when Sarah asked if she could stay there. When she told me about it, I had assumed you weren't coming back from New York until today based on our last conversation." Tony studied his face. "Is everything okay?"

Uncomfortable, Derrick shifted in his seat. "Sure. Same thing as always. I'm vermin. She hates me. You know the drill."

Tony held a hand out. "*Amico –*"

"It's fine." Derrick surged to his feet. "I'm fine. Listen, I need to talk to Peter. Let me catch him before he gets too involved." He turned to his nephew. "Dude, good to see you." They slapped palms as Derrick stepped passed him.

Peter saw him coming and finished a conversation in time to smile a big Irish grin and hold out his arms. Derrick hugged the older man and slapped him hard on the back. "My brother," Peter said. "I'm so happy to see you."

Peter had fostered a young Tony, and took on a father-figure style role with Derrick as well. Despite Tony taking Derrick in off the streets, the two of them had more of a brotherly relationship.

The older man's hair had grayed, turning the deep black into more salt than pepper. Laugh lines and wrinkles lined his eyes. But he looked fit, happy, an eternal smile on his face. "I'm happy to see you, too."

"Tony says you're home for good."

"I am. I start work tomorrow morning."

"Welcome home." He patted his shoulder. "Interested in serving?"

As head of youth ministries, Peter's job oversaw everything from infant rooms to high school classes. Derrick had always worked with high school boys, both here and in New York. He and Peter had grown very close during the years he mentored young men, and even recently, he would contact Peter when he needed guidance with a more challenging boy. "Absolutely."

"Great. I have a new group of boys who need a mentor. I've still not got a grip on their stories. I was just telling Caroline last week that I wished you were here because you'd be perfect for them." He smiled a huge smile. "They've been coming together for the last few youth activities." Peter's phone beeped and he unhooked it from his holster and read a message on it. "Next time I should see them is Wednesday night."

Derrick could see Peter's distracted look. "You go and do. I'll be there Wednesday."

"That is wonderful, my friend." He held out his hand and they clasped hands then beat each other on the back again. "Good luck in your new job tomorrow."

"Thanks." After Peter walked away, Derrick looked at his watch. He didn't really need to sit through another service. Deciding that he'd take the afternoon to just relax and mentally prep for the week, he turned and nearly barreled into Tony.

"Robin is expecting you for lunch."

With a self mocking laugh, Derrick nodded. "Of course. I'll be there. At the new place?"

"Do you know where it is?"

"Yeah. You showed me the site before you broke ground."

"Okay. We'll serve around one."

That gave him about three hours to do other things. "Great. I'll see you then."

He started to walk by, but Tony put a hand on his shoulder. "I'm sorry the reunion wasn't what you'd hoped, but if God has a plan, then it will be."

The thought comforted him. "Thanks, brother. I'll see you in a few."

"MOM, I really don't understand. At least help me understand." Sarah slumped into her father's recliner and toyed with the swath of lace covering the arm. She had come to her mom's house after church and had just tried to convince her to go visit her father with her.

Darlene Thomas fiddled with the locket that hung on her neck. She was nearing seventy, and her blonde hair had long since turned white. She was barely Sarah's height with a petite frame that made her seem frailer than she actually was.

"He doesn't know the difference."

"He might."

"Sarah, honey, I don't even know if I can explain it. When I look at him, a man I've been married to for forty-eight years, and see him stare at me blankly or rage and demand to know who I am, it breaks my heart. I can't handle it. I don't want my memories of him to be … that. I want to remember the man I knew before he was sick."

Sarah pressed the heels of her hands against her eyes. "It's so unfair."

"I know, honey, no one knows it better than I do."

"I wish you had kept him home. I could have taken a leave of absence from the hospital. I could have …"

"You could have, Sarah, but I couldn't."

Sarah surged to her feet and paced. "You didn't even discuss it with me!"

"Really, it wasn't your decision."

Sarah gasped and whirled around. "How could you say that?"

The telephone at Darlene's elbow interrupted her attempted reply. She looked imploringly at her daughter as she picked up the receiver. "Hello?"

Sarah threw herself back into the chair and watched her mother's face. She felt her stomach knot when her mom's lips tightened and the blood drained from her face.

"I see," she said, "thank you." As she hung up the phone, her lower lip trembled.

"No," Sarah rasped out.

"I'm sorry, honey." Darlene put a shaking hand to her lips and took a deep breath. She opened the drawer on the telephone table and pulled out a small book. "I need to call the pastor."

AS the cloud covering the sun shifted, Derrick pulled sunglasses out of his pocket and slipped them over his eyes.

"I love this house," he said, taking a sip of his iced tea while he looked beyond the deck to the beach and water.

"Tony had it built when I was pregnant with Madeline," Robin said as the maid set a tray of sandwiches on the table. "I was perfectly happy with the apartment, but he insisted. I still get lost inside."

Derrick cut his eyes to the massive stone and glass structure behind him. Dozens of windows spread throughout the three stories winked back at him, reflecting the sun. "Well, the plus side is that you have room for a couple hundred more kids."

She laughed. "At least." She handed him a plate and gestured at the beach below. "Look at him," she said as Tony lifted Madeline into a rowboat and knelt next to it, gesturing with his hands. On the sand next to them, TJ rolled on the ground with a black puppy. "He's such a good dad."

"He's teaching her to row?"

"Yes."

He paused lifting a sandwich to his lips. "I can't believe she's five." He gestured. "She's a little too small for the oars, isn't she?"

"It doesn't matter. She's down there on the beach with daddy. If he never takes her to the river, it won't matter to her."

Derrick watched the two as Tony put his hands over his daughter's and showed her how to control the large oars with her little arms. He lidded his eyes and saw a father with graying hair and a daughter with jet black hair and saw the love shimmering around the pair. Derrick felt a tug of longing.

He looked back at Robin and found her studying him. "Do you think you'll ever marry?"

"Absolutely." Pulling his eyes away from the perfect scene, he grinned and saluted her with his glass. "I just have to convince her."

She raised an eyebrow. "Convince her to marry you?"

"No. Convince her she doesn't really want my liver on a plate."

Robin threw her head back and laughed. "Oh, how fun. Don't worry. Tony convinced me, and you have all his charm, if not more."

He smiled. "I can't believe you ever hated him."

"Oh, I did. Purely and absolutely."

"So, what changed your mind?"

"He loved me. He loved me enough to introduce me to God." She propped her chin in her hands. "So who is this mysterious she? Someone in New York?"

"Long story. I'd love to tell you someday."

Robin grinned, "I'll find out, you know."

Derrick nodded. "Robin, I promise you'll be the first to know."

"Okay, I'll leave it then ... for now."

He heard a sound behind them and turned his head to see the maid step onto the deck. "Excuse me, Mrs. Viscolli, but there is a telephone call for you."

"Thank you, Maria." She gracefully rose to her feet. "I'll be right back."

Derrick raised his sandwich to his lips again. "No hurry." He watched Tony kiss the top of Madeline's head before he lifted her out of the boat. The little girl wasted no time jumping into the wrestling match between her brother and the puppy. Tony stood next to them with his hands on his hips, smiling.

Robin came back outside with Maria, who immediately started down the stairs toward the beach. Robin walked to the edge of the deck without even looking at Derrick. She gripped the railing with her hand while the wind blew her hair around her head and stared down at Tony. Derrick stood, sensing something was terribly wrong, about the same time Tony paused and looked up. The smile faded from his lips. He said something to the children and ran toward the house. Halfway, he met Maria, pausing long enough to hear her say something before he kept coming.

In two strides, Derrick stood beside Robin. He could see her knuckles turning white from the force of gripping the railing. The wind was drying the tears on her face as they fell, and she kept her eyes fixated on her husband.

"Robin, what's wrong?"

"Poor Sarah," she whispered.

"What?" Panicked, Derrick grabbed her arm and whirled her around. "What happened? What's wrong with Sarah?"

"Her dad died this morning." She covered her mouth with her hands. "Poor Sarah."

He wrapped his arms around her and let her cry until Tony reached them. She seemed to sense that he was near, because before he spoke or touched her, she turned to him and wrapped her arms around his waist. "He was such a good man," she said through her tears.

"I know, *cara*."

"Where's Maxine?" Derrick asked.

"En route to the Cape. They left immediately after church. I bet they're not even there yet," Tony said. He bent and lifted Robin into his arms, then carried her to a chair and sat down. "We'll need to call her."

Robin kept her head on Tony's shoulder, but seemed to have the tears under control. "I gave Darlene the number," she said. "Sarah's going to be devastated."

"Maria will bring the kids in, and we'll go over there."

Derrick swallowed the lump in his throat as he stood. "I'll leave you to it. Let me know if anyone needs anything."

Robin lifted her head. "You aren't going to go?"

He slipped his hand into the pocket of his pants and made a fist. "It's a family thing."

Tony scowled. "You *are* family."

His smile was tight enough to crack his lips. "To you and Maxi, maybe, but not to Sarah. She doesn't need me there to antagonize her."

"Derrick …"

"Just …" He closed his eyes and rubbed them. "Just tell Sarah I'm sorry. That I'll be praying. And call me if she needs anything."

He left before Robin could say anything that would make him stay. Since all he wanted to do was go to Sarah, to have her turn to him the way Robin turned to Tony, he knew it wouldn't take much to convince him to go.

TOPAZ HEAT - CHAPTER 6

DERRICK sat at the head of the long conference table. Heads of the departments in the hotel sat in the seats around the table, from the head concierge to the head chef to the kitchen manager to the head of housekeeping, and everyone in between.

He'd introduced himself to those who did not know him personally. Despite this being day three of this first week, he hadn't yet made it to every department, so there were still a few people he hadn't met. He'd taken reports from each person. He'd asked for specific areas of concern within the hotel and the emergency needs that had cropped up during the last few weeks during the decline of the previous manager's job focus.

And all the while, he thought about Sarah. Sarah whose heart had broken when her father died. His own heart ached for her, and he found it impossible to ignore her in this time of need. Regardless of anything, he needed to go see her.

As if on a perfect, divine cue, his secretary, Andrea, opened the door at the end of the room and stuck her head in. Derrick caught her eye and she nodded, so he gestured forward with his hand. "Lunch has arrived, friends," he said, standing as Andrea walked completely into the room and held the door wide for the waiters pushing the carts. "Let's go ahead and take a break and eat, rejuvenate ourselves for the rest of the afternoon." He looked through the sea of faces and picked the facility manager. "Don, can you please bless this meal?"

As soon as Don initiated a chorus of "amens" and the staff went to stand in the buffet line, Derrick looked at his watch and motioned Andrea aside. "I need to head out to Charles Thomas' funeral. I just want to quickly pay my respects then I'll be right back."

She nodded. "I was surprised you called this meeting during the time of the funeral. I know the rest of your family is there."

"Well, the timing of Bill Matheson's departure was out of my hands." He pulled his suit jacket off the back of his chair and slipped his arms into it. "I doubt I'll be thirty minutes."

SARAH stood next to her mother and shook hands, kissed cheeks, allowed people to hug her, and generally accepted the sympathies of what felt like half of Boston. Aunts, uncles, cousins, friends, church family – they descended on the memorial service in droves. All she wanted to do was pull covers up over her head and hide away from the entire world, and here she was exchanging platitudes with some third cousin with a bad hair dye job.

Why? Why did God take her daddy away when there were evil dictators in third world countries who could be taken in his place?

With a sigh, she accepted a hug from a 10-year-old in her church's children's choir. That kind of thinking was childish. She knew it. She also knew her father loved the Lord, lived for Him, served Him, and now was accepting his reward. To question the why of that seemed to lack a faith she always knew she possessed. Maybe she would have more acceptance of everything if he'd been mentally acute at his death and could assure her of his readiness.

That wasn't fair, either. The time she got to spend nursing him had been precious. She knew that so many children lost their parents suddenly, and she couldn't imagine what that must be like.

"I love you girl," a familiar voice said, breaking through her reflections. She looked up at the beautiful face of her roommate.

"Melissa." She gave her a real hug, tightly thanking her for being a friend. "Thank you."

"Let me know if you need anything." Melissa moved down the line to Sarah's mother. "Mrs. Thomas," she said, "I'm so sorry."

Darlene coolly stuck out her hand. "Thank you."

Sarah looked down the never ending line and steeled herself to be gathered into a hug by one of her father's brothers. He sobbed on her shoulder and she found herself comforting him.

Darlene had to peel him off Sarah, and at great sacrifice to herself, too. Sarah saw her mother trying to keep from collapsing under the sobbing weight of her brother-in-law as Sarah turned to the next person in line. She felt her smile freeze as she came face-to-face with Derrick.

"Sarah," he said, taking her hand in both of hers. "I'm so sorry. I know what you're going through."

She felt tears burn the back of her throat. "Thank you," she managed to whisper.

He squeezed her hand and stepped forward. "If I can ... if there's anything I can do…"

Sarah looked down at their joined hands and put her free hand on top of his. "You are a good friend to my family." Tears poured down her cheeks and she sniffed. "I really appreciate you."

Derrick opened his mouth and then closed it as if he didn't know what to say. This was a far cry from, "I *hate* you."

Sarah squeezed his hands and released them then turned to a nurse who worked with her on the weekends. Out of the corner of her eye, she saw Derrick pause before moving to her mother. What he said to her, she didn't know. She just saw her mom nod her head and thank him. She got distracted by the next person in line and the next, but never saw him again.

DERRICK watched the three boys as they watched the high school youth basketball team practice. He guessed their ages to be right around thirteen. They wore the typical baggy jeans that came down too low and showed off too much. They each had on baggy shirts that fell well below the low waistband of the jeans, tucked in to the jeans so that it made their torsos look extra long. Derrick noted the careful lack of any gang colors.

Two of the boys were African American, and one was something Mediterranean. In this neighborhood, it was likely Italian.

He discarded his jacket and picked up a basketball. He contemplated the best way to approach the boys as he crossed in front of the bleachers, spinning the ball on his finger, bouncing it up and down his arm, tossing it in the air. He reached them about the time they turned in unison to watch him.

"Hey," he said, pointing at the court. "You going to join?"

One of the African American boys sneered and tried to look tough. "What's it to you?"

Derrick immediately felt like maybe the direct approach was the best approach. "Because, son, you'll discover at this church that there are actually adults who care about you, your well being, and your happiness, and we want nothing from you in return."

The boy held his gaze for about a second before looking at the floor. Derrick read all he needed to read in his gaze. "I'm Derrick. I just moved back here from New York this week."

The lighter skinned boy looked him up and down, from his clean haircut to the toes of his shined shoes. "Back here? Yo, you ain't from here, bro."

Derrick snorted and spun the ball on his finger. "You think? I grew up in that apartment over Jake's Bar."

The kid who hadn't spoken yet stared at him open mouthed. "You?"

"Yeah," Derrick drawled. "Until my eighteenth birthday."

One of the other kids spoke up. "The man closed Jake's down. Said it wasn't fit anymore. They're going to demolish the building."

That surprised Derrick. He felt a little sad. "I lived there my whole life."

"My brother Jonsie's getting a job with the crew. He's going to start in two weeks."

"That's fantastic." He held his hand out to the kid. "My name's Derrick. Derrick DiNunzio."

For a long time, the kid stared at Derrick's hand. Then cautiously he took it. His hand was limp, returning no grip. Derrick filed that away to teach him one day how a man shakes a hand so that the next time he could do it in confidence. "My name's Benny. This here is Alfonzo, and that's Tyrone."

"It's nice to meet you, Benny." Derrick shook hands with each one of them, saying each name, looking each boy in the eye, giving the respect that they had likely never received before. "Do you want to play ball?" He asked.

"They ain't gonna let us," Tyrone said. "We've been here for three weeks now and we ain't played yet."

"Have you asked?" Derrick said.

Instead of replying, the boys all shrugged. Derrick turned and whistled to the youth playing the game. "Got room for four more?"

"Four?" The tall boy who had been playing center asked. Derrick had known him since he was half his height, when he first moved in with Peter and Caroline O'Farrell.

Derrick slipped his tie over his head and unbuttoned his top collar. "You heard me."

"Sure. We got room for four." He laughed as he tossed the ball to Derrick. Hard. "You're going to feel it though, old man."

"Keep talking," Derrick said. He tossed the ball back and unbuttoned his left sleeve. As he walked into the center of the court, he looked behind him. "Come on. Let's show these guys how to play ball."

The sweat and the exertion would be good for him. The funeral had unnerved him more than he would ever admit. Funerals always sent him back to his mother's funeral. As his body played ball, his mind wandered far away and he remembered the day she died very vividly.

TWENTY-two-year-old Derrick DiNunzio propped his elbows on his knees and rested his head in his hands. On the hospital bed in front of him the frail body of his mother remained as it had for the last two days. Inside he felt hollow, knowing he should feel something, hating himself for feeling nothing.

He hadn't seen his mother in three years. Since the day Antonio Viscolli, a legend in his old neighborhood, offered him a home and a job four years ago, he'd only returned home once.

He remembered her as a cold, hateful woman. He returned home and she had cursed him for selling out, for letting someone else pay for his education in exchange for who knew what. He hadn't bothered to defend himself. It would have done no good to say anything to her, to try to make her understand something even he didn't yet fully grasp.

He looked up as his mother's head moved on the pillow. Her eyelids fluttered and she frowned before she opened them. He leaned forward and touched her hand. "Mamma?"

Her head slowly turned toward him. The disease that attacked her heart had stolen years from her, adding lines to her face and gray to her hair. As far as the doctors could determine, she had never received treatment for it. Derrick knew without anyone telling him that she wouldn't be leaving the hospital alive.

"Derrick," she whispered. "*Mio figlio.*"

"English, mamma, I can't understand you."

She patted his hand. "*Mio figlio.*"

He had never learned Italian. She had insisted that they only speak English so that she could learn it too. "I don't understand."

"She said, 'my son.'" Derrick whipped his head around and saw Tony in the doorway. "Is this a bad time?"

Derrick's eyes went back to her pale face. "She's dying."

She gripped his wrist and tried to sit up. "*Non l'ho mai detto…*"

Desperate, he looked to Tony, who walked into the hospital room and stood on the other side of the bed. "'I never told you.'"

Derrick stood and gently pushed her shoulders back down. "Don't try to talk now. Just rest."

"*Non ero una madre buona.*" Her eyes fluttered closed but she opened them again.

Without waiting for Derrick's plea, Tony translated, speaking softly. Derrick never even took his eyes off his mother's face. "'I've not been a good mother.'"

"Don't say that. Just rest." He wasn't hollow any more. Something inside of him opened up and flooded his heart, making his throat ache and his eyes water. "Just rest, mamma."

"*Non ero una madre buona, ma l'ho amato sempre.*" Her eyes fixed unblinking on his. "*Lei capisce?*"

"No, no, I don't understand."

Tony cleared his throat to ease some of the tightness. "'I've not been a good mother, but I've always loved you.'"

His hand trembled as he brushed her hair off her forehead. "I love you, too. I'm sorry, mamma."

"*Capire che sono orgoglioso di lei.*" Her eyes closed.

"'Understand that I'm so proud of you.'"

"Mamma – "

"*Sono molto orgoglioso di lei.*" She barely spoke above a whisper. "*Devo andare adesso.*"

"'I am very proud of you.'" Tony's voice sounded harsh. "'I must go now.'"

"No." He grabbed her hand and held it to his wet cheek, letting the tears fall unashamedly down his face. "No, mamma, not yet. Not yet. I haven't told you about Jesus, yet, mamma."

She patted his hand back, her touch like that of a little child. Struggling to speak in English, she whispered, "I know Him, Derrick. You tell. I read every letter you send me. Over and over again, I read. *Mio figlio.*"

He didn't see Tony leave and didn't look up as the monitor attached to his mother's heart sounded the alarm.

DERRICK leaned against the wall of the gymnasium, one foot propped against the wall behind him. He'd shed his shirt and wore only a sweat-soaked white T-shirt. He'd battled hard for his loss against boys half his age, and let them mock him for being old while they each gathered belongings and went home.

He'd given Tyrone, Alfonso, and Benny his phone number, and business cards. He'd told them to call him if they ever needed him, or to come to the hotel if they couldn't call.

"You going to be here Sunday morning?" he asked as they started out of the gym.

They shrugged, almost in unison. But Benny spoke. "Maybe."

Derrick smiled. "Well, maybe I'll bring some doughnuts for breakfast."

He caught their pleased smiles as they left. The slamming of the gym door echoed through the empty gym. Derrick looked at his watch. Nine-thirty. No wonder he felt so fatigued.

He was glad he went to the funeral this morning. He fought the desire to go visit Sarah now, to offer her comfort, maybe a shoulder to cry on.

Instead, he slipped on his shirt and jacket, found his tie and shoved it into his pocket, and rolled his head on his neck. She didn't want to see him.

He would leave that to the rest of the family.

Instead, he headed home, walking the downtown streets of his home town. The night air had a chill, reminding him that the beautiful, warm weather would soon be leaving them for the harshness of a Boston winter.

Chapter 7

SARAH rolled over and looked at the clock. With a groan, she pushed herself out of bed and sat on the side for a minute, holding her head in her hands. For two weeks now, she'd had a dull, throbbing headache – stress induced, she knew – but annoying just the same.

Energy was a thing of the past. All of it seemed to have been sucked right out of her until she nearly stumbled around. She didn't have a choice. She had to go to work today. Two weeks off was long enough. Without a problem, she could spend the rest of her life in bed, grieving the man she loved so much, but she knew the only way to get her body moving again and her mind back on track was to plunge back into the real world.

She scooped her glasses off the night stand and trudged from the room, stopping to glance into Melissa's bedroom. The bed was empty, so her roommate must have had a seven o'clock shift. Sarah was scheduled for three, and it was already nearly two. It was a fight to keep from calling in sick. But she wouldn't do it. She would face everyone, accept the sympathies, try to keep from losing control, and help a few babies come into the world.

She turned on the water as hot as she could stand it and let the claw foot bathtub begin to fill. While it ran she popped a cup of water into the microwave to make a cup of tea.

Her apartment building had once been a house, and the last owners converted it into three apartments – two downstairs and one upstairs. Toys from her neighbor's two kids littered the fenced backyard. She stood at the kitchen window while she waited for the water to heat and watched a four-year-old boy play in the sandbox. It was beautiful outside, sunny and warm if she went by the way he was dressed, and she took a deep breath. She was starting to feel better, but she didn't want to feel better yet. She wanted to rail and cry and moan. She wanted to tear her clothes and put on sackcloth and ashes.

But life didn't work that way. Even good, godly men got sick with terrible diseases and died before their seventy-fifth birthdays.

"EXCUSE me Mr. DiNunzio, but Maxine Anderson is here to see you."

"Thank you. Please send her in." Derrick set his pen down and stood as the door opened and in breezed Maxine. Every time he saw her, he couldn't get over the fact that not only was she still alive, but that she could walk. After the horrible accident seven years before, her entire existence was a miracle, a gift from God.

The first thing he noticed was that she'd changed her hair. Instead of falling to her hips, it brushed her shoulders and framed her lean face, highlighting the strong cheekbones inherited from her Native American father. She wore an emerald colored pantsuit the very shade of her eyes, dressed to the tee as always. Carrying twins had barely disrupted her thin figure.

"Maxi," he greeted with a grin, coming around his desk.

"Sorry it's taken me so long to come see you," she said, kissing his cheek as he hugged her. "This whole thing with Sarah's dad was all-consuming for a while."

He took her hand and led her to the couch that sat against the far wall. "I'm sure. How's she doing?"

"As bad as I thought she'd do." She sat sideways to face him. "And where have you been through all the memorials and funeral?"

"The last thing Sarah said to me the morning her father died was that she hated me. I briefly stopped in at the memorial service. I really had no place there."

"Huh. You might be the only man who could tell me Sarah said that I'd believe. She's so mild-mannered." Maxine half grinned. "You bring out her argumentative side."

He sighed. "To be fair, I usually deserve it."

She cocked her head. "You push her until she can't help it. You never coddle her bratty attitude." Her eyes wandered around the office, taking in the sheer size of it, the mahogany furniture, the fresh flowers, and her own artwork gracing the walls. "How are you doing, Derrick?"

He knew what she was asking. "Great. The transition went without a hitch. We promoted one of the girls from the front desk to assistant manager, and between her familiarity with the staff and Tony's endorsement of me, I haven't had the first problem I couldn't handle."

"You're a natural at this. You wouldn't have had a problem anyway."

His smile was quick. "It helped smooth out a few bumps, though."

She toyed with the ring on her finger, making the emerald and diamonds catch the light. "I came here to ask for your help."

"Oh? How can I help you, Maxine?"

"Well," Maxine grinned, watching his face. "Sarah turns thirty next week."

That set Derrick back. "Wow."

Maxine grinned and nodded. "Anyway, we have the ballroom downstairs and we were in the middle of all the planning, then we got distracted. I was hoping you could tell me that you have someone on staff who can help. Suddenly I can't do it anymore. I don't have enough time to finish all the preparations, and I have a show in New York Thursday night. Robin was helping, but school's back in and work is crazy for her for at least another week since Tony opened that new place near the other campus."

He held a hand up when she took a breath. "Why are you so nervous about asking me?" he asked, reaching behind him to intercom his secretary. "Andrea, get me Maggie, please."

Maxine laughed. "I'm not – I'm overwhelmed. *This* is what the inside of my head is like right now."

He raised an eyebrow. "You're nervous about your show."

She put a hand to her forehead and laughed. "It's never gone away. I'm like this before every last one of them."

He grinned. "Don't take this wrong, Maxi, but I think that's cute."

She stood as she laughed again. "You're terrible, and I'm starving. Let's meet with Maggie in the restaurant."

"I can have something brought in here, if you'd prefer."

"Don't be ridiculous. My baby sister turns thirty in a week. I want to be seen in public with a devastatingly handsome younger than me guy to make everyone wonder if I'm going through a mid-life crisis." She waved her hand as if typesetting a headline. "Famous artist dumps ex-football pro for mystery man!"

"You're all of five years older than me, Maxi," he observed dryly.

"I know. I just want to raid the salad bar while we're waiting on food. I told you, I'm starving."

He lightly and reflexively touched the small of her back as they left his office. "How do you eat the way you eat and still look the way you look?"

Maxine schooled her face and asked, "Have you met my husband?" Her husband, Barry, worked out seven days a week and likely put his wife through a similar physical regimen.

Derrick paused by Andrea's desk, waiting for her hands to pause on the keyboard. "Have Maggie meet us in the restaurant, please."

"Absolutely, Mr. DiNunzio."

As soon as they were clear of the office, Maxine looped her arm into his. "I've been going to Sarah's church the last two weeks. Have you started back at our home church, or are you going somewhere else?"

"How could I leave that place? For six years I wished that I could commute back and forth on Sundays and Wednesday nights."

"That's fantastic. Have you seen the new buildings that they built since you were there last?"

"I did. Peter and Abram gave me a tour Sunday after lunch. I imagine the church will own most of Boston by the time it's all said and done."

"The bigger we get, the more people in that neighborhood we can help. Kids like you and Tony used to be, who would otherwise be hungry and cold, have food and shelter now."

Derrick paused inside the restaurant and let the hostess rush off in a panic to find an empty table during the lunch rush. He knew enough of Maxine and her sisters' story, knew that their mother was a heroin addict who bounced from man to pimp, carrying her daughters with her. "And little girls like you and Sarah might have protection now."

"That is our prayer."

As the hostess seated them, Maggie Rogers, the Viscolli Boston Event Coordinator, approached their table. Derrick stood and introduced her to Maxine, then enjoyed his lunch while he watched the two women wield their imaginations to finalize the remaining details of Sarah's birthday party.

"WHY can't you stay with me?"

Sarah stopped dreaming of a long bubble bath and gently pried loose the hand that gripped her arm while she spoke in soothing tones. "I wish I could, Mrs. Kline, but I just take care of you until your baby's born. The next set of nurses specialize in your care after the baby is here." She went to the window and pulled the blinds shut, blocking out the fury of the lightning in the night sky.

"But I know you."

"I know." She smiled and patted her shoulder. As she spoke, she crossed the room to the door. "But, trust me, you don't want me in charge of you and baby Jonathan. I wouldn't know where to even begin, and these ladies do." A bubble bath, maybe some chamomile tea.

"But ..."

"And your husband will be here any minute. You'll feel better once he's here. I promise."

She had the door opened and was almost out. "Can you come visit me?"

Her smile stayed in place as she turned around. "Of course. I come up here before every shift." Mrs. Kline bit her lip but nodded. Sarah let the door shut softly behind her and stopped in the hallway to roll her head on her shoulders.

There were four babies in their little beds behind the nurses' station. She smiled when she saw them. Some mothers knew this was the only chance for sleep they were going to get for the next several months, and let the nurses take them until it was time to feed them.

She leaned against the counter enclosing the nurses' station and propped her chin in her hands. Her roommate, Melissa, held a baby against her chest and gently patted its back. The baby would start to doze but then would jerk awake and whimper. Another nurse was rubbing the back of a baby that lay in one of the cribs while she spoke on the telephone.

Melissa modeled to get through nursing school. She was just under six feet tall, with skin the color of mocha and pale green eyes. Her mother was Nigerian, her father British, and she had been raised in Texas, giving her the oddest sounding accent Sarah had ever heard.

Babies loved her accent, though. She could soothe the fussiest one, and had always been able to. Sarah smiled as the baby fell into a deep sleep. Melissa adjusted it more comfortably against her shoulder and looked at the clock. "It's after midnight, kid."

"I know. We were pushing at ten."

"Kline?"

"Yes. She's going to need a little extra care."

"Okay. Any story?"

"Sure. Her husband decided he could risk a business trip and leave his pregnant wife alone for a week in a town where she doesn't know anyone. They just moved here a month ago, and she's so shy that she doesn't even know her neighbors. She was hysterical by the time she got here." She straightened and raised her arms over her head.

Melissa raised an eyebrow. "How early was she?"

"Does that matter?"

"Absolutely. I'd rather know all the facts before I demonize the husband." She slowly transferred the baby to the bed. "How early?"

Sarah sighed. "Six weeks."

"Well then, he's probably as hysterical as she was." She stood and brushed the front of her shirt. "I'll just go make her comfortable. Do you know when he's expected?"

"Any time."

"Good. Now, you go on, take a long bath, sip on a cup of tea, and try to get some sleep. Just take care going home. The weather is getting nasty out there. I think summer is finally over."

Melissa stopped talking and stared over Sarah's shoulder. "Oh my. Very nice. I pray that this isn't Mr. Kline and that my lipstick is still in place."

Her laugh surprised her. "You're awful."

"You haven't looked behind you, yet. Wait until you do."

"If I look, then he'll know we're talking about him."

"Shh, here he is." Sarah watched Melissa put on her best beautiful model smile. "Hello."

She felt his hand on the small of her back the second she heard his voice. Every muscle in her body that had slowly relaxed over the last five minutes immediately tensed up again. "Hello," he said.

Sarah turned her head and glared at Derrick. "What are you doing here?"

He looked too good. She hated him for it. Dressed down in jeans and a cotton sweater, wearing a leather jacket as black as his hair that only further darkened his eyes, he stood close enough for her to see the raindrops glistening in his hair. Close enough for her to smell the subtle spicy cologne that it seemed he and he alone ever wore.

His teeth seemed whiter against his dark skin and the black coat when he grinned at her. "I came visiting."

"Visiting hours are over."

"Not when the person I'm coming to see got off her shift an hour ago."

Melissa leaned forward and held out her hand. "I'm Sarah's roommate, Melissa," she purred. Sarah rolled her eyes. "And you are?"

Derrick grinned and took her hand, giving it a light squeeze. "Derrick DiNunzio. Nice to meet you, Melissa. I actually saw you at the memorial service."

"Ah, Derrick. The long lost Prodigal brother. Robin and Maxine speak of you so often. Sarah, not so much. You're back in Boston for good?"

"That's my plan."

A man in a soaking wet trench coat with wild eyes rounded the corner. He moved so fast Sarah thought he would run right into the counter, but somehow he managed to skid to a stop at the last possible second. He was out of breath, and had to pant. "My ... wife ..."

Melissa hurried around the counter and took him by his arm. "You must be Mr. Kline. You poor dear. Come with me, sir, and we'll take you to your wife and your little boy."

"I just ... I can't believe ... I ..."

She cooed to him as she led him away. "Shush, now. Everything's all right now that you're here. Try and take slow breaths, Mr. Kline. You don't want to upset your wife or the baby."

Derrick watched her walk away, deciding it was a shame that he found other women so pale in comparison to the one quietly seething next to him. "Poor guy," he said.

Sarah's shoulders came back so quickly that he was surprised he didn't hear them snap into place. "Poor guy? His poor wife just went through eight hours of hard labor by herself a month and a half early, and you say poor guy?"

She stormed away, and Derrick slipped his hands into his jacket pockets and grinned while he followed her. They made it to the bank of elevators before she whirled around and glared at him. "What are you really doing here?" she asked again as she jabbed at the call button repeatedly.

"Oh, I just came to see if I could get you into an argument."

That tripped her up, and for a moment, all she could do was stare at him. Then she blinked. "What?"

He shrugged and leaned his shoulder against the wall. "Maxi and Robin are both worried sick about you. I figured since you fly into a rage at my mere presence, I could help out."

"Help out how?"

"By giving you a genuine emotion other than grief." Then he smiled. He felt arrogant and hopeful all at once.

She hissed a breath between her teeth. "What I feel and what I don't feel is none of your concern."

"Of course not. But I'm not here out of concern for you. I'm here for them. They both told me they can't even get you out of bed. Is this really your first day back at work?"

"You don't even know. You can't know. He was my daddy. He saved me and now he's dead."

She'd started quivering so hard that her teeth nearly rattled. He grabbed her arm and gave her a small shake. "I'm sorry it happened, Sarah. I'm sorry. I've been there, remember? My mom died right before I moved to New York. I wish I could take the pain away, but I can't. No one can."

He expected tears, but none came. She just trembled hard enough to worry him and blinked them back. "Have you cried yet? Have you let yourself cry?"

They were cut off when the elevator finally arrived, and they had to wait while an orderly pushed a man in a wheelchair out before they could get in. "I'm exhausted, Derrick. Really, could we do this another time?"

"You haven't have you?" He put his hands on her shoulders and looked down at her. "Sarah, you have to let it out. Don't hold something like that in. No wonder you're such a wreck."

She jerked away from him and stepped with her back against the corner, putting as much distance between them as possible. "Stop it! Just leave me alone. Forget I even exist."

Derrick sighed and rubbed the back of his neck. "I wish I could. You have no idea how much I wish I could."

The elevator jerked to a stop so quickly that he lost his balance and fell against the wall as the lights went out. He retained his balance, but in the total darkness, he felt completely disoriented. "Sarah?" He panicked when she didn't answer, worried that she'd hit her head or something. He dug around in his pocket until he found his cell phone. The lit screen almost illuminated the entire small enclosure, and he turned around.

Sarah was crouched down with her back to the corner, sitting against her heels with her arms wrapped around her legs. She stared up at him with a pale face and eyes so inundated with fear that it wrenched his gut. He knelt next to her and started to reach for her but she shrank back and her breath started to wheeze. "Are you okay?"

The emergency lights came on, providing a dim but constant light, so he pocketed his phone. "Sarah?"

"Don't touch me!" she shrieked.

He jerked his hand back and held it up so that she could see his empty palm. "Okay. Okay, don't worry. The power must have gone out from the storm. Looks like the generators don't run the elevators."

"Get away! Stay away!" She screamed, gripping the sides of her head and burying her face against her knees.

He decided she must be claustrophobic. "Just take deep breaths, sweetheart. I'm sure we'll be moving soon."

Sarah could smell the dank mildew. It got worse the farther back into the closet they went, and her sisters always put her way in the back, blocking her with their own young bodies. Her back was against the wall, and she could hear something moving just on the other side.

Only it wasn't moving like a person. It was one of the monsters. One of the monsters she couldn't see because her glasses were gone again. They hid behind the walls or stayed just out of reach, just out of sight where she couldn't see, becoming blurry shadows that danced around her, taunting her, hitting her, pinching her.

She could hear her mother, screaming those horrible words to him. Other voices came, men and women, laughing, taunting. She was hungry. It seemed like she was always hungry. But the last time she complained, the man made her eat the raw meat right out of the package. Her stomach gave a greasy turn remembering having to swallow the raw, red meat. When she cried, he slapped her and told her never to complain to him again. That was the last time her glasses disappeared.

His voice stood out from the rest, and she cringed even further back, toward the monsters. They just scared her. He made her sister Robin scream in bed at night.

Maxine would come to her then, crawl in bed with her and they would hold each other until it was over. Sarah would close her eyes and try to block out the horrible sounds coming from the other bed, and sometimes

Maxine would risk attention by softly singing in Sarah's ears. Robin wouldn't let them touch her for a while after he left, so they would stay together and cry for her, because she never did cry.

The lights came on and she flinched away. That wasn't right. There wasn't a light in the closet. It was always dark. She blinked and the world came into focus. She wasn't in a closet – she was wrapped in Derrick's arms on his lap, buried against his chest, sobbing so hard her throat hurt. He was rocking her, talking nonsense in a soothing voice.

Horrified, she pushed away, but he hauled her back down. As the elevator came to a stop, he gripped her tighter and pushed with his legs, sliding his back up the wall until he was standing, still cradling her.

She took a deep breath and rested her head on his shoulder. She felt tired – so tired. "I'm okay now," she said. She patted his chest – his rock hard chest. "I'm fine."

He gave a harsh laugh as he carried her through the empty central lobby of the hospital and into the parking garage. "I'm not."

"Derrick, really …"

"When you can say that without sounding like a beaten puppy, maybe I'll believe you."

Her energy was shot. She'd argue with him about it in a minute. For the time being, she just relished the strength of his arms as he carried her.

TOPAZ HEAT - CHAPTER 8

INSTEAD of asking Sarah where she had parked her car, Derrick just took her to his. He set her down next to the car to unlock and open the door, and then gently helped her inside. It seemed like it took an eternity to get around the front hood and then to his door, to unlock it, and slide into the seat next to her. Sarah just leaned against the car door as huge tears slid down her face. He wanted to do something to help her, but he didn't know how or what. So he drove, through the light traffic downtown, darting cars and pushing limits on yellow lights, until they left the city behind them.

In minutes, he turned into Tony's neighborhood. As he drove up the winding driveway and cleared the last of the trees, the sight of the downstairs lights spilling out through the windows filled him with a sense of relief. He felt nearly happy when he pulled in behind Maxine's car parked in front of the door.

Sarah hadn't spoken throughout the entire drive. He guessed she knew their destination without having to ask. He parked behind Maxine's car and quickly hopped out and moved to Sarah's door. She kind of poured herself out of the seat, very wobbly as she gained her footing. "Let's go inside, Sweetheart," Derrick said.

"Don't call me, 'Sweetheart,'" she reflexively insisted.

Derrick couldn't help but grin at the rebuff, glad to hear her words spoken without any kind of slur. He didn't know what happened to her, but she exhibited signs of shock and he wondered if he should have taken her from the hospital at all.

She wrapped her arms around her middle, as if warding off a deep cold. As the lightning flashed around them and the wind whipped her hair free of the confines of her hairpins, Derrick thought she looked very lost, and very scared. He put a hand on her elbow to help her up the wide steps to the big double front doors.

An eternity passed from the time he rang the door bell to the moment Maxine opened the door. She had a coat in her hand and Barry followed behind her. Her smile grew wider when she saw them, until she looked directly at Sarah.

"What happened?" she asked, a half second before she turned her head and called for Robin.

Sarah stepped into the house and fell against Maxine, whose arms automatically came around her. As the first sob escaped, Robin and Tony entered the foyer and ran toward them. Derrick watched helplessly, relieved that the family all came together, as Sarah sobbed out, "I remember."

A shudder coursed through Sarah's body, starting somewhere in her stomach and moving in a widening radius outward, until even her toes clenched against it. She sat curled up in a leather chair, Robin on the couch next to her, leaning forward with her hand on the arm of the chair, and Maxine sitting on the end of the table in front of her, her hands rubbing warmth into Sarah's legs.

"What happened?" Robin asked.

"We were in the elevator." Her breath hitched.

Maxine paused then asked, "You and Derrick?"

Sarah nodded. "He'd come to check on me, because you two were worried about me. We were fighting about something when the power went out." She waved a hand in the air. "I guess the storm." Her hand fell limply to her side. She felt disconnected from the material world. Another shudder made her jaw clench.

Derrick spoke from somewhere in the room. "The elevator jerked to a stop and the lights went out. I don't know how long they were out. It couldn't have been more than a few seconds but it felt like longer."

Sarah rubbed her eyes. "As soon as the lights went out, it was like I was transported back in time." She looked at her sisters. Her vision blurred as her eyes filled with fresh tears. "I remember we were in a closet. We were hiding. And he ... he ..." With both hands, she slapped her palms over her mouth. Both of her sisters moved toward her at once, sitting on the arms of her chair and wrapping their arms around her, around each other.

Robin spoke. "Shh. Shush, now. It's okay, now." Her voice soothed, as it had twenty years ago.

Sarah's stomach hurt as more and more memories assailed her, flooding her mind and her senses until she could almost smell the burn of the cheap drugs, feel the harsh hands that slapped at her, and hear the terrible sound of her mother's voice. "How have you lived? How have you functioned with this in your heads?"

Maxine leaned back and lifted Sarah's face, wiping the tears off her cheeks. "Well, Robin worked. And I shopped. And we did those things mindlessly and soullessly until we found God."

Tony appeared at Robin's side, a glass of water in his hand. Robin took it from him and held it up to Sarah. "Drink."

Despite the fact that the last thing she wanted was a sip of water, the cool liquid felt wonderful in her parched mouth and soothingly slid down her aching throat. She accepted the glass from her sister and took another sip, then handed it back as fresh tears welled up in her eyes and tumbled down her cheeks. She ripped the glasses off her face and handed them to Maxine.

"I remember that night. Hiding. And gunshots." She put the heels of her hands to her eyes and pushed. "Up until now, my earliest memory was waking up in my parents' house. I couldn't see anything because I didn't have my glasses. I realized, even at nine, that for the first time in my life I was really safe."

Her stomach clenched painfully when she realized that her sisters had never really told her a lot. "But you two —"

Robin shushed her again, using a soothing voice. "We weren't little. I was fifteen, Maxine twelve. There was little hope for adoption. We were put into series of foster homes."

Maxine continued. "It was bad at one of them. The man —" She pressed her lips together, obviously struggling to speak.

Robin interrupted her. "There is evil in this world. The man there was attacking Maxi and I stabbed him in the back with a kitchen knife. He wasn't badly hurt but within a few days, Maxi ended up in another foster home and I landed in a girls' home."

"When she turned 18, she was released. Hank gave her a job at the restaurant and he helped her get custody of me."

"And a year later, we started appealing for you, but your parents had already adopted you."

Sarah nodded. "I didn't know about you, but I dreamed about you. When I saw you the morning of my fifteenth birthday, I recognized you from my dreams."

Maxine's eyes shifted to a distant and very private memory and she confirmed, "God speaks to us in dreams."

Robin pursed her lips and swallowed hard, but her expression was more angry than sad. "Your mom was just protecting you," she finally said, as if telling herself.

Knowing now, knowing the bond that held the three of them together, remembering the love she had for her sisters that surpassed anything she could have imagined, her heart gave a painful, tight beat. "It wasn't fair," she whispered. "Maybe if we had been together, I could have coped with all of it instead of just forgetting."

"Hey," Maxine said, gripping her hand. "Take it as a gift. Take it as a gift from God. You were able to live a normal life, all things considered. You found a family, with uncles and aunts and cousins. You had parents who tucked you in at night and read you bedtime stories. You went to church and had Christ in your life early when you were still young. God gave you that for a reason – either for them or for you, we can't know. But Robin and I don't begrudge any of that for you."

"You were probably the only person in the world praying for us," Robin said. "And look at us now. We are together, a family." She held her hand out, and Tony stepped forward to take it. Derrick stood next to him, and Barry put his hand on Maxine's shoulder. "We beat the system, and the odds, and God made us into a family. Our children will never have to worry about any of the things that we faced as children, as long as there is breath in our bodies."

Sarah leaned down until her head rested in Robin's lap. Her sister ran her fingers through her hair.

Tony spoke above her. "We should pray."

Barry affirmed, "Good idea."

Derrick cleared his throat. "I'll do it." Sarah felt her neck muscles automatically tense up, but she closed her eyes and did not object. In a circle, they held hands, closed their eyes, and bowed their heads in prayer.

"Father God," Derrick began, "I'm not sure what to say. There is so much pain in new memories, and it's on top of fresh grieving. I'm afraid that it's a little overwhelming right now. I would like to start off by thanking You for placing me in the elevator tonight when the power went out. Thank you for letting me be with Sarah when she experienced the return of her past."

His voice, once grating to her very nerves, now soothed her, caressed her, until she felt the fist that clinched her heart loose its grip, until she felt a sense of calm slowly overtake her. Her sister's hands felt warm against her cool skin.

"Mighty God, you are a healing God. Your word tells us that You can do all things and we have faith that it is so. We know that if it is Your will, You can erase the scars of the past and heal the pain of past wrongs as if they never even happened. God, we have faith that it is so. We petition You to touch Sarah, tonight. Even now, God, we pray that You hold her up in the very palm of Your mighty hand and comfort her through the Holy Spirit."

As he prayed for healing and forgiveness, Sarah just relaxed and felt his voice flow over her body. Her heart felt lighter and she knew that they were in the very presence of the Holy Spirit.

"God, we pray for all those who persecuted us in our past. We pray that we can be living witnesses to them of Your glory and Your promise. We pray that we can testify to the truth of Your word and Your enduring love. Father, let Sarah feel that love tonight and let that love fill her to overflowing. Let her see Your love shining in her sisters and her brothers in law. You know how long I have loved Sarah, Lord, and just how much." As Derrick suddenly quit speaking, Sarah's breath caught and she sat up quickly, turning to look at him. Without her glasses on, she couldn't see a lot of detail on his face, but she could see that he stood frozen.

She watched him take a step back. "I'm sorry," Derrick said. "I ..." His face looked into the eyes opening around him and he proclaimed. "Amen. Amen." Then he rushed from the room. Tony followed him at a more sedate pace. Sarah heard their deep, masculine voices, but could not make out what they said. She felt a burning flush cover her face and reached forward to retrieve the glasses Maxine had set on the table next to her hip.

"Well," Robin said, standing and rubbing her hands on the sides of her thighs.

She didn't say anything else, and Sarah felt her face burn hotter when Maxine smiled and said, "Well, indeed."

The older sisters said nothing else, as if sharing a long kept secret or a private joke. Sarah put her hands against her cheeks which felt hot and damp with tears. "Goodness."

Tony came back into the room and cleared his throat. "Derrick had to go."

Barry's bark of laughter made Sarah flinch. "I bet," he said. He immediately sobered up and looked at Sarah, "Sorry."

"No problem," she whispered as she stood, shakily, to her feet. Maxine stood with her, reaching an arm out to steady her. "Can you drive me home?"

"Stay here, tonight," Robin said.

"I don't want to." She had discovered that Maxine and Barry had dropped the kids off with Robin so that they could go to New York for Maxine's show. "I don't think I can face the kids in the morning."

"This house is big enough that you wouldn't have to," Tony observed dryly, by way of teasing Robin.

Sarah gave a curt shake of her head. "I need to go home."

"We can drive you home," Barry said.

"I left my purse in my locker at work," Sarah said.

"We'll go there first."

She hugged Robin then Tony. "I love you," she said to them.

Robin stepped forward and hugged her again. "I love you. Call me if you need me."

Sarah knew Robin meant it. Robin had taken care of Sarah from birth.

When she was six-years-old, Robin was the one to wake up in the middle of the night to feed the infant Sarah. She was her mother more than the woman who died at the hands of a drug dealer, or the woman who fostered Sarah for the last nine years of her childhood. "I will."

TOPAZ HEAT - CHAPTER 9

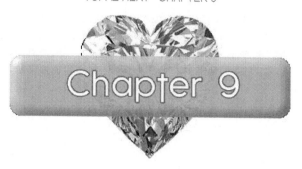

THE rain from a few days before ended any false hope that the mild autumn weather gave of a perpetual summer. Now a wind howled, blowing the remaining leaves from trees and sending people scurrying indoors. Several miles outside Boston, a cold, foggy mist settled around the mountains, making the world gray and dark.

Derrick looked straight up the imposing wall of rock in front of him and secured his backpack around his waist. He rolled his head on his neck and shifted his shoulders, shaking his arms and loosening up the muscles. Settling his gear comfortably, he stepped forward and started the climb.

Up and over, finding purchase for his fingertips and toes and sweating as he pulled his body upward and upward. Thankful for the unwelcoming weather, he had the mountain to himself. Derrick gripped a slate outcrop with the fingers of his right hand and pulled himself up, finding a toehold on the wet rock. The wind picked up a bit, shooting a misty rain against his face. Angry at the slip of his tongue the night before, he barely felt it and just kept moving up the mountain, gradually finding purchase on the wet rock as he made slow progress.

An hour later, he realized that he couldn't feel the rock beneath his hand anymore. The cold had numbed his fingertips. Despite the riskiness of coming out alone in this weather in the first place, he wasn't going to push his luck any further. He found a crevice in the small outcropping and stopped to put on a pair of gloves. He slipped his pack off his back and pulled out his thin cold-weather jacket. In each pocket, he had hand warmers, and he broke them open and shoved his hands into his pockets, immediately feeling the relief of the chemically generated heat.

He sat with his back against the rock wall and leaned back on his heels, temporarily sheltered from the icy mist outside. He needed to head back down before this rain turned to sleet, but he decided to just take another moment, get a little warmer.

Without the concentration of the climb, he thought back to the night before at Tony's house. Hope, horror, humiliation – strong emotions waged a battle inside his chest. He had prayed for Sarah for so many years that as he delved into the prayer the night before, he forgot himself. While he was certain God appreciated that kind of dedicated focus, the slip of the tongue destroyed just about any dream of the kind of future he had always hoped to find in Sarah. Not that he really harbored too much confidence that she would eventually come around to at least liking him a little bit, but there had always been that slim, sliver of hope. Maybe just a small glimmer – but hope nonetheless.

Derrick would never forget that first week with Tony. He would never forget appreciating the clean smell of the sheets and the warm room that greeted him when he got out of bed in the mornings, bitter cold ice and snow blanketing the city below him. He would always remember the shopping trip Maxine took him on, clothing him in good, brand new clothes – never before had he worn new shoes. Never had a pair of fleece-lined leather gloves warmed his hands.

It took him a long time to quit expecting the Viscollis to stop all this bluffing and play their real hand. It took him a long time to realize their love was real, genuine, and his for the taking. Their faith gave him a life, and once he started trusting them, he started trusting the one they called God. Once he started trusting God, his life had significance, their love had meaning, and he recognized that he had a purpose. He fell in love with Sarah gradually, deeply, and truly.

Late one Saturday night, he had stood in the kitchen of Tony's penthouse apartment wearing nothing but cotton pajama pants and a white T-shirt while sipping ice water and making a tuna fish sandwich on toast. Sarah had walked in and studied him from head to toe like he was some kind of anomaly for which she couldn't account.

Very precocious in appearance at perhaps half his size and at least a foot shorter than he, she had not smiled. Instead, her honey golden eyes – eyes the color of the richest topaz – had looked large and somewhat critical behind her glasses.

She wore an ankle length plaid skirt and a simple white blouse beneath a long sleeved button down sweater. She had an overnight bag slung over her shoulder. He remembered her reddish hair looking like it had a will of its own. "Hey," He stuck a thumb in the direction of his chest. "Derrick. Derrick DiNunzio."

Derrick was years away from elocution lessons and speaking in full and grammatically correct sentences. By contrast, the girl before him spoke with a cultured diction and nearly perfect inflection, sounding rather more like a Cape Cod Kennedy than a South Boston nursing student. "I know who you are. I'm Sarah. What on earth are you eating? It smells like an outdoor dock market in here."

Derrick shrugged. "Just tuna. Want I should make you a sandwich?"

Sarah had shuddered and her face had fallen in disgust. "Certainly not."

Her haughty tone nearly made him laugh aloud. Derrick had recently discovered a love for classic films. The teenage girl standing before him reminded him of a 1930s film noir movie matron, offended at the notion of this or that and uninhibited in communicating that offense to the world. He snapped his fingers. "Sarah. Right. Going to church with us tomorrow, yeah?"

"I'm going to church with my half-sisters, yes. Why?" Her chin jutted out.

Her arrogance made him want to tease her even more. He nodded and said, "Well, Sarah, it's just peachy keen to meet ya." He took an enormous bite of his tuna on toast and a spot of mayonnaise remained at the corner of his mouth as he chewed. With a cheek still full, he spoke, "I mean it. I'll remember it always."

Sarah had spun around muttering the word, "Disgusting," under her breath. Derrick had grinned, his teeth covered with tuna and bits of pickle, feeling nothing but mirth at the exchange as he watched her leave.

From the first moment they met, that initial dynamic had set a tone for their relationship that had only escalated through the college years and the years that followed. Through all that time, no other woman ever compared to her. Sarah had a fire and she never backed down. She never abandoned her principles and she never once, in all the time he had known her, stepped down off her high horse. While everyone else seemed to coddle her or tolerate her attitude, Derrick did whatever he could to throw her off balance and relish her discomfiture.

And he pined for her since the second they met.

The grief he experienced at his mother's death surprised him and nothing seemed to comfort him for weeks. Sarah continued to ignore him through the funeral and the days that followed.

In prayer he came to a place of equilibrium where he no longer experienced any feelings. The world turned silver and black and white like the old movies he watched and his heart beat a hollow rhythm in his chest. He started working more than he ever had before – sixty, seventy, even eighty hour weeks just to drown out everything else around him.

Tony, in his wisdom, sent Derrick away, with a new job, lots of new responsibilities, and new scenery. Derrick, knowing how much Sarah despised him, hoped that his absence would make her grow distant in his mind and, hopefully, his heart.

She had not.

He abided in her, prayed for her daily, and ultimately began to pray that God would soften her heart and let her feel the same way for him that he felt for her.

Now she knew his secret – now the whole family knew. His heart gave a painful twist at that thought. Would they treat him differently? Would they see him as an interloper, a predator in their midst all these years? Would he still be accepted as one of them?

He shifted and leaned forward, moving from a crouching on his heels position into a kneeling on his knees position. He felt he ought to talk to the One who got him into this mess in the first place. Hands still in his pockets to warm his numb fingertips, he bowed his head.

"God, I'm trying to trust my future to You, but I'm finding myself at an impasse…" As he prayed, the cold bit his cheeks. The wind whipped violently around him and the mist froze to little hard pellets of ice. He felt very alone and a little bit afraid. A part of his mind wondered if this is how David had felt waiting to see which way Jonathan's arrow would fall.

Finishing the brief but emotional prayer with a steadfast, "Amen," Derrick rose to his feet. He slapped his hands together and rubbed them hard, then stepped away from his temporary shelter and started, carefully, climbing back down the mountain face, racing the dropping temperature, while on the icy rock slipping too often for peace of mind as he made his retreat.

TONY met Derrick in the parking garage. He glanced into the back seat and spotted the climbing gear. His eyes shot angry daggers as Derrick pocketed his keys. "Tell me you weren't out in this weather."

"I came back down as soon as it turned bad." He stomped his feet and nodded toward the elevator. "Let's go inside. The heater's out in the car for some reason, and I'm freezing."

They rode up to the apartment in silence. Derrick kept his coat on, but shed his gloves and led Tony into the kitchen. He'd pre-loaded the coffee pot, so all he had to do was turn it on. Listening to the machine grind the beans and spit them into the basket made him already start to feel warmer.

"So, that was quite intense last night," Tony said without preamble.

"That's certainly a word." Derrick pulled two mugs from the cupboard and set them on the counter next to the coffee maker. He moved to the refrigerator and dug around inside, pulling out the makings of a turkey sandwich.

"Good thing you were there with her."

Releasing a breath, Derrick set the sandwich makings on the counter and leaned his hands against it. "I agree. I think I was supposed to be there."

The only sign Tony gave that he understood the deeper meaning was a slight purse of his lips. "Barry took her home after you left."

Derrick closed his eyes. "Tony…"

He felt the slap of his friend, of his brother's hand, against his shoulder. "Do you think for a minute that your feelings were not already known?"

Relief flooded his chest, choked his throat. He cleared his throat and opened his eyes, busying his hands with the twist tie on the bag of bread. "I thought I hid my feelings pretty well."

"Big giant pining brown eyes cannot be hidden."

Laughter bubbled up from the tightness in his chest, loosening the tension. "Okay. Okay." He pulled out two slices of bread and raised his eyebrow quizzically at Tony. At his nod, he pulled out another two. "Why didn't Sarah see it?"

"Derrick, for years and years, Sarah didn't see the love her own sisters had for her. God is still working on her."

Derrick pondered that. Then his hands abandoned their mundane efforts. "Tony, is this what it's like for Jesus? Does He just love us and love us from the time we are born and we disappoint Him over and over and just shun His love – and He never stops? He just never stops loving us even when we push Him away over and over again?"

Tony's fingers tightened on the younger man's shoulders. "Can you imagine how much it pains Him?"

Derrick felt tears threatening. "I don't have to imagine." His head hung and he changed the subject. "She knows, now. How many times have I baited her and teased her for no good reason? Just trying to get a rise out of her so she would think about me for the rest of the day. I've been so childish."

Tony grinned. "The good thing is that now there is at least a reason for her animosity toward you."

Derrick laughed again, knowing that Tony spoke the truth.

Chapter 10

SARAH tried to focus on the chart in front of her, but her mind kept wandering. So much at one time. For three days now, she had thrown herself into work, working overtime, extra shifts – anything to keep from thinking. She didn't want to think about her dad. She didn't want to think about her past. And she certainly didn't want to think about Derrick.

"Nurse!"

She whipped her head up and focused on an older woman. Mrs. Martinez. Her eyes were wild. "*Ayudame, por favor. Mi hija!*"

She knew enough Spanish to get by in this hospital with partial ease. She threw down her pen and ran to the room where Victoria Martinez lay curled into a fetal position. She clutched a bed pan, obviously feeling very sick to her stomach.

Sarah touched her shoulder and was surprised at the heat on her skin. She felt the young girl's muscles contract and rubbed Victoria's back as her body dry heaved.

"Have you been sick already?" Sarah asked, opening a drawer to get the thermometer.

"*Si*," Victoria said. "My little brother was sick two days ago. I have been sick since last night." She opened her mouth to take the thermometer. In seconds it gave a reading of 101.6. Victoria gasped and gripped her stomach.

Sarah glanced at the contractions readout coming out from the machine next to the bed. A pretty hard contraction hit the seventeen-year-old. She felt so bad for her. Labor was bad enough, but labor with a stomach flu would just be miserable. "Let me go call the doctor," Sarah said, holding her hand up to her ear like a phone. "*Teléfono médico.*"

"*Si*," Mrs. Martinez said, rushing back to her daughter's side.

Sarah returned to the nurse's station and paged the O. B. on call. After receiving an order for Zofran and instructions to go ahead and call the anesthesiologist to get an epidural going to alleviate her discomfort, she armed herself with ice chips and returned to her patient.

Zofran in her system, Victoria started feeling a little better, though very weak. She lay back with her eyes closed, opening them only to grab her stomach and moan with each passing contraction. The anesthesiologist finally arrived and Sarah groaned inwardly when it was Dr. Benson.

She intended to call him out about the weekend jaunt with his wife up to New York, but her father's death had interrupted her personal life to such an extent that she hadn't even thought of Dennis Benson the entire time. In fact, he had slipped her mind to such a degree that she hadn't thought of him until just this moment.

"Nurse Thomas," he said by way of greeting.

"Doctor."

After that, they both tended to the patient. Once the epidural was in place and the IV dripping, Sarah followed him from the room.

"I'm sorry to hear about your father," he said by way of preamble.

"Yes, all your phone calls, cards, and flowers were so encouraging," Sarah said sarcastically.

He put his hands in the pockets of his white coat. "I've been meaning to call you," he said warmly, leaning his shoulder against the wall.

Sarah cocked her head, as if studying him from a new angle. He looked like a plastic Ken doll. He had his perfectly sculpted hair sprayed into place. His fake tan looked wrong in Boston in October. The perfect starchiness of his clothing just added to the air of plastic facade. She wondered how she had ever found him attractive. She wondered how that saccharine charm had ever appealed to her. "What would your wife say to that, I wonder?" Sarah asked.

"My wife? I'm not sure I understand."

Sarah crossed her arms over her chest. "Listen, Doctor Benson. I have to work with you. But that's the end of our relationship. I don't really understand what you thought you would get from me, but go look elsewhere. Take your wife on another romantic weekend to New York. Or find some other nurse to butter up and deceive. It's not going to be me."

He visibly flinched back when she mentioned New York. His reaction alone informed her that Derrick had spoken truthfully, though she hadn't really doubted him. As much as she wished he had been mistaken, Derrick never forgot a name or a face and he had never lied to her. She knew that much about him.

She left the doctor leaning against the wall and went back to work. She made the notations she needed to make in the Martinez chart, answered a call from another room, and glanced at the clock. All of her patients were in good places right now, so she decided to go ahead and take her dinner break.

With an apple in one hand and her small purse-sized Bible in the other, she went to the hospital chapel and decided she would spend her hour regaining some focus.

SARAH spread her Sunday School material on the table in front of her. Freshly showered after working out with an exercise DVD, she swallowed half a bottle of water before sitting down to study the material. She hadn't led the class in weeks. When she read the e-mail from a friend who had been substituting for her asking if she should plan to teach the class this week, Sarah realized how much she missed her class, and her students. She realized how much she needed that back in her life right now.

Her table sat in the corner of her kitchen, looking out into the back yard. Ice rain pummeled the neighbor's swing set. Sarah looked out into the gray wet, worried about how dangerous the roads would be by nightfall, thankful she didn't have to work tonight. She wondered if there would even be church in the morning to teach.

The tea pot on the stove whistled and she flicked the burner off as she poured herself a cup of spearmint tea. Food didn't sound good to her. She figured she was way too tired to eat. Maybe after preparing her lesson, she could curl up on the couch with Jane Austen and hide from the real world for a few hours.

As she put together a lesson on positive body image, she got caught up in the research on college age eating disorders, suicide attempts, and emotional health matters as they related to a media driven world that projected a false god of ideal body shape. She thought of the eighteen girls in her class and wondered how many of them fell into the statistics she read. Her stomach rolled at the thought of purging meals, cutting skin, and anguish over normal, healthy weight.

A light sweat covered her body as she took another sip of spearmint tea, remembering how Maxine used to obsess about eating and exercising until Barry took her under his wing and taught her the healthy way to balance exercise with diet and fitness. She wondered if she could get her brother-in-law to come lecture her class about how to do it the right way.

Her stomach rolled again, making it hard to swallow her tea. Sarah suddenly realized the physical discomfort she felt might not have as much to do with her emotional reaction to the state of the world today as with the gastroenteritis suffered by her young patient, Victoria Martinez, two days ago.

She tossed her pencil down and pushed away from the table. As she rushed from the kitchen to the bathroom, one hand over her stomach, one hand over her mouth, she was certain she had diagnosed herself correctly.

SARAH felt certain she was going to die. She didn't think her body would take the violent dry heaving another time. Yet even as she thought that, she felt her stomach muscles rolling and felt the cold sweat break out all over her body. She laid half on and half off the couch, clutching the mop bucket she'd brought in with her. As her body wracked with the effort to dispel absolutely nothing from her stomach, her doorbell rang.

Heaving session over for the time being, she rolled over on her back and covered her eyes with her arm. She just wanted to sleep. The doorbell rang again and she moaned.

Muscles shaking with sickness, she barely made it to her feet. The room swirled around her and her vision started to gray. Drenched in sweat, she stumbled to the door. Leaning against the wall, she turned the doorknob and barely got the door open and saw a blurry half of Derrick's face before she collapsed.

The wind blew icy rain inside, reviving her as Derrick rushed in and knelt above her. "Sarah?" The concern on his face, the panic in his eyes, caused her heart to give a little tug even as her stomach rolled.

"Sick," she whispered. She rolled to her knees, arms shaking as she pushed herself up. Derrick knelt by her, putting an arm over her shoulders just as her stomach muscles started spasming. "Bucket," she got out just as the heaving started again.

He moved so fast, lifting her and taking her to the bucket instead of bringing the container to her. She sat on the floor, in between the couch and her coffee table and wished that death would just be quick so that she wouldn't have to face this man when she felt well again one day. As soon as she thought she could move, she pushed herself back onto the couch and lay down again.

"Please ... go away." Despite her whispered plea, she heard him shrugging out of his coat.

"Where's Melissa?"

"Work."

"Do you know when she'll be home?"

"Tomorrow morning." He didn't speak again, so she let herself drift away, dozing until she startled awake with the feel of a cool cloth covering her forehead.

"Think you can try some ice chips?"

Sarah pried open an eye, surprised at how dry her eyes felt, how much they ached. Derrick sat on the coffee table next to her, wearing a dark gray suit with a dark green shirt. His gray tie had green diagonal stripes and carefully camouflaged the three crosses at Calvary in what looked like a repeating houndstooth pattern to a casual observer.

She always saw that tough kid in the sweat pants making that disgusting tuna sandwich whenever she looked at him. She realized now that the kid was long gone, and in his place lived a very successful, very cultured man. Not a boy full of cocky attitude, but an accomplished man of God.

She closed her eyes again, curious as to the direction of her thoughts and certain that the reason must be because she currently ran a high fever. "Not yet." She ran her tongue over her dry lips. "Let me make sure my stomach will behave."

She heard him move, but didn't open her eyes again. Instead, feeling oddly secure, she slept.

DERRICK watched Sarah's face wrinkle into a frown, then relax as sleep took over. She was so petite, barely five feet tall, and so thin that he often wondered how she was able to handle the physical tasks of her job. He could never pinpoint her hair color to just one shade. Auburn and brown and blonde merged into a raging wildfire of curls that never stayed in place. Her naturally pale skin made her eyes stand out like the warmest honey, shine like jewels the color of the richest topaz.

Yet tonight, her hair lay in a sweaty, tame mass against the pillow. Her skin was so stark white that her freckles looked fake – penciled in. No light shown forth from her eyes as they instead looked dull with sickness. The violence with which she had gotten sick scared him, certain her bones would snap with the heaving.

Worried, he took the washcloth from her forehead and felt the heat on it. He touched her cheek and felt the burn of her fever. Moving quickly to the bathroom, he rinsed the cloth with cool water, then squeezed it dry and folded it into thirds, gently placing it back on her forehead, saying a quick prayer for healing as he touched her.

He moved through the small home and into the kitchen, spying her books and papers spread on the table. Her phone sat next to her teacup and without a shred of guilt he went through the contacts in her phone until he found Melissa's number.

The roommate answered on the third ring. "'ello, love."

Derrick paused before answering. "This is Sarah's friend, Derrick. We met the other night."

"Of course. What's wrong?"

Rubbing the back of his neck before loosening his tie, Derrick went back to the room with Sarah. "Sarah is really sick. Throwing up, fever."

"Ah. So she caught it then. It's been going around. Nasty bug. It really just has to run its course."

Relief relaxed his neck muscles. "Okay. Thanks."

"Can you stay with her? I can call her mom or a sister —"

Derrick cut her off. "I can stay."

"Okay. I get off at seven. If she's not improving by six, call me back. I'll bring something home with me."

"Thanks. I'll call either way."

Derrick pocketed the phone and heard Sarah moan. He rushed to her side and held the bucket for her. As she lay back against the pillow, he wondered if she had even woken up. He stood to refresh her washcloth again but she grabbed his wrist. Looking down at her, he saw her eyes open and gazing right at him. His heart felt like it paused for just a beat, before resuming its pace at a slightly quicker one.

"Thank you," she said.

He covered her small hand with his. "My pleasure, Sweetheart."

"Don't call me sweetheart," she said absently, then closed her eyes again. Her hand slid from his wrist and fell limply to her side.

TOPAZ HEAT - CHAPTER 11

SARAH opened her eyes and flinched in pain away from the bright sunlight streaming into her room. Her head ached, her stomach muscles ached, and it felt like dry cotton balls lined her mouth and the back of her throat.

As she rolled into a sitting position, she realized she was in her bed, not the couch. She didn't remember coming into her bedroom. Her last good memory was Derrick coaxing an ice chip down her throat around three in the morning. Squinting at the clock, she realized that was a good seven hours ago.

Sitting didn't seem to cause any adverse reactions to her digestive system, so she cautiously tried standing. Her legs felt a little bit weak and rubbery, but better than the night before. She still wore the yoga pants and long sleeved T-shirt she'd had on the day before. The cold floor felt good to her bare feet.

She found her glasses on the night stand and slipped them on, then used the loose rubber band she found to gather her hair at the nape of her neck.

She opened the door quietly and peered out. Across the hall, she saw Melissa's closed door, and guessed that she was home and asleep. The rest of the house appeared silent, so she went into her bathroom. Examining her face in the mirror, she still looked a little wan. After brushing her teeth and washing her face, she had a little bit more color on her cheeks, but not like normal. She needed a shower, but she needed something to drink even more, so she left the bathroom and made her way to the kitchen, pausing when she saw a gray tie with green stripes lying on top of a gray jacket that lay casually tossed over the back of her arm chair.

Realizing she tensed up as she mentally braced herself, she entered her kitchen and stopped short when she saw Derrick sitting at the table, a steaming mug next to his elbow, talking on his cell phone. He had on his gray suit pants, but no shirt and no socks. The tattooed wing of the dragon snaked over his shoulder. A rough tattoo of a knife dripping blood lay over his heart.

"Yeah. I'll take care of it. Thanks," he said when he spotted her. He set the phone down and stood. "Hi."

Nervously pulling the arms of her sleeves over her hands before wrapping her arms around her body, Sarah hesitated briefly before responding. "Why are you still here?"

Derrick raised an eyebrow as he looked at her, peering into her eyes until she was certain he could read her thoughts or something. "Waiting for you to wake up."

"Why?"

He crossed the room and stood in front of her. "Because, Sweetheart, you scared me to death last night."

"I didn't think anything could scare you."

Derrick shrugged and put a hand on her shoulder. "Apparently the thought of you sick does." Before she could shrug his hand away, he removed it. "Anyway, it's good to see you back in the land of the living. Maxine is back from New York and said to tell you she'll be by after church with vegetable soup."

Sarah couldn't help but smile warmly. "I'm surprised she didn't offer chicken noodle."

"I talked her down," Derrick said dryly.

Laughing hurt Sarah's stomach muscles. She rubbed her middle as she went to the refrigerator to get a bottle of water. She twisted the bottle cap and was halfway through the first wonderfully cool sip when she realized something. "Church!" She turned around and looked at Derrick in horror. "Oh no. I never called anyone to cover my class."

"Indeed."

Sarah spun around and saw her mother standing in the doorway to the kitchen. She had Derrick's jacket and tie draped over her arm. Sarah immediately thought of Derrick's car in the driveway, covered in snow and ice, obviously having been there overnight. A strange, guilty heat rose up her neck from her chest and she felt it fan her cheeks. "Mom."

"I tried calling." Her mother's lips thinned and she looked directly at Derrick with such a look of disapproval that Sarah wanted to step in front of her and block him. "You were apparently otherwise occupied."

"I've been in bed." She put a hand to her forehead and closed her eyes, realizing how that sounded and how this all looked.

She jumped when she heard Derrick's voice. "Mrs. Thomas, I'm Derrick DiNunzio," he said, holding his hand out.

Darlene looked at his hand but did not take it. Instead, she looked him up and down, from his disheveled hair to his bare feet, then laid the coat and tie over his outstretched arm. "I know who you are."

"Mom –"

Darlene's head whipped toward Sarah. "Not another word."

Sarah snapped her mouth shut and didn't say anything else. But Derrick obviously hadn't been as well trained as Sarah in the fine art of dealing with Darlene Thomas.

"We aren't lovers," he said bluntly. Darlene gasped and Sarah felt a guttural little desperate cry escape her throat. "I came by last night and found she was quite ill. Melissa was at work, so I stayed."

Darlene looked at Sarah and back at Derrick. "Ill? Sarah never takes ill."

He held up his jacket and showed a stain. "She sure was last night. Incidentally, that's why I'm not wearing my shirt. And I've been up most of the night. You'll pardon my appearance."

The older woman cleared her throat and adjusted the collar of her jacket. "I see." She stiffly turned to her daughter. "And are you feeling well now?"

Sarah pulled the sleeves of her arms over her hands and crossed her arms. "I just got out of bed a few minutes ago. But I think I'll be okay."

Darlene stiffly nodded. "Good." She looked back at Derrick. "Thank you for taking care of her, Mr. DiNunzio."

Derrick cocked his head, as if waiting for more. After the space of several heartbeats, he finally nodded. "Of course. I was happy that I stopped by when I did."

"And why *did* you happen to stop by exactly?" Darlene asked.

Sarah took a step forward. "Mom!"

"No, it's okay." Her step forward put her next to him and she jumped when she felt his hand on the small of her back. "I'd come by to declare my undying love for Sarah and to ask her to do me the very great honor of marrying me and becoming my wife."

Through thinned lips, Darlene said, "Now you're making fun of me."

"I assure you I am not." Derrick pulled a hand out of his pocket and opened it. On his palm lay a gold ring set with a square cut topaz the color of burnt honey surrounded by glittering diamonds.

Sarah gasped and started to reach for the ring before she stopped herself and crossed her arms again. "May I speak to my daughter alone, please?"

Derrick nodded. "Of course. I need to see if my shirt's dry, anyway. If you could both please excuse me." He stroked the small of her back in an almost reassuring manner before he left the room.

Sarah chewed on her bottom lip, completely at a loss. Her heart beat a little excited rhythm that she couldn't identify or explain, and the small of her back still felt the heat of his fingertips. She watched her mother remove her gloves, one finger at a time, then sit in the chair Derrick had recently occupied. She used the edge of a glove to move his phone out of her way and then set her purse down in its place. "I'd like a cup of tea, please."

"Of course." Sarah rushed to the stove and pulled a mug out of the cupboard above her head. She saw the jar of instant coffee she kept on hand for company and touched the side of the teapot that sat on a burner and felt the heat, guessing Derrick used it to make the coffee he'd been drinking when she came into the kitchen not more than five minutes ago. With surprisingly efficient movements, she poured her mother a cup of tea and set it in front of her at the table, then sat across from her.

"Mom, I really don't –"

"You know, I fought your father about you even learning you had half sisters. He won, of course." Darlene played with the paper hanging off the end of the tea bag string. "Your psychiatrist felt that getting you involved with your sisters in some facet of your life might alleviate some of the nightmares you were having. I fought it and fought it, because I knew the kind of influence they could have on you, but your father insisted. I never wanted them to be anywhere near you. I never wanted you to live with them and go to school. I certainly never wanted them to be such an important part of your life."

Darlene picked up her cup but immediately slammed it back down, causing the brew to slosh over the sides. "And now I see where it's led, just as I knew it would. I come to your house and find you with this filthy street hood covered in tattoos."

"Don't!" The words hurt, yes, but they also made her terribly, terribly angry. She fought it down, tried to get a grip on her temper and the urge to lash out. "Listen. I love you. You're my mom. You have been for over twenty years. But I love them, too. I'm allowed to love all of you. I just don't see why you can't accept that and be happy for me. I have two wonderful families. I'm incredibly blessed."

As tiny as her mother was, she had the ability to tilt her head just so, so that she looked down at the person with whom she spoke. Sarah's hand itched to slap the look off her mother's face, and she felt suddenly horrified with herself. "I don't see why you consider it lucky to have blood ties with women who would sell themselves off to the highest bidder."

She gasped and pushed her chair away from the table. "How can you say that? How can you say that when you've seen them with their husbands and know how they feel about them?"

"Money is a strong motivator, Sarah. It can bring out the strongest of feelings. And now I see you with one of them. I can't believe that you ..." She broke off and took a sip of her tea.

"That I what? What exactly do you think I did other than throw up my stomach lining every twenty minutes?"

Darlene's eyes welled up with tears. "Sarah, who knows what horrors you suffered as a child. Who knows what buried memories are going to surface and affect your behavior now, your interpersonal relationships."

"Well, you can put your mind at ease, mother. As bad as it was, it wasn't quite there. At least, not for me."

"How do you know?"

"Because I remember, now. I remember everything. And sitting here looking at you, I suddenly realize that you've been trying to put little things like that in my head all my life. Why? Were you worried that you and dad alone wouldn't be enough to make me love you? Do you really think that you had to make sure I was indebted to you as well? That I would be so appreciative even without really knowing what it was really like before?" Her stomach was twisting itself into little painful knots. "It wasn't necessary. I didn't have to be fed with guilt."

Darlene leaned forward and pointed a finger at her daughter. "You were starving. You were a skinny little waif who couldn't see ten feet in front of your own face and jumped at shadows. You were covered with bruises. You hadn't bathed in weeks. Your clothes were too small, and your shoes were three sizes too big. We took you into our home, knowing what you came from and gave you everything we had. But the second your sister, your half sister, waved a college education under your nose, you dumped us with barely a wave good bye. And I don't think even you know the price tag that was put on that education, what you were really reduced to." She stood as she finished her tirade, and Sarah forced strength into her legs to stand with her.

"I dumped no one and you know it. Let me tell you something, mom." She barely spat the word out. "I didn't need a motivator. I didn't need the little extras you managed to throw in. You two were enough for me, enough to make me love you. Safety, cleanliness, a home was all I needed. Robin and Maxine are to be admired, revered even, for doing what they've done without having what I had. They made it before they met their husbands, and I think that angers you more than anything. I think the thought that maybe I could have made it too, without you, makes you uncomfortable. And afraid. Afraid that I would figure out I never needed you in the first place."

"That's absurd."

"Do you really think so? Or is what's really bothering you the fact that the man in the next room isn't a wholesome good old American boy-next-door like Dennis Benson. It was okay that Dennis was married as long as he was blond haired, blue eyed, and clean cut. Is that it?" She stepped a foot closer. "If it is, let me make one thing very clear. I'm an adult. I'm fully capable of making my own decisions, just as you are. Whether I want to date an ex-street hood jailhouse tattoos or a crown prince with jewels on his head, it shouldn't matter to you. What should matter to you, and what seems never to have mattered, is whether or not I'm happy with the choices I've made."

Darlene held herself stiffly, her frigid stare doing nothing to conceal the heat of fury that seethed in her eyes. "I will not stand here and be spoken to like that by my own daughter."

Sarah pulled herself up to her full height and stared her mother down. "Then kindly leave. Feel free to return when you're ready to apologize for being so rude this morning."

They stared at each other until the older woman finally pressed her lips into a thin line and gave a stiff nod of her head. She retrieved her bag from the table and left the room without any further words being spoken.

Chapter 12

DERRICK heard everything. He couldn't help but hear. The apartment was a good size, but the hardwood floors and old walls did little to muffle sounds. He stood next to the closet containing the washer and dryer in the hallway and listened to every single word while sincerely trying not to overhear.

He had never fooled himself into thinking that most people would accept him with open arms if they knew his past. He had perfected the right accent, the right clothes, the right way to carry himself so that the clientele, even the employees, at his hotels would never suspect his roots, the things he had done, the way he had lived, the raw desperation that had driven every action and reaction for the first eighteen years of his life. The knowledge of such prejudice being likely didn't stop the churning of emotions he felt at Darlene Thomas' words.

He fought a mixture of pain, anger, shame …things he thought he'd put aside a decade ago. He closed his eyes and, with purpose and precision, addressed each emotion and fought it back. Losing his cool and transforming into the hood Darlene Thomas accused him of being would do no one any good. His past was forgiven – redeemed. He knew that. It didn't matter what she thought.

After the sound of the door slamming finished reverberating through the house, he debated what he should do next. Then he decided that he would let Sarah take that lead. She could either kick him out or fall desperately into his arms. He preferred the latter, but would accept whatever came. He slipped his shirt on and buttoned it as he moved through the house.

She sat at the table, facing the door, across from the seat he had occupied mere minutes before. He knew if he touched his cup of coffee that it would still be hot. Yet, somehow, it felt like a lifetime had passed since he made Sarah laugh.

Her face looked even more drawn than it had the previous night, and though tears threatened to spill from her eyes her cheeks remained dry. He could see the effort she was putting into not crying, not giving in to her emotions. Quietly, he pulled out his chair and sat across from her.

"I guess you heard," she said in nearly a whisper.

Derrick shrugged. "I didn't try."

"I know." Sarah took her glasses off and scrubbed at her cheeks with both hands. "She said terrible things."

"She's had a rough time lately."

Meeting his eyes, she tilted her head and looked at him quizzically. "How can you hear what she said about you and … and everyone and say that so calmly?"

"Do you remember when we first met?" The tinge on her cheeks told him that she remembered more than her shrug did. "You really, really didn't like the fact that I was there."

"Yeah. I'd had a bad day." Sarah ran her tongue over her lips nervously. "And you were …"

He filled in the blank for her. "Crude?"

She raised her eyes in surprise. "No. I …"

"It's okay, Sarah. It's what I lived with until the day I turned eighteen. I'd walk into a store and the clerk would wait for me to steal something. And the thing is, I was probably there to steal something. I didn't make the changes to my accent and appearance out of any sort of pride. I did it so that no one would suspect who I was or what I did or what I might have been willing to do at some desperate moment. The way your mother classified me in her mind – the way you thought of me that first day we met – was something I was used to and something I even expected."

Sarah cleared her throat and stood. With nervous movements, she grabbed her mother's tea cup and carried it to the sink. "I walked in that kitchen and was immediately attracted to you. But I knew who you were and where you were from."

Derrick felt his heart rate increase just a little bit. Of all the possible things she could have said, that was absolutely the last thing he expected. He stood and followed her to the sink. "And?"

She turned her body toward him and he could see the tears filling her eyes again. "And my mom had made me so afraid." A tear spilled out of her eye and ran down her cheek. "Afraid that I would become like her – like my real mom. She made it seem like I almost certainly would, so I did everything in my power to prove to her that I was good and perfect and chaste and clean." Another tear fell, and another, wetting her eyelashes and streaking her cheeks. "And I walk into a kitchen and here's this tattooed, unmannered, unchurched boy who made my heart go pitter-pat. Being rude was the only way I could battle the fear that everything I'd worked toward really meant absolutely nothing."

A little glimmer of hope sprang from the frantic beating in his chest.

Derrick reached forward, wanting to touch her but afraid to shatter the moment. Instead, he put his hand on the edge of the sink, gripping it, leaning toward her.

"You became my adversary." She admitted. "As long as I didn't like you, and you didn't like me, there was no worry that I could be like her. I never saw the change in you. I never saw Christ enter your life. I never saw the love you had for my family. I never saw your success. I just saw that barefoot, tattooed kid in my brother-in-law's kitchen."

Sarah took a step forward so that he just had to let go of the sink for his arm to be around her. He watched as she bowed her head and leaned her forehead against his chest. Certain she would be able to feel the furious pounding of his heart, he slowly brought both arms around her and breathed in deeply, both in an effort to control his heart rate and to smell her hair. She turned her head until her cheek lay against his shirt. He felt her arms go around his torso and for the first time in his life, felt utter and complete contentment.

"I've never treated you well."

Derrick turned his head so that he could lay his cheek against the top of her head. "It's okay. I instigated most of our arguments. I knew your buttons and how to push them."

Sarah pushed far enough away to tilt her head back and meet his eyes. "It doesn't seem fair. If I hadn't been afraid ..."

"Sshh." Derrick cut her off and put a hand on her damp cheek. "We have to trust God's timing, which is absolutely perfect." She stared up at him with her warm wet eyes and he felt himself drowning in their honey depths. Thoughts fled, and whatever he might have been talking about no longer made sense.

It was hard to say which one moved first. Derrick slid his hand from her cheek to the back of her neck about the same time Sarah stood on her toes and wrapped an arm around his neck. Before either one knew the decision had been made, their lips met. Derrick pulled her closer as Sarah stepped closer, and he lost himself in the perfect feel of her against him, of her lips on his.

Her body pressed against him felt so wonderful, so right. Her lips moved against his as if they had been designed for him. A buzzing started in his ears. Heat rushed through his body. He wanted to get closer to her, even closer, feel her skin against his.

Even as he deepened the kiss, he knew he needed to back off a little bit before he lost control all together.

"Oh, I'm so sorry."

Sarah jumped and pushed away from Derrick. She looked scared and horrified and incredibly sexy. He smiled and faced Melissa. "Good morning."

Melissa stammered and stopped, then took a step backward. "I heard the yelling and came out to see if Sarah was okay." Her eyes darted between the two of them. "I'll just go back to bed now."

"No worries. I need to leave anyway." He looked back down at Sarah and ran a finger along her cheek. "When you want to talk, you know where to find me."

Sarah licked her lips nervously and nodded.

"WOW."

Sarah looked at Maxine and took another sip of heavenly vegetable soup. She wiped her lips on the napkin and nodded. "I know, right?"

"So what are you going to do now?"

Sarah sighed and put her spoon down. "I don't know. He wasn't coming here to ask me to dinner Friday night. He had a ring in his pocket!"

Fighting a surge of panic, Sarah pushed the bowl away and took another sip of water. Maxine leaned across the table and patted her hand. "It's Derrick, honey. Just talk to him. He's like your brother."

"Is that remark designed to make me feel better?"

Maxine laughed. "I guess not." She stood and took the bowl to the sink. "Listen. Just go talk to him. Tell him you need time to get your feelings in order but would be open to dating him."

"You're assuming I would be open to dating."

Maxine turned and looked at her. "Tell me you're not. Be serious."

Sarah felt the heat that tinged her cheeks. "Maybe I am."

"Of course you are." Her sister came back across the room and knelt by her chair. "Listen. Derrick has loved you forever. He went to New York to try to forget you, but it didn't do him any good. He loves you like Tony loves Robin, like Barry loves me. But I'm sure he'll be able to tone it down a notch so that you can see if you reciprocate that love."

"I've never talked to him away from absolutely having to. There was a decade between private conversations. I don't really know how to approach him."

"He's waited for you forever, honey. His entire life, in fact. I have no earthly idea why you would want to make him keep waiting but he'll wait as long as you need, I imagine." She stood and rubbed her hands together. "In the meantime, we have to finish the final preparations for your thirtieth birthday party." She clapped her hands. "Hey! I know! Let's go look at the hotel ballroom and make the final plans. It's just four days away."

"I don't know —"

"Oh come on. How many times are you going to have your thirtieth birthday, anyway? I was doing this without you, but you might want to see what we have planned."

"Well —"

"And you can talk to Chef Rupert about your vegan cake. You can probably even convince him to let you sample it."

Her stomach rolled. With a hand pressing against it, she shook her head. "Uh, might be a little soon for tasting."

"Of course. You're right. But you can still talk to him about it."

Sarah pressed her lips together and fought an internal battle that lasted about two seconds. Then she nodded. "Okay. Let me take a shower and get dressed and I'll go with you."

Maxine clapped her hands. "Wonderful! I'll call Chef Rupert now and reschedule the meeting I'd set up for tomorrow."

\

TOPAZ HEAT - CHAPTER 13

DERRICK signed the letter in front of him and set it in his OUT box on the corner of his desk for his secretary to mail. As he reached for the next piece of correspondence requiring his attention, his phone beeped. "Mr. DiNunzio? A Detective Wilson and Detective Beaumont are here to see you."

With a quick flip through his mind seeking anything hotel related that might have recently warranted two detectives showing up, he looked at the phone quizzically. Nothing immediately came to mind, so he said, "Please send them right in, Andrea."

He stood and walked around his desk as his door opened. The first man who walked through the door wore black jeans, a black leather jacket over a white turtleneck, and boots. He had blond hair and a face that looked drawn and tired. Derrick guessed he was maybe fifty. The man held his hand out and smiled a smile that barely showed teeth and did not reach his eyes. "Mr. DiNunzio. I am Jerry Beaumont, Boston PD. This is my partner Nick Wilson."

Derrick shook his hand and turned his attention to the younger man who had just entered his office. He was tall, thin, smooth shaven with dark hair and dark eyes. He wore his blue suit well, pairing it off with a white collared shirt and a maroon tie. Derrick knew good fabric and custom tailoring when he saw it, and filtered his mental database, running through all the Wilsons he knew, stopping at Nicholas Henry Wilson, Sr., sailboat mogul. "Junior?"

Wilson's lips thinned before he nodded and held out his hand. "Mr. DiNunzio."

Something about his eyes tickled Derrick's memory, but he didn't take the time to explore it. After shaking his hand, Derrick said, "Please come in." He gestured to his sitting area. "What can I do for two of Boston's finest today?"

He took the armchair while the two detectives took the couch. Beaumont took the lead. "Mr. DiNunzio, we're here about Gianni Castolli."

Derrick felt his insides go cold, but kept the smile firmly on his face.

"I'm sorry?"

Wilson spoke. "I think you heard us."

"I did. I just don't understand. What do you mean?"

"There was a time when you ... worked ... for Mr. Castolli, is that correct?"

Derrick fought the urge to stand and pace. Instead he leaned back in his chair and folded his hands together. "That is correct. While I understand that exemplary wouldn't actually describe my life all those years ago, I'm certain that nothing I did would warrant two detectives from our fine city's police force to take time out of what must be a busy day to come talk to me."

"I wouldn't be so sure." This time, Beaumont showed some teeth. "We'd like to discuss in detail some of those things you might have done."

"To what end?"

"Justice, Mr. DiNunzio."

Derrick raised an eyebrow. "While I'd guess that any of my petty activities would be cleared by statutes of limitations at this point, I'm actually quite certain that I don't have to discuss any activities that took place prior to my eighteenth birthday."

Wilson pulled a notebook out of his pocket. "There is no statute of limitations on murder, Mr. DiNunzio."

His stomach twisted into a painful knot. "Murder?"

"Yes."

"Whose murder?"

"We recently discovered the remains of James Castolli. Gianni Castolli's son."

"What?" The word came out on a breath, barely a whisper.

"He had been missing for ten years. As far as our forensic pathologists can determine, he's been dead for that long, too."

"I don't understand. Why are you talking to me? I didn't even know he was missing."

Wilson said, "You were the last person to be seen talking to him when he was still alive."

Memories started crashing in. Cold. Hunger. Desperation. Hopelessness. Prejudice. Cops always looking his way.

Derrick closed his eyes and took a deep breath, praying for the memories to be held at bay for just a moment, just long enough to get through this interview. He opened them again and spoke very carefully. "If you will wait for a moment, gentlemen, I'm afraid I need to call my lawyer."

Beaumont said, "In my world, innocent people don't need an attorney, Mr. DiNunzio."

"Coming from my old world, Detective Beaumont, no one is really all that innocent, are they?"

SARAH pulled on the hem of her shirt as she got out of her car. She handed her keys to the valet attendant on duty and walked through the big circular doors into the grand luxury that was the lobby of the Viscolli Hotel, Boston. She couldn't help but feel pride at Tony for creating this beautiful environment and at Derrick for running it. It wasn't easy, his job, and she admired what he was able to do.

She nodded to the desk clerk, someone who had worked there for years and knew Sarah by sight, then went down a hidden corridor behind the front desk and into the administrative section of the hotel. She passed the event coordinator's office, the assistant manager's office, the housekeeping manager's office, and finally came to the end of the corridor. Double doors led into Derrick's outer office.

She tugged at her shirt one more time before opening the doors. She stepped in and nodded to the secretary. "Hi Andrea. How are you?"

"Why, Sarah. What a surprise."

In a way, she'd hoped that the secretary would jump up and claim that Derrick had been waiting for her to come and that no matter what he was in the middle of, he was to be interrupted whenever Sarah showed up. She was amused at her own flight of fancy and smiled. "Is Derrick in? I'd like to see him."

"He is, but in a meeting just this second."

The doors behind Sarah slammed open. She jumped and looked behind her, surprised to see Barry storming in. He stopped short when he saw her. "Sarah. What are you doing here?"

Sarah opened her mouth then shut it, confused by the aggressiveness emanating from the big guy in front of her. "I was just here to see Derrick."

He nodded and pulled the vibrating phone out of the front pocket of his suit. "Now's not a great time." He read whatever was on his screen, pushed a series of buttons, and then pocketed the phone.

"I'm not sure I ..."

The doors slammed open again and Tony rushed in. "Have you been in yet?" He directed his attention to Barry and Barry only.

"I just got here." Barry gestured at Sarah. Tony looked at her with a harshness in his eyes she didn't really understand. Sarah started to get a little bit worried about what was going on.

"Hi," she said, stepping forward for Tony's customary cheek kiss and hug. Instead, he gripped her shoulders and looked down at her.

"Now's not a good time," he said, parroting Barry's words. "Best go on home."

"Tony, I..."

He shook his head once, sharply, silencing anything else she was about to say. He squeezed her shoulders and released her. "Let's go in," he said to Barry. He looked back at Sarah. "Go. I'm sure Derrick will call you when he's free to talk."

As the door to Derrick's office opened, Sarah looked in and saw Derrick seated in a wing backed leather chair, his fingers steepled in front of his face, his eyes closed. One man sat on a sofa near him and another man, a younger man whom Sarah almost recognized, stood behind Derrick's chair, scowling at Tony and Barry as they entered the office.

As the door shut, Sarah saw Derrick's eyes open. He looked around Barry and saw her standing there. A look of deep surprise passed over his face before he could school his features. He stood and shook Barry's hand, then turned his back on the door as it shut all the way.

Sarah huffed out a breath and turned to look at the secretary. "Well."

Andrea grimaced and picked up a pen. "Would you like for me to leave a message?"

Sarah looked at the seats against the wall then looked at her "You know what," she said, "I think I'll just wait here."

"I really have no idea how long they'll be."

Sarah smiled. "That's okay. I'm off today."

She sat down in a cloth covered chair and picked up the news magazine that sat on the table next to her. She noticed Tony on the cover, and slowly flipped through the pages until she found the lengthy article about her brother-in-law. Absently, she wondered if she would learn anything new about him.

"THIS is absurd," Tony said. "Derrick never killed anyone."

"You can't know that, Mr. Viscolli."

Tony gritted his teeth and stepped forward. "Wanna bet?"

Barry stepped between the two men. "Okay. Tell me what you want us to do."

Detective Wilson hung up his phone. "We'd like to take Mr. DiNunzio down to the station and question him."

"Out of the question," Tony said.

Barry glared Tony quiet before turning his attention back to the detective. "Are you placing him under arrest?"

"Not at this time. But get Mr. Viscolli under control or I'll arrest *him* for obstruction."

Tony shoved his hands in his pockets and whipped around toward Derrick. "*L'ha fatto uccide quest'uomo?*"

Derrick smiled, torn between trying to decide if he was more amused at the fact that Tony asked if he'd killed the man, or if he asked the question in Italian. Derrick didn't speak Italian very well at all and it amazed him that he even understood the question. "No."

Tony whirled back around. "There. Asked and answered. You don't need to question him any further."

Detective Beaumont barked a short laugh. "As much as we appreciate your assistance, Mr. Viscolli, we need to conduct our interview in a little more formal surroundings." He looked at Derrick. "Are you willing to go with us voluntarily?"

Barry answered. "We'll go in our own transportation and meet you there."

Beaumont clenched his jaw but nodded. "Very well. But leave that one here." He pointed at Tony. "He won't help matters."

With a nod, Barry watched the two detectives leave. As soon as the door was shut, he looked at Derrick. "Tell me everything they said to you."

Derrick surged to his feet, free to show agitation now. "They didn't say anything except that I was the last person to be seen with him."

"Him who?"

"James Castolli." He swiveled his head and looked at Tony. "Gianni Castolli's son."

Tony whistled under his breath. "Heavy players."

"Yeah."

Barry asked him another question. "When did you last see him?"

Derrick scrubbed his face with his hands and paced around the office. "The night before I left."

Barry pulled out his phone and typed in some notes. "What were the circumstances of that meeting?"

Derrick shoved his hands into his pockets and pivoted on his heel so that he could face Barry. "He said he'd kill me if I didn't do something for him."

"What something?"

"Run some drugs from the Cape to the city."

Barry raised an eyebrow. "So what did you do?"

"I agreed to the deal. Then I took the money he fronted me and put it in an envelope with a note that gave him some crude instructions about what he could do with the money. I left it on his doorstep and took the Charlie to this building."

"What did the note say, exactly? Did you threaten him?"

"I don't remember, Barry. It's been ten years. I don't think I threatened him out of context."

Barry nodded. "Then what?"

"Then I spent the night out by the Dumpsters and when Tony arrived, I waited an hour before I got up the courage to head to his office."

"You talk to anyone in that time? Anyone see you?"

"Nah. I was good at not being seen."

"Do you have any idea who might have killed James?"

Derrick frowned. "I didn't even know he was missing but I've had time to think since the cops got here this morning. The truth is, the list of people who wanted him dead would be a very long list."

Barry sighed and put the phone back in his pocket. "Right. To the best of your recollection, did you ever threaten him?

"I don't remember ever seriously threatening him. His father could have made me disappear, after all."

Barry nodded. His eyes reassured the younger man and his confidence bolstered him even more. "Okay. We're going to go talk to them. Try not to lose your temper. And if I tell you to stop talking, bite your tongue off if you have to but do not say another word."

Derrick nodded and walked over to his desk where he got his suit coat and slipped it on. "Anything else?"

"Just tell the truth." Barry stepped in front of him, making him stop his forward motion. "All of the truth about everything, Derrick. Don't let a question about illegal activity or interpersonal relationships make you feel like you need to lie. If this is a murder investigation, they're not going to care about a VCR combo you stole and fenced a decade ago."

Tony interjected, "Remember something else. You are forgiven for all that. Remember that you serve a higher calling and truth and justice are in His very nature."

Derrick clenched his teeth and gave a curt nod of his head. He started from the room and paused by Tony. "I'll be back soon."

Tony grabbed him and enveloped him in a hug. "I'll be here if you need me, brother."

Derrick pounded his fists on Tony's back. "I know."

He let Barry open the office doors and preceded him from the office, stopping short when he saw Sarah still sitting in a chair outside. "What are you still doing here?"

Sarah stood. Derrick felt his stomach muscles clench painfully. "You said that I knew where to find you when I wanted to talk."

Barry and Tony stared at Sarah through narrowed eyes, their faces full of suspicion. She supposed she deserved that from these men. They had probably never heard her utter a kind word to Derrick DiNunzio in living memory.

Rubbing the back of his neck, Derrick released a breath and closed his eyes for a moment. When he opened them, Sarah was looking at him then Barry then back at him with a worried look on her face. "Listen, sweetheart," he said. He paused, as if waiting for her to object to the nickname, but she didn't. So he continued. "I have to go to the police station and make a statement."

"The police?" Sarah stepped forward and grabbed his arm. "What's going on?"

"I don't know everything yet. Can I maybe call you when I get back?" He cupped her cheek and stared down at her. "Is that okay?"

The shock Barry and Tony wore on their faces watching Derrick's intimate touch and Sarah's loving reaction to it could not have looked starker. The men glanced from the scene unfolding before them, then to each other, silently asking if either knew about any of this, then back again.

Sarah searched Derrick's eyes then nodded. "Yeah. Okay. I'll wait to hear from you."

Derrick pulled her forward and kissed her forehead. He closed his eyes and inhaled the sweet smell of her hair then released her. He looked deeply into her eyes one more time, then let Barry lead the way out of the inner office and down the long corridor to the hotel lobby.

He looked back briefly, his gaze taking in the details of this ship he captained that sailed so very smoothly before exiting the building and sliding into the waiting car. He barely heard Barry give the driver the directions of where to go. Instead he closed his eyes and prayed. And prayed.

Chapter 14

SARAH followed Tony out of Derrick's office. She ignored his bid that she go home and instead stayed close on his heels. "I'm not going anywhere, Tony, until you tell me what's going on."

In the elevator that took them straight up to the top floor, Tony turned to look at her. The intensity in his eyes and the aggressiveness of his stance made her more scared than anything else. Not scared. She'd never be afraid of Tony. But worried. Worried about what Derrick had to do at the police station.

"Why do you care?" Tony asked, surprising her.

"I ... I ..."

"You what? You don't like Derrick. You've always made that perfectly clear. So why are you following me instead of listening to me?"

Sarah opened and closed her mouth as she tried to form the words to explain why she cared. Her heart felt like it swelled inside of her chest and then burst, sending a deluge of emotions throughout her entire body. Tears suddenly burned the back of her throat and she swallowed several times, trying to work through the feelings to find her voice again. "Because I love him," she whispered.

She loved him? She loved Derrick? The more she questioned why she said that, the more her heart and soul told her that yes, she very much loved him.

Tony cocked his head and stared at her for a long time. Finally he nodded. "Very well then," he said. "Derrick's being questioned about the murder of an old ... colleague."

All of those emotions that were trying to overwhelm her froze. She felt like her throat was closing in on her. Shaking her head to make sense of his words, she grabbed his arm. "Murder? That's insane."

"I know."

"Barry needs to fix this."

"I know."

"Tony, you have to do something!"

"I know."

The elevator stopped and Tony stormed off, acknowledging the greeting by the receptionist with the wave of his hand. Sarah followed closely on his heels all the way to his office, where he waited for her to enter before slamming the door. He ripped his suit jacket off and loosened his tie on the way to his desk. It shocked Sarah. She'd never seen Tony with even his top button unfastened. He always looked like he was about to take to the runway of a modeling show for upwardly mobile young professionals.

Sarah took the seat in front of his desk and pulled her cell phone out of her pocket. She flipped it open to the keypad and sent a quick text to her sisters.

COME TO THE HOTEL. DERRICK'S IN TROUBLE.

She listened as Tony called Barry's office. "Elizabeth, this is Tony. Tell me who the best criminal defense attorney in the state is. Then have him call me." Sarah took her glasses off and leaned back in her chair. She rubbed her eyes and fielded returned texts from her sisters while Tony continued. "He already had you call him? Great. Good. Thanks."

Tony slammed the phone down and looked at her. "I don't like not being able to do anything."

Sarah shut her phone and nodded. "Me, either."

He stood suddenly and moved around the desk to sit next to her. "So, let's do something. Help me pray." He took her hand and bowed his head, and she followed his lead.

DERRICK sat at the metal table next to Barry and repeated his story for the third time. When he was done, he leaned back in the metal chair and waited.

"Do you remember what the note said?" Wilson asked.

With a sigh, Derrick rubbed the back of his neck. "No. I don't remember. I wasn't –" he cleared his throat, uncomfortable, "I wasn't exactly sober at the time."

Beaumont reached into a box next to him and pulled out a plastic bag that contained a piece of paper. He laid the bag in front of Derrick. "Does this look familiar?"

He picked it up and looked at it. Notebook paper – like one might find in any school kid's desk – was wrinkled and torn. But the bold sloppy handwriting in black marker could still clearly be made out. "You threatened me for the last time. Take your money and choke on it. DD"

"Yeah. That's the note. How do you have this?"

Wilson spoke, "We found it in the bag of money."

"Where?"

Beaumont answered. "Shoved down James Castolli's throat. He was asphyxiated with it."

The breath sucked out of Derrick's body. "What?"

"One might say that he choked on his money."

"Wait."

"Where were you ten years ago on the night of January eleventh?"

Derrick lowered his head and rubbed the back of his neck. "I told you, I spent the night next to the Dumpsters outside of the Viscolli hotel."

"You're telling me that you spent the night outside, in January?"

Barry interjected. "That's what he's told you three times, gentlemen."

Derrick held up his hand and smiled. "You think that was the first time I had to sleep near a Dumpster in the winter?"

"That isn't answering my question." Wilson opened a file in front of him and pulled out a picture the size of a sheet of paper. He slid it across the table to Derrick.

A skeleton lay folded inside of a wall. Some clothes still remained on the body. Derrick recognized the leather bag slung over the shoulder. He wasn't going to play stupid. "Where did you find him?"

"In the basement of the building where you had your old apartment. Jake's Bar. Demolition crews uncovered it three days ago."

Derrick looked at the skeleton, ever thankful Tony had provided a way out of that life for him, a way to avoid a death similar to what he beheld. "I don't know how he got there, but it wasn't my doing."

A rapping sound came from the mirrored glass. Detective Wilson stood and went to the door. He opened the door a crack then slipped out. Curious, Derrick watched Beaumont file the picture and the letter away. He put the lid on the box and slid the box down the table out of reach. "Let's go back to this meeting with Tony Viscolli."

Barry answered. "That isn't relevant to this conversation."

"I think it is."

"I don't see how."

Beaumont opened his mouth to speak again but the door opening interrupted him. A small man with a balding head and a bulging briefcase tumbled into the room. "We're done here, gentlemen," he said in a voice that sounded like a radio announcer.

Barry stood and held out his hand. "Clifford. Thank you for coming."

Clifford shook Barry's hand then took a handkerchief out of his pocket and wiped his sweating head. "You should have waited until I got here before any questions were asked or answered. Well, water under the bridge. Let's go, Mr. DiNunzio."

Beaumont stood. "Cliff, I haven't finished questioning my suspect."

"Are you arresting him?"

"Not yet."

"Then you're finished." He put a hand on the back of Derrick's chair and pulled it back as Derrick stood, following Barry's silent nod of assent. "If you decide to arrest him, contact my office and we'll make arrangements for my client to turn himself in. Make a spectacle of the arrest and I will make you experience lasting regret. I hope you hear me."

Derrick followed Barry and Clifford through the police station to the bright lights of the afternoon outside. Clifford turned to Derrick as soon as they were on the sidewalk. He held out his hand. "I'm Clifford Lowry. Barry's office called me."

"Nice to meet you. Derrick DiNunzio."

"Yes. Let's get to my office and go over this, shall we?" He turned to Barry. "I know you're friends. I don't need you, but I'll understand if you want to be there."

"Tony's coming, too."

"Mr. Viscolli is already there. Apparently, there are some women there, too. These friends of yours ... do they grasp the concept of attorney client privilege?"

Barry chuckled. "We'll do whatever you need us to do, Cliff. I'm really glad you're on this."

"You won't be glad to get my bill. My secretary's bringing lunch in. Viscolli's buying so I went all out. We need to get a lot done before dinner."

Despite the circumstances, Derrick felt light. He thought maybe everything was under control. He thought maybe God was going to use this for some good. "Lunch?" he said. "Good. I'm starving."

SARAH sat next to Derrick at the big conference table in the middle of the twelfth floor of the Lowry, Lowry, Beachum, and Parkinson law firm. He looked exactly the same as he had looked four hours ago. Somehow, she expected him to come back weary and worn.

She pushed her salad around on her plate but had no appetite to eat. No one else in her family did, either. Robin and Maxine had come as soon as they received Sarah's texts, and with Tony they all congregated at Clifford's office and waited for his arrival.

"I can't comprehend why anyone would think you would do this," Sarah said to Derrick.

Clifford shut the file he had in his hand and replied. "They have evidence. Mounds of it."

A surge of angry heat went through Sarah's chest. "I know he couldn't have."

With a flighty flip of his hand, Clifford said, "Love and sunshine and butterflies ... all that isn't going to mean anything in a court of law. The fact is that they have enough of a case that a law student could get him convicted."

Sarah gasped. "How is that even possible?"

"Obviously someone set me up," Derrick said.

"Who would do that?" Sarah asked.

Tony answered from the head of the table. "Sarah, I love your sheltered innocence."

Sarah bit her tongue to keep from countering with a sarcastic, angry retort. She felt her cheeks burn with embarrassed hurt while Tony directed his attention explicitly upon Derrick. "What can you remember about competition? Any personal enemies of yours? Any grudges?"

Derrick rubbed the back of his neck. "Nothing specifically bad is really standing out. I mean, before today if you'd asked me I would have said James Castolli. But other than him…"

The way Derrick paused made Sarah think there might be something occurring to him. "What?" she asked, reaching over and touching his hand. "What is it?"

"Well, maybe Gianni Castolli."

Sarah wrinkled her brow in confusion. "Isn't that his dad?"

"Yeah." Derrick turned his hand so that their palms touched. "Not a nice guy."

"No," Tony agreed, "not a nice guy. You think he's capable?"

"Of killing his son? Maybe. I overheard an argument they had once. If I were his son, I think I would have believed he could kill me at that moment."

Clifford interjected. "And you crossed Gianni?"

With a shrug, Derrick wrapped his uneaten sandwich in its original wrapper. "Sure. I refused to go pick up a drug shipment. Then I disappeared."

Sarah looked at Derrick. "I thought James asked you to do the drug run thing."

Derrick smiled at her. "James told me to do it."

"So James was working for Gianni?"

"Everyone was working for Gianni."

Clifford nodded. "Ah. Okay."

Tony spoke, "And in that type of environment, it's logical to assume that no one would do something as extreme as kill Gianni Castolli's son without his permission."

"Well, he might have been killed, but it would have been very public. A statement."

"We also have to consider something else," Derrick said. Sarah watched his face change with an almost excited expression. "I might have been able to kill James and run away. But I couldn't have killed James by shoving a bag of money down his throat. Not alone. That would have taken a couple of people helping me, then putting him in the wall and closing the wall back up. All the people I knew on that street, all my acquaintances and supposed friends, would never have had the courage to not only do that, but to stay around after. It's all about survival out there, and Gianni Castolli offered survival. At a cost to your soul, yes, but survival nonetheless."

"So we assume that this Gianni Castolli guy killed his own son?" Sarah felt a wave of helplessness. "If he's who you say he is, then there's no way we can do that, is there? In fact, he's sure to have witnesses to say you did it." She laced her fingers with Derrick's. "So what do we do about that?"

Derrick turned his body so that he could face her directly. "We trust God. We stay faithful and strong and trust Him. What will happen will happen, and we'll be able to get through it because that's what we do."

Emotion clutched Sarah's throat. "I don't like this."

With a squeeze of her hand, Derrick turned back to the table and reopened his sandwich. "Join the club," he said with a laugh, and took a hefty bite.

Chapter 15

SARAH rushed to the door when she heard the powerful engine of the Mustang as Derrick's car pulled into her driveway. She opened her door and saw Derrick coming up her walk. He had changed into khaki pants and a dark blue cable knit sweater. He looked up and smiled when he met her eyes. He held up some plastic bags. "I brought dinner," he said, "I didn't think either one of us would be up to going anywhere."

Guessing how grueling his day must have been, Sarah smiled and held the door wider. "It will be nice not to be interrupted every fifteen minutes by a waiter, too."

As Derrick brushed by her, she caught a whiff of his after shave. He smelled very masculine to her – something she had never noticed before. Then she smelled rice and vegetables and felt her stomach rumble. She knew it was pushing nine o'clock, and long hours had passed since the lunch she couldn't stomach in Clifford's conference room.

She followed Derrick into her kitchen and headed straight for a cupboard to get plates while he unpacked what looked like take out from her favorite Japanese restaurant. "Any news?"

Derrick's hands paused briefly before he shrugged and continued to remove cartons of sushi and rice. "Clifford expects a warrant will be issued for my arrest."

Sarah's heart gave a nervous flutter and she felt tears sting the back of her throat. "I don't understand how this can be happening."

When Derrick took the plates from her hands, he purposefully brushed the palms of his hands over the tops of hers. "It's okay."

With her hands free, Sarah slipped her fingers under her glasses and pressed them to her closed eyes, battling back the tears. "It's not okay. You couldn't have done this."

"You know, less than a week ago you would have helped Beaumont throw me under the bus, then brushed your hands off and walked away."

Pressing her lips together because she knew that her attitude and behavior toward him would have led him to believe such a terrible thing,

Sarah went to the refrigerator and pulled out two bottles of water. "I'd like to think that I would have at least trusted Tony's judgment if nothing else," she said. "I know I treated you terribly, but I never thought you were a bad person. Not once."

Derrick held her chair for her. "It's okay, Sweetheart. I know."

"Don't –" she started to give her typical reply to his calling her sweetheart, but she couldn't make her mouth form the words. With her brow knit in confusion, she sat down and set a napkin on her lap. She waited for Derrick to sit then held her hand out to him, knowing that he would want to bless the meal. He took her hand, the rough calluses formed by rock climbing scraping against her smooth skin. She bowed her head and listened to his petition for God to bless the food they were about to receive, and chorused his "amen" when he was done.

"Don't?" he prompted as he dished sushi onto his plate and started smearing it with wasabi.

Sarah cleared her throat. "Nothing."

"I see." He smiled as he popped a sushi roll into his mouth and chewed. Sarah busied herself with fresh ginger and began eating. The more she ate the hungrier she became. Soon the two of them cleared the boxes and bags, leaving behind a wasteland of empty containers and used chopsticks. They filled the meal time with conversations about their nieces and nephews. Sarah's sisters and their husbands had spent many weekends in New York for various reasons over the years, and Tony considered him as much a brother as he considered Barry a brother. Their children had always known Derrick as their "Uncle D."

Once the meal was finished and the bags and boxes disposed of, together they moved from the kitchen into the living room. Sarah sat in the armchair while Derrick sat close to her on the couch. Tired of safe conversations, Sarah broached the subject that still hung in the air between them. "What will you do if you get arrested?"

Derrick leaned back against the cushions and hooked an ankle on his knee. "Pay a hefty fee for Clifford, I imagine."

"How can you be so nonchalant about it?" Sarah said. "Your whole life hangs in the balance here."

"No." Derrick leaned forward and laced his fingers, resting his elbows on his knees. "My whole life is centered on God's love for me, on the feelings you have for me that you're still trying to figure out, and my place in this family. These charges, which will likely come sometime in the next twenty-four hours, are nothing more than my past trying to bring us down."

Sarah leaned forward too, and surprised herself by sandwiching Derrick's hands with her own. The backs of his hands felt warm against her palms. He looked at their joined hands then raised his head to meet her eyes.

"Sarah, I just want to say something. All I can think is how thankful I am that you remembered what you remembered, that I was there with you when it happened, and that while praying I accidentally let you know what my feelings for you are. I'm thankful that God provided us with the opportunity to spend some non-hostile time together before I face this."

He cleared his throat and Sarah squeezed his hands in encouragement as she felt a tear slide down her cheek. He continued, "I am going to need this evening. This will get me through it. Whatever 'It' is, I can face it. Your friendship –"

Sarah licked her lips and raised a trembling hand to Derrick's cheek. "Derrick, I –"

The opening of the door cut off whatever she'd started to say. Melissa came in but stopped when she saw them. "We need to stop meeting like this," she said to Derrick.

He laughed and stood. "Melissa."

She waved a hand. "I'm only here to get my security badge. I left it on top of my dresser." She rushed from the room and Sarah sighed and leaned back in the chair, rubbing her forehead. What had she been about to say? She couldn't even think. Melissa came back very quickly, holding a lanyard that clipped together her hospital identification. "Just pretend I was never here," she said with a wave.

Derrick shoved his hands in his pockets and looked down at Sarah. "Listen, I should go. Tomorrow will prove to be a long day."

"Derrick, wait!" Sarah stood quickly, panicked. "I –"

He put his hands on her shoulders and shushed her. "Listen to me. Don't feel rushed or pressured. I need you to just relax and let this out of your mind for a while." He squeezed her shoulders and stepped backward. "Thank you for allowing me to bring you dinner."

"I just want to spend time with you," she rushed out. He smiled and cupped her cheek with his hand, sending little excited flutters through her heart.

"There will be time. I promise." His gaze held hers for several heartbeats. Before he turned and left the house, he gave her a quick peck on her forehead.

SARAH stood next to her friends in the atrium of her family's church. She made small talk with some friends while people came and went, going to their respective classes for the midweek services. She held her Bible in one hand and her cell phone in the other. While she tried to pay attention to the conversation, she felt focused instead on waiting for the phone to ring. The last twenty-four hours had dragged on and on while everyone just kind of collectively held their breath and waited. But nothing happened. Sarah had started to think that nothing would ever happen, that Tuesday had just been a bad dream.

A hand on her elbow made her turn from her friends and face her pastor, Norman Bishop. "Pastor," she said with a smile, "good to see you."

"We missed you Sunday, Sarah."

"I know. I caught a bug that was going around the hospital."

"That's what your mother said." He nodded his head in the direction over her right shoulder and Sarah turned slightly to see her mother join them.

"Mother."

"Sarah." The pursed lips showed that nothing had been forgiven or forgotten. Sarah felt only a small amount of remorse.

"I just wanted to tell you," the pastor continued, "that Jean and I are looking forward to Friday night. It isn't often that we get to attend a function at the Viscolli's Grand Ballroom."

"Friday?" Sarah felt her brow wrinkle in confusion.

"Your birthday party."

She gasped as she remembered. "I'm sorry. That kind of snuck up on me. With everything that's happened in the last few weeks, time has just flown."

He put a comforting hand on her shoulder. "You and your mom have remained in our prayers. I know your father's passing was hard on you both."

Hot tears stung her eyes as a flash of pain cut at her chest. "It isn't real yet."

"No."

Her mother cleared her throat and Norman looked at her. "Will we see you there as well?"

"I'm afraid not." Darlene adjusted the collar of her coat. "I don't enjoy driving in the city for any reason."

Feeling a bit like a chided child, Sarah stepped out of character and said boldly, "I've taken care of that, mother. I have a car picking you up at seven."

She knew her mother would be trapped by the presence of the pastor and her insistence on etiquette and manners. Her response did not surprise Sarah, but it pleased her. "Very well, then. I guess you will be seeing me." She brushed at the tips of her bangs with the edge of her fingers. "If you'll excuse me, I'll get to my class."

As her mother turned away, Norman spoke again. "Is everything okay here?"

Sarah waved a hand but had to clear her throat around threatening tears. "Not necessarily." She surprised herself with her honesty. "We're at a bit of an impasse right now."

He squeezed her shoulder again and said, "I will pray that you two are able to mend things soon." As he removed his hand, his attention was once again behind her. "Hello there."

Sarah smelled him before she felt his hand on the small of her back. Suddenly feeling a huge weight of doom lifting from her shoulders, she turned her head and smiled at Derrick. "Hi." She felt her face light up, felt the silly grin covering it, but was too happy to see him to pretend otherwise. "Pastor, this is my friend, Derrick. Derrick, Pastor Norman Bishop."

Derrick held out his hand and shook the pastor's. "It's nice to meet you."

"You as well. Is this your first time here?"

"It is. The times I've had the luxury of worshipping with Sarah, she's met me at my church downtown."

"Oh?"

"Yes. Boston Central Bible – BCB."

"That is an amazing church. It does wonderful things for the disadvantaged in the area."

"That is our focus."

"Well, we're happy to have you here tonight." The pastor looked at his watch. "Excuse me, I need to get to my classroom."

Sarah turned and faced Derrick fully. "I'm so happy to see you!"

He smiled and put a hand on her arm, then ran it down the length of her arm, squeezing her fingers before relinquishing the touch. Sarah immediately felt comforted, calm, and steady. "So far, everything today has been normal." He gestured at her nursing uniform. "I see you worked today."

"Yes. I had a six to six shift, so I just came straight here." She tilted her head to look at him. "I left you a message at work when I got off."

"I know. I've been in meetings all day. Trying to prep the staff for my..." he paused and clenched his teeth. "...my absence without really letting them know there will be one."

"Derrick –"

"Sarah. It's okay; it's more important that I plan than ignore."

"I just –" She paused and licked her lips. She wanted to tell him that she loved him. She needed to tell him that she loved him. But she didn't need him to hear it standing in the lobby of her church. "I wish we knew what will happen."

Derrick smiled and reached for her hand. This time he did not let it go. "I have been doing a lot of reading in Psalms. It's amazing how much comfort can be garnered by reading the words of a man being pursued and persecuted. Here is one I've committed to memory to sustain me through this trial. 'The Lord is my strength and my shield; My heart trusted in Him, and I am helped; Therefore my heart greatly rejoices, And with my song I will praise Him.'"

He squeezed her hand and she felt the reassurance all the way up her arm. "I'm here to praise Him, and I would really enjoy doing it with your hand in mine."

Sarah felt lighter, calmer, less burdened. She nodded and righted her glasses on her nose with her free hand. "I'd like that very much."

As they turned for her to lead him to her class, she caught a glance at her mother, who stared at her with such firm disapproval that Sarah could almost hear the look. She resisted the childish urge to stick her tongue out at her mother, and instead looked up at Derrick and smiled.

TOPAZ HEAT - CHAPTER 16

AS the last notes of the birthday song died down and applause erupted, Sarah blew out all thirty candles on the three-tiered cake and accepted the kiss on each cheek from her sisters. The smile on her face was strained enough that her muscles started to hurt, but she kept it plastered on because she didn't want anyone in her family to think she wasn't having the time of her life.

Derrick wasn't there.

Minutes had clicked into hours and hours had clicked into days and still no word from the police. The last time she'd talked to Derrick, he'd been prepping for a morning meeting, but assured her that he would see her there at the hotel for the party. But the party had been in full swing for an hour, and still nothing. She laughed and cut cake and fought back the tears that threatened to mar the makeup Maxine had coated on her face.

What if they'd arrested him and everyone was trying to protect her so that she'd enjoy her party? Worse yet, what if they'd arrested him and he hadn't made his phone call yet, so everyone was here yucking it up while he sat in central holding, or whatever they called it?

She rubbed her hands on the shiny material of her dress and nodded a hello to a nurse friend. She wore a dress the color of tarnished bronze that fit tight and showed off her small frame. The sleeves hugged her arms to her wrists, the hem stopped just at her knees, and the neck scooped a little lower than normal. She had to resist the urge to tug at it. Around her neck she wore a choker of hammered gold – her birthday gift from Robin – and her hair was bundled loosely on the top of her head, allowing curly strands to fall and wisp along her neck.

"Do you want some cake?" Maxine asked, holding out a plate with a thin slice on it.

Sarah shook her head. "Not really."

"It's vegan." She smiled and handed it to a guest before she picked up another plate. "No dairy products at all. Not even eggs. Though how the chef did it is beyond me."

She took the plate because she felt like it would be rude not to. "You'll have to get the recipe," she said, forcing the fork to her mouth and taking a small bite. She gestured at the table loaded with gifts. "What do I do with those?"

Maxine laughed and slung an arm around her shoulders. Her sister, as always, looked stunning in a jade green sheath. A jade necklace and bracelet complimented the dress, and her hair swung unbound to her shoulders. "Open them."

"Do I have to do it here?" The thought terrified her, being the center of attention for just blowing out the candles was hard, spending the time it would take to open the presents was too much. "I thought the invitations said no gifts."

"No, you don't. And yes, they did. But people are going to bring gifts, anyway." She stopped to hand out more cake. "Tell you what, I'll have the driver load them into the car and you can come out to Robin's tomorrow right after breakfast. The twins are spending the night there, and the kids can help you open all of them. It will make up for the fit they all threw about not being able to come tonight. Barry and I will probably sleep there, too, and that way we can all see your loot."

Maybe she'd feel more jovial in the morning. "That sounds like a good idea." She set the half-eaten cake on the corner of the table. "I think I'll go out onto the patio for a while. I'll be back."

Maxine put both hands on her shoulders and stared at her face. "You okay, kiddo?"

"I'm fine," she said with a forced smile. "I'm just not used to all this attention."

Maxine shook her head. "No. That's not it. It's Derrick. I know that the stress must be terrible on you and him. But we'll just trust God that this will all work to His glory. Other than that, it's out of our control."

Sarah's breath hitched and she bit the inside of her lip. "Okay. Thank you." Taking another deep breath, she said, "I love the party Maxi, it's exactly what I wanted. I can't believe you even flew family members out, and I'm touched completely. I'm just a little off tonight. . Just let me get some air and I'll feel better."

Maxine hugged her and handed her a glass of punch. "Here. Go sit outside, drink this, get some air, and come back ready to dance."

Her laugh was real this time. "I will. I promise."

It took her ten minutes to get to the doors of the patio. She had to stop and speak with everyone in her path, and by the time she made it to the doors, she felt desperate just to get out of the room.

Outdoor heaters surrounded the patio, beating back the cold of the night. Even so, chilly air formed goose bumps on her arms, but she had no desire to go back inside and get her wrap. Instead, she wrapped her arms around herself.

"Looks like a good turnout."

Sarah whipped around to see her mother standing near the patio door, dressed in a beautiful satin gown the color of rich wine. "Mom."

Her mother pursed her lips. "I'm surprised you're still willing to call me that."

Sarah stepped forward, but didn't reach out. "Of course I'm willing to call you that. That's exactly who you are."

"I haven't been a good one."

"What?" Sarah reached out this time, and hugged her mom, her eyes filling with tears. "Mom, don't say that. I love you. I have missed you so much."

"I've missed you, too." Her mom hugged her then stepped back and gestured to a stone bench. They sat, facing each other, knees touching. "I know you were angry with me for putting your father in the home. I'm afraid that my defenses pushed you away rather than argue with you about it. You took his death so hard that I was worried about you, and when you didn't come to church that Sunday, when I walked into your house, I immediately thought the very worst of you and of your friend. Instead of graciously admitting that I made a mistake, I made it all worse."

She reached out and took Sarah's hand. "I love you, Sarah, and I am sorry about the last year. The worse about everything I felt, the worse I treated you. I'm lucky I didn't lose you."

"You didn't lose me." Sarah squeezed her mother's hand. "I'm so happy you're here."

"I'd like to speak to your young friend. I owe him an apology, too."

Sarah licked her lips. "He's not here right now."

Darlene cocked her head waiting for more, but Sarah said nothing else. "I see. I was under the impression that you two were close."

"We are. I mean, we want to be." Sarah huffed out a breath. "I mean, I love him."

"Considering he was at your apartment to propose, I'm sure that makes him very happy."

"Well, I haven't told him yet."

"Why?"

"Because –" Pulling her hand from her mother's, Sarah stood. "There's this thing that has been kind of getting in the way –"

"There you are." Sarah spun around and saw Derrick coming out the patio doors. He looked amazing in his black tuxedo and stark white shirt. "I looked inside for you and couldn't find you. I figured you came out for some air."

Sarah rushed to him and threw her arms around his neck. "I was so worried!"

Derrick laughed. "I had a meeting across town. Coming back, a massive wreck had me stuck for over an hour. I walked into the hotel and into a major crisis that dominoed into another crisis. I kept thinking it would just be a moment longer, or I would have contacted you."

Sarah stepped back and gestured nervously toward her mother, who had stood. "My mom came, too."

Derrick smiled and held out his hand. "Mrs. Thomas. It's good to see you again."

This time Darlene took his hand, warmly, with both of hers. "It's good to see you again, too, Derrick. I was just telling my daughter that I'd hoped we had a chance to speak."

"Of course."

"I just wanted to apologize for mistreating you and for anything I said that hurt you."

Derrick nodded. "I accept your apology. Thank you." He held out an arm. "May I escort you two beautiful women into the party?"

Darlene touched his arm but did not take it. "Why don't you two take another few minutes alone? I can see my brother right inside the patio doors. I think I'll join him." She turned to Sarah and put her hands on Sarah's arms. "Happy birthday, my darling daughter."

"Thank you, mom."

Sarah felt herself relax completely. Her smile beamed across her face, and her heart felt light for the first time in days. Derrick put his arm across her shoulders and hugged her to him. He smelled nice, she thought, masculine and clean.

"I hate that I missed you blowing out all thirty of your candles," he said.

"Nice," she teased. "Rub it in, young man."

"It's just that thirty is so far off for me."

Sarah laughed and playfully jabbed him in the ribs. "I sometimes forgot I'm two years older than you."

"I'll make sure to keep reminding you, old lady."

"Har."

Derrick hugged her tight to him before he released her and stepped away. He reached into his jacket pocket and pulled out a long box. "Happy birthday, Sarah."

Sarah gasped and started to reach for the box but then pulled her hand back. Derrick smiled. "Go ahead. Open it," he said.

This time when she reached out, she took the box. With hands that shook a little, she opened the lid. There, nestled in a bed of velvet, lay a stunning bracelet. Rectangular cut topaz stones the color of rich, warm honey lay surrounded by pearls, all twisted together in a beautiful antique silver chain. She ran her finger over the stone as tears filled her eyes.

"This is so beautiful," she said.

"You're beautiful. These are just rocks in comparison," Derrick said, taking the bracelet out of the box. He slipped it over her wrist and efficiently clasped the clasp. It felt heavy, the metal and stones cold against her skin. She moved her wrist around, admiring the way the stones sparkled in the lights coming from the ballroom, how the pearls warmed the stone.

She looked up at Derrick and the love she felt for him overflowed her heart. "Thank you."

He cupped her cheek and leaned forward, briefly brushing his lips over hers. "You're welcome, sweetheart."

Sarah smiled and stepped closer to him. "Have I ever told you that I like it when you call me that?" Her voice sounded husky even to her own ears. She dropped the box and slipped her arms around his neck, rising up on her toes while pulling his head back down to hers. She felt the bracelet slide down her arm as his lips covered hers.

Derrick wrapped an arm around her waist and pulled her close. The chill of the evening air completely faded away and her senses were pummeled with the feel of him, the smell of him, the taste of him. As he deepened the kiss, he gripped the back of her head. Sarah felt her knees weaken, felt her head spin.

She ripped her mouth away and gripped the lapels of his tuxedo jacket, resting her forehead on his chest as she struggled to catch her breath. His arms came around her, strong and safe, and he rested his cheek on the top of her head.

After several long moments, she heard the sounds of the party and realized that they needed to go back inside. She raised her head and stepped back just slightly, enough to look up at Derrick.

"I guess we better go back in."

With a smile, he cupped her cheek again. "Of course. Let's go eat cake and party."

Sarah gripped his wrist with both hands and turned her head so that she could kiss his palm. "I'd rather stay out here with you."

With a chuckle, Derrick put an arm over her shoulder and turned them so that they could walk to the doors. "Duty to your sisters calls. We'll have more time later."

Desperately hoping that was so, Sarah smiled and stepped back into the party.

She chatted with an aunt who had flown in from Nevada, and watched as Darlene introduced Derrick to her brother. He won over her family, making them laugh and smile and interact with him with seemingly little effort. Occasionally, he would come to her and talk to her, putting a hand on the small of her back or rubbing a shoulder. It felt right, to work the room with him this way, working together as they moved through the crowd. It felt right to be with him, paired with him, one half of a couple.

Eventually they stood near her sisters by one of the buffet tables. The entire menu was vegan, and Sarah loved seeing all the different dishes the hotel chefs had managed to come up with.

Barry popped an endive leaf smeared with tapenade into his mouth and washed it down with his customary Shirley Temple. "What's up with the no meat, anyway, Sarah? I've never asked."

Sarah started to shrug, but then remembered. "One of my mother's boyfriends force-fed me raw hamburger meat one time after I complained of being hungry." She rubbed her arms and shuddered. "I really couldn't stomach meat after that."

Barry paused in the middle of chewing his lettuce leaf and looked at her with wide eyes. "Wow." He finished chewing and swallowed. "Can we talk about introducing a little dairy to your diet?"

Maxine laughed and put her arm around her husband's waist. "Barry, my nutritionist and fitness expert."

Sarah smiled. "I know. I've thought about it and probably will start a little bit. Take some baby steps."

Barry nodded. "Let me know if you want some help with that."

With warm love flowing out of her heart, Sarah hugged her brother-in-law. "I will. Thank you."

Tony put a hand on Derrick's shoulder. *"C'è la venuta di difficoltà."* At Derrick's questioning look, Tony said, "Trouble." He gestured to the door with a nod of his head.

"Trouble?" Derrick turned in that direction, and froze. Sarah saw a fleeting look of alarm before it was replaced by steely anger. Her eyes followed their glance and she felt her stomach fall to her knees.

Detectives Wilson and Beaumont marched through the big double doors with two uniformed police officers flanking them. Derrick turned to Sarah. "Listen to me. Whatever happens, and whatever you hear, I want you to hear from me that I didn't do this."

Sarah reached up and framed his face with her hands. "I know. I want you to hear from me that I love you and I will see this through with you."

Emotion flared in Derrick's eyes. He reached up and gripped her wrists with his hands. "I'm not asking you to do that. I don't know what's going to happen."

"That's okay." Through nervous tears, Sarah smiled. "God knows what's going to happen, and He wouldn't have brought you and I this close together this quickly if He didn't intend for us to be together. You hang onto that. Let that keep you positive. And I'll be doing whatever I can for you."

He pulled her hands down, briefly kissing her palm. "Okay. I love you."

"Mr. Derrick DiNunzio," Detective Wilson said as he approached the group. "You are under arrest for the murder of James Castolli. You have the right to remain silent…"

Sarah felt her emotions kind of skid to a halt as she watched them pat Derrick down and handcuff him before leading him out of the ballroom. She looked around and saw everyone at the party stopped, staring, watching. She met the eyes of her mother, who simply raised a questioning eyebrow. She mouthed the words, "It's okay," across the room, then turned to Tony.

"Why in the world did they do that here?" She whispered.

"I guess so they could start the public opinion of his guilt before anything even gets out," he said with clenched teeth. "Lot of power players for the city in this room. They'll picture Derrick being hauled away in handcuffs from now on." He turned to Barry. "This is unacceptable."

Barry nodded with his phone to his ear. "Agreed," he said in a clipped tone. He turned his focus to the phone. "Clifford? Barry. They made it public. Yeah."

Sarah laced her hands together and felt her sisters close to each side. "We need to leave before people start asking questions."

Robin put an arm around her shoulders. "Let's go up to Tony's office. Maxine can disband the party."

The emotions she'd put on hold to keep a brave face for Derrick started to come back. Her knees knocked together, and it was all she could do to hold the sob in before she got out of the ballroom. She covered her mouth with her hand and picked up the pace, running by the time they neared the elevators. As soon as she was safely inside with just Robin, she collapsed against her and let the sobs out.

TOPAZ HEAT - CHAPTER 17

Chapter 17

BY the time they finished processing Derrick, it was early Saturday morning. Once they arrested him and transported him to holding, Derrick never saw the detectives again. They didn't ask him any questions, nor did they corroborate any of his previous statements. They simply cuffed him, put him in a car, and drove him to the station.

Once there, he was photographed, fingerprinted, given an orange jumpsuit to wear, and placed in a cell. Luckily, the jail chaplain was making his rounds shortly thereafter, and gave him a Bible. He spent the weekend in a cell with two other men. He left them alone, and they left him alone to sit on his cot and read or pray.

Monday morning, they let him shave but did not let him change clothes. He was forced to enter the courtroom shackled to a long line of other prisoners, who waited their turns for the bail hearing. He saw Sarah and the rest of the family in the courtroom, and gave a brief nod of his head so that they knew he saw them.

Sarah's face looked drawn and pale, but she seemed calm. He watched Tony lean over Robin and speak to Sarah, saw her speak in reply and look back at him again. She smiled, placed a hand over her heart in a silent gesture of affirmation. Derrick didn't realize how much tension he felt over her condition until he saw her and felt it slowly dissipate from his body.

He didn't feel concerned for himself. He only felt concerned for Sarah and for the rest of the family. What would a murder conviction do to them?

When his name was called, he waited for the bailiff to remove him from the chain gang train, then took his place next to Clifford at the table.

The judge originally denied bail, but Clifford fought and assured and fought some more until he finally relented. Derrick closed his eyes and raised his face toward the heavens, silently thanking God that he didn't have to wait out the time until the trial from a jail cell.

Three hours later, Derrick left the jail wearing his tuxedo. He went straight to his borrowed downtown apartment where he found his family congregated in the sunken living room.

After he showered and changed clothes, he joined them, his bare feet sinking down into the plush carpet. He walked toward Sarah, who sat in an armchair. She looked up at him, her face mostly expressionless. "Can we talk alone for a minute?"

Sarah hopped up. "Sure."

"We'll go make some coffee and come back out."

He put a hand on the small of her back and assured Tony he'd be right back. "Clifford will be here in thirty minutes," Tony said.

"Good. We should have something brought in. I'm starving."

Maxine waved her hand. "I've taken care of it. There's a pot of stew on the stove and biscuits just out of the oven. You two go talk. I'll get it on the table when you're done with the room."

He led Sarah through the dining room and into the kitchen. As soon as the door shut behind him, she turned and put her arms around his waist, her face buried in his chest. "It's so good to see you."

He wrapped his arms around her and rested his cheek against her hair, closing his eyes and breathing in the scent of her shampoo. "It's good to see you, too."

She pulled back a little and looked up at him. "Was it just awful?"

With a shrug, Derrick stepped back and put his hands in the pockets of his jeans. "Actually, not so bad. The food was pretty terrible, and the bed uncomfortable, but otherwise I was left alone. The chaplain got me a Bible, so I was able to spend a lot of time with God." He ran a finger down her cheek. "What about you? Fallout from mommy?"

"Strangely, no. She came up with me to Tony's office Friday night and asked me what was going on. Robin and I filled her in on all we knew. She asked if you'd done it, we told her no, and she said to tell you she'd be praying for you. The next morning, she even called me and told me if I needed to talk, to give her a call."

"Why the sudden change of heart?"

Sarah shrugged and tugged at the sleeves of her shirt. "Maybe she just loves me."

Derrick felt a warm glow in his heart. He tucked a strand of auburn curls behind her ear. "Easily done."

He pushed away from the counter and set about making a pot of coffee. "I'm glad that dealing with her is now off your plate. You have enough going on."

"Derrick," Sarah said, putting a hand over his, stopping him from measuring coffee beans. "Are you afraid?"

Derrick felt his jaw clench and cleared the emotion out of his throat. "Sweet Sarah, fear is not of the Lord." Every time he felt like the world was closing in on him, he referred back to that verse.

"I'm trying not to be afraid, but I just keep thinking –"

He pulled her into his arms, partly to comfort her, partly to comfort himself. "It's okay. I won't go down without a fight."

"WHAT will our strategy be?" Barry asked, file folder open in front of him. He turned a page and read the arrest report. Next to him, he made notations in his legal pad.

"According to our client," Clifford said, sipping his coffee as he turned a page in the book before him, "profession of innocence."

Barry raised an eyebrow. "Oh?"

Derrick clenched his teeth. "What else is there?"

Barry turned his head to look at him. "Nothing, really. But the way the police handled this, I'm sure they bungled something."

"If I want to continue to do what I do for a living, I'll need to be completely exonerated."

With a shrug, Barry made another note in his pad. "That is absolutely true."

"That may not even be enough," Tony said, lips thinned. "I'm still angry about the way they arrested you. There's no way to keep the covers on it now."

Derrick sighed. "You know I can't work until the trial. You'll lose customers."

Tony waved his hand. "*Non mi importa.*"

"Well, you should care."

"If I lay you off, or fire you, or send you on sabbatical, it will make it seem like I think you're guilty. Since you're not, you'll work." Tony stared intently at Derrick. "Tomorrow morning, be in your office. No excuses."

Derrick held Tony's stare for a long time before breaking it and laughing. "Very well." He pointed his finger at his friend and mentor. "But be prepared for a serious decline in clientele."

"Bah," Tony said, waving his hand in a dismissive gesture, "maybe for a while. Actually, I expect a spike of looky-loos. After that, well, people have short memories."

"Speaking of clientele," Clifford said. "Tony, I need you and everyone else to leave. Barry can stay, but we need to talk to Derrick alone. Your being here destroys attorney-client privilege."

Tony stood, his jaw clenched. "I understand." He turned to Derrick. "Call if you need me."

Derrick nodded. "Thanks."

After Tony left the room, Clifford stared hard at Derrick. "During your time alone," he said, "did you give any thought as to who might want to set you up?"

Derrick ran both hands through his hair. "Of course, but I can't come up with anything. I would have said James Castolli would set me up, or his dad. But if his dad did it, he would have done it out in the open, with cause, and to send a message to everyone else: I'm willing to kill my own son ... watch your step. There wasn't a single person in that neighborhood who would have had the guts to cross Castolli enough to kill his son."

"But they didn't do it with guts. They framed you."

"Maybe because I was already gone?"

Barry paused in his note-taking. "Who knew?"

"Who knew what?"

"Who knew you were leaving?"

With a shrug, Derrick said, "No one. I..." Memories flooded. "Wait. Maybe one person knew. Let me think." He closed his eyes and rubbed his forehead. "Yeah. Ginger knew. I asked her if she wanted to come with me, and she laughed at me and told me I'd be back."

Barry raised an eyebrow. "Ginger?"

"Yeah, uh," Derrick cleared his throat. "Ginger Castolli."

"Let me guess," Clifford said, rubbing his forehead. "Castolli's daughter?"

Derrick sighed. "She was seventeen. We'd been on and off for about a year. Right then we were on about to be off again. We'd had a huge blow up fight, but I saw her out that night and asked her to run away with me."

"Do you think she told anyone?" Barry asked.

"I don't know. She was pretty..." Derrick paused again, feeling ashamed for some reason. "She was pretty stoned at the time. There's no telling."

Barry scribbled something in his notepad. "It's worth following up."

"Following up?"

"Sure." Barry capped his pen and closed the cover of his notebook. "It might be worth a little bit of Perry Mason to poke around and see if we can get any idea as to who framed you."

"What good will that do? No one else is on trial here. All of the evidence points to me." Derrick pushed away from the table. "Go digging up old bones and everything I've worked hard to escape will come crashing back down on me."

Barry stood as well, towering over him. "You are a new creature in Christ. That doesn't mean we shouldn't investigate other possibilities. Bones are going to come out of the closet. We can't stop that. Just don't lie, stand firm, and you'll get through this."

"Easy for you to say."

Barry cocked an eyebrow. "Yes. It is easy. What else would you like for me to say?"

Releasing a heavy sigh, Derrick sat back down. "Nothing. There is nothing that can be said." He pulled his phone out of his pocket and made himself a message. "I'll go visit her. Talk to her."

"Not alone," Clifford said, making notes. "You take someone with you. Barry or Tony."

"Okay."

DERRICK rolled his head on his neck before lifting his fist to knock on the door of the apartment number six. The six had loosed itself from the nails holding it in place and swung downward, making it look like a number nine.

Tony looked around him, at the dingy hallway, the garbage strewn floor, the flickering fluorescent lighting, and said, "Not exactly Castolli's castle."

"I know. I heard Castolli got busted about a year after I left. Looks like he didn't leave Ginger with the fortune."

The door swung open onto a chain and a very haggard and prematurely aged face appeared on the other side, but he recognized her. Lines formed around her mouth, circles darkened the skin under her eyes, and a bad hair dye job made her once black tresses look sickly purple, but he recognized her. "Ginger?"

She spoke around a cigarette hanging out of her mouth. "Double D? Well, if this ain't all that be." The door shut in his face then opened wide, no chain. The smell of the apartment almost made him take a step back. The long forgotten smell of cheap gin and burning drugs assaulted his nasal passages. "What are you doing here?"

He gestured to Tony. "Do you remember Tony Viscolli?"

She drew hard on her cigarette, then removed it from her mouth. Her long fake nails were scarlet red. "I only ever heard of the legend. I've never had the honor in person." She smiled, showing a mouth missing too many teeth. "Pleased to make your acquaintance."

Derrick watched Tony slap on the charm. "I knew you when you were a little baby," he said. "I remember rosy cheeks and cute little black curls. Your daddy loved to bounce you on his knee."

Ginger laughed then coughed then wheezed in another drag of the cigarette. "Come in." She held the door wider and waved them into her apartment. "Ain't what you's used to, I'm sure."

Derrick surveyed the apartment: dirty, lone couch; fast food bags and boxes; empty bottles. A young girl of about ten sat in a beanbag in the corner, holding a handheld game system. She looked at them with bored, stoned eyes, and then went back to her game. "That's my Delilah. Don't mind her." Ginger coughed again, then put the butt of the cigarette out into an overflowing ashtray. "What's up, D? Why are you knocking on my door for the first time in forever ago?"

Derrick slipped his hands into his pants pockets. "It's about James, Ginger."

"You heard about that, eh? That was some freaky stuff there, man." Ginger grabbed a glass off the coffee table and took a swig. She shuddered, swallowed, then wiped her mouth. "Freaky."

"I heard about it." He rocked back on his heels. "Think back for a minute, Ginger. Do you remember the night I left?"

Her eyes glazed over and she looked at a spot above his shoulder. "Kinda."

"Do you remember me asking you to come with me?"

She shrugged, then grabbed a pack of cigarettes off the table and pulled one out. "Sure. You had a job, you said. You was going straight."

"Did you tell anyone else about my job?"

She grabbed a lighter off the table and tried to light it. She flicked it three or four times, then tossed it on top of the mess that lay on the table. She moved to an end table next to the couch and ripped the drawer open. She dug around among the various paraphernalia haphazardly stuffed inside before she found a book of matches. Her hand shook a little when she lit the cigarette. "I ain't got nothing to say."

Tony cocked his head. "What are you afraid of?"

"I ain't afraid of nothin', rich boy." She pulled the smoke out of her mouth and pointed at him. "I ain't afraid of nobody."

"Something." He stepped closer. "Someone has you scared."

Both of her hands shook, and she had a hard time getting the cigarette back to her mouth. "You just stay away from me, hear? I ain't losin' what little I get –" She slapped her own hand over her mouth, eyes wide.

Derrick looked around. "Getting a monthly check, Ginger? Is that what's keeping you and Delilah off the streets?"

She threw the cigarette into the ashtray and rushed to the door, ripping it open. "You get out!" She yelled. "You get out of my house. I ain't got nothin' to say."

Tony slammed the door. She whirled around to him and covered her ears with her hands. Tears streamed down her face, smearing cheap mascara. "What is it, Ginger?" he asked.

"He'll kill me," she whispered. "Or Delilah. She don't matter none to him, even though she's his. He pays every month, though. Money comes right as rain. Can't lose my baby." With jerky movements, she tried to open the door again but her hand slipped on the handle. "I ain't got nothing to say. You can't make me."

Derrick pulled a roll of cash out of his pocket. "How much for just a name?" He asked. He started counting bills. At one thousand dollars, he said, "Just a name."

Her eyes bugged as she watched the money being counted. When he reached two thousand, he started to fold them up and put them in his pocket, but she snatched at his wrist. "Twenty-five," she said.

He counted another five one-hundred-dollar bills, then held up the money in a fan. "Name?" She reached for the money, but he held it back from her. "Gotta give me the goods before you get the cash," he said.

Ginger looked over her shoulder, as if someone else might hear. She leaned forward and whispered, "Nick Wilson." Derrick was so stunned at the name that he froze. Ginger snatched the money from his hand and rolled it into a tight roll before sticking it down her shirt. "That's all you get outta me."

"You've been very helpful," Tony said. He opened the door and gestured toward the hallway with his head. Derrick followed as if in a trance. As soon as Ginger slammed the door behind them, Tony spoke. "Some things just started looking a little clearer."

Derrick shook his head. "It just got more confusing."

Chapter 18

"SO what does it all mean?" Sarah asked, shaking some oil and vinegar on her salad. All around her, the hospital cafeteria buzzed with lunch time traffic. She nodded a greeting at a friend then focused her attention back to Derrick.

He shrugged. "No idea. He looked familiar to me the day he came to my office. He must have been a narc way back when. Maybe undercover."

"What does he have to do with her?"

"Well, her daughter was about ten. This all happened ten years ago."

"There you are." Sarah looked up as Barry pulled a chair up to their table. He threw a file folder in front of Derrick. "You're going to be interested in reading that."

She watched him skim the contents. "What is it?" she asked when he glanced up at Barry with a look of surprise.

"Yeah," Barry said. "That's what I thought, too."

Derrick pushed the file toward Sarah. She took a quick bite of salad and opened the folder. Apparently, Nick Wilson had worked under cover for over a year, and in the end he took down Gianni Castolli and his entire empire. He did it at the age of twenty.

She shut the file folder and looked at Barry. "How could he do that so young?"

Derrick answered her. "Gianni preferred younger guys working for him. Easier to control, less expensive, usually no family."

"Vice recruited Wilson fresh out of the academy," Barry said. "Top of his class, very green. But, he dirtied up easily and slipped right in."

"I probably worked right with him, and didn't know him when I met him in my office," Derrick said. He scrubbed a hand through his hair. Sarah could almost feel the agitation coming off him in waves. "I thought maybe for a moment I recognized him, but I dismissed it because I know his father from work."

Sarah felt little excited bursts going through her stomach. "Could he have killed James?"

"Ginger is obviously very afraid of him." Derrick tapped the file folder. "And I bet that half of what he did didn't end up in here."

"Speaking of which," Sarah said, feeling the burn of tears in her throat as some memories crept forward. "Can we talk about the little girl?"

"Already taken care of," Derrick said. He put his hand over hers. "Tony made calls on our way back. She's going to be investigated. Peter and Caroline O'Farrell have offered to take her if she's removed."

"Good. Thank you."

"I wouldn't have been able to ignore it, Sarah. Don't worry." She smiled at him, feeling a glow of love fill her heart.

"Anyway," Barry said, smiling and rubbing his chin. "We still don't know what happened."

"Maybe we should ask him," Derrick said. He reached over and snagged a carrot out of Sarah's salad.

"I think it best not to tip our hand without more information," Barry said. He slipped on a pair of reading glasses and made some notes in his phone.

"I was just kidding," Derrick said. He smiled and winked at Sarah. "I'm just happy to see things looking up."

"Me, too!" Sarah said. She laughed as he reached for another bite, and just pushed the salad in front of him. "Eat. Enjoy. I'll go get something else."

Derrick picked up her fork and dug in. "Thanks," he said around a mouthful of food. "I didn't feel much up to eating before we went to her apartment this morning."

"I think we might be celebrating a little too soon," Barry said. He looked at Derrick over the rim of his glasses. "We don't know anything."

"It's all too convenient," Derrick answered.

"I agree. But, that doesn't change the fact that they have proof and we do not. So, slow down on the celebrating. We haven't beaten this thing yet."

Derrick took another bite then slid the tray back toward Sarah. "I have to go, anyway. I have a meeting at two with the managers at the hotel. Since most of them saw me arrested Friday night, I should go speak with them."

Sarah broke open her roll and spread butter on it. She looked up and saw Barry watching her. She smiled as she held up her knife. "Yes," she said. "Real butter. Baby steps."

"That'a girl," he said with a smile that made her laugh.

To Derrick she said, "Have fun. Do they even know you're back at work?"

"I haven't been yet. Went to Ginger's instead of work this morning. It's the regular weekly meeting. I'm actually curious to see who shows up."

He stood and put a hand on her shoulder, squeezing reassurance into his touch. "I'll see you later," Sarah said.

"Count on it," Derrick answered.

Sarah felt her cheeks burn at Barry's knowing look and smile. "You shush," she said, and took a bite of her roll.

SARAH put her arms up over her head and stretched. She'd worked a double shift – the price paid for skipping work for court on Monday. That meant she got to work at seven that morning, and was staring midnight hard in the face as she walked out of the hospital.

She walked with a friend and left her at her car, promising dinner and a movie the following week. Despite the nearly seventeen hours on her feet, she felt lighter, more energized than she had going into work that morning. Things might actually, possibly be looking up. Her future with Derrick might actually be a real possibility.

As she pulled her keys out of her bag, she walked past the concrete pillar near where she had parked. She looked at her watch, knowing full well that it was too late to call Derrick, but fighting the impulse to do it anyway.

When a rough hand grabbed her by the back of the neck and spun her toward the pillar, she was too shocked to react. The hand violently pushed her head forward until her forehead smacked against the concrete. White hot pain shrieked through her body, making her stomach roll with nausea and her knees go weak. The hand on the back of her neck held her upright, her face pressed against the cold concrete pillar and away from the person holding her there.

Fear immobilized her. She didn't know how to fight back – didn't try.

"Your boyfriend is looking in bad places," someone whispered in her ear. "He backs off, or he'll find your skeleton in a closet somewhere."

The hand on her neck suddenly released her and she crumpled to the ground. Her glasses were broken, her vision blurred, and she couldn't make anything out but a dark figure running quietly away.

Within seconds, her vision grayed, and with a sickening roll of her stomach, she blacked out.

SARAH fought against the headache that tried to keep her from opening her eyes. Something important – she had to wake up.

Bright fluorescent lights sent pain straight to her brain and she held up a hand to shield them. Through blurred vision, she recognized her own emergency room.

The nurse who came to her bedside was a friend – a floater who worked all the floors. Sarah had worked with her many times. "Stay calm, Sarah," she said. "You have a nasty concussion."

"Derrick?" Sarah whispered.

"He's here."

"I'm right here." It hurt to turn her head. It hurt a lot. But tears of relief at seeing him there, safe, stung her eyes. He gently touched her hairline.

Sarah reached up and grabbed his wrist. "Listen," she said, her stomach rolling with the effort it took to speak. "It was him."

Derrick shook his head. "Him who?"

"Wilson." As the dark look crossed his features, Sarah said, "He said to tell you that you were looking in bad places. He said I'd end up in a closet like James."

The anger in his eyes scared her. She didn't want him to lose control. "Listen," she said. "We might be able to do something with this."

"Did you see him?" Tony stepped closer from somewhere in the room.

She tried to remember, but nothing was clear. "I don't think so."

"Then there's nothing we can do."

"Wanna bet?" Derrick said.

"*Calmi giù, il fratello,*" Tony said. "Stay calm."

"Do not tell me to calm down. If that were Robin lying there, you wouldn't be advising calm."

This time, Sarah heard Robin speak. "No, but you would be. Nothing good at all will come of you going off and confronting the officer in charge with your arrest."

Maxine came out of nowhere, too. Sarah closed her eyes. All the movements and words were making her dizzy. "It will all eventually be handled."

Sarah felt Derrick take her hand. She loved the fact that she already recognized his touch. "Fine," he said. "I know you're right, so I'll listen. But Sarah needs someone to protect her right now."

"I don't need protection," Sarah said. But her tongue felt thick and the words sounded slurred. She kept her eyes closed as their voices sounded more like mechanical buzzing than her family.

The next time she woke up, she was out of the emergency room and in a regular room. Her mother sat dozing in a chair in the corner. Derrick sat next to Sarah's bed with his hand in hers, his head against her leg. He slept, his breath coming in and out in a steady rhythm. She wanted to reach over and touch his face, but she didn't want to disturb him, so she just looked her fill. His dark eyelashes lay feathered against his cheekbones. A curl of black hair teased his forehead. In sleep he looked relaxed, content, untroubled. She put a hand to her heart to try to control the flood of emotion she felt. How had she wasted ten years that could have been spent with him?

She closed her eyes again and the next time she opened them, only her mother was in the room. She came up to the bed and frowned down at her daughter. "Are you okay?" she asked.

Sarah raised a shaking hand to her forehead and probed around the tenderness she felt there. "I hope so."

"What happened?"

Sarah shook her head. "I have no idea. Someone came out of nowhere and just slammed my head against the pillar."

Darlene patted her hand. "I'm so glad it wasn't any worse than it is." She looked at her watch. "The police officer will be back here any moment. He went to get a cup of coffee."

"Okay." Sarah looked toward the door just as Detective Beaumont walked in. She felt her stomach clench into tight knots and her heart rate skipped then picked up speed.

"Miss Thomas," he said, coming fully into the room. "I'm glad to see you awake."

She cleared her throat. "I don't understand. Why is a homicide detective here for a mugging?"

He waved a hand at her. "Covering for a buddy. His wife is having a baby."

When she'd seen him in Derrick's office, his face had been hard and unfriendly. But tonight, he seemed at ease, warm, trusting. She knew his countenance must be a purposeful projection depending on the circumstances, but it was amazing the difference.

"Can you tell me what happened?"

Sarah held a silent debate with herself for about a nanosecond. The book of Mark told her to have faith in God. And so she would.

"Someone attacked me as I was about to approach my car."

"Did you see who it was?"

She pressed her lips together and shook her head. "No. But he said something to me."

The detective pulled out a notebook. "Oh?"

"He said that my boyfriend was looking in bad places and that if he didn't stop, I'd end up a skeleton in a closet, too."

With a frown, Beaumont narrowed his eyes at her quizzically. "What does that mean?"

Sarah took a deep breath, prayed for wisdom, then plunged forward. "My boyfriend is Derrick DiNunzio."

The detective had been writing, but his pen suddenly paused on his pad. "Really?" He said, pulling the word out to several syllables. "That is certainly interesting."

Sarah nodded. "I agree. I couldn't figure out why you were here, then I figured God must have sent you to me."

"What exactly do you mean by that?"

"Derrick remembered that one person knew he was leaving the old neighborhood that night all those years ago. His ex-girlfriend, Ginger Castolli."

Beaumont no longer looked confused, but he looked very interested. "Go on."

"So, Derrick went to visit her Monday. She said that she'd told someone else as well. Derrick asked her who, and she said that the father of her 10 year old child had known Derrick was leaving that night."

"Who was the father?"

Sarah stopped. "I don't know if I should tell you."

"Miss Thomas," he leaned forward, "if you have information in a murder investigation, you need to give it to me."

"Detective, I don't know if I can trust you." Hot tears stung at her eyes. "Derrick's life hangs in the balance, and telling you could ruin his chances."

"Listen to me." He capped his pen and put it in his pocket with the notebook. "Off the record, I didn't like the case against Derrick all the way. Things seemed too easy. To me, it was apparent that someone was setting him up, but the evidence against him was too great to ignore. If you know something that might change that, you need to tell me right now."

Sarah chewed on her lip and tugged at the blanket. She finally met Beaumont's eyes, and felt his sincerity. "It was Nick Wilson."

Beaumont sat back down and stared at her. "Well," he said, but he didn't say more.

"Well what?" Her voice sounded desperate even to her own ears.

"Well, some things make a little bit more sense now." He stood. "Please excuse me, Miss Thomas. Thank you for the information. I'll be in touch." He started out the door, but pulled a business card out of his pocket and came back to hand it to her "If anything else happens related to this, please call me directly."

Chapter 19

"I'M still not convinced that letting Wilson's partner know what we know was the best thing." Derrick sat at the end of Sarah's couch, her feet in his lap.

Sarah shrugged. "It felt right. That's really all I can say about it."

"You casually shrug as if my future doesn't hang in the balance of what you did or didn't do." Sarah pulled her feet out of his lap as he stood. He paced the room and rounded on her. "I wish you'd had him call me or something else. Anything else."

Sarah closed her eyes and covered them with her arm. "I felt led to talk to him, Derrick."

"He's a cop who is used to playing people to get them to talk, Sarah. He played you."

Anger burned in her chest. She felt as if he was treating her like a child, and she really, *really*, resented it. "You don't know that!"

Derrick's phone vibrated on the table. Sarah saw Clifford's name flash across the screen before Derrick snatched it up. "Yeah?" he said as he engaged the call. Sarah watched his face darken and slowly sat up straighter, fighting the pounding in her head. "I see … how?" After a pause, Derrick's face paled and he sat down. "Thanks, man. I'll talk to you tomorrow." He hit the button to disconnect the call and very carefully set his phone on the table in front of him. At the look on his face, her heart started to flutter nervously.

"Ginger Castolli was found in a Dumpster outside of her apartment building."

Sarah's stomach gave a sick roll. "What?"

"The money I paid her for the information she gave me was shoved down her throat."

Sarah gasped and covered her mouth with her hand.

"Exactly." Derrick stood. "What did I tell you?"

"You can't know that what I told the detective had anything to do with tonight."

His mouth thinned and he looked at her with just bare tolerance. "Can't I?"

"How do you know someone else didn't tell Beaumont that you'd been to her place? It could have been anything."

"Or it could have been you telling Wilson exactly everything by proxy."

"That's not fair!" She clenched her fists but stopped short of stomping her foot on the floor.

"Not fair? Not fair is you playing roulette with my life. You get a happy feeling in your little tummy about talking to a man who is trained to lower your defenses, and you think I shouldn't be upset about it?" He grabbed his coat off the back of the chair and in one fluid movement had both of his arms into it. As he passed the table, he snatched his phone up and shoved it into the pocket. "I have to go."

Sarah ran to the door and blocked his exit. "It's all fine and good for you to preach to me, to quote scripture, to assure and reassure. But the second I step out and make a move based on *my* faith instead of your faith, you stop trusting me."

Derrick narrowed his eyes. "Move."

She stepped aside and he wrenched the door open. A blast of icy air chilled her bare arms. She caught the door just as it started to slam behind him. "Derrick, wait."

"No." He stopped by the door of his car and looked at her. The glow of the porch light barely illuminated his face – made his eyes shine. "I can't be here right now with you. I'll see you later." He opened his car door and stopped again. "You shouldn't be alone. You should call someone to be with you."

She crossed her arms and huffed, "Do you think I'm a target? Need a babysitter do I?"

"No. Because of your concussion."

Sarah put a hand on her forehead and flinched at the tenderness. "I'll be fine."

He narrowed his eyes and she shivered at the directness of his cold stare. Finally he shrugged. "Your call. See you later."

His car door wasn't even shut before he gunned the powerful motor and started backing out.

DERRICK drove his mighty Mustang through the nearly empty streets of downtown. Within minutes, he pulled up front in the loading zone of his apartment building. A valet attendant met him as he got out of his car.

Instead of spending his normal time making small talk, he just nodded a greeting and went into the lobby. He didn't stop at the guard's desk. He waved hello and went straight to the elevator. The guard had activated it from his station, and the doors opened just as Derrick reached them.

He shoved his hands in the pocket of his leather coat and leaned against the corner of the elevator while it shot up twenty floors. Knowing full well the position of the security cameras and that he could be seen, he didn't pace, or punch a hole in the wall of the elevator, or throw his head back and scream in frustration. He just stared at the tips of his boots and waited for it to get him home.

He straightened as the elevator came to a stop. The doors opened and he found himself outside of his apartment door. The door held a combination key instead of a key lock, and he punched in the code and stepped into the first sanctuary his life had ever offered.

He walked inside the living room and expected to feel a sense of calm and security envelope him as it normally did. But, he felt nothing but anger burning a hole in his chest. Throwing his keys across the room did nothing at all to make him feel better. Kicking a chair over also made it worse. So he sat on the edge of the couch and put his face in his hands, struggling to control the anger, fighting back the wrath, knowing they could destroy him if he allowed them control.

He took deep breaths, reasoned with himself, talked himself down. How he wished the ice and snow outside would go away so that he could get out there and drive spikes into rock, throw his body weight into a physical task that would occupy his thoughts and center his emotions.

He looked at his watch. Nine-thirty. He wondered how long it would be before the police knocked at his door again and arrested him for the murder of another person he didn't kill.

Knowing he needed focus, he grabbed his worn Bible off the table next to his favorite chair and took it into the bedroom with him. He would read, focus on something else, until he couldn't stay awake anymore.

SARAH watched the sun rise over her back yard. She sat in her kitchen, knees pulled up to her chest, a cup of tea long cooled at her elbow, and watched through the kitchen window as the sun rose over the trees. Anxiety had settled like a fog over her whole body until she was nearly numb with it. She barely even felt the headache anymore.

She wasn't upset about talking to Detective Beaumont. She knew that the peace she felt inside when she spoke to him was real -- was God-given.

No other explanation existed for her. But what twisted her stomach and her heart into little knots of fear and hurt was the way that Derrick didn't trust that. Just like her sisters, when an adult moment presented itself, he treated her like a child – like a disruptive teenager. And he was very, very angry.

Once Derrick's car had gunned away, she felt the numbness settle over her. She went to her kitchen and made a cup of tea, then sat at her table.

As she sat there the rest of the night, eventually watching the sky gradually lighten in the winter morning, she decided that as unreasonable as Derrick's treatment of her was, she certainly wasn't going to go to him and say she'd been wrong, when she had definitely not. All she could do was continue to be there for him, to be present, and to pray.

The doorbell surprised her and made her stomach jump. As she got out of the chair, she stretched the muscles that protested at the first movement in hours. Rolling her head on her neck, she touched the edges of the bruise on her forehead and thought maybe some of the tenderness had gone away.

When she opened the door, her eyes widened in surprise to see Derrick standing there, the collar of his leather coat drawn up over his neck against the cold. She widened the door. "Come in," she said.

He came in and put his hands to his lips, blowing against them. "Temperature's dropped probably thirty degrees since last night," he said.

Sarah raised an eyebrow. "Okay." She waited, but offered nothing else.

Derrick shoved his hands into his pockets. "Listen," he said. "I'm sorry I got so irrationally angry with you last night. I was temporarily overwhelmed."

With a nod, Sarah gestured at the couch. "Have a seat."

Derrick unzipped his jacket and shrugged out of it. "What you said was completely true. That was terribly unfair of me to doubt your faith. Please accept my apology."

Sarah sat down against the corner of the couch and drew her leg under her. "Thank you." She expected Derrick to sit opposite her, and was surprised when he sat close. He picked up her hand. His fingers were cold.

"I don't know what my future holds," he said.

Sarah surprised them both by sitting forward, one knee on the couch, one foot planted on the ground. "I do," she said. She framed his face with her hands. Shadows under his eyes marked the fatigue on his face, but did nothing to take away from his handsome features. She stared into his eyes – eyes the color of the richest coffee. "Your future holds you and me together."

"We don't know that."

"I know that," she said. "I know with absolute certainty. And I'm here for you no matter what." She leaned forward and rested her forehead against his, gently to keep from irritating her bruise. His eyes looked deeply into hers, and she felt a tug in her heart like nothing she'd ever felt before. "No matter how long it takes," she said.

Derrick put a hand on the back of her neck. "I can't ask that of you," he whispered.

"You haven't." She gently pressed her lips against his and felt the cool skin warm under hers. He sat immobile at first, but very quickly deepened the kiss, pulling her toward him. Sarah shifted so that her thigh pressed against his, wrapping her arms around his neck.

Derrick moaned against her mouth. He moved, breaking the kiss as he stood. She looked up at him, dazed, and he laid his palm against her cheek. "I need to go," he said.

Sarah stood quickly and grabbed his wrist. "No, stay."

He gave a short laugh and hugged her to him. With his arms wrapped around her, Sarah felt wonderful, felt right. She laid her cheek against his chest and closed her eyes, breathing deeply in with a heavy sigh. "I have to go." With the squeeze of his arms, he kissed the top of her head. "When do you work again?"

"This afternoon." Sarah stepped back and watched him put his jacket back on.

"I'll pick you up and drive you. What time?"

"You don't have to."

He smiled. "Yes, I do."

With her fingers fluttering against her lips, she smiled back. "Two."

Derrick reached forward and took her hand. He raised it to his lips and kissed her palm, sending a warm shock up her arm and through her heart. "I'll see you at two."

Sarah walked him to the door and kissed him good bye. She fought the urge to drag him close to her and convince him to stay, and knew that was exactly why he had to leave.

He paused on his way out the door and turned toward her as he lifted his collar up against the wind. "I love you, Sarah Thomas."

Sarah smiled and laughed. "And I love you, Derrick DiNunzio. Have a good morning."

She didn't shut the door against the cold until he backed down the driveway. Rubbing the chill from the wind out of her arms, she moved to her bedroom and pulled the shades, determined to get a few hours of sleep before she had to work.

TOPAZ HEAT - CHAPTER 20

AT one forty-five, Sarah came out of her bedroom and turned toward her bathroom. The text from Derrick said that he was five minutes out, and she wanted to get her hair pinned up before he got there. She slipped her phone into the pocket of her scrubs and gathered her hair at the base of her neck.

She felt the movement behind her but nothing registered until a hand grabbed the back of her neck and pushed her forward, slamming her against the wall. Her hands, which were already at the base of her neck, were grabbed together and raised above her head. Before she even had time to react, the cold blade of a knife pressed against her cheek.

Sarah closed her eyes and concentrated on slowing her breathing. Breathe in through the nose and out through the mouth. As soon as she felt like she might not hyperventilate, she opened her eyes. A familiar voice spoke close to her ear. "Not a word," he said. "We're going to walk out of here nice and calm. No scene. Or I'll cut your pretty face to pieces. Understand?"

She gave half a nod and whispered, "Yes."

He released her hands but grabbed her again behind her neck. His hand on her neck kept her from turning around and seeing his face. He turned her body, propelling her through her house and toward her open front door. The security chain dangling, obviously cut, gave a clue how he broke through her meager defenses.

The shock of cold outside had her rubbing her arms, thankful that she wore a long-sleeve t-shirt underneath her purple scrubs. Her rubber shoes slipped on the ice on the edge of her sidewalk, but her abductor's hand on the base of her neck kept her from slipping and falling.

He half pushed her toward a black sedan. As they approached, the back door opened and, using the forward momentum of her body, he bent her and shoved her inside.

She landed against another person, who put his hands on her shoulders and settled her next to him. Before she could turn and bolt out of the car, the door shut in her face. The other passenger clucked his tongue and shook his head, and she saw that he had a gun pointed at her.

"Do you know who I am, little girl?" he asked.

Nothing about his appearance would suggest that he would have the murdering and thieving reputation that he had so rightfully earned. He had a small, lean frame. His once dark hair had gray peppered through it, and he had it combed off his forehead greaser-style. At a glance he just looked like an older man, heavy corduroy coat and thick pants blocking the cold winter wind. But as soon as she met his eyes, she felt very real fear. His light brown eyes pierced right through her.

"I've seen pictures of you."

Gianni Castolli laughed, a short, mean bark. "I bet. Plenty of pictures of my boy, too."

She could see the family resemblance. She imagined that, had he lived, his son would look very much like the older pictures of this man she'd seen. "Yes."

He looked her up and down, his eyes penetrating, almost as if they could look straight through her. Sarah felt a shiver shake her, but didn't know if it was his look or the cold.

"Go," he said to the driver – the same man who had dragged her out of her house. He didn't hesitate once the command was given to put the sedan into reverse and back out of the driveway. He sped quickly through the neighborhood and turned in the direction of downtown.

As soon as they were on the main road, Gianni looked at her again. "He killed my boy."

Sarah blew on her hands, then stuck them into the pockets of her scrubs shirt and almost started crying when she felt the slim lines of her phone. There was no way she could dial a number without looking at the screen, but she could answer it when it rang. Her only fear was that the setting was on ring instead of vibrate. She could only pray that she never changed it after her shift the night she was attacked.

"Who?"

Gianni narrowed his eyes. "You know who. He's going to pay, though." He leaned close to her, his nose almost touching hers. "She was a waste of breath. Wouldn't stand by her old man while I went through the mockery of a trial and the disgrace of prison. Ten years I rotted and never a word from her. Good riddance," he said, and for the first time Sarah saw the insanity in his eyes. "But my boy, now, he was my light. And he killed him. You're going to help me fix that."

Sarah prayed she gave no outward indication when her phone vibrated in her hand. She quickly hit the button to activate the phone. "Mr. Castolli," she said, "Nothing you do is going to bring your son back."

Another short bark of a laugh. "He owes me for this."

Sarah pulled her empty hands out of her pockets, and made a show of rubbing her arms, even though the warmth of the car had started to beat back the cold outside. She kept the phone on. "Where are you taking me?"

Instead of answering her, he sat back and looked out the window. "Oh, he'll pay all right. He'll pay what he owes."

DERRICK turned onto Sarah's street and nearly collided with the quickly moving sedan. He ripped the wheel to the right and skidded on a patch of ice, but narrowly avoided hitting the neighbor's car parked across the street.

Something started tingling in his subconscious when he saw the driver's sunglass adorned face, but he couldn't see any other details because of the darkly tinted windows.

Once the sedan was gone, he kept driving and pulled into Sarah's driveway. Tire marks on the snow had that subconscious tingling move from the back of his neck to grow into nerves in his stomach. He raced up the path and onto the front porch, ignoring the footmarks he saw in the snow.

The door stood partially open, the security chain dangling free, cut. Panicked, he pushed the door open and rushed inside. The house was empty. Every room echoed her name as he called for her. The sight of her purse hanging over her coat on the coat stand made the nervous flutterings in his gut turn into full blown panic fists.

He raced back out the door and pulled his phone out of his pocket. "Please God," he whispered. She answered the call on the first ring, but didn't say anything. "Sarah?" He said. "Sarah?"

Her muffled voice carried almost clearly through his speaker. "Mr. Castolli," she said, "Nothing you do is going to bring your son back."

He raced his Mustang to the exit of the neighborhood and sat there at the main road, trying to decide which way to turn. Closing his eyes, taking a deep breath, he headed in the direction of downtown, and prayed he'd made the right call. He knew he should call the police, but he couldn't risk disconnecting her call, so he just prayed for her protection and for his wisdom, and darted the race car through the heavy late afternoon traffic.

At a red light, he ripped open his glove compartment and dug around until he found the hands free device for his phone. He plugged it in as he accelerated and surged the car forward, darting in between cars and gunning the powerful motor, intimidating other drivers into moving out of his way. As soon as he had the earpiece in place in his ear, he pushed a button to activate the recording device on the phone, then dug through his pockets and found the business card Sarah had given him after she'd programmed Beaumont's number into her own phone. He prayed, fervently, that trusting her instincts was the right call as he sent a text to Beaumont, keeping the call to Sarah's phone engaged, listening to Gianni talking to her about his son.

THE driver stopped the car in front of a dilapidated building in Roxbury. Despite being mid-afternoon, the street around them appeared deserted. As Sarah stepped from the car, icy wind blew a flyer for a hip-hop show across her foot and sent a shudder through her body. She looked up at the building and said the name of the street out loud. "I think I used to live near here."

The driver pulled a heavy key out of his pocket and opened the old door. "Memory lane. It's a blast." Gianni grabbed her arm again and half dragged her into the building. The smell in the lobby made her knees weaken slightly. The smell of stale urine and God knew what else battled for the most prominent odor. Ripped carpet, trash, even a dead cat, lay on the empty floor. A broken chair lay against a far wall, and the frame of what was once a couch lay teetered back in front of a built-in desk.

This obviously had once been a hotel of some sort, but Sarah could only imagine the class of clientele based on the decor and the location. Before her ninth birthday, there was no telling how many similar buildings she'd lived in with her mother and her sisters. Now that she could remember her past, having actual memories to remind her of the salvation the Thomas' gave her made her appreciate them all the more.

The driver kept his glasses on, even in the dim interior of the building. He led the way to the stairwell in the back of the lobby, and Sarah walked between him and Gianni up three flights of precarious stairs. Halfway up the third flight, her foot went through the stair.

"Ouch!" She said loudly. The driver immediately stopped and turned around. Gianni gripped her arm and pushed her forward. "Wait," she said, "my shoe is caught."

Her comfortable slip-on nurse's shoe came off as the driver pulled her forward. "My shoe!" She said.

"You won't be needing it," Gianni said as she reached the landing of the fourth floor. Once they opened the access to the floor from the stairwell, she could feel the warmth coming from one of the rooms, spilling into the hallway. The unnamed driver pushed her into the room.

A man stood with his back to the door looking out the far window. He wore a tweed overcoat, leather shoes, but no hat. A kerosene heater sat in the middle of the room. Something about the warmth made the smell worse. Sarah swallowed against a gag reflex as the man turned around.

"I've met you here per your request, Gianni, but my reluctance is still very much present."

She immediately recognized him. She had never met him, but his son could have been carved out of the same mold. Nick Wilson, Senior's eyes widened when he saw her, then immediately flew to Gianni.

"What is she doing here?"

"She knows all about you. We have to get rid of her."

"All about me?" He looked at her again and stepped forward. White hair framed a tanned face, ice blue eyes penetrated hers. He stood a full foot taller than her, and as he approached, she resented having to look up at him. "What do you know about me?"

Praying her phone was still engaged, she raised her chin defiantly and started making a few calculated guesses. "I know you're Detective Nick Wilson's father. I know you're the head of one of the wealthiest families in the greater Boston area. I'm guessing that your wealth was accrued through some less than respectable methods, considering your association with Mr. Castolli here."

Gianni Castolli barked a short laugh. "She's smart, this one. Told you."

Wilson reached forward with a hand gloved in brown leather and grabbed Sarah's chin, forcing her to maintain eye contact. He moved her face back and forth and visually inspected her forehead. "Matty here did a good job on your head." She could hear the shuffle of the driver's feet but he didn't speak. "Obviously, you didn't get the hint as I intended it."

Refusing to be intimidated, she kept talking. "Maybe if you hadn't killed Ginger Castolli, things would have eventually died down."

"She could tie my Nicky to your boyfriend. All it would take would be some green waved in her face and she would have spouted anything to anyone." He squeezed her jaw hard enough to bruise before pushing her away. As she lost her balance, she felt Matty take her arm again. "As will you. DiNunzio needs to take the fall for all of it." He looked at Gianni. "What I don't understand is what she's doing here. Matty should have just taken care of her at her place and let her little boyfriend find the body."

"You killed my boy."

Wilson raised an eyebrow. "I beg your pardon?"

"You killed my boy then sent me to prison to rot while you took the money I made you and lived high and mighty."

"So what?" Wilson stepped forward, pushing Sarah aside as he did so. "What are you going to do about it? Threaten me?" He waved a hand at Matty. "Kill them both."

Gianni pulled the gun out of his pocket and pointed it at Wilson. "Oh no you don't. This is going to end here."

IF Derrick didn't have the ear piece in his ear, he would have missed Sarah saying the name of the street. He pulled over and sent Beaumont another text message, and as he did, received one from him. Carefully pushing buttons to keep from disconnecting the call with Sarah, he read Beaumont's reply to the first message and his immediate reply to the location.

He knew he was only a block away, so he left the Mustang parked and, grabbing a small knife and a screw driver out of his tool box in the trunk, he dashed around a couple of parked cars and into an alley that would take him to the street Sarah mentioned. But it would put him about midway down the street, and he wondered once he got there, which direction to take.

He emerged out of the alley, listening to Wilson's father greet Sarah and felt strangely sick. This man, who had spent many a night in the New York Viscolli hotel, was obviously a ring leader of Castolli's empire. But, how had he gone undiscovered? Then it occurred to Derrick. His son had been the one to bust Castolli. And, obviously, Castolli had been promised either money or survival if he kept his mouth shut about Wilson's part in the syndicate.

So, Wilson killed James, framed Derrick for the murder, bricked him into a wall, and walked away. Maybe it was a sign to Castolli to go down without a fight. Maybe it was because James wasn't going to let his father take all of the rap for the numerous crimes committed in the Castolli name. Whatever the case, by framing Derrick, it allowed him to be the suspect no matter when the body was found.

Ginger was obviously a loose cannon, and the one who could tip the scales on Wilson. Intimidation and a monthly allowance hadn't kept her mouth shut so they had to shut it permanently. But to do so, once Beaumont knew about it, they would have to frame Derrick once again. Piling Sarah's body into the count would only point the finger more firmly at Derrick, since Sarah was completely removed from any part of Derrick's past and anything to do with the Castollis.

He reached the end of the alley and looked up and down the street, praying for spiritual guidance. To his right, traffic picked up, pedestrian and automotive. A shopping district started at the end of the street, and several businesses operated above restaurants and boutiques.

To his left, the buildings slowly became more worn down, less attractive, less populated. A few beat up cars sat under a few inches of snow and trapped in the drifts created by the snow plows. Sending Beaumont a quick text, Derrick turned the collar up on his coat and started at a half-run, half-walk down the street, careful not to slip on patches of ice and, in one case, not to trip over a drunk's legs.

Three blocks down, he saw the sedan he'd seen in Sarah's neighborhood. He crossed the street and approached the building where it was parked more slowly, trying to appear casual. He paused at the corner of the block and looked up at the buildings and around him, seeing no movement, almost sure no one stood guard.

He cautiously approached the building and tested the door. It was locked tight. Looking around him, he knelt and inspected the lock, then pulled out his knife and the screwdriver. More than ten years had passed since he last picked a lock, but his hands remembered even if his mind tried to disengage the notion, and in seconds he cautiously inched the door open and slipped inside.

He held his breath against the stench and let his eyes adjust to the interior. As soon as he could see, he raced across the lobby and up the stairs. He knew from the time they entered the lobby to the time they started talking to Wilson, they were at least two floors up. So, he lost what he thought was precious time moving quietly and steadily over the second floor. Halfway through checking the rooms, he remembered. Her shoe! It hadn't been a full minute from the time she lost her shoe to the time she'd started talking to Wilson, so wherever he found it, he would also find the floor they were on.

Racing back to the stairwell, he moved as quickly as he could, as quietly as he could, until he came upon the stair where her foot had gone through. Reaching in between the rotten wood planks, he retrieved her shoe and went to the top of the stairs. His phone buzzed in his hand and he saw the message from Beaumont informing Derrick that help was minutes away. It seemed when seconds counted, the police were always just minutes away.

Through the muffled confines of Sarah's scrubs pocket, he heard Wilson say, "Kill them both."

Chapter 21

"THIS is going to end here." Gianni waved the gun between Wilson and Matty. "You're going to be implicated, and so is your boy."

Sarah's heart fluttered in her chest. Panic tried to gurgle up and choke her, but she forced it back down. Die or live, she wouldn't give in to hysterics. Watching Darlene's grace in even the most trying of circumstances through the years taught her how to put her back up and maintain an outward appearance of stoicism.

"Why kill me?" She turned toward Gianni. "Why not just give the authorities the information you have?"

His insane eyes met hers. "DiNunzio owes me. Nobody quits Gianni. Nobody gets to just turn in a two week notice and leave. I figure I kill you, then we're even, him and me. Besides, killing him wouldn't hurt him as much as losing you would."

"No," Sarah whispered, fear closing her throat.

"Do you even know who he is? Do you know the things he did for me?"

Regaining her control, she lifted up her chin. "I don't care. What he did is in the past. Who he was 10 years ago has no bearing on the man I know today."

Gianni threw back his head and laughed. "You're like a child. Let me explain something to you. You don't just get absolution for some crimes."

"You do from God." Derrick's voice startled everyone in the room. Sarah gasped and started toward him, but Gianni clucked his tongue and waved his gun. She stopped with her foot outstretched, then set it back down.

"Well, hello there boy. Been a while."

"Not long enough." Derrick held a knife in one hand, resting it against the side of his leg. "Sarah, come over here, sweetheart."

"You will stay put," Gianni said loudly. He waved his gun at Sarah and then leveled it to point at Wilson, who had started inching around the room. "You will all stay put."

"What are you going to do? Shoot everyone here?" Wilson spoke with authority as he nonchalantly straightened the collar of his coat. "Matty, let's go."

"Do not!" Gianni stepped forward and cocked the pistol in his hand. Sarah kept her eyes trained on Derrick. His face looked like it was set in stone, and he watched Gianni intently. When he lifted his hand and waved her forward, she didn't hesitate.

Derrick silently prayed that Sarah would move out of the line of Gianni's fire when he gave her the signal. He prayed she wouldn't hesitate, that she would react and come to him, to the door, to a close exit that would remove her from the madman's sight. Out of sight, out of mind, he thought. As he barely lifted his hand and gestured, not looking at her, he peripherally saw her move toward him immediately.

Gianni saw the movement too, and spun on his heel, his gun moving in a wide arc as he turned his body. Derrick let his knife slide down his hand until he clutched the blade instead of the handle. He tested the weight, remembering a decade gone by, recognizing its feel, measuring the distance.

As Gianni aimed the gun at Sarah's back, Derrick drew back and let his knife fly, watched it whirl through the air.

In the same breath, Derrick stepped in front of Sarah, shielding her with his entire body, using his other hand to push her behind him and toward the door. Gianni flinched toward Derrick and the room filled with an unbelievably loud noise as the madman pulled the trigger and fired.

Time slowed down.

Derrick saw the lightning bright muzzle flash fill every corner of the room with pale light. He smelled the burned cordite, the sharp smell of extinguished gunpowder that reminded him so much of burning orange peels. His ears filled first with the sound of echoing thunder then the high pitched whine of noise induced deafness.

He witnessed the business end of the pistol buck in the older man's hand as his thrown blade continued to tumble in the direction of his target.

Then something shoved him backward very hard and very suddenly, and he stumbled into Sarah's fleeing back. In the next heartbeat, Derrick's knife came to an abrupt halt, embedding itself into Gianni's forearm.

Time sped back up to normal as Derrick stumbled, turning and pushing Sarah into the hallway as they fled. With a roar of pain, Gianni dropped his smoking gun to the floor. Derrick turned his head to watch as Gianni reflexively gripped his wrist with his uninjured hand. He stared at Derrick in shock as he fell to his knees, trying desperately to retrieve his pistol from the floor with fingers that no longer wanted to respond to his mental commands.

Sarah felt nothing except for Derrick's arms wrapping around her, shielding her from any harm with his muscular body, protecting her and preserving her at risk of his own life. Behind them, she heard Matty attack Gianni.

In the hallway, Sarah saw Detective Beaumont leading a team of policemen in full body armor rushing toward them. In the space of a breath, she witnessed Derrick and Beaumont exchange some silent and very masculine communication, using only eyes and the nodding of heads to convey whatever message they conveyed.

Beaumont and his team rushed into the room with pistols drawn, yelling baritone commands to those within, commands that would be obeyed or else someone would pay dearly. Someone would pay with his very life. The ordered shouts that followed settled down until Sarah heard the metallic clicks of handcuffs in the sudden stillness.

Derrick winced and put his arm around Sarah's shoulder. He grinned stoically and said, "Let's get out of here, sweetheart."

"As quickly as we can," she said with a smile, her breath hitching as tears flooded her eyes and choked her throat.

Derrick's smile faded and his voice went low. "I'll try very hard not to lean on you too much, but we need to get to the street soon. I bet there's an EMT down there."

Sarah was confused but only for a second. She looked Derrick up and down and finally saw the crimson stain spreading on his chest, getting wetter and darker and wider with every heartbeat. "He shot you!" She breathed. "Derrick, he shot you!"

Derrick grinned. "Better me than you, sweetheart." The color had started to leave his face. Sarah recognized the early symptoms of shock. "I think I can make it if we hurry."

Sarah knew better. The wound looked dangerous. It looked like the bullet had entered through the front of his left shoulder, possibly shattering the clavicle, possibly puncturing the lung which could result in a tension pneumothorax, or splintering a bone that could possibly endanger his heart. If it wasn't a through and through, the bullet could endanger all kinds of vitals in his thoracic cavity and end his life in seconds. "Sit down and put your back against this railing."

"Sarah…" Derrick protested.

"Do it. Carefully." Her tone brooked no further argument. All of her medical training took over and her voice barked with authority. She pulled his shirt out of the way and yelled, "Beaumont! I'm going to need some help here!"

"Sarah," Derrick grinned, "I know you're a good nurse but I'm not having a baby." His head lolled backward and the grin faded from his face.

Sarah ignored his attempt to jest and became all business. She ripped his shirt out of the way then applied pressure to the wound with her bare hand.

"Sit forward for a second." Derrick leaned forward and she inspected his back. No exit wound. The bullet was still inside. He had taken the bullet instead of her. He had put himself between a madman with a gun and her. He had probably saved her life. "Sit back … slow. Easy does it."

Beaumont walked calmly into the hallway. "It's okay. We've got them all in custody." He saw Sarah's arm and Derrick's chest covered in bright red blood and his words froze. He drew his radio like a firearm and said, "I need EMTs to the third floor now! Right now! We have a man down."

He holstered the radio and his eyes met with Sarah. "How is it?"

Sarah didn't move. She said, "I'll tell you tomorrow."

Beaumont nodded and raced down the stairs.

Derrick leaned back and coughed abruptly. Sarah felt a tight dark circle of fear when she saw foamy blood tinge the corners of Derrick's lips with the cough. His lung had been punctured. "Derrick, listen to me. The bullet didn't go through. It's still inside. Your shoulder feels a little crepitus, which means that your clavicle is probably shattered. That means you have bone splinters and a bullet rummaging around in there. We need to get you immobilized and then they are going to need to operate. In the meantime, you need to take slow, shallow breaths. Okay? Slow and steady."

Derrick grinned, "My heart is racing but it isn't because I'm shot." Sarah's eyebrows knotted. She wondered if he was starting to lose his lucidity.

"Don't talk," Sarah ordered.

Derrick covered her hand with his own. "I love the way you touch me."

"Derrick…"

"I love you, Sarah."

"I love you, too, Derrick. Now please shut up!"

Derrick chuckled and it turned into three sharp coughs. Then he said, "Let's pray."

Sarah nodded. "How about if I pray and you be quiet and take slow, steady, shallow breaths?" She looked toward heaven and said, "Dear God, let us feel Your presence right now. Let us feel You lifting us in the palm of your hand."

She continued to pray as paramedics raced up the stairs with a stretcher.

SOMEONE had fetched Sarah's shoe and handed it to her before the doors of the ambulance closed. The paramedics let her ride in the ambulance, but they wouldn't let her help them. Powerless, she watched them work, never ceasing praying. Praying out loud, praying under her breath – she never stopped. Derrick lost consciousness long before he was loaded into the ambulance, but Sarah still constantly squeezed his hand, touched his cheek, spoke to him in soothing tones. It comforted her even if it couldn't comfort him.

The ride to the hospital was short. The emergency response team met them at the doors. A surgeon started assessing the situation immediately as they rushed into the trauma room. Sarah answered the questions pointedly, never missing a beat. This was her hospital. She knew the staff, and they knew her.

While the secretary at the administration desk called for an operating room, the trauma team stabilized Derrick. Sarah helped one of the nurses cut his clothes off so that monitors and IV's could be attached. A breathing tube was inserted. The second the surgeon gave the go ahead, they wheeled his bed from that room and headed toward the elevator. At the elevator doors, her clothes-cutting partner stopped her. "You can't go in with him, Sarah. You need to go to the waiting area."

"But –"

"Nurse!" the surgeon said, gesturing toward the controls. Every heartbeat of Derrick's outside the operating room brought him one heartbeat closer to a bullet fragment ripping apart a vital organ.

The nurse stepped back as the doors slid shut. Before they sealed completely, Sarah heard the alarm of the heart monitor signal a warning.

Stomach rolling and hands shaking, Sarah pulled her phone out of her scrubs pocket. With Derrick's dried blood on her fingers, she sent a mass text message to her family – Tony, Robin, Maxine, Barry – asked them each to check with each other to make sure everyone got the message and to meet her in the surgical floor waiting room.

She called her mom. Her voice started to hitch, but she swallowed the tears. Time for that later. "Please come," she whispered when she finished explaining where she was and why she was there. After she hung up, she called Peter O'Farrell.

"Sarah?" She turned and saw her roommate Melissa. She held her arms out and Sarah stepped into the hug, soaking in the reassurance. As Sarah stepped away, Melissa said, "Here, now, love. Go change. I'll rummage up some tea for you."

Sarah looked at her clothes and all the blood staining them. Derrick's blood. "Thank you," she whispered.

"Do you have a change of clothes?"

Trying to make sense of Melissa's words, Sarah finally nodded.

"Good. Okay. Go use our locker room. I'll meet you upstairs."

Feeling as though she moved underwater, she walked through a series of corridors. Even the staff of a hospital in downtown Boston looked at her, shocked expressions failing to hide their curiosity as to what she would have encountered to be covered in so much blood. Finally, she came to the OB nurses' locker room. Her fingers fumbled on the dial of the combination, but she finally got her locker open. Inside, she kept a spare set of scrubs and underwear. She grabbed her toiletries bag and the change of clothes, then went to the shower room.

She stood there under the lukewarm spray and watched the blood mix with water and spin down the drain. Tears burned in her eyes, but she closed them, took a deep breath, and gave her head a quick shake. Determined, she picked up a washcloth, soaked it with body wash, and scrubbed as quickly as she could. Time to breakdown later, she promised herself. She needed to put her back up right now – be there for her family, be able to answer questions and make sense when she spoke.

She didn't bother wetting her hair. She just washed the blood off her hands and arms, and cleaned the cuts on her ankle and leg from when her foot fell through the stairs. As quickly as she could, she dressed in clean scrubs, threw everything into her locker, then rushed upstairs to the surgical family waiting area.

Chapter 22

DOCTOR Jeremiah Woodworth picked another bullet fragment out of the lung of the young man on the operating table in front of him. He had done this too many times in his career at the hospital central to Boston's downtown, and it never got easier. It never got dull. So much violence tainted this fallen world.

The hand carved tattoos on the man's chest combined with the bullet ripping its way through the torso gave the doctor some indication of the type of lifestyle this poor soul likely led.

While he worked, while he asked for tools, sponges, light, while he explained things to the surgical intern watching the procedure intently, he prayed for this young man. He prayed for his physical body and his spiritual state. He knew he didn't know anything, but he knew the Holy Spirit did, and that was all that mattered.

He followed the path of a fragment to the outside of the heart. "Let me see that x-ray again," he said to the nurse at his right elbow.

She held up the x-ray to the overhead light. He squinted at it, looked at the chest cavity below him, and said out loud, "I hope this young man has someone praying for him. And for me. Because I think we're both going to need all the help we can get."

SARAH stared at the toes of her shoes. She didn't have a change of shoes and blood covered the plastic tops. Cleaning them didn't occur to her until she sat in the waiting room, away from access to water and towels.

Her mother sat on one side of her, Maxine on the other. Robin and Maxine sat with their heads bent together, talking in low tones. Barry stood, leaning against the wall, hands in his pockets, ankles crossed. He hadn't moved a muscle in an hour.

Peter came and went, taking phone calls outside the waiting room. For some reason, the silence wouldn't be penetrated. There seemed to be an unspoken acknowledgment of the need for utter silence.

Sarah concentrated on even breathing and maintaining control. So far, she'd relayed the story of what happened three times. Once Tony got there, she'd have to tell it all over again. She needed to keep control. She needed to not break down. Not yet. Tonight. Tonight in her own home in her own bed, when Derrick was safe and alive and well, she would break down.

Had she ever considered the magnitude of her love for Derrick? How empty her world would be without him? How had she allowed them to waste ten years they could have been together? If only she had quit looking at the outside package and seen the man inside, they could have had an extra decade together. Now they might not have another ten seconds.

The waiting room door slammed open and all eyes turned to look as Tony rushed in. He scanned the faces in the room and headed straight for Sarah.

Robin jumped up as he reached them, and he put his arms around his wife but spoke to her sister. "I got here as quickly as I could. Had to turn the pilot around. What happened?"

Sarah took a deep breath as she stood and wiped her hands on her thighs. "Gianni Castolli abducted me from my house today," she began.

With Tony's "What?" interrupting her without really interrupting, she continued with the rest of the story.

Long after she finished speaking, he stared at her. Finally, he stepped toward her and put his arms around her. "I'm so sorry, *mia sorella*."

"I know." She hugged him tight once then stepped back. "At least it's all over now. Derrick isn't facing a trial for murder anymore."

"Instead we're in here waiting while a doctor digs a bullet out of his chest." Tony ran his hands through his groomed hair.

Peter set his Bible down and approached his friend. "You and I both know that you can't wish away your past," he said. He took his glasses off and slipped them into the front pocket of his shirt. "We can be absolved for our sins, but the past still exists. Derrick handled himself like a champion soldier of God throughout this entire ordeal. He never faltered, he never wavered in his unshakable faith. For that he is to be admired. For that, we can lift him up as an example of how to persevere in even the most trying circumstances. Don't take his past from him."

Tony cocked his head while he stared at his mentor. After several seconds, he nodded. "Thank you."

Sarah rolled her head on her shoulders and watched as Melissa came into the room with a tray of coffee and tea. She was so thankful for her friends and family. Without them here in this room with her, she would be an emotional puddle on the ground.

She moved back to her seat, but instead of sitting in the vinyl chair, she sat on the floor between the feet of her sisters. Maxine leaned forward and hugged her. "I hate waiting," she said.

Robin took a cup of coffee from the tray. "I remember waiting after your accident," she said to Maxine. "It was a nightmare."

"I wish they would let me in there," Sarah whispered. "It's the not knowing what's going on that is so hard. If I just knew, I could be digesting it and coping with it."

Robin put a hand on her shoulder. "We'll know soon enough."

Melissa knelt behind Sarah. "Do you need anything?"

Sarah reached her hand over her shoulder. Melissa placed her hand in her roommate's. Sarah stared at her sisters, then her mother, and squeezed Melissa's hand. "Not a thing."

DOCTOR Woodworth grabbed another sponge as the machines around him screamed alarms. "I need another set of hands," he said through gritted teeth. "I can't stop this bleeding."

"Doctor –" the anesthesiologist said, the warning in his voice conveying all the information the doctor needed.

"I know. I know!" Woodworth said. He grabbed the intern's hand and said, "Here. Press right here. Don't move until I tell you to."

He grabbed the tweezers and a needle and thread and stitched the hole as fast as he could. Blood still poured out from somewhere else, though, and as fast as the nurse could replace the sponge, it filled up.

"Get some more volume in him," he ordered, gritting his teeth. "He's losing blood faster than we can get it into him." The nurse next to him wiped the sweat on his brow. "Clamp," he ordered, holding a hand out.

"Doctor," the anesthesiologist said, as the heart monitor next to his chair flat lined.

SARAH rested her head on Maxine's knee while her sister ran her hand through her hair. She closed her eyes and prayed, prayed for the doctor, for Derrick.

Her stomach muscles tightened, her heart paused for a moment and then beat furiously. Sarah gasped and sat up, hand to chest, while nausea swirled in her stomach. She pushed herself to her feet, shooing away Barry's hands that suddenly appeared, ready to catch her should she collapse.

"We need to pray," she said insistently. She gripped Barry's hand tightly and looked up at the giant, feeling a little bit crazed. "We have to pray right now. Something's wrong. Something's really wrong."

Robin stood and took Sarah's face in her hands. "Okay. Let's pray." She turned and gestured to her chair. "Looks like a good prayer bench to me."

Sarah collapsed on her knees and started praying, uttering words like, "Please God," and "I beg you, Father." Her spirit, though, spoke volumes to God, speaking for her while her mouth simply just couldn't form the words.

Her family knelt next to her and they all prayed together. Fervently. Passionately. Faithfully.

DOCTOR Woodworth stitched the hole as fast as he could, listening to the alarm of flat line. "Come on come on come on," he said under his breath, willing his fingers to work faster, more efficiently, more proficiently.

The second he could, he raised his hands out of the chest cavity. "I'm clear!" he said.

The internal paddles were placed on the newly repaired heart and a jolt of electricity was sent through it, hopefully to spark it back to life.

Every eye in the room was trained on the monitor. One breath. Then another. Nothing.

"Push an amp of epi and charge to 50."

While the defibrillator charged, he reexamined his work. Double checking to make sure that every hole had been sealed – that none of the life giving blood continued to seep from wounds. "I want another X-ray," he said. "Before we seal him up I want to make sure we got all the metal."

"Ready," said the doctor with the defibrillator. "Clear!"

AN hour went by. Then two. Sarah's knees started to ache before they finally went numb. Eventually, she shifted up into a chair, but she didn't stop praying. She held the hands of her sisters, who held the hands of their husbands, who held the hands of Peter and Melissa and her mother. In a circle, they prayed. Sometimes out loud, sometimes quietly.

The intensity of the feeling she originally felt started to abate. The grip on her heart loosened. Knowing she had started the praying and that they would end it only with her, she finally whispered, "Amen." Around the circle, a chorus of "amens" echoed and one by one, and hands were released.

Sarah rolled her head on her shoulders and stood to stretch. The she noticed the doctor standing in the doorway.

With a voice that screamed fatigue, he said, "I didn't want to interrupt, but I need to speak to the family of Derrick DiNunzio."

Sarah didn't recognize him, but she hadn't worked surgery in a long time. "We are his family."

The doctor scanned the faces in the room and finally slipped his do-rag off his head. "I'm Doctor Woodworth," he said by way of introduction. "I – I don't know how to explain this." He rubbed a hand over his eyes. "Derrick was in bad shape. The bullet fragmented when it entered his body, and there were pieces of metal everywhere."

Sarah focused on the word "was". Past tense. What did that mean?

The doctor continued. "We worked as fast as we could, but he lost a significant amount of blood. I couldn't…" Tears burned his throat and he had to clear it to continue speaking. "While we were in there, a fragment pierced his heart. I couldn't work fast enough to stop the bleeding."

Sarah's head started reeling. No. Not possible. "I couldn't," were **NOT** the words that the doctor was supposed to say, especially when speaking in the past tense. He was supposed to say something like, "It was a fight, but he's in recovery now."

The family let out a collective gasp. Someone started crying. Sarah reached forward and gripped the doctor's wrist. "Please," she whispered.

Male hands touched her shoulders, trying to comfort her or restrain her, she didn't know which.

"At some point, I was certain all was lost. As I worked, I started praying for God's help. As I came in here and saw you all in such intense prayer, I know how what happened … happened."

A glimmer of hope sparked to life in Sarah's heart.

The doctor continued. "All I know is that Mr. DiNunzio should be dead, and there is no reason why he's alive and in recovery right now other than God deemed that it would be so."

A loud sound of relief moved through the group like a wave. "In recovery?" Sarah said.

The doctor smiled. "Yes. I'm sorry. I am in such awe of what happened that I forgot to start with that information. He is severely critical. I'm not even going to guess his chances, medically. But he shouldn't even be alive and he is. So, let's go with that and trust God."

With a sob of happiness, Sarah threw her arms around the doctor's neck. She started crying and didn't know how to stop. All she could do was say, "Thank you, God," over and over again.

Sarah continued her prayer; ignoring the nurse who rushed in moments later, ignoring the deep sigh that the doctor breathed, ignoring the deafening silence that fell over the entire room.

Chapter 23

"PUT your foot here," Derrick said, gripping Sarah's slim ankle in his hand and helping her find a solid toehold. "Now reach above you and grip that piece of rock with your right hand."

"What piece of rock?"

Derrick pointed. "That one."

Sarah narrowed her eyes. "There's no way that's going to hold me."

Derrick grinned. "Trust me."

With a huff, Sarah reached up and grabbed the little piece of rock jutting out of the mountain face. She pulled herself up and Derrick followed, providing instruction and advice as he lifted, pulled, tugged, and maneuvered both of them up the mountain side.

Sarah stood in the small crevice and put her hands on the small of her back. The hot sun beat down on them, causing her face to glow with sweat. She pulled her canteen off her belt and took a small swallow. "You okay?" she asked him as he pulled himself up and over onto the rock next to her.

With a habitual movement, he rubbed his chest. "I'm perfectly fine," he said. "This is the best thing for me."

Her eyes narrowed. "I don't want you over doing it."

"Yes, doctor."

She threw her head back and laughed. "Just nurse. I'm only thinking about doctor."

"You can do it. You can do anything."

She offered him the canteen and he gratefully accepted it. "As long as you're rooting for me, I believe I can," she said with a smile.

Derrick turned and looked at the view. The magnificence of God's creation stared back at him from their vantage point high above the beautiful Massachusetts wilderness.

"You know, I stood here, in this spot, about eight months ago."

"Oh?" Sarah asked.

He walked up to her and slipped an arm around her waist. "Yes. I was distraught."

Sarah tilted her head back and grinned at him. "You? You're the picture of contentment. What had you distraught?"

Derrick shifted until he faced her. He slid his hands over her shoulders and down her arms until he held both of her hands in his. "My love for you," he said, looking deep into her eyes.

Sarah, whose heart had started beating double time with the touch of his hands, felt her chest clench and her breath hitch. She looked up at him, feeling like she would drown in the brown depths of his eyes. He was so strong, so handsome, and she had come so close to losing him that sometimes she had nightmares about it. "I wouldn't want our love to cause you distress," she said in a whisper.

With a crooked smile, Derrick raised her left hand and kissed the gold and stones that graced her ring finger. The day he got out of the hospital, long weeks after the bullet fragment pierced his heart, he took the ring with the square cut topaz out of a drawer in his bedroom and, in front of their family, knelt next to where Sarah sat on his couch and claimed his love for her, his adoration of her, and told her how much the topaz paled in comparison to her beautiful honey-brown eyes. He asked her to marry him, and he barely had the question out before she had her arms around his neck as she said, "Yes, yes, yes," over and over again.

Now here they stood on this beautiful mountain the morning after their wedding night. Sarah could not imagine a more perfect place to spend their honeymoon, learning Derrick's favorite pastime away from family, friends, and any kind of technology that might beckon him back to work.

"At the time it was simply my love. You hadn't yet realized that you returned it." He cupped her cheek and kissed her softly. "I climbed up here and prayed, begging for God's direction. Then I went to your house to ask you to marry me, but you threw up all over me instead."

Sarah laughed and stepped back. "I did no such thing. I never missed the bucket." With Derrick's cocked eyebrow, she waved her hand. "Well, maybe once."

His face sobered again and Sarah felt a fluttering in her stomach at the look on his face. "I have loved you from the moment I laid eyes on you, sweetheart. And I will love you until we reach the end of eternity."

Stepping forward and slipping her arms around his waist, she rested her head on his chest and listened to the beautiful sound of his heart beating. She vividly remembered sitting in the hospital room with him, breathing in time to the machines, listening to the beep-beep-beep as the monitor signaled the rhythm of his heart. "God has given us a beautiful gift in our love," she said. "He brought us together, then He healed you with a miracle. I sometimes feel like we can never do enough to be worthy of this gift."

Stroking her cheek with a finger, Derrick smiled. Then he shrugged out of his backpack and dug around it in until he pulled out a couple of energy bars. "All we can do is love Him and serve Him with all our heart." He winked as he handed her the snack. "Heart, not hearts. Did you catch that? Because we're one, now, you and me."

Sarah slipped an arm around his waist and looked out over the beautiful view, admiring the wonder of God's creation. "I'm blessed."

THE END

TOPAZ HEAT - EPILOGUE

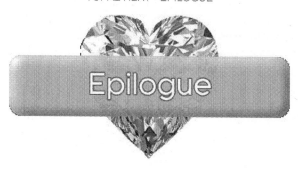

IT was October, but the Florida Keys varied little in the sense of changing weather. For a brief time, they worried that the tropical depression sitting a few hundred miles off the coast in the Atlantic would affect their plans. At the last minute, the storm veered in its course and allowed for the perfect day. The sky was blue enough to hurt the eyes. The sun was warm enough to allow short sleeves. The air was fresh enough that spirits felt rejuvenated just breathing it.

Across the sloping lawn that led to the beach, white covered tables nearly bowed under from the weight of the food. Every several yards, drink stations were set up, manned by a wait staff all in white who worked under the expert eye of Mrs. Tony Viscolli. In the kitchen, the army of decorators unwound with cool drinks after hours under the drilling command of Mrs. Barry Anderson. And the children were relaxed and refreshed after an afternoon spent with Mrs. Derrick DiNunzio.

All in all, it was a perfect party.

The guest list ranged from the country's most prominent to the bartender who ran the seediest bar on the south side of Boston, with dress ranging from black tie to black leather. An hour before, the crowd had buzzed with the surprise arrival of President Cummings, while some had shifted position to avoid being in the way of the big guy with the goatee who went by Hank. But the sisters saw neither political affiliation nor social status. They merely looked out at the hundreds of people and saw Tony's friends and associates, all those who had come to the extreme southern part of the country to pay homage to him on his fiftieth birthday.

Near the cake that rose six tiers, a lone microphone waited. Antonio Viscolli rarely let an opportunity go by without giving a speech, and his wife knew him well enough to know that and have it installed even under his protests. After the cake was cut and the champagne poured for the toast, she gave a secret smile to her youngest sister as he took the miniature stage.

He waited with a smile on his face as the applause died down, then cleared his throat while he scanned the sea of faces. "My wife worried that no one would come," he said, then waited until the laughter faded away. "I want to thank you all for being here. The honor I feel at seeing so many friends at one time is a great one, and I feel it deeply.

"Birthdays are a time of gifts, but this year I've decided to give rather than receive."

Robin sat at the table with the rest of the family and glanced up when she felt someone at her elbow. Surprised, she took the thin box from the uniformed waiter. Tony continued to speak. "In December, it will be eighteen years since I asked my wife to marry me. At the time I was willing to do anything at all to get her to say yes. As it was, all it took was offering her a trip to Italy."

More laughter followed Robin's surprised gasp. He grinned at her from his spot. "Small change compared to the joy she's given me over the years. For the two beautiful children. TJ, fourteen and already a championship rower, Madeline, my precious little girl who just became a teenager. It was just yesterday that you two were born, and here we are." He paused while his children looked at each other and grinned embarrassed smiles. "*Cara*, about three hundred people are waiting for you to open your present."

While Robin fought the bright paper, Tony explained his gift. "She's always complaining that the jewelry I buy her is too much. Too flashy. Too expensive. I'm afraid that she has nearly quit even opening the boxes, very frustrating for a man who enjoys beautiful gems, I assure you." He felt the familiar glow she always brought him as he watched her hold up the simple sapphire hanging from a thin gold chain. "Maybe this one you'll actually wear, my love."

Murmurs flew through the crowd as Robin secured the chain around her neck and clutched at the stone. Maxine was so involved in watching Robin, that she didn't realize a waiter holding an identical package stood at her arm until he tapped her on the shoulder.

"Maxine, my sweet. So many years ago we feared we'd lost you for good. You who lights up a room just by walking into it, and who has gifted this world with your magnificent art. To Maxi, the mother of my four precious nieces and nephews, to the wife of my best friend and brother. You are the one who always complained that you didn't get the flashy jewelry. Well, sweetheart, this was the flashiest I could find."

Other women would have oohed and ahhed over the emerald the size of a robin's egg centered in three strands of emeralds and diamonds. Maxine, though, threw back her head and laughed. She removed the thick gold band from around her neck and put the new necklace in its place. What should have been tacky and overdone somehow found its home as it complimented her black sheath perfectly.

Sarah's face fused with color when Tony turned his attention to her.

"This brings me to our little pixie Sarah, the one whose strength binds our family, who is our constant voice of reason. The one who has spent her career in service to others, helping deliver countless babies. She is the wife of the man who is my brother in my heart, and the mother of his almost three children." He grinned down at her while she hid the fact that she was having another contraction. She wondered if it would be rude to tell him to hurry up.

"Your husband has been about as bad as I am with my lovely wife in showering you with presents. So it was hard for me to find something you may not already have. But somehow, I managed it. The bracelet he gave you for your 30th birthday was a rare find. He wanted the topaz, but he wanted a certain color. He was so proud of it, and discovered during his search that it originally had a matching necklace."

Sarah felt the man at her shoulder and took the thin box from him. Her hands shook so badly that she worried she'd drop it, and she nearly cried in relief when Angela, her three year old, clambered forward to help her open her present. "After months of searching," Tony continued, "I finally located the matching necklace. To inspect it, my buyer had to fly all the way to Australia." Sarah lifted the necklace out of the box and barely saw the strand of pearls interlaced with topaz gems the color of honey through her tears. Maxine crouched behind her and removed her pearl choker, helping her fasten the new necklace.

"You sisters are the jewels in my life, in the lives of my brothers. You are the reason we are complete, the reason we greet each new day fresh, ready to tackle the next thing the world brings us.

"One day, we will receive jewels in our crowns in heaven. But, for now we will work for God's kingdom, together in our marriages that are to emulate Christ's relationship with the church. We will continue to fight the good fight and run this race. And the reason we can do it with such love and joy in our hearts is no doubt because we have you sisters by our sides.

"Without you, the three of us would be miserable old men with no joy or laughter in our lives. Because of you we have our children, we have our homes, and we have love.

"There was a time in my life I was as alone as a person could get. It was dark and cold both inside of me and out, and most of you out there would have written me off as no good, as having no hope. No other birthday present could compare in my heart to looking down from this spot at the table filled with my family. The table with those beautiful women and all those beautiful children, and knowing that they will forever keep that dark and that cold at bay, and knowing that the love at that table is real and it is absolute because that love all came from God."

He paused and smiled at his wife with love in his eyes so strong there wasn't a person who could see it who doubted him. He raised a glass and softly said, "*Grazie.*"

READER'S GUIDE MENU

SUGGESTED luncheon menu for a group discussion about *Topaz Heat*.

Those who follow my Hallee the Homemaker website know that one thing I am passionate about in life is selecting, cooking, and savoring good whole real food. A special luncheon just goes hand in hand with hospitality and ministry.

For those planning a discussion group surrounding these books, I offer some humble suggestions to help your special luncheon talk come off as a success.

Quick as you like, you can whip up an appetizer, salad, entree and dessert that is sure to please and certain to enhance your discussion and time of friendship and fellowship.

The appetizer:

Viscolli Hotel Caprese on a Stick

What could be better than a one-bit appetizer that satisfies all of the tastebuds in your mouth?

Here is a dish that is offered in Viscolli hotels worldwide.

INGREDIENTS:

¼ cup balsamic vinegar

½ cup extra virgin olive oil

1 tsp salt (Kosher or sea salt is best)

½ tsp fresh ground pepper

Fresh mozzarella balls

grape tomatoes

fresh basil leaves

PREPARATION:

Place a toothpick through a mozzarella ball, grape tomato, and basil leaf (with the cheese on the bottom, tomato in the middle, basil on top). Place in a shallow pan.

Make as many as 3-4 per guest.

DIRECTIONS:

Mix the balsamic vinegar with the salt and pepper. Slowly whisk in the olive oil until it emulsifies.

Drizzle over the cheese and tomato bites.

The Soup:

Maxine's Vegetable Soup

While Sarah is recovering from a terrible illness, older half-sister Maxine brings this amazing vegetable soup over to help restore her health.

INGREDIENTS:

2 cans diced tomatoes

1 large onion

2 large carrots

2 large celery stalks, with leaves

2 large potatoes

1 large parsnip

1 6-ounce bag frozen peas

1 6-ounce bag frozen organic corn

1 tsp salt (Kosher or sea salt is best)

2 tsp dried parsley

1 tsp dried oregano

1 tsp dried basil

$\frac{1}{2}$ tsp fresh ground black pepper

Water to cover

PREPARATION:

Dice the onion.

Slice the carrot & parsnip.

Slice the celery and finely chop the leaves.

Peel and dice the potatoes.

DIRECTIONS:

Place the vegetables and the salt and spices in a large pot. Cover with water. Bring to a boil.

Reduce heat and simmer.

You can serve and eat it as soon as the vegetables are fork tender, but for the best flavor, let simmer for several hours.

The Sandwich:

Robin's Roast Beef Sandwiches

Derrick lived under Robin's roof from the time he was 18-years-old. Robin learned very quickly how to feed a "growing boy". When he comes home, she knows exactly what to feed him.

INGREDIENTS:

1 3-pound Bottom Round Beef Roast

2 TBS flour

2 tsp salt (Kosher or sea salt works best)

$1/2$ tsp fresh ground pepper

1 TBS extra virgin olive oil

Onion rolls

1 large sweet onion

1 green bell pepper

2 TBS butter

provolone cheese

Mayonnaise

PREPARATION:

Salt and pepper all sides of the roast. Rub with flour.

Preheat the oven to 350° F (180° C).

DIRECTIONS:

In a skillet large enough for the roast, heat the extra virgin olive oil. Place the roast in the oil and brown each side just until browned.

Remove and place in roasting pan. Add about $1/2$ cup water. Bake at

350° F (180° C) for 2 ½ to 3 hours. Remove from oven and let cool.

Thinly slice the onion and the pepper.

In a skillet, melt the butter over medium heat. Add the onion and the pepper. Let cook, slowly, until the vegetables are soft. Remove from pan.

Split each onion roll in half. Slather with mayonnaise. Place cheese on one side of the bread and a generous helping of roast beef on the other. Top the beef with the onion and pepper. Serve with plenty of paper towels for this wonderful, messy sandwich.

The Dessert:

Sarah's Vegan Birthday Cake

Maxine works with the pastry chef at the Viscolli Hotel in Boston to make her baby sister the perfect vegan birthday cake for her 30th birthday. This recipe is so wonderfully delicious, you'll never miss the dairy or eggs.

INGREDIENTS:

FOR THE CAKE:
4 cups cake flour

1 ½ cup sugar

1 tsp salt (Kosher or sea salt works best)

2 tsp aluminum free baking powder

1 tsp baking soda

2 cups water

¼ cup coconut oil

¼ cup palm shortening

2 tsp vanilla extract

2 tsp lemon juice

FOR THE FROSTING:

¼ cup coconut oil

¼ cup palm shortening

3 cups confectioners sugar, sifted

½ tsp salt

1 tsp vanilla extract

2 tbsp coconut milk

PREPARATION:

Preheat the oven to 350° F (180° C).

Lightly grease two 8" round cake pans with palm shortening. Dust with flour.

DIRECTIONS:

FOR THE CAKE:

Sift the flour, sugar, salt, baking powder, and baking soda into a large bowl. Set aside.

In a smaller bowl, combine the in a separate bowl, combine coconut oil, palm shortening, water, vanilla extract, and lemon juice. Slowly pour the wet ingredients into the bowl with the dry ingredients and, using a mixer beat on low until well combined.

Pour the batter into the prepared pans and bake for 25-30 minutes or until a knife can be inserted into the middle and come out clean.

Remove from pans and cool on wire cooling rack.

FOR THE FROSTING:

Place the coconut oil and palm shortening in mixing bowl. Beat on high until fluffy. Gradually add in the coconut creamer, vanilla extract and salt. Mix for 3 minutes.

Turn mixer to low and slowly add the confectioner sugar. When it is fully incorporated, turn the mixer to high and beat for 2 minutes or until fluffy.

READER'S GUIDE DISCUSSION QUESTIONS

SUGGESTED luncheon discussion group questions for *Topaz Heat*.

When asking ourselves how important the truth is to our Creator, we can look to the reason Jesus said he was born. In the book of John 18:37, Jesus explains that for this reason He was born and for this reason He came into the world. The reason? To testify to the truth.

In bringing those He ministered to into an understanding of the truth, Our Lord used fiction in the form of parables to illustrate very real truths. In the same way, we can minister to one another by the use of fictional characters and situations to help us to reach logical, valid, cogent, and very sound conclusions about our real lives here on earth.

While the characters and situations in **The Jewel Series** are fictional, I pray that these extended parables can help readers come to a better understanding of truth. Please prayerfully consider the questions that follow, consult scripture, and pray upon your conclusions. May the Lord of the universe richly bless you.

Sarah's dislike of Derrick is evident in *Topaz Heat*.

    1. Do you think that dislike ultimately hurt her relationship with God?

Miriam wants to break off an engagement because her fiancé is not a Christian.

    2. How would you counsel a young Christian woman in this situation?

Derrick struggles not to give in to despair when facing criminal charges. Read Psalm 42.

>3. What example does David give in dealing with times of overwhelming trial in our lives?

Derrick comes from a past scattered with sin. Yet, whether or not we ran with an inner city gang performing thievery and thuggery or dealt drugs for a crime-lord, we are all stained with sin, and that sin is all the same to God. Read Hebrews 10:17.

>4. What does the Bible say about our sin when we accept Christ's sacrifice?

>5. Do you think it's "fair" that someone with Derrick's past is as forgiven and as washed clean as someone with Sarah's past?

Sarah felt judged and manipulated by her mother; however when the older woman sincerely apologized, Sarah forgave her immediately and let her back into her life.

>6. Do you find it easy to forgive? Why or why not?

Derrick and Tony have done things in their past they take no pride in now that they know Jesus Christ. Robin and Sarah demonstrate how we can emulate the love of Christ in wiping the slate clean.

>7. Do you find it easy to forgive others, particularly for actions they took before they came to know Christ? Why or why not?

TRANSLATION KEY

amico – friend, buddy
aspetto – be looking forward to; expectation
Ayudame, por favor. Mi hija! – Help me, please. My daughter!
bello – beautiful
Buon san Valentino – Happy St. Valentine's day
buona sera – good evening
Calmi giù, il fratello – Calm down, brother
Capire che sono orgoglioso di lei – Understand that I am proud of you
capisce – understand, comprehend
cara – dearest, darling, beloved
cara mia – dearest of mine, (darling/beloved of mine)
C'è la venuta di difficoltà – Trouble is coming.
ciao – hello or good bye
come tragica – how tragic (it's a tragedy)
devo andare adesso – I have to go now.
esatto – precisely, exactly
figlio – son (esp. beloved male child)
grazie – thank you
la ringrazio, Dio – thank you, God
Lei capisce? – Do you understand?
Lei parla Italiano – Do you speak Italian
L'ha fatto uccide quest'uomo? – Did you kill this man?
magnifico – magnificent
mi amante – my female friend of whom I am fond
mi amico – my friend

mi fratello – my brother

mia cara – my dearest, (my darling, my beloved)

mia sorella – My sister

mio figlio – My son (especially beloved male child or young man)

mise en place – French culinary term 'everything in place' or 'all in preparation'

Napoli – Naples, Italy

non ero una madre buona, ma l'ho amato sempre – I was not a good mother but I always loved you

non l'ho mai detto – I never said

non mi importa – It is not important

non ne parlano – don't speak it (don't mention it)

qualunque – any (whichever, whatever)

Seanmháthair – Irish for grandmother

Sei benvenuto – you're welcome (formal)

semplici – simple

si – yes

si un piccolo testardo – a little stubborn (pig-headed)

sono molto orgoglioso di lei – I am very proud of you

spiegare – explain

te amo con tutto il cuore e con l'anima – I love you with all of my heart and soul

teléfono médico – telephone doctor

ABOUT THE AUTHOR

HALLEE BRIDGEMAN lives with her husband and their three children in small town Kentucky. When not writing Christian romantic suspense novels or penning cookbooks, she blogs about all things cooking and homemaking at her Hallee the Homemaker blog.

Hallee loves coffee, campy action movies, and regular date nights with her husband. Above all else, she loves God with all of her heart, soul, mind, and strength; has been redeemed by the blood of Jesus Christ; and relies on the presence of the Holy Spirit. She prays her books are a blessing to you and would love to hear back from you.

FICTION BOOKS BY HALLEE:

Sapphire Ice, Jewel Series book 1

Greater Than Rubies (a novella inspired by the Jewel Series)

Emerald Fire , Jewel Series book 2

Topaz Heat , Jewel Series book 3

A Melody for James, Song of Suspense book 1

An Aria for Nick, Song of Suspense book 2

A Carol for Kent, Song of Suspense book 3 (coming soon)

COOKBOOKS BY HALLEE:

Fifty Shades of Gravy, a Christian gets Saucy

The Walking Bread, the Bread Will Rise

AFTERWORD

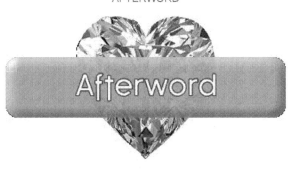

OUR sincere prayer is that reading *The Jewel Trilogy* by novelist Hallee Bridgeman has blessed you in some way. Years ago, Hallee had written 10 secular romance novels in less than two years before having the good fortune of finding an editor who saw her potential – and marrying him. After a few revisions she began submitting her work to various contests in the hopes of putting her work in front of an agent or "big house" publishing company editor.

After submitting *Sapphire Ice* in its secular form to a prominent contest, Hallee experienced a conviction in her heart that she had to rewrite her novels to more closely model and reflect her Christian worldview and she set about doing just that. Hallee had barely finished completely rewriting *Sapphire Ice* when she got the news back from a "big house" publishing agency. They wanted to pay her for the entire trilogy.

Hallee stuck to her convictions and wrote the agency back, informing them that she had gone through a spiritual change of heart and submitting the full (now fully revised) manuscript for their consideration. The big house turned the novel over to their inspirational line, who sent a hand-written note back informing Hallee that, her work was very good but too "edgy" for their subscribers.

In other words, Hallee's stories, while fiction, could very well happen in today's contemporary world. Looking at the Christian fiction market today, you can find a lot of Amish stories, and a lot of Victorian or Western stories. These environments that are far removed from the contemporary and popular secular culture of today's fallen world. Likewise, their characters are often plastic and inhumanly good – very far removed from anyone you might actually meet in your real life. Hallee's characters are flawed and imperfect and suffer temptation and confusion and emotions. No one is made of plastic and no one is inhumanly good.

In reading *The Jewel Trilogy*, perhaps you closely identified with some of the characters. Perhaps, like Robin, you once felt like you could take on the world all by yourself and had no need of anyone's help, particularly God's help. Maybe like Tony you have let anger bring you to a place where you want to visit evil upon someone who has hurt you or a loved one despite your life long convictions.

Perhaps, like Maxine, you just "played church." Attending was more of a social event for you than an expression of the fact that your life has been permanently transformed. Maybe, like Barry, you were once angry with God and considered life unfair.

Maybe, like Sarah, you have known the truth about God and His plan for you all your life but never let that truth transform your life or open your eyes to the greater good He had in store for you. Perhaps, like Derrick, you wear your past for all the word to see, like his tattoos, a bitter reminder of the lost soul you once were.

Perhaps you have a dark past. Perhaps loved ones have suffered or even died and you cannot understand why. Perhaps some traumatic memories haunt you. Perhaps you were abused or harmed by someone you should have been able to trust, someone meant to keep you safe.

The truth is that the fictional reality these characters echo is a reality with which many in this life are all too familiar. But the greater message of *The Jewel Trilogy* is that we are all worthy of redemption. In your real life, that real message still holds true.

Scripture informs us that no man is good, no, not even one. Only God is good (John 10:29). All of us are worthy of redemption. All of us can release the chains of the past, overcome temptation and our sinful nature, and claim the victory that God promises.

All we need to do is accept His help. All we need to do is lean on Him and believe on Him to see us through even our darkest hours.

If you feel like God isn't listening or God is powerless to hear you – if you feel like God couldn't possibly love you – take a moment and talk to him in prayer. Just talk to Him and listen when He answers.

Tell God how you feel and what is on your heart. Maybe start with something like, "God, as I was reading these books, I felt like You were speaking to me in many ways."

We would love to hear from you. Please drop us an email or a comment on the blog so that we can pray for you.

God Bless,

Gregg Bridgeman

SONG OF SUSPENSE SERIES

The *Song of Suspense* Series...

A MELODY FOR JAMES

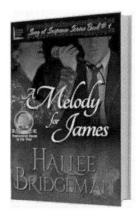

MELODY Mason and James Montgomery lead separate lives of discord until an unexpected meeting brings them to a sinister realization. Unbeknownst to them, dark forces have directed their lives from the shadows, orchestrating movements that keep them in disharmony. Fire, loss, and bloodshed can't shake their faith in God to see them through as they face a percussive climax that will leave lives forever changed.

♫ ♫ ♫ ♫

AN ARIA FOR NICK

ARIA Suarez remembers her first real kiss and Nick Williams, the blue eyed boy who passionately delivered it before heading off to combat. The news of his death is just a footnote in a long war and her lifelong dream to become a world class pianist is shattered along with her wrist on the day of his funeral.

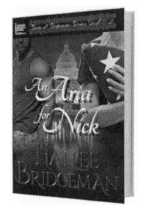

Years later, Aria inadvertently uncovers a sinister plot that threatens the very foundations of a nation. Now, stalked by assassins and on the run, her only hope of survival is in trusting her very life to a man who has been dead for years.

♫ ♫ ♫ ♫

A CAROL FOR KENT

BOBBY Kent's name is synonymous with modern Country Music and he is no stranger to running from overzealous fans and paparazzo. But he has no idea how to protect his daughter and Carol, the mother of his only child, from a vicious and ruthless serial killer bent on their destruction.

♪ ♪ ♪ ♪

A HARMONY FOR STEVE

CHRISTIAN contemporary singing sensation, Harmony Harper, seeks solitude after winning her umpteenth award. She finds herself in the midst of the kind of spiritual crisis that only prayer and fasting can cure. Steve Slayer, the world renowned satanic acid rock icon, who has a reputation for trashing women as well as hotel rooms, stumbles into her private retreat on the very edge of death.

In ministering to Steve, Harmony finds that the Holy Spirit is ministering to her aching soul. The two leave the wilderness sharing a special bond and their hearts are changed forever.

They expect rejection back in their professional worlds. What neither of them could foresee is the chain of ominous events that threaten their very lives.

♪ ♪ ♪ ♪

Hallee Bridgeman

VIRTUES AND VALOR SERIES

The Virtues and Valor series
The battle begins in 2013 ...

SEVEN women from different backgrounds and social classes come together on the common ground of a shared faith during the second World War. Each will earn a code name of a heavenly virtue. Each will risk discovery and persevere in the face of terrible odds. One will be called upon to make the ultimate sacrifice.

Introduction	Heavenly Heroines
Part 1	Temperance's Trial
Part 2	Homeland's Hope
Part 3	Charity's Code
Part 4	A Parcel for Prudence
Part 5	Grace's Ground War
Part 6	Mission of Mercy
Part 7	Flight of Faith

INSPIRED by real events, these are stories of Virtue and Valor.

A note from Hallee Bridgeman...

I'm so happy and honored that you chose to read *The Jewel Anthology*.

My sincere prayer is that it blessed you.

I'd love to hear from you. Leave a comment online at Hallee Bridgeman, Novelist. Your feedback inspires me and keeps me writing.

May God richly bless you,

Hallee Bridgeman

HALLEE ONLINE

Hallee the Homemaker blog
www.halleethehomemaker.com/

Hallee Bridgeman, Novelist blog
www.bridgemanfamily.com/hallee/

Ask your local library to stock fine Olivia Kimbrell Press titles. Consider purchasing a copy of this book for your church library or as a gift. This book and upcoming releases from Hallee Bridgeman are available in e-Book format and trade paperback wherever fine books are sold. For more information, visit us on the world wide web:

www.bridgemanfamily.com/hallee/book-samples/

www.oliviakimbrellpress.com

HALLEE NEWSLETTER

Hallee News Letter

http://tinyurl.com/HalleeNews/

Never miss updates about upcoming releases, book signings, appearances, or other events. Sign up for Hallee's monthly newsletter.

Made in the USA
Lexington, KY
27 March 2015